The SACRED MESSENGER

The Chronicles of Farro–Book I

M. D. PRIVRATSKY

PHOENIX SPOTLIGHT
PUBLISHING

The Chronicles of Farro: The Sacred Messenger

Edited by Erin C. Brenner
Co-edited by Kristin Geditz
Cover and interior design by Gene Mollica Studio, LLC.

ISBN: 0692186530
ISBN 13: 978-0692186534

Second Edition, Tade paperback

Library of Congress Control Number: 2014902434

PHOENIX SPOTLIGHT
PUBLISHING

To my father, Ben R. Privratsky, who inspired me to become a writer. To my brother, Roger A. P., - you continue to inspire me, you will always be my muse. To Mark S. - your hard work in this project was greatly appreciated! To Justin and Bridget B. - your hard work in this project will never be forgotten.

Graven

Barrens

Dajan River Valley

Bandare

Shadow Land

Sonja Mt. Range

Sonja Mt. Range

Desert of Gadluin

Female

Rahara

Sion

Port of Maji

Simone River

Tambecam

Sea of Tanja

Desevon

Mt. Somer Set

Zendra Isle

Serrigen
Mountains of Peril

Ramidus

Mendax

Faircrand

Plains of Galasand

Life River

Arnest

Kett

White Prawn

Eden-Glee

Adarah

Shandel

Abondrous

Timber

Devercinden Forest

Edenbury

Seamara Cypress Palace

Shoshon

Ivani

Mt. Jubaa

Misty Forest

Ice Isle

Mt. Cangan

Keyron

Isle of Rane

Sea of Emaian

Sable Isle

Kadera

Sea of Jenquis

Tamira

Afar
Dark Isle

Andora
Age of the Phoenix
10,021 11th Age

Map of the Known
Island Realms

Age of the Phoenix
10,021 14th Age

Aura
Upper World

Inferus
Lower World

The Great South Ocean

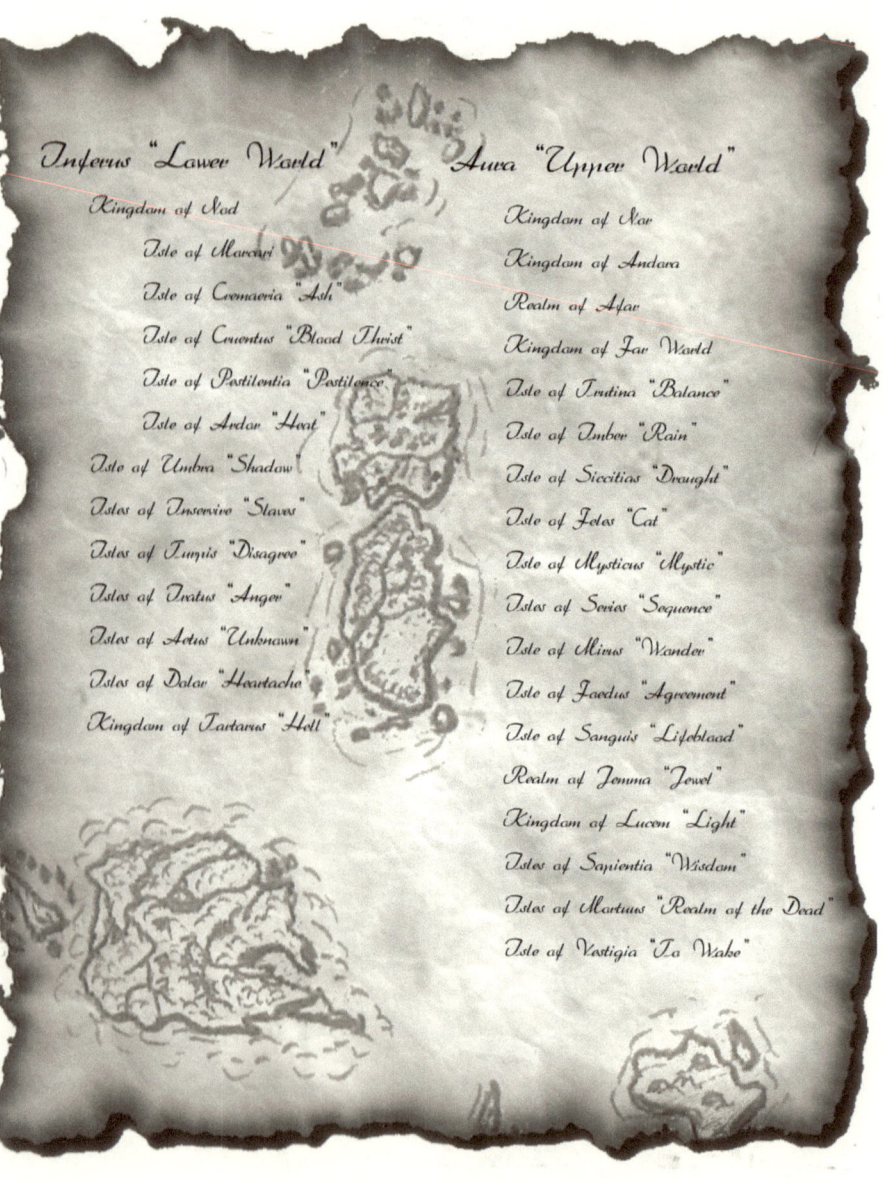

Inferus "Lower World"

Kingdom of Nod
   Isle of Marari
   Isle of Cremacria "Ash"
   Isle of Cruentus "Blood Thirst"
   Isle of Pestilentia "Pestilence"
   Isle of Ardor "Heat"
Isle of Umbra "Shadow"
Isles of Inservire "Slaves"
Isles of Turris "Disagree"
Isles of Iratus "Anger"
Isles of Actus "Unknown"
Isles of Dolor "Heartache"
Kingdom of Tartarus "Hell"

Aura "Upper World"

Kingdom of Nar
Kingdom of Andara
Realm of Afar
Kingdom of Far World
Isle of Trutina "Balance"
Isle of Umber "Rain"
Isle of Siccitias "Drought"
Isle of Feles "Cat"
Isle of Mysticus "Mystic"
Isles of Series "Sequence"
Isle of Mirus "Wonder"
Isle of Faedus "Agreement"
Isle of Sanguis "Lifeblood"
Realm of Jemma "Jewel"
Kingdom of Lucem "Light"
Isles of Sapientia "Wisdom"
Isles of Martuus "Realm of the Dead"
Isle of Vestigia "To Wake"

*"The greatest warrior one can have at their side
is one which we call a friend,"*

—M. D. Privratsky

Prologue

Dark was the night that settled over the land of Andora. It lay in quiet slumber as the surrounding seas ebbed and rolled with the tide. All was peaceful and serene, but not everyone found sleep on such a night.

Far from the mainland of Andora sailed the Mazu. She was a merchant ship that voyaged to and from Semara, a coastal port city of the Shandel, to Arnest, a coastal port city of Eden-Glee. Along her journey around Andora's southern shores, the Mazu would make stops at several port cities along the route. On this particular voyage, the Mazu and her crew would make an unscheduled stop at the remote and mysterious island only known as Ice Isle.

While in Semara, the crew received a passenger who paid them handsomely to take him to Ice Isle. Captain Ergos was most hesitant about taking a side trip to Ice Isle, even with the promise of getting such a grand payment. The passenger then introduced himself as Randye of Corpus. He was the royal advisor to King Jaspel, high king of the Shandel. The details of the mission were under terms of complete secrecy, so nothing more was uttered. Although still hesitant, Captain Ergos allowed Randye to journey along with them.

On the night of their second week out, Randye was up late logging his latest entry in his journal by lamplight.

It is the year 9000, at the beginning of the Age of Armageddon. Janyay 13:

Today, the weather was again most turbulent, the likes of which neither Captain nor crew has ever seen in their nearly fifty years of sailing these shores. They are most superstitious and say that such unusual weather is a very bad omen. I hear them speak at night, and they tell ghost stories about the murky Ice Isle. One of the sailors told of how the island came into being. It was said that thousands of years ago, the island was split in two by a violent earthquake caused by a volcanic eruption. Another spoke of how the spirits that govern the elements of earth split apart a mass of land known then as Pandera, thus creating Ice Isle to the north and Sable Isle to the south. I believe both theories hold truth and maybe something more. There is a piece of history that has been forgotten and wants to be remembered.

I am an old man; according to the high council, my time has been spent. They push to have me replaced, but my hope in this quest is to uncover this lost truth and bring my findings before my vexed king and secure my status as royal adviser. Images of evil times coming to the Shandel haunt the king's dreams. The scholars on the high council try to ease his worries and tell him such are things of the past. I sense otherwise. Word of this matter was even sent to the sacred order of Osarian Knights, but there has been no word from them. I do not know what I will find in my quest, but as surely as I am gazing out over the Sea of Tempus, I feel that my journey to find the truth will prevail as will my position.

———◆◆———

When the morning sun broke over the horizon, Randye, Captain Ergos, and the crew beheld a most spectacular sight. The horizon cleared for the first time in many years, and the sun shone brilliantly upon the snow-covered island. As they gazed upon the dazzling white isle, they were drawn to explore it. Sailing into Ice Isle's eastern harbor, the crew could not help but be fascinated by the shimmering island before them. However, before they could arrange a scouting party to go ashore, thick fog rolled in and enveloped the ship.

"This place is cursed," Captain Ergos said as he went white with fear. "O'foose sends us grave warning. He forbids us from venturing any further.

"Who or what is O'foose?" Randye wondered as he looked between the captain and crew.

"O'foose is the legendary spirit of fog. He was a sphinx of the ancient world, but that was before the Age of Set when all sphinxes were wiped from the earth," a fellow crewmember explained.

"We will leave this place and never return," the captain ordered as he turned to make his way to the bridge.

"NO! Captain, *please!*" Randye rushed over to the captain. "We cannot just give up! I have come all this way…."

"Then surely you can go all the way back from whence you came." The captain remained firm in his decision.

"No, I cannot," Randye said with growing desperation. "It must be learned what happened here. My king has to know.

"There are some things that should remain buried," an aged sailor offered as he stepped out of the crowd of gathered crew members. "The spirits of the world made this island forbidden for a reason.

"If I return empty-handed, my king will have no choice but to listen to the high council and put me out to pasture," Randye began to explain.

"Retirement does not sound all that bad," Captain Ergos offered with a sigh.

"Retirement for me will only be in shame. All I ask of you is to send me ashore. If I do not return in half a day, then you have my permission to leave," Randye bargained.

"What makes this island so special?" The Captain seemed a little startled as he looked in surprise at the aged man.

"It was said long ago that a mysterious spirit inhabits this island.

It is rumored that if the spirit is of goodness, then peace, prosperity, and immortality will be given to the brave visitor; but if the spirit is of evil, then the visitor will be given a most agonizing death. It is a test of faith. I am honored to do this for my king. He is a good man and deserves to have peace of mind," Randye explained calmly as he gazed through the thick fog towards the isle.

"What news are we to bring the king if the worst should happen?" Captain Ergos asked with concern.

"That the stories of old are true and that he is not to pursue this myth any further," Randye said simply.

Captain Ergos was silent for a moment as he studied the aged man before him. "I cannot say if you are the most loyal or foolish man I have ever come across, but I do admire your courage." He then took ahold of Randye's hand, "Godspeed."

"Same unto you, Captain." Randye nodded. He took one last look at the captain and crew before turning and climbing over the railing on the port side and lowering himself into a small rowboat below.

The captain and crew watched as the old advisor made his way to Ice Isle's shoreline. They watched him until his ghostly image disappeared into the thick fog. They stood there for a long moment waiting for the advisor's return. Their wait would not be long.

Pressing deeper into the fog, Randye could scarcely see the immense island before him. As he strained to see what was before him, he gripped the oars of the small boat tightly. Fear of running into some ravenously hungry monster kept Randye on edge. When his small boat finally ran aground, he could not help but jump. After a long moment of waiting and determining it was safe to move again, Randye climbed from the boat and slowly began to make his way off the rocky beach. As he climbed the rocky ridge, he found himself rising above the thick cloud of fog that loomed along the beach. As Randye looked on ahead, he noticed that the landscape was quite rugged and inhospitable, but still a good feeling stayed with him, and he continued.

"Maybe the omen of fog was merely a test of character," Randye thought to himself encouragingly. In order to cut the cold, he pulled his robes tighter and continued further inland. When he reached the summit of the mountain ridge and looked across the whole of Ice Isle, Randye lost his ability to breathe for a moment.

A vast wilderness of ice and snow-covered mountains formed the whole of the isle's interior. Turning his gaze, Randye saw the famous volcano of Ice Isle. Mt. Congoa was located on Ice Isle's northern coast and stood taller than any other mountain on the isle. Its dominating presence seemed to enforce its role as the island's sentinel. Mesmerized by the wondrous realm before him, Randye figured that surely heavenly creatures had to inhabit this island. Then at that very moment, a strangely warm breeze washed over him.

"You are strange to this place," a warm voice called to him from the breeze...

"Yes, I am. I come from the great kingdom of the Shandel, and I come in search of the truth about this lonely island and the spirit that lingers here," Randye announced as he tried to see where the mysterious voice emanated from.

"If it is truth you seek, then you have come to the right place," the kind voice spoke with assurance.

"Thank you...," Randye began to reply when the earth beneath his feet began to shake violently. "What is going on?" The calm tone in his voice turned to panic.

"The truth you seek is about to reveal itself," the voice explained.

The earth shook so violently that Randye stumbled and tried to grab onto some nearby rocks to steady himself. Suddenly, the entire ledge on which he stood gave away! A scream left his mouth as he slipped into the madness of rocks, dirt, snow, and ice that fell into the chasm below. He tried to call out, but the dirt and snow quickly choked him up. The chaos of madness around him seemed to last forever; as he prayed for this time to pass, he reached the bottom of the chasm. A sickening crack echoed through his ears, followed by sheer silence.

Lying at the bottom of the icy chasm, Randye regained

consciousness. At first, he thought he had died and had returned immortal; but then as his senses became clearer, the severe, excruciating pain of his broken body told him otherwise. He looked around for any sign of help, but there was none to be found on such a barren island. Painful realization told him that the myth had been true, but it was not as he would have hoped.

"I must get off this island…," he said to himself in a wince of pain. He tried to move, but the pain that coursed through his body was far too great.

"That will come soon enough," the warm voice replied seemingly out of nowhere. "But first there is something that you must know.

As chilling winds howled through the chasm, Randye shivered uncontrollably as he looked for the source of the mysterious person. Then out of thin air, a white, cloaked figure appeared before him. It kneeled on the ground before him, reached out its hand, and placed it gently on his shoulder. Soon, immense warmth washed over his body, and his excruciating pain melted away. Then the white stranger stood up and stepped back to allow him room to get to his feet.

"You are a heavenly being!" Randye exclaimed with relief as he took an unlabored breath of air. He rose to his feet and turned to the white stranger. "I thank you." The white stranger humbly bowed in response. "Now, what is this that you have to tell me?" he asked gently.

"You have been horribly used and insulted by your kingdom and especially your king," the white stranger spoke with fervor. "Your mission here was merely a ruse to get you out of the way while they replace you and wipe your name from the history of your people.

"My king would never! I have been a faithful servant for many long years and a good friend. My king needed to know the history of this island, and I bravely volunteered to embark on this mission. King Jaspel said that my place would be preserved until my return." Randye eyed the white stranger angrily as he defended his homeland and king.

"So certain, are you? Then why did your faithful king appoint your assistant to replace you in your absence?" The white stranger waited for Randye's answer.

"No such action has been…!" Randye started to protest when he saw the white stranger turn and lift its hand and magically create a ring of fog. There within the foggy ring, an image was revealed. It was King Jaspel talking to Randye's young assistant, Zerond. As Randye listened in astonishment, he heard the devastating truth. The white stranger had been right. When the image of the King and Zerond faded from sight and the fog ring disappeared, the white stranger turned back to Randye.

"What do you plan to do now?" the white stranger asked with intrigue.

Randye was silent. He searched for words to speak, but none came. He turned back to the ridge that he had fallen down. "I will return to the ship and…" His voice was stolen away when he saw his body still lying at the bottom of the chasm. "What is this?"

"You are at the bridge between life and death. Your body is so badly broken from your fall and your spirit too tired to fight its way back…you are dying." The white stranger sadly gazed at the broken advisor's body. "It is a shameful, tragic thing to happen to such a man. You deserved more than what you were given." The empathetic tone caught Randye's attention.

"Is there something you can do?" the heartbroken advisor wondered somberly.

"I can help you regain the respect that you truly deserve. Your king and country will remember your name for ages to come." The white stranger's voice was filled with promise.

Tears stung Randye's eyes as he reflected on all his long years of hardship in the palace. He turned to the white stranger and smiled. "Then let your will for me be done.

"It will be all that I have said and more…much more." The stranger then had the spirit of Randye return to his body. He laid a hand over the mortally wounded advisor's body and began to chant in a strange language.

"Let the spirit of this man's body be at peace forever more, but let my spirit take his place and walk the land as he did. If this body should be destroyed by a higher power, then let my spirit live on and wait until another comes…"

In that moment, the white stranger shed its cloak, and a dark spirit now loomed over Randye. The evil spirit known to the ancient world as Lord Jarden was most pleased by this chain of events. "I have waited six thousand years for this..." Then he disappeared into the body of the advisor as the spirit of the advisor was cast into the spirit realm. Rising to his feet, this creature returned to the Mazu and to the Shandel. His promise to Randye would be kept and much more.

—⋅⊰⋅⊱⋅—

Twenty and one years later.

Far from Andora's shores to the west lies a chain of islands known throughout the world as the Kingdom of Nor. Unknown to most of the world is that this exotic chain of isles is the location of the last dragon realm. It is a sacred sanctuary created for dragons by an elite member of the Osarian Knights.

In his journeys around Andora and the world, Rafar the Elder was grief stricken to learn that the race of dragon was nearly extinct. Assigning his duties in the Order to his four fellow companions, Rafar traveled to Nor where he could rebuild the dragon population. Out of all the isles that made up this beautiful realm, Rafar chose Lompoconi to be his home island.

There was not a day that passed that he did not think about his many friends in Andora or the mission that had been left to them some five thousand years earlier. Then, one day, some twenty and five years after his departure from Andora, Rafar found a sailor standing on his doorstep with a parchment in his weathered hands. The sailor only spoke a few words of apology for the parchment had been severely delayed due to the adversity within Andora as he gave Rafar the leather parchment, but it only took a glimpse at the seal on the parchment to reveal the identity of its sender.

In the year 9021
Marcen 5

Rafar,

I hope this letter finds you well, if it finds you at all. The news that I need to relate is most distressing and disheartening. I, myself, do not know how our beautiful Andora has come to this. In short, what we have feared since the time we took the oath to uphold Farro's words has come to pass! The ancient evil known as Lord Jarden has escaped from his icy prison and has brought the realm of Andora to ruin. Gone is the beautiful lush kingdom of Lani. Its foliage had grown back after the decimation of the sphinx empire. However when the peoples of the Shandel tried to stop Lord Jarden, they scorched the earth within Lani. This land will remain forever barren, for it was not magic but man that destroyed it. We are all appalled by the horror around us, but what is so much worse is the loss of life. Sadly, Pryor, Saxon, and Enoch have perished along with a multitude of others trying to stop this evil. You and I are all that remain of the Order, my friend, but I am afraid that my death is close at hand. I have taken what time I have left to try to get this urgent message to you. I hope and pray this letter reaches you in time. Farewell and Godspeed.

P.S.
The Caesaria will bring you to Adarah's eastern shores. Please hurry...

Your companion,
Sariff

As Rafar put down the parchment, he could still see the devastation that Sariff described: villages and towns decimated, families torn apart, and dark clouds blotting out the radiant sun, leaving Andora in a dim darkness. Gazing out across the Great Ocean, Rafar could almost see the troubled realm. Although Andora was in total ruin, it was not lost. He could sense several strong holds still resisting the darkness. It was these few places where survivors could seek refuge. However, this evil would never permit these fortresses of light to last. Rafar knew if something was not done soon, the brave few who stood against the darkness would suffer greatly before they succumbed to death.

In the hour of receiving the message from the Order, Rafar was ready to return to Andora. His return was necessary, but it would be most difficult. Many of the dragons he had raised were most saddened to see him leave, one especially: a brave young female dragon named Kiya. This gold dragon dearly loved Rafar and was always there to protect him if danger ever loomed close by. She enjoyed hearing the stories Rafar told about Andora. She wanted to accompany him to his home kingdom, but he could not allow it.

"You cannot go with me—not this time," Rafar said sadly as he stood on the beach and watched the crew of the Caesaria resupply for their voyage later that night.

"Did you not promise that one day I could go to see this realm you called home?" Kiya asked as she recalled one of their earlier conversations.

"One day is not today, my dear." Rafar turned back to Kiya and saw the sadness in her green eyes. "Please understand—Andora is overrun with darkness, and the evil that dwells there seeks to destroy all living things. I cannot put my children in the path of such danger, especially you, above all, my dear one," he gently explained as he stroked her head.

"Then I bid you farewell and that you are guided back to these mystical shores," Kiya said with a long sigh.

"I can only hope…," Rafar replied with uncertainty as he reached out to hug Kiya. However, before he could even take a step towards her, he was suddenly snatched away! A startled cry left his mouth as he was lifted high into the air. When his world stopped spinning, Rafar opened his eyes and found himself hanging upside down and only inches from Kiya's large green eyes. There was a moment of seriousness, but soon her bubbly laughter filled the air.

"Remember what we said about hope?" Kiya looked at Rafar knowingly.

A smile came to Rafar's face as he nodded in understanding. "Hope is underestimated, dashed, and most times scoffed at, but it always remains." This small reminder lifted his spirits about the mission before him and raised his hopes about returning to Lompoconi. "Thank you, Kiya. I will remember." As she gently turned him right-side up again, he embraced her nose while she nuzzled against him.

Later that day as the sun set on the vermillion-magenta horizon and evening fell upon the misty realm of Lompoconi, Rafar boarded the Caesaria. He looked out over the beautiful landscape as if for the last time. As the dark of night covered the land, there was a glorious spectacle of light and flame from all dragons that dwelled upon the misty island. It was their tribute to Rafar as they saw him off.

Tears ran down Rafar's cheeks as he gripped a special leather parchment and gazed out over the multitude that had gathered in his honor. The parchment that had been given to him contained this incantation:

> *To Our Father, Rafar the Elder,*
>
> *May the spirit of the dragon be with you always, that it may guide and protect you on your journeys afar. Let this spirit help you vanquish evil and let future generations remember the Great Dragon known as Rafar.*
>
> *Children of Lompoconi*

The voyage back to Andora was filled with unsettling anticipation for Rafar. His thoughts were focused on the mission that lay ahead of him. As he read over the letter sent to him, he could not help but be filled with great worry and dread.

On Abril 28th, 9021, the Caesaria was 1day out of Andora when she sailed passed Ice Isle. Rafar was fixed next to the railing as he studied the ice barren isle. Legend, according to the Osarian Order, said that when Lord Jarden was imprisoned on the isle during the

4th age, the isle was split into two islands. The northern most isle was mysteriously plunged into an ice age, which had lasted to date. It was feared by the sphinx, who imprisoned him, that this was a sign of defiance. This evil threatened to return. Now he has escaped, but Ice Isle remained an icy, barren wasteland. This omen bothered Rafar. It was a sign that this evil might prove impossible to vanquish, but his hope remained.

When morning came and Rafar came above deck and took his first look at Andora after twenty and five years, he stopped breathing for a moment. The absence of sun left a dim, gray darkness that reached far across the horizon. When his eyes adjusted to the bleak conditions, Rafar's heart fell into the pit of his stomach.

"Where are we?" he uttered in a gasp. The landscape's appearance was hostile and devoid of all plant life.

"This is Andora, sire. We are just off the eastern coast of Adarah and near the capital city of Shoshon." The captain gestured as he pointed out key features of Adarah's landscape that had not been destroyed.

The dream world he once knew as Andora had turned into a literal nightmare and hell on earth.

"Lord God, help us all!" he managed to utter as he grasped the railing in front of him.

"Do you still wish to make port here, sire?" The captain awaited his next order as he watched the prophet's face begin to pale.

Overwhelmed by the devastation that lay in front of him, Rafar could not think of anything else. Not once did the thought of returning to Lompoconi come to his mind, for now he thought of the many who had given their lives to stop this madness, including his companions in the Order. "There is no turning back. I cannot let this madness spread and ruin another beautiful realm. It has to stop with us!" Rafar took his leave of the captain and crew, and then entered this strange, dark realm with only his knapsack and walking stick for company.

Journeying deeper into Adarah, Rafar cautiously walked the road to the capital city. In natural times, Adarah closely resembled the majesty of Lompoconi, but the landscape that appeared before him now was a hellish nightmare. The rolling green countryside had been turned into charred ruins and darkened ash, the crystal sea-green rivers and streams were now only dry, cracked deserts, and even the sweet air that once rolled across the land was now rank with smoke and the odor of carnage. Adding to the burden that was already on his heart, Rafar would come across villages and homes laid to ruin and see the unfortunate many who were unable to escape.

Overwhelmed with grief from the atrocity around him, Rafar was unaware of the dangers that now lurked within the land. Stopping him dead in his tracks, Rafar heard a haunting wail call out from behind him. Lifting his sights to the dark sky above, he could not distinguish anyone or anything that posed a threat, but his instinct told him to fall to the ground. The very moment he did, he felt a "wisp" of stale air pass directly over him. When he looked up, he froze solid at the sight of the creature now before him.

It was a death phantom. These were creatures only known to the realm of the dead. They could take the life from any living being by flying straight through them. He guessed that since Lord Jarden had been unleashed, all foul creatures within the underworld had also been set loose. Much to his good fortune, the death phantom did not pursue him as its next course of business. Waiting a long moment before continuing onward, Rafar gave this creature ample time to move on.

Slowly rising to his feet again, Rafar looked on ahead and took notice of a shining light emanating from the other side of the mountains. Of all the darkness that the ancient evil had created to wash over this realm, he was not able to snuff out this brilliant light. He watched it with relief as it continued to shine in defiance of the surrounding darkness.

"Thank the heavens! Shoshon has been spared." His spirits began to lift as he quickened his pace for the grand city.

Finally nearing the outskirts of Shoshon, Rafar discovered the source of the brilliant light. All those of the elfin race who survived the assault from Lord Jarden and his minions now stood side by side to form a barrier of light to hold back the darkness and create a refuge for all survivors. Together, their magic produced such brilliant light. This power, however, was momentary, for even elves could not keep this up forever.

Picking up his pace, Rafar hurried towards the city when something out of the corner of his eye caught his attention. At first glimpse, Rafar saw a hellish-looking creature tearing at the remains of what used to be an old farmhouse, but a closer look revealed a more desperate scene.

A young boy trapped within the farmhouse was armed only with whatever was around. Finding an opportunity to injure the beast, the boy lit a piece of splintered wood and threw it at the beast. The splintered board flew through the air and lodged into the creature's shoulder. The roar from the creature was earsplitting, and it was then that Rafar realized that matters had just gotten worse. In the brief moment he had gotten a good look at the creature, he realized that this was a Rectera. This creature was born from the fires of hell itself. The only difference between an attack from the Rectera and the death phantom was that the Rectera would take its time, bite-by-bite, helping its victim pass into the realm of the dead.

Quickly reaching into his knapsack, Rafar pulled out the Armament Stone and slipped it into his walking stick. This razor-edged red diamond was a very dangerous weapon, and as such, it was only used during times of extreme peril. Turning his attention to the debilitated old country house, Rafar planned to take on this furious beast, but it had vanished!

"What? Do you not want to play?" Rafar said as he slowly approached the house. Drawing nearer, he looked through the doorway only to see a vacant house. Slowly stepping one foot inside the house, Rafar felt his heart sink as he expected to see the boy being eaten alive. Turning the corner and looking inside the main room, Rafar gasped and threw himself backwards. Out of nowhere, the boy came at him with a pitchfork! Rafar watched as the pitchfork was imbedded into the door and pinned his arm up against the wood.

"Who are you?!" the young boy demanded as he watched Rafar with wild eyes.

"I am someone who can help you," Rafar managed to reply as he focused his gaze on the boy, but strangely did not feel any pain from the pitchfork.

"LIAR! I have heard such talk before, and after trusting folk put down their guard, the wretched being took them to the realm of the dead, like my parents." Anger flared through the boy's green eyes.

"I am not here to bring harm to you or anyone," Rafar spoke calmly. "I am an Osarian Knight, and I have been sent to destroy the evil that poisons our land." He hoped this boy knew of the Order.

"Another lie. That Order died out after Lord Jarden came to power. However, if you have come to try and rid our land of this pestilence, then how about you start with that monster behind you?" The boy's words caused a cold chill to run down Rafar's spine.

Having no time to turn his head to look at the beast, Rafar tore his arm free as he jumped out of the doorway. As he hit the ground, the Rectera attacked and clawed the door where he had been standing, and its claw marks on the door turned to ash. The Rectera turned on Rafar and leapt for him. At the last possible moment, Rafar grabbed his staff just as the beast landed on him!

The boy could only watch as the fire beast came down upon the cloaked elvin stranger. He had seen many like him before pose as an agent of light and turn on the very people the being swore to protect. There had been something almost trusting about the stranger's brown eyes, but the thought quickly was dismissed as the fire beast clawed at the stranger. There was no hope to save this one—he was dead already.

There was nothing for the boy to do now but save himself. He turned and slipped out the back door of his tattered home and hurried to get on the road to Shoshon. Only—before he could make five steps out the door—he found himself face-to-face with another fire beast! Acting solely on instinct, the boy thrust the pitchfork into the creature's burning, red eyes. The night air filled with a shrill wail as the fire beast recoiled from the boy and tried to dislodge the sharp barbs from its eyes. Grabbing his moment to live, the boy began to dash down the road towards Shoshon when there was a thunderous crash behind him. On impulse, he turned to see what else was coming. His mistake, for now the fire beast was truly furious. This beast no longer had eyesight, but it mattered not. This beast could smell the living miles away. The boy whirled around to try and outrun the creature but ended up stopping still on the road. What stood before him was far worse than what was charging after him. A death phantom loomed just overhead waiting to make its next kill.

The boy could not get his body to move, for it was frozen in fear. The death phantom began to move closer towards him, and the thunderous sounds of the fire beast were rapidly approaching from behind him. Then before he could take a single breath, a dark blur rushed at him from the side and crashed into him, and together the two tumbled off to the side of the road. The boy managed to catch the precise moment when the death phantom and the fire beast collided. In a brilliant spectacle of dark, light, and flame, the two creatures vanished.

"They're gone? How is that possible?" the boy wondered to himself as he sat up and stared into black space where they had been only moments before.

"When it's evil versus evil and both are eliminated in the fight, the only winner is us," a familiar voice explained with a relieved sigh.

"YOU! You are not dead!" The boy could only stare in awe at the elvin stranger that was now sitting beside him.

"Not today," Rafar said simply as he brushed the dirt and ash from his cloak.

"But I saw the fire beast take you down. No one could have survived such an attack!" The boy watched in amazement as the elvin stranger picked himself off the ground and reached over to help him up.

"Do you believe me now?" Rafar asked.

The boy still could not believe his eyes as he studied the stranger before him. It was then he took notice of the staff in the elf's hands. "That is the Armament Stone! You are Rafar the Elder, a member of the Osarian Knights!" he exclaimed in astonishment as he took Rafar's hand. "I am sorry that I did not believe you, but it was said that the Osarian Knights had been killed when Lord Jarden sent the first wave.

"Wave?" Rafar's voice filled fear.

"It is the dark power of Lord Jarden. The wave consists of dark clouds of hot gas that will race across the countryside and scorch everything and everyone in its path. The first wave was sent at the end of Febro. The chaos that followed was crippling, and now rumor has it that another wave is overdue. This next wave might finish us for sure," the boy explained with a panic-stricken expression.

"Why do you say that?" Rafar turned back to the boy.

"Those who survived the last wave have been working with other elves to form the barrier of light. This barrier has lasted for two months strong, but the elvin people are exhausted. They will not survive another wave." The boy's voice was riddled with worry and fear for his comrades.

"Then I have come just in time." Rafar looked towards Shoshon with determination. "We will not abandon our kinsman at their most desperate hour.

"You will take me with?" Anticipation filled the boy's eyes as he gazed up at the prophet.

"And why not? I will need your help when we get to Shoshon," Rafar reasoned as he put a reassuring hand on the boy's shoulder. "Now it is clear that you have heard of me, but I cannot say that I have heard of you.

"I am Hosea of Roth." His eyes were filled with excitement for a moment but then saddened when he looked back to his home. "This… was where my family lived since the third age of the world.

"I am very sorry for your loss, Hosea." Rafar put a reassuring hand on Hosea's shoulder. "Although no amount of vengeance will bring them back, we can see to it that no more harm comes to our people." Rafar's words were hope-filled, but Hosea looked to the dark horizon and was dismayed.

"Lord Jarden has slaughtered thousands, and many more are in danger of perishing. It has been whispered that he has summoned the Draccen people from the realm of the Serrigen to march over

Andora to ensure that no one is spared after the next wave passes." As Hosea recalled the horrific events of the past few months, he gestured towards the eastern horizon. "How are we to defeat such evil?"

"In ancient times, the peoples of Andora looked to the sphinx for guidance and aid," Rafar reminisced.

"I was told the race of sphinx died out millennia ago," Hosea recalled.

"That is one way of putting it." Rafar lowered his head sadly.

"Then what defense do we have?" The boy looked at Rafar with worry.

Looking back at the brilliant light that emanated from Shoshon, Rafar felt the need of those suffering. "Me.

Hosea was a little puzzled, but he felt safe having the elder prophet near. Then before he could say anything in reply, there was a low and eerie rumble across the land. They both turned towards the eastern horizon and froze in fear at the sight of the coming horror.

"Is that the…?" Rafar stammered as he watched the black clouds boil over the eastern horizon.

"WAVE!" Hosea shouted as he whirled around and dashed down the road for Shoshon. "Hurry, we do not have much time before it reaches the city.

"Are the people ready for this yet?" Rafar called out as he quickly joined Hosea.

"I fear they are not." Hosea's expression was grim, and when they finally reached the grand city of Shoshon, it was discovered how right he was. One could easily see that the strength of the elvin people, who struggled to keep the barricade intact, was failing. "What can we do to aid them?.

Rafar saw panic in the people as they tried to brace themselves against the coming storm; even members of the royal family were standing side by side at the frontlines with the people. Prince Leondros Goldendragon and Princess Zation, along with the rest of their family, were struggling to help their friends keep up the barrier of light. The exhaustion in their faces matched the rest of the people's.

"Come, we must work quickly," Rafar spoke urgently as he ran towards the line of weary elves.

In the rush to reinforce the line with other elves that had made it into the city, a weary elf named Mahelia stumbled and fell. She fought to force her weary body back to the barrier, but her strength was spent. Seeing this out of the corner of his eye, Prince Leondros left his place in the line and scrambled over to help her. When he reached her, he noticed the dark wave was almost upon them. The barrier would collapse without them!

In the brief seconds, that remained before the wave enveloped the city, Leondros felt another pair of hands pull him and Mahelia to their feet and push them back into the line. Much to his sheer amazement, Leondros saw Rafar the Elder standing between him and Mahelia.

"Rafar! You have returned!" Leondros looked upon the elvin prophet with amazement and relief.

"In the nick of time, it would seem," Rafar offered kindly. "Hold on." In that moment, everyone held their breath and braced for what was to come. The fury of the dark storm quickly reached Shoshon; as the radiant light was blotted out, all went dark. The second wave sent by the ancient evil burnt the already-scorched land, turning everything into black glass. Yet for all its wrath, the second wave could not undo the unyielding power of the elves. When the dark wave subsided, the brilliant light from Shoshon broke through once again. The light from the city shone out even brighter—this was only surpassed by the cheers from the people within.

Following the second victory over the waves of darkness, Leondros, Zation, Rafar, Hosea, and many others began to help those worn to exhaustion from the wave.

"It is good to have you home again," Zation said as she hugged Rafar.

"We feared Sariff was the only one left," Leondros said with renewed hope as he welcomed his dear old friend with a hug.

"Does he live still?" Rafar had feared that since the letter, Sariff had met the same fate as Pryor, Saxon, and Enoch.

"He lives, but this war has taken its toll on him," Leondros explained with a growing tone of sadness as he motioned towards the center of town. Rafar followed his gaze and felt his heart hit rock bottom. Before the war, Shoshon center square was full of beauty and excitement, but now it was a makeshift morgue. Sensing the deep sadness within the prince, Rafar put his hand on his shoulder.

"You have my word: these will be the last days of darkness that our people will see in this age. Peace and happiness will come to Shoshon and Adarah again." Rafar's promise was heard by the many that gathered to listen, and their hope was renewed.

Later when Rafar and Hosea made it to the Temple of the Osarian Knights, Hosea was able to take in the grand sight within the temple. The walls were of the warmest mahogany, and the air within the long corridors was thick with the calming and relaxing scent of incense. It gave Hosea a feeling that he was safe from all evil. As he followed Rafar deep within the temple, he caught sight of a crest in the main temple underneath which a strange inscription was written.

"What does this crest represent?" he asked as he studied it closely.

Rafar turned and stopped still in his footsteps. He was silent as he looked upon the crest; when he finally spoke, there was immense reverence in his voice. "This is the crest of the Osarian Knights. The five smaller crests refer to the five prophets of the order and what their duty represents. The larger crest refers to Farro. We keep it to remember what took place so long ago.

"Who was Farro?" Hosea wondered as he turned to Rafar.

Although time was precious and the forces of evil were growing with every passing moment, Rafar knew that this story could not be forgotten. "Farro was a great and wise sphinx of the ancient world. This sphinx was guardian and protector of Berecyntia, the sphinx who held control over the order of the earth. During the fourth age of the world, there was a great battle between an evil creature from the distant land of Nod and Berecyntia. Although she was able to imprison this dark creature within the island of Pandera, Berecyntia had been fatally wounded and was not able to destroy this dark creature. In her last moments, she watched as the island was split into two, and the north half was turned into an icy, barren wasteland. Now it was on this half where the creature was imprisoned. Fearing for future generations in case of this evil's return, Berecyntia prayed that the world would know and remember how this evil should be defeated. Vowing to carry on Berecyntia's wish, Farro went forth and chose five noble persons to help carry on this legacy. They were told about how the ancient evil, named Lord Jarden, was imprisoned and how to defeat him should he ever arise again. Over the course of the age, these stories formed the code by which these five prophets lived. These prophets became known as the Osarian Knights. They had learned much from Farro in the ages that followed, but there was so much more our Order could have learned....

As Hosea listened with delight, he studied the crest on the wall. He could almost see the story of Farro as it happened. Then Rafar paused for a long moment. Turning back to him, Hosea saw immense grief in the prophet's face. "What happened?" he asked softly.

"In 8021, the race of men had grown bitter and jealous of the sphinx and had them annihilated for not turning over the secrets to their power. Farro was among the last to be executed. Fortunately, Farro sensed this dark time coming and prepared the Order. Since then, we have kept to our word, but it would seem that we are still learning..." As Rafar reached the end of his story, it was clear there was much sadness in his face. Then before he could utter anything more, something foul within the temple air caught his attention. In that short moment, his face lost expression as he turned towards the long, dark corridor just ahead of them.

"What is it?" Hosea studied his tanned face with realization.

"Evil tried to enter here, but it was stopped..." Rafar's voice faded once again as he marched towards the darkened corridor. Before passing under the archway of the corridor, he stopped and gazed at the floor. Kneeling down, he gently touched a spot of dark liquid spilt upon the marble floor and examined it.

"Blood?" Hosea guessed as he stepped up to Rafar.

"Whatever stopped this evil did not do so without being severely injured," Rafar detected as he studied the surroundings in the hall; then as he looked down the hall, some terrible realization came to him. "COME!" he gasped as he raced down the corridor. Following closely behind his new companion, Hosea was led through a series of tunnels and staircases and corridors. Finally, after many turns, Rafar made one last turn through a large pair of doors that led into a grand library and came to a sudden stop. Skidding to a stop himself, Hosea managed to stop before colliding into Rafar. They both saw a disheartening scene lying before them.

There, in the peaceful solitude of the dim library, a white-haired elf lay unmoved in a pool of dark liquid. Hosea stood frozen for a minute as Rafar rushed towards the motionless body. Gently turning the wounded elf on his back, Rafar quickly came to the sad conclusion that his companion would not last the night.

"Sariff? Can you hear me?" Rafar pleaded as he began to dress some of his friend's wounds with his own robe.

"Please...do not bother." Sariff's voice was a raspy whisper. "I will be dead soon enough." The cold bitterness of reality was written in the prophet's pale face as he slowly sat up with Rafar's help. Yet in spite of being mortally wounded, he did not wear an expression of defeat. "The ancient evil was most clever... He tried to have his minions secretly overtake the temple, but they failed..." Sariff pointed towards the broken library windows. The view from the broken windows revealed the interior courtyard of gardens and granite walkways on which hundreds of ash piles were neatly laid. "The task of defeating Lord Jarden...is now left to you, my friend...but there is one last thing I must do...," he managed to utter.

"You have done all that was asked of you and so much more. What more is there to be done?" Rafar tried to lift his dying friend's burden.

"The people...," Sariff replied weakly. He closed his eyes for a moment as if to allow a period of intense pain to pass. "The dark lord is sending a third and final wave...and this time...the weary souls of this city...will not be able to hold it back.

"Then let me help, my friend." Rafar could not let his wounded friend do this task alone.

"Help the people...by getting rid of this darkness," Sariff insisted earnestly as he put a reassuring, bloodied hand on Rafar's shoulder.

"Then please let my friend Hosea help you." Rafar gestured sympathetically.

Sariff turned his gaze to the elvin boy and managed a smile. "There is promise in your eyes...I am honored." Taking another labored breath, he turned his gaze back to Rafar. "Before you go...there is something that you need to know." Rising to his feet with both Rafar and Hosea's help, Sariff made his way over to the study area. On a particular table lay dozens of scrolls, manuscripts, and parchments. Shifting aside some of the clutter, the ailing prophet found a map and laid it out for all to see.

"What is this madness?" Rafar managed to say as he stared in horror at the newly designed map before him.

"This is what has become of our beloved Andora... The minions of darkness call it...Goratha. I guess it is rightly named...for this new dark realm lies under a sheet of darkness, ruin, and blood," Sariff explained softly.

"How did it come to this?" Rafar shook his head and stared in disbelief at the drawing of the black continent before him.

"It was over...before we realized it began." Sariff hung his head shamefully. "This evil was most deceptive...for he disguised himself as a minion of light." He lifted his head to Rafar, and his expression of shame was replaced with urgency. "What is important now...is taking back our home.

Inspired by Sariff's words, Rafar looked passed the broken windows and towards the dark eastern horizon. As he began to form a plan of action, he caught sight of the people outside the temple walls. As an elf, he felt the weight of their weariness and pain. Turning his gaze, he saw the prince and princess as well as their family, offering aid to the multitude that surrounded them, although exhausted themselves. Feeling the burden of their need, Rafar was driven to fight for them.

"This will end soon. I promise," he said as he turned, picking up his knapsack and heading for the door.

"Rafar... Wait!" Sariff rasped. "Beware of the dark creatures that roam the countryside. Their hunger for carnage is unquenchable.

Rafar nodded in understanding, but before he could turn to leave, Hosea walked up to him with an expression of worry.

"What is to become of me?" the elvin boy wondered with a tone of uncertainty.

"Help Sariff protect the people. Watch over them until I return." Rafar's instructions gave Hosea hope.

"You will return?" he asked enthusiastically.

"I need to teach you the laws of Farro. The Order of Osarian Knights must not end with me. Future generations have to be taught Farro's valuable wisdom," Rafar explained with a warm smile as he put a reassuring hand on Hosea's shoulder.

"HA! He is too stubborn to die," Sariff piped up as he joined them.

Rafar smiled as he turned to his dear companion and took the elf's hand. "Until we meet again, my brother, peace be unto thee." Both prophets gave a humble bow to each other, after which Rafar took his leave of them.

As he journeyed beyond the border of Shoshon's light, Rafar felt the cold chill of evil and darkness surround him. The menacing howl of the wind tore at him, and signs of a third wave were presenting themselves. Turning his back on the city of light, Rafar prayed for his people, that they might be spared the horrible atrocity of this next wave. Feeling the weight of his mission now before him, Rafar pushed deeper into the dark wilderness and plotted a course that would take him far into the Adarahian and Shandel wilderness.

In the time that followed Rafar's departure, Sariff was able to take a few hours with Hosea and tell him of the history and importance of the Osarian Knights.

"Over the ages, people from all across the realm of Andora have questioned the Order. They call us false prophets and say that this mysterious being called Farro was truly a demon sent to destroy the world. In spite of all the harsh treatment we endured, we continue to remain faithful.

"What telling fact keeps you strong in your faith? I mean, what was it about this creature Farro that moved you to such belief?" Hosea wondered as he looked over several sacred scrolls supposedly written by the legendary sphinx.

Sariff took a moment to reflect as he slowly turned to the window and closed his eyes to gather his strength.

"The night Farro died; there was such turmoil and chaos. An army of men from the Shandel seized all sphinxes and sent them to concentration camps located deep within the plains of the Barrens. Many were horribly beaten, some burnt alive, others..." Sariff's voice failed as it went hoarse with pain as images of that night haunted him. "Many of our people rushed the camps and tried to stop this atrocity, but the race of men was blinded by greed and quickly snuffed out the ancient race. In their rush to exterminate the sphinx, many elves, myself included, stormed the camps and tried to free those that were still alive. I searched for dear friends of mine that had been taken, but in my search, I found Farro instead. In the chaos of people fighting around us, Farro pushed a woman named Anyi into my arms and told me to get her out and keep her safe. The survival of our world depended on it. Then, seconds after that was said, Farro was taken and executed before our very eyes. We could only watch in horror from the other side of the fences as all other sphinxes were silenced. Those of us who remained nearby were forced to prove ourselves as elves. Several were killed because of lack of proof. However, those responsible for this outrage were quickly seized by armies of elves and men. The high kings and queens from both Adarah and the Shandel came to order the proper punishment. All responsible were sentenced to live out their remaining years on plantation farms. Solitary confinement would be their demon in life unto death." Sariff lowered his head to gather his thoughts. "The woman that Farro saved was the wife of Reymier of the Shandon, the judge and counselor for the high king of Adarah. It was said that she would bear a child that would be the key to salvation.

"I mean no offense, but what hope is there? Farro died...," Hosea started to say but was cut off.

"Farro's last words to me were '*I will return one day to free all peoples of this realm—believe in that…,*'" Sariff said with surprising strength. "I will never see that day, but I still believe. The sphinxes of the ancient world were a source of love and compassion, and when they were slain, much of that magic was lost. Today, our world only has vague reminders of such things, but I believe that a time is coming when love and compassion return with the sound of trumpets and a demonstration of true love and compassion that will stun the multitude. *That* is why I am moved to believe." As Sariff retold his account of the horrible night, he led Hosea down a grand torchlit hall. They came to two large doors at the end of the hall, and as Sariff opened them, Hosea beheld a most breathtaking sight.

"This is the chamber of the five swords. This is the cornerstone on which the Osarian Knights were founded and why we keep to our oath," Sariff began as he entered the large, dark marbled chamber, walked to the center of the room, stood before a magical display, and bowed his head for a long moment. Hosea stood in awe at the column of light that shone down from the ceiling and illuminated a large round altar built of white limestone. In the air, hovering just above the altar, were five golden swords that gently rotated clockwise over the altar. The detailing on the swords was exquisite and fascinating. Each sword had a symbol and a name etched into the metal: *Baron, Oracle, Cipher, Armament, and Marshall.*

As Hosea moved around the altar stone, he stopped at an inscription that was carved into the white limestone altar.

> *"Let the knowledge and magic of the fourth age of our world not be forgotten so that during dark times it will be at your side as will these swords. Let these weapons as well as your love and compassion protect those who call Andora home.*
>
> *Farro – Seventh day of Mayen,*
> *In the year of 4025*
> *During the Age of Enchantment*

"Farro built this?" Hosea asked, dumbfounded.

Sariff smiled and looked up at the glowing swords. "After the dark lord was defeated in 4021 and most of Andora was restored to its former splendor, Farro vowed that the knowledge and magic used to save a multitude from this evil would not be forgotten; and so five elfin prophets were chosen and entrusted to help carry on this legacy. This knowledge became their law, for they all had to be keen of sense when the time came to encounter evil again. Farro taught us that this knowledge was most sacred, and only those chosen as the prophets' replacements would learn of it.

"Us? You were one of the original five prophets!" Hosea exclaimed with astonishment.

"Farro taught Rafar and me much before...," Sariff tried to reply, but his voice failed him. He laid a gentle hand on the inscription in the limestone. "Afterwards, we truly understood, for the first time, how important Farro's mission was to preserve this knowledge. We embraced it, and thus the Order of Osarian Knights was created.

Sheer silence filled the room in which they stood for a moment; Hosea felt foolish for doubting this master. When he tried to utter an apology, his words were stolen away by a great shaking of the earth! Dust and debris fell around them as they staggered around.

"An earthquake? Here?" Hosea cried in panic.

Sariff waited and listened for a moment. Then, without warning, the violent shaking ceased. The silence that filled the room was far from peaceful. There was an unsettling, eerie feeling in the surrounding air. Sariff turned to a window and narrowed his gaze. It was in that moment he realized what was upon them. "No worse...come. I will need your help.

Together, they rushed through the temple and out into the city. The people around them were filled with fear and panic as they picked themselves up from the earthquake. Some of the people cursed at Sariff as he made his way to the edge of the city; others pleaded with him for answers. He said nothing but remained calm and kept moving. When Sariff and Hosea finally reached the barrier of light, they found Prince Leondros and his twin sister.

"Prince Leondros, I am going to need you and your sister's help," Sariff asked with a calm, but urgent tone.

"What can we do?" Prince Leondros asked as he was joined by Princess Zation.

"Tell all the people to gather in the center of the city, including those who stand in the barrier." Sariff's words took everyone by shock. "What is coming cannot be held back by our brethren—I must meet this alone," Sariff gently explained.

Prince Leondros took notice of the wounds that would claim the prophet's life. "You are gravely injured—surely there is another way.

"There is…I could do nothing." Sariff's point was made. Leondros nodded in understanding. "Farewell, my friends." He humbly bowed before the prince and princess; however as he stood up, they returned their gesture in a hug. When they finally let go of him, he spotted Hosea standing nearby with a longing expression. "I suppose you too?.

Hosea smiled and gently wrapped his arms around Sariff. "I will keep your belief alive." When he let go of the prophet, an expression of understanding passed between them. Then Sariff took one last look at his friends and turned and walked beyond the boundary of the city.

In the moments that followed, everyone watched in breathless silence as another wave, even more threatening than the previous two waves, came at the city. They watched as Sariff raised his arms towards the heavens as the dark angry clouds engulfed the prophet and bore down on Shoshon. What came to pass no one within this grand city had ever seen. Just as the wave reached the city limits, a magical explosion of light and sound came from deep within the wave. This magical blue light soon enveloped the entire dark wave and blew it back across the charged landscape whence it came. Daylight broke through the clouds and warmed the countryside.

Cheers erupted from within the city as the people celebrated the victory over the waves of darkness. The blue magic of Sariff went beyond Adarah and washed over the lands of Andora, healing the earth scorched by evil's magic. However, when the blue light faded, a hush fell over the crowd, for it was felt by all that the elvin prophet Sariff was gone.

Joining Hosea's gaze, Prince Leondros and Princess Zation looked out towards the east. There remained a darkness looming on the horizon. "What of the ancient evil?" Leondros wondered.

"Rafar journeys to stop him. Let us pray he is successful, for he is the last knight of the Osarian Order empowered to stop such evil." Hosea's words were felt by all who gathered near. The elvin people once stood together against the darkness; now they stood in prayer to pray their knight home again.

Crossing over a ridge and looking out at the dismal wasteland before him, Rafar could not tell if he had actually passed beyond the border, for the landscape was the same. The entire countryside had been turned into black glass as ash gathered like sand dunes in the distance. Then he came to a stone pillar and managed a sigh of relief, for they were markers to signify the border of Adarah. Setting his course for the northeastern horizon, he continued his journey with all haste. Only, before he could make another mile, everything went suddenly silent. Looking around, Rafar felt his blood run cold. There, just in front of him, came another dark wave, but this one looked far more intense.

"Dear God!" he gasped as he braced himself within a western-facing cave and waited. It took only seconds for the wave to pass over him and continue towards Shoshon. "Lord, watch over my friends." He felt frozen as he watched the third wave reach the capital city. He closed his eyes in prayer—only what came next was beyond what he expected. Moments later, Rafar watched a radiant blue wave wash over the entire countryside and continue on east. The aftermath of this wave delighted Rafar immensely. It had reversed the treachery that burned the land black. The land was as he remembered it and in some ways better.

Turning his gaze back to the eastern horizon, Rafar saw the dark clouds over the Shandel get even darker as thunder cracked overhead. "It looks as if our message has been received—lucky me." He took a deep breath and pressed on, even deeper into the gloom of the Shandel.

On the third night of his journey, Rafar camped at the edge of the plains of Golasand. He looked out over the plains to the southeast with the mountains of the Serrigen to the north. It was a grand sight, even with the darkened clouds hanging overhead. As he meditated, Rafar received a vision. He saw the earth brought to its end as darkness welcomed the dawn of a new age. He caught a glimpse of what awaited this realm and had to turn away. Awakening from the vision, Rafar jumped to his feet and turned his gaze to the eastern horizon. He was enraged and refused to sleep. Looking to the tallest mountain on the Zabor Mountain Range, Rafar saw the glow of torches on its slopes. He wanted to rush with all haste and confront the dark lord, but he was hesitant as he studied the dark plains below him. It was through a narrowed gaze and with great concentration that Rafar was able to see the plains of Golasand covered with armies of Lord Jarden's creatures.

"How nice—you even had a welcoming party all ready for me." Rafar smiled and prepared to counter this obstacle. However, before he had a chance to move forward with his plan, a terrible sense of dread came over him. In the light of his campfire, he caught a glimpse of an unnerving sight lurking in the shadows. It was Damacos, a fearful beast from the underworld that is part shadow and part something else, something only talked about in myths from the first age of evil. Now Rafar had the chance to fight one.

The awe of such a meeting caused Rafar to be hesitant. This was all the time needed for the creature to strike—and that it did. It lashed at Rafar with its bony tail; but for all its accuracy, it missed. Just as it intended to strike, the Damacos was hit broadside by a large gold blur. The creature tumbled backwards; but when it managed to collect itself to attack again, a pair of powerful jaws clamped down on its skeletal neck and shattered it. The Damacos let out a muffled wail as it vanished.

"KIYA!" Rafar gasped in utter surprise as he stared in disbelief at the gold dragon standing before him.

"I hoped I might find you here," she said with a relieved sigh.

"Why on earth have you ventured so far from home?" He was beside himself with concern.

"There was a rumor amongst the other dragons that you were going to face a dark creature from the ancient world. It was also said that this creature brought Andora to ruin in only a few short years. I could not possibly stay in paradise while you were alone in such a battle." The compassion in Kiya's voice melted Rafar's anxiety.

"I could say it was most unwise for you to follow me here, but that would be a lie. This battle cannot be won by a single individual. I am glad that you have come," Rafar replied gratefully as he walked up to Kiya. Only, before he could reach out to hug her, he was whisked up into the air. He then found himself staring right into her green eyes. They glistened with tears.

"You saved my kind from extinction—now let me return the kindness." She gazed across the dark valley towards the glowing mountain.

"I gladly accept," Rafar managed in a rough whisper as he wrapped his arms around her nose and held her tight. The tenderness of the moment was quickly lost when a loud crack of thunder echoed out over the plains, and the lights on the mountain glowed even brighter.

"The dark lord grows impatient," Rafar noted as he studied the mountain.

"Then it is best not to keep him waiting." She carefully placed Rafar on her back and took to the sky with all haste. As they sailed through the air over the dark valley, Rafar breathed a sigh of relief as he looked upon all the creatures he might have had to confront. Then, before he could look back to the mountain, Kiya let out a wailing roar of agony!

"KIYA!" he screamed as he feverishly looked to see the cause of her pain, but it was too late. They were on a crash course into the glowing mountain! In the last moments before colliding with the face of the mountain, Kiya was able to set down upon the summit without causing harm to her rider. "Kiya!" Rafar cried as he scrambled to aid her, but the young dragon took her last breath and was gone. In his frantic search, Rafar stopped in his tracks as his heart crashed into his stomach. A giant spear pierced her chest, went through her heart, and stuck out her back. Collapsing to the ground, Rafar wept bitterly as he clung to her neck.

"There must have been a strong bond between you and the dragon for her to save your life, even after she was dead," a strange voice spoke up from nearby, but Rafar cared not.

"More than mere words could describe." Rafar placed a gentle hand on her head and prayed that her spirit may find peace.

"I despise such things," the voice hissed.

Finally collecting himself, Rafar rose and turned to the being behind him. It was a cloaked figure, but as it walked into the light, he saw a horrific image of the Shandel's old advisor, Randye. His body was badly decayed as flesh hung from his bones.

"What is it that you seek besides dominating our realm and making it devoid of all life?" Rafar asked angrily as the grief of Kiya's death fueled his rage to confront this dark foe.

"Domination will only be the start. I am preparing this realm for a glorious dawning." Lord Jarden's voice filled with excitement and anticipation.

"The dawn of ruling a dead realm?" Rafar eyed the dark lord coldly.

"You have wisdom, but no imagination," Lord Jarden sneered. "I am merely a scout in the eyes of my kind, but they look to me with hope. I have been sent to make this realm ready for their coming." Lord Jarden's news coincided with Rafar's vision.

"Why Andora? Why not be content with your own realm?" Rafar tried to find a point of reasoning.

"Our realm cannot support our mass numbers. Your realm was the weakest—thus, the struggle to take it over would be less time-consuming," Lord Jarden continued with a sense of superiority.

"Life means nothing to you, does it?" Rafar felt infuriated by this being's senselessness.

"Why should it? My people are not amongst the living, but then we can use them for our own purposes." Lord Jarden looked towards the western horizon and glared at the bright light coming from it. "Those who refuse to die for us will be taken to our world and sold.

"Not if my kind have anything to say about it!" Rafar retorted angrily as he pulled out his trusted sword, the Sword of Armament.

"Your kind does not worry me." Lord Jarden's simple reply drove Rafar to attack.

The battle between these two extreme forces was nothing short of Armageddon. Mountains crumbled, deep gorges were formed in the Shandel's landscape, and many of the dark lord's minions were caught in the middle of the massive battle. Their battle reached as far as to the Sea of Naira. Then in the last moment, when Rafar was on the verge of claiming total victory, Lord Jarden inflicted a fatal injury on Rafar and sent him to the depths of the sea. In spite of the excruciating pain of his chest wound, Rafer he refused to let his people be tortured and sold into slavery. Summoning the last of his strength, Rafar emerged from the sea and sent a radiant ball of energy into the dark lord. An ear-piercing shriek of agony cut through the air as Lord Jarden fell from the ridge overlooking the coast and landed on Zendro Peninsula.

No longer possessing the strength to destroy this great evil, Rafar had one plan of action. With his remaining moments of consciousness, he walked over to the paralyzed dark lord.

"Your world will have to wait a while longer before you can dominate us," declared Rafar, glaring at Lord Jarden. The evil being remained defiant.

"It matters not. I will escape—and when I return, none of your kind will be able to stop me. Best of all, none of your pathetic knights will be around to teach others. I will…" Lord Jarden's ranting had severed Rafar's last nerve. Using the last of his magical power given to him by Farro, he created a deep chasm on Zendro Peninsula and entombed the ancient evil in solid granite. Then he engraved an incantation of warning on the stone blocking the tomb so no mere commoner could accidentally set this evil loose again. This incantation was made in the language of the sphinx. It was, sadly, on the verge of being a dead language—thus, no one in the distant future would remember it. After all that had been done to ensure this ancient darkness was sealed far away from the world, Rafar still felt uneasy about this lingering evil; so he climbed from the chasm and caused an earthquake to separate Zendro from the rest of Andora. When the land crumbled into the sea, Rafar was caught in a landslide and was buried underneath the waters of the new harbor!

When the earth was still once again, evil's grip was broken. The dark magic that had held Andora and her peoples prisoner was undone, and the hellish minions of the dark lord were sent back to the underworld. Although the land of Andora had been restored by the great prophet Sariff, the land of Lani remained charred. While Andora remained whole, this charred remnant would be forever known as the Barrens.

As a multitude raised their voices in celebration over the defeat of Lord Jarden, there were still a small few who could not celebrate yet, for their victory was not complete. They watched, waited, and prayed for their dear friend to return home to them.

In the days that followed the defeat of Lord Jarden, life for many of Andora's people was better than most had hoped. Many of the loved ones thought to be dead returned home again. Celebrations were held to honor the elvin prophet, Rafar the Elder, for defeating the ancient evil. In addition to the festivities, it was announced that every one hundred years from that time hence, such celebrations would take place so as to not forget what had been done for the people of Andora.

Yet, for all the joy and happiness that could be felt, there was also grief. Some loved ones did not return home. Among the many lost, it was widely believed that Rafar was one of these lost souls. Hosea dwelt within the Temple of the Osarian Knights, uncertain what to do next—but something deep down told him that he had not seen the last of the great master Rafar.

Far from the white city of Shoshon lay the newly formed island of Zendro. The waters that surrounded the isle were turbulent and dangerous. Nature herself protected the island from curious spectators that might try to venture upon it. As the rough waters that would later become known as the Bay of Panthea crashed upon the Shandel's northeastern shore, they brought with them a body.

Somehow, reality became real again, and Rafar opened his eyes to the world. Although he was gravely wounded, something spurred him to rise to his feet and return home. When he turned and looked out over the new bay and saw the misty isle of Zendro, he was able to breathe a little easier. However, something bothered him about the ancient evil's last words to him.

"...I will escape—and when I return, none of your kind will be able to stop me. Best of all, none of your pathetic knights will be around to teach others. I will..."

In his pondering, Rafar received a vision of future times. It was a glimpse of the future without the knowledge of Farro. The sight of the horror before him caused Rafar to fall to his knees as tears ran down his face. The realm of Andora had been reduced to a burning wasteland. It was here that millions lay dead and decomposing. Hellish creatures feasted upon their remains. As he reeled from the atrocities before him, he caught another heartwrenching sight. He watched as those remaining of the Goldendragon house rushed to reach the kingdom of the Shandel. Grief and desperation filled the faces of King Doran and Princess Zation as they raced for Akendron. Their journey took them deep inside the broken castle of Avdima; their journey ended tragically. Zation sank to her knees and wept uncontrollably as she looked up at the body of her brother, Prince Leondros, hanging before them. He had been horribly beaten and left to die as he hung by his wrists in the cold, damp tower cell. King Doran and Princess Zation were captured and taken to the dark realm of Lord Jarden's people.

The treacherous rule of Lord Jarden was merely the laying of the foundation for his people, who came to Andora's shores and settled upon the graves of the many that died, and renamed the realm Goratha. The dark lord then gave his rule over to his king, thus sealing the realm's fate forever.

Awaking from his nightmarish vision, Rafar realized he could not leave the world yet. There was one last thing he needed to do.

"Lord, grant me strength to live long enough to pass on my wisdom." Rafar closed his eyes, took a labored breath, then climbed to his feet and set out from Adarah.

Two weeks had passed since Hosea had watched Rafar leave to confront the ancient evil. He had put his time into looking through old texts and studying some of the history of the Order, but many of the texts were in other languages that he could not read. He also took time to watch over the city and was surprised that hardly a trace of the darkness was visible.

Then late one evening as Hosea turned down the lights within the temple, there was a knock at the door. He stood still for a moment wondering if he had actually heard it. When the knock sounded again, Hosea took a lamp and hurried through a corridor and down several flights of stairs before coming to the front temple doors. As he opened the doors, the light from his lamp fell upon the road-weary stranger standing on the landing. When Hosea looked upon the stranger, he dropped the lamp in sheer shock.

"I know my appearance must be something of a shock, but seriously…," Rafar said humbly as he leaned heavily upon his walking stick.

"Forgive me, my lord!" Hosea exclaimed as he collected the fallen lamp and reached out to assist his master. In his hurry, Hosea caught sight of the fatal wound that would claim his master's life.

"Please, 'Rafar' will be fine. I will not be around long enough to have need of such a title." Rafar spoke with a weak voice, but it was still gentle and kind. When they walked to a room where Rafar could sit from his journey, he looked to Hosea. "There is something you need to do for me now.

"Yes, anything," Hosea replied eagerly for he was glad to have his friend back again.

"I will need for you to write something down, and then there is something you must learn. It is dire that what you write be kept safe at all costs. Now hurry—my time is nearly spent," Rafar instructed as he rested his sore back against the chair.

In the next few hours, Hosea was made a knight of the Osarian Order and entrusted with their knowledge as well as the vision foreseen by Rafar. As it was told to him, Hosea wrote down the vision into five separate scrolls. They were to be kept secret, for if the minions of evil ever learned of them, the future of Andora would be at stake. These scrolls were to give the people of Andora hope, but this was only if a child from an ancient realm survived long enough to read the scrolls. If not, then the third age of evil would begin and bring about a world so horrible that no nightmare could describe it.

Then, during the midnight hour, Rafar and Hosea sought council with Reymier and Anyi of the Shandon. In spite of the late hour, they were glad to see their dear old friend and his apprentice. They were given one of the five scrolls. A scroll was given to Reymier's father, Teloan. The remaining scrolls were secretly concealed within the vast realm of Andora. A fifth scroll would be entrusted to King Doran. They pledged never to speak of these scrolls as Rafar insisted. Before they took leave to return to the temple, Rafar was able to speak with Anyi.

"I foresee you having a beautiful daughter. Guard her well, for one day she will save a multitude and a son of the elvin realm." His words were pleasing to hear but held much deeper meaning for the future.

In the days following Rafar the Elder's death and burial, Hosea of Roth took a pilgrimage to the Shandel's southeastern forests. The mission before him required him to keep the knowledge of the Osarian Order alive and the prophecy safe. He would journey forth, build a new temple, and recruit four other wise and trustworthy souls to rebuild the Order. Along with him, Hosea took the first scroll of the ancient prophecy, a letter from Rafar, and the swords of the Order. They were to be hidden and only revealed to the next man, elf, or dwarf that would replace him.

Crossing the border between Adarah and the Shandel, Hosea gazed at the green, lush fields and forests that ran on for as far as the eye could see. He breathed in the sweet smells of the earth and gladly took in the wonder of the landscape before him; but, still, the image of the devastation that charred the earth was still fresh in his mind. He remembered some of Rafar's last words, which still haunted his mind. *"Today peace prevails and though the darkness still lingers and will search for a way to bring our world to ruin, we will be defiant, we will press on with steadfast trust…for our hope will return!"* In that thought alone, a wave of determination came upon him.

"Rafar, the lesson of the great sphinx, Farro, will never be forgotten, and the evil will never see his kinsmen take over this realm—on this promise, I swear." Then setting out again, Hosea entered the land of the Shandel as a soft breeze found him. A time of peace was at hand, but preparation for what was to come would begin, for there lingered a shadow in their future, but also a great hope.

A Word from Sala of Antioch

They call me Sala of Antioch. I am a member of the sacred society known as the Osarian Knights, and the story I am about to relate has to be told, for if history is not passed on to others, it will be forgotten.

At the beginning of the eleventh age, my order sensed that a time of great unrest and strife was at hand. Our world has known evil times before, but none such as what was to come, so much so that we have named the age "Phoenix": although we fear what is to come, we have faith that we shall rise from it.

The evil of which I speak overtook Andora during the third and tenth ages of our world, slaughtering all in its path and claiming the lives of nearly one-third of Andora's population. This evil would have continued to spread its wrath, but Adalai, the Lord of the heavens, summoned a warrior from each age to stop it. The first was a sphinx known as Berecyntia. She imprisoned the dark spirit on an island, which later became known as Ice Isle. The second was Rafar, an elfin prophet and trusted member of my order. After their great battle, Rafar banished and imprisoned the evil to Zendro Isle.

Although I am now the only remaining member of my order, it was beyond a comfort to know that Andora has been safe and at peace since that time. The evil remains locked away in the depths of the earth, where it waits to be unleashed back into the world. I fear this evil will return from its long imprisonment to hunt our children. At the beginning of this age, there are very few who can repel such darkness, but I continue to have faith...

Chapter 1

Seer's Warning

Peace and prosperity once again flourished throughout the realm of Andora. All memory of death, darkness, and evil had faded over the course of nine centuries and now only vague stories of such things existed. A sparse few still remembered the tales of old, for these things had been written in scrolls and passed on from one generation to the next. Sadly, most of these existing documents had been destroyed in fires over the course of the age. Now only two known archives still existed. One remained hidden within the elfin kingdom of Adarah; the other was protected by a sacred and mysterious order known as the Osarian Knights. It was clear to many that during such an extended time of peace, the people cared not for knowledge about distant and dark times. Yet what if the ancient darkness returned? Would anyone take heed of such warning? Or would pride and ignorance be humanity's undoing?

—◈◆◈—

Age of the Phoenix
Juna 10, 10021

Looking down from a stone balcony that was perched upon one of Avdima's highest towers was good King Alabaster. His athletic build and strong form stood tall against the railing made of sparkling gray granite, and his deep brown eyes looked out over the city below. The evening breeze lightly blew at his shoulder-length dark-brown and gray hair. It also found the long tails of his burgundy robe and cream-colored sash and gently tousled them. His dark-brown eyes stoically gazed upon the beautiful lights that emanated from the city below. Deep in thought, King Alabaster could all too easily remember what his kingdom was like before the scene that now played out before him. He had often stood here over the long course of his reign, dwelling on the troubles that plagued his kingdom. This night, though, was much different. Marveling at the sights and sounds that were coming from the streets, Alabaster could hear the wondrous sounds of laughter, rejoicing, and music filling the city once again. The shops and the markets along all the city streets within Akendron were decorated with colorful banners and streamers of reds, purples, golds, and other brilliant colors.

As the crowd within the streets hustled back and forth between the shops near the castle, Alabaster noticed a flute player, dressed in a dark-purple and white tunic with a purple turban that almost covered his curly red hair; though it sat slightly tilted on his head, it never distracted his focus as he slowly weaved his way throughout the crowd playing his aged wooden flute. The kindness that shone from the flute player's freckled face was reflected in his music, which seemingly could lift any burdened spirit. People walked by him and smiled wistfully as they admired the beautiful, harmonious music. Several small peasant children ran from the crowd to play around him; they laughed and played to the fast rhythm of the tune played with the greatest of ease. The mood that existed amongst those who passed by the flute player was festive and enchanted.

The king again sighed in relief. Too many long years had passed where the only sounds he heard were the cries of starving children within the city and around the Shandel. Drought, pestilence, and conflict ran rampant throughout his kingdom for nearly fifty long years as he struggled to bring aid to his suffering people. Food became so scarce that people had little choice but to feed on horses, mules, and other livestock. Fear grew as rampant as hunger. Rumors of overthrowing the royal family were everywhere. Breathing in the warm evening breeze, Alabaster thanked Adalai, the Lord of the heavens, for the hundred-years' miracle rains that were first received in Janyay and continued to bless the lands of the Shandel. These miraculous rains first occurred in the year of Rafar's death and had repeated every one hundred years since. These special rains were more than a usual passing shower, for they brought great bounty to the harvests of the farmers and plantations so hunger and need were scarce.

It was late, past the hour of ten as Alabaster continued to observe the festive celebrations in the streets below. Other gifted musicians had joined the flute player, and soon their boisterous music caused those who listened to dance in the streets. It was a wondrous sight to behold. King Alabaster took delight in seeing the people laugh, play, and dance. Then, out of the corner of his eye, he caught a glimpse of his son and daughters dancing in the streets with the people. Prince Alon-Settie and Princesses Minta and Kosta were a delight, not only to him and Queen Elanza but also to the people of the Shandel. The two princesses bore a strong resemblance to their mother; their radiant green eyes, ivory skin, and ebony-black hair made them the talk of the kingdom. Princesses Minta and Kosta greatly cared for the people and brought to them much happiness through their tireless efforts. The king was very proud of his children for playing such an active role in the people's lives. However, it was Prince Alon-Settie who had worked especially hard in helping the people recover from the many years of famine. The prince, who looked like a young Alabaster, had earned the respect and gratitude of his people and peers. The title of "king" was not far from his grasp. Smiling as he breathed in the warm Juna air, Alabaster lifted his gaze to take in the splendor of Akendron and the lush realm surrounding her gates.

"Nearly four hundred years have passed, and the Tabor line lives on," Alabaster proudly reflected on his family lineage and the accomplishments spanning nearly half a millennium. "Lord, please bless my family and lead us into the next age of the world," he prayed. As he did so, he did not know what events had already been set in motion.

Still lost in the excitement that went on in the streets below, Alabaster did not hear someone slip into the room. Soft footsteps quickly came up behind him as the shadowy figure took hold of a heavy object and raised it high overhead. Crack! The sharp sound echoed throughout the room. Alabaster's thoughts raced with alarm as he whirled around and caught sight of his beautiful queen. Elanza stood still, watching him with a calm but loving expression. On the floor beside her was a heavy leather-bound book.

"Good Lord!" he gasped as leaned back against the window ledge. "Please can you warn someone before you scare the life out of them?" he pleaded, but this was an old argument that he could never win. She only smiled as she stepped up to him and kissed his slightly tanned cheek.

"What, and take all the fun out of seeing your beyond-terrified expression? I would not dream of doing something so drastic." As Elanza spoke, her soulful green eyes glistened with delight. Alabaster slowly relaxed as his smile returned. He could not help but gaze at her beauty, which was only accented by the beauty of her dark-green and gold-laced gown. Her raven hair was streaked with slight locks of silver, highlighting her cream-colored face and green eyes. The delicate gold crown studded with diamonds that she wore sparkled in the chamber's torchlight. Returning his smile, Elanza reached out, wrapped her arms around him, and held him tight. Together they turned their gaze to the lively city streets below. As Alabaster rested his head against hers, he thought how lucky he was to have someone so special. Most people of nobility would never pay a moment's interest to a commoner, but Alabaster remained ever thankful that he had broken with tradition when he chose Elanza to be his bride.

"If someone told me a year ago that today we would be celebrating the Year of the Great Dragon with harmonious festivities, I would have flogged them for telling such a cold-hearted joke," Elanza said as she shook her head with disbelief.

"You are too hard on yourself. We endured many long years of famine and plague without respite. Those years were tough on everyone. Someone would have flogged that person long before you could have gotten to them," he offered reassuringly as he held her tight.

Smiling, Elanza breathed in the scent of a cool breeze thick with rain as it blew through the window. It brought back a memory from her childhood. "When I was a child, I would see it rain, but Mother would tell me of the miracle rains that occurred every one hundred years. I always dreamed that I would live to see it, but I never imagined that the Shandel could be so green and beautiful," she said.

"It is indeed," Alabaster replied as he sighed in relief. He could not put to words how great it was to have peace and tranquility back in his land again. It was a perfect moment. Lowering his gaze into the lively street below, Alabaster watched the people dance merrily with each other. Judging by the boisterous feeling that hung over the crowd, King Alabaster thought it seemed impossible to think that these people had endured fifty long years of pain and suffering. Looking amongst all the smiling and happy faces, Alabaster saw one face that caught his attention.

A haggard old man dressed in tattered sackcloth slowly walked down the street toward the crowd. His features were rough and worn, and his wild gray hair signified that he had lived among the wilderness, but his facial expression stole the lingering heat from the night air. This gray-bearded old man walked with a staff that came up to his chin. Although he stopped and took notice of the crowd, he was not interested in the festivities going on around him. He searched the crowd for something specific until he finally lifted his gaze to the castle and fixed them on Alabaster and Elanza. His dark eyes held their gaze as his face changed into a look of warning. The old man's expression was so intense that soon Alabaster and Elanza did not see or even hear the pandemonium from the surrounding crowd. Then it was that the old man began to shout at the top of his lungs so that all who surrounded him could hear. People who stood nearby looked upon him in great alarm.

"You saw the end of those dear to me. Now it is your time at its end. I tell you this: the Evil is coming..."

A wave of fear washed over Alabaster's form as he felt his whole world crash in around him. The old man's raspy voice uncovered a deeply hidden dread. Looking down at his wife, they exchanged looks of horror.

"What does he mean?" she asked with an unsettled tone in her voice.

Alabaster looked back at the old man only to find that he had vanished. Searching the crowd wildly, he could not find any trace of the old man.

"Alabaster? Alabaster, what is it?" Elanza asked again with worry as she firmly took his muscular arm.

"I-I have seen that man before. I wish to God I had not," Alabaster replied, sounding almost shaken by the experience as he lowered his head shamefully.

A terrible feeling came over Elanza as she looked into Alabaster's pale face and saw the worry in his eyes. "When *did* you see that man before?" The king paused a long moment before answering his wife.

"A little over a year ago," Alabaster said slowly as if he were lost in the memory of what had happened. "I was touring the northeastern coast of the Shandel when I came upon Mendor and Farasand. They had been hit the hardest by the plagues and famines, and barely anyone was left alive. The few remaining people told me that out of the fifty years of hardship, famine, and plague, that year was the worst. They were desperate to take ships and leave the Shandel for better lands. I told them not to lose faith, for better times were ahead. I gave them what provisions we had with us and sent for more to sustain them for another year." Alabaster took a long and labored breath, for the weight of the story burdened him greatly. "The people's worries were calmed, and once again they were filled with hope from my message and supplies that had been given to them as they went back about their business. I was relieved that I was able to give them hope during such a bleak time.

"You offered them hope and gave them aid during their most

desperate hour. Why does this burden your mind so?" she asked as she saw the great worry in his eyes.

"Six months after my visit, my sources tell me, all the remaining people were slaughtered by savages from the Kingdom of Graven." Alabaster's horrific conclusion seemed to hang in the air, preventing anyone from speaking. "I rushed back in hope to find survivors, but no one was spared. Not even the children," Alabaster said and then swallowed hard, reliving the horrific scenes of the cities.

"If no one was spared, then how did you come to see that man?" Elanza's face was fixed in thought.

"He did not live within the city limits of Mendor or Farasand. He came from the wilderness, but all he had for family perished in Farasand," Alabaster explained with a heavy heart. "When I made it to the city, I saw him carrying his granddaughter's lifeless body. He looked up at me as the tears ran down his dusty face. I did not see anger within his eyes, only disappointment. He dropped his gaze, overwhelmed with grief. I approached him and tried to offer some comfort, but he did not reply. After my soldiers and I helped bury the dead, I offered him a chance to come back with us to Akendron; he shook his head and then slowly lifted his gaze and looked at me with an expression of terrible realization.

"'Look to your own, for the peril that awaits you and yours will be a hundredfold,'" he said.

"How dare he threaten the king!" Elanza replied with anger.

Alabaster shook his head knowingly. "He did not threaten me..." His voice trailed off as his thoughts were clouded with great worry. "He gave me a warning.

"Warning? What warning?" A wrinkle formed across Elanza's brow as she struggled to understand what this could mean for their kingdom, but as she searched Alabaster's face, she saw a fear like she had never seen before.

After a long moment of hesitation, he finally lifted his head. "Do you remember an old myth that spoke of an evil that had been imprisoned within the earth by an elfin prophet?"

"I thought it was only a ghost story told to impress travelers," she said, looking at Alabaster in disbelief. Judging by his petrified expression, this was not some mere ghost story. In fact, his lingering silence and fearful expression only confirmed the growing suspicions that lingered in the night air around them. "What are you going to do?"

Deciding that he was not about to let fear rule him, Alabaster turned and headed for the door. "I must consult Solarous about this matter. I need to hear what insight he can give. Maybe there is a chance…" King Alabaster said as he reached the door.

Queen Elanza clenched her jaw tightly but could not keep her concern to herself. "I do not share your level of favor for Solarous," she said. Alabaster stopped and turned back to her. "He has dark and mysterious motives. There is more to that man than he wants us to see. Do not trust his words, for I feel that his aid comes from lies," she warned as she folded her arms across her chest, a look of genuine concern radiated from her eyes.

"Dark and mysterious? Solarous? Surely, you jest. He rivals our court jester every night at banquet," Alabaster said chuckling as he looked at her in disbelief. "Do not worry, my queen. He has been the royal advisor since my grandfather was king.

The king's words did not dispel Elanza's fears concerning the suspicious royal advisor. "All the more reason to be worried. He has almost completed his second century of life. How many men have lived so long?" she asked. He shrugged, uncertain of the answer. "Only those who have consorted with the dark powers can live such long lives." It was clear what Elanza was accusing the advisor of, but Alabaster could not betray his ever-loyal servant. Angered by her distrust of Solarous, he looked away for a moment to collect his thoughts.

Elanza looked at her husband a moment and realized that he was not the source of the problem. "I am sorry," she said, letting out a frustrated sigh. "I do not mean to argue. I just do not want you or our family hurt by that man—or anyone else," she apologized as she walked up to him and looked up into his gentle and handsome face. Alabaster understood his wife's concern, but hearing her words warmed his heart.

Wrapping his arms around her, he held her close. "I, too, am sorry. I will keep your observations in mind. We will talk later. Now I must go. I will inform you about what I have learned upon my return," he said, leaning over and kissing his wife's forehead. She nodded and bade him farewell. As she watched him slip out the door, Elanza remained in deep thought.

Turning and walking back through the stone archway onto the balcony outside, Elanza took in the moment, seeing such a calm and peaceful evening. It was the most beautiful night that she had seen in a long time. She breathed in the fresh night air. It was filled with the thick scent of trees and freshly cut grasses, combined with the smoke from nearby campfires and the coming rain. It truly was something to be celebrated, especially for all the people she knew who had toiled for so long in the hot, burning fields. This night seemed to have been chosen just for them. Letting out a short sigh, Elanza wanted to enjoy this night, but her mind was haunted by what she had heard.

"Seers are often not taken seriously, but I sense that shadows are creeping over this land. Let the king go to his advisor. I will go to mine. Surely I will get to the bottom of this!" she said to herself as she pulled on a hunter-green cloak, its large hood nearly concealing her entire head. Silent as the night, Elanza made her way through Avdima's secret passages. The winding stone corridors soon led her through a brick tunnel that ran deep underneath the castle and into an abandoned back alley in Akendron. The queen's way was set before her as she quickly passed through the large city and onto a winding trail that would lead her to Misty Forest and, ultimately, Sala of Antioch's palace.

Chapter 2

Solarous

Descending into the lower levels of the castle, King Alabaster peered through the darkness to find his footing along the damp stone stairwell. Even with the torches lit, the corridor seemed dark, cold, and hostile. The darkness of this corridor overpowered the torches' light as if it could snuff out every flame's light and warmth. As he pressed on deeper into the lower level, Alabaster fought to catch a breath of fresh air. The musty, damp odor of Avdima's lower level loomed in the passageway and clung to the inside of his nose. As he approached Solarous's chamber door, Alabaster could not even distinguish the sound of his own footsteps echoing down the hallway. All he heard was his breath in the lingering silence. He did not know why this part of the castle had always been so dark and eerie. Deciding that it was mainly because the lowest level of Avdima was built some one hundred feet below the ground's surface, Alabaster shrugged off the eerie chill that ran down his spine. He did not read anything into this strange daily occurrence because Solarous was a wise and kind soul and would not knowingly subject him or his family to harm. The sorcerer simply did not have it in him.

Coming up to Solarous's chamber, Alabaster pushed against the large wooden door that was damp to the touch. As it opened, its large, rusty hinges loudly creaked, echoing down the corridor. Ignoring the chills that it gave him, Alabaster slipped inside and looked around the warmly lit chamber for his advisor. After a moment of searching, he finally spoke into the silence of the room.

"Is my good advisor around, or have I lost him to another enchanting spell?" the king asked, hoping to see Solarous's face. Looking around, Alabaster only saw cobwebs and dust on almost everything. At the far end of the torch-lit chamber, he saw an old wooden table with an assortment of glass vials filled with colorful potions that ranged from deep red to ocean blue. A few of the potions were in beakers with a flame directly underneath. Solarous took his work seriously, for he found many elements in nature that could cure everyday illnesses. Moving farther into the chamber, Alabaster noticed a strange smell. He followed it into a small hallway that led to a smaller room. In this room, the king saw a pool built into the floor. Slowly walking up to the pool and looking into the green water that filled it, he was startled to find that it was churning by itself. White foam mixed with the green water, and at one point he could almost make out images of people and landmarks within the Shandel. As chills ran down his spine, Alabaster felt that once again his wife had been right.

Then, Alabaster heard a terrible commotion within the advisor's chamber, sounding as if all hell had broken loose. Thunder from an explosion filled the small chamber until it became deafening. Unsure of his own safety, Alabaster ran from the small chamber and made it out of the sorcerer's chamber door and back into the eerie hallway. After a moment or two, the king heard his advisor yelling profanities from within the chamber. Cautiously sticking his head back into the chamber, Alabaster searched until he found Solarous. The short, chubby man was dancing around the chamber frantically, quickly tearing off his black robe. The king watched as the robe sailed through the air and burst into flames as it landed on the floor. Dressed now in only his white undergarments, Solarous hurried to get a bucket of water to save his poor robe. Dousing the robe with the entire bucket of water, the advisor watched in dismay as the flames continued to consume the robe, despite the water that he had thrown on it. After it was burnt to ash, Solarous looked up at King Alabaster with a weary expression on his soot-covered face.

"Remind me never to mix spirits with flame. The results are disastrous," Solarous said, sounding a little worn and weary from the excitement. Alabaster could not help but smile at his advisor, who was half-covered in soot from his obviously failed experiment.

"I take it you have been having a rough night," Alabaster said as he glanced at the remains of the robe. Solarous gave him a look. His small, button-like dark eyes seemed almost angered as they shone out from his soot-covered face.

"'Rough' is nicely putting it. Such has been my day since dawn. Mere moments before the charred robe incident, I had a vial of potion explode in my face!" he exclaimed as he threw his hands into the air.

"You should not let your work get the better of you," Alabaster responded with a sly grin. Solarous shook his head and sighed.

"I will keep this in mind. But now, what can I do for my king on this lovely evening?" the balding sorcerer asked, the tone of his voice changing as he turned his attention to Alabaster. He sensed that his king seemed troubled.

"I have come seeking your wisdom on a very disturbing matter," Alabaster began discreetly. Solarous nodded curiously and encouraged his king to continue as he slowly walked over to another wooden table within the chamber to pour himself some wine. As he listened, Solarous picked up a round glass carafe that sat on a silver tray, poured its red contents into a silver goblet, and brought it to his lips to take a swallow. "I need to know what insight you can give me on the myth concerning the ancient darkness known as Lord Jarden," Alabaster continued. At the mention of the dark lord, Solarous choked on his wine.

"W-W-What?!" he gasped as he spit out the wine. Looking at Alabaster's troubled expression as he wiped his mouth with his hand, Solarous knew the king was not kidding. Quickly collecting his thoughts, the advisor tried to offer an equally discreet answer. "You look troubled, my king. Why does this matter concern you so?"

"Near a year ago, I was approached by an old man whose family had been slain in the Mendor and Farasand massacre. He told me, 'Look to your own, for the peril that awaits you and yours will be a hundredfold.' I had nearly forgotten about him, and then tonight I saw him again for only a moment. All he said was, 'You saw the end of those dear to me. Now it is your time at its end. The Evil is coming.' Then he vanished from all sight," Alabaster said as he paced back and forth. "I cannot think of any reason we should see such trouble in the Shandel. All that comes to mind is the story my father told me about this dark lord, who took hold of this land two thousand years ago. Are we in such peril now and do not realize it?"

Solarous was silent for a long moment, lowering his gaze to the floor. The portly sorcerer's brow wrinkled as he thought deeply on how to respond. "My lord, the myths of this dark being are just that—myths," he began calmly as he raised his gaze back to Alabaster. "We are protected by the same magical powers that protected our ancestors one thousand years ago. The magic of Rafar the Elder is still with us as we have seen in the rains that have blessed this land. We are safe in this city from any such force," Solarous said reassuringly. "This man you saw, was he a seer?"

Alabaster thought for a moment as he recalled the old man's demeanor as he stood in the crowd of people. "He seemed terribly grieved, almost as if he were burdened by more than just his family's death." As Alabaster offered his description of the seer, Solarous thought for another long moment before looking up and smiling.

"I see no trouble here, sire. The old man is not who he claims to be. His reaction is only natural after experiencing the trauma of such a massacre. Do not be alarmed, my lord. In several days' time, you will see peace and quiet again, of this I am sure." Solarous's recommendation was accompanied with the warmth of his voice.

Taking a deep sigh of relief, Alabaster felt the stress melt off his shoulders. "I thank you, Solarous. Your insight is most welcome." He began to turn toward the door as Solarous took his arm with reassurance to accompany his king. The sorcerer calmly veered their conversation toward more pleasant matters to further ease the king's mind as they left the lower level of Avdima and casually walked to a large patio on the first level of the castle that overlooked a serene hanging garden.

When Alabaster finally took leave of his advisor and began to head back to his bedroom chamber, he thought about the night's events. He was comforted by his advisor's reassurances, but he sensed there was still something to be wary of. He kept playing the seer's warning in his mind and found himself more confused than before.

Chapter 3

Sala of Antioch

Midnight approached as the festivities within Akendron came to a close. People wearily left for their homes and did not notice the dark-cloaked figure moving through the streets. Wrapped in her dark-green cloak, which was slightly frayed and ragged so not to draw attention to herself or her royal status, Queen Elanza blended in with Akendron's commoners. Although few people knew it, she had been born and raised in this style of life. Elanza put aside all proper etiquette and took up the behavior she had learned as a child while living on the streets of Endenbury. She transformed into a shadow in every sense of the word. As she passed through the iron gates of Akendron and made her way into the surrounding tree-covered hills, Elanza's mind was not on her silent departure from Akendron; it was burdened with deeper, more troubling matters.

The old man's haunting words mixed with her own feeling that something was terribly wrong. She knew that her husband did not sense the shadow of evil that was beginning to drift across the kingdom. True, it was not something that one could see, but one would have to be dead not to feel it. Elanza did not know how it was that she could feel such power, but she knew that something had to be done, and done quickly. Definite action needed to be taken before the myths from ages past came back to haunt them with a vengeance.

Looking back at Akendron, the queen saw a quiet, peaceful city, but a chill ran down her spine. Something made her feel uneasy. *There is more at work here than what mere mortals can sense,* she thought. *Something is coming...* Her thoughts drifted back to the old man's warning. His dark, soulful eyes told of the unspeakable horrors he had witnessed at Mendor and Farasand. More unnerving, though, was his warning of a far worse fate.

Turning around and heading deeper into the dense forest, the queen walked into a thick fog that swallowed everything around her. The air now smelled damp but sweet. Rose and jasmine fragrances filled her nostrils. Taking a deep breath of relief, Elanza knew she had entered the beautiful and mysterious Misty Forest. It was here that Elanza would find her long-time friend and counselor, Sala of Antioch. He was a mysterious but wise advisor. Rumor had it that he was the last remaining member of a secret society known as the Osarian Knights. Neither the people of Akendron nor the scholars of Avdima had certain knowledge of this secret order, only rumors and speculation. Nevertheless, Elanza believed in Sala and knew that he would never let any harm come to her or her family.

Guided by secret marks in the trees, Elanza made her way through the thick mist. Staring straight ahead, Elanza watched mesmerized as a silver-leafed cypress tree almost seemed to materialize from the fog itself. Its tall branches reached high into the air above Elanza's head. Its pale green leaves seemed to shimmer, even in the dark of night. This tree was more than just mesmerizing to the naked eye; it symbolized the passageway into Cypress Castle, Sala's enchanted palace. Holding out her hand, she touched the mist in front of her and watched as the fog gently moved and began to form into a misty archway. Soon the fog under the archway cleared to reveal a magnificent wooden bridge, which led to the enormous palace. The most beautiful poetry could not begin to describe what Elanza saw. Cypress Castle was a fortified palace of immense power where no dark force of man or spirit could enter. Only members of the Osarian Order and a rare few individuals knew of its existence.

Passing through the magical gateway, Elanza watched as the thick mist began to close behind her. Her skin tingled as the magic moved around her. Turning back to the shimmering castle of radiant white granite, she could not put into words how much she loved coming here. Its massive towers stood tall, offering anyone coming to this place a feeling of protection. The palace was also a place of purity and reflection. It was here that she came whenever problems weighed down heavily upon her.

Passing through the castle's golden gates, Elanza caught sight of the lush, mist-covered hanging gardens that filled the inner court of the palace. There were no other gardens like these in the world—or at least not from what she had seen. Not even the grand gardens of Avdima could compare. These gardens were even greener and more breathtaking than the fields and trees that surrounded Akendron after the miracle rains. Although it was dark, the gardens seemed to glow with a heavenly light. The light had no source. It was just there. Turning her gaze to the middle of the hanging gardens, she saw the sacred pool and the most beautiful sea-green water that she had ever laid eyes upon. At the center of the pool was a heavenly water fountain constructed of dark stones that formed a pile from which the water flowed. Water gently cascaded down the dark stones and rained into the pool below.

"Sala, if you make this palace even more wondrous, Heaven itself will be jealous," she whispered as she walked up to the pool and sat on the rock ledge to wait for her dear old friend. As her gaze fell on the water, Elanza saw her reflection, and then, startlingly, she found herself lost in a vision.

The pool was first overcast with white mist and rolling clouds. Then it showed her an image of the haggard old man from the festival. He stood all alone among the bustling crowd. Although he didn't speak, his dark eyes screamed for someone to listen. Wanting to understand his grief, Elanza looked into his eyes and suddenly found herself standing in the streets of Farasand. The horror Alabaster had described to her was greatly understated. Blood mingled with the brown dirt in the streets as the bodies of Farasand's own lay dismembered and discarded on the ground. No man, woman, or child escaped this brutal fate. The smell of death and rotting flesh found her nose. Swallowing hard and trying to keep the contents of her stomach down, Elanza covered her mouth and turned her gaze away. Upon doing so, she saw the old man kneeling in the dusty street and gently putting a hand on the body of a child. Then he slowly picked up the bloodied child and lifted his tearful gaze out over the decimated street.

Elanza clearly understood the heart-wrenching pain that he felt, but as she turned and joined his gaze, she saw something against which even this horrific experience paled.

Together, they looked into Andora's past and saw an evil that had brought disease, death, and darkness during two ages of the world. Horrific scenes of pestilence, torture, war, and evil flashed before their eyes. Elanza was desperate to turn away from the awful images that were revealed before them, but she could not move her body to do so. In both ages, they were relieved to witness the fall of this great evil to a valiant warrior, but Elanza was left with an unsettled feeling when the dark spirit was only imprisoned, not vanquished. She felt the eyes of the dark evil watching them as it waited to be released again. A sense of impending doom crept into her thoughts.

"The evil will come again," they said together, for both sensed it was only a matter of time. Elanza's heart broke when she thought of her children and loved ones being left at the mercy of this evil. Looking down at his lifeless granddaughter's bloodied body and then up at the bodies that lined the street, the old man managed to find his voice again. "If the evil returns this time, there will be nothing left. He will finish us all." Then, before the old man could utter anything more, a dark image arose in front of them and rushed toward them. Recoiling backward, Elanza went rigid with fear as she covered her face with her arms.

"Your majesty?" A familiar man's voice calmly asked as it cut through the intense vision. Gripped with fear, she managed to lower her arms and look up at a man standing before her, dressed in a royal deep-purple robe with a black sash wrapped around his round belly. Daring to look up at his face, Elanza saw a brown-bearded man with shoulder-length brown hair that had several steaks of gray running through it. His face was tanned and weathered from the elements, but the immense kindness in his blue eyes put her at ease. Elanza's fear melted into a half relief as she looked up at Sala of Antioch. Although he was her royal advisor, he was also her friend and had been for many years. His was a kindhearted nature, and he had the patience of a grandfather.

"Many apologies, my queen; I did not mean to alarm you," Sala said in a worried tone as he clasped his hands together humbly in front of him. His aged face was filled with deep concern as he studied her. Standing near the pool and watching her with his wisdom-filled blue eyes, Sala seemed to sense something troubling about her reaction.

"No, it is all right. I was just daydreaming," Elanza said, trying to dismiss her alarmed reaction. As she did, she glanced back to the pool for a moment. She sighed in deep relief, for this time both their reflections could be seen.

Sala raised his eyebrow with suspicion. "Then it was quite the daydream for you to react so violently." One simply could not hide truths from Sala. He was a very insightful man, reading expressions of the body and soul accurately. Elanza took great comfort in his presence and tried to relax. Sala's very soul seemed to generate warmth and comfort for all those who knew him.

"You are truly a man of vision and insight. However, this is something I pray will remain only a vision and nothing more," Elanza uttered weakly. Tears welled up in her eyes as she fought for composure. Her gaze fell back upon the sea-green pool again.

Seeing the queen's pale and grief-stricken expression as she peered fearfully back down at the pool, Sala came to an interesting realization. "Elanza, no mortal has ever looked into this pool and seen anything but his or her own reflection." He looked down into the pool for a moment and came to an unnerving realization as he raised his gaze back to her. "Unless you were granted a vision." Judging by her unsettled expression, he knew she had seen something horrible. "What have you seen?" he asked as nervousness washed over him.

"How can I speak of something so awful?" Elanza swallowed hard;

she tried to find her voice again as she raised a delicate hand to her forehead. Concern increasing, Sala slowly sank to his knees to look her directly in the eye.

"If this is news of grave warning, then it would be far worse to remain silent," he advised gently.

Thinking of how much she loved her family, Elanza looked at Sala and knew that this danger would affect him too. As Elanza nervously wrung her hands, she retold the events that had transpired in Akendron, what she had learned from Alabaster, and what she had seen in the pool. All the while, Sala listened quietly but felt a growing sense of dread.

"The pool revealed a terrible evil that overtook Andora during two ages of this world. In both cases, the evil was banished and imprisoned within the earth, but it came back. I fear its rage will not be able to be contained for much longer and it will rise again," she said.

When Elanza thought about what she had just said, she shook her head, for she knew how ridiculous this sounded, especially during a time of such prevailing peace. "Am I letting my suspicions get the best of me?" Sala stared at her a moment before dropping his gaze. A burden of great dread seemed to drop upon his shoulders.

"Your suspicion is not unfounded," her advisor replied heavily after a moment of deep thought. His reaction was that of one finally accepting a horrible truth that must be dealt with. "I, too, wish that this was only our imagination. This is a most unfortunate premonition." He lifted his eyes and looked at her with a serious gaze. "We must act fast with the little time that remains," he said in a hushed voice as he rose to his sandal-covered feet. "Come. You had better follow me." His face was stone-like and void of all expression. Elanza rose to join him, and together they walked quickly toward the majestic palace, illuminated by the moon that shone despite the thick clouds passing overhead.

Walking with him, Elanza felt an uneasiness wash over her. She had never known Sala to be worried about anything. Normally he wore a tranquil smile, but tonight his look was one of fear. Passing through the stone courtyard into Cypress Palace, Elanza and her advisor walked quickly through a series of beautifully wood-lined corridors lit with torches. Despite the ambiance of the palace, Elanza could not stop to enjoy its elegance.

At last they reached a darkened hallway at the top of one of the palace's four main towers. Elanza caught her breath, coughing a little from the thick, musty air. Dust covered the walls and floor. As she fought to see in the dim corridor, Sala continued slowly through the shadowy hallway, guided by a single torch that he had taken from a lower level in the tower. Its orange light seemed almost smothered by the prevailing darkness that surrounded them. Sala held the torch up to an object as high on the wall as he was tall. It took a few moments for the object upon the wall to catch the torch's fire, but when it did, it flickered until it burned brightly within the darkened hall. Being able to see now, Elanza saw the high tan walls of the corridor and many large pillars that lined both sides of the hall, stretching its full length. Between the tan pillars hung beautiful paintings. Looking up, she saw the ceiling arching upward. Looking back at the paintings and judging from the story the ones closest to her told, Elanza knew that this hall was different from all the others she had seen on past visits. She sensed great history in the paintings. They spoke of war, great triumphs, disheartening losses, and love. Altogether, this hallway gave Cypress Palace a very special purpose.

"This place feels old, almost as old as history itself," Elanza quietly remarked as she looked back at Sala, who had taken a skeleton key on a leather cord from around his neck and gently inserted it into the black keyhole under the door's dusty knob.

"In that assessment, you are correct," Sala replied with a wink and turned the key until they heard a loud click echo down the hall. Pulling the key out again, Sala took hold of the doorknob and put his full weight on pulling the large wooden door open. The creaking sound that emanated from the large metal hinges echoed down the hall, driving chills down both their spines. When he finally got the door open, he gently took Elanza's hand in his. "This is a sight you will not want to miss," Sala advised, sounding almost excited. At the same time, they stepped inside the darkened opening; Sala whispered something under his breath and Elanza' suddenly glimpsed heaven.

Before them a heavenly blue glow seemed to ignite almost out of the darkness itself. It started in the center of the room and touched the ceiling in mere moments; it quickly chased all darkness from the room. The queen gasped at the sight of the warm coffee-colored walls and the green marble floors and pillars of the library. The heavenly blue light came from a round crystal orb in the center of the most beautiful, grandest library she had ever seen. The orb itself sat upon a pair of outstretched hands belonging to a beautiful metal sculpture of a strong woman dressed in a long flowing toga. Elanza found herself marveling at the sculpture and that it was a woman and not a man standing there. Sala noticed the queen's concentration upon the orb's statue.

"I call her Clio," Sala began warmly. "It means 'muse of history.' Fitting, yes? What better place for a muse of history to call home than in a library?"

"Very impressive," Elanza forced herself to utter at last as she struggled to take in the grandeur of the extensive library. Smiling at the expression of wonder upon the queen's face, Sala continued with the tour.

"This is where the knowledge of Andora's darkest secret in history sleeps. Judging from your vision, it will soon be awakened, however," Sala said. The eerie tone in his voice forced Elanza back to the reason he had brought her here. The seriousness in Sala's voice remained with Elanza as she watched him slowly make his way over to a large wooden desk at the far end of the room. As she followed him, Elanza noticed almost instantly that the room was not dusty the way the hallway had been.

"Why does the air seem so clear and...?" she began to ask as she breathed in a lungful of mysteriously fresh air.

"Fresh?" Sala offered as he combed through piles of aged manuscripts and scrolls on his desk without breaking concentration. "The magic that resides in the palace keeps this room from the elements of nature and thus keeps all these documents from aging. Dust has no chance here. Which is a relief—as I can barely keep up with managing the books, manuscripts, and scrolls that reside here," he said. There was no lie in this, for Elanza saw that even his desk had long ago become overrun with paperwork, books, and artifacts. She saw that all the large wooden bookshelves that stretched to the far back of the huge chamber were overfull. Yet every other book, sheet of paper, and scroll that Sala could not find room for had found a home on the green marble floor. The piles of literature that lined the floor of this massive library were almost mountainous. As she slowly made her way toward Sala's desk, she noticed that the library was in disarray from many years of use. Out of the corner of her eye, the queen watched as Sala navigated from his desk and weaved throughout the congested piles that cluttered the library floor with the greatest of ease. Looking down at several piles of aged manuscripts lying on the floor, she found to her sheer amazement that some works dated as far back as 5,000 years and others were dated during the first age!

"This place is a wonder," she said slowly as she gazed in awe at her surroundings. About the time when she wondered if Sala was coming close to finding what he was looking for, there was a thunderous crash that echoed through the chamber, and Sala screamed. Elanza dashed through the maze of aged manuscripts and scrolls, desperate to find her friend. "Sala! Where are you?" she called. Looking around frantically, she began to fear that he would be lost under a mountain of fallen manuscripts. At any other time, it would all seem rather humorous. Listening closely for any sound of the aged advisor, she began to hear something muffled far underneath one mountain of manuscripts. "Sala! Can you hear me?" she called. No answer.

The entire room started to shake. Books and manuscripts from all over the library began falling from their shelves. Fearing for her life, Elanza took cover next to a bookshelf. She nervously watched for anything that could come down on top of her. The bookshelves within this library reached twenty feet to the ceiling and were jammed with thousands upon thousands of works from centuries past. Some were quite large and very heavy. If dropped with precision, they would render a person unconscious or worse.

When the shaking came to an end, Elanza looked up and around for any sign of Sala. In all the chaos, she feared that her advisor had been completely buried under the library that he dearly loved. At that moment, she heard the sound of Sala coughing. He was alive and, what was more, the mild quake had disturbed the manuscripts just enough to uncover him. Scrambling over the heaps of fallen books, manuscripts, and scrolls, Elanza quickly spotted Sala sitting half buried by a mountain of books and scrolls. When she finally reached him, he was a little bruised and slightly shaken but all right. As she looked directly into his blue eyes to see if he was really all right, Elanza realized that being buried alive by his own library was the farthest thing from his mind at that moment. Sala's face was white as a sheet and drained of all expression.

"What is wrong? You look as if you have just seen a nightmare," she asked with concern.

Looking up at her, Sala nodded his head slowly. "You are more right than you know," he said as he picked himself out of the heap.

Elanza quickly began to clear away a pile of books that kept him from moving and took hold of his hand. When Sala was finally free, she noticed something in his hands. "What is that?" she asked. It appeared to be yet another yellowed scroll, but this one seemed very strange. It was made of leather instead of paper. Its red seal of wax had never been broken. The seal had a crest of six symbols on it. She had seen this same seal on the scarlet banners that hung within the palace corridors. Sala gazed down at the scroll with a grave expression of concern. "Sala?" she asked again, hoping to break him out of his trance-like state. He finally looked up at her with an expression of dreadful certainty.

"Long ago, my master entrusted this scroll to me. He said it contained the prophetic incantations passed on to us by an elfin prophet who had warned to never let them fall into the wrong hands——hands that were in the service of evil. Since the prophet's time, my order has kept the scroll safe behind these walls until we should need its secrets to defeat the evil once again.

"So the rumors are true? You are a member of the Osarian Knights?" she asked, her eyes filling with wonder, seeing her advisor and friend in a whole new light.

"Unknown to the common world and far from the reach of any rumor, the Osarian Knights were a select group of prophets chosen by a sphinx of the ancient world. All members pledged to uphold the instruction set down by the sphinx, who first began the order. All the prophets of the past guarded and protected their world from evils that tried to destroy it. Although I am the last knight of this ancient order, I keep my oath still. I remain fervent in my mission, for what is written within this scroll will come to pass eventually and we must be ready!" Sala's bold reply caught Elanza off-guard.

"Forgive me for not understanding, Sala, but what you speak of sounds like a prophecy," she said as she looked at the scroll with great interest. Sala shook his head.

"It is not *a* prophecy, it is *the* prophecy. Rafar the Elder himself wrote this prophecy." Sala's words caused Elanza to freeze in wonder. She looked at the scroll with a reverent gaze.

"Not… *the* Rafar?" she managed to utter. Sala nodded assuredly.

"Yes. It was he who gave my order the signs of terrible times to come. A thousand years prior, the elfin prophet had fought an evil spirit in a great battle. Defeating the spirit, he asked the heavens to rain upon the earth every one hundred years and bless the farmers with bountiful harvests. The Andorans call him 'The Great Dragon' and honor him annually by celebrating their independence.

Sala then closed his eyes and began to quote from his teachings: "Although my rains will nourish the land every century until all the ages of the world have been spent, beware of the latter years, for drought, hardship, and plague will run rampant throughout the realm of man. After this time, peace will be short lived, for an even greater threat lies waiting to be unleashed.

"Then the vision, the old man, and everything that has happened in the Shandel over the past fifty years were signs that some great evil was about to be unleashed again," Elanza said as the color drained from her face. These vivid clues gave Sala an uneasy feeling as he carefully broke the seal and began skimming through the prophet's writings.

"According to my teachings and what is written in these sacred lines of text... the third time of evil is almost upon us," he said, sounding uneasy and overwhelmed.

Although she feared the thought of some evil creature wreaking havoc upon her kingdom, Elanza dreaded even more the thought of her loved ones being at its mercy assuming it even knew of mercy. "What does Rafar tell us we should do?" she asked, taking the aged scroll from Sala's hand and reading it.

Chapter 4

The Letter

They moved to the lounging chamber, which Sala used as a reading room, to inspect the sacred scroll. The chamber was much smaller than the grand library. The walls were painted deep mahogany, with silver etchings throughout. Vases of the deepest shades of purple and gold decorated the room. The scent of lavender emanated from fresh flowers that had been placed within the vases. The ceiling was arched but not as high as the one in the hallway outside. The floor, on the other hand, was constructed of the finest cream limestone known to the natural world. Sala and Elanza sat in comfortable cushioned chairs made of rattan and soft white velvet fabric and were positioned before a glorious fireplace as Sala read the mystic lines of text from the letter. For all the comfort and warmth that the chamber gave to ease their minds, Sala and Elanza could not relax.

Mayen, 15, 9021, The Tenth Age

> *Today, peace prevails once again, but tomorrow is uncertain, for what I have foreseen is terrible beyond all imagination! How*

I long to tell you of these things myself, but I will not live to see tomorrow's dawn. Instead, I entrust my knowledge to you through this letter so that you may be prepared for what is to come.

On the distant isle of Zendro, I have imprisoned an evil known to the old world as Lord Jarden. The precise place where he resides will remain secret, but in due time it is very likely that this evil will escape again.

Plague, famine, and death have run rampant throughout Andora since the year 9000. The atrocities of the past twenty and one years that those remaining of my order and I have seen have not been witnessed in 6,000 years. We do not known precisely when the evil escaped from Ice Isle, but we know that it overtook the body of the advisor Randye. Thankfully by the grace of our Lord, I, Rafar the Elder, have managed to imprison the evil within the earth, but I worry for the future. He vows to return, and by this promise, I know he will.

In my visions, I have seen the evil creature known as Lord Jarden and his true mission. He is but a messenger for his people. He comes from a distant land across the ocean known only as the Kingdom of Nod. It is a dead realm. The annihilation of Andora and her people is only the beginning of what Nod's king has in store for this realm and the poor souls he lets live. The scorched earth that will be left behind after Lord Jarden's people finish with it will never support life again! However, we have the faintest of chances to overturn his plan.

Unknown to Lord Jarden, I have foreseen times in the future where if certain people are rescued or certain events changed, you will be able to stand up against all the dark armies of Lord Jarden and destroy them completely. Adding to this brief glimpse of hope, I have foreseen a dark and mysterious warrior whose return from the ancient world can lead you and all you hold dear to victory. You must seek him out to tell him of the task that awaits him!

The visions do not reveal much about this warrior, but this much I can tell you: the ancient warrior will not be born of man but will be of an ancient royal line. This chosen one will not be a sight for the wealthy or political eyes, but their heart will be like no other.

They will be guided by a strong will and a quest for right amidst a sea of wrong. The warrior has an eye for compassion, and stronger still are the bonds of truth, friendship, loyalty, and love.

You will not know this warrior by mere sight. This warrior has been chosen, not by man, but by the god Adalai. It is not the great that can claim this title but rather the meek of the earth. The warrior will be called Farro.

In the time that you read this, all knowledge of what I have seen will be lost through the course of events. This is why I have written the details of my visions in four scrolls, taking pains that such knowledge not be discovered by the dark realm. The prophecy that I have written is in a text that only the chosen messenger will be able to understand. Each scroll has been hidden carefully throughout the whole of Andora.

There is wisdom in the lines of prophecy; let them be your clues to the three remaining scrolls. They will be as clues to a map. These are indeed instructions that you will need to save your world.

Beware of your eyes, for they will be deceived,

Beware of your ears, for they will not hear truth,

Believe what your heart tells you.

Only this path can lead you to glory.

In the final days of the Great War in Andora, an awesome transition is to take place. If the events have been altered enough, the dark and mysterious warrior will gain the full measure of their true power. This can be achieved only by the healing of another soul and by breaking the chains that bind the multitude. It is not known who, but this other soul is elf in origin. This achievement of power can be successful only if the bond is true and from love. If it is not, the warrior will perish from all existence. Fear not! Great truths will come to pass.

Rafar the Elder

After Sala finished reading the letter aloud, the crackle of the fire from the fireplace was the only sound. At first, there were no words to speak. The weight and grandeur of the prophecy that now loomed before them was staggering.

"Are we too late?" Elanza asked, sounding unsettled at the notion that they might be past the point of all help. Sala looked at her for a moment and thought deeply about her question. "Has the ancient evil already been unleashed?" Her question caused Sala to be gripped with a moment of fear.

"Has it really come that far without our realization?" Sala asked, with a tone of dread in his deep voice.

Elanza thought a moment about all the strange events that had been going on within and around the castle and within Akendron. She reflected on the fifty years of plague and famine that had run rampant throughout the kingdom. *Maybe these were signs of this dark lord gaining his power to take over Andora,* Elanza thought but dared not utter yet. "I cannot say for sure," she said aloud. "I sense evil is growing not only within Avdima, but it is spreading throughout the rest of the kingdom as well. Many do not see it yet, but I know it is here," Elanza said with conviction as she sat rigid in her soft-cushioned chair.

"You are right. I, too, have felt this. Yet I do not believe we have missed our chance. The ancient evil is still imprisoned within the depths of the earth; his rise to power would be quick enough that even a commoner would take notice," Sala offered thoughtfully as he put a hand to his mouth to think. "Besides, we have not received the first sign of the evil's return," he said knowingly as if from experience as he replaced his index finger on the aged letter and continued to gaze thoughtfully to try to understand its cryptic message.

"What is the first sign?" Elanza wrung her hands nervously as she studied Sala's expressionless face for answers. After a long moment of almost eerie silence, Sala finally raised his head to look at his queen. There was something almost haunting in his blue eyes.

"Lord Jarden will take over the body of a palace official to better infiltrate the current government. According to my order, he has done this twice before. He is not likely to veer from a course that has worked before." His words were almost a whisper, but Elanza understood. Her heart sank.

"I was afraid that our fifty years of plague, famine, and death were Lord Jarden's regaining his full power to return again," Elanza said, letting out a short sigh and dropping her head. But she still felt unnerved. Looking up at her advisor with concern, the queen noticed that he was no longer looking at the manuscript in his lap but at the fire that continued to burn. His expression was almost sad. "What is it?" Elanza managed to ask softly. There was horror in his face as if he remembered a certain atrocity in his past that their conversation had uncovered.

Sala sat quietly for a moment. "In the year 4021, when my order was first ordained, the elders wrote down their own accounts of the battle with the ancient evil, thus describing the conditions of the land and people." His voice was riddled with immense grief as tears stung his eyes.

As Sala summoned the courage to retell what his peers wrote, Elanza felt her throat tighten, for her mind flashed to the hardship that the Shandel had faced for so long. Though she feared the details Sala might give her, Elanza asked anyway. "What did they see?"

"You said we have seen fifty years of famine, plague, and death, but after reading just a few of their accounts…" The solemn advisor shook his head. "We have seen nothing." Sala's words hit Elanza hard. "If we are to truly *do* this and not just speak it, than we need to follow what Rafar left us," Sala said boldly. His blue eyes were almost piercing and his words caused Elanza to sit back. "He foresaw a great war between the forces of good and evil. An army must be raised to fight this war. Men from all parts of Andora will have to be assembled and trained for battle. Andora hangs in a moment of peace. We must make the most of that moment." His words reassured the queen, but she knew that grave peril was imminent and could not easily put it out of her mind.

Sala took a deep breath, looked down at the still-sealed first scroll of the prophecy in his lap and then carefully began to open it. The leather manuscript that was Rafar's letter to them had been wrapped tightly around the first scroll of the prophecy and sealed with wax. Once the scroll was opened, the old Osarian Knight studied it closely, desperate to make out the strange markings on the page. He held it up to the flame's light, and then after a long moment, he let out a heavy sigh of frustration.

"Are the events Rafar foretells that horrific?" Elanza asked, wringing her hands again and sitting on the edge of her chair.

"I do not know; I have yet to read them. The lines of text are written in a strange language," Sala answered simply, looking up from the cryptic text.

"You cannot read it?" Elanza asked with growing concern. Judging from his blank response, this was one language that escaped even Sala's vast knowledge and understanding. The queen began to feel the odds were already stacked against them.

"We are fortunate to have the first of the four scrolls in our possession, but it does us little good if we cannot understand the language it has been written in," he replied, trying to remain optimistic as he scratched his head thoughtfully. "Long ago, our order knew all the languages of Andora, but I am ashamed to say that some have long since been forgotten.

"Did Rafar not mention a chosen messenger? One who would be able to read this strange language?" At Elanza's question, Sala perked up, skimming back over the leather text again, and began to nod his head.

"You are right. He did," he replied with an assured tone of voice as he scanned over the text with his long index finger. "*The prophecy that I have written is in a text that only the chosen messenger will be able to understand,*" Sala reread. "My guess is Rafar foresaw a person who could already read this language. Our search to understand these scrolls begins when we find this chosen one.

"Where and how do you begin to look for such a person? Andora is a vast nation, and within her, there are millions of people that call her home," said Elanza fearfully.

"Faith," he calmly replied. Elanza was confused and impatient. Sala could also sense that she was worried about what was to come. She dropped her head, frustrated by the path that stretched before them. They would have to find the scrolls of the prophecy with the meager clues Rafar had left for them, and they would have to find the one called Farro with equally meager clues. But the advisor was patient with his queen. "We need to let our god handle such matters," he said with a nod of insistence. "Rafar the Elder went through too much hardship and toil to give us this prophecy for us to just give up. Its message, if carried out as written, is the best possible course for Andora. Right now, we have an advantage over the darkness, and we must protect it," Sala spoke calmly to Elanza as he held up the first scroll. "I will keep it with me at all times, so it will not slip into the wrong hands, even by accident." She nodded in agreement and knew that they were all in good hands. It was then that Sala gazed at the scroll, and a thought crossed his mind.

"Have you discovered something?" she asked. Although she had more patience this time, she was still edgy.

The tired and worn knight sat back again and rubbed his blue eyes for a moment. "Maybe, but it is not for certain yet. We have to be patient with this. In time, the answers will present themselves to us."

Elanza finally took his word for it and nodded. "You are right. We must be patient, or we will rush into this and risk missing something important. Since the dark forces are already at work, we could easily be caught off-guard, and who knows where that will lead us?" she said sincerely.

"Or someone," Sala interjected thoughtfully. Elanza looked at him with interest. "It may be that the sacred messenger is not of great wealth or stature," he started again, but then his voice trailed off. A look of grief came over his face. The queen grew concerned. When he looked at her again, only a wan smile came to his face. "My fear is that we will miss them, because they may appear to us most unexpectedly. It is good that so many Andorans live in wealth and prosperity, but there are a great many poor among us."

"People of wealth do not wish to look at those they consider beneath them, but little do they realize that those they spurn are often the worthiest among us." The queen's words touched Sala and he found his warm smile again. "Lord willing, someone will spot them," she said hopefully.

Sala nodded in agreement as he slowly returned to examining the ancient text and continued trying to make sense of it. "I do believe that the Lord has already taken care of this matter and has summoned the perfect person to find our sacred messenger," Sala said, still studying the ancient manuscript.

These words somehow reminded Elanza of the old man. "I cannot help but think about the safety of my people and the people that reside within the neighboring kingdoms. What is to happen to them? There is no one to protect them." Then Elanza gasped in surprise. "That is it!" she exclaimed, jumping from her chair.

Startled by her outburst, Sala fell back into his own chair. "What is it?" he asked with uncertainty.

Fearing for those living in the far reaches of the three lower kingdoms of Andora, also known as the Tribunal, Elanza's mind had quickly birthed a plan that would offer these individuals protection. "I am going to start work on a secret alliance of knights who will protect all those of the Tribunal. When this evil rises again, at least my people and those within the neighboring kingdoms will have a chance at survival.

Knowing that the Tribunal was a vast and not-always protected realm and judging by the enthusiasm in the queen's eyes, Sala knew that he could not sway her from this decision. Then again, it was not an ill-conceived plan, for Andora would need protection when the ancient evil escaped again. "This does sound quite promising. You will need the best archers and warriors from all Andora to set up such an elite force of men to do what you are planning," Sala advised thoughtfully as he resettled himself in his chair.

Inspired by her advisor's support, Elanza began to think of whom she could recruit for this army. "I will have Alon-Settie help me. He is the finest warrior within the whole of the Shandel. We can begin work on recruiting other warriors from the other kingdoms within the Tribunal," she said, beginning to plot out this scheme in her mind as she paced the floor.

Sala's thoughts turned to someone who would also be ideal for this secret alliance. "Send for Prince Leondros Goldendragon as well."

The elfin prince from Adarah was renowned throughout Andora as a skilled warrior and an excellent archer. More than that, Leondros was a trusted and dear friend of his whom Sala could not pass up the chance of seeing again. Many long years had passed since their last meeting. "He is a friend of your son's, and he is renowned warrior and archer," he said. Elanza nodded as she listened intently. A smile came to her, for she also knew of the great friendship that the two princes shared.

"It will make Alon-Settie glad to see Leondros once again. They are as close as brothers. So many times each has saved the other's life. It is a real treasure to see such a friendship exist," Elanza said with great tenderness, recalling the many adventures they had shared. Then something else came to her mind which also made her smile. "If only I could find their matches for this life, then I could say my work is done." As the queen spoke these words, Sala also could not help but smile.

"It may be easier to find a lady for your son than it will be for Leondros," Sala said with a warm chuckle. He loved Leondros as if he were his own son, but in the 2,300 years that Leondros had walked the earth, he had yet to find the one chosen for him. Sala was glad that the elfin prince took this well, for the young prince did not seem to mind the single life. Yet Sala never lost hope for his dear friend.

"Yes, you may be right about that, too," she said, with an understanding nod. Elanza then caught a glimpse of the moon falling into the western sky. "Oh dear! It is very late. I must return. There is still much I have to do," she said, and she started to hurry for the wooden door of the lounging room. At the door, she stopped and looked back at him. "Sala, please pray for us. Even though peace still rules Andora, I sense that it will not last long. There are many out there who are going to be battling much tougher battles than we will. They will need all the help they can get." Her words were genuine and heartfelt.

"I will, my queen," he promised with sincerity. As he watched Elanza rush to tend to her business, he too, thought about the pressing matters of his own schedule that lay ahead and that sleep would, unfortunately, have to wait. His meetings with the high council throughout the week demanded his presence, and he could not be late. "Worry not. I will not rest until I reveal some crucial answers to our questions. Good luck to you, too. Lord knows we are both going to need it," he finished as he got to his feet and walked with her out of the lounging room to escort her out of the palace. As they walked, Sala felt relieved that he finally had someone he could confide in about this dire issue. Before she passed back over the bridge that would take her back into the kingdom of the Shandel, Elanza pulled the hood to her cloak over her head to conceal her identity. "Be safe, my queen. Evil can take many forms," Sala warned as an uneasy feeling came over him.

"Worry not; I have made this journey many times." Elanza's confidence almost reassured him, yet there was still something about this time that felt wrong. He nodded in reply and watched as she silently walked back over the bridge. Sala waved to her as she passed beyond the cypress tree. He continued to watch with concern from behind the curtain of white mist until he could no longer see any trace of the queen.

Chapter 5

Sphinxes

When Sala returned to the warm lounging chamber and began to pore over the ancient language again, something seemed to jump out at him. Looking closer, Sala realized what language the prophecy had been written in. Though he still could not understand the text, he could discern that the strange language was that of an ancient, mysterious race called the sphinxes. At the time that the scrolls were written, there were only a few elfin scholars and prophets who could understand the language. These scholars and prophets had been taught this language many thousands of years before Rafar's battle with Lord Jarden by the sphinxes themselves.

Sala had never laid eyes on a sphinx, let alone one from the ancient world. However, he remembered some of the tales of old that spoke of these great and wondrous beings. It was said that in early times, the god Adalai made sphinxes the guardians of every creature within the world. They were entrusted with such awesome power because their hearts were righteous and filled with profound love. Among their powers, the masters of their race possessed the ability to heal the sick and dying. There were stories that they could even reverse death. Their great power was matched by great beauty as well. The sphinxes sought to spread love and goodness throughout Andora and became close friends with the elves. They shared their knowledge and wisdom with the elves, for they were the only creatures the sphinxes knew could be trusted with such knowledge. Over the course of the ages, the sphinxes and elves tried to teach this knowledge to the race of man. Sadly, the race of man was not ready for such power and wonder.

Over the passing few millennia, many rumors as to what really happened that brought about the fall of the sphinx people surfaced. One of the more likely versions told of how the race of man grew greedy and jealous from some unknown act that spawned immense bitterness towards the sphinxes. These men tried to enslave these beautiful beings to obtain the power of the sphinxes for their own use. Over time, many of these powerful beings were killed from experiments done on them in an effort to gain that power. Some who resisted and tried to escape were also slain. Even sphinxes who tried to befriend man were hunted down, for man's greed could not be stopped. When the elves heard of the tragedy that had fallen upon their dear friends, they rushed to save them before it was too late, but it was not to be. The entire race of sphinxes was gone from the world, never to be seen again. Sala was silent for a long moment as a great wave of sadness came over him.

"This could not have come at a more unfortunate time," he said to himself. Sala's heart began to ache with bitter grief. "If the ancient scrolls were written in the Sphinx language and now the only ones who could possibly read it are gone from the earth, then..." Sala's voice faded as grief overtook him. Then he slammed a fist into the wall next to the fireplace. "Man's greed did not just kill the entire race of the sphinxes; it sentenced everyone else to the same fate as well!" he shouted angrily as tears filled his eyes. Finally giving in to his grief, Sala sank to the floor and began to weep bitterly.

While in the depths of his grief, Sala had a vision. He saw something that the elders had neither spoken or written of. He saw a female sphinx going into hiding. Under the cover of the night's darkness and dressed in a dark-gray cloak, she moved as silently as a shadow through what appeared to be city streets. There, safe within her arms, was a child. No one knew of their presence. Moments later, she vanished into the night. When Sala awoke from his vision, he raised his head and gazed down at the aged scroll and the leather manuscript still in his hands.

"Could it be possible?" Uttering these words, Sala regained his composure and hope. He would not speak of this vision, for like Rafar and the mother, he realized that the child was their only hope and must be protected. Looking at the last lines that Rafar wrote, Sala was inspired. Hope was not gone; it had just been hiding, waiting for them all along.

"The chosen one would not be of wealth or stature. They would be far from any public attention," he thought aloud. Sala slowly nodded his head in understanding. "The meek of the earth..." he said slowly, with realization. A smile came to his face, for he knew how true this was. "I would trust my life to the meek rather than to those within this land claiming and boasting to high heaven that they are good," he said, again nodding. Gripping the scroll, he rose to his feet and raced back into the library.

There was much more research that needed to be done! He needed to reread his peers' old journals for what they might have learned of Farro. He would not rest while it remained undone. Looking at an oil painting of Rafar that hung upon the wall closest to his desk, Sala was regretful. The image of the elfin prophet held both a sword and a scroll. His face was handsome and stoic, his dark eyes looking straight ahead and seeming to pierce through the very soul of the viewer. The athletic-looking elder wore red and black armor and had his black boot firmly resting on the body of a reptilian creature that he had just slain. The caption below this captivating painting read, *"Always vigilant, always ready."* Sala looked down at his round belly and sadly shook his head. Looking back to the painting, he nodded to Rafar with promise. Long years with no evil to vanquish had left Sala's skills mute and his senses dull. It was time to regain what he had lost. Sala began to haul out journals and books and prepared to relearn the history of the sphinxes and retrain himself as an Osarian Knight.

Chapter 6

Seed of Evil

Juna 10th

Walking back into Akendron through the cool night air, Elanza went over the plans for her kingdom. Her mind was everywhere except on what she was doing. As she neared Avdima, Elanza snuck by a local pub still full of people celebrating, although by now they were too intoxicated to remember why they were celebrating. When she ducked into a small alley, Elanza saw a drunken crowd of people stumbling and laughing as they were trying to leave for their homes. Not too concerned if they recognized her, for they probably would not remember seeing her when they sobered up, Elanza continued to hurry on her way. Just as she watched them stumble onto another street, Elanza felt someone large crash into her. Fighting to keep her balance, Elanza whirled around to see a heavyset drunken man struggling to remain on his feet. His balding head shone brightly in the moonlight, but in Elanza's opinion, that was all he had going for him. Beyond the rank odors of sweat and spirits, he looked like he had not changed out his ragged sackcloth in at least a week. In his fight to remain on his feet, the man stumbled forward and grabbed her shoulders to steady himself.

"There is a reason they call it *last call*," Elanza remarked as she worked to push his heavy hands off her shoulders. She saw the glazed look in the man's cold brown eyes and realized he was just moments from collapsing from his night of heavy drinking. Shoving his drunken and clumsy form away, Elanza started to walk on when he ran into her again. This time his grip on her shoulders was like iron.

"Hey!" The man mumbled loudly as he looked at Elanza for the first time. His focus was now on her. Taking notice that she had a beautiful face and had great strength, he slurred, "Y-you... f-f-f-face... pretty. Y-y-you... m-man...need.

"I am dreadfully sorry, sir. I am not out for a date," Elanza said as she tried to pry his hands off her to continue her journey.

"Y-y-you... man n-n-need!" he slurred again as his voice rose angrily. In his awkward movements, he leaned his sweaty, pasty face near her own to speak. Elanza turned her head away, for the smell of spirits was heavy on his breath. When he swayed back again, she glared at him through narrowed eyes.

"And just how would you fit into that role?" she scowled at him as she began to pull from his grip. Her eyes took in his hanging flesh with disgust. Feeling the pain of the insult, the drunken man became frenzied. He grabbed her and drove her back into the dark stony wall of the alleyway and held her from escape. The sudden impact of being slammed into the hard stone wall took her breath away.

"Y-y-you... need man," he said roughly. His words drove chills down her spine as he looked down upon her with a lustful smile. Terrified, she began to fight against him harder now, desperate to get away. This did not deter him. His hot and sweaty face began kissing her neck. He used his sheer weight to hold her against the stone wall as one of his hands ripped aside her cloak and felt her skinny waist; his right hand quickly slid down the folds of her gown and tried to feel her legs. She felt his hot sweaty hand caress her thigh and begin to pull at her gown.

"HELP! SOMEONE HEL-!" Her frantic screams were instantly silenced as he put a rough hand over her mouth. She felt him press harder against her with his large flabby body. In another attempt at freedom, Elanza reached up and scratched his face with her fingernails.

He let out a yell of pain and recoiled from her and she took her chance to escape. Ripping herself away, Elanza broke free from the man's steely grip. Whirling around, panicked and confused, she bolted down the trash-littered alleyway in hopes of finding the closest means of escape. Ducking into another side alley, she did not turn back to see if he was pursuing her. Convulsions of panic overtook her as she ran frantically through the darkened alley. She had no thought of where she was going. All Elanza knew was that she had to get away. Then she felt herself trip over something in the street. Falling to the ground and striking her head, Elanza ached as she watched the world spin out of control. Fighting to come to her senses, Elanza tried to clamber to her feet when a rough pair of hands grabbed the hood of her cloak and ripped it off her head and then grabbed her hair and pulled her to her feet. The heavyset man shoved her into another wall and forced his body against hers again. This time, he covered her mouth before speaking. He seemed to be sobering, for his speech was improving.

"I said you need a man. I am that man. You will enjoy this or you will hate this; either way, you will be mine tonight," he whispered in her ear with rancid breath. This time there was no escaping for he quickly pinned her arms with his huge body. A second later a moan left his mouth as he hungrily began kissing her neck again. Using his left hand to cover her mouth, he used the right to tear the fabric around the bodice of her gown. Tears welled into her eyes as she felt his hot and sweaty face against her neck and shoulder. His kisses became more forceful. She couldn't struggle enough to stop him. It only made him angrier. He pressed her head harder against the rock wall behind her as his other hand snaked inside the bodice of her gown and groped the skin of her waist. She felt his mouth quickly sliding down her throat, edging closer to her chest.

Knowing there was nothing she could do, Elanza looked away. Doing so, she saw a shadow appear from behind the man. Before she could understand what was happening, a dark object was quickly raised into the air and swung at the man's head. Elanza heard a sickening crack as the object slammed into the man's skull. The assault stopped and her attacker released his savage grip on her as he lost consciousness.

Elanza watched his eyes rolled back into his head as he crumpled to the trash-littered street.

The queen was out of her mind with fright and gasped for air, remaining close to the wall. She wrapped her arms tight around her and stared wildly at her rescuer, whose dark shadow loomed over the unconscious man. He was tall and wore a dark robe with a hood to cover his face. Her rescuer looked down at the man for a moment and then at her. In his hands, he held the long wooden staff that had successfully knocked the man out. Then Elanza noticed his hands. They were not a man's hands! Looking closer at her rescuer, Elanza realized her mistake.

"You are a woman!" Her words came out shaken and hoarse as she tried to swallow. Her throat was sore and dry. The person looked at her a moment in silence before she spoke.

"As are you." Elanza heard the comforting sound of a young woman's voice. The woman pulled back her hood to reveal her identity. Elanza had never been so happy to see another person. "He had better remember that next time. No one deserves such treatment, no matter who they are." The woman's words were truly those of someone from a noble family. The queen marveled at the young woman's beauty. She had tanned skin and a thick braid of brown hair streaked with gold. The braid disappeared under the young woman's cloak. More radiant were her eyes. They were bright and the color of the sea. Judging by her build, no one would have expected such strength coming from her.

"Are you an angel?" Elanza asked as the young woman reached out and offered her arm to her. Showing no fear or reluctance, she gladly took the arm of her heroine and stepped over the large body of the unconscious man. Dropping her arm, the young woman only smiled humbly and shook her head.

"I am of flesh and blood, just like you, my fair queen," she replied, bowing her head respectfully. The young woman replaced her hood and cautiously looked around for any more danger. When she had made sure the way was safe, she turned to the queen. "May I escort you home? This night is not a good night to be out and about," the woman offered kindly. Her advice was well taken. Turning back to her attacker, the queen nodded.

"I would be most grateful to you," Elanza said. Then narrowing her eyes at the man, Elanza raised her foot and kicked the man in the skull.

When she turned back to the young woman, a smile came to her face. Taking the queen's arm again and leading her away, the young woman spoke again. "He will have a headache tomorrow, and it will not be just the spirits at work," the mysterious woman noted as she studied the unconscious man before quietly moving on. Elanza found herself chuckling at the remark and realized how safe and secure she felt in this young woman's presence. As they walked back into the street, Elanza found herself clinging to the young woman's strong arm. They quickly left the place where the man attacked her. Her mind remained tortured from the brief and frightening experience. She then felt a kind and reassuring hand touch hers. "Are you all right?" the young woman asked in a warm whisper.

"I fear my mind will never forget such a wicked experience," Elanza replied, sounding shaken. She could not help but wonder how this brave young woman knew that she was in trouble. "How is it that you knew I was in danger?" she asked. The young woman continued to eye their surroundings as they walked.

"I heard your screams," the young woman replied finally. Elanza found this strange.

"But how? I got out only a few words before he covered my mouth," she said, still shaking from the attack.

"My hearing has always been very keen," she said. Her words continued to comfort the queen as they made their way to the castle. Elanza watched the young woman with great interest, who reminded her of Leondros Goldendragon. He was the only other person she knew who had the same strange yet kind and compassionate nature. It brought her great comfort that there were still good and righteous people in the world like Leondros.

Looking to the east, Elanza saw the first moments of morning slowly spread across the horizon. She was even more anxious to get home; people within the palace would note her absence. The young woman graciously took the queen's directions to sneak them undetected inside the castle. Even though the young woman asked the queen which way to go next, she walked the underground passage with confidence. Finally, the young woman led the queen safely to her own chamber door. Pulling her dark hood down over her eyes, the young woman humbly bowed and turned to leave. The queen hated to see such a wondrous person leave her sight.

"Please…" she said, causing the young woman to stop and turn back to her. "I have not thanked you for saving me tonight. How can I ever repay such kindness to you?" Elanza offered as she walked up to the young woman and took her strong arm again. The mysterious young woman thought for a moment, pulling back her hood to see her clearly; she smiled warmly at the queen. Placing her hand gently over the queen's, the young woman finally spoke.

"Do not let the memory of tonight haunt you forever. The world still has good people in it, and many of them suffer in the chains of bondage. Their taskmasters are even more cruel, foul, and sadistic than the man who attacked you tonight. You can repay me by showing them kindness, breaking the chain of pain and suffering that will only harm more innocent lives. Do this and though what has happened is done, your mind will find the healing it needs." The young woman spoke softly but with strength and courage. Then the sounds of someone approaching caught her attention. Turning back to the queen, she bowed her head one last time. "Farewell, my queen. God be with you." With that, the mysterious young woman recovered her head, whirled around, and bolted down the dimly lit hallway. Servants would soon come to light the torches that burned in the hallways during the daytime, but the current dimness aided the mysterious woman's escape.

Standing outside her chamber door with her arms wrapped around herself, Elanza looked down the hall almost in a trance. Although morning's light had yet to break through the colorful stained-glass window at the far end of candlelit corridor, Elanza would always remember the last images of the brave young woman silently darting down the hallway and disappearing like an apparition.

The queen found herself still standing outside the chamber doorway some long moments later as she was awoken from her trance-like state by the sounds of servants entering the corridor. Frightening images of the night came quickly to her mind, but she found that the courage displayed by her mysterious heroine seemed to block the ghastly images. It brought her incredible comfort that God had provided such a compassionate and kind soul to protect her at such a horrendous moment in her life. The young woman's voice lingered in her mind, and the words she had spoken gave her healing. It reminded Elanza of her own mission. The young woman inspired her to show others the same kindness and compassion. "I promise I will not let you be the only one fighting the darkness that surrounds us," she said aloud. Speaking the words filled the queen with iron-clad determination. She quickly and quietly entered her chamber where Alabaster lay fast asleep; she quickly bathed and clothed herself with a royal-purple robe. The queen did not otherwise take care with her appearance, for it was still early morning and most were asleep at this hour. Marching stealthily through Avdima's corridors, Elanza was on a mission, and no one would stop her.

As Elanza made her way down the long corridor to the wing where her children's rooms were located, her silver satin slippers kept her footsteps quiet as she walked over the bare stone floors where the purple hallway carpets did not reach. Hurrying up to her son's chamber door, the last one at the end of the hall, she quickly and quietly pulled it open and slipped inside the room without anyone seeing or hearing. Once inside the dimly lit chamber, Elanza was greeted with warmth from the fireplace and her son's musky scent.

A large canopy bed was the focus of the room, with two beautifully crafted wooden chairs lined with the softest velvet positioned in front of the fireplace upon a large rugs midnight blue and gold. Alon-Settie was a simple man; he had only knives and daggers on display, along with his silver battle armor. Both Elanza and her husband were pleased that their son took such an active role in the Shandel's defenses.

As her eyes adjusted to the dimness of the room, Elanza saw the prince sleeping soundly under thick, dark-blue satin blankets. He had not stirred from the slight sounds of her entrance. It brought a warm smile to her face to see him safe and sound as she tiptoed close to him.

"Alon!" she whispered loudly. He did not stir. Elanza whispered his name even louder, but there was still no movement from her son. Coming back to the reality of her family and their routine, she momentarily forgot about the nightmarish event of the past evening. She rolled her eyes and shook her head sadly. "Just like your father. You sleep like the dead," she said in her normal tone of voice. Her patience was not as deep as her son's sleeping, however. Taking a deep breath, she shouted at him. "ALON!" Her shout echoed off the rock walls within the chamber.

Prince Alon-Settie wearily opened his eyes and groggily raised his head from his pillow. Looking at his mother with a dazed expression in his dark-brown eyes, the prince slowly propped himself on his bare elbows.

"Mother? Did you say something?" he asked in a very groggy tone. His mother watched him for a moment, before she dropped her head in sheer frustration.

"Only about three times. Now get up and get dressed. I need your help," she instructed as she strode across the chamber and grabbed his black and gold velvet robe from the back of one of the chairs facing the large fireplace and threw it at him. The black robe settled over his dark-brown hair, which stuck out in every direction. The dark robe draped over his head until Alon-Settie realized that he was not dreaming and reached up to remove it.

"What is it?" he asked as he slowly worked through the pull to go back to sleep. He pushed back the thick covers and dragged his bare muscular legs out of the warm bed one by one and pulled on his robe. When there was no response from his mother, Alon-Settie looked up still in a slight daze to see that his mother had already left the room. Jumping up and running barefoot for the door, which was slightly ajar, Alon-Settie quickly looked down the dim candlelit hall and saw Elanza marching toward the staircase at the other end of the corridor. Her ebony hair hung wet down her back and bounced as she moved further down the hallway. His mother marching this early in the morning meant something was up or wrong. Darting barefoot down the cool hallway, Alon-Settie fought to tie his robe around his waist and struggled to catch up to his mother. "Mother?" he called after her. She turned around and motioned for him to remain silent and follow her. Thoroughly confused by this point, Prince Alon-Settie had no choice but to follow his mother. She silently led him down the winding staircase that led to the lower levels of the castle. The only revealing attribute of their secret departure were soft sounds of her slippers and his bare feet pattering against the cool, damp stone steps as they descended deeper into the castle's lower level to a secret meeting chamber that only royal family members knew of. Prior to entering this secret darkened passage, Elanza grabbed a lantern from a hook off the wall, concealing the lantern's light to prevent anyone from detecting their presence and continued on her way.

Upon reaching the isolated meeting chamber, Elanza was quick to open the dark, heavy wooden door with the greatest of ease, letting Alon-Settie in, and then quickly closing the door behind them. It creaked and moaned as its immense weight bore down on the hinges. It closed with a slam that filled the room and the hallway outside for but a moment. The door shut, they stood in a world of complete darkness; the only sound was the fading echo of the door closing. The sound made no difference, for they were far enough down in the castle that no one would hear anything even if they were listening. The lower levels of this palace always creaked, moaned, and made odd, eerie noises. Their sudden departure was still secret.

"Now, I can tell you." Elanza spoke in a normal voice as she unveiled the metal lantern and slowly walked over to the meeting table in the middle of the cool, stone chamber and placed the lantern upon the table, thus centering the dim lantern light within the room. The smell of the chamber was slightly musty from the damp. "I had to be sure no one was around. What I have to tell you is sensitive and very important." Remaining silent for a long moment, Elanza ensured that they were totally alone and that they had not been followed.

Turning around, she quickly walked to a wooden bookshelf that contained many blank parchments, quill pens, and ink bottles. "We have a lot of work to do, and we have little time to do it, so we have to start now," she said, speaking quickly. Alon-Settie had remained standing just beside the large meeting table in a drowsy state and seemed too tired to grasp her revelation at such an early hour. But he saw something unsettling in her face that caused him to become fully awake if not startled.

"Slow down a bit, Mother. I am not ready for such an attack so early in the morning." His words made her stop and almost seemed to freeze her where she stood. Recalling a true nightmare, Elanza slowly turned and looked at him for a long moment in silence. The expression of her face was of grief and trauma.

"I pray we never see such a thing," Elanza said in raspy whisper. Alon-Settie looked at her strangely.

"Mother? I was only saying…" His voice trailed off as he saw tears in her eyes. He became concerned and walked over to her slowly. "Mother? What is wrong?" he asked. Now he was fully awake, and he looked at her closely. He could see that she wasn't herself. Her eyes were slightly puffy from crying, and there were red marks on her neck. She dropped her gaze to the floor for a long moment, trying desperately to regain her composure. He looked again at the red marks on her neck. "Mother, were you out of the castle grounds last night? Did someone hurt you?"

Elanza felt her face grow hot and lowered her gaze in reply. The vague clues of what had happened to her began to come together for Alon-Settie. Reaching out to her, Alon-Settie found that his mother was very hesitant to get near him. Then he gently took her shoulders and looked at her. "Mother, please…" He tried again in a soft whisper. The gentleness in his gray eyes pleaded for her to tell him. Taking what courage she had, Elanza looked up at him with tears running down her white face.

"Tonight, I was walking and…this beast of a man tried to…" Her voice failed and she covered her mouth with her hand and began to weep uncontrollably. Alon-Settie reached out to hold his mother. She still seemed hesitant to let him hold her, but then she stepped into his arms and broke down completely. He wrapped his strong arms around her but could not stop her from shaking as she sobbed. After she had calmed down, he continued to hold her and attempted to speak to her again.

"Tell me who did this, and I will make sure he pays," he said with great determination. Instantly, Elanza raised her head and looked at him through her tear-filled eyes.

"No, son. He has paid the first part of his sentence tonight. A young woman bashed him in the head with her staff, and I gave him another testimonial from my foot." Her words truly surprised Alon-Settie. Looking at his mother, he smiled with awe and wonder. "In time, Adalai's retribution will be more just. It may not be now, but he will not escape his deed." Although her voice was still riddled with grief, her depth of understanding of what had happened to her was remarkable.

"Beyond this terrible thing that has happened, I can see there is a light that shines from your face. I have not seen it in years. Where did you find such strength?" he asked, dumbfounded. She smiled back at him as she wiped the tears from her face.

"I was reminded of the strength that I had in me all along from the young woman who saved me tonight," Elanza said in a reverent tone.

"Who was this brave woman?" he asked with curiosity. He could not even imagine such a thing.

"She did not give her name. But she was a mysterious and wondrous person. She spoke with a kind, soft voice, but it was also firm and strong. She had great strength. I would say that she was of noble blood. Somehow, though, she reminded me of your dear friend, Leondros Goldendragon." As the queen spoke, Alon-Settie listened intently. He still could not envision such a woman but was glad that such a brave soul fought to aid his mother.

"In any case, I am not going to let the perverse things that are seeping into my kingdom go unchecked. Alon, I called you down here at this unseemly hour because our kingdom is in great danger. Indeed, all of Andora is in great danger. I have been sensing that a strange darkness is falling over the land, and I fear that if something is not done about it, it will rise up destroy everything that we hold dear." As she spoke, Alon-Settie could not help but feel the renewed strength that was radiating from his mother's kind voice.

"What is it that you want to do, Mother?" he asked, uncertain of how to take on such an elusive enemy. She smiled at him with a confident expression.

"I want to create a secret alliance that will be sent out to protect the kingdoms within the Tribunal." Alon-Settie raised his eyebrows in awe of his mother's vigilance.

"That is truly an awesome feat. How do you propose we do this, and why?" he asked as he rubbed his weary head.

"I have had a vision," Elanza began slowly. "There is a terrible force heading in our direction, and we must be ready. We will need to gather warriors and archers that are known throughout the land of the Shandel and throughout Andora who can help us in our quest. We will then need to send conscription notices to all warriors able and ready and tell them that we are in desperate need of their help. Upon their arrival to Akendron, training will begin, for we do not have much time." As Elanza spoke of her plans, Alon-Settie slowly took a chair and found himself in continued awed. As the prince listened to his mother's elaborate plans and thought about the extremes of her night and the instance that drove her, Alon-Settie was not about to try to talk her out of it. He had tried this before, without success.

All he could manage to do was stare at her in wonder. Elanza placed a handful of parchment, a quill pen, and a small glass ink bottle in front of her son.

"While you wait for the awe and wonder to wear off, please start taking down names," she gently instructed with a tone of urgency. Shaking off the stunned feeling that plagued him, Alon-Settie fought to catch up with his mother.

"All right then. Where do you want to start?" he asked as he shook his head and proceeded with his mother's wishes. Placing a blank parchment before him, Alon-Settie took up the quill pen, dabbed it in the inkbottle, and readied himself to write. He looked at his mother after she was silent awhile. Elanza was lost in thought.

"Well," Elanza began slowly as she paced the dimly lit chamber. She got her tired mind to remember the grand list of young men who would be good candidates for this mission. "I know that this army will not be successful unless we have the best men suited for the job. I am quite sure that you and Leondros would begin to fill those rolls nicely." The seriousness of the problem they were dealing with began to settle on Alon-Settie. Leondros Goldendragon was a precision shot with a bow and deadly with a sword. With the mention of his friend's name, Alon-Settie knew that his mother meant business. He was inspired by her strength and by the thought of fighting at his dear friend's side once again. Alon-Settie began to write on the blank parchment; he no longer felt the weariness of sleep nagging him. He was now compelled by his mother's mission too, but he was also driven by another pursuit. There would be justice served to the man who had attacked his mother. He would not rest knowing that such a man could just walk away from committing such an act of treachery against a queen. He would not allow it.

Chapter 7

Close Call

As the night deepened in the kingdom of the Shandel, the peace that had existed within it for a thousand years was slowly being taken over by a dark force, the same force that had left the Shandel in ruin twice before. Although its full power was still contained deep within the earth, its essence was present, finding its way into the hearts of the people, who displayed it as anger, bitterness, and hatred. Peace and tranquility were now only illusions, nothing more than masks for this rising dark force. That very evening, evil's stronghold over the land was sealed. It would not be long before the full force of evil was unleashed.

In the comfort of his darkened chamber, Solarous looked up from his work to see a green haze rising from the cooled mixture in the cauldron at the back of the room. He stopped for a moment and stared at it.

"Strange," he murmured as he slowly got up and approached the green mist. Studying it for a moment longer, he slowly passed his hand through it. When the mist dissipated, Solarous shrugged his shoulders and turned to go back to his work unaware of the haunting presence that caused the room to become almost cold. As he headed to the chamber door, the green haze returned. It was much more concentrated and loomed close behind him. He stopped again and listened, for he had heard a hissing sound within the room. Then as quickly as it had started, the strange hissing sound stopped. He shook his head and assumed that he seriously needed sleep. Reaching for the door, Solarous felt something seize him from behind. It was not a pair of hands but an invisible force. He cried out of fear and began to struggle against it. He lunged for the door, mere feet from his reach. The force seized its opportunity to overtake him. It picked Solarous up and threw him across the room, slamming him against a damp stone wall. He was aware of his skull striking the hard wall. His body instantly went limp, falling to the cold stone floor. As the portly advisor lay sprawled on the ground, unconscious, the green haze quickly settled over him and silently enveloped his body. In a moment, it disappeared within his body and became a part of him. Evil now controlled Solarous's every move and waking thought.

When Solarous finally awoke, he found his assistant Zudoo looking down at him. Zudoo was a Drac, or of the Draccen people. Draccens resembled small dragons able to stand on their rear legs and were blessed with the beautiful coloring of their dragon cousins. The Draccen who lived within Andora were either a solid color or a blend of black, brown, or green. Zudoo's particular race was colored red, blue, silver, or gold. Zudoo's family had journeyed from across the ocean, and he knew that many others still dwelt in distant island realms, Mountains of Peril, otherwise known as the Serrigen. The blood-red scales that covered the small creature's body shimmered in the chamber's torchlight. Zudoo wore only a light black robe, which did not come past his waist. The silken robe was tied with a crimson sash around his small waist. This uniform was a way for the palace servants to not be as fearful of his presence.

"Are you all right, sire?" the small dragon-like assistant asked with a warm tone of worry. His large green eyes examined his master, and though he seemed all right, minus a bump or two, Zudoo sensed a change within Solarous.

"I am well," Solarous said as he slowly sat up and rubbed the sore spot on the back of his head. As he did, a sudden thought of clarity came to him. "Very well, in fact.

"You worried me for a moment, sire." Zudoo said, letting out a sigh of relief. "I was coming to insist you take your rest when I found you like this," the small Draccen messenger explained. Solarous smiled and shook his head as he put a reassuring hand on his assistant's shoulder.

"Thank you for your concern, but while I was passed out, I received a revelation and an answer to my purpose here." As Solarous spoke, Zudoo remained still and listened to his master's words. "Earlier tonight I was reminded of a prophecy that was predicted for our time. There are many that fear this coming to pass, but the vision that I was given tells me something different. I believe it needs to be released upon the world so that we are made a part of the glorious dawn that it holds in store for anyone willing to aid it. Lord Jarden will reward his subjects handsomely when his king takes power over this land." Solarous's words and voice were soothing as he spoke of his vision. Solarous rose to his feet with ease and, quickly taking his place at his writing desk, resumed work. "We must work quickly, for there is little time.

"Is there a task you would have me do for you, my lord?" Zudoo asked, continuing to watch his master with amazement. In the few years that he had worked for Solarous since being taken from his homeland, Zudoo had never known Solarous to openly talk about his plans.

"There is indeed, but you must follow my instructions to the letter," he said, giving Zudoo a detailed list of arrangements that needed to be carried out within the next three days.

Three days later, a moonless sky allowed Solarous and Zudoo to depart from Akendron unseen. They had purposely waited for the new moon before starting their secret mission. Both royal advisor and assistant were dressed cautiously in black cloaks to avoid detection.

They kept to the shadows, scurrying through a maze of clay walls, shops, and countless markets that stood between them and the city's outer stone walls.

As they hurried toward the front gate, Solarous's mind raced with anxiety, for if they were captured and their mission discovered through the notes in his shoulder bag, they would both be killed. As he rounded a corner and began down the next street, Solarous crashed head-on with another scholar in passing. The collision caused books and papers to scatter and fall to the sand-covered ground. Zudoo was quick to disappear from sight, so as not to be noticed. After landing on the ground, Solarous, reflexively climbed to his knees, leaned back, and pulled back the hood that had fallen over his head. He looked around. It was still predawn and the city streets were dark, with only randomly placed lanterns to light the streets. His gaze fell to the ground as a cool breeze gently passed between him and the other scholar he had collided with. From a large city lantern that was nearby, Solarous glimpsed the other scholar. To his horror, it was none other than Sala of Antioch!

"Good Heavens!" Sala blurted out in surprise, fighting to adjust the warm brown robe he had thrown on as he had rushed out the door to make it to an early-morning appointment. Struggling to regain his wits and the papers that he had lost, Sala realized whom he had crashed into. The surprise in his face drained into bitterness. "Solarous! Even a fool would have heard someone coming down an otherwise empty street! How could you have missed me?" the prophet said angrily at his rival. Solarous froze as if unsure what to say. The expression on the king's heavyset advisor was blank for he felt his mission all but lost.

"I do apologize! I must have been lost in thought," he tried to explain as he fought to keep his emotions in check. Leaning over, Solarous helped pick up the papers that had been strewn about from the collision. In doing so, he picked up an aged scroll with a strange red wax crest upon it. Solarous's apology had caught Sala completely off-guard and it was enough to make him stop what he was doing and look at his adversary.

"What are you up to, Solarous? You have never apologized so

quickly, except when you have gotten away with some sinister plan," Sala said, seeing the first scroll of the prophecy in Solarous's grasp. The air seemed to freeze within his lungs and his body went cold, but Sala managed to keep his stern expression.

"I am only on my way to carry out my master's wishes, nothing more," Solarous explained as he looked up at Sala.

"Of this, I am sure," Sala replied sarcastically as he gave the royal advisor a dark look and leaned over to nonchalantly begin to pick up some of Solarous's books and papers. Solarous understood the reason behind Sala's anger toward him.

"Please let your anger die. The king's choice for a royal advisor should have been you, but he changed his mind at the last moment. I had nothing to do with it," he said innocently as he took his papers from Sala. The prophet only eyed the sorcerer with a festering distain.

"You may deceive the king all you like, but I know where your allegiances truly lie. I will be watching you and waiting for your true intentions to be revealed!" Sala said, his voice filled with promise. Sala's blue eyes seemed to bore right into Solarous's soul and made the dark sorcerer fidget uncomfortably. As he did this, he took back the first scroll of the prophecy and the other books and papers that he had dropped, without letting his alarm seep into his voice.

"You do not know the half of it," Solarous muttered with an evil smile as he walked away and disappeared into the shadows of the city's back alleys, where he reunited with Zudoo.

Arriving at Avdima Palace, Sala cautiously stepped inside the large wooden doorway to the grand council chamber. Dawn's light had yet to filter through the chamber's three main windows, thus the usually bright tan chamber was cast in a dim shadow. The room itself smelled of polished wood and freshly scrubbed stone floors. After checking to make sure no other public official or scholar had arrived before he did, Sala quickly sprinted down the wide darkened stone steps to the third of the ten terraces that made up the meeting chamber floor, which was shaped like a coliseum rather than a typical meeting chamber. Resting on each stone terrace was a row of wooden chairs. Upon finding his usual seat, Sala leaned back against the wooden chair, closed his eyes, clutched his knapsack with the scroll safely tucked inside, and fought to control his breathing. Although his hair was disheveled from his run-in with Solarous and was not appropriate for such meetings, at the moment he didn't care. As he leaned against his wooden chair and continued to breathe heavily, Sala reflected that his scheduled meetings in Akendron were not supposed to be this stressful.

Regaining his composure, Sala opened his eyes to focus his mind on the day ahead. Slowly turning his head, Sala realized he was not the only who had arrived early for the meeting. He froze for a long second, staring in horror at the royal dignitary sitting on the other side of the stairwell he had just scampered down. The elderly man sat up straight, with his wrinkled hands properly folded in his lap over his books. Dressed in a black-and-gray royal robe, the white-haired man almost blended into his surroundings. A long moment of silence passed between the two men as Sala struggled to explain his child-like behavior. "In-laws," he offered simply. Out of a stoic appearance that seemed like the man's usual expression, a faint smile came to the old man's lips; as the alarm in his face faded, the man nodded slowly in understanding.

Chapter 8

Finding Zendro

Among the tasks that Zudoo had been assigned, he was to charter a ship to take Solarous and him from the harbor just east of Akendron to the shores surrounding Zendro Isle. He found that the journey itself was a bit odd as did the shipping company merchant who owned the ship Zudoo had hired, for the sea that surrounded Zendro Isle was turbulent, and no one sailed near there for that reason. Many ships that sailed into those troubled waters, while trying to press their luck and increase their fortunes, often crashed upon the sharp rocks near Zendro's rugged shoreline. Still, under the cover of a dark hooded cloak, Zudoo made the charter according to Solarous's wishes. After their silent and almost incident-free flight out of Akendron, Solarous and Zudoo made it aboard a newly built ship called The Tamrika. The crew and captain were proud of their new ship, for she was built with an iron-clad hull that would keep breaches from occurring as often happened when they sailed through seas like those surrounding Zendro Isle.

"So you wish to press your luck, eh?" the tall captain inquired in a low gravelly voice as he limped up to Solarous and his oddly small assistant. They had just left the port of a small shipping village east of Akendron. The captain was dressed in a coat trimmed with gray and blue that hung to his knees, a beige loose-fitting shirt, and worn dark-blue pants. The flaps of his coat hung open and easily caught in the breeze that passed over the ship. The gray in his coat nearly matched that in his long beard. The large-brimmed hat on his large head seemed to do little to protect his face, for it was sunburnt and weathered from his time on the sea. As the captain studied the royal advisor and his companion cautiously with his storm-gray eyes, Solarous began to feel uneasy. He hesitated before replying.

"Our journey is one of great importance, and judging from what your employer boasted about you and your crew, I know we will meet our destination safely. What better way to test the capability of your new ship than sailing around the waters of Zendro?" The large royal advisor spoke with great anticipation, scanning the ship and crew and patting the sturdy wooden railing beside him. Nodding slowly, the captain continued to stare at the odd couple aboard his new ship.

"There is a tale that seamen tell during their time on the sea. It has been told for hundreds of years. It speaks of a man, an advisor such as yourself, sailing to find some treasure or mysterious truth. It is said that he boarded the legendary Mazu and set a course for a distant isle, forbidden and treacherous. The man's mission, they say, was folly and brought much misfortune to him and to anyone who crossed his path. Do you know what happened to the crew who granted this unfortunate man passage?" the old sea captain asked as he cocked his head slightly, his gaze dead set on his new passengers.

"I would hope that they were compensated for their troubles," Solarous answered as he began to fidget. A cold expression filled the captain's rough face.

"Their compensation was a grand one, yes," the captain said with a strange smirk. "On the trip back to Akendron, no more than a few miles out of port, the advisor rose up against the captain and crew and butchered them. Only one poor soul, mortally wounded, managed to slip unnoticed over the side of the ship and swim to safety. His dying wish was that no seafaring man ever forget this story. It is a reminder to any crew who sails the seas to beware of any traveler who pays them a handsome price to sail them to some God-forbidden place. Do you know why I told you this tale?" the captain pressed as he continued to watch his new guests.

"Travelers' delight?" Solarous lightly reasoned.

"To warn you that the story gives us the right to leave such a traveler at sea." Solarous and Zudoo both felt the seriousness of the captain's warning. "Be advised, that same course of action applies even now. When we return to Akendron, be on your way with your business and leave us to ours." The captain bowed his head as if promising Solarous and Zudoo that he was a man of his word. He then pulled his coat open to reveal a dagger and a bloodstained sword. With that, he turned and quietly walked away. Solarous and Zudoo were left to ponder what he had said as the captain and crew went about their work.

"Does the captain's message concern you?" Zudoo whispered. Solarous turned to the open ocean before him and smiled.

"It tells me I am on the right path." The advisor took a deep breath of salty air.

Early in the morning of the second day of their voyage and the eighth day of their mission, Solarous and Zudoo were dropped off on the shores of Zendro Isle by means of the captain's personal dinghy. As the two strange travelers made it through the choppy waves and over treacherous rocks that reached out of the dark sea, they turned back in time to see the iron-hulled ship sail off down the coast.

"They are leaving us!" Zudoo gasped as he tried to wave them back.

"Leave them to their superstitions; let us be on our way." Solarous said, glaring at the ship as it disappeared into the mist that surrounded the island's coast. Turning around, Solarous and Zudoo took in their first sight of the forbidden Zendro. The island was dead. The trees on this island had long ago stopped growing any leaves, leaving eerily naked branches. There was no grass but merely hardened clay and dirt. Animal skeletons could be seen half buried in the hardened earth. Looking at the path ahead of them, Zudoo could only watch as the morning's light quickly disappeared under a strange veil of dark clouds that loomed over the isle. As they moved deeper into the dark island's interior, Zudoo fashioned a torch for them to see the dusty, barren trail ahead. As they slowly moved toward the island's interior, a pungent breeze greeted them. It was rank with alkaline earth. Not even the air was fresh; all upon the isle was dead.

"No wonder this place is forbidden. There is definitely a curse upon the island," Zudoo said in a whisper.

Overhearing his assistant as he inspected the murky island, Solarous smiled. "Well, then, it looks like we came to the right place.

"How is it that you knew where to find this place, sire?" Zudoo asked with curiosity and dread.

"From a dream," Solarous began, sounding a little confused. He stopped walking and fought to remember how he knew to come to this particular isle. "Or a nightmare. In any case, my dream vision cannot be mistaken. This is where our dear lord was wrongfully imprisoned. He beckons us to release him. It is a mission of great urgency, so we must not linger." The portly advisor spoke with renewed fervor and strode past Zudoo. Solarous seemed very eager to find Lord Jarden's prison.

"Come, Zudoo, the time of the next glorious kingdom is almost upon us!" Solarous called in an excited tone. Zudoo remained silent as he followed his master. He sensed that this was an awful mistake in the making. They continued on through a narrow path that was barely visible through the thick brush and thorn-riddled bushes, all of which had died long ago, until they came to a part of the trail that grew even more treacherous. Dead vines and thorny bushes had once grown wild over this path. It was as if nature herself did not want anyone to go down the path. Solarous did not let this deter him. He pulled out his sword and started hacking through the sharp and twisted vines that prevented admittance. After several hours of cutting and hacking through the dead foliage, Solarous stopped and stared in amazement. Zudoo ducked his head around his master's body to see for himself.

Just ahead of them was a very large stone of the darkest ebony that he had ever seen. Next to the stone, even night looked like day. Large vines had long since grown over it and died. They seemed to be the chains that barred everyone from what was lurking on the other side.

Eagerly tearing aside the thorny foliage, Solarous could see a strange inscription etched into the rock. He held the torch close to the stone to examine the writing.

"Clever, very clever," Solarous offered sarcastically, glancing down at Zudoo, who looked on in anticipation. Solarous looked back up at the strange lettering. "Rafar, it is going to take more than a language barrier to stop me," he laughed as he set down his shoulder bag on a nearby stone. He handed Zudoo his torch and began to dig through the greenish bag. As he did, Zudoo began to grow nervous.

"Sire, I do believe that..." But before the warning went out to his master, a shadow from the edge of the darkened forest reached out and snatched up Solarous. "SIRE!" Zudoo screamed as he watched his master helplessly thrown about by the wild creature.

In the dimness, Zudoo squinted to see what had taken his master. His heart stopped as he made out a Gradon. This ancient-world creature looked like a dragon with two heads and two tails. It breathed both fire and ice and was very difficult to kill. As Zudoo stood in dismay watching the wild scene before him, he heard his master's blood-curdling scream cut through the air.

"Hang on, master!" he called out into the darkness that surrounded them like night itself. Agonizing moments passed for Zudoo as he dug through his master's belongings. Finally, he found his master's sword and ducked through the dense brush until he caught up with the Gradon. Managing to avoid being trampled, he tumbled underneath the dark-green and brown beast's belly and thrust the sword into its heart. The monster thrashed violently, catching Zudoo in the midsection and knocking him backward into the thorny brush nearby. The Gradon's dying wail echoed across the island and far from Zendro's shores.

When Zudoo opened his eyes and shook off the dizziness in his head, he looked around. It took him a moment to get his bearings. Thanking his night vision, he quickly jumped clear of the prickly mess he had found himself in and ran to the scene of the battle. He climbed over the dead body of the Gradon and searched for any sign of his master in the thick dead brush beyond. "Master?" he called out with growing anxiety. After a long moment, he heard someone walking toward him. Hurrying into the thicket of dead brush, Zudoo was overwhelmed with relief to find his master alive and only slightly shaken. "Are you all right, master?"

"No, but I will be shortly," Solarous said in a selfish rage as he stormed back to the rock that stood between him and the new regime that was desperate to be unleashed. Zudoo felt a slight stab in his heart as he watched his master walk away without any recognition of his valiant deed. Hanging his small dragon-like head, Zudoo slowly followed after his master. Digging through his shoulder bag again, Solarous finally found a black leather roll and carefully untied it. Opening it and studying it closely under the torch's light, Solarous smiled. "Rafar, you used the power and language of the sphinxes to seal this prison," he laughed. He then spoke the words written on the scroll to lift the enchantment from the large rock. "Your power is undone!" he announced in a loud voice.

The earth then began to shake violently as the black stone came loose from the mountainous cave that it had formerly concealed. Solarous and Zudoo watched in silent amazement as the dark magic dwelling within this place moved around them. Once the stone had moved on its own several feet from the cave, a large hole of sheer blackness remained. When all was quiet again, Solarous looked at Zudoo and then began to walk toward the cave entrance. Before entering the cave, he looked back to see his aide lingering behind nervously.

"Go on ahead, master. I will remain here until your return," Zudoo said. He could not make himself take another step.

"Come, Zudoo! Do not stop. Your glory is at hand!" Solarous tried to force his aide to follow him.

"Master, do not ask me to follow. Not this task. I fear that my death awaits me on the inside. Go and complete the quest that you have journeyed so far for. This is *your* quest. When the orders are given to bring a new empire over Andora, I will be there to see it with you. This treasure is for your eyes alone," Zudoo replied humbly, slowly backing away from the cave. Solarous looked at him a moment and then nodded in agreement. In the moments before entering the darkness of the cave, Solarous wound up some rags upon a stick and whispered a few words of his ancient teachings under his breath and created fire. The Draccen servant watched as his master disappeared into the eerie darkness of the cave, but he sensed he would have his own mission awaiting him.

Chapter 9

Lord Jarden

Walking down a long, dark tunnel with only the light from his torch to guide him, Solarous chose his footsteps very carefully. The tunnel floor was uneven and treacherous and becoming more so the farther he went. Suddenly, Solarous heard a voice call to him from deep within the cave.

"Solaroussssss! Come!" The voice sounded like a loud raspy hiss. He could not fight the chills that ran down his spine, but he continued on, determined. Moving forward, he could now miraculously pass over the treacherous path with the greatest of ease. It was as if someone were helping him to make the journey deep within the cave. Then, he reached a dead end, barring any further descent. With the aid of his torch, Solarous looked closer at the cave wall, finding sphinx writing had been etched into it also.

"Rafar, your magic is as old and dead as are you," Solarous scoffed under his breath.

"The prophet, like his order, are a plague to me and my kind," the raspy voice spoke from the darkness.

"Lord Jarden, would it delight you to know that the Osarian Knights are no more?" Solarous asked the voice. "My sources say that the last knights perished some six hundred years ago.

"This is indeed good news. They can no longer interfere with my plans." The voice sounded joyful at this news.

"Sire, I have come to free you from your prison. What must I do in order to achieve this?" he asked with anticipation, awaiting his next instructions.

"Read the text that has been inscribed on the wall but speak only its opposite meaning," Lord Jarden said with more energy and clarity. Solarous brought his torch up to the incantations and read its meaning to himself, careful not to utter it aloud. The translated text read:

Beware of this place for a great evil has been contained within these walls. DO NOT release this evil, for he will bring great peril to Andora.

Solarous took a minute to think of an opposite meaning in the same language. Standing back from the wall, Solarous began to speak the opposite meaning of the text.

"Welcome to this place, for a great wonder has been contained within these walls. Please free the great wonder, and he will bring much wealth and bounty to Andora.

Solarous then began to hear a great rumbling from within the wall. Soon the entire cave shook violently, and he staggered to another wall to brace himself. A great crack cut through the sacred inscription that Rafar had etched himself, and from the crack sprang heat and flame. As the flames neared the royal advisor, he found much to his delight that the intense heat had no effect on him. Solarous watched as the entire cave lit up from the orange and red flames that spewed out from the other side of the crack. In a moment's time, the entire area became consumed by the heat, and the eruption continued, forcing the crack to become a gaping hole. Backing farther away from the heat and flames, Solarous watched in anticipation for his lord to be freed from his prison. The magic enchantment that held power over this evil had been broken, and now it would be free once again.

Solarous knelt down humbly as he waited for his new master to come forth from the heat and flames. He heard the sound of someone walking toward him. "Rise up, my humble servant." Lord Jarden's voice was deep and resonating. Solarous slowly climbed to his feet and tried to look upon the face of his new master. However, Lord Jarden's true appearance was shielded from him by a hooded scarlet robe. Jarden was truly an eerie sight, but Solarous did not care, for his heart was glad. Lord Jarden put his hand on Solarous's shoulder. "I have great plans for you," he said promisingly.

"What are the orders you have for me and my aide?" Solarous asked eagerly.

"Have your aide go to the Mountains of Peril and summon all the Draccen who are imprisoned there. With them, I will build the greatest army Andora has ever seen," the dark lord instructed. "You, my friend, shall return to Akendron." His words caused Solarous great worry, for his return would not be a pleasant one. Jarden saw the look of fear in his new servant's black eyes and understood. "Fear no mortal being or the weapons they possess. There is much that I expect of you, and great power will be given to you to accomplish it. "

"It brings me great comfort and pleasure to hear this, my lord. Is this all that you request of me?" Solarous asked, feeling that he could do so much more for his lord.

"Patience, Solarous. Our rise to power will be quick and as silent as the night. Still, we must plan our rise very carefully for there is still goodness lurking about, and this force can get a foothold into our plans most easily. We must be wary of all agents of light. When you have completed all that I have asked, no one within this realm will be worried about what I have in store for them. It will occur to them only when it is too late to stop us." Lord Jarden's words hinted of a failsafe plan.

Solarous's thoughts drifted to those who could stand in their way. "What if there are agents of light that are strong enough to stand in our way?" he asked. Silence passed between them as Lord Jarden took a moment to think carefully. Then, without saying a word, he turned to the empty space on his left and, with a wave of his hand, created a huge ball of flame. It glowed with vibrant oranges and yellows. Tossing it into the air, he turned the ball into a great fiery ring. As it transformed, Solarous saw images appear within the fire ring. An image of Prince Alon-Settie came into view.

"This is our current problem. He must be dealt with quickly," Lord Jarden warned.

"Why is Prince Alon-Settie such a threat?" Solarous asked with uncertainty as he tried to look beyond his own understanding to foresee any such threat.

Lord Jarden was quick to change the image within the fire ring to show Solarous the threat that the prince could be to them if not stopped. "Even as we speak, the queen is constructing a massive army. This alliance will be comprised of men from the Tribunal, including Prince Alon-Settie. Many men look up to him and will gladly follow him into battle. That kind of power could easily disrupt our plans for a new empire." Solarous found himself amazed that the queen had taken such a bold move already.

Solarous's faith, however, in their Draccen allies was not diminished. "The queen's army could never be a match for our Draccen army.

"True, but we cannot let pride be our downfall. We must bring the forces of good to their knees. We will crush them by taking out key players. Their forces will lose their courage to continue after they see their leaders fall," Lord Jarden explained, showing a ghastly image of the Prince Alon-Settie's death in battle.

Dreading the thought of the young prince's death, Solarous thought of a way to spare his life. "Allow me to offer an even more enticing plan," the royal advisor said humbly, lifting his gaze to the scarlet form standing head and shoulders over him. "Wouldn't Prince Alon-Settie prove to be of more use to us alive if he were lured over to our side?" the royal advisor suggested. "He just might prove to be an even more powerful ally.

Solarous's idea pleased Lord Jarden, but then the dark lord remembered that Prince Alon-Settie had many powerful friends. "You are right. However, we might have an even greater problem on our hands than Prince Alon-Settie. He is a friend to the elfin prince of Adarah. Their bond of friendship is very strong, and it will be most difficult to break. This bond must be broken, or your great Draccen army will not stand a chance against such a force. The queen secretly intends this elfin warrior to become the general of her army. If this were to happen, we are already marked for failure," Lord Jarden said, for he greatly feared this elfin warrior. "Solarous, I give this task to you. Eliminate this elfin warrior by any means necessary.

Solarous grew nervous again. "If I may ask, why is this elfin warrior such a threat to you?"

"There is a spirit of light surrounding the elfin warrior. Why he is being protected by this spirit is a mystery, but this is a bad omen for us. He *must* be dealt with quickly." Lord Jarden seemed most unnerved by this potential threat.

"Let this trouble you no more, my lord. I will see to this personally," Solarous replied in a confident and reassuring tone.

This brought Lord Jarden great comfort, and he nodded his head. "Return to the Shandel. There is much work for you to do," he said as he caused the ring of fire to disappear.

"What of you, my lord? How will you get to the Shandel or anywhere else?" Solarous asked as he studied the eerie form of his master.

"I know this land well. Worry not, I will find you. Solarous, remember all that we are planning needs to be accomplished before the grand ceremony of The Great Dragon," Lord Jarden advised as he raised a bony hand. The skeletal hand still had remnants of skin upon it.

"This does not give us much time, but it will be done," Solarous said. Lord Jarden then vanished before an unsuspecting Solarous.

Zudoo watched the cave from a safe distance, listening to the conversation. He could not help but feel a great sense of dread.

"So many lives are now at the whim of whatever it is that we have unleashed," he said to himself. "What have we done?" he asked with an immense sadness weighing down his heart. "If I am able, let me set things right," he prayed. He saw his master reemerging from the darkened cave. He cleared his thoughts for the moment and approached Solarous. He attempted to speak but was quickly discouraged from doing so.

"There is little time for us to do the task Lord Jarden has given to us. Our jobs are quite clear and must be followed precisely for this great conspiracy to work," Solarous explained.

"I await the orders that you have for me," Zudoo offered humbly.

"Return to your home in the Serrigen. Lord Jarden will empower you to free your people from their captors. Rally them to rise up against the peoples of the Tribunal. Lord Jarden will have more instruction for you at that time. Do not wait. We have very little time, and there is still much that awaits us. After you set your people free, return to Akendron. I will expect you within a day," Solarous informed him. He sounded almost impatient as he walked with Zudoo back through the narrow path he had cut through the thicket. The small dragon-like assistant felt the air freeze in his lungs for a brief moment; such a task was truly asking the impossible. The Draccen race had been in prison for thousands of years, but to answer anything other than "yes" would be unwise. Zudoo still bore the scars of his first days in Solarous's captivity.

"This task that you have given to me does not sound all that difficult. Freedom to my people sounds like a dream come true, but I sense that there is a greater problem that you do not speak of," Zudoo replied carefully, hiding his doubt.

"The queen of the Shandel is secretly forming a great alliance that will be sent throughout the Tribunal to protect its people. Lord Jarden says that this alliance will not fall as long as Prince Alon-Settie and his elfin friend lead it. They must be dealt with accordingly," Solarous said, lowering his voice to a whisper. The coldness in his voice suggested what was to happen to Alon-Settie and his elfin friend.

"Why does Prince Alon-Settie have to die?" Zudoo was suddenly overwhelmed with fear by such a ruthless decision.

"It is not Prince Alon-Settie that Lord Jarden is concerned about. I have my own plan for the prince of Akendron. It is the prince's elfin friend who is the real threat. Rally the Draccen soldiers to hunt him down. He must be eliminated quickly." Solarous's intentions were clear, and Zudoo nodded in understanding.

"I understand the mission that lies before me, but in what way is an elf more of a threat than Prince Alon-Settie, one of the finest warriors in the land?" Zudoo asked.

"This particular elf has a spirit protecting him. We do not know how or why, but any creature with such protection will be impossible to defeat. We cannot allow this elfin warrior to live," Solarous explained, understanding the fear that his lord had concerning this elfin warrior.

"It will be done, sire. Who is this elfin warrior?" Zudoo did not want to take the chance of killing the wrong elf. Lord Jarden did not seem like the type who would lavish his subjects with immense forgiveness for such a mistake.

"Prince Leondros Goldendragon. You must see that he never reaches Akendron. He will already have been summoned and will be on his way to Akendron. The son of King Doran must not be allowed to live, or we might find ourselves at the edge of his sword." As Solarous spoke, Zudoo could not help but notice the intense and serious look in his master's cold, dark eyes. Even if the Draccen war party made it into the lower kingdoms in time and was still unable to stop Leondros, it was only a matter of time before this elfin prince would be killed.

Chapter 10

Draccen Revolution

F ar from the turbulent shores of Zendro Isle lay the treacherous and hostile kingdom of the Serrigen. It was a morbid landscape of dark, rugged mountains ash, and dust. No vegetation grew within this vast, desolate wilderness. The Serrigen was wide and shallow, with its eastern and western borders stretching from coast to coast and its northern and southern borders acting as a natural boundary between the once tropical region of Lani, which was now an endless barren wasteland, like the realm of Graven to the north and the tropical kingdoms to the south. The Draccen people who resided here had been prisoners in their own homeland for many thousands of years, trapped by the rugged mountain ranges, their only food was the game that could be hunted and the vegetation that could be gathered.

Around 5800, the Draccen leaders began expanding their search for food and had led hunts down to the lower kingdoms to provide for their people. Some of the Draccen abused this privilege, however, and lay siege to entire cities to further their people's prosperity. The lords of the Draccen people protested this action, but when they openly opposed those who led the savage attacks, they were butchered in their sleep. Thus, these new Draccen warriors were promoted to lords, and the raids continued upon the lower kingdoms until the year 6897, when a Draccen raiding party was captured in its attempt to ransack the elfin city of White Tower. The band was forced to take their captors back to the Serrigen, where the Draccen nation was finally held accountable for its crimes. One leader from the new Draccen regime was allowed to live on one condition: any creature of the Draccen race must remain within the confines of Romulus, a great city deep within the Serrigen realm. It was said that the city was so massive that its subterranean tunnels housed over a million Draccen. Fear ran deep amongst the few men who guarded the massive hoard, and they ultimately decided that if any Drac was caught outside the boundaries of the city or was discovered trying to escape, they would be executed on sight.

The guards soon grew tired of having to provide food for the multitude but wanted to a humane solution for their prisoners. In 6904, they called upon a group of sorcerers from far and wide to come up with a humane solution to this problem, thus the sorcerers banded together to put an enchantment upon the imprisoned Draccen. Each man who guarded the Draccen city was given a white talisman that glowed with an emerald-green light. The light from the talisman put the Draccen in a constant state of slumber. As the long years passed, the guards began to notice that their Draccen prisoners did not age during this time of slumber, and thus their massive numbers remained constant. These men remained ever cautious, for they feared that if the green talismans ever lost their enchantment, the Draccen would awaken and start a rampage across the whole of Andora to satisfy their thirst and hunger.

Thousands of years passed. As new men were trained to guard this dark realm, they were taught to be vigilant in case a massive army ever came to free the Draccen prisoners. The guards had built up several high walls that circled the city of Romulus to protect them from any such onslaught, either inside the city or outside of it.

The stone blocks that made up this huge barricade were overwhelming. One block was double the size of a six-foot-tall man, and ten of these blocks made up the height of the wall while six more made up the depth. The walls encompassed Romulus completely. Guard towers were constructed along the wall so the guards would have the chance to signal for help should an attack on the fortress happen. However, it had been over 3,000 years since the Draccen people were first placed into incarceration, and no attempts from any party outside the Serrigen had ever been made to free these people. Content with this knowledge and believing that no harm would come from their actions, some guards secretly sold several Draccen prisoners to traveling sorcerers and merchants. They never suspected such actions would come back to haunt them.

One particularly dreary day, an armored guard of Romulus was slowly making another uneventful round while on his watch of the fortress's southern wall. His walk was slow and even. He carried a bow and quiver upon his back and other handy weapons upon his person, should an occasion call for it. He was average in size and appearance, physically in shape and mentally prepared for any incursion that could take place. As he walked, this red-haired man longed to leave this seemingly useless position. From under his rounded metal helmet that sat heavy on his head, his green eyes carefully studied the dark mountains that loomed along the horizon and took in the gray clouds passing over the desolate land. He hoped these clouds would bring rain, for the land was unbearably warm and had hardly seen any precipitation. This thought alone made the guard uncomfortable with the region's heat, for his black tunic was thick and coarse and shiny armor plating covered his chest, arms, and back. To take his mind off of his discomfort, the guard thought about his family within the Shandel. The guard had accepted this solitary station when the King of the Shandel offered it to him over five years ago. Although it took him away from his family, he felt he could earn more money to support them from afar; however, now he was beginning to feel that he could do more good if he was actually with them.

In the course of his weekly routine, the red-haired guard walked the entire length of the immense wall's southeastern quadrant. It was a grueling trek of some fifty miles. Deep down, he thought that they were severely undermanned should the worst happen, for the citadel had only a couple hundred men to tend the wall's entire outer perimeter. Still, he remained firm in his duty.

Nearing the guard tower of the citadel's eastern wall, the guard noticed a lone stranger walking up a rugged mountain trail toward the eastern gate. The stranger was covered in a dark cloak that almost completely covered them. The guard leaned closer and blinked several times to make sure he was not seeing things. His eyesight was not failing him. It was indeed a small Draccen, slowly approaching the huge fortified gate. Although the Drac was wearing royal robes and jewelry, signifying status, the guard's training warned him to be wary.

"Stop! Do not come any further! Return to where you came from and I shall not alert this fortress of your presence!" the guard shouted down to the Draccen stranger. The Drac stopped silently before the gate, which was constructed of heavy timbers and metal hinges and took several strong men to open. A long moment passed as the Drac stood under the dark cover of his cloak. The guard felt shivers of fear and dread course down his back. "Turn back! I am warning you! You will be shot if you come any closer to the gate!" the guard's thundering voice echoed throughout the surrounding mountain range, but the cloaked Drac only lifted his deep-red scaly head and looked up at the guard with searing green eyes.

"This is something I cannot do, but you must do something for me, if you give any regard for your own life!" the small Drac shouted back. The creature's voice was gentle but filled with genuine concern. "Open wide the gates to Romulus, destroy the talismans that hold power over my people, and set them free!" the request of this seemingly polite Drac was unimaginable.

"Are you insane? I would be dead long before my king would have the chance to fire me!" the red-haired man yelled back, totally taken aback by this request.

"Then take your chance and flee this place. Go find your family, and leave Andora altogether!" the small Drac advised. There was a moment of silence as the lone guard contemplated this tempting choice.

"I will not live a life away from Andora in shame! Do what you must, but I will do my duty!" The guard's response caused the small Drac to lower his head sadly. When he lifted his head again, he was looking down the blade of an arrowhead aimed right at him!

"I pray your soul finds mercy, for I have given you your chance!" the small Drac called out as his searing green eyes met the red-haired man's. Something in the Drac's small face unnerved the guard. A second later, the Drac took out a shiny black orb from under his cloak. The small Drac gripped it tightly with his dark little claws and quickly knelt down and slammed the orb into the rock-hard ground at his feet. The orb shattered, and a thick, red smoke rose from the shards into the air and quickly dispersed through the heavy timbers of the massive east gate. A wave of fearful suspicion gripped the red-headed guard as he looked down at the green talisman that hung around his neck. A small cloud of red haze passed near the charm that hung and was absorbed into the talisman. The glowing green light went out. The talisman, which had glowed green for as long as he had had this job, was now nothing more than a necklace.

"WHAT HAVE YOU DONE?" the guard screamed hysterically as he turned and saw the same red haze quickly passing into the sleeping city of Romulus. When he snapped his head back to the small Drac still standing at the gate entrance, the guard felt fear truly grip his heart. The Drac was now pointing up at him with a single talon.

"I have awakened my people. Sadly, your life will end..." The small Drac's voice was drowned out by a terrible noise rising from the city behind the fortified wall. The guard turned his eyes slowly back to the shadowy city. Crazed howls and screeches accompanied an eerie thunder that grew louder with each passing moment.

"No, you have just unleashed hell!" the guard replied in horrible realization. He felt himself sink a level on the food chain as he caught his first sight of a true Draccen citizen from Romulus. Her features were more dragon than human, her flesh a bluish-black color. Her disheveled black hair came to her muscular shoulders. Her clothes were ragged and torn, revealing her gaunt, muscular form. She lifted her pointed nose to the air and sniffed the air with intense satisfaction. Wild with hunger, the Draccen woman's keen nose smelled the lone guard, and a haunting roar left her mouth. The guard watched for only a second as the Draccen woman tore through the deserted streets toward the fortified wall of the citadel on all fours. Her claws quickly gripped the stone blocks, and she scurried up the wall with no effort.

It was not supposed to end like this, the guard thought as he took his still-drawn bow and shot the arrow at the crazed Draccen woman. The arrow caught her in the throat, and she fell. Her agonizing wail filled the dimming night sky as her claws feverishly tried to dislodge the arrow. Hitting the hardened ground below, the Draccen woman did not get up again.

The guard watched the darkened city streets in the distance begin to move and shift. From the darkness, he saw the colorful shimmering eyes of the Draccen people who had been awakened. Never before had he laid his eyes on the million Draccen souls that had slept beneath the city streets. Fear now stirred in his heart as he looked upon the glistening ocean of shimmering eyes looking at him. The guard looked down the long road of rock wall ahead; no other guards were around or coming to his aid. Taking a deep breath, the guard reloaded his bow as a raging storm of Draccen rushed toward the base of the wall far below him. He made sure his swords were close by and prayed that his family would be spared from this coming horror. The guard shot several arrows before the first wave of ravenous Draccen reached him. The dutiful guard never hoped to meet death in the magnificent glories of battle, but knowing now that he would never see his family again, he made his last moments count. In a valiant array of stunning moves, the guard held his station for several long moments. The guard's fight for survival was short-lived as the mob swarmed over him and restrained him from further movement. His inhuman screams were drowned out by the ferocious wails of these creatures fighting over their first meal in ages.

Turning his head away from this atrocity, Zudoo felt glad that his people were free for he knew they were truly good at heart, but this savage demonstration of his people would not win any favor with the kingdoms of this age.

"Man made them this way." a low resonating voice spoke softly to the small Drac. "They are truly wondrous beings if they are given the chance." the dark lord had silently appeared beside Zudoo and watched the crazed madness going on overhead.

"I know," Zudoo replied simply. He then felt Lord Jarden gently lay a comforting hand on his head.

"You have done well today," Lord Jarden said. "I will lead them now, but first I will honor my part, for I could not have accomplished this without you," the dark lord said with sincerity. "Just as I brought you to the gate of your home city, I will take you back to your home in Akendron.

"I am grateful; Solarous does not like to be kept waiting. My mission in this is far from over," Zudoo confessed as he rolled his large green eyes with frustration. Lord Jarden nodded his head slowly and waved his hand over the small Drac's form. Zudoo's image faded under a deep green haze until he had completely disappeared.

Left alone, Lord Jarden turned to the ravenous horde pouring through the massive gate that had been forced open. A moment before they overran the dark lord, he waved his bony hand through the air in front of them. A cloud of purple haze left his hand this time, and its effect on the savage crowd before him was instantaneous. The rampaging people came to a dead stop and slowly stood on their hind legs and looked up at Lord Jarden in awe and wonder.

"I have taken your hunger and thirst, but your anger for those who imprisoned you will remain with you. You will need it for what is to come," Lord Jarden announced to the massive group now standing before him just outside the gate of the citadel.

"Why should we listen to you?" a Draccen man dressed in ragged clothes asked with a growling sneer as his golden eyes glared at the red-cloaked figure before him.

"If you follow my plan accordingly and leave no room for mistakes, not only will you have earned freedom from man's grasp, but you will have received your revenge." Lord Jarden's words caught the attention of everyone who stood before him.

"Then I guess our next question is what is your first order of business?" said another Draccen man, stepping forward. It was clear this Drac had been a military leader. Lord Jarden nodded his cloaked head in approval.

"I will need several bands of warriors to take people from the lower kingdoms under the cover of night. Start with farmers, hunters, and anyone caught outside after dark. If anyone sees you and tries to tell others of you, kill them but leave no evidence behind. You must be as swift as shadows. If the people of the lower kingdoms want a war, they will have a hard time trying to raise an army big enough, if their people keep vanishing." the dark lord's plan pleased the Draccen leader, who nodded in approval. "While the bands are out, I will need several hundred of your people to build compounds that can house thousands of people. These compounds will be located all over Andora. Those whom we have kidnapped need to be imprisoned until they are ready to serve my purposes.

"This is far worse than what put us in prison the first time," said the Draccen leader, seeming agonized over the duties that awaited him and his people. Then his brownish-red eyes shimmered with excitement and a toothy smile appeared. "I love it.

"Then you will love this: gather a regiment of your finest men who can travel with great speed. They are to take out a key piece in this glorious revolution. If my suspicions are correct, you will intercept a lone elfin warrior heading to the capital of the Shandel. He must not make it out of the Divervandon Forest alive," Lord Jarden added, and his tone became serious and threatening. The Draccen leader's smile never left.

"Then we are wasting valuable time," the Draccen leader said. Many Draccen soldiers stepped forward from the crowd that now stood upon the 120-foot-high wall. "We make for the shadows of the Divervandon Forest!" the Draccen leader told them. The hundred-plus soldiers let out a ferocious roar that echoed far across the land surrounding the citadel. A revolution was beginning as the Draccen allied themselves with the darkness of Lord Jarden.

Chapter 11

The Tomblock

S everal days prior to the excitement caused by the seer's message of
warning, another individual was already sensing change for her
was close at hand. The sweltering sun burned in the afternoon sky.
There was no escape from its intense heat, not on this day, especially
not for the people who worked on the Shandel's plantations. A
great many of them were slaves forced to work long hours doing
rigorous labor in their masters' fields and could not just retreat into
the cool shadows of their homes. Life on the slave plantations was
an ongoing nightmare. Most slaves were not treated well; they did
hard work in extreme conditions with no rest, little to no food, and
decrepit living conditions with brutal taskmasters ensuring the work
was completed. Many slaves died from the experience.

A small band of slaves had worked to find ways to escape the barbed
wire and high rock walls of their plantations to look for food and the
necessities they needed to live. For many months, when darkness fell,
these brave souls had tunneled under the ground to a spot beyond
the protective fences and watchmen that kept them confined to the
plantation. Once accomplished, these slaves began to make nightly
escapes to Akendron, searching only for the things they desperately
needed. The risk was great. Several of them had been caught and taken

from the plantations. They had never been seen or heard from again.

Once away from the plantation, a slave might be tempted to abandon the plantation entirely. But slaves who were successful in their escape did not live long afterward. Once it was learned that someone had escaped, the taskmasters would pay trackers to hunt down and kill the escapee. No one had escaped from these dreadful places with their lives yet.

People became slaves by falling into debt; they were then bound to their plantations until their debt had been paid in full by working in the fields for a determined number of years. The greater the slave's debt, the longer the sentence. Over time, many plantation masters had grown greedy and dishonest, not wishing to give up their easy life. So they made it impossible for slaves to leave. The slaves were given a goal to work toward, but one by one each slave had their goal revoked as a result of some misdeed the slave was claimed to have committed and the sentence lengthened accordingly. For many slaves, hope became too expensive to own, but some spirits will not be broken or contained.

One such brave slave was Tahari of the Shandon. Orphaned from the age of three, Tahari had spent her entire life on the plantation that many called the Tomblock. She barely remembered her parents or what it was like to have a real family. All she knew was the life of a slave, working long hours beside others under the scorching sun. Unknown to her, when she was just a small child, she had been left with the Dancar family, owners of the Tomblock plantation. When they realized that no one would come back for her, they made Tahari a slave and gave her to Saratee, an old black woman who lived on the slave plantation. Though she had endured a hard life, she freely loved the child. Frail in appearance, Saratee was strong in spirit, which was reflected in her weathered brown face and her warm light-brown eyes. Her positive presence could intimidate even the strongest taskmaster at the Tomblock. Saratee cared for Tahari as if she were her own daughter, but their time together was short. When the Dancar saw how happy the old slave woman was to have the orphan child in her keeping, they put Saratee in the fields and worked her even harder.

The poor woman could not last in such overburdening conditions, and on Tahari's eighth birthday, Saratee died in the cornfields that she had worked in much of her life. Although Tahari was still very young, she knew what had transpired and was greatly devastated by the loss. The Dancar family held little compassion for the grieving child and pawned her off on other slaves to care for her. Saratee was quickly forgotten, but Tahari never forgot this spirited, loving old woman.

As Tahari grew up, all the people that had become a part of her life ended up dying in the Tomblock's various fields or was taken to other plantations. She was often told by the master's wife that she was the reason these people had died or were taken away. Tahari never believed the mistress's hurtful words, but as she grew older, she could not help but wonder why she always felt so alone, even amongst the other slaves who had grown quite fond of her. In fighting these demons, Tahari refused to believe the Dancar family's lies. She came to believe that she was not like the other slaves and that she had a special purpose. Until she found out what her purpose was, she would be determined to help the other slaves in their labors, for Tahari greatly cared for them and could not bear to see them suffer.

The life she was forced to live from day to day was difficult, but Tahari carried herself with dignity. The other workers saw in her a wisdom that seemed as ancient as the land itself. The people around her took great comfort in her presence—except the Dancar family. They were spiteful of Tahari for she took her burdens without a care and gave hope to others. They could barely stand the sight of her for they saw that, compared to their own daughter's beauty, Tahari possessed something much more. In truth, Tahari stood out from amongst the slaves. She was as dark from working long hours under the burning sun, and she possessed features that were both delicate and strong. The regal beauty that shone out from her tanned face made Tahari seem almost angelic. Everything about her seemed to give off a positive energy that easily infected the other slaves. In seeing this, the Dancar family increased her burdens many times over, doubling and often tripling her workload. Tahari remained unfazed and looked upon these injustices as opportunities to make her stronger.

Nearing her eighteenth birthday, Tahari began to feel trapped within her life and longed for freedom. She grabbed at a chance to join in the underground movement to search Akendron for food and supplies. She soon saw a better life waiting beyond the Tomblock's high stone walls. Tahari dreamed of the day she would no longer be a slave. Yet the long, hard days continued as she and the other slaves were subjected to the taskmasters' whippings and cruel beatings. At times, it seemed impossible that there could be life outside of this horrible place, but refusing to give up her dreams, Tahari remained unbroken in spirit. Although she could not explain it, she sensed that the Tomblock was about to undergo a great change.

One evening, like many before it, Tahari secretly climbed into a large oak tree not far from the barracks where the Tomblock slaves slept and sat high in its branches. Under the dark blanket of night, Tahari looked out at the universe of stars stretching from one side of the horizon to other; she sat between heaven and earth and felt at peace. This was a sacred place where she could be free from the troubles of the land. On this night, though, a new problem plagued her mind.

It was not the excruciating pain of searing sunburn, the taskmasters' daily threats, or the worry over the other slaves' whippings that concerned her. This was a new and unexpected burden. As she sat facing the vast countryside, Tahari closed her eyes and breathed in the cool night air, hoping to rid her mind of several strange premonitions that had flashed before her eyes earlier that day before starting the day's chores. Yet these haunting visions did not leave. Resting her weary head in her hands, Tahari thought about an earlier conversation she had with Senti, a white slave who had been both mother and dear friend to her since she was ten.

"You are a very special individual, Tahari, one that I am glad to call my friend," Senti had said. "These visions that you experienced are a valuable sign. My parents used to say that the seer has a great responsibility. One can choose to help those concerned or to do nothin' Either way, the choice is one that only you can make, but you have a good heart and I can see it in your eyes that you long to help these people. These visions may just help you do that.

Senti's words were as vivid as the sparkle in her hazel eyes when she smiled. The old woman was thin but strong. Like Saratee, she had spent many long years on the Tomblock, and yet somehow she did not show the hardship she had endured. Tahari knew it was because of Senti's positive attitude and laughter that not even the taskmasters could beat. Many times when the taskmasters would threaten Senti, she would return the insult and laugh, thus causing the other taskmasters and slaves to laugh at her accusers. Beatings would follow, but she was never broken by them; rather they seemed to strengthen her. Senti was now the closest thing that Tahari had to a mother, and she dreaded the thought of losing her. Tahari cared about all the slaves that she worked with, and it caused her heart to ache when she would see a fellow worker being beaten in the fields by a taskmaster but even more so when she saw dear Senti being thrown to the ground and beaten. How she always longed to stop it! Maybe now she had her chance.

"If I have been given such a wondrous gift, then maybe its purpose should be to do as I have always wanted to do. If it calls me to someone's aid, I will not deny them such divine intervention. I pray that when such visions are sent to me, I will have the wisdom to use them for the good that is intended," Tahari said to herself in a hushed whisper. Watching the night around her, she saw a falling star brightly arcing across the sky overhead. In that mesmerizing moment, a voice whispered on the cool breeze that blew gently against her sunburnt face.

"You will save a multitude."

The voice sounded like a woman's. Realizing what the words meant, Tahari lost her balance from the thick branch she was perched on. Looking around and finding herself still alone, the slave girl sensed an immense mission was awaiting her. She looked at the high stone walls of the Tomblock and the taskmasters on night patrol. Narrowing her gaze, Tahari grumbled under her breath, "Your days of torture and cruelty are drawing to an end, and I will be there to see you fall."

Chapter 12

A Slave's Life

The morning sun had yet to rise from its bed when the horns sounded in the foggy courtyards of the Tomblock. The blaring horns cut through the cool morning air and reached the weathered barracks where the slaves slept. Another day had come for the slaves, but as Tahari had sensed, great changes were coming with it. Many of these changes would be unexpected and downright brutal for those in charge.

The bellowing sound of the great horns through the plantation cut sharply through Tahari's dream world again, this time bringing her fully awake. She noticed the other slaves pulling on their worn sackcloth as she leapt from the floor. The Dancars saw to it that slaves had only the coarse sackcloth on their backs, sackcloth tied to ankles for shoes, and a dark robe for the cold season. However, Tahari found this to be an advantage: she did not have to take time to dress and was able to get out to the fields quicker. The beige sackcloth she wore was severely torn from working in the fields, but she made the best of it. Quickly grabbing her only brown leather strip for her long brown hair, she pulled it into a tight ponytail and ran out of the rickety barracks into the cool morning air. The sun's intense heat had not yet burned through the thick mist that hung in the morning air. She breathed in the cool fresh morning air, for she loved this time of day. The cool air was thick with the scent of flowers and freshly cut grass. She almost felt like she wasn't a slave but as free as she was in her dreamland.

As Tahari made her way toward the dusty courtyard, she looked back to see the rest of the workers filing out of the gray barracks. It stopped her for a moment. Her heart sank to see such solemn faces. New slaves find it easy to hope for freedom when they first arrive, but they lose that hope the longer they are here. Most now seemed to have so little life left within them as they staggered toward the center of the courtyard. It almost seemed as if their spirits had left their bodies long ago. It was hard to believe that there had ever been happiness on these hardened faces—but there had been, and she would help them to remember it. Seeing them sparked an idea within her. She thought of a way that she could make them smile again, but it would mean performing another nightly escapade and bringing back more food. Taking this spark of enthusiasm with her, she joined the other workers as they formed lines to wait for roll call and then take their turns to get their hoes and rakes from the taskmasters for the day's work.

One by one, each worker was issued their daily chores from the prime master, who stood in front of the large group of slaves before him. The prime master made himself known by the bright red sash that he wore over the black shirt and leggings that all the taskmasters wore, along with the black turbans that kept the sun off their heads. These harsh men never spoke their names to the slaves, for they did not want to know them; they were as cattle to be used for their labor. Some of the older workers were given light work around the buildings and the main house; others were sent to tend the vegetable and flower gardens. The rest of the men and a scarce few women, Tahari included, were sent to the far fields. These fields were some ten miles from the main plantation and consisted of various crops, including corn, oats, wheat, and potatoes. It was in these fields that much of the Tomblock's brutality occurred. The taskmasters who were sent to supervise the workers got away with murder—sometimes literally.

Taking up her hoe and starting the long walk to the far fields, Tahari lost herself in thought. She looked forward to the long walks out to the fields and being in the fields themselves, for it was here she had a slight taste of freedom. Even as she worked in the various fields, she could always find time to dream, though she had to be mindful of her progress in the fields or the taskmasters would be out for blood.

The morning sun quickly rose higher in the sky and burned off the thin layer of mist that lingered in the air. Tahari looked up and saw that today the sun would be as intense as ever. The air around her already felt hot and sticky. By the feeling that she had deep inside, she knew that they would see a good-sized thunderstorm before the day was out. As Tahari lowered her eyes to shield them from the sun, she happened to gaze at her browned arm. It almost took her breath away. Although she was an immensely strong individual compared to most of the people who worked here, Tahari noticed just how thin she had already become. Although the slave's life has never been easy, recently it had grown worse. At the beginning of this year, their food rations went from three healthy and filling meals a day to one meager meal a day, served at night after the work was done. In the brilliant morning sun, Tahari could see that her arms were still very muscular, but it scared her a little to see her bones. Things had to change, or even she would not be able last much longer in this place.

Upon reaching the far fields, they felt the sun beat down on them with intense heat. A group of them were chosen to work the cornfields. Taking up their hoes, they quickly disappeared into the tall rows of corn. Because the fields were so large, each group split into two and started at opposite ends of the cornrows. This was done so that by the end of the day they would all meet in the middle of the field. Tahari stared in awe at the height of the stalks of corn, which were twice the height of any average-sized man. It had indeed been the best year for their crops. "I guess the *miracle rains* really do make a difference," Tahari said to herself.

As Tahari reached the far end of the cornfield, she saw her dear friend Rami. Of the same ethnicity as Saratee, Rami had lighter skin than Saratee's dark brown and large brown eyes. His pitch-black hair was short enough so one could see beads of sweat glisten along his brow and scalp. He seemed old and worn from the many hard years of slavery, but in spite of his tired, almost hardened features, he had a kind soul. Tahari could see it in the soulfulness of his eyes. It usually would come out when he greeted her in the morning, and his whole face would brighten when he saw her.

"Good morning, Rami," Tahari said with a cheerful tone. Looking up from his work, Rami saw her, but his smile was not as cheery as usual. Tahari could see that he was deeply troubled by something. "What is it?" she asked in a softer tone as she came up to him, her expression filled with concern. His gaunt face looked around the immense cornfield to keep a keen eye on the taskmasters. Rami usually didn't reveal what was concerning him to anyone, but he knew that Tahari was not like other people. He also knew that there was not much he could keep from her because Tahari usually guessed it anyway.

"There is much trouble in the air," he said, his deep voice hushed and low as his gaze drifted to the main plantation in the east and then slowly came back to her. "Be careful, Miss Tahari. Evil is lurking' about and has descended upon the master's house." his words worried her, and Tahari kept a watchful eye out for the taskmasters.

"What happened?" Tahari asked with great concern, seeing same look of worry on other slaves' faces.

Rami's features filled with great sadness. "Our families are slowly starvin' to death, and the prime master has taken the liberty of cutting food rations again." he lowered his voice to a whisper so that it wouldn't carry on the breeze. As he paused for a moment, Tahari caught the worry in his large brown eyes. He was clearly upset by the news, and he had good reason. It also angered Tahari, but she continued to listen intently. "That is not all," he said, the muscles of his jaws tightening. "Before the horn sounded this mornin', Master Dancar had the taskmasters gather a few of us from the barracks to inform us of these changes and to spread this message to everyone within the plantation. The daily work load for the entire plantation has been doubled." as Rami uttered this disheartening message, Tahari felt the burden of this added load already on her shoulders and more so on everyone else's.

"This is madness! Why would they do such a terrible thing?" Tahari asked in fatigue and frustration as she turned her attention to the taskmasters. They were standing around, eyeing other slaves working nearby. The mere sight of these lazy taskmasters infuriated her. The life they led was anything but hard, and their bodies illustrated it. They were sunburnt like uthe rest of the slaves, but the only burden they had to haul around was their overgrown bellies that rolled over their belts. Tahari then felt an eerie silence from Rami. Turning back to him, Tahari saw him lower his gaze to the ground. She sensed that he was trying to protect her from something. "Rami, what are you not telling me?" Tahari asked as she fought off the tears that were forcing their way to the surface. Something about this new decree gave her the feeling that in some strange way she was responsible for this.

"It is a sad thing to see when Adalai grants the Dancars the miracle of another beautiful baby girl only for them to be jealous of her and make her a slave in their fields." his words seemed almost mythical, but it hit home and it hit hard, for Tahari's past was never an easy story to tell. Tears welled in her eyes for a brief moment before she quickly blinked them away. Rami's empathetic gaze settled on her, his dark eyes glistening with his sadness for her. "It is their bitterness and hatred of you that has brought about these changes. The master has said that you are the reason he has done this." his words were riddled with grief. Immediately Tahari sensed that everyone's eyes were burning into her back.

"Why do they make so many suffer because they hate me?" Tahari asked. She was filled with hurt and anger.

"I do not understand the reasoning for such madness," he said slowly as he wearily shook his head. "Still, master has decreed that if you alone can outwork the strongest man on the plantation, then everyone will have to meet this standard." Tahari's gaze wandered over to the other workers and she shook her head sadly. It was beyond staggering to think the Dancars would place these demands on these weary workers. Half of these people could barely stay on their feet, they were so weak. Rami saw Tahari's sadness melt into anger and put a comforting hand on her shoulder. "Please go about your day. Do not push their anger any further, or you will have more than just the taskmasters on your back." his words gave her fair warning. Tahari nodded as she picked up her hoe and moved on to start her work.

The long hours passed slowly under the scorching sun. Tahari felt its hot rays pierce through her thin sackcloth shirt and further burn her already sunburnt back. The day had been a long one, and she stood for a moment to stretch her aching back. Looking through the tall rows of corn at the other workers, it was not hard to find truth in what Rami had told her earlier. The gazes from the other workers were the equivalent to the sun's scorching rays upon her back. Tahari quickly went back to her work as she heard the slow meandering sound of a taskmaster walking by. Their work was never done, for this was just one of the twelve fields that they worked. After one field was finished, they were moved to the next field that needed to be weeded, watered, or harvested from. There were only about fifty workers able to work in these distant fields. The workload was tremendous for the few of them, but they would either work these fields or be severely punished.

The taskmasters had several ways to get people to work. If a slave did not want to work in the fields, they could send them to the rock mines to split rocks all day. There were other forms of punishment, but the most dreaded was the cross. A slave would be taken to caves that were just south of the Tomblock, close to the Misty Forest. Inside the caves, the slave was chained to the walls and then whipped and beaten. After two days of this treatment, the slave was sent back into the fields to work—if they survived.

Tahari had not been subjected to such treatment, but she had witnessed it many times over. Trying hard to pull her mind out of the depths of such morbid thoughts, she straightened her stiff back again and took a deep breath of a cool breeze that blew against her. Trying to focus on happier thoughts, Tahari remembered that she would turn eighteen years of age this month. Even though this was not a long time to have lived in the world, Tahari could not help but feel old, ancient really, on the inside. In some ways, Tahari felt that she had not been a slave all of her life.

"Daydreamin' again, Miss Tahari?" a woman's kind voice broke through Tahari's drifting thoughts. Blinking herself back to reality, Tahari looked over to see Senti walking up to her. She always wore a faded light-purple scarf to cover her curly gray and white hair to keep the sun off her head. Even though it was incredibly hot and they were all weary from working many long hours in the large cornfield, she greeted Tahari with a loving smile as she always did.

"Afternoon, Senti. I guess so, but it is hard not to do when you work in the fields of toil and despair," Tahari said with a sigh as she motioned with her chin to the long faces that could be seen throughout the field. Senti turned and nodded slowly in understanding. Her warm brown face seemed saddened by this, but when she looked back at Tahari, she found her smile again.

"Yes, you are right, especially on a day with such dreadful news. Just be mindful, my dear. Today, the taskmasters will be working' harder than ever." she spoke gently, but Tahari actually found her words amusing.

"If they do, it will truly be a first," Tahari remarked sarcastically. Senti's eyes went large as she coughed and laughed, caught off-guard by Tahari's sudden humor. Putting a delicate, dirt-covered hand to her mouth, Senti tried to clear her throat to breathe normally again, her eyes following Tahari's to a portly taskmaster who was contentedly basking in the sun.

"Just be careful. They are out for blood, and right now, you are not sitting too high on their good list," she cautioned Tahari.

"I am not sitting too high on anybody's good list at the moment," Tahari said with a somber expression. It was hard to be in these fields knowing that everyone around her seemed almost pitted against her because of the plantation master's decree.

Senti reached over and put her hand on Tahari's sunburnt shoulder. "Tahari, we all know the intense hate the Dancars have for you. At the moment, the workers cannot help feeling the way they do. Life for all of us has just gotten worse." her words caused Tahari's chest to tighten.

"If they hate me so much, then why do they torture everyone else from day to day? I would rather bear the brunt of their rage than see everyone else suffer from their cruelty," Tahari said in a tone of anger. Senti and Tahari looked at each other in sudden and horrible realization. The Dancars wanted the workers to rebel and secretly get rid of Tahari, so that her blood would not be on the plantation master's hands.

Senti was greatly saddened by this revelation, but she gently touched Tahari's hot cheek with her palm. "Tahari, there is somethin' very special about you. Whatever it is, it inspires the rest of us to live on day to day with hope. If you were not here, many of us would have lost our will to live long ago." Tahari found her own will to go on again in her words. She smiled encouragingly at Tahari. Then something caused her hazel eyes to lose all expression. A taskmaster had been eyeing them and was approaching. "We will talk later," she said in a rushed whisper. Senti quickly went back to work hoeing weeds from within the long rows of corn as did Tahari. The portly taskmaster came close to them and looked at them with dark, scolding eyes. Tahari did not look up at him as she worked without appearing distracted by his looming presence. Tahari could feel his eyes burning into her back. Finally, he turned and left, though she felt his eyes occasionally looking back at her.

The burning sun finally sank below the western horizon and a warm breeze drifted through the cornrows, causing them to gently sway. The breeze felt cool on Tahari's tired, sunburnt body. She fought to shake the weariness from her head for although the day had been very long and tiring, they were not done with their work yet. They still had to clean out the Dancars' main livestock barn back at the plantation. The taskmasters eagerly reminded them of this with the cutting lash of their whips. The lashings had gone on throughout the day, and Tahari had received several strikes across her back, though she had not faltered with her work once. Perhaps they were trying to make a daily quota.

Tahari felt her mind grow weary again from the intense heat and hard work. She stood for a moment to get her bearings. As she gazed into the setting sun, she became lost in its red and flaming glow.

Everything around her faded, and Tahari felt herself drift away from her body and the intense heat and pain of the day.

Strange images turned from blurry to painfully clear. Tahari took them in with confusion and disbelief. She was looking at what used to be the Tomblock Plantation, except what she saw looked as if an explosion had ripped it apart. Fields had been swept barren and trees stripped of bark, debris filling their leafless branches. All was silent. As Tahari walked through this nightmarish scene, she realized why everything was so quiet. There were no bugs buzzing in the late afternoon air. No birds sang. The normal sound of people talking over supper, discussing their day, was absent.

As Tahari continued to walk through this silent world, she began to feel very anxious and her heart raced. Then on the still air, she caught the smell of what had happened here. Death. Swallowing hard, Tahari came to a pile of debris, grass, and mud that had collected near a tree that had been uprooted. The bodies of some of the workers lay impaled by wood or other objects from the plantation yard. The rancid smell of blood caught in her nose, and she backed away to look for survivors, if there were any. Going from one pile to the next, Tahari found that all who had lived and worked on the plantation had been killed, including the whole Dancar family.

Tahari then came to a small concrete bunker that seemed intact. Summoning her courage, Tahari looked inside. Ironically, there was life within this old prison cell where many slaves had died at the hands of taskmasters. Rushing inside, she came upon her three dear friends: Almari of Trensa, Rami, and Senti. Of the three, only Senti remained alive, her chest barely moving. Cradling Senti's broken form in her arms, Tahari watched her weakly open her brown eyes.

"It was a tornado. They left us. They left us!" she frantically said in a raspy gasp, grabbing Tahari's shoulder. The excruciating pain that emanated from her hazel eyes told the horror of her story. Tahari watched the strength drain from her face as she succumbed to the severity of her wounds. Her grip on Tahari's shoulder weakened and her whole body went limp. Senti died in Tahari's arms.

Tears ran down her face as she slowly stood up, turned, and walked back to the silent world outside. Tahari made it only a few steps before breaking down. Sinking to her knees, Tahari covered her face with her hands. Tahari wept for her friends. She looked up as she heard thunder in the distance. Lightning flashed and blotted out the world around her.

When the blindness cleared, Tahari found herself on the road that led to Akendron in one direction and to the elfin kingdom of Adarah in the other. Again, everything was completely silently. Something was terribly wrong here as well.

Looking down the road to the east, Tahari did not see anything out of place, but when she turned her gaze to the west, her heart sank. On the road as it disappeared over the hill, Tahari saw the body of soldier lying on the ground. When she reached the body, she stood for a long moment staring at it. The soldier had been a large man, reptilian in nature, almost dragon-like. As if calling to mind a very distant memory, Tahari realized that the soldier was a Drac, a member of the Draccen race, whose people dwell within the Serrigen's dark mountains. Tahari's distant memory told her that they had been imprisoned and put under an enchantment to keep them in a deep sleep until it was finally decided what to do with them. This decision never happened.

"If you are here, then your people are free from their prison. This bears ill for us all," Tahari whispered to herself knowingly, but how she knew of these things, she could not say. The Drac had been slashed with a sword. Tahari felt confused looking at him. Then a breeze found her, and her stomach churned as her nose filled with the stench of more death. Raising her gaze, Tahari looked down into the surrounding valley and saw fifty-some Draccen soldiers lying dead.

"What happened here?" Tahari asked herself as she stared in wonder at the horror before her. As Tahari surveyed the valley floor, she caught sight of one of the dead who was not a Draccen but an elf. His shoulder-length blond hair was disheveled and his handsome face was dirty and scratched, telling the tale of his valiant struggle. Dirty and broken was the silver-plated armor designed to look like dragon's scales covering his chest and midsection. Even his deep-green and brown tunic was stained and torn from the battle. Something beckoned Tahari to his side. As she carefully made her way down to him, Tahari felt sudden grief for this elfin soul. He had been speared through his midsection. She knelt down beside him. "Why were you all alone?" Tahari asked aloud, looking upon his pale face. Her heart hurt as if she had known him in a past life. Reaching over, Tahari gingerly touched his head with her fingertips. A jolt passed through them.

The elf awoke with a start and gasped for air. His brown eyes were filled with alarm, and he looked around wildly, expecting to be attacked. In spite of the spear, he scrambled to a nearby tree. He coughed up blood and watched it drip from the corner of his mouth; he fought to remain focused.

Tahari took hold of his shoulders. "Take it easy, my friend. What is wrong?" she said as she searched his pale face for the answer. Swallowing hard and fighting to breathe, the elfin warrior looked at her with great urgency.

"They were waiting for me. They knew I would be here. More are coming." his voice was warm and gentle but was growing weak. Tahari quickly scanned the surrounding forest but could not see any other Draccen soldiers. When she looked back at him, she saw death on his face. "He comes for me. He will take my head; his lord will want proof of my death." seeing the harsh truth of this in his regal face caused her heart to ache.

"They will get no such thing," Tahari promised him with certainty. He looked at her with disbelief, but hope began to fill his face as he began to understand that Tahari would honor her word. Something caught her attention. A huge Draccen soldier approached them, and he carried a huge sword. When Tahari looked back down at the elfin warrior, she could only watch in dismay as he shut his eyes and his head sank back against the tree as death took him. A passing breeze caught his hair and gently blew it across his handsome face as if to signify death's victory over him. Anger passed over Tahari as she felt the devastation of his death and the reason for it. Reaching up, she touched his cheek. "I will protect you, my friend, to whatever end," Tahari promised. Raising her gaze, she saw the large Draccen solider standing before her. He raised his sword over his head.

"His head is mine as will yours be!" the soldier's voice was garbled and rough. As he brought the heavy sword down, a rage came out of her that she had never known in this lifetime.

CRACK!

A sharp pain cut across her back, awaking Tahari from the intense imagines. Still wanting to protect the fallen elfin prince, she lashed out at her attacker. As the portly taskmaster loomed over her, wearing an angry look and poised to whip her again, Tahari whirled around. She took a firm hold of his arm and in one swift move sent him flying over her shoulder. As the taskmaster sailed through the air, Tahari grabbed ahold of his rod-like whip and broke it in half.

When the taskmaster landed with a thud, he looked at her with true fear in his dark eyes. She glared at him. Then Tahari heard the sound of other taskmasters yelling and running through the field, anxious to put down the disturbance. They stopped in front of the downed taskmaster and stared at Tahari with disbelief. Many of the field workers were staring at her in amazement. Tahari began to realize that she was no longer in the dream defending an elfin prince. Tahari let the broken whip slip from her hands. She feared what she had done, but Tahari was still of a mindset to protect someone. One of the taskmasters came up from behind her. His presence alone was enough to infuriate her, but she grew angrier as she heard him mutter, "Slaves will never learn they have no right to harm the upper class.

The taskmaster raised his whip and brought it down toward her. Reacting with a speed that Tahari had never known before, she turned and snatched the whip in midair. Yanking the whip from its master's hands, Tahari watched as he tumbled forward. He was desperate to regain his whip and, with it, his power over the slaves. Instead, he caught Tahari's best-ever front kick. The taskmaster somersaulted backward and remained on the ground. A third taskmaster marched over to stop her with the back of his hand. He quickly swung his arm back to hit her when he went sailing harmlessly through the air. The massive taskmaster got to his feet quickly and felt someone tap him on the shoulder from behind. He turned around to see the blur of a fist coming at him. Pain filled his senses as his world went dark, and he crumpled to the ground. The slaves, watching from the edges of the cornfield, enjoyed the sight. They, too, had felt as Tahari did after all the times these arrogant men beat them with their whips.

Strong arms suddenly restrained Tahari from behind, and she was quickly dragged from the edges of the cornfield. As Tahari was being dragged off, she heard several more taskmasters threatening that if this were ever repeated by anyone, they would be sent to the cross. They dragged Tahari up a nearby hill, shouting and threatening her for her treason.

At the top of the hill, they tied Tahari to a pole overlooking the fields. Her hands were bound in front of her and tied around the pole. Then the beatings and whippings began. Yet she still felt the adrenaline from her vision coursing through her veins. The searing pain of the beatings and whippings did not faze her. One of the taskmasters grabbed her hair and forced her head back. Tahari was momentarily blinded by the sun, but then she saw the evil in the prime master's eyes staring at her.

"You have committed very serious crimes against us today. Punishment for such an outrage is death," he growled at her.

"Really? Then what is taking so long?" Tahari asked defiantly. She could not stop the words from coming out. The prime master was stunned for a moment, but then he quickly slammed her head against the pole. Tahari's skull made a sickening crack when it struck the pole. Dizziness and pain overwhelmed her world. She struggled to stay conscious as her body went limp.

"We refrained from doing so because you have ties to Master Dancar. We cannot kill his prize. However, we can leave you here to contend against the forces of nature. Let's see how you fare after several days in the burning sun with no food or water," he said in a menacing tone. The other taskmasters laughed and sneered at her. With that, they left her alone to hang from the wooden pole by her wrists.

Now Tahari felt the full measure of the torture that she had received. Immense pain screamed throughout her body. It did not help that the last remnants of the hot sun burned against her wounded, sunburnt back. Still, Tahari managed to find strength in the midst of excruciating pain. The visions that she had received stayed with her. They gave her a reason to stay alive. Many lives were hanging by a thread, and Tahari would not leave this world until they were safe.

Chapter 13

The Elfin Prophecy

Far from the growing troubles of the Shandel was the peaceful kingdom of Adarah. It was a mystical land covered with the greenest and lushest grasses and trees. Crystalline blue rivers ran throughout this vast tropical paradise, ending in misty waterfalls. It was truly an enchanted realm, for the power of the elfin people protected it. This power kept out all who intended harm and treachery to those who lived within it. Only the elfin people could pass in and out of the realm at their leisure. No one else could enter it without an elfin escort.

The elfin people were long-lived, ageless, and wise. They had lived in peace for hundreds of years with all those who called Andora home, but they were not strangers to war and conflict. Adarah's people had endured centuries of war and strife with other kingdoms. They were a skilled race in all the arts of warfare, but, for all their power, they were not immune to death's cold grip.

At the beginning of the Age of the Phoenix, the elves were in a state of tranquility and peace, but unlike their neighbors, they had not forgotten about the threat of the ancient evil's return for they kept safe one of the sacred scrolls of prophecy. No one was more aware of this prophecy than the royal family of the Goldendragon house.

Doran Goldendragon was High King of Adarah and had ruled for over two thousand years. King Doran had witnessed many difficult and dreadful times before and during his long reign, including the annihilation of the sphinx race, the scourging of the beautiful realm formerly known as Lani, and the second unleashing of the evil Lord Jarden. Lani, now known as the Barrens, had a sacred haven developed deep within its interior called Rahara. Despite the current peace, something haunted this good king's mind even more than the horrific images of the past. Upon the death of Rafar the Elder, King Doran was given the fifth scroll of the prophecy. In it, he read of several omens that overshadowed the Goldendragon family.

In the Age of the Phoenix, an ancient evil will be returned back into the world. Peace and tranquility will exist only for as long as it takes for the armies of good and evil to be gathered.

Since the dawning of the eleventh age, King Doran had been filled with worry and concern. Although many of his friends and most trusted allies promised him that they would protect his family, King Doran still felt uneasy. Unable to sleep late one night, King Doran made his way down to the grand library to look over the scroll once more. As the still athletic but aged elf quietly made his way through the palace's grand candlelit halls, he looked in on his sleeping family. He longed to spare them from the curse that could easily steal them away from him. Determined to find an answer within the cryptic text, he entered the library and looked at the scroll fervently. This time he discovered that another page had been tightly pressed against the original page of the scroll. When he managed to pry it free with his long fingers and began to read over the contents of the new page of the prophecy, he went numb with worry and fear. It was worse than he had imagined:

*A grand alliance will be summoned from all parts of the Tribunal. Be cautious and vigilant.

*The secret alliance cannot fall with the spirit of the dragon present. Be sure the son of Goldendragon is not alone.

*Evil will spread its deception and turn people against each other. Keep

bonds of friendship strong.

*Betrayal and death will fall upon a prince of the Goldendragon house who is destined to be king. Grant a brave soul permission to look in on the dead.

*The house of Goldendragon will be overrun with peril and grief as a grand city of white is turned to ash. Escape to havens north.

*Hope that still lives in the smallest of chances will become the bringer of life. Look to the orphan child whose wisdom is ancient.

Looking up from the newly found text, King Doran remained frozen, uncertain of his next course of action. He looked out the clear glass window onto his city of white limestone and crystal. Paracity Palace had been designed to be a beacon of light to all who entered Adarah's capital city. The same great care went into the design and construction of the rest of the city of Shoshon. Beautiful temples of the finest elfin craftsmanship were scattered throughout the city skyline. The streets were paved with gray and white stone, and statues of the elves' ancestors stood throughout the city so that no one forgot their immense efforts in establishing the society the people currently enjoyed. The minds of the people were even more beautiful than the city they lived in. The elfin people were rich with literature, art, music, and heritage.

The king turned his pleased gaze toward the busy markets within Shoshon's downtown square adorned with vibrant banners and streamers. Preparations for the Celebration of the Great Dragon had recently been completed. Life within this grand city was festive but civilized. He was overwhelmed with the fear of losing such a grand city. Suddenly, a flash of lightning from a passing thunderstorm lit up the entire grand library. Startled, King Doran turned his gaze back into the room. On the wall next to the colorful stained-glass windows was a painting of his children. In that moment, everything was clear to him.

"Forgive me for my selfish thoughts. Thank you for showing me my mistake," he prayed in a whisper. Walking up to the painting, King Doran touched the faces of his children tenderly. Above anything else, he knew that it was his children he needed to protect, for cities of stone could always be rebuilt. He would gladly give up the city and even his life for them if it meant that their lives would be spared. This was a lesson that he had learned from his dear friend, Reymier of the Shandon.

Reymier was a judge and counselor who had fought bravely to protect his family and friends from a ferocious beast that had attacked the grand city almost eighteen years ago. Although Reymier and his family perished in the siege, the elfin judge had managed to save Shoshon and his friends by taking the great beast with him into a deep gorge just outside the city. It was Reymier's love that saved the people of Shoshon.

King Doran stood for a long moment gazing at the portrait of his four children. Normally, only one child was born to an elfin family. The Goldendragons considered themselves blessed to have had four children born unto them. Their hope was that these children would carry on the name of Goldendragon, for they were the last of their lineage.

Twenty-three hundred years had passed since the birth of their twins Zation and Leondros. They had four in all, Dreyhon, Gwenth, Zation, and Leondros. As he watched his children grow in strength and wisdom, King Doran had put the troubling prophecy out of mind. As Prince Dreyhon would one day succeed him as king, he had the young prince learn about the important matters of the kingdom.

The daughters of the Goldendragon house, Gwenth and Zation, possessed the delicate beauty of their mother, Inya. They both had long, flowing hair that came down to their lower back. Gwenth, like Dreyhon, had the dark brown hair and brown eyes of their father. Zation had golden blonde hair, like her mother and brother, Leondros. These princesses were kind and gracious, but they too were well-educated in the warfare of their people. They were the hope for their people, and as Prince Dreyhon was destined to follow in King Doran's footsteps, they were destined to become queens in their own right. In the passing of the new millennia, all the Goldendragon children had grown in strength, spirit, and wisdom. Their love for each other was especially strong. The immense bond of love was strongest with Zation and her twin brother, Leondros. Together they shared a strong sense of each other's feelings and thoughts; it became the link that always connected them, even when Leondros was separated from her by great distances.

Prince Leondros played a lesser role within the palace, barely residing there. Under the watchful eye and wise tutelage of his only uncle, Tonious Goldendragon, Leondros learned to be an excellent archer and swordsman. He had traveled with his uncle throughout Adarah, Andora, and even abroad to other island realms around the world. After several long years of living in the wilds of Andora, word of the elfin prince began to spread throughout the realm. He had become renowned throughout Adarah and Andora as one of the most skilled warriors in the land. Leondros found true contentment, though, within the grand mist-covered forests of Adarah. It was here that he could find peace and solitude. He never seemed to be lonely, for he found much joy and contentment in the time that he spent in the wilds of Adarah and Andora. Still, Leondros could sense that he was missing something in his life, but he never knew what for certain.

"This is most terrible," King Doran whispered to himself after reading the new page of the prophecy. He feared that the dreadful events of the prophecy would fall upon his first-born son. It was for this reason that he kept Prince Dreyhon close to home. Even when the prince ventured abroad, tight security was near him at all times. Prince Leondros was left out of matters that most concerned Prince Dreyhon. Doran knew that Prince Leondros preferred it this way, for though the youngest prince cared for his brother, he cared little for politics. Long years had passed since the reading of the elfin prophecy and the pandemonium that resulted within the palace. It was during these times that the high king noticed his youngest son seeking refuge from the bickering of palace life in the tranquil forests surrounding Shoshon. Leondros, however, was not without friends.

In fact, Prince Leondros had made many friends throughout the Tribunal. His most trusted friend was Prince Alon-Settie, someone with whom he could relate about many matters. Even though their ages greatly differed, he found a kindred spirit within the Shandel's young prince. Many would swear they were brothers, they were so close. They had incredible adventures together and more than once had found themselves in life-and-death situations in which one had saved the other's life. It was truly the best of friendships.

As King Doran reflected on this new passage of the prophecy and became more concerned with Prince Leondros's safety, it caused a memory to trigger from long past. It was a memory he had long since pushed out of all conscience thought. It was a bizarre turn of events that occurred when Leondros was but a small an infant. There had been a lowly sphinx woman who had caused much disruption during the ceremony that decided which sphinx citizens would become Zation's and Leondros's rightful guardians and protectors. Rumor had surfaced that she secretly watched over the elfin prince until the annihilation of the sphinx people. King Doran did not see the relevance of this memory, but it gave him a sense of peace.

Chapter 14

Leondros

Zation stood gazing out the window of her cozy green bedchamber. Sunlight splashed into the room and warmed it. Her long blonde hair, rustling in the breeze, seemed to almost glow in the radiant sunlight. The intense light even caused her purple and white beaded gown to glow. She carefully scanned the tree covered mountains that spread across the distant horizon. She had been waiting by her windowsill for several long moments already this morning. This was the given day that her dear twin, Leondros, would return from his journey abroad, which had lasted well into a third month. Zation's large window, framed with gray stone, overlooked the thickly forested road that led east out of Shoshon. She had been watching every day for Leondros's return, but now she knew for certain that he would return today; she could sense it. Her gaze fell upon the green canopy of trees below her window. Breathing in the thick scent of the trees and the warm air, Zation felt the peace and quiet that filled the moment, understanding why Leondros loved to spend so much time in their kingdom's forests. The soft scent of the trees and rosemary in the hanging gardens would often drift into her window on nights that Leondros was gone and remind her of her brother. Unlike their siblings, Zation and Leondros were not caught up in the fame and riches that their titles destined them to; they found it easy to be amongst the kingdom's common people and genuinely felt concern for those in desperate need. They would gladly offer their help and insisted that no payment would be accepted.

Leaning out the window for a moment, Zation heard the sound of light footsteps coming down the hallway toward her bedchamber's door. The footsteps slowly approached the chamber door, sounding almost hesitant. She turned her attention away from the window for a moment and listened carefully to the footsteps coming toward her room. A smile came to Zation's face as she turned back to the open window.

"Come in, mother," Zation said loudly. There was a moment of silence before the heavy oak door opened slowly. Her mother, dressed in a beautiful orange-and-cream gown, peeked her head around the light-beige door and gave her daughter a dumbfounded look. Zation could not help but smile. Inya looked suspiciously at her and then looked at the door for a long moment. Then she turned back to her daughter.

"I will never understand how you and Leondros do that!" she said as she shook her head in wonder. A matching cream-colored veil gently covered her long blonde hair, which had been neatly pinned into a spiral bun at the base of her neck with a beautifully crafted bronze barrette. Inya's gold and crystal crown sat snug upon her veiled head and sparkled in the morning light that beamed through the large window.

"How are you today, Mother?" Zation asked, greeting her mother in her usual way. Inya smiled and shook her head. It amazed her that Zation and Leondros always seemed to have a sixth sense about them. It caught her off-guard much of the time.

"I am well," Inya said hesitantly, knowing full well that Zation would be able to pick up on her worry regardless of how much she tried to hide it. She looked at her precious daughter in the early morning sunlight that beamed through the open window. Inya felt herself gasp suddenly. Zation's features were so close to Leondros's that she could not help but see an image of her son in Zation. She shook her head slightly and managed to find her voice again. "I guess a mother cannot help but worry about her children. I am worried for your brother." her words were also riddled with deep concern as she returned her soulful gaze to Zation.

"Worry not, Mother. I know that Leondros is safe and sound. I sense that he will return today from his trip to the Barrens. More than that, I feel that he is longing to come home again." as Zation spoke in her soft voice, Inya listened intently with a loving and concerned gaze. It brought her great relief to know that her youngest child remained safe.

"Bless you, child. Through all my years on this earth, I have never before seen such a strong bond between two siblings," Inya said with great kindness and affection. She joined Zation at the window. Inya felt the sun's warmth upon her as she stepped from the shadows of the cool stone chamber. Zation put a loving arm around her mother's slender waist, but then she noticed something sad in the queen's usually strong features.

"Mother? Why so sad?" Zation asked as she turned her head to look deep into her mother's sad brown eyes. Inya lowered her head a moment as her brow wrinkled with some great unknown sadness that seemed to burden her heart. "Mother?" she asked again as she reached up and took her mother's hand firmly in hers. Finally, Inya was able to find the courage to raise her head again. When she did, Zation saw tears running down her pink cheeks.

"Forgive me," Inya said at long last. Her white face felt hot with the sun beating against it and the cool tears seemed to bring some relief. "I fear that I have not been the best mother that I could have been to all my children," she continued after a long pause. She looked sadly into Zation's dazzling brown eyes, which were fixed with concern.

"Why do you say such a thing, Mother? You have always been there for us. What more could you have done?" Zation asked as she took a hold of her mother's slender arms. Inya shifted her sad gaze to the window. She longed to see Leondros again.

"Sometimes I fear that I have missed out on Leondros's growing up, and I dread that I have missed my chance to be there when he really needed me." Inya's words greatly concerned Zation as she watched her mother turn to the window and rest her arms on the warm stone sill. Inya breathed in a lungful of fresh air. "I take great comfort that you are as close to Leondros as you are. Through you I can know for sure that he is safe." she paused for a moment and then looked at Zation inquisitively. "Have you dreamed anything about him?" she asked with a concerned look.

"I have not. Have you?" Zation replied slowly as she studied her mother's worried expression. Her mother's words unsettled her, and what was more unsettling was that maybe a mother's intuition about her child was more powerful than a twin's.

"Yes, and they give me grave warning. The things that I have seen are terrible, and…" Inya paused and kept herself from saying anything more as her softened voice began to crack with grief. "I can only pray that Adalai is watching over him because I fear that I will not be able to. I just wish I had more time to tell him." Inya's words failed completely as her beautiful white face fell, and she began to weep. Zation took her mother in her arms and held her for a long moment.

"Mother, Leondros knows that you love him and would not trade your love for anything," Zation said, gently reminding the queen of the genuine love between mother and son. "I have watched you when you were with him. Even as a child, you always took him up in your arms whenever he came to you. His journeys abroad only made it seem that you never got to show him the love you have for him. You've always loved him and shared that love with him freely." Zation's words melted a part of Inya's worry. Pulling away to look at her mother's tear-streaked face, Zation sensed there was something else that was troubling her mother. "There is more, is there not? Is it news from the Shandel?" she asked with a curious look. Inya lifted her tear-streaked face to look at her daughter and just marvel at the foresight gifted to her.

"There is no hiding anything from you, is there?" Inya said as she found her smile again. "Yes, both times," she affirmed with a strange look on her face. Her daughter's intuition was even stronger than hers. "A messenger has come with utmost haste from the Shandel. He has brought with him a letter from the Queen of the Shandel for Leondros. They are asking if he will be a part of a secret army that is being put together." As Inya explained this news, Zation now understood why her mother had such nightmares about Leondros. Still, she did not worry about Leondros, for she held great faith in her brother.

"Mother, Uncle Tonious taught Leondros everything he knows, and Leondros's travels have taught him even more. Uncle Tonious told me once that when Leondros was still very young, he already had a dead aim with a bow. He told me what skill Leondros already seemed to have with a sword. It was as if Leondros was born for the life that he had chosen. Have faith in him," Zation reassured her mother.

Suddenly Zation froze. Inya, too, stopped as she watched her daughter's expression go blank. The princess had sensed something approaching the palace. It was a familiar presence that Zation knew well, for she quickly turned to look out the window. Instantly, Zation's expression changed into one of pure excitement. Her beaded gown spun around her strong yet delicate form as she turned quickly toward the door, and Zation bolted barefoot for the chamber door. "Mother! He returns!" she opened the door and bolted barefoot from the chamber.

Inya was quick to follow her daughter from the room. They ran through the halls and almost flew down the steps, eager, if not desperate, to see Leondros again. Zation and Inya emerged a moment later from Paracity Castle out into the warm summer day, hurrying down the long staircase of white marble that led into the street below. As they ran, holding onto the white marble railing, they could see Leondros riding in on his white horse, Aton. He wore a desert-brown tunic with black leather armor covering his head, chest, and arms. He had had a long road back, for dirt covered his clothes and armor. Even from a distance, they could see that his dusty face looked slightly sunburnt and weary from the long journey. When he caught sight of them rushing out to meet him, the road-weary look melted from his face and a tired yet welcoming smile replaced it.

Stopping just inside the golden front gate, Leondros slowly climbed down from Aton's back. The elfin prince walked in front of the strong white stallion and gently stroked his head, whispering something to him before giving the horse's leather reins to a servant who had quickly hurried out to greet his prince and take his steed to the stables. Turning toward the palace, Leondros pulled off his black leather helmet, revealing blond hair tied in three small braids. Taking a deep breath, he took in his first real feeling of being home. He saw his mother and sister running to meet him. Inya reached him first and threw her slender arms around him, holding him tightly. He sensed that she was worried and to see him again brought her great relief. Though her intense hug surprised him a little, Leondros was glad to receive such a grand welcome. He saw Zation standing nearby with a very pleased smile on her face. Inya's grip around him was uncommonly strong, but he did not mind as he rested his weary head against hers.

"To what do I owe the honor of this grand welcome?" Leondros asked finally, stepping back a bit to look down into his mother's loving face. Inya smiled at him with such warmth. How she had longed to look into the beautiful face of her son and to have him safe in her arms again!

"I cannot say what it means to me to see you return again safe and sound," she said in a warm, soft voice. When she finally let go of him, the warm smile on her face and the sparkle in her brown eyes never left. "Now, come in, eat, and rest. I can only imagine the journey that you have had. You will tell us of all the happenings on your journey tonight at our banquet," Inya exclaimed excitedly. "Your father will be glad to know that you have returned. I will bring word to him of your arrival," she said as she began to make her way toward the palace.

"I will be in shortly, Mother," Leondros said with a smile and a nod. The queen mother smiled back as she turned and walked back up the long white marble staircase that led through an exotic garden of various flowers, ivies, and palm trees and eventually to Paracity Palace. He watched his mother disappear into the garden before turning to Zation. "What was all that about?" he asked in a whisper. Leondros felt puzzled by such a warm greeting as if something were about to happen to him.

"Mother felt that she might have neglected you somehow when we were growing up. She just wanted you to know that she has never stopped caring about you," Zation replied. A peaceful look came over Leondros's dusty face.

"I have not been around the palace much; in that she is right, but this welcoming will be something that I will always remember," he said quietly, lowering his gaze thoughtfully. Zation smiled at him and slipped her arms around him. Giving her brother a warm hug, she whispered to him, "It is good to see you again, brother." she rested her head against his shoulder for a moment. It was a relief beyond measure that her twin brother was standing next to her again. Leondros held his sister tightly, for he too understood the special bond that they shared.

"Just as good as it is to see my sister again," he replied in a whisper also as he continued to smile. Their hug lasted a long moment before she let go of him and began to walk with him back to the palace.

"Now, what have I missed since I have been gone?" Leondros asked as he looked at Zation, for he could see that she longed to tell him of the family and life within the palace. Zation was quick to give him details on the current happenings of court life and the mild issues concerning Adarah as they retreated to a lounging chamber. The chamber was made of beautiful dark-wood walls and offered chairs cushioned with spun burgundy silk. Around the large chamber were various types of ivies and palm trees, which added to the room's serenity. Many came here to relax and enjoy late-night conversations in front of a warm fire while sipping hot tea. Here Leondros and Zation had spent many hours talking whenever he returned from his long journeys through Aura and its surrounding isles. While Zation talked of the latest news from court, she noticed a messenger leave a scroll on top of a curio cabinet near the door. "Business as usual, then," Leondros said with humor, settling back in the soft chair. He gazed out the large window, taking in the heavenly sight of the mist-covered mountains that surrounded Shoshon. He relaxed into the peace and quiet of the room and began to fall asleep, until he heard Zation speak again.

"Not all of it," she said in a tone that seemed tense and greatly concerned.

Fully awake again, Leondros turned his attention back to his sister. He saw the genuine concern in her eyes. She rose from her chair with a silent grace and walked across the room toward the wooden curio cabinet near the entrance of the room. He sensed great trouble in what she had to show him. When Zation returned to her chair, she handed him a scroll. He looked at her with a puzzled expression as he reached out and took it from her. "The messenger who brought it did not know many details but guessed that the matter deals with strange happenings that have been occurring within the Shandel. Father shares the queen's fears and thinks something dark is coming." Her words added to his growing dread. Zation looked up to see her mother at the doorway. The queen was silently summoning her to rejoin her. Zation nodded and got up again. "Please excuse me for a moment," she said as she took leave of Leondros. He acknowledged her departure with a nod of his head and began to open the scroll.

"This is most unusual," he said to himself as he read. It had been a thousand years since he had received a request for help from anywhere. There had been such a long time of peace and serenity throughout Andora since the evil had been imprisoned a second time that it was hard to believe the news. He read through the scroll and then laid it in his dusty lap and let his gaze drift to the brown stone floor. Try as he might, Leondros could not shake the chilling and disturbing feeling that came over him. There was something more to the notice that had been sent. Although his thoughts told him that he could take on this adversary without failure, his powerful intuition gave him grave warning. "There is more lurking in the shadows, and I do not believe they can even see it," he said aloud. He knew that the Shandel was in serious trouble.

Chapter 15

Secret Alliance Scroll

E vening's shadow finally fell over Adarah after what seemed a long day. On this night, song and celebration could be heard throughout Shoshon. News of Prince Leondros's safe return had spread throughout the city and into the far reaches of the territory surrounding Shoshon. A large feast was held in the prince's honor to celebrate his homecoming. Leondros visited with the many friends who had come to see him. The festivities went until late in the night. As people left for their homes, they spoke blessings of good fortune for Leondros. The prince was greatly admired by many within the kingdom. He enjoyed talking to all who came to see him and thanked them for their kindness.

The night passed into the early hours of morning, and Leondros was still awake as he waited for the opportunity to talk with his father privately. He stood in the lounge where he had been with his sister that morning. Now he did not feel quite so relaxed. He looked out the window at a spectacular waterfall that was illuminated by the moon's soft, heavenly light. Surrounding it was the soft shadows of the flowers growing near the palace and the dense forest beyond. It felt like heaven on earth, but Leondros could not appreciate it because of the suspicions that haunted his mind.

Leondros caught the sound of heavy footsteps coming toward the study. They hit the floor so that they echoed in the airy corridor. He listened as they stopped just out of eyesight of the open door.

"Father, please come in," Leondros said, still in deep thought. He heard someone gasp slightly and then enter the room slowly.

"Leondros, you and your sister startle me sometimes." King Doran's deep, warm voice filled the small, dimly lit study. The king had finished seeing out the last of their guests and had taken a moment to change into his white cotton evening robe before retiring for the night. As King Doran stepped into the room, the candles scattered throughout the room caused the golden thread embroidered into his white robe and along the storm-gray sash at his waist to shimmer. Although he sensed that Leondros was glad to see him, King Doran could see that something greatly troubled his son. King Doran approached Leondros, catching sight of the white scroll that was sitting on the windowsill in front Leondros as he came nearer. He remembered what word the messenger brought about trouble arising in the Shandel. His son gazed into the moonlit night, his arms folded over his chest. The young prince had long since cleaned up from his dusty journey and changed into a dark-green and silver robe. He seemed a little rested from his long journey, but there was definitely something troubling his youngest son. The king's slightly aged face radiated genuine concern, and he waited patiently for his son to speak.

"The Shandel sends for warriors, but do they not know the enemy they are going to be facing?" Leondros asked, turning to his father. King Doran could see that Leondros was troubled over the few details given to warriors selected to face the troubles bearing down on the Shandel. He saw the great concern in Leondros's brown eyes.

"Some of them must. Otherwise they would not have sent word so far for help," King Doran offered, glancing down at the scroll. The king stood a few inches taller than his youngest son, and his trained eyes easily noticed the concern in his child. Leondros's features were rigid. He knew that his son sensed something deeper than the mere evil that was prophesied.

"I agree with their decision to send for help. It is the only sensible thing to do," Leondros said, sounding hesitant as he took hold of the notice and looked thoughtfully at it for a long moment.

"But...?" King Doran asked as he watched Leondros lift his gaze back to the moonlight. He saw something in his son's face that actually scared him. He realized finally what concerned Leondros: the fear of death. King Doran knew only too well that if Leondros were to fight in this battle, the only danger he would run into was burying his dear friend Alon-Settie. All too often, he watched as Leondros saw his friends die before him, and it was often Leondros who had to return their bodies to their parents. It broke King Doran's heart to see the effect it had on his son, but Leondros always managed to find a positive way of dealing with it. He saw a blessing in every new friendship, and he would try to protect them as much as he could. It was truly a noble thing to do.

"If this is the same evil from the tenth age, will the secret alliance be enough?" Leondros asked as he looked back at his father. King Doran thought for a moment before speaking.

"You may be the chance this alliance needs, but only if you choose to take your place among them," King Doran said with an encouraging smile. "You are one of the most renowned warriors in the whole of Andora. There are many who would be honored to fight at your side." Leondros listened intently, but the chill of worry did not leave. "The prophecy of our people says that the time of the ancient evil is close, and it will affect more than the Shandel. If it is not stopped in the Shandel, it will continue to march across Andora. After that, there will be no stopping it, and all will be lost to its madness." Leondros nodded slowly.

"Whether I go or stay might make the difference in the battle ahead, but I fear what might happen to my family in my absence. What if this is the chosen year that our prophecy has forewarned us about?" Leondros said thoughtfully. King Doran agreed with that possibility and appreciated his son's concern for them.

"It may be, but we have seen many armies over the millennia form for battle. There has often been some unknown threat to the kingdoms throughout the years. Yet here we are, still thriving and living in peace. Many parts of the prophecy have yet to transpire," King Doran said, reassuring his son for the moment.

"This too is true," Leondros replied thoughtfully. His mind made up, he said, "I will leave for the Shandel at first light." Leondros then looked out into the peaceful night. This enchanted place was his home. He could not bear to see any part destroyed or to see anything happen to his family. They seemed to be the only constant in his life. "Father," he said, turning to face him, "if anything should happen in my absence, please do not hesitate to send for me." King Doran was surprised by the worry in Leondros's face. He had never seen such concern for his family than he did looking into the worry-filled eyes of his son. Smiling, he put a reassuring hand on his son's strong shoulder. Looking down into his son's concerned eyes, King Doran said, "I will not wait a single moment. Now take some rest, son. You have a long journey ahead of you. I know that you will encounter much on this trip.

Leondros nodded in agreement, suddenly realizing how weary he was. He took the scroll and left the lounge's warmth. As he made his way to his chamber on the far side of the palace, Leondros felt good about his decision to go to the Shandel. He knew that his god would watch over him as he went through his trials. It brought him some peace to think that he would see his most trusted friend, Alon-Settie, again.

As King Doran watched his son disappear down the candlelit hallway, he felt a sudden pang of fear. Although he had often seen his son go off to war, this time seemed different. "Why?" the king wondered to himself. It should be like any other time Leondros had gone off to battle, but a strange feeling passed over King Doran.

"Do not worry," a woman's voice said quietly behind him, nearly sending King Doran into the ceiling above him. He turned to see Inya standing silently behind him. She too had changed into her evening attire: a dark-peach robe with a burgundy veil over her long hair.

"It is no wonder where Leondros and Zation get their ability to scare me to death like that," King Doran said, putting a hand on his chest and leaning slightly to catch his breath. As he did, Doran's dark-brown hair slipped past his broad shoulders. Inya smiled sweetly as she stepped close to his side. She gazed at the doorway that Leondros had just passed through.

"Leondros will be all right. After all, Tonious reassured us that Leondros was a one-elf army." she took King Doran's arm and held it.

"This is true, but there is something that bothers me about this mission. Leondros also senses it," King Doran whispered so that his voice would not carry.

"Leondros is not like many of our elfin kinsmen. There is something special about him. I cannot explain it. He can sense things that no one else can see or touch," she said as she walked to the doorway and peered down the dimly lit corridor. Though she could no longer see Leondros, she knew he had been there. "Whatever it is that watches over him will bring him home to us again. I am sure of this." her words reassured King Doran, who joined her at the doorway. He took her arm and led her down the dim hallway toward their bedchamber.

Peace settled over the Goldendragon household, but Zation found that sleep eluded her. Something bothered her, but she could not say what. She dressed herself in her light-blue satin robe and paced around the room many times. Finally, she stopped at the window and gazed out at the calming night that surrounded the palace.

Maybe my mind worries for Leondros, she thought. Leondros had come to her before retiring, telling her that he would be leaving for the Shandel in the morning. She turned from the window and slipped into a pair of light-blue satin slippers and walked across the cool stone floor to her closet. Zation opened the door and slipped into the small darkened room. Through a maze of clothes and garments, she felt along the back wall for a lever that would open a secret passage door. Finding it, Zation pulled the lever and heard a low rumble as the back door within the closet slowly opened before her. She pushed her way through the drapes of her many gowns and slipped into the darkness of the brick-and-stone passageway. It smelled slightly musty, but she had placed stocks of lavender and other flowers along the route to drive away the smell. Few knew of the door or the passage behind it. Zation walked through the dark passageway without problem, for she could see perfectly in the dark. The passage led her through many turns, but she finally came to another heavy wooden door and opened it cautiously. Slipping through the door without a sound, Zation took in Leondros's room.

As children, they'd had their father put in this secret passage. This way, they could go to each other's room without anyone else knowing. They often pretended they were on secret missions. The passage had another purpose for Zation and Leondros. They had always been close, and many times, they could sense when the other was troubled. Many nights during times of distress, one had gone to the other's room to comfort their twin. Zation often used the passage to keep a watchful eye over her brother. Of the two, Zation was older, and she felt it her responsibility to watch over Leondros.

When Zation poked her head out of the wooden closet and looked into her brother's bedchamber, she saw that Leondros was sitting in a chair with only the moonlight and a single candle on a nearby nightstand for company. He was leaning forward with his hands clasped together on his knees and his head hung in deep thought. She sensed his mind was greatly burdened.

"Leondros?" she asked in a whisper as she walked over to him and touched his shoulder. He was not startled by her sudden appearance, and he slowly looked up at her. "Your mind is troubled about the journey that is ahead of you." it wasn't a question. "How is this different from the other missions that you have been on?" she asked with great concern as she sat in the green-satin cushioned chair that faced his. Zation studied his features with deep concern.

"I cannot help but feel the evil that I am heading into. This is like no other mission that I have been on before. There is much danger in the path of the secret alliance and much more waiting in the shadows. Will this mission bring more hardship than I can contend with?" he said, and Zation heard the fear in his warm voice. She took his hands in hers and held them tightly.

"Leondros, I have always sensed that there is a kind, compassionate spirit that watches over you. It has been there on all of your past journeys. I can feel it even now. I know that it will be with you, and it will be that warm and loving spirit that will bring you home to us again." as Zation spoke softly, she could see that her words brought great comfort to Leondros. He was quite tired, and she knew that he would let sleep come now.

"Thank you. I needed your words tonight," he said wearily. Zation smiled as she reached over and touched his cheek.

"Sleep now, little brother. Let your mind be at peace. My prayers will be with you always." Zation's words continued to calm Leondros's mind. As he sat back in his chair and rested his weary head against its tall back, Zation went to the window and opened the bamboo shutters to allow the cool night breeze to enter. When she turned back, Leondros had already fallen asleep in his armchair. Zation smiled. Tiptoeing across the dark stone floor, she picked up a light-cream blanket from a curio cabinet near the corner of his room and covered him with it. She also found chamomile incense in the cabinet and carefully lit some. Its scent was soothing, easing her mind of the troubles that weighed heavily upon her. Taking her place in the chair that faced his, Zation sat down and prayed silently until she too fell asleep. She wished that he did not have to go on this mission, but she knew that much devastation would result if he did not.

Chapter 16

Bête Noire

As Zation slept soundly in the armchair next to Leondros's, she dreamed. Her dream was anything but peaceful. Instead, Zation found herself in a nightmare.

Walking down a long and dark corridor, Zation heard only her own soft footsteps on the stone beneath her. As she walked, the eerie patter echoed off the cold corridor's hard surface. The floor itself was cold and damp beneath her bare feet. She had no idea where she was, but she seemed to know exactly where she was going. It was as if something were guiding her through the darkness. She heard haunting sounds of someone crying, their moans drifting toward her, seemingly from above her. She heard great pain in the voice, and her heart broke. Suddenly, a metal screech rang out in the damp night air, causing her heart to skip a beat. The voice was abruptly silenced. Zation stopped and considered turning around, but she felt as if someone was calling out to her, almost begging her to find them. Stepping out of the long corridor, Zation now found herself climbing up a murky winding staircase. Zation could barely see in front of her. There was no light, only darkness, but as she moved forward she saw a faint orange light up ahead. It was barely noticeable, but she set her gaze on it and followed it.

The light led her safely up a set of damp spiral stairs constructed of stone. Climbing upward, Zation reached the source of the orange light. A small candle sat on a plain metal stand rusted from time in a damp nook beside a doorway. Its light illuminated the small stone doorway. Looking through it and seeing another dim hallway ahead of her, Zation's nose was greeted by the smells of mildew and disease. The gloom of this place easily reminded her of a prison block. She sensed pain, suffering, and death in this hallway as she stepped through the archway. At the end of the corridor was a small torch whose flame did little to brighten the room. Zation narrowed her gaze and searched the corridor, noticing five doors on each side of the short corridor. The wood doors were gray with age and had small, barred windows at the bottom.

"Why am I here? Why have I been led to a prison?" she asked herself. She sensed that many souls had been imprisoned in this foul place and many more had died horribly within these cells. The damp sank into her body. She had never felt the chill of winter before, but here, within this dark place, she trembled from the eerie cold that surrounded her. Looking around the corridor, Zation wondered for what purpose she had been brought to this terrible place. Then she heard a heavy door creaking opening as its immense weight pushed against its rusty hinges. The chills down her spine increased. Curiosity called her over to the door on its own, almost pleading for her to look inside, yet the darkness that dwelt within warned her to stay out. She ignored the warnings, and taking a deep breath, she walked into the cell.

A pungent odor hung thickly in the air. In the shadows of the room, she could just make out moldy straw that was the only source of bedding and rain that had collected upon the floor. Near the stone ceiling, she saw a small square hole that was used for a window. There was nothing to bar the harsh elements of nature from entering. Prisoners were at the mercy of both nature and man.

"Death is in this room," she whispered to herself, stopping while her eyes adjusted to the dim light. Once her eyes adjusted, Zation saw a body hanging from a large timber overhead, its back to her.

The body was suspended by ropes tied around the wrists. The body itself dangled just above the damp floor in the middle of the room. The man hanging there had endured much cruelty and torture. His clothes were almost unrecognizable as such. She stepped toward the man, seeing that he had been whipped and beaten bloody. "No one deserves such torture," she said sadly as she walked around him so that she could look upon his face. Zation gasped in horror at what she saw. A wave of negative energy passed through her. The trauma of what the man had endured hit her hard. She staggered backward and fell to the ground.

Waking with a start, Zation looked up, dazed for a moment. The dream's horror was still vivid in her mind. Looking over at the green armchair in front of her and then quickly scanning the bedchamber itself, she discovered that Leondros was gone. Jumping to her feet, Zation hurried to the window and saw that dawn had come. She caught a glimpse of her twin for but a moment. Leondros was riding out of Shoshon on his way to the Shandel. He was wearing his silver armor and a desert-beige tunic for the journey ahead. When he was out of sight, Zation was gripped with a terrible fear.

"Beware, my dear brother. There is great danger ahead for Alon-Settie and I fear, for you, too," she said aloud. Zation began to pray for her brother. Only Adalai could see to it that he came back home again.

Chapter 17

Winds of Change

The hot afternoon sun sank slowly behind the distant mountains to the west. Evening was on its way, and Tahari was still bound to the wooden pole. The remnants of the afternoon's sun beat upon the wounds she had received earlier that day. The only pain that hurt worse was remembering the unsettling details of her visions. Tahari was compelled to go beyond anything she had ever done to save her friends and the elfin warrior, but how? Resting her aching head against the pole's coarse surface, Tahari tried to think of a way that she could save them. Suddenly, Tahari sensed that she was no longer alone. Her aching body went rigid, for the presence was not friendly.

"Well, well. Now this is an interesting position you've gotten yourself into." the nasally, high-pitched voice of Master Dancar's daughter, Tana, was not hard to identify. Tahari turned her head to see the cruel and almost-pleased look on her pudgy face as she slowly approached her. Her easy, food-rich life had made her seamstress's job difficult, for her wardrobe was designed to make her appear thin and delicate, yet with one grimacing look, it was a lie. Tana's presence was almost insulting, for Tahari sensed that she enjoyed watching her suffer. Her small hazel eyes seemed to sparkle in the twilight. The warm evening breeze caught her long, sandy-colored hair, and she worked to keep it in its place. Tahari next caught a glimpse of her mother approaching. There was no mistaking Thera's appearance, for her wiry frame seemed to radiate her spiteful personality. Her dark brown hair was streaked with vivid strands of white, fitting the bony structure of her face. Her mere presence could bring a chill to the hottest day on the plantation. Thera and her daughter's occasional visits were never short enough, and the time between them was never long enough. They were her adoptive family, but in the years that Tahari had known them, they treated her worse than did the taskmasters.

"I rather like it. You are free to join me if you wish. I am quite sure they can find room for you," Tahari replied with disdain, glaring at them. Tana sneered and pulled her nose up at her.

"This is not a place for the future queen of the Shandel. It is fit only for trash like you and all those you call friends," she said, not sounding convinced by her own words. Tana glanced at her mother, who gave her a reassuring nod. The pair stared at Tahari as if she were not deserving of even the air she breathed. Tahari narrowed her eyes, for she could not see Tana as the ruler of anything except pain and misery.

"Now that is too bad, isn't it?" Tahari said, sounding truly saddened by her discomfort. "As a future queen, you should be aware of just what your reign stands upon. A kingdom is nothing without the people who live there." Tahari's response caught them both off-guard. Tana set her pudgy mouth stubbornly and turned to her mother with an offended expression.

"Are you going to let her, of all people, talk to us that way?" Tana demanded of her mother with disgust as she pointed to Tahari. "I mean, just look at her! What right does a slave have to use such language in our presence?" As Tana spoke, Tahari saw the anger grow in Thera's black eyes. Tahari's jaw tightened. They had come here for a reason, and she was about to find out what it was. Thera looked at Tana with a calming but cruel smile. Tana seemed to understand and turned to Tahari again with a look of sinister pleasure. She began to dread what they had in store for her.

"Slave? I do not see a slave here," Thera said with a cruel tone, slowly walking around the pole Tahari was bound to. "What I see here would not even be considered with such regard." her words bit into Tahari's heart, and she stepped closer to her. Leaning close enough to whisper into Tahari's ear, she said "You are less than the dirt that has to endure the weight of you walking upon it. Why would we care about the words you utter? You are nothing to us." her cold, high-pitched voice was salt in Tahari's wounds. Seeing the pleasure in their faces, Tahari knew that Thera was far from finished. "If I would have known of the troubles that you would plague my family with, I would have drowned you after your mother abandoned you on our doorstep." As Thera spoke these crushing words, Tahari turned her head away. The very sound of Thera's voice next to her caused her skin to crawl.

"How dare you! Look at us when we speak to you!" Tana shouted angrily as she reached out her chubby hand and grabbed Tahari's hair, forcing her to look at both of them. Glaring at them with a stern expression, Tahari was not through giving them a piece of her mind.

"I am glad that I am here where you have placed me," Tahari managed to say as she fought the overwhelming feeling of defeat. "I may live with the trash of the world as you call them, but there is a simple happiness that your wealth could never afford. In the life that I have lived, I have never seen such creatures as foul as you. Judging by your description of me, I pale in comparison to you both." Tahari's answer was enough to enrage them.

"Wretched child!" Thera spat as she grabbed hold of Tahari's hair. "May God have pity on you, for I have none! If he lets you live or die, I care not. I am done with you!" Her words came out in a resentful hiss. Then, with all her strength, she drove Tahari's head into the pole. Tahari's ears filled with the sickening sound of her head hitting the pole. Thunder filled her senses and her body went limp, hanging by the coarse rope that bound her wrists.

Time passed as Tahari helplessly hung from the pole. Tahari could not tell whether she was awake or not. Her head spun and ached. Thunder loudly rumbled in the distance, finally waking her. Tahari lifted her aching head up slowly and looked around to see if her nemeses had left yet. Doing so brought on the full weight of her headache. Resting her pounding head against her arm, Tahari looked out at the dark horizon. Her gaze fell upon the moonlit plantation. As awful as she felt inside and out, Tahari found the courage to hope for a better life away from all this pain and misery. Others had become complacent with this hard life and had long since given in to the lie, that told them that there was nothing better to hope for. Tahari refused to let herself believe this, for she knew that if she stopped right now, this would be all that she would get.

Tahari realized then that she was alone and that no one would be coming back for her. Tahari was struck with an inspiring thought: if no one cares enough to want me back, then let me never return. Tahari found the strength to get to her feet. Looking at the rope that cut into her wrists and the wooden pole, Tahari realized how worn both really were. They were not strong enough to keep her from freedom. Easily tearing herself from the pole, Tahari staggered backward. Never before had she tasted true freedom. For a moment, Tahari was unsure what to do with it. But the next thing she knew, she was bounding over the soft grass of the hillside, heading straight for the Divervandon Forest. Not a single soul was around to stop her from escaping, and she did not pause to think about her decision. As Tahari approached the southern edge of the Divervandon Forest, she basked in her new-found freedom. Her spirits soared beyond the treetops as she ran. All she wanted to do now was just keep running and never return to this awful place. Why would she possibly go back now? But as Tahari reached the edge of the forest, a loud clap of thunder startled her back to reality.

Tahari skidded to a halt, a feeling of dread overcoming her. She turned and looked up at the evening sky. The wind began to blow harder, and the dark clouds blotted out the moon, moved quickly toward her. Lightning flashed, and the sticky night air became thick and uncomfortable. Something did not feel right about this storm. Tahari's senses screamed at her to flee the area for they knew something horrible was coming. However, if she took this chance at freedom, people would die—and not just those poor souls from her vision.

"I hate being right all the time!" Tahari grumbled, feeling greatly disheartened as she dashed back toward the Tomblock. After the near-marathon run, Tahari reached the plantation's main yard. Gasping for air, she looked wildly around at the workers resting near the barracks. "Go for cover! Go! A storm comes!" She yelled as she waved her arms wildly. Reaching a worker walking slowly through the main yard on his way back to the barracks, Tahari grabbed hold of his strong brown arms and warned him of the coming storm. His sunburnt face looked back at her blankly, and then he slowly lifted his dark eyes toward the cloudy sky overhead. "A tornado comes! Get out of here and find shelter!" Tahari yelled as she pointed toward the stormy horizon. Then as if the god Adalai himself came to help her with this evacuation, a powerful lightning bolt struck the ground just beyond the main yard. The energy of the radiant white flash sent the message of danger throughout the camp, and cries of horror rang out. Almost at once, the field workers started rushing around and began running for the stone barracks just east of the plantation, built especially for these storms.

Seeing these people hurrying to safety, Tahari turned her attention to finding the three she most feared for. Rushing over the dusty ground to the small stone bunker that served as a jail at the center of the yard, Tahari watched the bunker's guard take notice of the coming storm and quickly abandon his post. She could watched as his chunky figure hurried toward the main house.

"I figured as much," Tahari grumbled, and she charged up to the bunker. When she had forced the door open and entered the makeshift jail, Tahari saw Almari, Senti, and Rami locked behind the prison bars.

"Tahari! Please help us!" Almari cried as she reached out for her. Tahari could not miss her friend's horrified expression, her face now white with fear. The fear almost gripped her as well. Looking at her, Tahari did not see her friend, who was the same age as her, with her almost-blonde hair hanging in locks around her sunburnt shoulders and her tattered sackcloth garment; Tahari saw a little child. "The guard told us that a storm was comin' and then he left us!" These words were almost haunting. Tahari took hold of her hands firmly as she tried to comfort her. Tahari realized then that this building had gaping holes for windows, which would offer little protection from flying debris. As she looked at the metal bars that kept them from leaving, she became angered that they were even here.

"Why have you been imprisoned?" Tahari demanded as she peered around the room, unsuccessful in finding the keys that would open the lock to their cell.

"Do not waste your time tryin' to find the keys. The prison guard took them when he left for shelter," Rami explained, the tone in his deep voice saying that he had already made peace with his fate and was just waiting for death to come. Senti stood near Almari and watched Tahari nervously. She did not speak of her immense fear, but her large hazel eyes spoke of the death that was close. Despite her own fears, Tahari was not about to stop finding a way through the bars.

"They figured that we might try to free you from the torturin' pole, so they locked us in 'ere," Almari explained as she clung to the bars and watched Tahari look for another way to get them out. Then a confused expression came over her face. "Wait... how did you get free?" she asked.

"Mere rope cannot stop me," Tahari said with a sly smile as she held up her rope-burnt wrists. Studying the iron bars that were not going anywhere and knowing there was no key to use in the lock, she looked down at the floor to think for a moment. A shiny piece of metal wire caught her eye. A wild thought crossed her mind. "I will try you," Tahari said aloud as she began her attempt at picking the lock of the prison door. Rami and Senti had their doubts about what Tahari was tryin to do, but Almari gazed at her friend with a hopeful smile as she watched her work on the lock.

"Tahari? What on earth are you tryin' to do?" Senti asked Tahari nervously. Never had she seen a lock opened in such a manner.

"Give her a moment. Tahari has learned the magic that has power o'er these metal locks," Almari said in a hushed tone, trying to give Tahari room to concentrate. She continued to work the lock, determined to get it open. Then Tahari heard the wondrous click that opened the lock. She looked up at her friends with a wide smile. A second later, she pulled the cell door open with the greatest of ease.

"The magic lies within the wrists and the knowledge to use your surroundings to your advantage," Tahari said as she watched their amazed expressions. They walked out of the prison cell almost in disbelief but quickly gathered their thoughts as they saw the warning in Tahari's face. She was looking out the prison door at the blackened skies overhead. The wind that had swept through the yard only moments earlier had died and now was not even a noticeable breath of air, but her heart continued to race.

"Is the storm over already?" Senti asked as she joined Tahari at the open doorway. She shook her head slowly.

"It has only begun," Tahari said. Then there was a strange wail far in the distance. Its haunting sound gave her sufficient warning. "Come! Quickly! We do not have much time!" she shouted, running outside just as the wind began to pick up again. They were quick to follow her, and she led them to one of the plantation's storm bunkers. Unfortunately, they had to run across the entire plantation before they would reach them. Glancing back over her shoulder, Tahari caught sight of the dreadful twister that was only illuminated by the flash of the lightening that lit up the area. It was passing over the distant wheat fields, the twister's long column turning a dark tan. Senti had also turned back to look at it, but Tahari took her arm and kept running. "Do not look! Run! It will be upon us in moments!" she yelled as the wind began to pick up around them. They felt the sting of dirt hitting their bodies, and they continued to run to the bunkers.

This was not a time to become distracted, but something caught Tahari's eye. Looking over at the main house, she saw the house lights burning and people standing around seemingly unconcerned with the events outside. They finally reached the bunker, and Tahari let Almari, Rami, and Senti go in before her. Tahari stopped at the doorway. The Dancar family was in serious trouble. Turning toward the main house, Tahari did not stop to think about what she was doing. No one would blame her for leaving them to a well-deserved fate, but there was one witness watching. Tahari could never turn her back on His ever-watchful gaze.

"Tahari! What are you doing? Come inside!" Almari cried hysterically. The wind was now beating against her with an intense force, and thunder cracked overhead. Tahari turned back to her for a moment.

"I have to go back for someone! Stay there! I will not be long!" Tahari yelled. Almari did not approve of her friend's decision, but she could not force herself to go after her either.

Running headlong into the storm, Tahari heard thunder crack overhead, and lightning lit up the ground around her. Rain pelted her on all sides. Tahari wrestled with the driving wind and rain to make it across the courtyard and reach the main house in time. She dodged a piece of debris only to lift her head and have a dark blur come at her. Stars exploded all around her, and lightning and thunder filled her senses. All went dark and silent.

Chapter 18

Measure of Kindness

Thunder shook the earth as Tahari slowly came to. Looking up into the stormy night sky, she remained lost for a moment, trying to get her bearings. The rain that fell upon her was only a gentle shower, and the wind that blew against her wet skin was merely a strong breeze. Her thoughts were unfocused and scattered when a faint cry broke through. It grew louder and more mournful. Shaking her head, she slowly picked herself out of the mud and debris and climbed to her feet to look around. The main house was gone! Only a pile of debris remained.

Tahari's heart dropped into her stomach. She raced toward the wood splinters and timber that had been left behind. As she drew near, Tahari saw someone battered emerge from the rubble. It was Lord Dancar.

"Where are Tana and Thera?" she asked as she grabbed him by his mud-soaked shirt. He looked at her with a face smeared with mud. The rain and mud had also matted down his short brown and gray hair; he was almost unrecognizable. His gray eyes were filled with great sadness as he shook his head. He turned and walked in a daze back through the upheaval that used to be his world.

Tahari was not about to give up that easily. She did not know what kept her looking for the two people who probably hated her the most, but she could not give up. Tahari searched through the ruin of their home, looking for signs of life. She caught a movement in the debris just ahead of her. Stumbling over the broken, mud-covered timbers and boards, Tahari clawed her way to where she had seen the movement. She managed to move several large beams. In doing so, Tahari watched Tana slowly climb from beneath the ruins of the house. She was also soaked and completely covered in mud. Her forehead bore a large scratch, and blood ran down the side of her face. Taking hold of her arm, Tahari helped her out of the debris. She seemed grateful for the help until she saw who was helping her. Rage filled her hazel eyes, and she yanked her battered arm out of Tahari's grasp.

"Take your hands off me!" Tana hissed at her angrily. She quickly adopted the smug look that she gave Tahari when she was still tied to the torturing pole. Tahari did not have the time or the energy to waste with this senselessness.

"Where is your mother?" Tahari demanded, looking around the rubble. Tana glared at her a moment without saying a word. Tahari could see the worry for her mother seeping into her face, but she refused to ask for Tahari's help. Shaking her head slightly, Tahari turned back to her search. Climbing around the ruins, Tahari felt a presence among the debris, mud, and grass. Peering through the murky darkness, she made out someone lying in a heap, trapped under heavy timbers. Cautiously, she made her way over to the mud-covered body. It was Thera Dancar without mistake.

When Tahari reached Thera, she cautiously leaned over the huge beam to check whether she was still alive. After pressing her fingertips to the skin of her neck just below her chin, Tahari was blessed with a half relief. Thera was still alive and awake enough to recognize who was at her side. She cried and pleaded for Tahari to free her. Tahari was glad that she was awake and hysterical; getting her out otherwise would have been much more difficult. Tahari struggled to move the heavy beam off her. Try as she might, though, there seemed to be no way for Tahari to free her. She thought about the last thing that

Thera had said to her. It in itself gave Tahari no real motivation to get her out of this situation, but the anger she felt gave her another idea. Tahari looked at her angrily.

"Live with this knowledge," Tahari said as she glared deep into her coal-like eyes, and then she let out an angry yell and with all her strength pushed the heavy beam aside. The huge pile of debris she was trapped under shifted enough for Thera to climb out. Tahari grabbed her just as the debris shifted again.

Taking a firm hold of Thera and pulling her bony body over her shoulder, Tahari began to make her way out of the ruins. The debris groaned and shifted with each step. Tahari fought to keep her balance, and more rubble collapsed behind her. Praying earnestly with every step, Tahari steadied her pace until she was free of the remains of the house, safe on solid ground again. The feeling of solid earth beneath her feet was never so welcome. When Tahari made it a fair distance from the ruins of the Dancar mansion, she stopped and turned back to see just how close she had come to meeting her own end. Lord Dancar and Tana rushed up to her. Tahari gently laid the older woman on the muddy ground and turned to give them time alone with Thera. Tahari felt this was her time to leave, so she quietly made a retreat into the thick mist that had settled around the plantation. Only Tahari did not make it as far as she would have liked.

"Wait!" Tana cried out after her. Stopping and turning around, Tahari looked wearily at Tana. Her expression was a mix of confusion and anger. "Why did you do this?" she demanded, gripping her arms tightly. The heavy-set girl was covered head to toe in mud, but her hazel eyes still saw Tahari as the one who looked out of place. Tahari looked at her and then at Lord Dancar. She shook her head slightly and smiled sadly.

"If you do not know now why I did it, then you never will," she replied in a soft and weary voice. Tana looked at her for a moment and seemed more confused than before. Then she looked at her father. He lowered his head in shame.

"What is that supposed to mean?" she demanded, turning back to Tahari and began shaking her. "Only you would seek fame like this!"

she shouted at her. Anger surged through Tahari's exhaustion, and she shoved her away.

"Honor your family and see to their needs. Leave me alone," Tahari replied tightly as she gave her a look of warning. Tana stopped and stood like stone before her as if shocked that Tahari had actually given her an order. Looking at her a moment longer, Tahari then slowly walked past her and began to head back to the slave barracks. She wanted no reward from them, for she had seen all the goodness they could ever offer her. At this moment, Tahari wanted none of it. Her concern now was for her friends, and she prayed that they had fared better than the Dancar household had. Tana was about to pursue the matter further, but her father walked up to her and put a firm hand on her shoulder to stop her.

"Daughter, leave her be." Lord Dancar's words were almost startling for Tana, but when she looked back at her mother, she did as she was told. As Tahari walked away from them, she noted that this was the first time that they had ever showed her some kindness. Tahari could only wonder how long it would last. On her way back to the bunkers, she was beginning to feel the full impact of her exertions and injuries. Tahari felt almost overwhelmed with exhaustion and barely able to walk anymore. Dragging herself onward, she forced herself to reach the bunkers. It was here that she would be able to find rest.

Chapter 19

Visitation

The rain had lessened by the time Tahari had reached the bunkers. She found herself lost for words. There had been no damage to the bunkers. It was as if there had not been a tornado. Just to see the buildings, which were built halfway into the ground, still standing was a wondrous sight. Lanterns in the windows of the weathered barracks burned brightly through the humid darkness. This was a truly heavenly sight! Standing silently for a moment listening to the rain patter around her, she observed the people gathered around the bunkers. They were still slaves bound to this land, but somehow they were given a moment of equality. Tahari saw spirit and pride return to their faces and, most importantly, life. She could have stood there forever enjoying this view. As Tahari took in a deep breath, she heard someone call her name from the crowd that had gathered around the door to one of the bunkers. It was Almari.

"We were so worried about you!" she exclaimed in relief as she broke through the crowd and rushed toward Tahari. A second later, she wrapped her up in a huge hug. Tahari managed to smile weakly in her loving embrace in spite of the pain she felt as Almari held onto her bruised body. Senti and Rami came running from nearby. Their expressions of happiness shone through their disheveled appearance.

There was relief and happiness in their welcoming eyes as they, too, took turns wrapping their arms around Tahari. They all looked a little weather-beaten from the storm but, thankfully, were alive and unhurt.

"Thank the Lord! I prayed that he would keep you safe." Senti's warm voice was soothing to hear. As she held Tahari tight, the young girl collapsed to her knees. Senti gasped and then dropped to her knees to examine Tahari for any serious injury, her hazel eyes looking intently into Tahari's bruised face. Senti saw her pain and utter exhaustion. "What possessed you to go back into that storm?" she asked, causing concerned looks from both Almari and Rami. There were even a few others nearby who looked like they wanted to know the reasoning behind such madness.

"To accomplish the impossible," Tahari said in a weary tone.

"And what was that, child?" Senti asked kindly, resting on her knees and patiently waiting for the answer. Few people understood Tahari or her strange ways, but Senti always seemed to understand her no matter what.

"To be merciful to those who have never given mercy, for they have never learned to understand its value," Tahari said, smiling wearily at Senti. Tahari knew that she understood, for she did not utter a reply, only gave a wistful smile. Not many around them understood what Tahari meant, exactly, but that was all right. In time, they would. Senti touched Tahari's face gently.

"One day, child, you will travel beyond this bitter land and bring life and all its wonders back to this kingdom and its people," she said. Her words of wisdom filled Tahari with great hope that she might be able to have the chance at freedom again. Tahari could listen to her forever. When she looked up at the people who gathered around the bunkers, Tahari motioned for Senti to follow her gaze.

"I believe that it has already begun. It may not come with the sounding of great trumpets or some massive army but rather with the kindness of one soul spreading love and compassion to others," Tahari said in a faint whisper, but Senti heard her words clearly. After Rami helped Tahari to her feet again, Senti put a loving arm around the weary girl and led her through the crowd of people toward the bunkers.

"Come, it is time for our heroine to rest," Senti said softly as Almari and Rami followed closely behind them. They too, had heard their conversation, and Tahari could sense that they had indeed understood what she had said. They seemed almost amazed that she had such a positive conviction about the bitter life that they led, and a spark of hope lighted in their eyes. They did not have any idea when they would see their freedom, but they knew that this bitter life could not go on forever. After helping Tahari clean up from the night's adventure, Senti found her a warm place to sleep. It was no more than worn ticking on the building's dirty stone floor and a holey blanket for warmth, but as worn and beaten as Tahari felt, they were a touch of royal life. Senti gently wrapped the blanket around her, looking thoughtfully at her for a long moment.

"Why such a thoughtful look?" Tahari asked, drowsily looking up at her. Her curly gray hair was starting to frizz from the humidity, creating an odd halo effect. She smiled kindly, gently stroking Tahari's hair behind her back.

"It was what I said to you earlier and your reply. You are going to leave this land, but it won't be your strength that saves many. It will be your love and kindness, just like it was your love that saved us tonight. Know that you are blessed, and anyone who receives the gift of your friendship is equally blessed. Now go to sleep and dream good dreams, for all of us." Senti's warm whisper lulled Tahari to sleep, and she leaned over and kissed her head. Tahari basked in Senti's loving presence, closing her eyes and listening to the rain gently falling on the roof and on the ground outside. Its fresh scent drifted in on the cool breeze. Slowly Tahari managed to find sleep and drifted far from this world.

Later that night, lying unmoving and in a deep sleep, Tahari sensed something going on in the room around her. Then a voice spoke to her.

"Tahari," she heard it say though she was still in a sound sleep.

The voice called to her again, and Tahari heard such warmth and compassion in the voice that she was not afraid to answer it. She sat up and saw a column of white mist drift into the room from the open doorway.

"I am listening. What is it that you ask of me?" Tahari asked with uncertainty. The voice seemed to be coming from the white column. It was a woman's voice and seemed almost familiar. An image appeared before Tahari: a woman with dark flowing hair and sea-green eyes kneeling before her poor bedding. Her skin looked beautifully tan and contrasted with her white gown, which shimmered with iridescent beads. The bunker glowed from her radiant light. Her presence did not wake any of the other workers. Her regal facial features were eerily familiar, but Tahari could not put a finger on it.

"I do not ask anything of you. I have come to tell you something. It will not be easy to understand, but you must hear me out, for there is much that is depending upon you," she said with grave seriousness. "Tahari, you are of the ancient race known as the sphinxes. Long ago, they existed in this realm of men, elves, and dwarves. They had the bodies of mortals, but they were so much more. They were one of the most powerful creatures in the world. Their power was matched only by their wisdom and love. The ancient sphinxes guarded this world. Because they were creatures of such immense compassion, love, and wisdom, Adalai entrusted each sphinx at birth to be the keeper of a single element of the world or a living creature within it. The more powerful the sphinx, the greater their responsibility." the woman's words were incredible, but as Tahari thought about how out of place she felt among the other slaves on the Tomblock, she found it easier to believe and understand. "A sphinx's life span could be an eternity if they did not see war or become victims of violence. If one were killed, its power was passed onto another—it could only happen when the dying sphinx touched another sphinx at the time of their death. In some cases, their power was absorbed by the creature or element they were protecting. However, the rarest occurrence that has ever transpired with the transference of a sphinx's power happened when a sphinx mother was allowed to pass on her abilities to her unborn child. This has only happened two times in our history.

"Every sphinx that ever existed was a guardian of one element or creature of the world, including each other?" Tahari asked with amazement. The dark-haired woman nodded kindly. Images of these heavenly creatures came to mind, though Tahari really had no idea of what they looked like. Her best guess was that they could have been beings of light given earthly forms so they could reside in the world unknown.

"Yes. One of the most powerful Adalai made the guardian that could reach out to all the sphinxes from all the ages, living or dead, and call them to battle with a whisper. She was called Shamira, which means 'the guardian.' Adalai saw something else within this sphinx. He saw her passion to help those in need, and thus he gave to her a special mission. She was told that in the ages to come there would be an elfin child born unto a king. Shamira was to watch over the child and protect him from the unseen darkness that would try to endanger him.

"How sweet it must have been for Shamira to watch over and protect an elfin prince," Tahari said with a gentle sigh. The story sounded wonderful to her. The woman said nothing for a long moment.

"It did not happen as we would have liked," the woman said, her voice filled with grief. "About 300 years after the child was born, the race of man became engulfed in blind, rage-filled greed and wanted the immense power of the sphinxes for themselves. When the sphinxes refused to release the knowledge of their power, they were slain by the very creatures they were trying to protect. Soon, all but a rare few perished at the hands of man." The woman's story caused Tahari's heart to plunge deep into her stomach.

"What about Shamira? What happened to her?" Tahari asked with growing dread.

"This great sphinx was one of the last to perish from man's greed." The woman's words were very disheartening to hear. However, seeing Tahari's saddened expression, the woman smiled hopefully. "Do not despair, for man had forgotten one thing about Shamira: her love continued on even after her death. Upon her death, Shamira asked Adalai if her spirit could linger behind to watch over the child. He not only granted this prayer, but spoke comfort to her. 'The elfin child that I have chosen you to protect will never be far from your comforting presence. In the ages that are to come, he will be caught in the middle of a great revolution between darkness and light. He will also be the key to winning the great battle that is to come. The mission to protect him will continue, for in the time to come, his enemies will become great in power, and he surely would be lost to the darkness if there was no such being to watch over and protect him.'"

"What happened to the elfin child?" Tahari asked with a tone of wonder. A spark of hope dazzled in the woman's sea-green eyes.

"Tahari as I have said before, you are a sphinx of the ancient world. You are the last sphinx born from that ancient race. Adalai found favor with you upon your birth and made you the possessor of the spirit of Shamira, the great sphinx of the ancient world. This is why I have come to you now. I must help you remember who you used to be so that you can set out on your mission. You must find the elfin child Adalai has entrusted to your care, for this child's life holds the key to the future of Andora.

Though awestruck, Tahari fought to speak. "If I possess the spirit of the great sphinx of the ancient world, then why do I not remember my life before? And if I am this elfin prince's protector, who has been watching over him while I have been locked away in the Tomblock?" she asked, feeling great confusion overwhelm her thoughts, trying to understand what this all meant.

"There are those of us who still watch, even in death. We have been guarding the chosen one until you are ready to take on the role as his true protector," the woman responded gently. "As for your memories, you must be patient. They will come to you in time. Do not worry, for there will be things to come that will trigger the memories to return. However, I am afraid that when you wake from this dream, you will not remember anything that has been said here." the woman's words sounded very defeating.

"How will I know…?" Tahari began to ask, growing anxious again.

"Shhhh… You have a young mind, but your heart will remember the lessons of old in time. This visitation is only meant to be the spark that stirs your heart to remember who you were before. Soon you will know not only who you are but also what mission lies before you." her words brought some comfort, but Tahari could not help but wonder about these unanswered questions.

"Is there something that you can give me that I will be able to remember when I wake?" Tahari asked with a hopeful tone.

"The only thing that I can say now that you will remember is that you must seek out and find the son of Goldendragon. He is the child you were sworn to protect long ago. His life is in grave danger, and you must help him or the future of Andora could be lost to the coming darkness." when Tahari heard these words, she felt a heavy burden weigh down upon her. "Tahari, do not worry. You have all you need to find him and help him. Adalai would not have given you this task unless he knew you were the right one to complete it. Now, rest, for there will be much to come in the days that follow. Your time on the plantation is almost done, and you soon will embark on a great quest. Always remember that your heart will guide you through your troubles. Listen to it closely; Adalai uses our hearts to speak to us, for they are the best way for him to reach us." as she spoke these last words to her, Tahari felt herself drift away into a dream-like slumber.

Soon all that was told to her became tangled into a dream. Tahari tried hard to hold on to what she had learned, but the harder she tried to remember everything the dark-haired woman had said, the more she began to forget. Then everything got confused with reality and the dream world. All Tahari could remember now was the vision of the wounded elfin warrior and the need she had to protect him. Tahari felt, for the first time in many years, a renewed sense of purpose.

Chapter 20

He Will Rise After Being Slain

Under the cover of darkness, Solarous made his return to Akendron. His solo journey had taken him just three days. Armed with dark powers given to him by Lord Jarden, Solarous literally walked from Zendro isle back to the main land of Andora. It gave him greater strength and speed. No natural force knowingly dared oppose him, for Solarous's new power coursed through his veins and grew with intensity. Deciding to save his feet, Solarous passed a farmstead and found a midnight-black horse for the journey ahead. By chance, the farmer stepped out of his wooden cabin for a breath of fresh air and to stretch the stiffness out of his back and aching muscles. The man yawned as he scratched his balding scalp, his thoughts on the past day's toils. Although tired, he did not miss his prized stallion being ridden away by a stranger. Dressed in a soft white nightshirt that hung past his knees, the farmer rushed barefoot from the porch and across the cool grass toward the darkly cloaked stranger.

"Hey, you! Thief! Stop!" the farmer shouted. His thin form raced up to Solarous to pull him off the dark stallion. Solarous merely raised his hand and a blue bolt of energy leapt from his palm, striking down the defenseless farmer. The body crumpled lifeless to the dusty road beneath him. Hearing the commotion, the farmer's wife emerged from the cabin dressed in a white and blue flower print nightgown and matching nightcap. Her eyes went wide with horror, and her mouth dropped open as she suddenly went running to her dead husband's side. She made it only half the distance before she met the same fate.

"Impressive," Solarous said to himself as he examined his hand with interest. After this, the sorcerer soon learned the full extent of his new powers. This was most noticeable when he passed through the thick forests that lay north of the Shandel's capital city. The forest air was filled with the sounds of night creatures and insects. As he entered the dark forest, the wild sounds faded until there was only silence. Even the cool breeze that had gently stirred the lush green leaves had turned into a dead calm. Only the sound of his horse's hooves upon the ground echoed through the forest. Looking about the forest, Solarous could see some of the creatures trying to hide from him. He heard their very thoughts. They greatly feared him and the evil that dwelled within him. Solarous was pleased by this, for he knew that he would soon have the power to control more things and people as well.

When Solarous finally reached Akendron's stone streets, people returning from late-night outings sensed the evil in Solarous as he passed by and were afraid. Though he made no sound, onlookers could feel the darkness within him. Normally, Solarous would have feared a large group, for they often mocked him, but no more. His dark power was far beyond any of them, and they would be afraid of him instead. Still, Solarous did not let pride turn to foolishness and remained ever watchful, for the eyes of goodness would be searching for evil's darkness. His master told him to be aware of the forces of light, for even if their numbers were not great, they would have the power to defeat him easily.

At the palace's grand gates, Solarous stopped his dark steed for a moment to gaze at the brilliant white palace that reached high into the night sky. Avdima's massive stone walls and high towers stood strong before him. The sheer magnitude of the palace had been the greatest achievements of its architects and builders. It had stood for countless years as a symbol of justice and goodness. A smile came to Solarous's pudgy face as he nudged his horse on. He would become greater than this mere pile of cleverly constructed stone. Solarous felt his darkness cause an eerie shadow to creep over the castle, and the feeling was growing. Lord Jarden would be able to take over this kingdom easily. Then, just before he made his way across the palace's main courtyard, he was overwhelmed with an uneasy, fearful sensation. It could mean only that the forces of light were in his midst. Looking around, he saw several men dressed in long dark robes with red sashes draped around their shoulders. The palace counselors and scholars were returning from late-night services, and even in the shadow of night, Solarous knew, they had seen him. Their eyes pierced the murky night, and they sensed exactly what he was now. Gripped with great fear, he yearned for the safety of his subterranean chamber.

Whipping his horse, Solarous hurried across the palace grounds, hoping to quickly disappear into the castle's dark corridors, losing the scholars and elders. He did not make it that far. The men began yelling at him, and everything turned into a blur.

"You bring darkness to Akendron! You bring the ancient evil to our door!" one of the scholars cried. The men quickly surrounded him and his horse. Enraged by the great evil they sensed, they grabbed hold of Solarous's cloak, pulled him to the ground, and began to beat him. They feared what the legend said about how the ancient evil would return to the kingdom. They feared it so much that they would do anything to stop it. In the heat of the moment, one of the elders tied Solarous behind his horse and slapped the horse's hindquarters. Startled by the strike to his body, the horse bolted and ran throughout the courtyard, Solarous helplessly dragged behind him over the hard ground. His body quickly became bruised and bloodied. The elders watched on with growing relief, for they felt the evil presence dying. Solarous's torture continued as his bruised and broken body was dragged over the rough cobblestone footpaths that ran throughout the palace grounds before death claimed him.

Meanwhile, Prince Alon-Settie had been walking down a candlelit corridor when he saw someone being dragged by a horse around the courtyard. He ran to the window for a closer look. Peering into the dimly lit night, the prince recognized Solarous as the one being dragged behind the horse. Alon-Settie knew that Solarous was notorious for upsetting the elders with his theories. He could only wonder what Solarous had done this time to tick off the elders as he raced through stairwells, desperate to reach the palace grounds before the old advisor was seriously harmed.

The prince was quick to reach the palace grounds and saw the crowd of six scholars and counselors gathered to watch Solarous. After observing their reactions for a moment, Alon-Settie realized they were pleased with this unusual demonstration. The horse returned to the group, close enough for everyone to see the broken and bloody body of Solarous. The prince became alarmed and enraged by this transgression. He rushed up to the dark horse to try to calm him down. As he did, he got a good look Solarous. The royal advisor had been beaten and trampled to death. His features were no longer recognizable. Snapping his head back to the crowd of elders, Alon-Settie glared.

"What is the meaning of this outrage?" he demanded. The elders did not hear him over their own angry conversation. Taking a whip from the horse's saddle bag, Alon-Settie cracked it in the air above him. The sound echoed across the courtyard, successfully catching everyone's attention.

"Y-your m-majesty," one of the elders stammered as he finally saw the prince's angered expression. At that moment, the elders fell silent as they saw Alon-Settie for the first, unsure what to say or how to explain their actions.

"I say again, what is the meaning of this outrage?" Alon-Settie said in a fierce tone, motioning to the broken body of Solarous. The prince's dark eyes flashed with rage. The counselors and scholars looked at each other, still not knowing how to explain what had occurred. Finally, one scholar came forth to break the heavy silence that had grown between them.

"My good prince, you do not understand what has taken place here. Solarous was about to bring about the evil that we have all feared for these past thousand years.

Alon-Settie looked at the group doubtfully. "This is also the man who tried to make himself disappear and ended up giving himself and half the royal court rashes that lasted for a week." Alon-Settie's point was well taken, and the elders shifted guiltily. "You killed the king's own advisor!" the prince continued, pointing at the six men before him. "I hold all of you responsible for this treachery! Do not look to flee Akendron. Consider yourselves under house arrest until this matter is settled. You will all be severely punished for this!" There was promise and certainty in his face as he then turned toward the dead body of Solarous. The elders wanted to plead for Alon-Settie's forgiveness, but then courtyard went strangely silent, and an eerie breeze swept across it. Alon-Settie looked around the courtyard and saw a white mist rising from the blood trail that led to Solarous's body.

"The evil is still here!" one of the elders said, whirling around and fleeing the scene. The other scholars and counselors quickly followed suit. Alon-Settie was left to watch this strange proceeding alone. He didn't believe the palace elders' suspicions about Solarous, even as he watched the white mist rise out of the blood that had been smeared across the courtyard. The mist drifted toward the royal advisor's broken body and gently settled over it. Alon-Settie watched in awe as Solarous's body began to glow. Then, just as quickly as it came, the white mist vanished. A moment passed before the prince could force himself to approach the royal advisor's body. Solarous started to move again! Alon-Settie watched in amazement as the advisor rose to his feet with ease and began to walk toward him.

"Solarous?" Alon-Settie managed to ask the portly advisor, who was walking toward him as if nothing had happened to him. The prince was relieved to see Solarous alive, but his father's royal advisor seemed different. Still, it did not concern Alon-Settie—the man was alive again! That was all that mattered to him.

Solarous gave Alon-Settie a warm smile. "I am glad that someone came to stand up for me. Otherwise this could have taken me longer,"

Solarous said as he stretched the stiffness out of his shoulders and brushed the dirt from his dark cloak. Alon-Settie was mute in disbelief of the resurrected advisor. "I owe my thanks to you, my good prince," Solarous said kindly, patting the prince's shoulder.

"What I have done is nothing compared to the feat that you have just preformed," Alon-Settie said, finding his voice at last. Solarous chuckled at the prince's dumbfounded expression.

"True enough. However, there is much that you can help me with now," he said with an encouraging look. "Come, we have much to talk about." he took Alon-Settie by the arm and led him back into the palace. As the two men walked toward one of Avdima's many doorways, Solarous noticed from the corner of his eye that several people were eavesdropping from nearby palace windows. Even strangers who had been passing by the palace gates had seen the resurrection. They had lingered for a long moment, but now were quick to move on again. He knew that word of his "miracle" would spread like wildfire. A twisted smile came to Solarous's lips, for he knew that everything was going according to his master's plan.

Chapter 21

The Corruption

"Now, how can *I* help you?" Alon-Settie asked as they finally reached the royal advisor's dimly lit chamber. He followed Solarous into the chamber and slowly shut the heavy door. As he did, a ghastly image of his mother being attacked in the dark street by the vile man flashed through his mind. He shook his head to rid his mind of these horrible images. The prince forced himself to focus on the conversation he was having with the royal advisor as he watched the aged man move almost gracefully around his dimly lit chamber, lighting torches to brighten the damp room. His mind continued to offer potent images of his mother being assaulted by the beastly man. Holding his head and shutting his eyes, Alon-Settie tried to force the images out of his mind, but they only became more intense. He began to gasp for air as he felt darkness crowd him.

Solarous looked at him strangely. "Are you all right, my prince?" he asked with a tone of concern. The prince could not answer; his mind was being assaulted nonstop by the images of what had happened to his mother.

"Maybe it is I who need your help," Alon-Settie confessed, holding his head in his hands.

Taking one of the prince's arms, Solarous sat him down in a red feather-cushioned chair. "What is it that you see?" Solarous asked, looking at Alon-Settie with expression. The prince looked at him strangely at first.

"How did you know that I saw something?" he asked with a cocked eyebrow, feeling his head begin to ache. Solarous spread out his hands and just looked at the prince.

"I can see when someone has a vision by the expression on their face," the royal advisor replied simply.

Alon-Settie realized how foolish his question was, especially to a man who had just returned from the dead. Nodding in understanding, the prince thought for a moment before revealing the horrid visions. "I see my mother being horribly attacked in the street by a large drunken man. This does not surprise me, for it actually happened, and..." he wanted to continue but decided against it.

"You want to see this man pay. Do you not?" Solarous guessed carefully as he watched the prince's reactions. The advisor stood nearby with his index finger on his upper lip and listened intently. Alon-Settie didn't say a word, but he nodded his head. "If you let me, I can help you seek your revenge on this man for the terrible deed that he has committed against your mother and our queen.

Alon-Settie looked up with renewed interest. "Can you really help me?" he asked with a pleading tone as a yearning expression filled his dark eyes.

Solarous smiled, for he knew that he now had Alon-Settie's trust. "I can empower you to make this man suffer for his actions. I know that many would refuse such tactics, but this man will never see justice if something is not done." Alon-Settie realized that he was right. As Alon-Settie began to plan what he would do to the man, he felt his head ache worse than before. The prince felt the room begin to spin around him and the pain intensify as he gripped the chair's wooden arm. Alon-Settie went limp and collapsed in a heap on the floor.

The royal advisor slowly walked over to the fallen prince and stood over him. The advisor's shadow fell over the prince's body, and a cruel smile came to his face. Solarous knelt and put a hand on Alon-Settie's soft tan robe. A green mist left Solarous's hand and disappeared into the unconscious prince's body. Solarous remained on his knees, smiling as he gazed upon his new disciple. "I can help you now, for you have paid the price of my services. Though I failed to mention that once you make a bargain with me, it is binding for life. You will help me overturn this kingdom, along with the rest of Andora. You will hurt those close to you, and this, my dear prince, will be only the beginning for you," Solarous said in a low voice. Then he rose to his feet, crossed the chamber to the dark wooden door, and opened it.

Chapter 22

Revenge

*Five days before the celebration
of the Great Dragon

In the nights leading up to the celebration of the Great Dragon, Akendron was full of life and excitement. Festivities ran late each night; stories were told, dances were held, and food and drink were served. In addition to this, the people of the Shandel were still counting their blessings for the rains, for they had endured too many long years of plague, famine, and death. As most people were heading home for the night, the excitement continued within one bar. Patrons had been drinking heavily, enjoying the night. One large man in particular was continuing to drink more than his fill when he spotted a dark, short-haired woman leaving the tavern. Catching sight of her purple gown and shawl as she headed toward the back alley, the drunken man was determined to get something more than just drink this night. Rising from his barstool and pushing it aside, the large man staggered toward the door. Emerging through the already open door, the man saw the woman disappearing into the alley. He was quick to follow, and when he entered the dark alley, he saw the woman trip and fall to the ground of the dirty alley. Running up to her, the man struggled to unfasten his belt and then grabbed hold of her and rolled her onto her back. She looked up in horror. The drunken man held down the next thrill of his night when he saw a large figure step out of the shadows.

"You again!" the man hissed as he pointed a fat finger at the dark shadow standing now near woman's head. The woman tried to scramble away, but her attacker forced her back to the ground. "Finish with y-you when I am d-done," the man managed to stutter. But before he could look back at the shadow before him, something smashed into his skull. He fell backward on the dirty ground, dazed by the blow to the head. The short-haired woman quickly scrambled away from her attacker, who now could not get up.

"See how you like it!" she spat at the drunken man and then whirled around and fled down the alley.

"Y-you will, w-hen I get…" The large man paused to spit blood from his mouth, which only dribbled onto his ragged, sour-smelling shirt. Looking up again, he realized that the dark-haired woman was gone. Narrowing his eyes, the man saw the tall black figure still turned in his direction. He remembered all too well what had happened the last time a shadowy figure attacked him in this alleyway. Suddenly, the man felt a wave of anger wash over him. "YOU!" he bellowed and angrily climbed to his feet to charge the tall shadow. The shadow easily moved aside, and the man crashed into some garbage-filled crates standing next to the building.

Recovering his senses, the man turned onto his back and looked up to see the tall shadow standing over him. There was no face to this person. It was just a shadow standing in front of him. "What the—" he said, his words suddenly cut short. The shadow brought down a heavy club onto the large man's skull. The savage beating continued long after the man had died. When the deed was over, the shadow disappeared from the alleyway, unnoticed by anyone except for one person.

"Now you are ready for what is to come, my prince," Solarous said to himself. As he watched on with delight from the misty haze of his black caldron. No one could have fathomed what he planned next, or so he thought.

Chapter 23

Prophetess Revealed

D ays had passed since Queen Elanza had visited Sala of Antioch
about the seer's warning and thus the discovery of the scroll
of the prophecy. In that time Sala took little time, for eating or
sleeping, or even tending to his appearance, for too much was at
stake. Sala had sat secluded in his library searching for answers. As
Sala stoically combed through the mountain of literature concerning
Andora's past, the small, wiry glasses that rested on the edge of his
nose shimmered in the light from the candle that burned brightly
on his desk. Over the past several days, he had pored through old
journals, manuscripts, and letters from previous members of the
Order. Sala had also reread the prophecy; he had discovered that
a sphinx from the ancient world might still live, and he had set to
work trying to find them.

"It has been foreseen that a sacred messenger will be able to
read the ancient text, but who will be able to read this?" Sala asked
himself, lifting his studious gaze from the aged parchment. As he
did, Sala remembered the seeing pool that Queen Elanza had looked
into several nights before. Jumping up from his cluttered desk, Sala
sprang for the door and dashed toward the hanging gardens just
outside of the palace. Hurrying through the dimly lit corridors of

Cypress Palace, Sala felt the tails of his worn gray robe flutter behind him and nearly get caught on the statues that populated the long hallways. When he finally reached the enchanted sea-green pool, he gripped the stone ledge and gazed into the water. His silver-streaked hair fell past his shoulders when he leaned over the edge of the pool. "Reveal to me the identity of the sacred messenger," Sala said and waited in anticipation.

The sea-green pool did not move at first, but Sala was patient and waited calmly. Continuing to gaze into the pool of enchanted water, Sala watched his reflection disappear and the water churn and become clear with its first image. Sala found himself staring at the plantation known throughout Akendron as the Tomblock. It was a most horrible place, to be sure. Very little regard was given to those who worked long hours in the fields. Sala felt a pang of guilt, for he had intentionally avoided places such as this. He felt great pity for those who were treated so cruelly but never took the time to look into what really went on behind the plantation's high walls. Now, Sala refused to turn away to search elsewhere for the sacred messenger. He knew the seeing pool had shown him this plantation for a reason. No sooner had he wondered where in that horrible place he would find the sacred messenger than a face appeared before him.

Sala saw a slave of about twenty years. She had warm, tanned face. The girl's hair was long and dark-brown. Her features were darkened from working long hours in the scorching sun. He marveled at her sea-green eyes, which were the same color as the water in the enchanted pool. Already he could see that she worked as hard as most of the men in the Tomblock, yet she had an unblemished appearance in comparison to the rest of the plantation's workers. It was as if she had never seen the whip or club before. Sala hoped for her sake that she had not, but he knew this was highly unlikely. The slave greatly interested Sala, for he sensed that she was different from those she worked around—and for.

"This has to be the one that I have been searching for," Sala said, still watching the enchanted pool. He saw images that greatly worried him. He saw what conditions the plantation's head taskmaster had forced the girl to work under. The image changed again, and Sala's heart sank as he could only watch as this poor girl was tied to a large wooden pole and viciously whipped and beaten in the scorching afternoon sun. "My word! What deed deserved this degree of treatment?" he agonized, wanting to reach out and offer some aid to the poor girl. The scene within the sea-green pool changed yet again. Sala watched in disbelief and at times found himself cheering the slave girl on as she retaliated against the taskmasters who were trying to "discipline" her. He could only wonder what would keep such a strong, valiant girl from freeing herself and escaping. "What is keeping you from freedom?" he whispered aloud.

The pool's image changed again, and Sala watched the girl, dressed in her ragged sackcloth, take the chance to be free. He found himself rejoicing as she dashed toward the dark forest of Divervandon. Only she stopped and stood still for a long moment, deep thought. She had every reason to continue on and never return to her cruel world, but he watched as she did the unimaginable. She turned around with an expression of horror on her face and ran back to the plantation!

As the images changed, Sala found out exactly why she had returned. The girl rushed back to warn the workers that a horrible storm was quickly approaching. No sooner had she spread this news and helped people to safety than a deadly tornado swept right through the Tomblock's main yard. What amazed Sala even more was how this girl chose to go into the storm to see that her master's family was all right. Though little thanks were given to her, Sala could not help but, awed by the depth of her compassion. At least he learned her name, being able to read the other slaves' lips as they spoke her name.

"Tahari has a heart like I have never seen before," Sala marveled, sitting back in disbelief. "She chose to ignore freedom and risked death itself to return to her cruel world to save the lives of her friends. She even saved the lives of the very people who mistreat her." He spoke reverently as he found himself humbled at Tahari's valor. Then he realized that she had not seen the approaching storm until she had returned to the Tomblock. "How could she have known about such events?" he asked himself aloud. The enchanted pool heard his request and granted it. Soon the image within the sea-green pool before him began to change again.

Sala saw the vision that been given to Tahari to warn her of the coming tornado.

"She is a prophetess," Sala said in awe and admiration, pulling back once more from the water and resting his tired form against the pool's stone wall. "Long have been the years since I have seen someone bearing such a gift." he took a moment to breathe a sigh of relief. He had been right that there was still a sphinx from the ancient world alive to translate the ancient scroll of the prophecy. Rising to his feet, Sala walked slowly around the enchanted pool. He lifted his hand to his mouth and thought deeply. He did not dare get too excited just yet. Tahari was still a slave of the Tomblock, and he could not say how long she could survive in such dreadful conditions. "I need her help, but getting the family to release her could take a long while. How long could she possibly last in such conditions?" he wondered aloud. When Sala realized that he had asked the question openly, he looked back into the pool. There waited another image. It caused him to stop in his tracks. "It cannot be..." he gasped, taking in the vision of the future, and he sank slowly onto his knees to stare more deeply into the glimmering pool of water.

Sala watched in horror as the enchanted pool revealed to him the cruelty that would befall Tahari if she was not taken from the Tomblock as soon as possible. In the silence of a night yet to come, Tahari was taken from her sleeping quarters and dragged across the plantation by two large, rough-looking taskmasters dressed in black. Tahari was forced to stand alone before a line of taskmasters and the head taskmaster. Sala felt his heart sink as a trial proceeded. Judging by the grim posture of Tahari's body, her trial and sentence were over before they started. Judging from the motions of the plantation master the sentence would be death. Sala did not know the reason why she was about to executed, but here the reason did not matter. Tahari was a serious threat to the survival of the plantation, and she was being dealt with quickly. He watched as she was led away from the plantation and brought into the surrounding wilderness. They took her deep into a nearby cave and tied her to the rock wall so that she could not escape. Then they began to beat her. Sala could barely watch this compassionate girl being violently killed. When they were finished, Tahari hung lifelessly from the rough ropes that bound her wrists to the rock wall. Sala's eyes stung with tears as he looked at her a moment longer. Even after the image clouded over to show him his own saddened reflection, Sala could not remove the image of what was about to happen to Tahari from his vision.

Chapter 24

Rise to the Moment

The enchanted oil that provided light for the magical palace of Cypress burned long into the night and well into the next day. All the while, Sala sat in the grand library deep in thought. He realized that he had little time to rescue Tahari from the Tomblock. Although the fate of Andora now rested in his hands, tied up with Tahari's fate, he did not dare rush to the plantation to try to rescue her, for it would result in a disastrous chain of events. He had to be patient and calmly plan his strategy for getting past the taskmasters and getting Tahari away before they followed through on their plans to kill her.

Sala was out of the athletic shape the Osarian order had molded him into, age having settled into his bones and muscles. He wished his dear friend Leondros could be the one to get Tahari out of the Tomblock, but Sala knew it was too much to wish for. Leondros was far away in his homeland and unaware of these events. Taking a deep breath, Sala rose slowly to his feet and paced the grand library's floor. Even though he was an aged man and fluid movement was not as easy for him, he still had some agility and fight left in him. He glanced over to a far corner of the room. Hidden by the shadow of a large bookcase stood a long wooden staff that Leondros had given to him long ago.

He recalled the first time he met the young elfin prince. At that time, he was just a youth himself. Sala had journeyed to Shoshon to be apprenticed to the elfin scholars, who resided there. Leondros befriended the young Sala and instructed him in tasks that were still quite strange to him. As their friendship formed, Sala was quick to learn under Leondros's tutelage. Later, Sala would happen to find himself alone and at the mercy of villainous bandits on more than one occasion. It was only because of Leondros's valuable teachings that he was able to survive these sudden and dangerous encounters.

A warm smile came over Sala's tired face as he walked over to the aged weapon, wading through the piles of papers to reach the beautifully carved staff. The staff rested horizontally on the same metal pegs that he had put into the stone wall himself many years before. The iron pegs kept the staff above the paper mess that covered the floor in this corner of the library. As he took up the staff carefully, Sala was filled with the memories of his time spent with his dear elfin friend. As his fingertips felt the impressions of the script that had been burned into the wooden staff, Sala looked closely at the engraved script that Leondros had placed there:

May this rod be your comfort even when I am absent from your side. Remember that I am never far from your memory. Safe travels, my friend.

Leondros Goldendragon

His friend was still encouraging him, even now. He nodded as he held the staff firmly in his hands and took a deep breath. "All right, my friend, once again you have inspired me to go beyond my abilities and help me prove that I can stand against darkness." Sala quickly left the grand library, cleaned himself, and prepared for the night that lay ahead. Dressing in a dark battle suit accented by silver armor plates covering the shoulders, forearms, and chest, Sala reminisced. He gazed reverently upon the Osarian knight's official battle armor. He had a renewed sense of purpose, remembering what it meant to be a true knight of the order. The armor's stunning beauty and the suit's conformity to his body, a little tighter than he remembered, were inspiring. The silver plates were etched with detailed symbols. Each of the order's five knights had armor specially designed for his purpose. Sala's role in the Osarian order was specific and full of great meaning. As he looked at himself, Sala tried to blink the tears from his eyes. He sensed the purpose he still had—not only to the order but also to those who needed him.

Stepping from the comfort and the safety of Cypress Palace to embark on his mission, Sala pulled the dark chain-link hood of his battle suit until it came over his forehead. Armed with his staff and other weapons, Sala stepped into the warm afternoon sun with great determination. He took in the day's warmth and breathed in all the wondrous smells. Only when he turned in the direction of the plantations was Sala of Antioch confronted by the reality of the mission before him.

The thought of actually taking on the Tomblock's taskmasters, by himself, scared him to his core. It had been many years since Sala had been in any confrontation, let alone a battle. Now he felt far too meek for such a task. He felt useless. He closed his eyes, sadly shook his head, and was about to retreat when he felt a jolt of lightning strike him.

Thrust into a vision, Sala opened his eyes upon the Tomblock plantation during the night. He watched the events he had foreseen in the sea-green pool coming to pass. Tahari was brutally murdered in the secrecy of a cave. Her corpse was left in the cave, which was sealed like a tomb. The taskmasters prided themselves on their craftiness, for no one would ever search for her here.

Closing his eyes to block out the heart-wrenching scene, Sala began to fully understand what would happen if he gave in to fear. Finding the courage to open his eyes again, Sala found that it was still night, but now he stood in a dense forest. He guessed it was somewhere within the Divervandon Forest near Endenbury. It was quiet a night until something started charging through the dense ground foliage. Leondros and several other men on horseback, wearing battle armor, broke through the foliage, searching for something or someone. Leondros caught up to one of his men, who led him deeper into the dense forest.

"Did you find the traitor?" Leondros asked as his dark-brown eyes searched his surroundings frantically. The man beside the elfin prince searched a thick patch of bushes and trees a moment longer before turning his horse around and looking calmly at his general.

"Yes," the man slowly answered, a cruel smile forming upon his lips. Leondros looked at him strangely. Before either man could move, a spear was driven deep into Leondros's back! He could not breathe, and his body was flooded with searing pain. The elfin prince toppled from his white horse and collapsed on the ground. Quickly, more of the armored men restrained him so that they could finish him. Leondros weakly lifted his gaze to look in disbelief at the men he had put his trust in. Another man, this one shrouded in a dark cloak, joined the traitorous soldier, who stood watching in delight as the life faded from Leondros's face. The cloaked man walked up to Leondros, who writhed in excruciating pain. The cloaked man revealed himself to Leondros, drawing close enough to whisper in his general's ear before taking a firm hold of the spear and snapping it in half, leaving the spearhead in his general's body. This time, the agonizing pain emanated from his heart. He fought to rise and back away from these men, but he succeeded only in stumbling into a nearby creek. All the color in Leondros's face drained away as the life within him began to leave. The crowd of soldiers only watched as their dying general was washed away by the current.

In the last moments of Leondros's life, he floated near the village of Endenbury. The unpaved streets that surrounded the simple thatched-roof homes and markets of the pleasant village were strangely quiet. Then, without any warning, an incredible flash of heat and light tore through the middle of the village and blinded the elf's fading senses. The flame and heat ripped through the forest that surrounded Endenbury, successfully finishing off the general of the Secret Alliance.

The flash of intense light blinded Sala as well as he watched on in horror. When he awoke from the heart-wrenching vision and opened his eyes again, Sala found himself back on the bridge outside of Cypress Palace, still facing the road he needed to travel to reach the Tomblock. The warm sun still burned brightly in the sky. He breathed out a huge sigh of relief. Everything was as it had been before. Sala reeled from what had been revealed to him. He angrily pushed aside his fears. He had a mission before him, and he would not fail. Departing, Sala began to realize that Leondros and Tahari were important links in the prophecy.

The knight's journey to the Tomblock was short. The sun was beginning to set when he arrived, and the newly inspired warrior sensed that it was time for the Osarian Knights to fulfill their oath to their founder and master, Farro. "I will keep to my oath!" he said. Coming out of the thick forest that surrounded this awful place, Sala felt his heart skip a beat as he saw the barbed wire strung along the high stone walls that made up the plantation's outermost perimeter. Looking within the compound's main courtyard and nearby fields, Sala saw the guards that were overseeing the workers, ready to pounce on anyone trying to escape. There was no way in or around this tight security. Sala grumbled to himself as he scrambled up a small hill and took cover in some bushes from where he could overlook the whole plantation. He would have to wait until full dark or risk being discovered, destroying Tahari's only chance of escape. The only thing that Sala could do now was pray that the god Adalai would let him be successful in his endeavors tonight.

As he waited, Sala felt the future of Andora settle on his shoulders. "No pressure or anything," he said to himself inaudibly, trying to shake off the anxious feeling that the whole world was watching him in that one moment. In spite of what he felt, Sala could also feel goodness working hard on this day. It was with him every step of the way. He knew in his heart that he would be successful. Sala continued to sit silently, watching the happenings within the Tomblock from his secret post on the hillside. The day's shadows gradually grew longer, and night was fast approaching.

Chapter 25
Destiny Calls

In the days that followed the tornado that swept through the Tomblock, the workers were put to work picking up the debris that had been scattered throughout the plantation. Despite the heroic actions of others and Tahari, life on the plantation returned to normal. Some had hoped that she would be shown some kindness in return for saving the life of the master's wife. What Tahari received was not what they or she had anticipated. Master Dancar remained cold-hearted and forced even stricter rules on the workers. He claimed that the storm had caused a major delay in their productivity, so workloads were doubled. None of this surprised Tahari. What did surprise her was that when she showed up for work, the taskmasters restrained her and brought her before Master Dancar. His gray eyes stared at her coldly, and then he sentenced her to a full day of work in the rock pits. Tahari was to remain there alone until day's end. The reason he gave for the sentence was that she had aided the slaves before him and his family. In spite of his outward cruelty, Tahari sensed that it was really a gesture of thanks rather than a punishment. The thought of spending the day alone in the rock pits seemed much more pleasant to her than working in the hot fields with taskmasters stalking her every move.

The sweet smells of the morning gradually burned away with the scorching midday sun. Soon the sun's warmth began to burn through Tahari's clothes and beat against the nearly healed cuts on her back from the taskmasters' whips. Standing up and stretching from her work to rest every once in a while, Tahari quickly found the enjoyment of being here. A day without the taskmasters was a true blessing. Still, she clearly understood why they would trust her to be all by herself with no guard or shackle to keep her from escaping. Even if she managed to escape, it would not be for long. She would be hunted down, quickly dealt with, and left dead somewhere in the wilderness. They were only looking for a reason to do away with her. Tahari would enjoy making their efforts unsuccessful.

As Tahari headed into the long hours of her day, her thoughts began to drift. Something from deep in her memory was struggling to be remembered. Whether it was because of the recurring dreams that she had been having or her longing to have a true family, Tahari began to wonder about her *real* family. As Tahari thought about something Senti had said to her when she was young, another memory emerged, words that had been said to her long ago.

"Do not be afraid, my daughter, for I will be with you always. Take care of those around you; it is your mission in life. Farewell, but never goodbye.

Coming back to reality, Tahari looked wildly around, with fists clenched, prepared for any taskmaster that might be hiding nearby waiting for an excuse to beat her. Much to her surprise and good fortune, there was no one else around. Tahari was still very much alone. "Strange…" she said as she looked cautiously around her and made sure that she was truly alone. Finally, Tahari realized that she was free to let out her emotions without worry. Taking a deep breath, Tahari thought about these beautiful, strange words. She repeated the words slowly and said aloud, "My mission in life.

Tahari remembered then the dream she had on the night of the tornado. She remembered the nickname from her past life, Shamira. "Guardian," Tahari said to herself as she recalled the vision of the dying elfin warrior. Her visions and dreams didn't seem to be from an overactive imagination, they felt more like memories of her true self. This was the *real* her.

Tahari tried to put the vision out of her mind for there was much work that still awaited her. Looking back at the rocks that remained and needed to be split, Tahari sighed sadly and continued on as before. The reality of this harsh place told her that all her childhood dreams would pass her by and she would be powerless to catch up to them. Just before she fell into despair, something in the air caused her to stop in her tracks. A strange feeling passed over her and stirred her heart. A feeling of a coming danger and a fear for someone dear overwhelmed her. Tahari listened closely to the air around her. It became still, and her senses told her trouble was quickly approaching. Turning around slowly, Tahari sensed that it was coming from the Divervandon Forest. Tahari went numb with fear.

"It is time," Tahari said to herself as she swallowed her fear, laid down her hammer, and ran out of the rock valley. As she did, she felt her heart leap into her throat. Tahari sensed that if she did not hurry, the vision of the elfin prince's death would become a reality. Suddenly, Tahari stopped and realized that by doing this, she would be giving the taskmasters the weapon they needed to get rid of her. Tahari would be forfeiting her life by leaving the plantation. Taking a moment to look back at the rock pits that she had been working in all day and then back at the forest, she knew of only one course of action. There was no glory in saving these rocks. If doing this one thing were her last moments to be alive, then she would live them being truly alive.

Making her way into the southern edge of the Divervandon Forest, Tahari found herself in near darkness. The trees within this massive forest had grown so close together that light was barely able to pass through its thick canopy. After letting her eyes adjust to the dimness, she sensed strangeness about this place. It caused shivers to run down her back and her skin to crawl. Tahari listened for the wild sounds of the forest, but all was eerily silent.

Evil has come to this forest, Tahari thought, scanning the thick green brush around her. The evil wanted her to leave, but this only made her more determined. Tahari defied the evil presence and pressed on, the image of the fatally wounded elfin prince vivid in her mind. She would not abandon him to that horrible fate or to this evil. As she fought to make her way up a steep embankment, she heard strange noises around her. The evil was close now. When Tahari finally reached the top of the embankment, she looked down into a deep-forested valley below. She saw a narrow road that cut through the middle of the surrounding trees. It was one of the few known ways into and out of Akendron. Thinking that this would be an excellent place for an ambush, she caught sight of the evil that she had felt. It surrounded her!

Scattered in the surrounding trees overlooking the valley below was an army of the dragon-like creatures that Tahari remembered from her dream. These were the Draccen soldiers of the Serrigen realm. Many people who lived within the Shandel had never heard of or seen such creatures before, for they had been closely guarded and not much talked about. As she studied their reptilian features more closely, she somehow felt that she had fought their kind in her past life.

Judging from the movement around her, Tahari reasoned that an army of about a hundred soldiers waited just out of sight. "A lot of Draccen soldiers for one elf; they are taking no chances. But why?" she wondered.

Not about to let their numbers scare her, Tahari looked around for a suitable weapon. The only thing that she had was her bare hands; she needed something more covert and silent. Tahari looked at all her options. Granted, there were more than a few in the bushes and trees that were scattered in the hillside around her, so she narrowed it down to a Draccen soldier a few feet downhill from her. The soldier was holding a long war bow in his hands and had a light brown leather quiver full of arrows on his back. Those would do nicely. Tahari silently made her way down to the Draccen soldier.

The dark-green–skinned Draccen soldier intently watched the

narrow road below and trained his arrow on the spot where his unsuspecting victim would soon be. His black eyes were wide and alert. Tahari picked up a small rock and threw it squarely at the back of his head. Fighting to muffle his angered response through clenched teeth, the Draccen soldier bent over and picked up the rock, rubbing his sore head and looking around to repay the favor. Scanning the surrounding foliage, the Draccen soldier found another soldier nearby who wore a suspicious grin on his face, angering the Draccen soldier Tahari had hit even further. "Funny, is it?" he growled as he gripped the stone and prepared to fling it at the grinning Draccen soldier. Behind him now, Tahari used her new-found speed and power to knock out the soldier with one punch, and he fell into some nearby bushes. No one seemed to take notice of his collapse.

Quickly, Tahari grabbed his bow and put the quiver on her back and just as quickly settled back into the thick foliage of a nearby tree. She was now ready for battle. Glancing down at the soldier, she was amazed that she had actually executed the lightning-fast punch to the back of the Drac's skull with such ease and accuracy. She wondered about her past life as a great sphinx warrior. However as Tahari remembered the soldiers surrounding her, she decided to think about her history later. Loading her bow, Tahari took a deep breath, focused her aim, and systematically took out the Draccen soldiers positioned farthest from the road. Her one hope in this silent operation was that the soldiers were not expecting company from behind. After Tahari ran out of arrows, she crept between the thick green foliage and borrowed what weapons she could find from a fallen Draccen solider and then moved on to the next to keep her silent war going strong. Tahari also had to impersonate Draccen soldiers at times when signals were given to keep a vigilant watch on the whole group.

"Talk about being at two or three places at once," she mumbled to herself as she threw rocks and shot arrows to mimic the movements of Draccen soldiers within the heavy brush.

Chapter 26

Help From Above

Approaching the last great stretch of the dark Divervandon Forest, Leondros Goldendragon found himself anxious to reach the other side, for it had been long since he last entered this immense forest. It covered nearly half of the Shandel and was a wild, untamed place. People journeyed through these wild regions escorted by expert hunters or excellent marksmen. Countless stories had been told about the lives that had been claimed by the vicious creatures that lurked within Divervandon. Leondros knew this dark forest and the dangers that awaited him well. He knew that no one should dare such a trip alone unless they knew what they were doing. However, unlike his many previous trips through this forest, Leondros sensed that this trip would be much different.

Despite its dangers, Leondros usually found himself at home within Divervandon. Yet something about the entire trip to Akendron bothered him. Leondros focused on his surroundings. A fair distance within the dark forest, he finally began to understand what was bothering him. His blood ran cold as he identified what awaited him.

Evil dwells here and is close at hand, he thought, guiding his white steed, Aton, down the winding dirt road that cut a small path through the wild forest's thick underbrush. The narrow road would eventually lead him out of the great, dark forest and straight to the stone gates of Akendron. Leondros continually shifted his gaze along the dark brush that was all around him. Fighting the anxiousness that bubbled up in him, he also ignored the part of his mind that screamed for him to turn back. As he journeyed on, the unsettling feeling grew more intense.

Leondros realized suddenly that it was more than just a feeling that bothered him. A strange odor floated on a faint breeze. The odor itself almost stopped him in his tracks, for he had not smelled such an odor since he passed through the desolate Serrigen mountains with his uncle. His uncle had told him that the strange rancid swamp scent came from the Draccen race, who were mostly reptilian in nature. At the time, Leondros was a little unnerved, for the odor was almost overpowering when they passed by the grand city of Romulus, where the millions of Draccen people slept. The smell was a nightmarish awakening for the elfin warrior, and he scoured his surrounding with an intense gaze.

"What in all creation possessed someone to awaken the Draccen people now?" he wondered as a nervous chill passed through him. The scent of the Draccen people was thick in the air. Now, Leondros knew for certain that an ambush was imminent. Stopping Aton and jumping from the tall steed's back, Leondros was about to take cover in the trees along the north side of the road when he realized he was too late.

He glanced at the tree-covered hills that towered high above him on each side. There were Draccen soldiers entrenched in both hillsides! They had been silently waiting for him, just out of sight. Their numbers were hard to determine, for they were scattered throughout both hillsides. Smacking Anton's hindquarters, Leondros caused the horse to bolt and run from the coming onslaught. Running back toward the bend in the road, he hid behind a huge oak, pulled out his bow, and quickly fitted it with an arrow. No sooner had he done that than he heard a shrill scream cut through the eerie silence. The shrill scream of arrows flying through the air caused Leondros's blood run cold, and they embedded themselves into the thick bark of the oak tree he had hidden himself behind.

Leondros quickly poked his head out from around the tree and then ducked back just as more arrows embedded themselves into the already arrow-riddled tree. Having picked out his targets, Leondros moved to the right side of the tree. With lightning speed and precision, he slipped out from behind the oak to take out his marked targets and then return behind the tree. Before he could let loose an arrow, four large Draccen soldiers came charging down the north hillside. They were almost upon him. Leondros leaped into the thick branches above him, avoiding the first wave of soldiers, who were left puzzled as to where the elf had gone. Their confusion was followed by severe headaches as Leondros jumped down from the branch he had been perched on and landed on one Drac, driving him to the ground. The other three got his bow handle upside their heads and joined their unconscious companion on the ground.

More soldiers began springing up from their hiding places, weapons in hand. Their chilling cries filled the forest. Far from being overwhelmed, the elfin prince took up his bow and began to fire upon his enemies without worry. Being sharp of eye and having even sharper arrows, there was not much Leondros could not bring down. Once he had spent his arrows, he leapt into the brush on the north side of the road, where he could get close enough to his attackers without their noticing him or his daggers. Moving swifter and faster than the Draccen soldiers, Leondros watched as their numbers quickly dwindled. He had not known how many had actually been hiding in the surrounding hills, but he sensed that many of them had perished.

When all was silent once again, Leondros remained wary. Cautiously, Leondros emerged from the thick brush and slowly walked down the dirt road. The road was littered with bodies. He counted thirty in all. As he moved down the road toward the next bend, he listened closely. Though Leondros did not hear any more soldiers, he could still smell the rancid swamp odor. The evil was still present, and the closer he got to the next bend, the stronger the scent became. Moving cautiously forward with his bow drawn and ready, he picked up used arrows to refill his quiver. Leondros knew this attack was far from over, but when he came around the next bend, what he saw dismayed him.

In front of him stood a small army of Dracs. These soldiers were nearly double in size and covered with armor. At least fifty were ready to charge him. Swallowing his fear, Leondros took up his bow once again. He had no choice but to face the odds that were stacked against him.

"Oh Lord, please be with me," he managed to say before the Dracs rushed toward him. Forcing himself to focus, Leondros began to fire upon this sea of charging giants. A good majority of them were armed only with swords, which allowed him to take down several with his bow. Those armed with bows tried to target him, but thanks to Leondros's speed and agility, the Draccen archers only succeeded in taking out their comrades. Out of arrows, Leondros abandoned his bow and took up his sword, remaining steadfast in cutting down any Draccen soldier that got close. Dueling with two large Draccen soldiers at once, Leondros was suddenly grabbed from behind by a large pair of iron-like arms. Seconds later, he was driven to the ground and pinned!

Kicking at the Draccen soldier who pinned him to the ground, Leondros fought to get to his feet again. Two more Draccen soldiers grabbed his arms and drove him back to the ground, thus pinning him helplessly. There seemed to be no chance for escape as another large dark-green Draccen soldier stood over him. He looked down upon the elfin prince with an icy glare.

"We will get a good price for your head when we bring it to our new master!" the large Draccen soldier said in a deep and heavy voice. Fear overwhelmed Leondros for a moment as the soldier looked down on him with a menacing expression. The Draccen soldier picked up a thick spear and swiftly raised it to impale his elfin prisoner. Before he could bring it down, an arrow cut through the air and impaled itself into his muscular wrist. Pain coursed through the creature's face as he fought to hold on to his weapon. The shock of the moment was intensified when the soldier on Leondros's right side cried out in pain, an arrow sticking from his chest. The Drac was frozen in pain and fear as he fought to breathe.

Taking the opportunity, Leondros ripped his right arm free and drove his fist into the face of the Draccen soldier who restrained his left arm. The Drac's eyes rolled into the back of his large head and his enormous body collapsed to the ground behind him. The elfin warrior lurched to the side, just as the large spear was driven into the ground next to him. Leondros scrambled to his feet and grabbed his sword. Leondros could not miss the lost expression on the reptilian beast's face. He stood dumbfounded that he had missed a target that was only three feet away.

"Tell your new master that I am keeping my head!" Leondros said in a raspy voice as he impaled the soldier with his sword.

The odds were still stacked against him; death hovering nearby, but Leondros battled on. He knew now that someone was aiding him in this overwhelming attack. Several Draccen soldiers stumbled over each other, colliding with Leondros and driving him to the ground. Feeling his weapons ripped from his hands, Leondros was desperate to get free of the massive bodies tangled around him. He scrambled to his feet, and four Draccen soldiers took their aim to fire upon him. With no chance to run, Leondros felt death upon him. Instead, he watched three of the four soldiers fall to the ground in quick succession, arrows sticking out from their backs. The remaining Draccen soldier was stunned and just looked blankly at Leondros. Leondros quickly threw a black dagger and watched the last soldier fall.

Strength renewed, Leondros fought to win the battle. A short while later, he looked around and realized that the grand Draccen army that had been dispatched to stop him was now lying dead before him. The enormity of what he had been through began to sink in. He thanked his good lord for seeing him though such an ordeal. However, it was not his skill alone that had brought him through this battle unscathed. His skills in battle were unmatched, but he knew that without the aid of the mysterious archer, he could not have survived the ambush. He looked in the hills surrounding him, but Leondros sadly realized that he was once again alone. Still, a weary smile stayed on his face.

"My thanks to you, whoever you are. I pray that the Lord allows our paths to cross again and that I can repay your kindness," Leondros said aloud, bowing his head respectfully. As Leondros paid homage to this angelic being for their assistance, Aton returned to find his master. It was all the signal the elfin warrior needed to keep moving. He took up his sword and bow, mounted Aton, and quickly set out again for Akendron. He did not linger a moment longer in this dark forest. Divervandon still harbored other dangers, and it was not safe to dwell too long in one spot. But though Leondros left this place behind, he would never forget what had transpired here. The memory of this miracle would linger with him always.

Chapter 27

Sentence to Salvation

L ooking down onto the road, Tahari felt relief. The vision that had caused her heart to sink was altered. The elfin warrior had lived through the intense attack. She started to make her way down the steep embankment to reveal herself. Tahari had not made but a few steps when she stopped abruptly. The great horn of the Tomblock sounded over the fields and drifted into the Divervandon Forest. The horn's deep sound reminded her that she was still a prisoner of her own world and that her demons had yet to be dealt with. The resonating sound of the horn overwhelmed her with alarm. More time had passed than she had realized! The sounding of the horn meant the end of the day, which meant time for the counting, a process that happened twice a day and let the taskmasters know if all the slaves were accounted for.

Oh, no, Tahari thought, dread washing over her. She saw the elfin warrior warily looking at his surroundings for any further signs of danger. She felt relief for him, for she knew he was safe now, but her hopes for their meeting quickly faded.

"Farewell, my elfin warrior. May you be accompanied by a kind spirit in your journeys to come," Tahari whispered. She wanted him to hear these words, but the moment had passed. The great horn sounded a second time. There was not much time, for when the third and final sounding of the horn came, those late would be severely punished and those absent would be immediately hunted for. Charging back up the steep embankment, Tahari forced herself through the overhanging branches and bushes that got in her way. Urgency washed away the weariness that had been weighing her down. Her need grew into burning desperation. Darting from the thick trees of the forest, she quickly made her way into the rock valley, picked up her sledgehammer, and rushed onto the road that would get her to the main yards of the plantation. Hearing the third and final sounding of the horn caused a horror such as Tahari have never known before. It was as though she heard the sound of her own end in the air around her.

Still determined, Tahari continued to run in spite of the horn being sounded. As she ran her full speed, her worn sackcloth shoes became torn to the point that they fell off her calloused feet. She paid no heed. Edging closer to the main yards, Tahari could now see the hundreds of field workers already gathered in the main courtyard. Her heart sank deeper as she drew closer to the group. There would be no hiding the fact that she was extremely late for The Counting. Then, just as she skidded to a halt behind the large group of workers already gathered, Tahari looked around to see that the taskmasters themselves were late for The Counting. Tahari began to hope that her tardiness would go unnoticed. Standing on her tiptoes, Tahari managed to glimpse the taskmasters finally walking down the stone footpath from the main house. One could see the taskmasters talking amongst themselves about other matters. Her spirits rose slightly, as it seemed that no one had realized that she had been gone. Trying to look worn and dazed like the rest of the workers, she hoped to blend in with her surroundings.

Tahari heard heavy footsteps behind them. Master Dancar had made it to The Counting and was now taking the roll call. This was her moment of truth. The hairs on the back of her neck stood on end as she heard him come to her, stop, and then slowly walk on. When he reached the end of her row of workers, she let out a silent sigh of relief. Then his slow and steady footsteps stopped. Tahari turned her head slightly to glance over at him. Suddenly, she heard his footsteps come marching back to her. This time they were quick and fixed on a target. Before Tahari saw his face, she heard the air around her grow still. A brilliant array of stars appeared before her eyes as something heavy connected with her skull. The ground rushed up to meet her, and she was quickly overwhelmed by darkness.

Tahari awoke to a soft breeze blowing across her face and a throbbing pain in her head. Dizziness kept her from picking her head up off the ground, but she managed to open her eyes. Tahari found herself in a dim, dreary place. Judging from the sour smell and the little she could see by the moonlight that found its way through boarded up window, she was in the far prison. This prison barracks had one distinguishing feature that separated it from the one on the main grounds. The iron bars that formed the prison cell had been painted red. It was a sign to the prisoner that death was near. Workers under the severest of punishments in the Tomblock were sent to this small prison barracks. Most workers never survived the punishment that was to follow, once placed within this barracks.

Tahari had been unconscious for many hours. Her heart was in her throat. Stories of slaves being taken here and never returning had long been whispered throughout the Tomblock. The prison consisted of a fortified building on the plantation's southern side. Her end was most definitely in sight now. Rising to her knees, Tahari wearily hung her aching head, her hair hanging tangled and snarled behind her. The thunder of heavy feet came up to the prison. It did not take them long to reach her cell. The clang of iron keys knocking against the metal bars as the taskmasters unlocked the heavy door made her head pound even more. The metal hinges groaned as the heavy door opened. More of the moon's light found its way inside her cramped cell. Tonight, the taskmasters were dressed in black robes. The two largest taskmasters stormed into the cell, took Tahari up by her dirty arms, and dragged her from the sour-smelling cell out into the night's fresh air.

Tahari was quickly dragged away from the prison and away from the plantation. As she looked back towards the main grounds, she saw a great fire burned within the middle of the main courtyard. Not far from it, many slaves were bound and shackled, and the taskmasters stood before them. One taskmaster grabbed Almari. She was bound and gagged, and they pushed her closer to the flames. Her deep blue eyes met Tahari's. Every moment that they spent together from the time they met until now passed before her. Before Tahari could utter anything, the moment was gone. She was quickly taken down a grassy hill, and Almari vanished from her sight. The taskmasters dragged Tahari out into the dark wilderness. The land seemed so strange to her, for everything around her was disappearing. At long last, they stopped her before a dark cave. They stood silent and unmoving as if they were waiting for something. Soon, Tahari heard heavy footsteps walking against the hard ground toward them. It was apparent who they were waiting for.

"So it comes to this." Master Dancar's familiar voice broke the silence. He stepped out of the dark cave. He, too, wore a black cloak with a hood covering his head. He pulled the hood back so that Tahari could get a good look at him. In the moonlight, she saw the look of cruel satisfaction in his dark, cold eyes and the smile that formed upon his lips. He gazed at her a long moment before saying anything. "I can still remember the night that you first came to us. It was a night very much like this one. The moon was full and bright, but there was something foul looming in the night. There had been talk that beasts of unknown origin and immense terror were sweeping over the land. Rumor said they were seeking something. Then, we found you upon our doorstep. We were quick to take you in, for we feared for you. Our hope was that we could raise you like our very own daughter, but..." as he told the story of her past, she became angry.

"You did not spare me for my sake, nor did you ever think of me as anything remotely close to a daughter!" Tahari snapped. "You merely saw another slave for your fields and another target for your taskmasters to torture and beat!" Her answer was complete and true. She saw only coldness and unconcern in his face.

"If only your mother had been as smart as you," he said. Then he stopped as if he remembered something, and began to laugh. Tahari glared at him. When he looked at her again, an evil expression flickered in his eyes. "The night she left you with us, she was killed by those foul creatures. Fifteen years ago this very night." his words hit hard, forming a painful knot in Tahari's chest. Her mind raced with what he had said. He moved away from the cave and motioned to the taskmasters. "I hear that it is your birthday today," he said, turning back to Tahari, "and I have a special birthday present for you. Trust me, it is to die for."

The taskmasters shoved Tahari through the cave's entrance. This would be the last time Tahari would see Master Dancar, she knew. The cave's darkness enveloped her,f and she found herself blind. The taskmasters had not pushed her very far within the cave before she was thrown up against a rock wall, her right side bearing the brunt of the impact. There was no light to see anything, but Tahari could hear the taskmasters coming after her. She felt the full weight of a heavy club catch her square in the chest and drive her back against the wall. As the air was forced from her lungs, Tahari collapsed to the hard cave floor. She felt death creep close to her.

In the dark, Tahari heard the clanking of shackles and the snickers made by the taskmasters as they prepared to chain her to the wall. She knew the obscenities they were going to enjoy doing to her before they killed her. As one approached her, he passed close to the wall of the cave and one of the shackles he was carrying scraped against it. The metal sparked against the rock, which ignited some old rags that had been left from an earlier execution. The sudden appearance of light shocked the taskmasters, but in that moment, Tahari caught a glimpse of a dark-haired sphinx woman. The image stood beside the stunned taskmasters, who had no awareness of her presence. This sphinx woman resembled her so much, Tahari sensed it was the person she was from a past life. This was of Shamira! She was dressed in dark dragon-like armor and stood ready with her own sword. Looking into the woman's desert brown eyes, Tahari saw potent memories of the sphinx warrior that she had been.

It was as if Tahari was that warrior once more. She looked at the taskmaster directly in front of her. He was unbuckling his belt. She charged into him with her shoulder, driving his fat body against the side of the cave. He let out a raspy cry as his back was driven into the wall's sharp rocks. Several other taskmasters raced to aid their fallen companion. The taskmaster closest to Tahari kicked her in the stomach. Landing on her knees, Tahari saw him pull out a sword. She again drew on her strength to stand and send her foot into his chest. He gasped as the air was driven from his lungs and fell to the ground.

As he fell, his sword fell against Tahari's leg. She quickly leapt over him and ran out of the cave. Emerging into the wide-open night, Tahari noticed that Master Dancar was nowhere to be seen. When she looked back towards the inferno that raged upon the plantation, she caught sight of Master Dancar racing back to the main grounds. There was pandemonium; upon the grounds, the workers were retaliating. This night would not end well for the workers should Master Dancar regain control of the Tomblock.

Tahari had no plan for where to go; she just ran. Anywhere but here was good enough. She found herself heading toward the Divervandon Forest. That was good; she would be safe from these men in the forest. Suddenly, she felt something sharp bite into her back. Tahari stumbled slightly, but she managed to whirl around to face her attacker. Looking back at her were the taskmasters who had taken her out of the fields and whipped her after her slight disagreement with them.

"We knew that you were trouble. Tonight, we are free to kill you," the portly taskmaster said, the whip he had used to stop Tahari firmly in his grip. The five other taskmasters each seemed to be ready to settle their issues with her as well. They charged toward her. She was tempted to turn and run from them, easily outdistancing the overindulgent taskmasters, but she did not want them to see her leave and follow her later. Any pain that she would have to endure was well worth a permanent freedom. And any pained she endured would be miniscule compared to what they would, for they were standing between a slave and freedom.

Tahari came at them with a fury that she had never known. They were not prepared for her rage and quickly found themselves on the ground. As Tahari backed away from them, she suddenly felt all her energy drain from her body. Staggering now, Tahari watched them climb back to their feet. A retreat was now in order, for she knew she would not be able to survive another attack.

Whirling around, Tahari ran as fast as she could. The taskmasters overtook her again near the rock valley and brought her down upon the sharp jagged rocks, beating her viciously. The beatings took her breath away. One of the taskmasters kicked her in the stomach. The force of the kick sent her over the embankment and down into the rock valley. Tahari's world spun as she rolled violently down the hill, pain seeming endless. When Tahari finally came to an abrupt stop at the bottom, she lay in a battered and bruised heap. Surprised at still being conscious, Tahari wasn't sure she could climb out of here on her own. She heard the taskmasters hurrying down the rocky embankment. They would not leave until she was dead. Laying there, Tahari chose not to contend with this life anymore. She had had enough of it.

Then Tahari witnessed something miraculous. A silver-and-black-armored figure was suddenly before the taskmasters, and with profound efficiency, he dropped them to the ground where they stayed silent and unmoving. He walked up to her, lifted her off the hard ground and carried her away. Tahari was too weak to keep her eyes open any longer, let alone struggle, but she could sense immense kindness from this man. It seemed so strange that someone would be rescuing *her*. She felt the overpowering need to give in to unconsciousness, but Tahari fought to stay with this world just a little longer. Then, she felt a gentle hand touch her aching forehead as a warm voice spoke to her.

"Sleep, my child. Your body needs rest, and so does your mind. It will make you strong for the journey that is ahead of you. Do not worry, for you are safe. Be content and sleep. There will be time to talk later." the voice reassured Tahari that she no longer had to fear her surroundings. Darkness came then, and she no longer feared what she would wake up to. It would be all right now, would it not?

Chapter 28

To Save a Hero

S ala had waited for darkness to execute his plan before leaving his hiding place upon the hill. Before he left, he saw something that broke his heart: a huge bonfire was built, and several slaves were taken from the crowd, killed, and thrown into the fire. He did not know what had transpired that day to provoke the taskmasters enough to start killing their slaves. Sala could only watch helplessly if he were to save Tahari. Then all the slaves rose as one and began fighting the taskmasters. They were not going to allow the taskmasters to harm their friends and loved ones any longer.

Sala searched desperately for Tahari in the crowd. He could not see her anywhere. Rushing down the hillside, he made his way into the plantation. No one noticed him, busy as they were with their own battle. Sala began searching the plantation. He had not realized what a large place it was, with so many places that he would have to look in. His desperation to find Tahari grew into a crazed obsession. He searched like a madman, but there was still no trace of her. Then as he stopped for a moment to catch his breath, he remembered something Leondros had told him a long time ago: "Be patient. Listen to your surroundings. Calm your thoughts. They will speak to you.

He smiled with understanding and nodded. "All right, we will try this your way," he said aloud as he closed his eyes and began to clear his mind of the panic that he was feeling.

Reopening his eyes, Sala looked around the plantation and took everything in. In the distance, he heard the chaotic sounds of the slaves fighting off the taskmasters. He felt torn, for he wanted to help these people, but Tahari was his mission, and he was not about to let her down. Sala continued his search for the girl.

Spying her emerging from a cave a short distance away, Sala knew that Leondros had once again been right. She looked around wildly, trying to avoid being seen and then broke into a dead run. She headed toward the Divervandon Forest, but he saw that she would have problems doing so. Six taskmasters also emerged from the cave and ran after her, soon overtaking her. Sala then saw the girl take on all six taskmasters. He stopped for a moment in awe and then came to his senses and sped toward her.

It was as if all her strength had vanished. The amazing force that she had used to fight with was spent. She whirled around and tried to make a break for the forest. The taskmasters rose up to go after her. Sala fought to close the distance between them and him. When he finally reached the place where the taskmasters had overcome Tahari, he felt a sudden stab of panic. The girl was nowhere to be seen, and the taskmasters were now alone, starting down the side of a steep rocky embankment. Sala sprang in front of them, unwilling to let such treachery go unpunished. Armed with only his wooden walking staff, Sala made short work of the six taskmasters, taking advantage of their surprise. When they finally began to fight back, it was too late. Soon, all six were lying unconscious upon the ground.

After making sure that his opponents would no longer be a problem, Sala looked over the steep embankment to the rock valley below. At first, it was hard to distinguish a body amongst all the moonlit rocks, but after a long moment, he caught sight of Tahari's beaten form. Scrambling down the steep embankment, Sala could see that she was in bad shape. When he finally reached her, he felt his heart sink.

"Please be alive," he whispered as he reached down to touch her neck for signs of life. Much to his relief, Tahari's pulse was strong. Still, she needed medical attention and rest. She was badly bruised and beaten. Picking her up off the ground, Sala felt concern for the girl, for she barely weighed anything. She was like a doll in his arms. She tried to speak, but he calmly reassured her that she would be all right, and she closed her eyes. Looking at her for a moment, he wondered if the taskmasters knew what she was. Why else would they go to such lengths to kill her? It was a question to be answered later. "Your time as a slave is over, my dear," he said, taking comfort in the knowledge that he had this chance to help Tahari win her freedom. After seeing the kind of person she was in the Tomblock, he could only wonder what she could bring to the wider world.

Chapter 29

A Kindly Man

Tahari awoke slowly to the sound of someone humming nearby. She wearily managed to open her eyes. She found herself in a strange place. As her new world slowly came into focus, Tahari wasn't sure if she was alive. Then she saw an aged man with brown hair tightly pulled back in a ponytail standing next to her. He wore a black robe with a gray sash tied at his waist. Tahari saw kindness in his tanned face as he tended the wound on her leg. Feeling intense pain as he worked on the wound, Tahari guessed that death had passed her by again. Tahari winced, and the man looked up at her.

"She awakes. How do you feel, child?" he asked her in a kind voice, his blue eyes meeting hers. Tahari looked at him for a moment and realized that he was the man who had saved her from the taskmasters. Tahari felt that she could trust him.

"I hurt, but I will live," Tahari said slowly, trying to endure the pain. He smiled hopefully. His features were softened by the candle that burned on a table next to the bed on which she lay. Tahari was lying on a soft bed with white sheets! She took in the rest of this new room. It was an enchanting stone bedchamber with a stone fireplace in which a glorious fire burned. The gray stones were decorated with burgundy and white tapestries. Candles were cleverly placed throughout the room. The overall grandeur of this bedchamber overwhelmed her, for such pleasures were found only in dreams. The cold reality of where she came from refused to let her mind accept this new situation and passed it off as a dream.

"It is good to hear you say that, for you have been through quite a lot tonight," he replied warmly, sitting down slowly on a polished wooden stool next to the bed. He seemed as stiff as she was.

"You helped me escape the Tomblock, did you not?" Tahari asked groggily, slowly realizing that she was *not* dreaming.

The kind man nodded. "May I be so bold as to ask why the taskmasters were trying to kill you?" His voice was filled with concern.

Tahari looked away, overwhelmed that a stranger worried so much for a plantation slave. After a long moment, she looked back at him. "Slaves are bound to the Tomblock. Slaves are not permitted to leave unless they are being shipped off to another plantation or killed. They were going to kill me because..." she paused for a moment as she replayed the events of the night in her mind. "Because I left to bring aid to someone who was in great danger of dying," she finished softly, feeling the tug of sleep begin to overwhelm her again. The kind man took great interest in this and moved himself closer to the bed to hear her better.

"Tell me, child. Who was this person?" he asked curiously. Tahari did not see what significance there was in the question, but she managed to speak.

"I know not his name." she said softly as the strain of talking added to her weariness. "He was an elfin warrior. The evil was coming for him. It wanted him dead, but I could not let it happen. I would not..." Tahari's voice faded, and her eyes closed. Tahari could no longer fight the darkness.

Tahari felt him lean closer to her and gently pull a blanket over her.

"Sleep...just sleep," she heard him whisper as she faded into unconsciousness.

Chapter 30

Weaving Darkness

As Sala cared for Tahari, Solarous worked in his chambers in the dim candlelight, to bring about his dark lord's rise to power. After gaining a new ally in Prince Alon-Settie, Solarous was ready for the next step in his plan.

The silence of Solarous's chamber was broken only by the yellow liquid boiling in a cauldron and the fire that crackled beneath it. Solarous sat at his old wooden desk writing the memoirs of his dark master's life and the people he came from. The story of Lord Jarden was a striking tale that he had become familiar with after his transformation. Finishing another page of the epic tale, he gently picked it up and looked at it in the chamber's orange glow. He smiled wistfully as he looked upon the freshly inked words on the yellowish page. He took a deep breath and gently laid the sheet aside. Solarous then took up his quill again, intending to continue his work, when he stopped and lifted his gaze from the paper to the dark-brown tapestry with gold etching that hung on the wall behind his writing desk.

"Come in, General," Solarous called out as he heard footsteps cautiously approaching his door. The heavy wooden door creaked as it was opened. Someone dressed in a chain-linked suit of armor cautiously entered. Solarous smiled as he turned in his seat to face his guest. The appearance of the Draccen general was a wondrous and yet strange sight, for no Draccen soldier had ever set foot in Avdima Palace. "You made good time.

"It was no easy feat to make such a journey, but we hope that our efforts have found favor with the dark lord. The main body of the Draccen army waits encamped in the mountains north of Akendron. I have sent a small band to take out the elfin warrior as he makes his way through the Divervandon Forest; a scout will return to give us word when the elf has been taken care of," General Sabin said sounding weary from his long trek. However as he spoke one could feel the battle-seasoned soldier's wisdom and experience. Solarous managed to hide the smile that threatened to come out as he studied General Sabin's features. Even though the dark coloring of the general's armor toned down the brightness of his features, his very appearance still seemed to light up the dim chamber, for the dark green of his scales had turned pale, almost white, with time. The harshness of his marred appearance suggested he had been in many battles and that keeping him waiting was not wise.

"Your efforts have pleased Lord Jarden more than you know," Solarous said as his small dark eyes studied the scar that was all that remained of the general's right eye. "How, may I ask, are the rest of your people doing?"

"Upon the reaching Akendron and setting up camp, we received word by carrier pigeon that ten compounds are being secretly constructed around the whole of Andora. They have much work ahead of them, but with our mass numbers, completion of these compounds should be within days and will be ready before the first prisoners arrive." as the general reported these crucial details, Solarous smiled with great pleasure.

"Most excellent!" Solarous said with barely contained excitement, clasping his large hands together with satisfaction. The portly man's dark button eyes sparkled for a moment, and then he looked at the general for a long moment, his excitement fading away. "Does it seem strange to you that your people are asked to make concentration camps for people who dwell in the same country as you?" Solarous's question did not seem to faze the aged general.

"I am ordered to follow Lord Jarden, for he freed my people from the endless sleep we were cast into thousands of years ago, and if I am ordered to capture a city and burn it to the ground, then I will make sure all my men carry torches. If I am asked to take human prisoners to these camps and keep them restrained, I will post guards on round-the-clock watch. If I need to execute them in front Lord Jarden himself, then I would only ask which weapon he prefer I use. I serve Lord Jarden and will do what I am ordered." General Sabin spoke without expression, his remaining brown eye focused on Solarous. "Now, what is it that you require of me and my men?" the general asked with a cock of his head.

"Except for a few soldiers, you and your men will make your presence nonexistent. No one can know that you are here. I will do my part to make sure that the soldiers do not patrol north of the city. You will wait until the word is given five nights hence, during the Celebration of the Great Dragon; then you will silently start your march into Akendron," Solarous said in a low voice.

"Understood," General Sabin replied.

"As for the few remaining men, they will create some havoc outside of Akendron," Solarous said thoughtfully. General Sabin forced himself to hide the smile creeping onto his stern face.

"What do you have in mind?" the general asked, a hint of excitement in his deep voice.

"Something insulting." Solarous lowered his head in thought for a moment. He thought about the queen and how much she despised him. Then he remembered that she had been born in Endenbury. An idea came to him. "Endenbury. Destroy it. Take its people prisoner; kill all attempting to escape, except for one. I want word to reach Akendron on the eve of the celebration. The king and queen will have no choice but to call out this precious Secret Alliance. This will give you and your men room to work at your leisure." the reptilian general nodded approvingly.

"Consider it done." General Sabin's features were relaxed and unconcerned with the tasks before him. "We will wait for the signal to take Akendron." he bowed his head humbly and turned to take his leave of the dark royal advisor. However, just as General Sabin reached the door to leave the chamber, he stopped and turned his pale head back to Solarous, who could now see the short dark spikes that ran the course of his back.

"Your master will have no problem taking this realm. If he wants to keep it, however, he will have to work a little harder." the remark caught Solarous off-guard and something in General Sabin's large brown eye caused him to be uneasy. "There is a deep magic that lies within this land and those who used to dwell here. Beware of it." General Sabin held Solarous's gaze briefly before turning and leaving the dim chamber. Solarous was left to ponder what the old war general could have meant.

Chapter 31

Darkness Foreseen

Music and celebration filled the air surrounding the grand palace of Akendron. The people who surrounded Avdima's high walls were full of excitement and anticipation. This was the annual Great Dragon Celebration to honor the beloved prophet Rafar the Elder. Here, people could find peace from the problems of the world for a time. There was no concern or thought about evil.

Walking through the immense crowds that had been invited to the palace, Tahari found her way from the front palace gates to the main meeting hall where the royal family was appearing. The gray stone walls were richly decorated with colorful banners and historic artifacts. Colorful streamers hung high overhead. Torches had been placed throughout the grand hall, adding to the night's warm and inviting feel. She saw women dressed in stunning gowns of every color imaginable. Their men were dressed in dark tunics and turbans. Everyone in the crowd could have been mistaken for royalty. Though the atmosphere should have lightened her mood, something bothered her. She sensed great evil intertwined within the festive air. Trumpets sounded within the grand hall causing a hush to fall over the crowds as the royal family made their entrance. Cheers and applause erupted from the crowd as they shifted and moved to get a better view of the royal family. In all the chaos, Tahari glimpsed someone standing in the far corner of the room. Looking upon this eerie individual who was adorned in royal robes, she was immediately repulsed by the darkness about him. His cold expression was strangely out of place. A cold chill ran down her back.

Great evil emanated from him, but Tahari could only watch in silence. He blended in with the shadows, and she could see him moving his lips. Then, all hell broke loose within the meeting hall.

The chill of evil filled the room as six men and six women overtook the bodyguards with supernatural strength and charged toward the royal family. Some people within the crowd panicked, and others fled the hall. The king was the first to be attacked, and as the children tried to protect their father, they too were killed. Taking up a sword, Queen Elanza tried to defend her family, but she met the same fate as her family. When the deed was done, a hush fell over the hall. Solarous smiled as he approached the gruesome scene. Looking at the twelve men and women with great approval, he nodded with satisfaction and then pointed to the door. "Go now. Finish them all!" he commanded. A crazed look appeared on the twelve's faces, and they screamed and howled, whirling around and charging at the remaining crowd.

Chapter 32

Last Sphinx

Three Days before the celebration of the Great Dragon.

"No!" Tahari gasped, sitting straight up in bed. She realized that, like the elfin warrior, the royal family as well as the whole of the Shandel were in grave danger. Feeling overwhelmed, Tahari lowered her head for a moment and prayed for guidance. She would follow whatever course her prayers guided her to, but she feared that a time of evil was upon them. A long moment passed before she could put these thoughts aside and focus.

When Tahari raised her head to look at her surroundings, she was caught off-guard. What was this place that she had been taken to? The beauty of her room was breathtaking. The floor of the bed chamber and the furniture were constructed of the warmest oak that she had ever laid eyes upon. The bedding was white silk, which matched several of the tapestries that hung alongside deep burgundy ones within the chamber. The walls were made of gray stone. The white seemed to glow with the light of the sun shining through a large window, the shutters of which had been opened to let in the fresh air. How had she come to this place?

Lifting the soft bedclothes and climbing out of bed, Tahari found that she had been wounded, but her wounds had been tended to and dressed. She was wearing a white and silver robe and had never been so clean before. The plantation seemed only a vivid dream, not a reality. As she rose to her feet and began to move around the room, Tahari could feel no pain. Looking into a mirror on the wall for the first time in many years, she saw a true reflection of herself. Tahari was amazed. Her tanned face glowed, and her sea-green eyes dazzled brilliantly. Her long, dark-brown hair was cleaned and brushed, hanging freely down her back. Although she was painfully thin, her muscles were toned and strong. A minor bruise on her forehead, along with the rest of her bruises, had all but healed. How strange this ability to heal so quickly was! Tahari had thought that her health and healing on the plantation were just luck, but she was beginning to see that they were part of her power.

By the doorway was a stunning pair of white satin slippers. Tahari slipped them on so that she could check out her new surroundings. She wandered out of her room and down a long, warmly lit corridor. The oak continued down the corridor. Many large pillars rose from the oak floors to the ceiling high above. This was truly a wondrous place! Her wanderings led her down a tall staircase, through a large, beautifully decorated room, and out into daylight and lush hanging gardens. Tahari soaked up the warmth and spirituality that she felt in the very air. Even in the bright afternoon sun, a soft mist surrounded the trees and bushes of this enchanted garden. Maybe she had died and journeyed to heaven in her sleep. After some exploring, Tahari finally came to a mist-covered pool. She walked over to it and gazed into the sea-green water. The mist began to clear away from the pool, and she noticed how clouded the water seemed. Looking deep into the pool, she saw images coming into view. Tahari knelt down, wanting to get a better look. Then she froze. The face that was looking back at her was no longer her own!

The face before her was that of an elf. Tahari studied his features for a moment, and then he spoke to her.

"Be brave, my daughter. There is greatness in your future. Though you might forget what has been said today, remember there is something great that lives within you. Not many will see things as you do, but do not be disheartened. The power that lives within you is beyond imagination, and when that is combined with love, anything is possible. You will save many.

It was truly her father!

His warm, loving voice was at once familiar. Tahari sat for a long time trying to make sense of her life. Between the lies, half-truths, and bits of memory, she could not begin to piece her life together. Feeling her head begin to ache, she looked away from the pool and felt someone standing behind her. Turning around, Tahari saw the kind man who had saved her the night before.

"Forgive me for startling you, Tahari," the man kindly apologized as he slowly approached Tahari. There was genuine concern in the warm expression on his face and even more emanating from his deep-blue eyes. She watched as a soft breeze played with several strands of his shoulder-length hair.

"It is all right," she said, looking up at him curiously. "How is it that you knew my name?" She asked. He slowly took a seat on the other side of the small pool.

"One can see and hear many things within the enchanted waters of the mystic pool," he said, motioning with his bearded chin toward the pool. "It was how I knew that you were in danger three nights ago. I was able to help you escape, and I brought you here, to my palace. You've slept almost constantly for the last two days, waking only enough to take a little water before falling back to sleep again.

"Then may I ask the name of my rescuer?" Tahari asked politely. The man looked up at her in surprise and shook his head as he smiled humbly.

"Forgive me. My name is Sala of Antioch, but you may call me Sala," he said with a humble bow. "There was not much time to offer it the other night, for you needed rest after your ordeal," he continued as he looked at her with concern.

"I am not questioning the miracle that saved me, but what makes me more important than any other worker within the Tomblock?" Tahari asked Sala. A hint of sadness washed over his face.

"If I had no knowledge of what I am to tell you, then I would not have left with just you last night, for no living person deserves the treatment that happens within the Tomblock," Sala answered sadly. "I wish I could have saved more than I did." Tahari was now worried as she watched his expression fall along with his gaze.

"What has happened?" she asked with dread. His eyes were filled with tears as he looked at her.

"When I went to save you, I saw huge bonfires within the plantation's main yard and many slaves gathered around it. I did not know the final outcome until yesterday. Rumor in the streets says that many slaves died that night.

His words were hard to hear, and Tahari sat silent for a long moment staring again into the mystic pool. Her mind was filled with grief and uncertainty. She needed to know if her friends had been spared from these horrific events. "Did anyone survive?" she finally managed to say.

"There are no names yet. The slaves retaliated hard against their taskmasters. It is rumored that several have indeed escaped, however." Sala spoke in a gentle and remorseful voice, giving the best explanation he could.

Tahari looked up with a hopeful expression. In spite of her sadness for those who had died, she was encouraged. It was inspiring to hear that some of the workers took it upon themselves not only to fight back but to escape. "Thank God," she whispered as she lowered her head wearily and closed her eyes to pray for all those from the Tomblock.

"Forgive me," he said after a short moment. Tahari lifted her head and took a deep breath to fight back the tears that were threatening to spill. She studied his pleasant features and realized that he had something of great urgency to say. "Forgive me for not giving you more time to pray for your friends, but there is something that I must tell you. It is vital for all our sakes.

"Very well, then. What is it?" Tahari asked in understanding as she turned her attention to him.

Sala was surprisingly silent, despite his urgency. The kind man before her seemed overwhelmed with perplexities; he fought to find a good starting point for what he had to tell her as he put a hand to his mouth to think. Then he rose to his feet and looked at her, his blue eyes filled with urgency and truth. "Come, there is no better way to tell you than for you to see for yourself," he said as he motioned for her to follow him. Jumping up, Tahari hurried after him as they left the breathtaking gardens. She followed him through an arched doorway that led into his beautiful white palace. He led her through winding corridors and eventually into a huge library. Tahari froze at the door, for she had never before seen such a collection of aged books, manuscripts, and scrolls. Sala calmly entered the library and carefully made his way through the mountainous piles of books and scrolls lying upon the floor. He saw her still standing within the doorway, smiled as he saw her overwhelmed expression, and motioned for her to come in. Walking into the grand library, Tahari carefully made her way over to him. Until now, she had felt like she was in a dream, but as she joined Sala at his large wooden desk and saw the seriousness in his face, another grim reality took hold.

Sala picked up a particularly aged scroll in his hands. "This must be something very important, for I see fear and uncertainty in your face," Tahari said. "Then again, this could be the thing that my life was destined for," she continued, sensing the reason why she was there. "I have always known that I would never die within the Tomblock." When she looked back at him, Sala seemed uneasy about revealing the contents of the scroll. She smiled encouragingly. "Whatever awaits me within that scroll—it holds the promise for a better life than the one I have been living," Tahari said, thinking painfully about all the years that she had had to endure the tortures of the Tomblock.

Sala brightened and put a comforting hand on her shoulder. "There is no doubt in my mind that you are the one chosen for this task." his words gave her courage, and she lowered her gaze to the scroll that he was holding.

"Tell me of this task that you speak of," Tahari said, and she took a deep breath to ready herself for the next part of her life.

Sala slowly sat down upon a wooden stool near his over-piled desk and gazed at the aged scroll in his hands. "Do you know the legend of the Great Dragon?" he asked her with a curious look.

"It is why there is a celebration every one hundred years. To honor the memory of the elf who saved the Shandel and Andora from a great evil that wanted to overtake them," Tahari repeated the answer that had been taught to her. Sala nodded as he looked down at the aged scroll.

"This elf's name was Rafar the Elder. When he was finished with his great task, the god Adalai granted him visions of the far future. He foresaw that the ancient evil would return, but he also saw something that gave him great hope. However, none these hopeful things would have come to pass if no record of them were made. Therefore, Rafar spent his last hours writing down these events in four separate scrolls. They were written in a cryptic language to protect their precious meaning and to shield those it concerned from the great evil that would come to haunt this land again." Sala fell silent then, and Tahari could see the distress in his face. There was much weighing on him, and she felt that weight settle on her, too. "Adalai's ways are truly his own," Sala mused as he put a hand to his forehead. "The language that Rafar chose to write these sacred scrolls in belonged to the ancient race known as the sphinx. This language protected the prophecy, even after it was lost.

"Lost?" Tahari asked with uncertainty, but as he spoke of the sphinx, she was reminded of her dreams.

"One thousand years before the battle between Rafar and the ancient evil known as Lord Jarden, the race of man had become jealous of the sphinxes for the awesome power they possessed. Man wanted this power for himself. The sphinxes refused, for the request was unwise and dangerous. Consumed by their greed, man annihilated the sphinxes for not relinquishing their power. Over the course of two thousand years, their language was gradually forgotten until one day it was gone." as Tahari listened to Sala's story, she realized the truth of her dreams; she was indeed a part of this wondrous race. Tahari's heart hurt to hear this, and she could not help but grieve for her ancestors.

"Will the world ever learn?" Tahari asked angrily. Sala looked at her with worry. She shook her head sadly. "I was told just recently that

I am a sphinx of the ancient world. I just did not know that I was the last," she said, feeling suddenly all alone.

"You still have purpose here, my dear," Sala replied as hope radiated from his blue eyes and kind, tanned face.

"How much difference can one slave girl from a plantation make against a coming storm of evil?" she asked with doubt.

Sala smiled knowingly as he slowly opened the aged scroll. "Not a slave, a sacred messenger. Rafar spoke of a chosen one who would be able to understand the language of the prophecy. Thus, there had to be a sphinx still in existence to accomplish this task," Sala said as he handed her the scroll. Taking the scroll, Tahari knew that he hoped she was the sacred messenger he had been searching for. She looked down and studied the strange language for a long moment. At first, she could not make any sense out of the words. Tahari tried to decipher them, but she could not.

"I am sorry, Sala, but I'm afraid that..." she started to say in a tone of disappointment, preparing to give him back the scroll, but she recognized something about the text that caused her to study it again. Tahari could not explain it, but the strange words seemed to jog her memory. Suddenly, a memory flashed in her mind. Tahari remembered a life that seemed to be a dream in comparison to the life she had upon the Tomblock. Tahari saw her mother and the people who kindly watched over her. She remembered the love, laughter, and joy they brought into her life. She remembered their compassion. In this former life, the loving people in her world not only taught her the sphinx language, they also taught her the common language of Andora. Focusing on the present now and the scroll before her, Tahari watched in amazement as the words' meanings seemed to reveal themselves before her eyes. "I can understand it," she finished in simple disbelief.

"You can understand what it says?" Sala asked in growing anticipation. Tahari nodded in response as she continued to examine the old script before her. As Tahari did, she did not see Sala's face fill with excitement.

"Yes," Tahari affirmed simply as she continued to study the scroll and read from it. Sala let out a yell and jumped from his seat. Looking up, Tahari could only watch as the kindly aged man danced merrily around the cluttered library. A dumbfounded smile came to her face as she watched Sala rejoice in this unexpected discovery. Then he ran up to her and caught her up in the largest hug that she had ever been in. When Sala finally looked down at Tahari's lost expression, he laughed.

"You will have to excuse me," he apologized as he let her go and fought to contain his giddiness. "I have been searching so long for a sphinx of the ancient world, and when I thought the race of man might have succeeded in their nightmarish quest, I started to despair," he said. He took a deep breath and slowly sat back down on his stool. "You, my dear, are the sacred messenger chosen to carry this quest." Sala's words completely caught her off-guard.

"How will I be able to accomplish this when I have been locked away within a plantation for eighteen years? I know little to nothing of the outside world," Tahari said, feeling self-conscious. Sala looked at her with a warm and understanding expression.

"Tahari, listen to me," Sala said in a comforting tone, putting his hands on her shoulders. "Your people were a powerful and wondrous race. More than that, they were the guardians of the earth. It is said that those who have passed into legend still whisper and give guidance to their descendants. Quiet your mind and listen. They will guide you." his words stirred Tahari and caused her to remember her dreams and understand that they were memories from her past life yearning to be remembered. Hearing this brought clarity to her confusion, but it too was overwhelming.

"If I am a sphinx of the ancient world, then why was I trapped within a place like the Tomblock?" Tahari asked with confusion. He thought for a long moment before speaking.

"No doubt you were placed there to acquire strength for what is to come. You said it yourself: the life that awaits you now holds more promise than the life that you knew, but it is going to take someone of immense strength to live it." As Sala spoke, she began to understand how her mixed-up life was beginning to fit together.

"Can you tell me more about the ways of the sphinx of the ancient world?" Tahari asked with renewed spirits. He smiled kindly at her change in attitude.

"I know of their history and the miraculous things they did while here, for it was said that they were creatures made by Adalai himself, but beyond this, I have no knowledge of their rituals or culture." He shook his head in sadness, but there was still hope in his eyes. "Maybe when you embark on this journey, you will discover these things for yourself." Tahari smiled, feeling encouraged as she slowly nodded in understanding.

"Speaking of journeys…" Tahari said as she held up the scroll and began to translate the ancient language of the sphinx. Sala sat back and listened in anticipation.

Chapter 33

The First Scroll

I. The Secret Alliance will go forth in battle. *Do not look for lost men;
search out your friends.
II. A long-awaited night of celebration turns foul. *Rise up to stop this
assassination.
III. A betrayal and a tomb await a prince. *Do not leave him in towers
high, but bring him home.
IV. The key to finding Farro will lie within a tomb. *Be of courage to
make a sacrifice.
V. A dark dragon will deliver unpleasant tidings. *DO NOT bring
down his murderers.
VI. Flame and spear will fall upon the kingdom of the elf. *Escape will
depend on all.
*Look for a stone within a tomb that is marked with the crest. This is
where you will find the second instructions.

After Tahari finished reading from the first scroll of the prophecy and its instructions, she slowly laid it on Sala's desk. She felt overwhelmed with worry and concern. When she looked up, Sala, who was quickly writing down the translation, showed worry and great stress in his face.

He finally laid aside his quill and looked at her. "Maybe there is still time before this all starts to try to decipher what it is trying to tell us," Sala finally said as he climbed to his feet and began to pace the room. Tahari looked back at the scroll and read the instructions that it gave. After studying the lines of the prophecy and its instructions as well as the letter that Rafar wrote to his order, she realized something.

"Rafar was brilliant!" Tahari exclaimed. "The lines of prophecy are like points on a map. We are to look for the event that is described—for it is a clue to finding Farro. The lines of instruction that are given after each line of prophecy show the course that we are to take to lead our world away from Lord Jarden's plan of destruction," she outburst with excitement.

"This is good," Sala said distractedly, starting to comprehend what Tahari had said, but he still looked puzzled. "So we are to let these things come to pass?" he said with deep concern. Tahari understood of what he spoke.

"True, it speaks of many unsettling and tragic things coming to pass, but war is coming to Andora regardless. Once Lord Jarden is free again, he will scorch this land if he is not stopped. If ruin is to fall upon this land, then let it happen with the knowledge that we have found Farro, and that he has vanquished this evil once and for all, and that this land is still ours," Tahari explained with courage. Sala sat silent for a moment but soon began to nod his head with acceptance and understanding.

"Forgive me, for I have never looked upon the face of warfare or the horror of great battles. I was trained to prevent such atrocities from happening." Sala sat back and gave serious thought to her words. "However, you are right. Lord Jarden's defeat means we keep our land and our home." Slowly lifting his gaze to hers, a look of promise filled the features of his face. "Where are we to look for the second scroll of the prophecy?" he asked, glancing over his translation. "It says we are to look for a crest upon a stone within a tomb. This is a most cryptic text to be sure. There are hundreds, if not thousands, of tombs within the Shandel alone.

"I do not think we should concern ourselves with this matter just yet. All these clues will follow a delicate timeline. We dare not perform any one task out of the order that is given. I believe that the event needed to find the second scroll will come to pass, and then we will be able to find the tomb that Rafar speaks of," Tahari explained. A twinge of pain washed over her as she looked at the scroll in her hands.

"Tahari?" Sala asked with concern as he watched her face fall.

"This will be a quest of great hardship for everyone, but if we stay this course, and stay strong in our faith, I do believe victory will be ours," she said as she continued to examine the scroll. Tahari could almost feel the entirety of the journey ahead of them, and she had to take a moment to collect her thoughts and emotions.

"You are a motivating speaker," he said with a sly smile. Feeling inspired by this, she gazed around at the disarrayed library.

"Now for the truly impossible: cleaning up your library." Tahari looked at Sala with a serious smile. He looked at her and began to chuckle. Somewhere, Tahari found the ambition to start putting order to his chaos.

"I do not think even Rafar had the foresight to take on *this* quest." he shook his head. As he was about to lend a hand to help her, they heard a loud knock echo from the main door of the palace. Sala smiled at Tahari knowingly and held up his hand to excuse himself for a moment. She nodded with understanding and went back to her quest. Her ambition grew with every moment that he was gone, for she could not wait to see his surprised expression when he returned.

Chapter 34

Uprisings and Disappearances

S ala left the library and made his way down the long staircase and to the front door. He did not have any concern about who it could be, for there were only a few who had permission to enter through the sacred gates that led to Cypress Palace. Opening the door, he was greeted by Queen Elanza. Her presence was unexpected, and her expression said that something truly awful had transpired.

"My queen, this is a surprise," he said slowly, studying the concerned expression on her face. Her dark-blue cloak covered her royal gown and the large draping hood almost concealed her face. "I sense the news that you bring is not pleasant.

"Dearest Sala, how I hate to bring such dreadful news, but I felt that you should be aware of the happenings within the kingdom—especially those incidents taking place within Akendron," Queen Elanza said in a voice riddled with grief. It was clear by her weary expression that she had found very few hours of sleep the night before. Sala heard the seriousness in her voice and could not help but think the worst.

"What is this dreadful thing that has happened?" he asked with a tone of worry as he led her into the grand hall.

"It is so horrible. I, myself, cannot begin to understand how such things ever came to be. Three nights ago, there was a great uprising at the plantation just south of here. There is talk that many slaves were trying to escape when their taskmasters tried to stop them. The slaves retaliated and began to kill the taskmasters. Master Dancar is said to have been suddenly overtaken and given a most horrible death. I will not even speak of the things that were done to him," she said as shaking her head sadly.

"Those that are left are now trying to pick up the pieces and continue on with everyday life as much as possible. Master Dancar's son Abalan has stepped up to carry on in his father's stead. He and some of the taskmasters have spread the word and made sure everyone within the city and surrounding villages knows about the escaped slaves. If anyone sees or hears of the escapees, they are to report to the plantation taskmasters right away. It is said that these slaves who escaped are the ruthless instigators of the uprising." she handed him a list of the escapees.

Hearing these outlandish lies from the queen's mouth was hard for Sala. Grief filled his features. Looking down at the list, Sala read over some of the names of the slaves who had been caught or killed and then read the names of those who had escaped. Sala felt his throat go dry. Tahari's name was on the list of escapees.

When he looked back up at the queen, Sala found himself trapped between right and wrong, truth and lie. He loved and honored the queen and would give his life to save hers, but he could not make himself turn Tahari in. Sala felt everything in his very being scream at him not to reveal the sacred messenger.

"How unexpected to hear of such dreadful things," he managed to utter in a weakened tone, shaking his head disappointedly. "It could not have come at a more unfortunate time for us," he said, referring to the ancient prophecy and the mission they were both on.

Queen Elanza eyed him with an understanding gaze and nodded slowly as there were other troubling matters haunting her mind. "Have you made any progress in finding the special one who can translate the strange language?" she asked with a genuine concern, but Sala once again found himself caught in between loyalties and truths. While he pondered what to say, he glanced down at the list in his hands. He could only imagine what would happen to Tahari if she were discovered by anyone within Akendron or even within the Shandel. It would easily mean her death.

"I am working diligently on our current situation," Sala said, choosing his words very carefully. "I have faith that a messenger will come forth to help us with the translation of the sacred scrolls. Still, I sense that when they are found, they will need protection, for the agents of darkness will be searching for them."

As he spoke these words, a pained expression washed over Elanza's white face, causing the advisor to worry anew. "Forgive me, did I say something wrong?" he asked. The queen shook her head; her white veil bounced slightly as it caught in the gentle breeze. He saw great sadness in the delicate features of her face.

"No, it is only that you are quite right as usual." she sighed deeply. "There are rumors surfacing around the palace that people within the Shandel have disappeared. Not so much as a trace of them is left. It is as if they have just vanished. This is happening all over Andora, too. Farmers, travelers, hunters, traveling merchants, even whole villages have been reported missing." Elanza's strange news drove chills down Sala's spine.

"This is not good. Keep this news secret," Sala said as he felt great warning in what she spoke. "There is no need to cause a panic, but be mindful of those around you," Sala advised in a whisper, nervously scanning the forested area through the palace windows. "I will hasten my search, for we must expedite our plans to find Farro," he offered with determination and a nod of certainty.

"Very well, and Godspeed," Queen Elanza encouraged her advisor and once again nodded. "I know that you will succeed in your search. It will be only a matter of time now. Do not stop searching, Sala. They are out there somewhere," she replied with a hopeful expression as she put a comforting hand on his shoulder. Then, managing a kind smile, she took her leave of Sala.

"Good day to you, my queen, and thank you," Sala said warmly as he bowed humbly to acknowledge her departure. When he stood up again and saw that she had disappeared into the mists that surrounded and guarded Cypress Palace, he took a deep breath of air. The news of the vanishing people bothered Sala greatly. It said that time was indeed running out, but the only thing that could be done for those missing now was to help Tahari find the other three scrolls. Looking again at the notice in his hands, his heart sank, for he knew that this would not be easy for Tahari to see. Closing the palace door, Sala slowly made his way back to the grand library.

Upon reaching the doorway of the library, he could see that Tahari had accomplished the impossible. He stood for a moment to marvel at the clean and orderly library that was now before him. He was relieved to see her in his presence, but troubled as well.

Chapter 35

Pain Renewed

As Sala walked into the library, Tahari noticed the grim expression clearly written on his face. She also noticed a piece of paper in his hands. The news that he had received from his visitor was not good, then.

"Sala, what is the matter?" she asked. He looked at her with his blue eyes full of worry. She slowly put aside the crate of papers and journals and patiently waited for Sala to speak.

"There is much turmoil in the land after the other night's events," he said in a low and even voice. "I never saw this coming, but I am afraid that you are in danger even as we speak." guilt washed over his face.

"What further danger is the plantation to me? They must believe that I am dead by now. Do they not?" Tahari asked as she looked at Sala with a sudden pang of uncertainty.

Sala slowly shook his head sadly. "I believe they look for you still," he said grimly, handing her the paper. "This has just come from the palace. The other night's events were tragic enough, but I believe that the taskmasters within the Tomblock are stating that the slaves premeditated the uprising. The slaves' uprising resulted in several taskmasters getting killed as well as Master Dancar." Tahari's jaw dropped open in shock and horror.

"Master Dancar? Killed?" She looked over at the paper and could not help but feel that she was being targeted. "Sala, please tell me that you believe me," Tahari said, feeling exposed and guilty as she searched his blue eyes for his trust.

"Yes," he said with assurance. There was great strength in his face as he gazed at Tahari. "I was there that night and witnessed these happenings. What they are saying now is false. The slaves revolted only after they realized that they were going to be annihilated." his words greatly comforted her. Then Tahari gently took the list from his hands and read it over. Her eyes scanned over the writing until she ran across her name. "Is there someone else other than Master Dancar who held a grudge against you?" Sala wondered as he looked at Tahari with concern.

"Lady Dancar and their daughter. They have held nothing but distain for me." Tahari thought back to the many occasions where she had to endure their presence. "One death was not enough for them," Tahari reasoned with a bitter whisper.

"Tahari, is there anything that I can do? I will go to the Tomblock and speak with them myself," Sala offered as his face filled with sympathy and concern for her. Tahari looked upon the list and then back at Sala as she shook her head.

Tahari knew that he would try to figure out something to try to help her, but she merely shook her head. "Lady Dancar and her daughter are the sour core that made the Tomblock into what it is today. It will just be best if I lie low for a while, maybe in time, I will see the disbanding of the wretched plantation," Tahari said, looking down at the list again. Her eye caught something it had missed before. Sala looked on with concern.

"Tahari? What is wrong?" he asked, stepping closer to her. She felt her whole world cave in on itself.

"It is worse than I thought," Tahari said as she felt the sting of tears in her eyes. "If it was just me they wanted dead, so be it, but this…" Her voice faded from her throat. Tahari slouched in agony as if someone had rammed a sword through her heart. Sala slowly took the list from her loosened grip and tried to guess what had upset her so.

"I had several dear friends in the Tomblock," Tahari managed to whisper, trying to keep her grief at bay. "But from what this list says, none of them lived to see the morning. They're gone. They were among those executed." her voice now completely failed her as she felt her throat become tight and painful. "Please excuse me," Tahari said in a raspy whisper. Lowering her head sadly, she quietly walked out of the huge library and down the long corridor.

Tahari somehow found her way through the palace corridors to the beautiful hanging gardens again. The afternoon's warm light created a heavenly glow upon this wondrous sanctuary of green trees, colorful flowers, and flowing fountains of sparkling water. Tears blinded her and kept her from running over the stone footpaths. As Tahari finally stumbled against a tree on a nearby hill, she felt her strength fail her completely. Collapsing against the large oak tree, she could no longer stop the hot tears from streaming down her face. Tahari wept bitterly for her friends.

All throughout her time within the Tomblock, the Dancars had always tried to hurt her every chance they got. When they realized they could not do it physically, they turned to those closest to her. Tahari watched time and time again as her dear friends were badly hurt or killed. In the end, the outcome always entailed her praying for those friends of hers that had passed into the realm of the dead. Once, she thought about refusing to care for any other living being. Maybe more lives would be spared from the Dancars' wrath, but this decision was against her nature. Tahari could not deny kindness, compassion, and friendship to others.

"Let those lost to us be safe in the realm of the dead," Tahari prayed aloud. "Whatever comes my way, I pray that you will guide me through it. I know that I do not have the strength to do this alone. However, if it is right that I should receive the blessings of having another friend in my life, then help me to watch over them. The very gift of having a friend is a responsibility that I am fully aware of and will give anything for. After these tragic events, it could not have been made any clearer." She felt a gentle breeze touch her hot, tear-streaked face, and she rested her weary head against the rough bark of the tree. As the breeze blew through her hair and pushed it over her face, she was lulled to sleep. Closing her eyes, Tahari saw vivid images of Almari, Senti, and Rami flash through her memory. They had been the dearest friends that she could have ever had in her life. Now, they too, were gone. Tahari hoped that when she woke again, they would still be alive and all of this would be only a nightmare. As she slipped off into sleep, Tahari remembered all the times that she had helped her very dear friends in some way. How she longed to do that again and see the warm glow of happiness that filled their faces when they received her help! It made her days truly complete. Yet a strange feeling came to her, almost as if someone was speaking to her. *Your empathy and compassion for your friends will be the key to saving those around you.*

Chapter 36

Elijah

*Hours before the uprising
within the Tomblock.*

Arriving in Akendron just hours after his escape from the Draccen in the Divervandon Forest, Prince Leondros Goldendragon was thankful to see the grand city. It was not home, but he was counting his blessings that he was alive to see it again. As he rode into the city, Leondros found the shops, homes, and streets brightly decorated with banners and flags that flapped lazily in the afternoon breeze. Although it was late in the day, the city's marketplace was still bustling with excitement. People were busy preparing for the upcoming Celebration of the Great Dragon. He could not help but feel immense pride and honor when he saw this. It was not every day that an elf was so highly recognized and honored in human society. The people in the marketplace noticed him making his way toward Avdima Palace. Expressions of reverence and kindness came to people's faces, and they stopped their work in admiration and to clear an easier path for him. Leondros acknowledged the people kindly as he continued on his way. He had not been in Akendron for some time, and he wondered whether anyone would recognize him.

Whether they did or not, these people were glad to see an elf in their grand city again.

When Leondros finally made it past the palace's high stone gates, he took in Avdima's grandeur. He had seen it many times and knew it was a wondrous palace, but to look upon it once again made it seem so much more wondrous. It was one of the grandest palaces in all of Andora and was equal to his family's palace. The entirety of Avdima Palace—from the hidden underground tunnels to the high light-brown sandstone walls that made up the palace's furthermost exterior to its many exquisite temples and chambers located within the main building or found along beautiful cobblestone footpaths that ran through a maze of enchanting hanging gardens—covered over five square miles. The enormous white granite palace itself was nestled among hundreds of lush trees and hanging gardens. Leondros felt that he might have been wrong and that perhaps he was home after all.

It was not long before two servants of the royal court dressed in royal blue and red tunics noticed Leondros slowly walking beside his faithful white stallion up the wide cobblestone path that led into the palace's main courtyard. These servants had been ordered to welcome and tend to the needs of all officials arriving for the summit meeting. They were quick to greet him cordially as they kindly reached to take Aton's brown leather reins. The large white stallion jerked his head back with a grunt as he seemed a little edgy. Sensing his partner's uncertainty about the two servants before them, Leondros turned to his four-legged friend and gently stroked his silky head and looked into the horse's dark-brown eyes.

"I hear you: there is something about this place that feels wrong. But I trust you to be resourceful," Leondros whispered with a sly smile. Aton's white and gray ears relaxed as he exhaled with a huff. Leondros's eyes caught his companion's strange humor. "Just be nice…" Aton eyed the two servants closely and snickered as Leondros slowly gave the reins to one of the servants. The elfin prince watched as Aton let himself be led away to the royal stables.

Leondros relaxed for the moment and enjoyed the peaceful gardens that surrounded him. The path Aton had disappeared down was dim from evening's growing shadows, and the humidity hung in the air like a faint mist. The soft insect buzzing helped Leondros take his mind off his near-death experience in the forest. Finally making his way toward the palace itself, the elfin prince noticed a young messenger boy with short, curly blond hair approaching him from the main doors. The boy quickly and quietly made his way to Leondros. The young messenger clearly took his duties seriously, conducting himself with etiquette and restraint. His light-blue robe and black sash and his leather shoes were worn and faded but were otherwise in pristine condition.

"It is a great honor to have you here with us again, Prince Leondros," the boy said with a humble bow. The boy's eyes showed his tiredness, but his concern was not for himself or his needs but for Leondros.

"I do apologize for my lateness. I met some resistance on my way here," Leondros kindly apologized, glancing over his silver armor, which bore some of the story of his near escape.

A warm expression filled the boy's young face. His green eyes showed his concern. "You have made it safely; that is all that should matter. The king will be greatly delighted to hear that you have arrived," he said as he motioned for Leondros to follow him toward the palace. He led Leondros through Avdima's towering main doors and into the large spice-scented hall of wood and stone. "We are blessed to have you here with us tonight. This is our greatest hour of need," the boy said in a low voice. It was clear that he did not want to cause alarm to spread. "It is said that a strange darkness is returning to take Andora by force, and there is a rumor of people being taken from all over the kingdom. I have heard only a little of the story as the scholars and elders do not speak of what keeps them from sleep at night. I can sense that this will be more terrible than many can possibly know. However, I sense that there still is a light in our future. I have never seen a night that had no day.

Leondros listened intently to the boy as they walked along the long torch-lit stone hallway toward the chamber where the king, advisors, scholars, and elders were meeting. The soft clank of his armor followed after the boy's quick steps. The boy seemed to greatly fear this strange darkness but continued to hope with fervor.

"You have a courageous heart. That is admirable. Tell me your name," Leondros said with interest as he looked at the humble messenger. The golden-haired boy stopped in his tracks, looking up at the elfin prince, dumbfounded.

"I-I am Elijah," he answered with surprise. This servant boy knew that it was acceptable etiquette for noblemen, dignitaries, royals, and other high officials who dwelt in this land never to associate with commoners, servants, or slaves. The boy had long since accepted this behavior as the normal routine that accompanied his station.

"Elijah, I am pleased to meet you," Leondros said with a bow of his head. "Do not lose that courageous heart, for it will strengthen you for the things that are to come." Leondros's kind voice caused the boy's rigid posture to relax. Elijah's face brightened with a hopeful smile, and his green eyes lit up.

Elijah led him to a large limestone corridor and eventually to a pair of oversized brown wooden doors that led into the grand meeting chamber. "The high council is already in session on this subject. You are invited to join them," he said encouragingly as he slowly opened the polished wooden door to the meeting chamber and peered into the room. Gesturing for Leondros to wait outside for a moment, Elijah quietly slipped into the chamber. Leondros listened closely as the royal messenger announced his arrival.

"My king, Prince Leondros Goldendragon from the kingdom of Adarah has arrived at last." Elijah's voice echoed throughout the chamber as he spoke. The chatter of voices fell silent.

"Excellent. Please do not keep the poor elf waiting. Kindly let him in." the sound of King Alabaster's loud voice could not to be mistaken. Elijah slipped back out of the meeting chamber, turned to Leondros, and smiled.

"You may go in now, Prince Leondros," Elijah said in a soft tone and bowed. Leondros took joy to see renewed life in the servant's soulful green eyes.

"I thank you," Leondros said in a whisper as he entered the grand meeting room. The boy gently closed the large wooden doors behind the elfin prince. When he finally pulled shut the large heavy wooden doors, Elijah was still dazed by what seemed to be a simple, almost meaningless gesture. Still, it was the first time today that someone had actually talked to him as if he were a real person. In that briefest of moments, a special bond of friendship was formed. Little did Leondros realize just how big an effect his seemingly trivial kindness would have on the servant boy.

Chapter 37

High Council

Walking into the brightly lit grand meeting chamber, Leondros looked out upon a round room of white. The many torches that burned in sconces drove the shadows from the chamber. Sixteen large white pillars encircled the large chamber like giant sentinels watching over the chamber's eight terraced levels, where wooden chairs with deep-purple velvet cushions were strategically placed. Each level that descended toward the main floor was made of dark granite. Some two hundred noblemen were scattered throughout the levels, and all had turned to look upon the newcomer. Many were gray-haired men dressed in brown or black robes. Their aged faces said that they really didn't know what was going on outside of the city's walls. As their cold eyes studied Leondros, the elf could tell that they were more concerned with what he was rather than the help he could offer, for they looked upon him uncertainly. The silence was now intermittent as some of the men began whispering to each other. This lasted but a moment before the whispers were drowned out by a familiar voice. Out of the crowd of strangers came the most welcome face of Prince Alon-Settie.

"Prince Leondros! It is an honor to have you here among us," Alon-Settie said in a grateful tone as he stood up from a chair on the second terrace and motioned for Leondros to join him. Leondros silently descended the terraces as the nobles eyed him cautiously. When the elfin prince finally reached Alon-Settie, they exchanged hugs. Leondros quickly took in his long-time friend's features. The Akendron prince was dressed in a red and black robe that showed his athletic form. The robe was accented by a thin gold crown upon his dark hair. An expression of great relief showed on Alon-Settie's bearded face as he looked upon his dear friend again. Among all those who sat in council, Alon-Settie was the only one who was truly aware of the great warrior that stood in their midst.

"My friend has asked for my help, and now I am here," Leondros announced as he bowed his head humbly before his dear friend and the high council. He, too, was relieved to see his dear friend's face again. It had been ten and five years since their last meeting, and now before him was a man where a boy once stood. Prince Alon-Settie looked upon his friend with a warm smile, and then his dark eyes shifted around the eight rings of cold, noble faces.

"Noblemen of the high council, many of you have never heard of the legendary elfin warrior from the distant realm of Adarah. In spite of the uncertainty we are facing, Prince Leondros has come to help us in our time of need," Prince Alon-Settie said to remind the high council that all help offered should gladly be accepted. "If it would be your will, Your Highness?" he asked humbly, turning to King Alabaster, who was sitting with several other nobles on the lowest level of the chamber. His attire matched Alon-Settie's except for the gold trim of his robe. Alabaster almost mirrored Alon-Settie, but along with the regal features that shone in his aged face, there was a certain essence of wisdom that made him stand out. In the room's bright light, the gems upon the king's gold crown sparkled with every slight movement the king made. All heads turned to the king and waited for his answer. They waited in silence and anticipation, for during the course of this one meeting, they would decide whether they truly needed the Secret Alliance and, if so, approve the warriors who would make it up. King Alabaster sat with his hands resting on the arms of his chair, which was slightly elevated and adorned with a tall back. The wise king gazed thoughtfully at Prince Leondros and then looked back at all the nobles awaiting his next word.

"This is a very crucial time for all of us," King Alabaster began as his voice rose from the lowest level of the terrace. "As we have been discussing here tonight, do the strange occurrences, abductions, and stolen property around the Shandel warrant the forming of a secret force of men to deal with these areas of concern?" At this question, Leondros noticed many heads shaking their answer.

"I make an objection, my Lord!" A wiry older man stood up in the fourth terrace, looking harshly upon the princes. "This is hardly the time for rash actions!" His voice was raspy and even, and he gestured wildly as he spoke. "Our fragile kingdom has just emerged from fifty years of drought, famine, and plague. Resources are thin. Are we to take what we have been blessed with and throw it to the four winds?"

"My fellow councilman makes an excellent point," said a man far to the left of the wiry councilman as he stood. "Are we to waste valuable resources on mere hunches? These strange occurrences should not be ignored, but let us use what resources we already have." the short, gray-haired man calmly looked around. His features were well-proportioned, and he seemed to speak with a charismatic charm that eased the fears growing within the room.

"Do you expect injustice to wait until our own soldiers receive the authorization to look into it?" asked another gray-wigged man loudly from the other side of the room, rising quickly. The man's dark eyes almost burned into the souls of the other men. "Just this past week, an old couple in the mountains that overlooked Akendron were slain upon their own land, right in front of their home! Do you know when this occurrence was discovered and finally reported to the soldiers of Avdima?" the enraged man pressed.

"I do not receive such—" the second councilman tried to answer before he was interrupted.

"It never did!" the third councilman snapped angrily. "This atrocity would have gone unnoticed, and no honor would have come to them in death. There was no paperwork, no messenger. There was nothing!" The cold truth of this startling news gripped the room.

"If no one knew, how did you?" the second councilman scoffed. The third councilman did not back down or shy away from the confrontation as his dark eyes continued to glare across the room.

"They were my parents! I regularly go up the mountain to check on them and the farmstead they managed, but no longer!" The air within the meeting chamber had become heated and uncomfortable.

"That is quite enough!" King Alabaster said loudly as he stood. There was a hint of anger in his voice, and his dark gaze looked back and forth between the three men, who were all still standing and angered by the strange occurrences that were happening within the kingdom and the decisions that still needed to be made. His stern gaze caused the men to be mindful of each other and return to their seats. "You all have stated excellent points. I am glad that these opinions have been addressed, but we are hard-pressed for a solution. It is clear that something strange is going on in this kingdom. I notice it more and more every day. The reason to form a specialized group of men is to ensure the safety of not only the people of the Shandel but of all kingdoms of the Tribunal. It was only due to the Queen's intuitions about this matter that such actions have been taken." The king's last words struck an unsettling nerve with some of the men gathered around the meeting chamber.

"Surely you jest, Your Majesty!" a man spoke up haughtily as he rose to his feet. "The motivation driving the idea to form this grand alliance of men from all three kingdoms comes from some idle woman's thinking?" The tall, broad-shouldered man's smug expression suggested that he would like to dismiss the subject altogether. His pale gray eyes seemed to laugh at what he had just heard. "Are we to jump every time our women have a hunch or an idea?"

"You will remember to hold your tongue before talking about the Queen in such a dishonorable manner!" King Alabaster shouted, turning to the tall councilman.

"Our King is right; such remarks have no place in this chamber." A fifth councilman stood to face the fourth man. "It is a valuable thing for people to have the foresight to warn us of grave and impending dangers, no matter the color, race, or even gender.

"Intuition, idle thoughts, some random happenings within the kingdom and we all go crazy!" the first councilman rose to his full height, and though he was a frail man, he stood firm on the granite floor beneath his feet. "We have no *real* proof that there is any danger coming our way! Do not let fear or some stray fantasy be the pebble that tears down the mighty walls of this kingdom. It is time for this council to get a hold of itself!" he shouted, gesturing angrily.

As Leondros listened to the councilmen and their king, he struggled to mind his own anger. The last words returned him to the adrenaline-filled moments he spent in the Divervandon Forest fighting for his life due to a very real threat.

"Blind men of the world!" Leondros shouted angrily as he stepped out from his place next to Alon-Settie. The men of the council were quickly silenced, either from astonishment that this newcomer was daring enough to speak to them or out of curiosity as to whether he actually had proof of some threat to the kingdom. "Maybe you have grown too comfortable with peace, for war is knocking at your very door! Believe me when I tell you that there are more than just some strange occurrences going on in your kingdom. Coming here was by no means easy for me. An army of Draccen soldiers attacked me in the Divervandon Forest. I tell you now that the evil has been awakened!" Leondros's words caused a great stir within the council chamber.

"You lie! The Draccen people have been imprisoned for over three thousand years! We are in no danger from their kind. Where is your proof?" the first speaker shot back defensively, pointing a bony finger at the elfin prince with his last words. His cold, light-brown eyes bore down on Leondros. "All we have is your words. What trust can we put in them?" the aged man sneered at Leondros. Leondros was about to reply to the accusation when Alon-Settie put a comforting hand on his shoulder to try to cool his friend's anger.

Alon-Settie tried to smooth the ruffled feathers of the council members as he could see various heated glances raining down upon them. "My lord councilman, please understand that my elfin companion has ridden a very long way on this night, and—" his words were cut short as Leondros, who could no longer stomach the insolence of the old men of the council, decided not to remain quiet. Reaching into the leather quiver that still rested over his shoulder, the elfin prince pulled out a brown menacing-looking arrow; quickly taking out his bow, he fitted the strange-looking arrow and shot it past the first speaker. The arrow's wisp cut the sudden silence of the room like a knife. The impact of the arrow lodging into the first councilman's chair echoed throughout the large meeting chamber.

"THERE IS YOUR PROOF!" Leondros yelled angrily as the features of his face hardened. "The Draccen people are awake, and they have been turned loose upon the Shandel—or would you prefer that one of them stand where I am and take the same shot as proof? I assure you, they would not have aimed for your comfortable chair!" Gasps of shock and horror echoed throughout the chamber as the realization was made by all attending the meeting that war was coming.

"It cannot be…" the first man managed to utter, shocked by the arrow that had just whizzed past him. "We… we are in a grand time of peace and prosperity. War cannot come here!" The old man shook his head, desperate to deny the evidence that was lodged in the back of his chair.

"Your peace ended when the Draccen people rode into this country, free to do was they wished!" Leondros revealed the cold reality of the Shandel's situation before all two hundred council members as well as King Alabaster and Alon-Settie.

"It is no matter!" the councilman responded, waving his hand through the air to once again dismiss Leondros's testimony. He pulled the arrow from the chair and tossed it on the stone floor at his feet. "Their forces, no matter how many, cannot breach the mighty walls guarding Akendron. Beyond that, the people of the city could still seek refuge within the walls of Avdima. We are safe here." The aged man spoke with resounding reassurance, smiling and gesturing at the architecture of the meeting chamber. As Leondros listened to the foolish man's words, his anger was replaced by horror. He looked directly at King Alabaster. Leondros shook his head with immense grief and then looked at the floor.

"I pity you, and all of those who dwell within your house."

Leondros said as he lifted his heavy gaze to the white-wigged man. The councilman seemed unsettled by Leondros's grave tone, and he looked back at the elfin warrior. "You would never know death, even long after it passed over your doorstep." Leondros's words struck the councilmen of the chamber with a cold sense of reality. He turned back to the king. "Ask it of me now, and I will stay and do what I can to defend you and yours, or I will respectfully take my leave. This threat will not stop, and there are other kingdoms in dire need of word of these happenings." Leondros's words were sad and heavy as his soulful gaze stayed on the king. Although the minds of the councilmen were unsure whether to believe this elf's testimony, King Alabaster was more than convinced. A look of realization had long since filled his features.

"Anyone who has the words to humble a nation is guaranteed a place at my side," King Alabaster said with warmth as he slowly lifted his strong form from the throne he had been resting upon. "No man of this kingdom would have gone half as far to deliver such tidings. We—I—am in your debt." King Alabaster paused, reflecting on the great trial the elfin prince must have gone through just to make it to Akendron. Leondros humbly bowed his head in gratitude to the king. "I know you, Leondros Goldendragon; your experience in battle and knowledge of this country are paramount. One would have to be a fool not to ask for your aid in what is before us. The Queen and I have already decided that you would be a prime candidate to be General of the Secret Alliance, but this time of adversity has humbled me, so I ask for your help, Prince Leondros Goldendragon." As the king spoke, the councilmen sat in silence and disbelief at the king's humility.

"I would be honored, and I promise to protect this grand city and her people until my last breath." the prince's words warmed the hearts of the surrounding spectators, who were awed by the elfin prince's promotion. King Alabaster smiled as he looked upon the brave elf before him. One of the councilmen rose from his chair and began to clap. As everyone turned to him, they saw a look of admiration and reverence upon the elderly man's face. One by one, more members of the grand council stood and clapped. Soon only the first speaker remained seated, dumbfounded. Yet, he too, was moved to show his appreciation for Leondros's courage. Only one soul did not rejoice, standing without movement. In the shadows of this glorious celebration, Alon-Settie's facial expression was stoic and fixed, for he was moved not by gladness for his friend but by jealousy.

Chapter 38

Chilling Realization

After Prince Leondros was declared the General of the Secret Alliance, a place was made for him to sit with the members of the high council. King Alabaster knew that his wisdom was desperately needed. When Leondros spoke of the Draccen people being awakened, it had shed light upon the mysterious disappearances throughout the kingdom, but it had also raised more issues than it solved. Most of the pressing issues of the safety of the kingdom would be solved with the formation of the Secret Alliance. The rest of the pressing issues were less easily solved. The meeting lasted into the night and well into the next day, and the servants saw to the council members' needs for food and drink. When the meeting finally adjourned, all of the members were weary from the lack of sleep. Palace chambers were set aside for the council members who had traveled a great distance to attend the meeting in Akendron. Thus, Leondros slept fitfully that night, awakening uneasy and tense, for his new responsibility hung over his head. He spent the next day trying to make plans for the new alliance, but something in the air continued to unsettle him. On the second night of his stay, he slept fitfully in spite of all the responsibilities that rested upon him. Upon rising the next morning, he decided to walk around the palace to clear his head.

Walking aimlessly down corridors, he finally came to a stop at a window that overlooked the palace grounds. Gazing out, Leondros saw many men in the far courtyard training to become warriors for the Secret Alliance. He wondered what vision of horror Queen Elanza had seen to orchestrate such a master plan.

"Whatever the Queen foresaw moved her enough to lay the groundwork that was needed to prepare the kingdom for war. But if she did not see the coming of the Draccen armies, what was it that she foresaw?" he said to himself as he eyed the men training for hand-to-hand combat.

"I believe Mother said it was a warning to be prepared for a coming darkness." Alon-Settie had come up quietly behind Leondros. He wore a warm but concerned expression as he held out his hand to the elfin prince. Taking his hand, Leondros wrapped an arm around his friend in a welcoming embrace.

"It has been too long, dear friend. How have you been?" Leondros asked. His features relaxed at the sight of his long-time friend as he let go of Alon-Settie.

"Well, my friend. Better now that you are here. I do not know that I could have commanded the Secret Alliance by myself. I want to congratulate you on your appointment to the Alliance. Come, walk with me. I need to fetch some maps before I consult with the war council," Alon-Settie explained warmly. He rolled his eyes and led Leondros down a series of long corridors and stairwells that put the two princes in the lower levels of Avdima near the old map room.

They talked as they walked. Passing by Solarous's chamber, Leondros stopped in midsentence, suddenly overwhelmed with weakness. The elfin prince felt the cold chill of evil in the air around them. He stopped next to a dimly lit door and for a moment could not find the energy to continue. Leondros had never felt anything like the chill that seemed to emanate from the darkened doorway.

"Leondros? Are you all right?" Alon-Settie asked with concern as he turned back to see why his friend had stopped talking and was no longer by his side.

Leondros fought to keep standing, warily looking at the darkened doorway of Solarous's chamber. Refusing to give in to the evil that surrounded him, Leondros slowly backed away from the shadowy chamber door. "There is something very unsettling about this place. I feel the chill of evil. It lingers close by," he said with warning as he looked up at Alon-Settie. Leondros hoped that his friend would feel the same strange chill and would want to look into this, but Alon-Settie did not seem affected by the eerie chill in the air. Leondros guessed that it was his heightened senses that allowed him to pick up such things and that Alon-Settie would never fully understand this, for men could sense only a small part of this spectrum.

"Come, my friend. You been through much the last few days," Alon-Settie said with a warm smile, gently taking his friend's arm and continuing toward the map room. Leondros hesitated for a moment before moving any farther. He knew that what he was feeling was more than ordinary weariness. Shaking his head, Leondros forced himself to start walking again. As he got farther from the darkened chamber door, Leondros felt the chill in the air gradually recede without completely disappearing.

Walking into the dark map room, Alon-Settie went to light a candle. Left at the entrance to the map room, Leondros took in the room's essence. It smelled of old papers, parchment, books, and dust. His eyes quickly adjusted to the darkness and could see bookshelves lining every wall. He watched Alon-Settie stumble around, trying to light a candle.

"This place has been undisturbed for some time," Leondros commented as he slowly made his way across the dusty stone floor to the table in the middle of the room.

"Until recently, the map room had rarely seen visitors, if at all," Alon-Settie said, wincing as he ran into a chair and knocked it over. He rubbed his shin and continued. "Now, though, there has been so much going on within the kingdom." Alon-Settie finally lit a partially burnt candle that rested on the edge of the table. As the flame began to grow, Leondros sensed that Alon-Settie was uneasy about being in this room. As Alon-Settie searched for a particular map, Leondros caught a glimpse of something interesting. In the far corner of the map room was a bookshelf that had wooden boards nailed over it. A few books were still visible from underneath the boards. They appeared to be religious texts. This added to his suspicion about the mysterious evil presence dwelling within the palace.

I wonder why? Leondros thought. He heard Alon-Settie rummaging through piles of old manuscripts, and by the sounds of his grumbling, he was unsuccessful in his search. "Have you found what you're searching for?" he asked.

"I have, actually," Alon-Settie said as he pulled out a long, yellowed map, laid it on top of the large dusty wooden table, and unrolled it. It was a map of Andora. "We are hoping that we might have something more than just weapons to use against the Draccen soldiers. In the three thousand years since the Draccen race was laid to sleep in their tunnels under Romulus, the land features of Andora have changed slightly. This could serve as a valuable tool in our fight against the Draccen armies. I know that what has been planned…" Alon-Settie's voice trailed off. Leondros looked up to see his friend was staring off into space. He felt the eerie chill creep into the room and evil's power growing around them.

"Alon-Settie?" Leondros asked, hoping to break his friend out of the trance. Failing, he reached over and touched Alon-Settie on the shoulder. As soon as he touched Alon-Settie's shoulder, Leondros felt a painful jolt of chilling energy hit him. When he jumped back, Alon-Settie snapped out of his trance.

"Leondros? What is it?" Alon-Settie asked as he awoke from his trance and looked at his elfin friend with a worried expression on his face. Leondros studied him for a moment before saying anything. He wanted to believe that his dear friend was going to be all right.

"Do you not feel what is going on around you?" he asked with concern. Alon-Settie's blank expression answered his question. "There is evil here. It lingers in this palace, within this very room. Do not be taken by it. You must fight it at all costs. I do not want to lose you to it," he warned, gripping the prince's strong shoulders. Alon-Settie listened closely as he looked around, seeming to pay more attention to of the eeriness in the room. He finally felt evil's chill, and he cringed. He looked up at Leondros, grabbed the map, and quickly left the room. The elfin prince followed his friend into the warmly lit corridor. When Alon-Settie turned back to the dimly lit chamber, he seemed to notice a change in the air around him.

"You are right, my friend. I do feel it," he said with astounded realization. He tried to shrug the cold chill out of his limbs. Leondros looked back into the room for a moment.

"You must be very cautious from now on, for the darkness is growing within this place. Be on your guard. It will not stop here," Leondros warned as he turned back to his friend.

Alon-Settie nodded with understanding. "I will make sure others are aware of this." he eyed the map room cautiously. "Thank you, my friend. I am very glad that you have come. Otherwise, things might have been quite different," he said with a warm, genuine smile. He began to walk away from the map room with Leondros following him. The elfin prince took relief from the fact that he was able to pull Alon-Settie back from the corrupting darkness. Yet as they walked through the palace, Leondros could still feel the eerie chill of evil. He wanted to leave this place before it could influence him.

"Please, go ahead to the war council without me. There is something I must take care of before I can join you and the others," Leondros gently instructed. The elfin prince looked out a window in the direction of the Misty Forest, for he was eager to meet with another long-time friend, an old Osarian knight. "Beware, my friend. The darkness lingers here still. Stay strong," Leondros cautioned. Alon-Settie nodded and smiled kindly.

"I will, my friend," Alon-Settie said warmly as his elfin companion took leave of him. Then, he turned back the way they had come to attend the "war council" in Solarous's chamber. A sinister smile widened on his face. It would not be long now.

Chapter 39

Secret Alliance

*Two days before the celebration
of the Great Dragon.*

Entering into the bright afternoon, Leondros walked from the palace grounds toward the busy streets of Akendron, breathing in the warm breezes that blew past him from the city ahead. His adventurous journey from Shoshon, the all-night meeting with the high council, the stresses and responsibilities of being the General of the Secret Alliance, and the strange occurrence with Alon-Settie had left him terribly drained. Breathing a deep sigh of relief, Leondros stopped for a moment to take in the festive sights and sounds and the delicious smells of the coming celebration. The farther he got from the palace, the more the evil chill faded until he could no longer sense it, and his energy returned. He knew that when he returned to the palace, he would have to deal with the growing evil that dwelt there, but for now he welcomed the respite.

Leondros quickly made his way through the city's hustle and bustle to the quiet footpath that would lead him to Cypress Palace. He had never seen the people of Akendron in such festive spirits before, yet he could not help but feel that they would see much more than fireworks and grand parties.

Disappearing into the Misty Forest that bordered Akendron to the south, Leondros felt true peace. The forest was untouched by the darkness that was looming over Akendron. He felt such tranquility within this forest that he sometimes believed that Adalai himself lived here. Whenever he visited this forest, he never wanted to leave. Walking through the thick mist that hung close to the ground, Leondros slowly made out the silver-leafed cypress tree that was the magical gate between the known world and the realm where Cypress Palace existed. He was grateful to have the chance to return to this sacred place. When the thick mist in front of him started to churn and clear away, he could see the stone bridge that led to the gleaming white palace in the distance. Waiting on the bridge, wearing a long dark robe, was his dear friend Sala.

"Leondros Goldendragon. Long has been the time since you have last stepped in the Misty Forest." Sala's voice was warm and inviting. Leondros watched as his old friend stepped out of the mist toward him. "It is a wonderful blessing to see you again," he said with a welcoming smile on his face. He walked up to Leondros and welcomed his elfin friend with a warm hug.

"It is a blessing to see that you are well," Leondros replied kindly. He saw that the years had aged his long-lived companion, who was in fact mortal. However, Sala was special, for since he took the oath be a Knight of the Osarian Order, Adalai had blessed him with long life. Their first meeting had been well over a century ago, and he knew that the kind man was far older than he let on. Still, for all that time, they continued to stay the best of friends. Leondros had at one time felt like a father to Sala, but with the troubles he was now facing and the elderly prophet's warm bearded face, Leondros found that Sala was the father this time. It was something he did not mind, for this was a time when he needed someone to help him. The enemy he sensed within Avdima Palace was not going to be brought down by a mere arrow or sword; it would take more than he had to offer. When Sala let go of him and looked into Leondros's face, he smiled knowingly.

"Come inside. I can see there is much that is weighing on your mind," Sala said as he put a reassuring hand on Leondros's shoulder. Once they passed through the magical gate and the thick white mist closed behind them, they knew that it was safe to engage in conversation on the troubles at hand. "I know that by now you have felt the darkness of evil in the Shandel," Sala said.

"Felt—and seen. The Draccen people have been awakened, and they are in the Shandel. Yet the darkness that I experienced on my journey here is nothing compared to what I sensed within Avdima itself. Something must be done to rid the land of this evil, and it must be done now," Leondros replied as they passed over the stone bridge leading to Cypress Palace. Sala listened intently, the reality of their deteriorating situation beginning to sink in. He shared the troubled expression that was on Leondros's weary face, but he had reason to hope.

"You are right; we must act quickly," Sala said. He stopped them before the colossal front door of Cypress Palace. "But what you do not know and what the Queen herself is very discreet about telling anyone is that the darkness that she had envisioned coming to Akendron's door was the ancient evil Lord Jarden himself." The seriousness of the moment was not just in the tone of Sala's voice, but in his stoic expression as well. At Lord Jarden's name, Leondros went pale. "However, we are not without hope," Sala continued. "I have obtained something just recently that will greatly aid us in this battle to stop this evil." Leondros was not sure what his friend had in mind, but knowing how resourceful Sala was, he knew it would be worthwhile.

Leading Leondros into Cypress Palace and to his grand library, Sala easily made his way through the large study chamber to his oak desk, unhindered by any fallen books or manuscripts. Leondros stood at the doorway in awe of the sight that lay before him. Sala's grand library had always been in disarray. He had never known that such order could be established in this room.

"I expected this would be a time of change. However, I was not expecting this," Leondros commented as he made his way into the now-clean library. As he took in the room's orderliness, he remarked, "I am impressed.

A mischievous expression filled Sala's blue eyes as he looked back at his friend from his desk and chuckled slightly. "I, unfortunately, cannot take the credit for this miracle. That honor would be more properly placed with my new friend, Tahari. It was she who decided to help me organize after a little catastrophe," Sala explained as he dug through the papers on his desk. Leondros could not help but give him a look that said, *A little catastrophe?* "It was amazing, really. In the aftermath of my library nearly falling on top of me, I found an ancient scroll and document left by the old, wise prophet Rafar." At the mention of Rafar's name, Sala had the prince's undivided attention. No one who lived within Adarah was unaware of who Rafar was. Leondros had even met this legendary elf once long ago.

"Rafar the Elder?" Leondros asked as he looked at Sala somewhat in disbelief. He watched Sala pull out an aged scroll and, with it, a new piece of paper with his handwriting on it.

"The very same. Did you know him?" Sala asked as he looked at him with curiosity.

"I remember very little about Rafar, but my father knew him well. It is said that he gave my family a sacred scroll that contained prophecies about the Goldendragon family." As Leondros explained, Sala unrolled the scroll and laid the new page alongside it so that he could read them.

"Rafar was a wise and compassionate man. In his last moments, he wrote the prophecy entrusted to your family, but he also wrote another prophecy and with it, a set of instructions. This prophecy was entrusted to the Osarian Knights," Sala said as he moved to let Leondros read it.

"How is this possible? I have never heard of a second prophecy written by Rafar," Leondros asked, gazing at Sala with a perplexed expression.

"It was kept secret to safeguard it. It needed to survive two thousand years in order to protect this generation from the ancient evil," Sala explained as he slowly walked across the great library floor to the window.

Leondros remained in disbelief. Looking down at the aged scroll, he saw the strange language written within the aged scroll, and though he could not understand it, he did recognize it as the language of the sphinx. Focusing his attention on the new page that lay beside it, he read from the translation. As he read, Leondros grew concerned. When he was finished reading the text, he looked back at Sala, who leaned against the wide sill of the window and silently gazed out of the large library window.

"Much of what has been written here is just beginning to transpire. It speaks of the forming of a Secret Alliance, and it foretells of death awaiting a prince…" Leondros's voice trailed off. He initially thought that it might be his life that was in danger, but remembering how close the evil was surrounding Alon-Settie, he greatly feared for his best friend's life instead. "Is our fate already sealed?" he asked Sala with worry. When Sala looked back at Leondros, he could not miss the defeated expression on his friend's face.

"The prophecy foretells of unfortunate things that *may* happen, but the future is yet mutable," he replied with a determined tone. "This is only the first of four sacred scrolls that make up the entire prophecy. Recognizing that the events described in the prophecy are the clues we need to follow, we then need to follow the instructions that have been given. If we follow these scrolls precisely, they will lead us to the ancient warrior Farro." Leondros looked at his dear friend with a wide-eyed expression.

"Farro? The one who began the Osarian Order itself? He died, did he not?" Leondros asked while trying to grasp this startling news.

"According to the scroll, he will return," Sala affirmed with a hint of excitement in his voice. "It says that he is the one who will defeat the evil of Lord Jarden. Until then, we must be patient and remain close to our friends through the great peril ahead.

As Sala explained the details of this secret mission, Leondros gazed over the aged scroll for a moment. "Sala, I did not know that you could read the sphinx's written language. I thought all who could read its meaning had long since passed away," Leondros said with a tone of surprise.

The old man gently shook his head. "It was not I who made

the translation. Our good friend Rafar made mention of a sacred messenger. This person would be of sphinx origin and would be the only one able to read the ancient scrolls. That messenger has been found, and it was she who translated the scroll for me," Sala replied.

Leondros listened intently, but he still could not believe his ears. "A sphinx of the ancient world still lives?" he asked. "The sphinxes of the ancient world vanished from existence during the eighth age. How is it that one survived?" he asked as haunting images flashed in his mind. He, along with his family and friends, had fought to save the sphinxes but to no avail. They could only watch in horror as these beautiful creatures were wiped from the earth. The sadness of that loss still grieved him.

"I do not know the answer to this, nor does the messenger. It is my friend, Tahari," Sala said as he looked back out the window. Leondros noticed the sadness growing in his friend's face. "I found her a slave about to be executed by the Tomblock's taskmasters. She barely survived as the slaves revolted against their masters. Slaves and taskmasters alike were killed, and now the remaining plantation's taskmasters are searching for her. It is surely a miracle that has brought her this far." Sala recounted the previous evening's events at the Tomblock. Leondros was taken aback by the news, for this work farm was but a few miles from Avdima Palace where he had sat in council.

Leondros felt sympathy for this last sphinx known as Tahari. "Is she still here?" he asked in a hopeful tone. More than knowing that Tahari was the last of her race and that such a discovery was worth protecting, he hoped to learn more about where she came from.

Sala nodded and motioned toward the window. "Since I smuggled her out of the Tomblock, Tahari has been recovering from the hard life that she was condemned to and trying to heal from the horrors of the other night," Sala explained. Leondros joined Sala at the window. It was hard to see anything through the thick trees and bushes of the hanging garden, but he glimpsed a girl with long dark hair in a white robe resting against a huge oak. Leondros noticed that her skin was dark from the sun and that she seemed young, maybe less than twenty.

Yet something about her stood out. Even though she had been a slave for the majority of her life, Leondros did not see the worn, weathered face of a slave. He sensed that she was wiser than most mortals twice or even thrice her age. He read her tired expression and knew it all too well.

"I feel as she does; standing against an entire army and looking around to see that you are the only one fighting against it," Leondros said in a whisper as his memories of the Divervandon Forest came back to him.

Sala saw the look of concern in Leondros's face. He remembered how torn Tahari had been over the loss of her dear friends from the plantation. Leondros lived his life in the company of good friends who eventually succumbed to death. Turning from the window, Sala headed for the door of the library. "Come, I think she is someone you need to meet," he said, looking back over his shoulder.

"I do not wish to trouble her at such a time," Leondros said hesitantly.

Sala smiled warmly and motioned for him to follow. "It may be just the thing to help her get past the tragedies that befell her. It was she who reminded me that we need to stay close to our friends to get through what is to come.

Leondros realized that Tahari was right. It gave him courage to go forward and meet her. He felt a measure of anticipation, for it had been two thousand years since he had last seen a sphinx of the ancient world.

Following Sala through the winding passages that led through Cypress Palace, Leondros emerged into the beautiful hanging garden. They navigated their way through the garden's foliage-ensconced passages. When they reached a small opening, they saw Tahari sitting under the oak that was atop a grassy hill. Leondros watched her for a moment.

"She seems so sad," he whispered softly as he glanced at Sala.

Nodding in response before speaking, Sala said, "A natural reaction for anyone who loses someone they care about. However, sphinxes are beings of immense kindness and compassion. Their bonds to those around them are incredibly strong. When they lose someone close to them, they feel the grief acutely." he studied Tahari's expression with understanding before he turned back to Leondros. "You see, when the Tomblock began executing slaves last night, Tahari's friends were among those killed. It would appear that they were the closest thing that she had to a family." he sadly looked down and closed his eyes as if to block something horrible from his mind. "The images of that night will linger with me forever." Sala's words seemed to hit Leondros hard.

Looking back at Tahari, he could not help but feel an instant connection with her. Most races did not understand the life of an elf. All his life, Leondros had made friends from other realms only to see them perish from age and unforeseen events. Sala alone understood this, but perhaps Tahari might be another one to understand.

Chapter 40

The Growing Darkness

Sitting in the shadows of his chamber, Solarous was taking his notes for Lord Jarden. Only the scratching of his quill against the parchment and the bubbling of the yellow liquid in the nearby cauldron broke the silence of the chamber. Finishing yet another page of notes and gently laying it aside, the keen-sensed advisor stopped and lifted his head. Someone was now standing on the other side of the door, and the dark power that had consumed him told him who it was.

Lifting his head, he called out, "Come in, Prince Alon-Settie. I have been waiting for you." A moment passed before the door opened. When it did, Alon-Settie walked in wearing a black and red robe, accented by a dumbfounded look on his face and a map in his hand. He searched the dimly lit room until he found Solarous.

"How did you know that it was me?" he asked, slowly shutting the heavy door behind him.

Solarous smiled with an evil grin and gazed into the fire beneath the cauldron. "How did your little test work on the elf?" the advisor asked curiously, turning his gaze to his new servant.

"Perfectly. He is very vulnerable to the evil. It will not take much to overwhelm him," Alon-Settie replied as he gently set aside the map on a nearby table. Getting the old map had only been a ruse to lead Leondros close to the source of evil to test his tolerance to the evil. Solarous looked up from the papers he had been working on and smiled with satisfaction.

"What other news do you have for me?" he asked. The prince was about to deliver his news when the yellow liquid within the cauldron distracted him. There seemed to be wormish tendrils churning in the hot yellow potion.

"Is that something new Lord Jarden has given you to use against our enemies?" Alon-Settie asked, intrigued. Solarous looked at him evenly, before uttering his answer.

"It is chicken noodle soup. Now, tell me the news you have for me," the dark advisor replied without humor. Alon-Settie turned his gaze sheepishly back to him. The prince felt uneasy about the news that he had to deliver to this dark advisor, but it had to be done.

"When Leondros had had enough of the high council's squabbling, he told them he was going leave if they didn't want his help. His courageous actions impressed Father so much, though, that he made Leondros General of the Secret Alliance," Alon-Settie reported evenly. There was a clear hint of jealousy in the Akendron prince's voice. Solarous smiled. He was more impressed with Alon-Settie's reaction than with the actual news that he had brought.

"What do you think of his being made general?" Solarous asked as he clasped his fingers together and put them to his lips to think.

"Leondros senses the evil within the palace. If he suspects what we are up to..." Alon-Settie trailed off. His mind was in a whirlwind of suspicion. "He has my father's favor and will have no trouble reporting these findings to him." the prince was silent a moment, deep in thought. Finally, he said, "I fear that Leondros will become a great threat to our plans." as he spoke about his fears, Solarous listened intently and smiled.

"This complication works perfectly with my plan. Worry not," Solarous replied easily and calmly, his dark button-like eyes once again gazing into the flames beneath the cauldron.

"Worry not? If you plan on getting rid of Leondros, will not the men of the Secret Alliance show concern for their general and come to aid him and apprehend those who seek to harm him?" The stress in Alon-Settie's face was clearly visible as he pointed out these facts.

Solarous looked up at him calmly. "The men within the so-called Secret Alliance are not as strong-minded as their new general. The dark powers will easily consume them. They will have no such regard for Leondros once the darkness takes hold of them," Solarous explained simply as he sat back in his chair. "Our energies must be put toward getting rid of the Queen. That is where the real challenge lies.

"The Queen? How will getting rid of her be of any help to us? Should we not be concerned with bigger problems, like...?" Alon-Settie stopped. All he could see was Leondros being the imminent threat at this point.

Solarous turned to the prince and glared angrily. "Be silent, small-minded fool!" he hissed angrily. "If you attack the leader first, you will quickly be surrounded by his followers. That is the way of things. You must look beyond the most apparent source of conflict. Yes, Leondros is a matter that we need to rectify, but that will happen in good time. We must look at the other points of conflict. In this game, there are many pieces that must be silenced. Since my return to Avdima, Lord Jarden has told me of the Queen, a general, and a stranger. They all must be silenced. Then and only then can we work at our leisure," he explained with renewed patience.

"A stranger?" Alon-Settie asked, lifting an eyebrow. "Who is this stranger? For all you know it could be a filthy peasant from the streets. Surely this cannot be a point of conflict?" He sneered at the thought of a peasant being a threat to them and the grandeur of their scheme. "How dangerous can a mere peasant be?"

"Very," Solarous replied, glaring at the prince. "What have your years of training taught you about fighting an enemy?"

Alon-Settie thought about who stood in the way of the new empire. "If the Queen, the general, and the stranger are dead, there should be no one strong enough to contend against our forces. The rise of the new kingdom should be quick," he said. Then he remembered how strong both his mother and Leondros were. "But only the Queen and Leondros will not go down easily. It is because they are so strong that they have to be eliminated. This must be done carefully and cautiously, or as you have said, we will be overrun by their followers," he reasoned thoughtfully. Looking back at Solarous, he realized that the royal advisor had already foreseen this.

Solarous gazed back at him with a sinister smile. "Now you have got it!" He climbed to his feet and walked across the room to a bookshelf tucked just out of sight behind a tapestry. The prince guessed that the books were dark and sinister in nature, thus their being hidden from sight. He watched as Solarous searched for a certain book.

"What is your master plan for getting rid of them?" Alon-Settie asked. Finding what he was searching for, Solarous pulled the book from its place high upon the shelf. After blowing the dust from its dark leather cover, he opened it and gave a sinister smile.

"During his days as the conduit of Lord Jarden's powers, Randye of Corpse wrote several useful things we can use in our plans. He has already given us the first step in how to take down our enemies. You search out your strongest enemies. The next step is to find and then exploit their weaknesses. Let us take the Queen. It is quite obvious that she is not renowned for being a fierce and cunning warrior. It will be no trouble to physically overpower her," Solarous said as he paced the room, reading suggestive hints from the small leather book in his hands. "Enter the stranger. I have heard rumor that on the night the Queen was attacked, someone came to her aid. No one knows who this savior was, but my guess is that if the Queen's life falls into peril, then we shall see this stranger again. It is then that we must make our move.

Alon-Settie was beginning to like the design of this plan, but he could only wonder how they would bring someone like Leondros Goldendragon down. "All this sounds most promising, but what about our last point of conflict?" he asked.

Solarous stopped pacing a moment and looked at Alon-Settie. "It will have to be something very special indeed," the advisor reasoned thoughtfully. He did not know of any known weaknesses that existed which would bring Leondros down. "He is a very cunning warrior, and it is impossible to catch an elfin warrior off-guard.

"Several thousand years of training and tactics govern Leondros's actions. No matter what we throw at him, he will only keep on coming until his opponent is defeated," Alon-Settie replied. "Well, at least this is one battle I do not have to help him fight," he said, sounding discouraged. A phrase caught Solarous's attention.

"What did you say?" he asked as he looked at Alon-Settie with sudden realization.

"Just that Leondros will not have any help from me in preventing his demise. In the past, I would have come to his aid without question, but after the other night," the Prince paused as anger crept into his features. "The right to be General of the Secret Alliance should have been mine," Alon-Settie's anger was clear. "He stands in the way of the very thing that we are trying to achieve. Why would I help him?"

Solarous knew then of a most treacherous demise for the elfin General. "You have just concocted the plot that will lead to the death of the General, my dear Prince," Solarous said with great approval, for he marveled at Alon-Settie's brilliant idea.

"How did I manage to do that?" Alon-Settie asked with disbelief.

"You know your enemy's strengths, and you also know his weaknesses," Solarous explained. "Your skills will prove most beneficial in the rise of our new empire.

"All right then," the Prince said as he agreed to Solarous's plot. "Just know that he is quite resourceful in unpredictable situations.

"That is why I have set my plan in motion. Taking down Leondros will come in two parts. First: the corruption of the Secret Alliance," Solarous said as he glanced over at the bubbling cauldron of chicken noodle soup. "The queen's plan for a Secret Alliance will horribly backfire on her, the army that she wishes to protect her people with will be the weapon that cuts them down." Alon-Settie joined Solarous's gaze and began to understand.

"Soup enough for an army," the Prince offered slowly with realization. The advisor gave a sinister wink and nod of certainty.

"They have yet to ask for seconds, but it should be any minute now." Solarous anticipated as he leaned an ear towards the doorway for the sounds of servants returning to fetch more soup. "Second: the fall and eventual death of Prince Leondros Goldendragon. The master plan I have already crafted for Leondros's demise is cruel to be sure, but you have intrigued I may yet…have need to concoct something truly heart-wrenching." Alon-Settie gave him a look of renewed interest.

"What are the details of this master plan?" Alon-Settie asked as he crossed his arms over his chest as he was eager to learn how Leondros's death was going to play out. "Besides, I am more than willing to suggest a few ideas." the tone of Alon-Settie's voice suggested his bitterness towards the elfin prince from Adarah.

"Patience, my Prince. When the time comes, all you have to do is show up and do what you do best. Besides, with all that is at stake, it is imperative not to rush the timing. We are on the verge of the greatest celebration in the kingdom." Solarous refrained from revealing the intricate details of his sinister plot for Leondros.

"Your plans still sound vague to me," Alon-Settie pointed out. "However as long as Leondros dies, it is what he deserves for taking what is rightfully mine." Solarous listened intently, for he wanted Alon-Settie to truly savor his revenge.

"Death, is that all?" the advisor asked in tone that suggested there were untold possibilities. He put the book down upon his desk and walked to the black cauldron and breathed in the soup's pleasant aroma. "Alon-Settie, by now I am sure you know that there are many ways to inflict great pain on your enemy. Very soon, you are going to find out that there are many ways to defeat your enemy other than death. Death is merely the kiss goodbye." Solarous spoke with a low whisper, and Alon-Settie stepped closer to hear him better.

"You have renewed my interest. Tell me more," Alon-Settie insisted.

Solarous nodded slowly, a smile on his lips. Now he was certain that Alon-Settie had chosen his side in the coming battle. "You study your enemies' weaknesses. All of them. In the case of these three, it is a fair assumption that if they are brought together, they will be virtually unbeatable," Solarous said as he reached for a long wooden staff that was leaning against the dark cauldron. "Take this wooden staff, for example. It is almost impossible to crack because it is all one piece," he said as he slowly examined it and handed it to Alon-Settie. "Here. Try to break it." doing as he was told, Alon-Settie took the wooden staff, and using all his strength, he tried to break it against his knee. Much to his dismay and pain, Alon-Settie could not break the wooden staff. "All right, we know that if we allow these three people to join together, they will be unbreakable. What now?" Alon-Settie asked as he winced from the bruise growing on his leg.

"When you have successfully severed one from the rest, you cut down the group's strength. You are then free to cut them down on a more personal level," Solarous said as he took back the wooden staff and began puncturing small holes throughout the staff with a small metal punch in his hands. "Alone, one cannot stand up against such intolerable treatment. Try to break the staff now," Solarous instructed, handing the wooden staff back to Alon-Settie. Alon-Settie took a firm hold of the staff and slammed it against the ground. The staff splintered into several smaller pieces.

"You see, no structure can stand if key pieces are missing. The integrity of our enemies' strength will be as this wooden staff: broken and shattered," he said as he bent down and picked up three pieces of splintered wood. "Once you have achieved this, nothing can stop you from reducing them to nothing." he took the three pieces of wood and threw them into the fire, watching them catch and burn into ashes.

"They will die quick deaths, I promise," Alon-Settie said with assurance. "But what about the other kingdoms? Once Leondros has been killed, his family, indeed the entire kingdom of Adarah, will be in an uproar. News of this will surely reach the other kingdoms, and people will come to stand against us," he said thoughtfully. "I do not want to imagine the army that will await us then." Alon-Settie knew that although not all of the kingdoms had friendly alliances with each other, they would have no trouble banding together to stop the evil that had come to take over the entire land of Andora.

"Ah, yes!" Solarous said as if he had just been reminded of something. "You make a very excellent point. That is where you will come in, my Prince. From every kingdom that has to come to join the Secret Alliance, these men have eaten of my chicken soup. Of the whole army, I have convinced several men to join our side, and I then empowered them with the ability of persuasion. During the Secret Alliance's first campaign, these men will vanish into the countryside and will be reported to have been mysteriously taken by the Draccen soldiers lurking in the area. In the General's concern, you will catch him off-guard and strike him down. Once Leondros is dead, you will take charge of the Alliance and send these men back to their homelands, where they will spread the glory of our new kingdom to their people, none of whom have yet been attacked by the Draccen raiding parties. They will be convinced about the dawn of this new empire, and then there will be no more threat of armies rising up against us," Solarous explained as he put a hand on Alon-Settie's shoulder.

"Brilliant. Food poisoning on a new level; I like it." Alon-Settie said thoughtfully as he eyed the yellow mixture before him cautiously. "I especially like how you will use his compassion for others against him. Very clever. When Leondros goes to search for these men, it will be a perfect time to catch him with his guard down," Alon-Settie noted in agreement. "Still, Leondros is a true leader in every sense of the word. He will not go down easily.

As the prince spoke from experience, Solarous nodded. "The more he resists, the worse it will be for him. In time, you will see the full measure of my plan," Solarous said with assurance. He slowly waved his hand over the red flames that licked the bottom of the cauldron, causing the flames to go out and a thick white smoke to rise from the embers. Solarous peered into the smoke, seeing how certain events would transpire. "Everything will happen as we have planned here," he said as he showed Alon-Settie a glimpse of images of future events.

"Truly? We can foresee what is yet to come?" Alon-Settie asked in amazement, looking more closely at the smoke.

"Yes. Much more than that," Solarous affirmed as he cleared the thick white smoke away with his hand.

Alon-Settie pondered on their plans to bring about a new empire and began to wonder if there was anyone who could possibly oppose them. Of all the legends he had heard of, there was one that came to mind, and it concerned him.

"What if—in the course of getting rid of the Queen, the stranger, and Leondros—what if by some chance the legend of Farro comes true?" Alon-Settie asked with concern.

Solarous became most angered by this. "WHAT?!" Solarous demanded. The advisor was rigid with anger, and he glared at Alon-Settie. "What did you say?" he asked again, sounding almost ready to explode.

"I just asked…" Alon-Settie started to explain himself as he backed away from Solarous. However, before he could utter another word, Solarous held up his hand to stop him from saying anything more.

"Do not utter another word!" Solarous hissed through clenched teeth. "Never mention that name again, here or anywhere!" he scolded Alon-Settie as he continued to glare at him. "If such a name is ever mentioned where people could hear you, it would destroy everything that we have worked so hard to achieve. If you have any regard for your own life, never mention that name again," Solarous threatened.

"But, surely, it is only a folk story, a myth that I heard once, somewhere. I haven't heard it since. I can only assume that it must mean nothing," Alon-Settie explained, hoping to calm the advisor down.

"Do you want to know why no one has mentioned it? Because there was never any reason to bring it up! I have led these fools to believe that the ancient evil has been locked away for all time and, thus, there is no need to look for some ancient warrior to save them. Praying that this information does not get out, we may just have enough time to overthrow those in power. Once the glorious splendor of the new kingdom has been established and Lord Jarden is ruler of all Andora, there will be no chance that any such being will overthrow him. The myth that you spoke of will stay that way: a myth," Solarous said, pacing the floor near the cauldron.

Alon-Settie could see that this matter really concerned his new master. "If this myth is so threatening, why not learn about it? Find its weaknesses, and destroy any chance of such a myth ever coming true." Alon-Settie offered hopefully.

Solarous looked up at Alon-Settie and slowly nodded his head in agreement. "You are right," he said, though he still seemed deeply troubled by this myth. "But you must be very cautious with *this* enemy. It is not like trying to defeat an elfin warrior by any means. It is said that this being will possess great and unlimited power, such as the world has not seen in many millennia." As he spoke, Solarous felt a stirring within his own dark soul.

Chapter 41

Dark Insight from Within

The stirring in his soul became a dark voice that came from within but could be heard by others.

"Solarous, be aware of the stranger that you have spoken of, for they are a great threat to you. Be aware of the one who sees with the eyes of an elf", said Lord Jarden said through Solarous.

"My lord, how am I to know of such a person? There are many elves who reside within the far kingdom of Adarah and who travel through the Shandel," Solarous asked aloud, trying to picture this stranger in his mind.

"You will know by what you sense. Be mindful of your feelings, for they will reveal this stranger to you. They will not be who you think," Lord Jarden advised him, for there was a foreseeable danger to their plan if this stranger was left to do as they would.

Alon-Settie watched his master with a mystified expression. He sensed a dark presence within the chamber. He had backed away from his master when he began to talk to himself and an even darker voice conversed with him. It sent chills down the prince's spine to hear a dark voice coming from deep within the advisor. As he continued to watch from the corner of the room, Alon-Settie began to understand that the cold chill in the air was the presence of Lord Jarden himself.

After several moments passed, Alon-Settie felt the heavy presence lift from the room. Looking back at his master, he wondered if he would be the same as he had been before. Standing for a long moment in silence, Solarous finally turned around and faced him.

"Well, that was a mind full," Solarous said with a strange smile on his face. Alon-Settie was not sure if he should laugh at the remark or not.

"It was Lord Jarden, wasn't it?" Alon-Settie asked in a cautious tone as he eyed his master carefully.

"Yes, it was," Solarous replied as he thought about what his lord had been telling him.

"The stranger is an elf, then? An elf other than Leondros?" Alon-Settie asked with a tone of confusion.

"Not an elf, but someone who has the ability to sense evil, like the elves. If such a person does exist, they would also be trying to fight against the coming darkness," Solarous replied.

"Well, that narrows down our search to just about anyone who is not an elf," Alon-Settie offered sarcastically. He did not want to think of the search that would await them. The race of men greatly outnumbered the elves. He shook his head, but seeing the disapproval in Solarous's face, Alon-Settie felt compelled to make a good effort in finding this stranger.

"We must not assume anything at this point, my Prince. Assumptions can be the deadliest fault in people," Solarous said as he turned back to the steaming cauldron.

"Whoever this stranger is, I will search them out and see to it that they are eliminated. If they are so dangerous, then we do not want them joining forces with the Queen or Leondros. Such a bond would be impossible to break," Alon-Settie said assuredly.

"Then you have a plan in mind for this stranger?" Solarous asked with an inquisitive expression.

"Just give me the word, and I will take care of the problem at hand," the prince promised without any doubt in his mind that he could handle this elusive threat.

"Leave the stranger to me." Solarous interjected as he cringed at the prince's over confidence. "You need only concern yourself with Leondros, but I hope for your sake that you are not caught off-guard by something unexpected," Solarous warned him as he gave the young prince a cautious look.

"What do you mean? If we swoop in and eliminate these enemies before they have a chance to realize what is going on around them, then do we not have the upper hand?" Alon-Settie asked with a tone of certainty.

"Never mind," Solarous replied, not wishing to instill doubt in his servant who would bring some of his greatest enemies to ruin. "Just be observant of those around you and of the ones that lurk within the realm of light. They are stronger in the face of adversity than we realize. You must break them of this spirit before it is too late," Solarous warned strongly.

"Consider our battle to overrun this kingdom and Andora won," Alon-Settie replied with incessant overconfidence. Solarous watched as the prince gave one last look of certainty before he was out the chamber door. He wondered if such pride and assurance would not lead to their eventual downfall.

"If you fall due to your own pride and overconfidence, it will be you and you alone who will fall. I will not be caught up in your faults," Solarous said in a hushed whisper as he turned back to the smoking cauldron to see what else the future held for them.

Chapter 42

Chance Meeting

Feeling the warm sun upon her face gave Tahari some comfort, but it could not dull the pain she still felt within. Tahari had long since forgotten the time as she sat thinking about her friends who perished during the revolt against the taskmasters. She was somewhat glad that the workers found the courage to stop being complacent and rise up against the injustice they were facing. However, it would seem that this came with a price.

Taking a deep breath of fresh air, Tahari lifted her head to look out over the beautiful hanging gardens that surrounded her. She realized this was the next chapter in her life. It was very strange in comparison to her past life. Tahari could only wonder what this life had in store for her now. A warm breeze gently blew against her face, offering comfort. Suddenly, she sensed that she was no longer alone. It would not have surprised her if it had been Sala coming to find her, but there was another presence, too. This other presence was much different. Looking around the garden, Tahari could not see anyone. While she listened and waited for someone to appear, she could not help but think that she had felt this presence before.

Then Tahari saw Sala's familiar features as he talked with someone in the trees surrounding the palace. Tahari smiled, for she was glad to see him. He looked her way and seemed to want to know if she was ready for company. She nodded. Smiling in return, Sala made his way toward her accompanied by a guest. At first, Tahari did not recognize the guest. It was a man of the elfin race dressed in a desert-brown tunic with silver armor that reminded her of dragon scales. The armor itself and the warrior looked as if they had seen time in battle prior to their arrival. As he came close, Tahari began to sense something familiar about him. Then the sunlight caught the edge of his war bow, which was carefully placed near his quiver. She had seen this elfin warrior before. When she looked into his warm brown eyes, Tahari froze for a moment. How was it that their paths were to come together again so soon? Still, looking upon this elfin warrior's face, Tahari was enormously relieved. He had indeed survived the attack and was now standing at Sala's right side. She silently thanked Adalai for the divine intervention that saved both of their lives.

"Lady Tahari," Sala said softly as they approached. Tahari noticed the look of concern on his face until he saw her smile in return. "I wanted to introduce you to a very special friend of mine," he said in a warm voice. "This is Prince Leondros Goldendragon. He comes to us from the distant kingdom of Adarah." he turned and gestured to his elfin companion. Tahari smiled contentedly as she finally had the chance to learn this mysterious elfin warrior's name. Leondros bowed his head humbly. It almost caught her off-guard that a warrior and prince was bowing before *her*.

"I am honored to finally have the chance to meet a sphinx of the ancient world. Long ago, our cultures existed together in peace and friendship," Leondros said in a reverent tone.

Tahari felt somewhat undeserving of such admiration, but she sensed great truth in the words that he spoke. In this moment, she somehow caught a glimpse of her past. Then she remembered that the elves had been the only ones trying to fight to save the sphinxes. Sadly, all their efforts failed them and the sphinxes were lost. Looking into Leondros's soulful eyes, Tahari realized that he had been there through all of it and wished that such peace and friendship could exist again. She nodded her head slowly and smiled with understanding.

"The honor is also mine. For it was known that the elves had been the sphinxes' closest allies, especially during the dark times. Such deeds will never be forgotten," she replied as she too bowed her head humbly. Leondros was surprised that Tahari was able to remember such details that went on well before her birth, but it also seemed to give him great comfort, too. Judging from his pained expression in regards to the sphinxes culture, she sensed that he knew only too well the tragic fate that fell upon her entire race. As they spoke, she could not help but feel a strange power in the air around her. It was both unsettling and calming at the same time. Tahari felt as if she were in the presence of a caring and compassionate soul. Oddly enough, this was not new to her, for she had felt it once before. It had come to her while she was in the Divervandon Forest, aiding this elfin warrior.

As they spoke, Sala looked pleased to see such a warm meeting between two of the oldest races. Then he seemed to notice something.

"I have to admit that you are looking better than when you first came to the palace," Sala commented. An expression of genuine concern came over Leondros's face.

"I am feeling more myself than I did," Tahari assured them with a warm smile as she continued to rest her back against the large oak tree.

"You may be more right than you know. I have never seen anyone heal so fast before ," he said. His blue eyes were filled with amazement as they looked from Tahari over to his elfin companion. "Well, almost never," he added in a thoughtful tone. Leondros had noticed his friend's surprised expression and looked back at me with interest.

"Lady Tahari?" Leondros asked as he stepped toward her, slowly sank to his knees, and looked at her with a hopeful glance. "*Do you remember this language?*" he asked gently in his native elfish tongue. At first, it was as strange to Tahari as the sphinx script that Sala had handed to her earlier. Only before she allowed herself to reply, she thought about it for a moment as she lowered her gaze to search her clouded memory. Then somehow, the words that he had spoken became as clear and familiar to her as when she first heard them.

"*Yes, I do remember. I do not know how it is, but I remember,*" Tahari replied back in the same tongue. She saw an expression of surprise wash over both Sala's and Leondros's faces as they exchanged glances. However, she did not believe they were more surprised than she was.

Turning back to Tahari, Leondros looked at her with an inquisitive expression. *"Do you remember your true parents? It may have been a very long time, but please try to remember. It is important,"* he asked, again in Elfish. Tahari had never been asked this before. Lowering her gaze again, she dug deep into her past. It was a place that she did not visit often, for it was always too vague to comprehend. Still, something about Leondros's presence helped her to remember the fragmented details of her past.

"My... father's name was... Reymier of the Shandon. He was the high judge and counselor of the royal elfish court and a member of the high council. Sadly, I can barely remember my mother or what she looked like," Tahari replied slowly as the pieces of her long-forgotten past started to fit together clearly. She was beside herself at remembering this much of her past, but she knew there was much more. Leondros offered a kind smile, and then he looked back at Sala for a moment.

"She is beginning to remember her past," Leondros offered in the common tongue. As he spoke to Sala, Tahari remembered the last memory she had of her father. Everything that Reymier had told her and everything that had happened to her after they were separated came back to her. More than just remembering these awful events, she felt them. The intense pain of these memories hit her with a vengeance. Tahari fought to remain composed as she lowered her head sadly. When Leondros turned back to look at her, he froze in horror. Tahari felt Leondros take her hands with his, hoping to offer some comfort. Looking up at him and seeing the understanding in his Bthe soulful expression of Leondros's face, she knew that he sensed the harshness of her past. It caused a pained look in his brown eyes. *"No wonder you had no memory of such things. Such trauma was never meant for any child,"* he said sadly in Elfish. *"I, too, remember that dreadful day, but what happened after that? What led you to the confines of the Tomblock?"* His voice was merely a whisper. In spite of the sadness that she felt from knowing how her father died, Tahari was encouraged to try to remember even more of her past. Taking a deep breath, she lowered her gaze and began to think. As she did, Tahari felt a cool breeze gently blow against her face. Then, a vision appeared before her.

Chapter 43

A Past Remembered

Lightning flashed, hurting Tahari's eyes, and thunder crashed, deafening her. Rain battered down on her, stinging as it pelted her skin. Everything around Tahari was dark and strange. The only thing that seemed familiar was the woman who held her in her arms. The woman was tall and skinny with dark hair that had been tied back in a long braid. Her eyes were sea-green, and her face was the color of brown sugar. Tahari was wrapped up within her dark cloak. This woman was her mother, and Tahari could sense that she was scared. Yet Tahari did not believe it was the storm that scared her. There was something even darker and deadlier following them, some dark force that would not stop until it found them.

Much of that fateful night was a blur, but Tahari remembered how tired and exhausted they both had been, for they had traveled so far. Tahari also remember being hungry, for they had little food with them. Mother refused to give up, though, and she continued to assure her that everything would be all right. Her consoling words sustained Tahari for the entirety of their trip. Their journey by day had been warm and pleasant, and they had been given food by an old couple they had encountered. By the time the next evening had fallen over them, though, they were far from their homeland and deep in the

Divervandon Forest. The night was once again filled with a violent thunderstorm. Tahari sensed a great fear within Mother. The danger that had been following them was quickly gaining on them.

Finally, Mother stopped at the first house that had lights burning within it. The people who opened the door seemed to welcome them with open arms. They wanted to take them in out of the wind and rain, but Mother refused to go in. She asked them to watch over Tahari, for she had something still to do. Then, before she left, she bent down and wrapped her arms tightly around Tahari for a long moment. Tahari recalled her last words to her.

"My precious child, how I wish I could have given you a better life. Tahari, never forget how special you are. You will go on to do great things. Do not be restrained by those who say you cannot. Believe that you can, and you will see mountains move. More than anything, remember who you are, for it is your love that will heal a multitude."

Mother's words were as clear now as if she had just spoken them. Then with one last warm and loving embrace, she kissed Tahari's forehead and walked back into the storm. The people were quick to change Tahari into warm clothes and feed her, but in Tahari's mind she was watching as her mother went out to confront the danger that she no longer feared, for the love of her life was now safe from harm. Mother never returned to get her, but then neither did the danger that had followed them.

When the vision cleared, Tahari remembered everything. Raising her head slowly, she looked up at Leondros and Sala with a sad smile. After a deep breath, she began to explain in the Andora common tongue the traumatic events that led her mother and her to the Tomblock fifteen years ago and the stroke of good fortune that brought her before them today. As the incredible events of her story were laid out before them, Tahari watched the amazement on their faces grow. She gave Sala a grateful smile. Leondros followed her gaze and nodded with understanding. It was apparent that he had heard about her rescue.

There was true understanding in his warm brown eyes. He turned his gaze toward the Tomblock for a moment. He murmured something under his breath. He seemed angered by what these people had done and how such cruelty went unnoticed for so long. When Leondros looked back at her, Tahari saw guilt and sorrow on his kind face.

"Your memory has not failed you, but we have. Any search parties that we had sent out never recovered anyone or any trace that led us to believe that there was hope to keep looking," Leondros said.

Tahari reached over and put a comforting hand on his arm. "No apology is necessary," she said with an understanding smile. "There was a reason I was meant to live within the confines of the Tomblock, and I sense that it can only help me with what is to come. However, it's still good to hear that such noble people had put forth such effort to find us. For this, I thank you." the relieved smile that came to his face eased her mind also.

"Tahari, after my task is done here, you are most welcome to accompany me back to your home in Adarah," Leondros offered kindly.

"I would be honored and most thankful," Tahari replied. The thought of seeing the place that she once called home lifted her spirits greatly. It was then that Tahari remembered something else that had transpired within the Divervandon Forest. She was now given the chance to reveal something to him that she had not thought she would get.

"Leondros…" Tahari paused, for she did not know how it should be put into words. He watched her patiently. "It is a blessing to see you alive after the attack within the Divervandon forest," Tahari managed to say at last. Leondros stared at her with a mystified expression. Tahari knew he was puzzled as to how she knew, but she knew that it would eventually come to him.

"It was you?" Leondros asked, sounding dumbfounded. An expression of sudden realization washed over his face. "It was you," he said again with certainty. Tahari smiled a little. "How did you know that I was in danger?" he asked with a mystified curiosity.

"I had a vision of you being attacked in the Divervandon Forest. The outcome that I had foreseen was most unfortunate, though," she said. "My vision gave me a chance to change what I saw," she said.

"What made you decide to help me if you didn't know me?" Leondros asked. Tahari smiled kindly as she pondered how to respond.

"Compassion does not need a reason to be given away. Our world has seen too much time without it." as she spoke, a warm smile came to Leondros's face. Such a gift had never been given to him by a complete stranger before. However, it was highly doubtful that they would leave this day as strangers.

"I do not know what I have done to deserve such favor, nor do I know how to repay such a favor." Leondros sounded a little beside himself. "All I can offer is my friendship." he seemed overwhelmed by the grandeur of what had been done for him. She smiled warmly, treasuring the moment. It may have seemed like so little to offer one's friendship to another, but for her, it was something truly special.

"Then I am the one who is honored. The gift of friendship is very precious, and it is something I hold in high regard. Thank you, my friend," Tahari replied. She had lost all the friends that she had ever known, so to have this elfin prince as a new friend greatly warmed her heart. It reminded her that her life still had worth and that she had a great responsibility to others. Tahari was so overwhelmed that she could not keep the tears from stinging her eyes.

"Never in all my long years have I had such a friend. You are right. Friendships are very precious things that I would be lost without," Leondros replied with a warm smile, resting a comforting hand on her arm. Then Tahari heard someone sniffling above them. In the moment, they had forgotten Sala, and she lifted her gaze to see him wiping the tears that were streaming down his face. Leondros followed Tahari's gaze and also noticed Sala's emotional state. The elfin prince looked at his friend as a smile spread across his face.

"That was so beautiful," Sala finally said. He used his long, sweeping sleeves to wipe the tears that were running down his face. Tahari could not help but chuckle. She looked back at Leondros, who smiled. He seemed amused by his friend's teary-eyed reaction.

"I thought that the Osarian Knights were regarded for their steel emotions and cool thinking under pressure?" Leondros playfully nudged his old companion.

"We did and always will," Sala replied with a sniffle. "But I can see a good if not great friendship is formed. It is a very beautiful thing." he paused to regain control of his emotions. "Now," Sala continued, "Leondros, please fill me in on the particulars that you have discovered about where Tahari comes from." the aged prophet waved his finger between Leondros and Tahari. Leondros sighed, for he knew this would take a great deal of explaining. It was a bittersweet tale to tell. Slowly sitting back on the soft grass behind him, he began to explain the mystery that had overshadowed Tahari's past.

"Tahari comes from Adarah. Her father was Reymier of the Shandon. He was the High Judge and counselor of the royal elfish court. He was also on my father's royal High Council." Leondros spoke with such reverence; it was clear that he thought Tahari's father a very good man. However, there was a definite look of sadness in his eyes. "Reymier had lived within Shoshon for many thousands of years before the day that would change all our lives. A large, dragon-like creature came to the city that day. It clearly intended to do great harm to the people. Father sent our soldiers to fight this beast. I went out to try and stop it as well. But it was Reymier who ended up vanquishing the dark beast," Leondros said. Tahari watched him tighten his jaw and lower his gaze. She sensed the grief that he was feeling and wanted to interject, but Leondros found the strength to lift his head again to continue.

"When it was clear that so many were in danger, Reymier fought like a warrior poet. He charged the mysterious beast, driving it back toward the ravine that surrounded the city. He drove the beast over the cliff's edge, falling in after it." his voice gave out then, choked with emotion. Putting a reassuring hand on his arm, Tahari picked up telling the rest of this story that ended with her mother stealing her away to the Shandel. Tahari had been only a child at the time, but somehow she did remember.

"No one ever asked me about my past, for they really did not care, and with the passing of the years, I, too, forgot these events. I had forgotten who I really was," Tahari explained as she relived her entire past as if it had happened yesterday. Leondros's and Sala's expressions had fallen as she told her story. Except this was not where her story ended. "But I remember now," she said hopefully as she looked over at Leondros. He caught her look of hope and smiled. It was his presence that stirred the elfin part in Tahari to life again.

"Well, one thing that is certain. Adalai has been watching over the both of you—and for good reason," Sala said, hinting at something. "Just before he died, my master told me that one day there would be an intense search for the one who started our order.

"You speak of Farro," Leondros said. Sala slowly nodded his head. "He died so long ago—is it possible that he can return?" As the brilliant sunlight shone down on the aged prophet, he smiled, and his blue eyes glistened with excitement.

"The powers that exist within the sphinxes are great and beyond our understanding, but what I was told was that in the Age of the Phoenix, I would see a strong friendship between a sphinx and an elf once again. This friendship would be the key to finding Farro. After so long, I did not think that I would ever see it, but today I have witnessed it with my own eyes." pausing, Sala looked around cautiously and then pulled a very old and aged scroll from a deep pocket of his dark robe. "This is a letter from Farro himself." Leondros and Tahari froze in awe, staring at Sala and the aged scroll.

Chapter 44

Farro's Origin

Sala opened the scroll carefully and began to read.

Abril 27, 8021
Age of the Set

    This will be my last word to you, my dear brothers of the Osarian Order. Although my race is strong and wise, we are few now. The price of man's greed has been paid for in our blood. As I write these few memoirs, I am being held within a prison camp along with the last remnants of my people. Every day they torture us in hopes that one of us will give them what they want. Each day one more of us greets death with open arms. We cannot give them what they ask, for it would be as giving up a part of one's own soul.
    In spite of the tragedy all around me, I am writing this to offer you hope. I have foreseen that in an age far from now, Andora will once again see the rise of the evil agent called Lord Jarden. He is but a messenger for his people and will not stop until he has enslaved Andora and turned her beauty into ash and fire. If there is one promise I can make to you and all who call this realm home,

he will not see his people again to deliver you to them.

I have been chosen by those who passed on before me to fight for this world. I will protect you all as long as there is breath within me. Yet I know that my body will die soon. For this reason, I have chosen you to follow in my stead and to watch over this land and her people after I am gone. The hope of which I speak will come with my return.

Upon accepting guardianship of this world, I was told of the great power that accompanies my race. Many of these properties are found only after death. I am bound by my word to keep these things sacred. My return is certain, for I cannot allow those whom I love to suffer and die.

I hear them coming for us now. They believe that we are weak, but they see only flesh. We are more...

As Sala read the words of the legendary sphinx from the ancient world, Leondros and Tahari were silent and captivated. He then pulled out a smaller note that also had yellowed with age and had been tucked inside the scroll.

Abril 28, 8021

Dearest all,

This day will never be forgotten. Our founder and teacher, Farro, has perished, along with the last remaining people of the sphinx race. In spite of all our efforts to save them, we were too late, except for one. Farro was able to conceal a woman by the name of Anyi. She was pushed into my arms, just before Farro was taken and executed before our eyes. I am told that in the ages to come, she will bear a child and that child will save a multitude. I am also told that Farro will return to save the people of Andora.

Take Farro's words to heart. It is said that in a time to come, there will be a bond of friendship between a sphinx of the ancient world and an elf the Adarahian realm. These two warriors will find Farro, and these warriors will lead the final war against Lord Jarden. Take care, my brothers, and believe!

Sariff the Wise

Sala carefully tucked the scroll away again and looked at them with anticipation. "Finding this scroll and seeing you two meet are signs that we must be fervent in our search for Farro. His time is close." as Sala's blue eyes sparkled with excitement and growing anticipation, he looked to Leondros and Tahari eagerly. Tahari felt excitement for the mission that lay ahead, but as much as Sala talked about the mission, his Order, and Farro, she still did not know the full history.

"May I ask a basic question?" Tahari asked, thinking how to word the question without feeling foolish. Sala smiled, nodded, and awaited her question.

"Who was Farro?" she asked, eager to know about this warrior that lived so long ago and began an Order to protect the people of Andora. Sala's smile faded.

"Forgive me for my thoughtlessness." he lowered his head to think. Looking up, he said, "In our training to be Osarian Knights, we learn of Farro and his teachings over forty days. It is a slow process to better absorb what is being taught. It is not something we expect to teach in a day. Hosea himself did not learn the full extent of his knowledge until long after Rafar and Sariff were dead," Sala explained, slowly walking back and forth over the soft grass, an index finger to his lips. He remained silent for a long moment. Then he smiled, but there were tears in his eyes. He lifted his head to the sky, and his whole body straightened. Taking a deep breath and slowly sinking to his knees, Sala finally looked upon Tahari and Leondros with an expression of reverence and pride. "Farro of Aiden was a simple farmer who came to Andora and dwelt within the kingdom of Lani around the end of the first age. As far as where and when Farro was actually born our history is a little vague." Sala began slowly as if combing through his memory of this story. "Although the sphinx kingdom had fallen upon difficult times, Farro remained steadfast in his love for his family, found peace with his neighbors, and worked very hard to farm his land. He was also a teacher; of the entire sphinx race that dwelt within the kingdom of Lani, he was the only one who remembered the ways of the old kingdom. Many of the old scholars, who had taught these valuable lessons, had passed away since the first sphinx pioneers had come to these shores during the first age." this intriguing concept aroused Tahari's curiosity.

"Where did the first sphinxes come from?" she asked eagerly.

"The first sphinxes came to Andora from far across the Great Ocean, from the island realm of Far World. They brought advanced knowledge of nature, architecture, and literature to the people of Andora. They also brought the love of Adalai with them, to whom they prayed. However, they did not force any of their ways upon their neighbors. The sphinxes were creatures of immense love and compassion, and they lit up the lives of the people who knew them. Peace and laughter soon filled the air where there had been an everyday world of work and toil," he explained with delight.

"You said that Lani had fallen upon difficult times," Leondros said. Sala's expression went blank and then filled with great sadness. The old prophet lowered his gaze sadly.

"Sala?" Leondros asked with concern as he saw the disheartened look in his dear old friend's eyes. Sala looked up at them again.

"I am sorry," he apologized as he shook his head. "It is said that the sphinxes were a race of immense love and compassion, a race that we could look to for guidance and understanding, but not all of them were and not always," he reported sadly as he shook his head.

"What happened?" Tahari asked, feeling a sour pit grow in her stomach.

"Around 2015, some of the younger sphinx generations began to tire of the teachings from Far World. The magic that dwelt within their race had never been seen, so they found it impossible to believe that it could ever exist. They rebelled against their teachers, overturned the educational system, forgot their beliefs, and put aside their traditions. They even killed the high elders who ruled over Lani. Their actions caused the sphinx empire within Andora to fall. Driven by this new-found freedom, the younger sphinxes encouraged others to follow them and promote this new life. They preached that the old sphinx regime was based only on controlling others and hoarding the great power that they had been given. They did not understand that without balance in society, life would be an upheaval. Still, the great majority broke with their beliefs for the freedom that these sphinx radicals promised." in Sala's words, Tahari could see the beautiful realm of Lani overturned in hellish moments of fire and chaos and consumed by treachery.

"What became of the radicals who overthrew the sphinx empire?" Leondros asked with concern.

"They became consumed by all the dark parts of life: arrogance, selfishness, vengeance, and intolerance. They committed terrible acts, acts forbidden by the old ways. They left behind everything that made them sphinxes. They were on the verge of becoming what were becoming known as dark sphinxes. If left unchecked, they would have become a plague to the known world," Sala explained half-heartedly. Tahari noticed out of the corner of her eye Leondros's face filling with horrible realization.

"It was said that when they left their beliefs behind, they were stripped of their power to protect their kingdom and the rest of Andora," Leondros offered. Sala nodded in agreement. Tahari looked at the elfin prince with uncertainty. Leondros explained. "Since coming to Andora, the sphinxes had built a strong alliance with the other kingdoms. They had agreed to help the other peoples keep the whole of Andora safe from outside evils who would try to overrun the land. The new life that was adopted by the sphinxes put the whole realm in jeopardy.

"Such a reckless decision would mean war with the other kingdoms, plus leaving Andora vulnerable to outside attack," she rationalized.

"You are more right than you know," Leondros replied.

"In 2021, Andora fell prey to just such an attack," said Sala, picking up the tale again. "In the far reaches of the world, there lies an island realm called Nod. Our order has heard only cryptic tales from the sphinx elders who dared to speak of what they had seen in their travels. They spoke of islands teaming with corpses ash, slavery, brutality, and death. Evil dwelt here. As bad as our world had become with the sphinx race turning their kingdom into chaos, it paled in comparison to what dwelt within that hellish island nation.

"This is where Lord Jarden came from, then?" Tahari asked with dread, for she saw an expression of certainty on Leondros's face. Sala nodded slowly.

"Lord Jarden was sent to seek out and overthrow other realms for his king and people. He came with a legion of his finest soldiers. They were heavily armed men who, although physically dead, moved as fluidly and easily as anyone of the living realm. And although their armor was heavy and cumbersome, slowing them down, they made up for their lack of speed with their stealth. They could strike down any target without any sound and be gone like a breath of wind. This legion of dead warriors was able to break down what defenses Andora had left and were able to gain a solid foothold. The only things able to stop them were the enchanted blades of the sphinx people, but since they had left the old ways, they had decided that if there were no weapons within the lands of Andora, no one would bring harm to them or each other. So they had destroyed all of their weapons. They were not missed until the sphinx people were defenseless.

"The dark lord's revolution was short. It took him only eight months to overcome the whole of Andora. No one kingdom was powerful enough to stand against him and no one would stand together, so his reign lasted a thousand years. Thus began the Age of Decimation," the old prophet said, sighing sadly. "Nothing changed until 3012, when a brave messenger finally managed to escape from Andora's dismal shores and brought word of this atrocity to Far World and the rest of the sphinx empire. The sphinx king was outraged and called upon ten warrior-prophets to go forth and reeducate the sphinx people of Andora. Those ten warriors were also generals in the king's army. Their skills and knowledge would be vital in raising armies within Andora in order to put down the dark lord's regime.

"These sphinx warriors were not only skilled in battle; they also possessed control over different elements in life. One such warrior,

Berecynthia, held the balance between good and evil. In addition to the general mission, the king gave her a most important second one: 'Look for the one who still holds true to the beliefs of old, for they are of my own bloodline and possess all the power of my family; protect them, to whatever end.' The king went on to tell her how this person would help her complete the rest of her special mission. Then, before she left on the mission, he said one thing more: 'If one has the heart to fight for their country, how much stronger is the warrior who fights for the one he loves?'"

As Sala explained the exciting events that gripped Andora, his words shed light on the first ages of the sphinxes, who struggled to save Andora and her people from Lord Jarden's wrath.

"How could the sphinx king be sure that his descendant would remain steadfast to the traditions of the old world when almost every sphinx within Lani had freely accepted the new life?" Leondros asked.

"There was a special magic that dwelt within the sphinx king's family. It not only made them stronger, wiser, and keener to their surroundings, but it also made them honorable people. They were loving and compassionate to all. Such traits ran strong in his family and would surely show up in his descendant." as Sala answered, the warmth in his voice could not be missed.

"It was Farro the king spoke of, was it not?" Tahari guessed as she looked to Sala to find the answer in his face. He did not give up the name, but his face brightened in response.

"In 3018, after sailing through much adversity caused by the off shore defenses set up by Lord Jarden to keep Andora under his control, the ten sphinx generals finally reached Andora's shores with their massive armies and took back the realm of Lani and established a new sphinx empire upon Andora's soil. Shortly thereafter, they joined with elfin people to free the kingdom of Adarah from the oppression of the dark lord. Under the guidance of their generals and their new-found vigilance to save all who dwelt within Andora from Lord Jarden's grasp, the remaining good sphinx people rose up against those sphinxes that had overturned their empire and banished the good laws of their people. After more than two years of intense battling, the sphinx generals had nearly overrun all of Lord Jarden's strongholds scattered throughout Andora. The loyal soldiers who kept the strongholds held sway with the dark lord's strict rule, and it took great skill and cunning to bring them down. However, the last stronghold could not be taken down as easily. It was a fortified castle within the Shandel, a fortress like no other." as Sala spoke, Leondros slowly nodded in understanding.

"The fortress of Grimlock." Leondros's voice was a whisper of dread as if he recalled a terrible memory. "It was one of the largest and most impenetrable fortresses within the Shandel. I have heard of it only from my uncle's teachings, but Grimlock's history is a very bloody one. Many souls died within its walls and many more died trying to save those on the inside.

"After Lord Jarden's defeat in 3021," Sala continued, "the king of the Shandel had Grimlock torn down; its presence only marred the green lands of the Shandel. It was located in Akendron, where Castle Avdima now stands." as he revealed this startling piece of history, Leondros and Tahari looked to the east toward Akendron and Castle Avdima. The vast expanse of the castle, its temples, walking paths, and grounds could easily be its own city.

"It is no wonder why certain pieces of history are buried," Leondros uttered softly as he cringed. Sala nodded in agreement and then continued his story.

"After much planning with the other kingdoms, the sphinx generals summoned all the people within Lani to prepare for battle. Farmer or soldier, royalty or peasant, it did not matter—all would be needed in this battle. In this campaign, they would be considered equals. Since landing upon Andora's shores, this massive army and its generals had been smiled upon by fortune, but during their march to the Shandel, fortune looked away. While the army took rest within the Serrigen, all of the sphinx generals but Berecynthia were slain by a secret group of Lord Jarden's elite soldiers. It was amidst this sudden attack, however, that a brave soul stopped the elite soldiers from slaying Berecynthia herself. Amazed by this mere farmer's skill in battle, Berecynthia asked for his name. 'Farro of Aiden,' the farmer replied humbly. Sensing something very special about this warrior, she asked him, 'If I would not have been one of the ten generals, but a mere page in this army, would you still have come to my aid?' Farro replied simply, 'It would have mattered not; my actions would have been the same.' This answer pleased Berecynthia, and she made Farro her personal bodyguard." in hearing these words from Sala's lips, the history of Berecynthia and Farro became as close as a recent memory for Tahari.

"How did she carry on after losing those who had been with her for hundreds if not thousands of years?" Leondros asked with a pained expression.

"Grief for her comrades was felt soul-deep, and their loss could be seen in the eyes of the men and women who made up the army. Berecynthia, however, refused to let this army falter. With great determination, she rose up and encouraged the others to continue on. 'I have not traveled so far or lost so much to give up now. If we quit now, this will be our future. We can do better!' she shouted to the multitude that stood before her as she pointed to their surroundings. The crowd looked to the barren, mountainous wastelands and to the graves of the fallen generals before them. 'I tell you this: I come from a beautiful green island nation where there is peace, prosperity, and plenty for those who dwell there. In our land, we may not always agree, but we still treat each other with respect and decency. I want that for you here, but you have to want it. DO YOU WANT IT?' She asked this last question repeatedly to the crowd before her and each time the crowd cheered, 'YES!'

"In those moments as the sun shone down upon her dark-red hair, lit up her green eyes, and dazzled upon her black and silver armor, Berecynthia looked upon the people before her with determined anger. She lingered only for a moment before she started marching toward Grimlock. And the crowd, with raised hopes for a brighter future and a home that would be theirs again, were rallied to follow her. They marched into battle without fear. When they reached the Shandel, they prepared diligently for what was to come. Their attack on Grimlock would be made on several fronts. The sphinxes used their control over nature's elements to subdue many of the dark lord's finest soldiers that hid in the surrounding countryside; the elves marched to face Grimlock's ground troops head on in battle using both sword and arrow; and the dwarves, who had by now joined the cause, led an attack through the tunnels that had been used to smuggle in new soldiers for Lord Jarden's regime. All the while, Berecynthia proceeded on with the secret mission that the sphinx king had entrusted her with. She was to take on Lord Jarden himself," as Sala continued this story, Tahari and Leondros eagerly awaited the ending.

Chapter 45

Berecynthia's Sacrifice

Sala continued the story of Berecynthia's battle with Lord Jarden that took place on Seprice 10, 3021:

I n the eerie, silent moments before the siege upon Grimlock began, Berecynthia and the Andoran army were hidden deep within the surrounding Divervandon Forest. They had already moved in and silently taken out the assassins that were entrenched within the surrounding brush and trees; they now waited for the sign from four scouts who had volunteered to sneak into Grimlock and take out the guards who watched over the fortress's seven gates.

As the army waited in silence, Berecynthia donned her armor for this last battle. As with all sphinx warriors, Berecynthia's armor consisted of a sheer black tunic, a black chain-linked suit, cloth boots to keep her steps quiet, and silver and black armor that covered her torso and arms. Her overall appearance was fearfully beautiful. As the sphinx warrior pulled her long red hair into a braid, she took a moment to give some last instructions to her loyal bodyguard.

"When the battle begins," she said in a hushed voice to Farro, "do not look for me. Go with the army and join the fight." The instructions struck Farro as odd.

"Why do you send me away from my assigned duty? The duty you gave me yourself," Farro asked with uncertainty, studying her face.

"This is something that I, alone, have been assigned to do for my king; I dare not bring you into it. You *must* follow my instruction," she told Farro firmly. He would have refused, but something in her dazzling green eyes made him agree with her wish. He nodded hesitantly in understanding.

"It will be as you wish. I will be but a moment away when you need me," he replied. Berecynthia smiled thankfully. Before she could say anything more, someone yelled over to them.

"There! Look! The signal!" The men and women of the army looked to Berecynthia for her next order.

"May Adalai grant us victory this day! Whatever may happen, we ride doing Adalai's will!!" she called out and then lowered her helmet's silver face shield and led her army into battle. Her black and silver armor glimmered in the torchlight, adding to the command of her presence. The Andoran army charged out of the thick Divervandon Forest, spreading out across the plains that surrounded Grimlock. Quickly, they bore down upon the fortress of brick and stone. In a matter of moments they stormed through Grimlock's seven large gates and brought the war against Lord Jarden to his front door.

The first moments of the battle were chaotic and Farro fought to stay with Berecynthia. It wasn't long before the Andoran army had overrun the elite soldiers of Lord Jarden's dwindling army. In the last moments before victory was declared, Farro glimpsed Berecynthia in the warring mass of soldiers. They made eye contact and nodded, for they knew the battle was won. A second later, a spear pierced Berecynthia through the chest of her armor. Farro could only watch in horror as the sphinx general fell to the ground. Jumping over bodies and pushing through the crowd, Farro managed to reach Berecynthia and quickly pulled her helmet off. When he looked upon her face, however, it was not Berecynthia he saw but her second-in-command! The woman who died in his arms did so honoring her people and her general.

"What is your *true* mission, my lady?" he asked himself as he held the dead commander and lifted his gaze to the highest tower of Grimlock.

After switching armor with her second-in-command, Berecynthia had disappeared into the warring mass of Andoran warriors and elite soldiers. She moved freely through the crowd, dressed now in just her tunic, making her way to a secret doorway. Berecynthia combed Grimlock until she finally located Lord Jarden in a tower chamber which overlooked the main battle. He stood near a window, his red-cloaked form intently watching the battle below. He was attended by one armed bodyguard, who stood nearby. The gray metal spikes that covered the guard's armor and helmet added to his ferocity. Seeing her, the guard raised his large sword and rushed at her. Berecynthia used her power to blow the guard out a nearby window. Lord Jarden remained unmoving at the window. Only when she raised her hands to repeat the task did he calmly speak.

"Do you really think that your people have the power to stop us forever?" He turned to face her, his red gaze searing out from under his dark hood. Although concealed in the shadow of his hood, Lord Jarden's true appearance was ghastly. He seemed to have been human at one time, but now the flesh that hung from his face was decomposing and falling off.

"You know nothing of our power!" she scoffed angrily and readied herself for the fight ahead. Lord Jarden merely laughed.

"You call having control over rocks and twigs power?" he teased.

Berecynthia was taken aback by Lord Jarden's ignorance of her race, but she knew she could use this to her advantage. Refusing to give in to anger she said, "Not just control over the elements but the power to hold the balance between good and evil," she said evenly.

"Impressive, truly," Lord Jarden sneered.

"We possess the power to summon all legions to rise up against you with a mere whisper," she said, still hoping to shake her opponent.

"That one could hurt and combined... I dread the thought." He sounded worried now, almost fearful. He lowered his concerned gaze to the floor, but after a moment, his searing gaze returned to her.

Instead of worry and fear, there was laughter in his eyes. "I admire your effort, really," he said sarcastically as he chuckled and shook his head. Judging from his lack of concern, Berecynthia knew that these properties would impact him greatly, but they would not destroy him completely.

"What do you fear, then?" Berecynthia pressed as she continued to eye him cautiously. Lord Jarden studied her and then spoke to her in a calm and serious tone.

"That which *you* do not possess. You fight because you are ordered to. I would fear someone who dives into the fray to fight for something much greater than themselves, someone who is driven to die but is empowered to live." Lord Jarden had finally given her something she could use.

"You speak of love. Well, today you have met such an opponent!" she declared, and she raised her hands for the battle ahead. Lord Jarden's eyes doubted her.

"As you wish." He shrugged and prepared for her assault. She shot a blast of white energy at him and quickly pulled out her sword and attacked. Dodging the blast, Lord Jarden had just enough time to draw his own sword and block her advance.

They were almost evenly matched. Lord Jarden cast a bolt of black energy at the sphinx general, who lay on the ground. Acting quickly, she pulled a mirror from her pocket and held it in front of her. The mirror sent the black energy bolt back at a very surprised Lord Jarden. His mouth opened in alarm, but he was hit by his own ball of energy before he could utter a cry. The hit drove him to the ground. Seizing her chance, Berecynthia scrambled to her feet, grabbed his sword, and slammed her foot down upon his chest. Raising the sword over her head, she was not going to give this demon any time for any last words.

"NO!" a new voice cried out, and a second later, Berecynthia felt the stabbing pain of something sharp rip through her left side. Staggering away, she turned to see the bodyguard she had shot from the window. Gone was his helmet, which had successfully hidden a hideous face, flesh well advanced in decay. He had pulled his burnt body back through the window of the chamber and thrown his dagger. It had hit its mark but did not have the result he had hoped for. Adrenaline coursed through Berecynthia's veins as she retrieved the sword and sliced off the bodyguard's head. The excruciating pain of the wound finally overwhelmed her and drove her to the ground, her chance to stop Lord Jarden slipping from her grasp for good.

Looking over at Lord Jarden, Berecynthia felt her strength failing. She watched in horror as Lord Jarden easily picked himself off the ground and brushed himself off. As he looked down at her, he casually approached. His hood had been knocked back, and Berecynthia could see a pleased expression grow upon his rotting face. Slowly leaning over, he grabbed her head with a violent jerk as if he intended to snap her neck, but he hesitated.

"I leave you with this knowledge," he whispered. "You were right, I fear the properties of which you spoke, but as I said before, you lack the *one* that would mean my death." He watched for the realization to hit her.

"Not love itself, but someone in love," she trembled in a pained whisper. He cocked his head and smiled sarcastically. Berecynthia realized that for all her power, she did not possess this quality. The one who must battle Lord Jarden and finish him was someone else, someone in love.

"Precisely!" he hissed. Then he tightened his grip to finish her. As he did, Berecynthia saw clearly a way to stop Lord Jarden.

As she thought of the many sphinxes who had the power to contend with Lord Jarden, herself included, Berecynthia recalled the sphinx king's words: "Look for the one who still holds true to the beliefs of old, for they are of my own bloodline and possess all the power of my family; protect them to whatever end." She now knew who this message was intended for and understood the plan the king had conceived. A blending of several sphinxes' power would finish Lord Jarden, but it would have to be the right blend. There was one last thing that she could do.

"You want to challenge that which you fear?" she piped up with a hoarse whisper. Lord Jarden stopped and looked at her a little dumbstruck by the strength that now emanated from her face.

"That is what I have asked for, to prove that love can be extinguished once and for all, but there is not one amongst your race that is so strong," he replied smugly, but he seemed unsettled by her question.

"If it is a challenge that you want, you shall have it!" she declared in a raspy hiss as she ripped her head free of his grasp, drove her fist into his chest, and expelled her white energy.

"No... it cannot be!" he gasped in horror as his joints began stiffening. "NOOOOO!" he yelled, his voice echoing through the corridors of Grimlock. Berecynthia watched as Lord Jarden's rotting corpse stiffened and transformed into a small, dark crystal. The power used to encase the dark lord knocked the sphinx general backward, but the deed had been done.

"This may not be the end of you," she said weakly as she pulled herself back to her feet and walked over to the dark crystal, which now cast a purple light within the dim chamber. "But one will come to finish what has been started here today. This I swear: you will never return to your home again," Berecynthia rasped as she fought the agonizing pain that burned in her side. Then, with the last of her immense power, she cast the dark crystal prison that contained Lord Jarden into the air and sent him to a distant island near Adarah's southern coast. She had a vision of the cataclysmic effect the crystal had upon the island. The small landmass split into two halves: one remained green and lush, while the other became cold and icy. Lord Jarden was contained, but he would find a way to return. As the vision ended, Berecynthia hung her head sadly and asked Adalai for forgiveness.

Hours later, Farro still searched throughout Grimlock and its surrounding grounds for Berecynthia. He was in a state of alarm. It had been the first time that someone had entrusted him with a special task, and now he felt that he had failed miserably. After many agonizing hours of Berecynthia's absence, Farro finally caught a glimpse of her as she weakly made her way through the crowd toward him. Concern and relief battled inside of him as Farro watched Berecynthia as she took hold of a wall to keep herself from falling.

"My lady!" he called out to her as he hurried to her side. Berecynthia looked up and offered a weary smile, but her expression quickly changed to alarm.

"Farro, DROP!" she screamed as she pointed to something behind him. Automatically Farro fell to the ground. A lone soldier of Lord Jarden's army, covered in a hooded gray cloak, swung a sword where Farro had been standing a split second before. Suddenly the man was gasping for air as a dagger lodged into his throat. As the cloaked soldier fell to the ground with a look of both surprise and horror on his almost-fleshless face, Farro watched the strange creature until his body turned to ash and blew away, leaving only his clothing behind. Turning back to the brave sphinx general, Farro was humbled by her indomitable spirit and quick reflexes. Seeing the soldier fall dead to the ground, Berecynthia was overcome with great relief. As she took a breath, her strength gave out; she slowly leaned against the stone wall behind her and weakly sank to the ground.

"My lady!" Farro gasped as he scrambled over to her in alarm. On her dark suit, he spotted the darker splotch spreading across her left side. He lifted her shirt and saw the wound that was claiming her life. Looking up at her, Farro saw not concern but relief and joy.

"I have nearly fulfilled my purpose," she whispered softly, her eyelids growing heavy.

"I thought I was supposed to protect you?" Farro asked as he looked at her in disbelief.

"No… I did not choose you to defend me; I was chosen to defend *you*," she said with a warm smile. "The sphinx king sent me to find his descendant. The night you saved my life I realized that you are of the king's bloodline." Farro was speechless. "The king had a plan to stop the evil of Lord Jarden once and for all. I thought it was me, but I was only meant to contain him until the time was right for the chosen one to vanquish him for all time," she said sadly.

"Then who does this task fall to?" Farro wondered with deep concern. He then saw the look of pride and reverence in Berecynthia's eyes. "This task falls to me?" Farro shook his head. "I am only a farmer." Berecynthia smiled and put a reassuring hand on Farro's shoulder.

"There *is* greatness within you…Farro of Aiden," she said. Her words became fainter as Berecynthia's life seeped from her body. "The power of the king's family is within you as is something else.

"How do you know what power I have?" Farro asked as he looked at her strangely.

"My power," Berecynthia said weakly. "Along with the power to govern the balance between good and evil and a few other things, I can see into a sphinx and see their power." Her words were a whisper now, but Farro heard them perfectly. "The sphinx king wanted to blend the powers of several sphinxes to create the one sphinx who could bring down Lord Jarden and the evil he brought with him. He knew that someone of his bloodline would not be corrupted by this immense power." She took a labored breath and then gave him his mission. "You will go forward and tell a select few what has happened here. You will empower them to stop any evil that lurks upon these lands. These lessons must not be forgotten. There will come a day when our kinsmen will be hunted down. Search out and find a woman named Anyi—protect her, even if it means your own death. Protect her!" she commanded in a firm whisper. Farro nodded in obedience to all the things that were asked of him but was overwhelmed with uncertainty. Berecynthia smiled. "Worry not; the spirits of old will guide you as will I. Let love and compassion govern your actions, and you will have no regrets.

"I will do as you command. I will trade my life for what needs to be done." Farro accepted his new fate wholeheartedly, but there was something within his voice that caught Berecynthia's attention. It was the slightest tone of disappointment. A realization of something truly special that had just passed him by: the chance to meet the love of his life. The beautiful sphinx general smiled weakly as if she had foreseen something in the far distant future.

"You will not walk this world alone forever; one day you will meet the love of your life. That love will be the focal point of your mission. Believe in that, and then you will experience the fullness of your power." Farro smiled contentedly but did not reply. "Now you must take my power and continue on." Berecynthia spoke in a faint whisper as she fought to cling to life for a moment longer.

"I cannot take your power; I do not know how," Farro replied with worry as he watched her fade before his eyes.

"If they choose to, a sphinx can pass on their power through reincarnation or at death." Berecynthia looked at Farro with sadness for she knew the burden that lay ahead of him. "I am so sorry. You must bear this burden now, but you will make us proud." Then she pulled off her black glove and placed her delicate hand on his chest. Instantly, Farro was knocked backward several feet as a bolt of white energy surged into his body—the power to balance good and evil, along with Berecynthia's other talents. When Farro regained his senses, the brave woman was dead. As he looked upon her lifeless form in a state of shock, the midmorning sun slowly broke through the thick clouds that drifted along the horizon. A single ray of sunlight washed over Berecynthia's lifeless form. Farro felt the power of the words that she had spoken, and he was determined to live them until his last breath. The elves, sphinxes, and dwarves who had witnessed this great happening began kneeling on the ground before Berecynthia and Farro.

Pulling himself to his feet and returning to Berecynthia's side, Farro said simply, "I promise." Kneeling before her and bowing his head, he pledged in his heart to do everything that was asked of him. When he rose to his feet and turned to those bowed before him, Farro began the quest that founded the Order of Osarian Knights, which would keep the knowledge learned alive and safe.

Chapter 46

The Beginning of a Quest

"Thus began the Age of Affirmation," Leondros recalled from his teachings after Sala had finished the story of Berecynthia, Farro, and the victory over the First Age of Darkness.

"Farro's love for his people and Andora must have been immense," Tahari said as she tried to comprehend such love.

"It was said that it was this love that drove Farro to fight even harder to keep his family, friends, and people safe. So much so that in 8021, Farro gave up his life for this cause and joined the rest of the sphinx race as they walked beyond the borders of this life," Sala added sadly. He gazed past them at the hanging gardens. "It was here that the brothers of the order first called themselves Osarian Knights," Sala added with a small smile that was belied by the tears in his blue eyes. This reminded Tahari of something he had said earlier.

"If the sphinxes of Andora were close to extinction, why did no one send word to the sphinx king in Far World, especially when Lord Jarden managed to return in the Ninth Age?" Tahari inquired. Her hope rose, for she prayed that she was not truly alone. Sadness filled the kind prophet's face, and he shook his head sadly. A soft breeze filled with the scent of rosemary blew past them, causing strands of his shoulder-length brown hair to cover his bearded face as if to conceal his grief.

"Word was sent. Long before Sariff got his message to Rafar the Elder in the kingdom of Nor, two messengers had been sent to Far World. Only one returned some months later with the same message in his hand. The remaining messenger said that he had encountered a huge storm on his way to Far World. His traveling companion had been washed overboard. When the storm passed and he finally reached Far World, nothing remained of the island kingdom. All that was left were barren islands of white sand and a thick fog that hung over the seas without relent. The island kingdom of the sphinxes had vanished." Sala's words hit Tahari hard, and her shoulders sank with disappointment. Now she felt truly alone.

"You said that Farro would return when Lord Jarden returned for a third time—would there be any description of him, so that we could know what he looked like?" Leondros asked hopefully.

"When Hosea took over the Order, he feared that evil would find a way to hunt down this promised being, so he removed all mention of Farro's description. In some cases, he even disguised aged texts that spoke of Farro to further protect his identity," Sala explained as he straightened his back for a moment; he had joined Leondros and Tahari on the soft, cool grass and now stretched his stiff muscles. His reply added another layer to the mystery surrounding Farro.

"Farro could be anybody?" Tahari said, a little overwhelmed.

"A search for such a vague warrior sounds like trying to find a seed in the sands of the Barrens," said Leondros. "There could also very well be other persons who have heard of this myth and will try to say they are the true Farro. How are we to know who is the real Farro? Surely there are some details given to clarify who it is that we are searching for."

"Did not Rafar leave us a few clues to help us in this matter?" Tahari asked thoughtfully as she recalled the leather manuscript in Sala's library. Sala nodded as she said this, for Tahari's memory was correct. "Rafar made mention of the characteristics that describe the inner traits of Farro. He will possess a true heart guided by a strong will and quest for right amidst a sea of wrong. He will have an eye for compassion. Stronger still will be his bonds of truth, friendship, loyalty, and love. We must look beyond the physical means and properties to find Farro, for he will not be what we are expecting.

"Rafar was very careful not to give too much detail about this person, for he, too, wanted to protect Farro," Sala replied. "It was only right that he did. If the ancient evil discovered Farro's identity before we did, Farro would be slain, and then our one hope would be lost and we would be doomed to Lord Jarden's coming world of eternal darkness.

Leondros's dark brown eyes watched them closely as he listened intently. The soft breezes blew through his shoulder-length blond hair, but one could see that he was in deep thought. "All right then, we have the first scroll. How do we go about finding the second?" he asked, looking from Sala to Tahari.

"At the end of the first scroll, there is a clue to where we will find the second," Tahari began as she gestured for Sala to pull out the first scroll of the prophecy. As they reviewed the sacred lines of text, Leondros looked upon the last lines of the prophecy and blanched.

"This foretelling is not for my people or Adarah." His voice was riddled with worry, and Tahari felt driven to help him in some way.

"What may I do to help?" she asked as she looked at Sala earnestly and then back to Leondros. The elfin prince looked at Tahari with surprise. "Adarah had been my home once—I am willing to fight for it, so that I may know what it is like to have a true home again." A smile came to Leondros's face.

"Tahari, you are the sacred messenger that Rafar the Elder spoke of," Sala instructed Tahari with a serious look of caution. "You and you alone are able to translate the scrolls of the ancient prophecy. You must find them and piece together the clues that will lead us to Farro. Remember, we three and Queen Elanza are the only ones who know of these scrolls. That is how it must stay." she saw that something else troubled him.

"There is more, is there not?" she asked. Sala looked upon Tahari and slowly nodded as concern filled his aged face.

"The forces of the dark lord will seek all who are agents of light and hunt them down. Leondros and I will hold back this flood, but

I fear that we may need help," he admitted, an overwhelmed look coming into his blue eyes. Looking at Leondros and then back at Sala, Tahari felt a warm wind blow over the hillside. As it played with her hair, Tahari yearned to do more than just be a prophetic scholar. She sensed that her ancestors were trying to tell her something, but she had already made her decision. Tahari was compelled to join Leondros and Sala in this mission.

"You are right. It would mean death for so few to undertake this," Tahari reasoned as she looked at Leondros and then at Sala. Although she could not find the words to speak of it, Tahari's oath as Leondros's guardian meant she would not let him or Sala fight this war alone. "I will join you both in this fight. I will not let you stand alone to face this coming darkness, and I will not rest until the enemy has been defeated and all are safe," Tahari said determinedly. Leondros and Sala looked at her with pride and encouragement.

"I could choose no other to be the eyes that watch my back in battle," Leondros said with a humble expression on his face as he held out his hand to her.

Taking hold of his outstretched hand, Tahari suddenly realized that this was the next chapter of her life and that this meeting had not been by chance; her ancestors had led her to these new friends so that they could work together to find Farro. More than this, Tahari knew that they would look after one another, for there was great darkness heading in their direction, and if one should fall, another would be there to pick them up again. This was their promise to each other.

Sala's attention was suddenly drawn toward the palace. A man dressed in a dark-brown hooded cloak humbly walked up to the foot of their little hill. Although Tahari could not distinguish his features clearly, she could see urgency upon his face. Sala jumped to his feet and quickly went to the messenger, alarm on his face. She could not hear the conversation between the two men, but seeing the weight of the news that fell upon Sala's strong shoulders caused her concern. Sala slowly nodded and bowed to the messenger before giving him leave to go. As the messenger turned and left, Sala walked back up to where Tahari and Leondros were sitting. The grave expression that had settled into his features and the furrows of grief that now wrinkled his forehead told her something terrible had just occurred. Tahari could not help but sense that our troubles had just started.

"Well, I am afraid our meeting has been brought to a close," Sala began as distress filled his voice and trouble shone on his face. As he spoke, Leondros and Tahari slowly rose to their feet. "Leondros, Prince Alon-Settie sends word from Avdima. You are to return as soon as possible. An attack on the town of Endenbury has been reported, and the people there need the Secret Alliance's immediate attention," Sala said urgently. Leondros's face set with a look of duty. He had a great responsibility to the kingdom of the Shandel, and it could not be denied or put off. It was in that last moment before he left to return to Avdima that Tahari was suddenly filled with the gravest of concerns for him.

"Be careful while I am gone. I sense that there will be much more than mere celebration going on within the kingdom," Leondros cautioned both Sala and Tahari. "When I return, we will discuss more about this secret mission," Leondros promised as he shook Sala's hand. As she watched him about to turn and leave, Tahari remembered reading a line of text that concerned him.

"And you also, my friend," Tahari spoke up with concern as she took a step forward and looked at him in the eye and put a hand on his arm. "I sense danger and deception in this mission. Do be careful and remember what you have read today. I feel that it will help you through what is to come." she tried to clarify what she was really sensing, but there was no real way to explain this feeling that she had deep down. As Tahari looked upon him with worry, she could not decide if it was because she was watching a friend heading into the heart of evil, or if it was because of her secret oath to be his guardian, or if it was because there was something more in Tahari that refused to let him go.

"I will, my friend," Leondros said with an understanding expression as he covered her hand with his. He smiled kindly. "I am honored by your concern. Know that it will go with me when I ride out of Akendron with the Secret Alliance. I thank you." His words gave Tahari comfort as she felt sincerity and promise in his words. Tahari released her gentle grip on his arm and nodded slowly. Then he bowed humbly before taking his leave of them. As Leondros headed down the grassy hill and walked back alone through the gate that led into the surrounding mists of the thick forest and on toward Akendron, Tahari watched him until the thick white mists swallowed up first his armor and then the brown cloak that hung from his shoulders. His form slowly faded in the white mists surrounding Cypress Palace until it vanished completely.

Chapter 47

New Discoveries

"Why such an expression?" Sala asked, his voice breaking through Tahari's thoughts long after Leondros had vanished from sight. The western horizon was filled with the warmest colors of vermillion that Tahari had ever seen as the sun slowly set. Returning to the present, she looked up and saw deep concern in his soulful face as he reached the top of the grassy hill. Tahari hadn't moved since Leondros had left. "Do not worry. We will see Leondros again. He is the finest archer and warrior in the whole of Andora. I believe that he will do some amazing things with this army—you will see," Sala reassured her as he joined Tahari's gaze out over the western horizon. Together they looked upon the small shadows of the temples and palace of Avdima that could be seen beyond the trees of the Misty Forest. The certainty in his features gave her comfort as he put a warm hand on her shoulder.

"Seeing the faith that you have in Leondros," Tahari began softly as her gaze lingered on the distant shadows of the palace, "I, too, believe this with all my heart, but when you sense danger in any friend's path, one cannot help but be concerned."

"Yes, this is true. The powers of darkness are indeed growing, even as we speak. However, what I felt when we sat together and talked was so much more powerful than all of that combined. It was like feeling an awakening within." He shook his head slowly, for he, too, was overwhelmed by the magic that filled the moments of their meeting with Leondros.

"*Awakening* would definitely describe it," Tahari said slowly as she nodded in agreement. "What I felt was very strong indeed, but why?" she asked as she looked over at Sala with wonder.

"You never knew that you were also of the elfin race, did you?" Sala asked as he looked at Tahari in disbelief. Tahari slowly shook her head.

"The pieces of my past slowly faded from memory with every passing day that I took to the fields of the Tomblock. The hardships that plagued us were so burdensome that it was impossible to believe I could have been born someplace so wonderful," Tahari explained with a saddened tone.

"My dear, your elfin half is so much more than those who bound you to such a terrible life. Elves are very intuitive people. Their senses are sharper than those of a mere man, and they possess knowledge and wisdom that no man can know. I do not know how to explain it, but they can sense when one of their kind is close. When you met Leondros, what you felt was that kinship that elves have for each other." As Sala explained with a warm smile, Tahari realized that she had inadvertently used these qualities when she ran toward the Divervandon Forest and the danger that threatened Leondros's life.

"That explains how I knew that he was coming through the Divervandon Forest when I was still in the rock valley," Tahari said aloud to herself, reflecting on the events that had played out earlier in the week. A look of confusion washed over Sala's face. It was clear that he had no idea what she was talking about. "I had a premonition that Leondros would be killed in a surprise attack by a Draccen army that was sent to stop him in the Divervandon Forest. Even though we had never met before this, I was compelled to help him," Tahari said as she remembered the heart-wrenching vision warning her that Leondros was in grave danger. "When I felt Leondros's presence while I was in the rock valley, I left quickly and prevented the vision from being carried out. This was the reason my taskmasters needed to execute me. By leaving to aid Leondros, I forfeited my own life," she admitted as she looked over at Sala. He looked amazed and yet proud. "I felt that my life was passing me by and that I had never really lived it. But by going to aid Leondros, I felt that I could at least truly live those next few moments," Tahari recalled as she found her smile again. Sala was silent. Looking at him, Tahari saw that he still wore a dumbfounded expression.

"My dear…" Sala at last managed. "You truly have lived if you helped Leondros take on an entire Draccen army and forgot about yourself," he said with awe and wonder as a smile slowly spread across his face. Tahari too, smiled at what he said as it reinforced what she had done.

"Two really are so much more than one. Leondros and I ended up taking *out* that entire Draccen army," Tahari slyly corrected him as her smile grew. Sala stared at her with a blank expression. He stood for a moment in silence and thought. When he finally found his voice to speak again, Tahari could not help but chuckle at the answer that managed to come to his lips.

"Adalai grant mercy to our enemies, for their opponents will show them none," he said with a serious tone as he lifted his gaze to the sky. Sala then looked at Tahari with a hopeful smile. In that moment, he realized that she was a lot tougher and stronger than she had let on. A thoughtful expression washed over his face. "Let us go. It is time to prepare for the coming darkness," he said and gestured for her to follow him. As Tahari joined him, Sala turned to her with his own sly grin. "However, perhaps it is the coming darkness that needs to prepare for us.

"Pride goeth before a fall," Tahari said with caution.

Sala nodded in agreement. "I stand corrected once again," he said with sincerity. "We must see what our enemies are capable of and not what we think." With that, they walked into the palace, and Sala eventually led her to a very large training room. The walls were made of warm wood accented by pillars of bamboo. The wide open floor was covered with a soft tan fabric that cushioned each step one took upon it. Sala walked out into the middle of the floor and stopped.

"Sala?" Tahari asked, a little uneasy. His even expression and his stance did not change.

"I feel that I should give you a few pointers before you go off into battle. I do not want to lose you to this evil," Sala said with a sincere tone. "It was here that I received many lessons from Leondros. It was he who taught me to become a fierce warrior in battle." Tahari could not help but feel the immense history that spanned between Leondros and Sala. As she slowly stepped onto the training room's soft mats, Tahari noticed that the room's wooden walls were covered with a wide assortment of weapons. She had never seen so many different styles of swords and daggers before, and these were just some of the weapons that decorated the room's interior. She watched as Sala walked over to the far wall and stopped in front of a long black sword that was resting on wooden pegs protruding from the wall. He put his hands together and bowed humbly, honoring the sword. Tahari guessed that this particular sword had seen him through many battles in the past. Sala stood again to his full height and gently took the black sword from its resting place. "Leondros told me long ago that a warrior may become familiar with all types of weapons, but there will always be one particular weapon that he will attach himself to. The sword or weapon of their choosing becomes the warrior's most powerful ally in battle." He spoke with reverence. Tahari nodded in understanding, but she felt that something should be added to that statement.

"Except for one thing," she said. Sala looked back at her with wonder. "Our friends." He smiled and slowly nodded.

"I thank you, Tahari," he replied in a softened tone. Warmth emanated from his face, and his blue eyes shone with appreciation. "Thank you for saving Leondros's life. He is the closest person that I can call family. Especially now, he seems more like a son that I never had." Sala's voice was filled with such tenderness and thankfulness that tears stung her eyes. He then shook his head as if to clear it and began the training session. They began with swords and moved on to other weapons that would be useful in hand-to-hand combat.

When the session was finally over, Sala was left bruised and sore.

Tahari's skills had more than matched his. She found herself feeling dumbfounded. As they trained, Tahari came to feel as if she had always had these combat skills. Some of these maneuvers Sala had never seen before, he told her. They wondered if Tahari had picked up something from her sphinx linage. After this, Sala had no doubt that she was ready for whatever was to come.

When they left the training room, Tahari noticed the proud look in his blue eyes. It was as if he knew that she was someone who would do more than keep her promise. It was the same look that had been in Leondros's eyes before he had left. Tahari had earned his trust, and now she had earned Sala's as well. Tahari would do what was necessary to keep that trust.

Afterward, she spent several moments in the hanging gardens in the evening's darkness. Tahari sat beneath the tree they had all sat beneath earlier that day. As she breathed in the cool air, Tahari felt like a whole new person. It was a strange feeling, but also a very good feeling. She felt stronger, aware of her surroundings, and aware of the warrior that she was quickly becoming. Sala, too, had noticed this extraordinary change within her. But as impressive as her newfound skills and abilities were, Tahari had to remember that the forces of darkness would use everything in their arsenal against them. They would use them against each other if they had the chance, so they had to stay strong in mind, body, and spirit. Their enemies could not be underestimated.

Tahari looked toward Akendron. She thought about Leondros and wondered where he was and what he was facing at that moment. The ancient evil was taking over Akendron, and her friend was in the midst of it. Leondros was fully capable of taking on any opponent, and she had faith that he would be all right on this night. But Tahari knew she would not find rest until he was safe amongst friends again.

Chapter 48

Watchful Eyes of the General

E ven before his return to Avdima, Leondros knew there was trouble within the Shandel, but as he neared Akendron's outskirts, he could feel that this trouble was far worse than the messenger had let on. Passing through the city streets, Leondros heard a very distinct moan in the air. It was not the cry of wind or some foul beast but of men, women, and children. Villagers wandered everywhere, looking as though they had barely escaped some disaster with their lives. They were scorched, dirty, and wounded. Many had lost loved ones. Leondros's heart sank into his stomach at the sight of the bloodstained streets and villagers. Terror filled the eyes of those who looked back at him. Swallowing hard, Leondros realized just how blessed he actually was. How he survived an attack from an entire Draccen army was still beyond him. If it had not been for Tahari, he would have been seriously wounded or even dead by now.

Searching the masses of soldiers and wounded villagers, Leondros finally found Alon-Settie talking with several soldiers. He walked toward his friend, who was now dressed for battle in his gray armor, marking the terrified expressions in the eyes of the soldiers who had arrived at the same time as the survivors. The harsh reality of what they were getting into was sinking in. Leondros, too, realized the weight of what lay ahead of him. As general of the Secret Alliance, he had to pull these men out of their fears and ready them for what was ahead. When he reached Alon-Settie, the prince wore a slightly overwhelmed expression on his bearded face; his dark eyes looked to Leondros for help as he welcomed him with a relieved expression.

"Draccen soldiers have banded together and are now attacking local towns and villages. The King has dispatched several scouts to these troubled areas. The few who have returned report that the Draccen soldiers have laid siege to the peaceful town of Endenbury," Alon-Settie explained in a slightly panicked rush, gesturing toward the soldiers who were either seeking medical aid or were aiding those who had been wounded in the siege.

"Endenbury?" Leondros said thoughtfully. Somehow, an attack on this quiet village seemed fruitless. There was nothing that made this village a target. "Endenbury lies close to Akendron. If the Draccen soldiers are so close, they could be planning an attack on Akendron herself," he said as he looked at Alon-Settie. The Akendron prince was filled with urgency and great worry as he headed for his brown horse, which had been saddled and readied for the mission ahead. "Alon-Settie...Wait, there is something that we must do first," Leondros insisted as he put a patient hand on his friend's shoulder.

"Leondros, our time is fading fast! We must hurry before the Draccen soldiers execute any more people of the Shandel, or as you just said, before they march on Akendron herself," Alon-Settie pointed out earnestly.

Leondros looked into his friend's dark-brown eyes. "Listen, my friend. We must be patient and talk to our men and help them to find their courage, or we will lose more men to fear than to the Draccen soldiers." But his words did not seem to affect Alon-Settie.

"Leondros, please—there is no time for such talk. The time to ride is now!" he replied with a hasty tone. He was intent on going without wasting time on nonsense. Leondros gazed at his friend with an expression of disappointment and sadness.

"Men of little faith have few encouraging words and even fewer meaningful actions," Leondros said softly and strode past Alon-Settie to the group of soldiers. He stared calmly at the two hundred men before him. The command of his presence silenced the crowd before him and stretched out to the villagers around them. Soon not even a breath of wind could be heard. "What we are about to do might not come easily to you, but let me remind you what you will be fighting for. You will be fighting for your homes, your wives, and your children. You will be fighting to keep your way of life. If you leave here fearing for your lives, you will walk into a losing battle." Leondros's voice echoed off the buildings. In his voice, one could hear a whisper of anger. Chills ran down the spines of all who watched and listened. "Now look at the man next to you. When we ride out, your responsibility is to see that that man returns, and he will do the same. No weapon is greater than the man who watches your back in battle." The general eyed his troops closely. He could see a change already taking place in these men. "Be mindful of your surroundings, for they will tell you much. Listen to everything that goes on around you. Be alert. These things you must always remember, for they will save you and the man standing next to you.

Standing in silence for a moment, Leondros took one last gaze into the eyes of his men before he turned and found that Elijah had come forth from the crowd with Aton. The boy looked up at Leondros with his green eyes shining with sincere admiration. Leondros put a thankful hand upon the boy's shoulder and gave him an encouraging smile of approval. Then Leondros climbed upon Aton's strong back and rode out. In the moments that followed, the thunder of two hundred following their general echoed throughout Akendron. The men had cast aside their fear; they took to their horses and quickly rode out to meet their enemy head on. The soldiers rode for their families and for each other, but not for themselves. Fear did not exist here.

Chapter 49

Mission of Deception

After leaving Akendron, Leondros led the Secret Alliance around the Divervandon Forest on a road that took them out of the way of the main road. He would not risk his men's safety by returning to the place that had nearly claimed his life so recently. Although they passed by the dark forest unnoticed and were making good time to Endenbury, Leondros felt darkness lying in their path. He sensed evil and danger waiting for them. They rode throughout the night and through most of the next day through the valley bordered by forest. With the passing of every mile, Leondros felt increasingly uneasy about their mission. There was something about it that eluded him. When he stopped for a moment to take in his surroundings, his elfin soldiers noticed their general's suspicious expression.

"Do you sense something, my lord?" one of the elfin soldiers asked him, quietly riding up beside him. It was Amon-yen, one of his father's best warriors from the Shoshon's royal army. He was dressed in the same blue and green tunic and lightweight armor that all the elves from Adarah wore. The men from the Shandel were fitted with sheer black tunics with iron-clad armor. Dwarves were also part of the army, dressed in brown tunics and dark chain-linked suits. Each contingent represented their land, but they would fight as a whole.

"Danger lingers close. Do you sense it?" Leondros asked quietly as he suspiciously searched his surroundings.

Amon-yen's dark blue eyes looked at his surroundings. He bore almost the same features as Leondros, but his long hair was light brown and he was a couple thousand years older than Leondros, for he had served in King Doran's army long before the elfin prince was born. Still, the older elfin warrior served Leondros with the same honor and loyalty as his king. "I sense it also, my lord. This land is quiet—too quiet," he replied in a low whisper as he slowly eyed the surrounding trees. "Evil *is* close," he added as he turned back to his general and patiently waited for his next order. Leondros knew for certain that they were being followed. An encounter with the enemy was close at hand.

Alon-Settie rode his horse up to Leondros. He could not help but notice the exhaustion that was in Leondros's face.

"I hate to be the voice of reason, but you have not taken rest since your arrival at the palace. Please, I urge you to…" His voice trailed off. He knew that Leondros was not about to rest. The expression in the elfin general's brown eyes was one of suspicion as he focused on the precarious situation they would soon be facing. This was clearly not a time to rest. "Perhaps not," he said to himself as Leondros continued to study his surroundings. "Well, then, what is our status?" Alon-Settie asked.

"Now is not the best time for conversations," Leondros said after a long moment of silence as he gestured subtly with his head to the gravelly path they had just traveled down. "We are about to have company," he warned Alon-Settie as his steely gaze looked back past his men, along the eerily quiet path and into the thick trees to the left and right of them.

"I take it that it will not be pleasant," Alon-Settie remarked as he followed his elfin friend's gaze into the thick trees. Leondros did not reply, for the silence of the forest that surrounded them spoke for him. There were no chirping birds, no buzzing insects, not even fidgeting squirrels dashing from one branch to another. All sound had died. Still, none of these things gave the prince of Akendron reason to worry. The reason was made clear in Leondros's stone-like facial expression as a strange crackling sound filtered through the stiff air around them. As all color drained from Leondros's face, Alon-Settie finally realized that danger was indeed coming to meet them.

"Move into the trees. Get the men out of sight. The enemy is almost upon us," Leondros whispered to Amon-yen, who awaited his next command. His gaze did not leave the path they had just traveled down. Amon-yen nodded and was off to pass the word along. Alon-Settie watched as a signal was silently made and passed along to all men within the army, who silently stepped into the surrounding trees and bushes. In seconds, the Secret Alliance had vanished from sight.

Gesturing to his faithful steed, Leondros motioned for Aton to hide himself in the thick foliage that shielded the road side from all view. Before retreating behind a nearby oak tree, Leondros had lingered a moment to ensure that all his men had safely taken cover. He could hear no approaching footsteps, but he sensed the dark presence approaching them. Soon, he could hear barely audible footsteps that became louder and unmistakable until they were like thunder from an approaching thunderstorm. As he looked through the trees, Leondros glimpsed Alon-Settie. The Akendron prince seemed greatly angered by something. Draccen soldiers emerged onto the path they had just left. The elfin prince watched as these reptilian soldiers charged down the path toward the Secret Alliance's former position. Moment by moment, the elfin general watched in dismay as over one hundred Draccen soldiers charged down the gravelly path and more of these beastly soldiers following behind them. The army was nearly five hundred strong, and they were on the path that would take them to Endenbury.

They must be reinforcements for the Draccen army that attacked Endenbury, Leondros thought, but still something about this mission bothered him. He continued to watch the Draccen army as they came closer to where his men were hiding. Quickly and quietly, he readied his bow and fitted an arrow. His men were quick to follow suit and began searching for their targets. The moment of opportunity came when Leondros saw the Draccen army marching right past his men. Drawing his bow taut, Leondros aimed and fired the first shot, which started a rain of arrows on the Draccen army. Many unsuspecting Draccen soldiers fell before their comrades' dismayed eyes. The sudden attack left them momentarily paralyzed, thus giving the Secret Alliance time to cut down the majority of the five hundred soldiers. Only a fourth of the Draccen soldiers were quick enough make it passed the intense fire. Leondros watched as doomed soldiers returned fire so that their companions could break for Endenbury. Their determination made Leondros wonder what was so important about getting to the already ransacked village. He silently issued the order to cease fire upon the Draccen army. The rain of arrows stopped and the Draccen soldiers who escaped the assault ran without hesitation toward the village.

Watching the Draccen soldiers run off into the distance, Leondros thought hard about their actions. His men grew impatient for action. Gesson, a black-haired dwarf from Eden-Glee, came to his general with this concern.

"My lord, why do we linger here? The enemy is all but finished. Give the word, and we will see to it that they harm no other innocent person," Gesson offered with an enthused tone, shifting his eager black eyes between his general and the retreating army of Draccen soldiers. As the Draccen soldiers began to put distance between them and the Secret Alliance, Gesson's portly brown face and stocky features began to reveal his impatience.

"Gesson is right, sire. This Draccen army is weak from our ambush. The time to finish them is now," Amon-yen said as he approached. There was an air of wisdom about his father's most trusted warrior that the elfin prince wanted to trust, but something told him to be slow in his actions. Leondros sat still and continued to watch the Draccen soldiers for a moment longer. He thought about their counsel but shook his head.

"We will not pursue them," Leondros replied in a low and thoughtful tone. "This battle was most unusual..." He turned his steady gaze back to the dust that lingered where the remnants of the Draccen army had passed. This portion of the road was hardly used, for it was a long way around the forest, which was generally safe for passage. This fact alone caused Leondros to wonder if these soldiers had not been actually following them.

"What was so unusual about it?" Gesson piped up impatiently. "We caught those Draccen beasts off-guard, and now all we have to do is finish them!" The dwarf waited for a moment before replacing his sword and throwing his hands up, for he knew from the patient expression of his elfin general that the fight he longed for had passed.

Amon-yen walked up to the dwarf, put a firm hand on Gesson's shoulder, and glared at him. "Do not speak in such a manner to the General. He has lived through many more battles than you, my friend. Be mindful." Amon-yen spoke in a hushed tone as his slightly aged face bore stern warning. Gesson clenched his jaw to contain his anger. He did not utter a word in response, but his silence spoke of anger and impatience.

"Dracs are not surprised so easily. Their senses are as keen and sharp as that of our elfin kinsmen. It is strange that these Draccen soldiers were unaware of us," Leondros spoke slowly, making his way back onto the trail where many of Draccen soldiers lay dead. Leondros knelt down and examined the aftermath of this battle. Amon-yen and Gesson joined their leader, and the rest of the soldiers gathered around them. While he was searching for the real reason these Draccen soldiers were going to Endenbury, Leondros picked up the faint sounds of someone running through the trees toward them. He raised his head, becoming more alert. His sudden reaction caused all who watched him to do the same. It sounded as if they were coming from Endenbury. His men were quick to take up arms and prepare to fight the unsuspecting soldiers coming toward them. Leondros rose to his feet and sensed that this newcomer was no enemy. "Hold your fire!" he commanded as he held his hand out.

Eyes focused and arrows pointed toward the sound that lay just ahead of them. When the source of the sound finally came into view, immense relief washed over all those watched. Their general quickly rushed over to the exhausted soldier of the Secret Alliance, and everyone lowered their bows. Judeas, another of his father's elite elfin warriors, bent over to catch his breath. Judeas's long black hair hung past his face, disheveled from his rush to return from his scouting around Endenbury.

"Leondros, thank Adalai I found you," Judeas gasped. It was clear from this elfin warrior's wounds and the dirt and sweat that covered his slightly tanned face that he had barely escaped Endenbury with his life.

"Judeas, what did you see?" Leondros asked as he looked at his elfin companion with deep concern. The rest of the Secret Alliance gathered around the weary scout to hear the news that he had brought.

"There was a traitor amongst us!" Judeas gasped as he stood to his full height and pointed toward the ransacked village. At the word *traitor*, the men of the Secret Alliance were fueled with rage. "He told them of us and our mission to Endenbury; that is how they knew we would be here. I overheard those Draccen beasts on the way into Endenbury. They are planning to meet up with the traitor once they reach the village," he said. The elfin general turned toward the village. Everything around him told him to take the Secret Alliance into the village, but he ignored the need to stop the traitor and the Draccen army and was compelled to follow Tahari's advice. In response to his inaction, he saw disappointment wash over all who gathered around him and were forced to continue waiting. Leondros felt the weight of this disappointment in his men as he overheard the mutterings of Gesson.

"I tried to tell him. But that elfin pride will always be their greatest downfall." Gesson's words were a mere whisper, but Leondros's keen ears heard them. The criticism was blunt and painful. Leondros tightened his jaw stubbornly. He would refuse to give in to failure, for he knew that there was a darker purpose for the siege upon Endenbury. He sensed that the force of darkness was stirring nearby.

Swiftly taking to a nearby tree, Leondros made his way up to the tree's higher branches. Peering through the canopy of the dense Divervandon Forest, he could make out the village of Endenbury in the distance. He could see that Judeas was right: the Draccen army that had escaped their ambush had indeed made it into the village. Leondros watched in disbelief as an explosion tore through the heart of the Draccen army, leveling everything in its path. Smoke and dust billowed high above the place where the village used to stand. When it cleared, Leondros could see nothing of the village or the Draccen army.

When he climbed back down and turned to his men, they looked at him with alarm. They had heard the intense explosion and were unaware of what had taken place.

"My lord, what has happened?" Amon-yen asked as he walked up to his general. His dark-blue eyes were wide with shock and fear.

Leondros looked at his men and thanked his blessings for their safety. "The Draccen army has been destroyed in the explosion that you heard," he said in an even tone, studying the expressions of his men. Looks of shock and horror filled their eyes.

"We are blessed, for that would have been us if we would have listened to our dwarven brother," Amon-yen commented, glancing coldly at Gesson. The dwarf lowered his saddened gaze with regret. In his shame, he managed to look at Leondros with an expression of apology and shame. In a gesture of forgiveness, Leondros put a hand on the dwarf's strong shoulder.

"Those Draccen beasts set a trap for us," Gesson said in a gruff tone. "What of the people still in Endenbury?" he asked with genuine concern. Leondros shook his head slowly.

"They are in Adalai's hands now," Leondros explained sadly as he lowered his head to pray for the poor souls lost in Endenbury. Then Leondros had an unsettling thought. *Those Dracs had a higher purpose for us, but then so did those who dispatched us.*

All at once, Leondros realized how wrong it was for them to be here in the growing darkness near the vast Divervandon Forest. It was now the night before the Celebration of the Great Dragon, and they were a day's ride from Akendron. A bad feeling came over Leondros as he began to realize that this mission had been just a very elaborate diversion to keep them away from Akendron at such a crucial time.

"What is wrong, my lord?" Amon-yen asked as he noticed Leondros's haunted expression.

"We should not be here." He looked at Amon-yen with growing dread. "Come, we must hurry. We make for Akendron with great haste," Leondros called to his men as he quickly whistled for Aton to come to him. "We must return to Akendron as soon as possible. There is little time before the Celebration of the Great Dragon, and it is vitally important that we be there," he said with urgency in his voice. Amon-yen nodded and quickly relayed the order to the surrounding men. There was little commotion as the army quickly assembled themselves for the journey back to the capital city.

"What about Endenbury?" Alon-Settie's voice came out of almost nowhere. Leondros turned to see his friend's face and realized that he had not seen him during the actual attack on the Draccen soldiers. It was something that concerned him, but there was little time to press the matter.

"Endenbury is no longer in danger, but Akendron is. We must be quick, or we just might lose her, too," Leondros replied with urgency as he looked back at the smoke rising above the remains of the ruined village. "I can only pray that we are in time," Leondros whispered to himself as he prepared himself for the long ride ahead.

"My lord!" Judeas's voice called out to him. The elfin scout was looking around and seemed to be missing something.

"What is wrong?" Leondros asked with concern as he saw the alarm in his soldier's dark eyes.

"Several men have gone missing. The rest believe they have been taken during the attack," Judeas replied with a deep expression of worry.

"Do you know who has gone missing?" Leondros asked as he gazed over the men before him.

"Theron and Aceon from Adarah, Kutalas and Dornos from Eden-Glee, and Jaran from the Shandel," Judeas replied with certainty. All who listened could not help but feel fear for their lost companions. Try as they might, Leondros and the remaining men could not find any traces of these lost men.

"This is most strange..." Leondros said thoughtfully as he felt their problems beginning to get more complicated. "Dracs never take prisoners. Anyone who fell victim to their wrath never lived to tell about it," he said in a puzzled tone. This was a very strange move on the part of the Draccen army.

"Shall we send out search parties to try and find them?" Alon-Settie asked as he climbed on his horse and readied himself for an intense search for the missing men. Leondros was torn with indecision. He wanted to make sure that no man was left behind, but he suddenly remembered the first line from the prophecy.

The Secret Alliance will go forth in battle. *Do not look for lost men; search out your friends.

"No. We will not find them here or anywhere close by," Leondros replied as he sensed that these men were no longer close by.

"We cannot leave them behind!" Alon-Settie pointed out with a concerned tone. Feeling tension between him and his friend, Leondros struggled hard to focus on the best course of action. Leondros lowered his head and took a deep breath.

"Alon-Settie, believe me when I say that I can sense that they are still alive. We will never stop our search until they are found, but right now there is grave danger in store for Akendron if we do not act," Leondros explained in an even and calm tone.

"How did you come by this knowledge and who would dare threaten the grand city of the Shandel?" Alon-Settie demanded as anger flashed through his brown eyes.

"Call it a hunch," Leondros answered simply, but judging from the anger that filled Alon-Settie's features, this meager answer would not do. "How strange is it that we, the Secret Alliance, are dispatched from Akendron just before the largest celebration in the country? What better way for an opposing force to take over an unguarded kingdom?" The anger that filled Leondros's response caught Alon-Settie off-guard and silenced him. Leondros looked at his friend with great disappointment, for he knew that this answer did not please Alon-Settie, but he could not let it concern him now. Akendron was in grave danger and was defenseless; those who dwelt there were going to need help.

Chapter 50

Premonition

Juna 24, 10021
Celebration of the Great Dragon.

I n the moments that followed, Leondros and the Secret Alliance set out under cover of night to return to Akendron. Time was not in their favor; it would take most of a day to get back. All they could do was press on and hope they reached the capital city in time. As the long hours passed, night gave way to day, and soon the hot summer sun began to bear down on the weary soldiers already exhausted from a lack of food and sleep. Leondros could see the weariness growing in his men's faces. The need for them to return to Akendron was very great indeed, but if these men did not get some rest soon, he would lose them long before the real battle began. He motioned to his father's trusted man.

"My lord?" Amon-yen asked in a parched voice as he rode up beside his general. Leondros had stopped Aton at the edge of a high, grassy hill. The elfin scout glanced down the hill and saw a lush field stretching all the way to Akendron. Here and there on the tree-studded plain were several small ponds where water could be gathered.

"We will take time to rest here. There is much waiting ahead of us, and the men will need to be fresh," said Leondros in a sympathetic tone. He could not help but feel his men's exhaustion and weakness, for he was feeling it, too. Leondros had not slept since he left Shoshon. It was only his determination that kept him alert to his surroundings, but like his men, he too would need rest for what was to come. When the word was given, Leondros heard his men breathe sighs of relief.

In the warmth of the afternoon sun, Leondros watched his men from a nearby maple tree. Many of them had quickly fallen asleep. He could already see a great difference in these men. They not only put aside their fears, but they were already bonding well. It was clear that they had taken his words to heart, and more than that, they were looking out for all who fought at their side. Leondros was proud to be serving with such brave men.

Leondros rested the back of his head against the tree and let his mind wander. The warm afternoon settled around him, and his eyelids grew heavy. He looked over the grounds where his men slept and saw they were safe from danger for the moment. Leondros closed his tired eyes, drifting off to sleep.

The white mist of the dream world appeared before his eyes and then began to turn gray. An image of a city appeared before him. Leondros recognized it as Akendron. It seemed to be a clear and peaceful day, but storm clouds were moving in from the coast. As the clouds built in the sky, they turned an ominous black. Soon, lightning flashed over Avdima Palace. As the storm grew, he heard thunder in the distance. Leondros stood atop a hill overlooking the city. He realized that he wasn't alone.

Alon-Settie was standing nearby, watching the coming storm with a forlorn expression. His soulful brown eyes were sad as if he knew what was about to happen and could only watch with growing dread. Then, Alon-Settie slowly looked back at Leondros with a sad gaze and shook his head.

"Leave while you can," he said, his dark-brown eyes filled with anguish. Leondros did not know whether to escape or stay with his friend. Then, panic washed over the Akendron prince's as he suddenly grabbed hold of Leondros's shoulders. "He is here!" A dark cloaked figure rose up behind Alon-Settie and put a bony hand upon his shoulder. Leondros watched as intense pain coursed through his friend, his whole body convulsing from the touch. Alon-Settie cried out in agony. The pain finally drove the young prince to his knees. Leondros tried to aid his long-time friend, but the dark cloaked figure raised his bony hand toward Leondros and knocked him back with a blast of blue energy. Landing on the soft grass behind him, Leondros looked up and saw a face emerge from under the black hood. It was Lord Jarden in his new form. His face was no longer shadow but flesh. As his eyes glowed with intense fire, a pleased look grew upon his face.

"He is mine." His gravelly voice drove chills down Leondros's spine. Then he leaned forward and pointed at the elfin prince. "I am coming for your people next!" Before Leondros could move, Lord Jarden unsheathed a sword and drove it into Alon-Settie.

Leondros awoke to find himself still perched within the same tree he had retreated to earlier. Looking around, he saw that everything was as before. His men continued to sleep soundly on the ground below. There were no signs of danger on the horizon. The images of what he had witnessed, though, stayed with him. He sensed that danger was now looming over his dear friend as well as Akendron. The Celebration of the Great Dragon now held a double meaning. The feeling that lingered with Leondros told him that the night's events would be more than just mere festivities and celebration.

What better night to come back from a thousand-year slumber than on a night of immense celebration, when darkness and evil will be the furthest thing from everyone's mind? Leondros thought.

Judeas approached the tree he was sitting in with a curious expression. "My lord? What is wrong?" he asked with concern, for he sensed that his prince was greatly troubled.

"We must break camp and return to Akendron at once. I feel that tonight we will see much more than a celebration. There is great evil ahead of us," Leondros said with a tone of urgency as he leapt down from the tall maple tree.

"My lord, you speak of the prophecy that foretells of the coming ancient evil, do you not?" Judeas asked in a whisper. Leondros at first seemed a little suspicious of Judeas, for not many knew of such things, but seeing the sincerity in the warrior's dark eyes, the elfin general took relief that someone else sensed the trouble that was awaiting Akendron.

"There is very little time before the Celebration of the Great Dragon begins, and we must reach Akendron before this night is over," Leondros explained quietly as he looked over all the men, who were still asleep or resting.

"I will help you wake the men. I, too, sense that there is darkness on the path ahead of us. However, I will be ever close to your side—and when you need me, my lord, I will be there," Judeas promised as he gave a humble bow to honor his general. Encouraged by this, Leondros began waking the men with Judeas's help. It was not long before the Secret Alliance was once again setting out for Akendron at their best possible speed.

Night fell only a couple of hours before their arrival in Akendron. As they rode hard across the land, Leondros's concern weighed even heavier on his mind. The images of the vision burned behind his eyes, and there would be no rest until he knew that both palace and people were safe from the dark lord's malicious plans, especially his dear friend Alon-Settie. He eyed Alon-Settie cautiously during the hard ride back to Akendron, but Leondros did not notice anything out of the ordinary. He sensed that his friend was in more trouble than he was sharing and thus, Leondros would not give up on his friend as long as there was breath within him. There was too much history between them to just give up on their friendship. As they reached Akendron, Leondros remembered his other friends and thought to look in on them first. Figuring that Alon-Settie would be safe with the Secret Alliance, the General of the army decided to take his leave of them.

"There is not much time now. You must be quick to move in on the shadow that has swept over this city, or we, too, will fall into its darkness. Go on ahead and confine all who attempt to bring harm to anyone, peasant or royal. The people within this city will have our protection; I will join you when I can. There is an issue of vital importance that calls for my attention," Leondros instructed his men. He saw looks of concern from his men, but he gave them a nod of assurance. Nodding in reply and honoring his orders, the Secret Alliance made for Avdima. As they began to ride past, Leondros stopped Alon-Settie. "Be safe, my friend, and do not be taken by surprise, even by those close to you," he instructed his friend, who listened with understanding and nodded.

"You too, my friend; be most careful tonight." Alon-Settie's expression was filled with sincerity. The friends nodded and then turned their separate ways. As he left his friend and hurried for the Misty Forest, Leondros prayed that somehow he would be given the ability to save his friends and his men from the shadow of the ancient evil. As the Secret Alliance began to ride into Akendron's brightly lit outskirts, Alon-Settie looked back to see Leondros already gone from sight. He spoke not a word, but an evil smile came to his face.

Chapter 51

Call of Duty

Hours before the Secret Alliance reached Akendron, the Celebration of the Great Dragon had already begun. The festive air over the city was filled with music, singing, and laughter. Baskets of food and wine were given to the people of Akendron and all visitors who came from afar to join the grand festival. All of the high council members and scholars of the royal court were expected to attend the festivities; King Alabaster wished for the people to meet the men who honorably gave counsel to him, his family, and the people of the kingdom. As the hour of seven quickly approached, Sala of Antioch rushed to prepare for the evening's gala, where he was to make his public appearance. Prior to this evening, he had warned Tahari not to attend the celebration, for he deeply feared that the Tomblock's taskmasters were still hunting her.

"I am going to take my leave of you now. The Queen needs me to make an appearance at tonight's celebration," Sala told Tahari as he hurried down the long set of stone stairs to Cypress Palace's main hall. In this grand hall was a modest closet cleverly hidden behind several tall pillars that stretched to the high ceiling. She followed quietly behind him. The door to this closet was designed to look like an exquisite painting of the ancient sphinxes so as not to mar the hall's breathtaking grandeur. It was here that Sala stored a variety of cloaks for many different occasions. He carefully pulled the oil painting away from the wall and reached inside the darkened closet to grab his cloak and walking stick.

"Sala, are you sure that I should not join you?" Tahari asked him again, watching him pull on a deep orange cloak over his white robe. "I fear that more will happen at tonight's celebration that mere festivity," she said.

He turned to Tahari before hurrying out the large main doors of Cypress Palace. There was deep concern in his blue eyes and face. "If that is so, I do not want you anywhere near there. I have just found you, and I cannot risk losing you now. You have a great quest ahead, and without you, the realm of Andora could be lost to the ancient evil," Sala said. He sighed deeply. "Tahari, I promise to keep an eye on things in the palace and those who live there. Besides, you are still healing from your time in the Tomblock. I do not wish to see you hurt again," he said as he gently took hold of her shoulders. The caring expression that radiated from his aged face kept her from pushing him further. Tahari sighed and nodded in understanding. "Please stay here, and if you should hear from Leondros, do not hesitate in sending me word of his arrival," he instructed her.

"I will not let you down," Tahari replied with a weak smile, for she understood his concerns ran deep.

"Very well, I am off then. Somehow, I do believe a few of those stuffy elders will be a little shocked by my attire," Sala said, a sly smile breaking through the seriousness on his face.

"You are a wild man, Sala of Antioch, and, dare I say, *fruity*," she reasoned thoughtfully as Tahari took in the loudness of his cloak. A grin came across his bearded face, and he began laughing while he took up his wooden walking stick and headed for the door.

"Good night, my dear," Sala said as Tahari opened the large wooden door for him and he stepped out into the evening mist. She watched him make his way across the wooden bridge and vanish into the lingering fog.

Watching him disappear from sight, she felt the need to follow him. Flashes of the vision Tahari had earlier came back to haunt her. The Queen was in grave danger as well as the rest of the royal family. There was more than good reason for her to go to the palace tonight. Danger was coming, and it would do so with or without her. The difference between her staying or going would be that many people might survive if she went. Tahari thought about her real past and who she actually was. "I am half elfish and half sphinx, and from that I possess the power to heal quickly. I cannot say what other characteristics I have, but I know for certain that I am not fragile," Tahari said aloud as she gazed out the open door at the thick white fog in the direction of Akendron. The need to leave could not be resisted, for she recalled the line of prophecy along with its instruction:

*A long-awaited night of celebration turns foul. *Rise up to stop this assassination.*

Tahari thought for a moment and smiled. "After all, I did say that I would not let him down," Tahari said to herself in a whisper as she quickly went to the concealed coat closet and pulled on her new black cloak and quietly headed out the large heavy door. Walking from the concealed boundaries of Cypress palace and its heavenly grounds, Tahari watched as the thick overhanging fog enveloped the bridge that she had walked over to leave the grounds. She now had but one course before her. Turning eastwards, Tahari listened to the sounds of the Misty Forest and the softness of the evening. It was in that moment that she heard the faintest of voices within the breezes that blew past her. Tahari felt a strong connection with it and sensed that it was her sphinx ancestor, if not a few of them. They reassured her and gave her direction to Akendron. Picking up her feet, Tahari started for the grand city of Akendron. However as she neared the city, she felt the tranquility of the forest fade and began to sense the chilling presence of evil growing around her. As Tahari walked unnoticed through the deep forest and silently made her way into the city and heard the roar of celebration, she sensed another force slowly moving into position.

Chapter 52

Darkness Moves In

Music and laughter filled the night air as the Celebration of the Great Dragon continued on. Hundreds gathered in the town square and on the palace grounds. There was not a sour face among the many that had come out for the celebration. Though dark clouds formed overhead and the air began to smell of rain, no spirits were dampened. Yet there was a shadow darker than any coming storm or darkness of night looming over the castle and awaiting its moment to strike. In just a few more moments, an unbelievable chain of events would transpire and allow that shadow to begin his rise to power.

Standing in a dreary tower chamber, Solarous gazed out a window at the crowds gathered in the courtyard below. He waited patiently for his moment of glory to come. Everything had been planned perfectly, and the moment would be flawless.

"Tonight, after our dear royal family falls, the people of the Shandel will have no other choice but to accept me as the next king of the Shandel," Solarous said to himself. He fantasized about what his time as king would be like. Then a voice spoke to him in the darkness.

"S-Sire..." the gentle voice hissed in an eerie whisper. Solarous turned quickly to see who it was and was relieved when he saw that it was only Zudoo.

"Ahhh, Zudoo. How good it is to see you, my friend," Solarous said as a smile slowly returned to his thinned face. His short time under Lord Jarden's power had caused the royal advisor serious weight loss, but the once-portly man did not mind; he greatly admired his thinner form. "What news do you have for me? Something in our favor, I hope?" he asked as he watched his dragon-like servant slowly creep out of the darkness of the chamber's doorway.

"Yes, more of my people have secretly arrived within the city walls. But I bring unfortunate news as well," he said. There was uneasiness in the humble servant's green eyes. "The Secret Alliance never arrived in Endenbury," Zudoo said with a careful tone with just a hint of sadness in it. Solarous thought about this news, and an evil smile spread across his lips.

"So our great Adaran general was no match for our small Draccen army, eh? I am actually quite surprised by this," Solarous replied with humor, clasping his hands behind his muscular back and lifting his gaze to the ceiling. "No matter. Now that General Goldendragon is..." He stopped when he noticed Zudoo's concerned expression. "Zudoo? What are you not telling me?" he asked, his dreams of a quick takeover beginning to wane. The dark-red Draccen was slow to answer, but he finally found the courage to speak.

"The scouts from Endenbury found no trace of the Secret Alliance in the town. All they found were the remains of several hundred Draccen soldiers that had been ambushed on the road to Endenbury. They believe the rest of our secondary army was in the village when it was blown up," Zudoo said carefully, for his master's expression was going from pale to red quickly. "The Secret Alliance has vanished.

"Vanished?" Solarous repeated in a tone of disbelief. "How does an entire army just vanish?" The royal advisor began to pace the room uneasily, kicking the tails of his long black-and-red robe with his feet as he walked. "This is not good. It cannot be overlooked. One cannot just simply overlook the fact that the greatest threat to the ancient evil is out there somewhere." The tone of worry grew in Solarous's voice. Zudoo took pity on his master and remembered something that would offer him some comfort.

"Sire, all hope is not lost," Zudoo began in a meek voice. Solarous looked at him doubtfully. "We must remember that Alon-Settie is still with the Secret Alliance. He will carry out the orders he has been given. The prince's heart is cold and frozen. It is no longer open to the warmth of compassion. He does not feel or care for anything but our purposes. He will not fail the special task that you have given him or let his men fail their night's mission." Zudoo's reminder was good medicine for Solarous's worried mind. The royal advisor glanced out the window at the courtyard below and smiled an evil smile as his small dark eyes sparkled with delight.

"You are right, my friend. Thank you for reminding me of our secret weapon. If it were not for you, my friend, I would be lost in worry," Solarous said. "No matter what the Secret Alliance does when it returns, *if* it should return, its general will not." Zudoo was pleased that he was able to offer some comfort to his master, but when the young Draccen aide thought about what would transpire, he was genuinely concerned for the Secret Alliance's general.

"I am glad for your happiness, sire…" Zudoo said, but his voice weakened and trailed off. There was something within him that told him this was not the right course to take.

"Come, Zudoo, the hour grows near. Tonight you will see many amazing wonders. The dawn of a new empire is almost upon us!" Solarous exclaimed. He took one more look at the festivities in the streets below and then left for the main ballroom, where the royal family was to appear. After his master left the room, Zudoo went to the window. He took in the sight of the people gathered in the main courtyard below.

"Amazing wonders…" he said in a whisper, his thoughts dwelling on the danger that awaited the good general of the Secret Alliance. "Let us hope so. I fear the night ahead, for it will be a time of great calamity. And calamity is often closely accompanied by death." Zudoo saw the darkening skies becoming more threatening. A great storm was approaching. He lowered his head sadly. "Tonight will mark the end of peace for this land," he admitted sadly. Zudoo did not know what hope he could cling to as he gazed sadly out the window. In the midst of his grief, he saw someone cloaked and unrecognizable moving through the massive crowds and toward the castle. Zudoo watched them enter the castle through a passage only known to the royal family. He did not know who this person was or what they were planning to do, but he felt a spark of hope ignite in his heart.

"The forces of darkness may have already claimed victory on this night, but the forces of goodness have not given up yet," he said to himself.

Chapter 53

Grave Danger

At nine, the royal family finally arrived in the grand ballroom. All those who were specially invited to see the royal family quickly crowded into the large ballroom. All were dressed in their finest gowns and robes, and mulled spices and candles warmed the air. Decorations glittered from the walls and crossed the large span of the room. The guests' excitement and anticipation of the royal family's presence hummed through the room: it had been rumored that the king and queen had planned a special surprise for their special guests.

The torches and candles were suddenly snuffed, out and a silent blackness fell over the room. The crowd grew uneasy, uncertain of what was going on. A few moments later, a single candle was lit in the front of the room. The crowd turned its attention to the solitary flame. Then a second candle was lit, and then a third and a fourth. Soon, the entire room was filled with the tranquil orange light from hundreds of candles. The King stepped out from behind a red velvet curtain on a stage before the large crowd. He was dressed in a midnight-blue robe tied with a white sash. The crowd erupted into deafening cheers and applause that echoed beyond the palace walls. The crowd's reaction grew as each member of the royal family stepped out from behind the curtain. People gasped at the elegance of their wardrobe. Soon, the entire royal family, excepting only Prince Alon-Settie, stood before the delighted crowd. King Alabaster noticed the looks of excitement changing into ones of concern as the crowd realized their prince was nowhere to be seen. The king stepped out to the edge of the stage and motioned for the crowd to be calm and silent.

"A warm welcome to all who have come out tonight to celebrate this wondrous occasion with us. I cannot help but notice your looks of concern, however, over the absence of my beloved son. Although he has been unavoidably detained, rest assured that he is safe. He will be with us again before the night is out," King Alabaster said in a warm and reassuring tone. The King's charming words, combined with his calm expression, helped soothe the crowd. "Tonight, we have gathered together to remember a very special day, a day that will live forever in history. On this day, one elf took a stand against evil. This elf looked beyond his own needs and ensured that those who resided within Andora would be safe forever. Tonight, we celebrate that elf's victory. Tonight, we honor the Great Dragon!" King Alabaster spoke with immense reverence. When he had finished, the crowd began to shout and cheer with great excitement.

Then, startled cries began drowning out the crowd's excitement. Guests looked around to see what was causing such a disruption. Suddenly, twelve seemingly ordinary people armed with deadly spears charged from the crowd. Their eyes were anything but ordinary, however. Their clothes were torn, foam came from their mouths, and they were covered in deep scratches. They charged straight toward the royal family.

"Guards, restrain them!" King Alabaster cried out in horror, fear washing over his handsome face as he backed away from the front of the stage. The royal bodyguards, who had been dressed in black robes to blend into the background of the room, were quick to surround him. Almost immediately, more royal palace guards filed into the overcrowded hall. The crowd moved back to give the palace guards enough space to apprehend these mad citizens. The twelve, however, swiftly killed the palace guards with their razor-sharp spears. The crowd gasped and began to panic. There was nothing between the attackers and the royal family.

Queen Elanza positioned herself in front of her daughters to protect them from four women who were charging at the princesses with blood-soaked spears. The queen had never seen such wild hatred in anyone's eyes before. Fear-stricken, Queen Elanza froze. She closed her eyes and waited for the spear to be driven into her body. Screams rang out from the crowd. King Alabaster turned in time to see what was about to happen to his beloved wife. He wanted to protect her, but he could not reach her. Chaos filled the grand ballroom.

In the midst of all the pandemonium, a dark-cloaked stranger had entered the ballroom unseen. Now, the stranger swiftly tackled the four enraged women who were ready impale the Queen and her daughters. The women quickly scrambled over each other to turn on their attacker. The stranger punched and elbowed them. One by one, the women let out a shriek and fell heavily to the floor.

Sensing their mission was in grave danger, the other attackers turned their attention to the dark-cloaked stranger. The crowd watched in awe while the dark-cloaked stranger faced the oncoming danger. The first man to reach the stranger struck with his spear. Sidestepping, the stranger grabbed the spear and head-butted the man. As the man tumbled backward and crumpled to the ground in a heap, the stranger was already whirling around to block the next attack. The stranger drove the blunt end of the first man's spear into the new attacker's stomach. The man doubled over and tried to back away from the stranger, but with a swift kick to his head, the stranger sent the man backward. He did not get up again. The stranger dealt with four more men in quick succession.

Turning around, the stranger faced the last two women. Grasping the spear's shaft, the stranger knocked both women back and onto the ground. When they tried to get up, they were met with the stranger's fist in their faces. Looking around and finding no more foes to fight, the stranger bowed toward the king.

More guards finally arrived and began restoring order, and the Queen and princesses quickly escorted to safety. King Alabaster pushed his way through his bodyguards to meet the brave soul who had stopped the attack on him and his family.

"Please, come forward so we may look upon the guardian who has protected us from this unforeseen peril," he requested kindly as the stranger was about to leave the ballroom. Silence filled the large room as everyone watched as the stranger turned back toward the king. The stranger bowed and, straightening again, pushed back the cloak's hood. The entire crowd gasped as long dark hair tumbled down. There standing before King Alabaster was a woman!

Chapter 54

A Hero Revealed

At the king's request, Tahari pushed back her hood. She could hear the crowd gasp at the shock of finding a woman had saved the royal family. King Alabaster seemed to be lost for words as he looked from her to the crowd and back again. Silence hung in the air.

"Excuse us for our response to your presence, for surely we stand in your debt," King Alabaster managed to say at long last, a warm smile coming to his face. "May we have the honor of knowing your name?.

"My name is Tahari of the Shandon," Tahari said, still feeling relief that the king and his family were safe.

"Tahari of the Shandon, tell me how is it that you knew that our lives were in danger?" he asked with a look of curiosity. She sensed that he was still shaken by what had just transpired.

"My lord, tonight there is great evil lurking near and abroad. I sensed that it was here, within the palace, and that those who lived here were in grave danger. This evil is working hard, especially on this night. It is why I am here, my lord. I am merely a humble servant, and I owe my allegiance to you. I am willing to fight for you and your family, my lord," she replied, bowing her head. King Alabaster's kind face was filled with a pleased expression.

"It is a rare sight indeed to see one such as yourself with such loyalty and devotion toward their king. We are fortunate that our youth still carry with them such wisdom and have the sense to use it," he said with a warm smile. Turning to address the crowd that surrounded him, he said for all to hear, "We will bestow upon you this honor: join me and my family in this grand celebration. It is a night of remembrance. It is only right that we honor you the same as we honor those who protected us before." The crowd's eyes beamed with excitement and gratitude.

Before Tahari could utter her reply, a loud and obnoxious voice shattered the moment. Everyone turned to see a shockingly thin man running through the crowd shouting out something at the top of his lungs. Tahari had never talked with this man face to face before, but already she could see that he was trouble.

"STOP THEM! DO NOT LET THEM ENTER! THEY ARE POSSESSED BY EVIL SPIRITS!" The words echoed throughout the room.

The crowd stared at the dark-robed man with a blank expression. When he finally broke through the crowd, the man stopped in front of the guards dragging the intruders away to the dungeons. He seemed lost for a moment but quickly collected his thoughts enough to ask. "What has happened here?" He approached the king, bowing quickly, and then looked over at Tahari. His dark eyes bore right through her, it seemed as he shot her an accusing gaze.

"All is well, Solarous. We truly appreciate your concern for our safety, but your warning comes to us a bit late. We are in good hands tonight." He gestured toward her. "This brave young woman has put her own troubles aside and kept us safe from these crazed citizens. We were just about to pay her our gratitude." King Alabaster smiled at Tahari. She smiled back at him, but she felt this Solarous was not about to let the issue rest. His very presence seemed to defy everything that she had accomplished.

"My lord, I must advise against you doing any such thing!" Solarous proclaimed with an alarmed look on his pasty face. "On my way to warn you about the great evil I sensed stirring within the palace, I saw thirteen citizens sneaking into the palace. I got close enough to hear them planning a conspiracy to assassinate the royal family. I could only make out twelve of the thirteen conspirators. The thirteenth one was covered in a dark cloak." As Solarous spoke, he pointed at Tahari's black cloak. Everyone's eyes turned toward her. Solarous pointed his large finger in her face. "She is the thirteenth member of that conspiracy. She is not here to save anyone but to assassinate you and all whom you hold dear!" The crowd started talking amongst themselves; Solarous's words seemed to be swaying them. Doubt and uncertainty grew on their faces.

Tahari turned to Solarous and glared at him. She could feel the overpowering evil emanating from him. How could the crowd believe him? What proof did he have? Tahari had taken out the twelve, had she not? A rage of anger welled up within her.

"Be silent, foul creature of darkness!" Tahari retorted angrily, standing up to his dark form as she had never been able to stand up to the taskmasters. Solarous gasped, his button-like eyes growing wide with the realization that he was not dealing with a mere human. "Your place here is temporary. It is not I but you who have been plotting works of evil!" Tahari declared in an angry voice as she approached him. Solarous shrank backward and sank weakly to his knees and cowered in her shadow.

"Sire! Help me, please, sire!" Solarous cried out as if in great intense pain. Tahari watched as his white face twisted in imaginary pain. "Stop the witch! She is killing me! She will put a spell on all of you next and you will all suffer my fate!" His cries seemed to shake the king.

"I order you to release him!" King Alabaster commanded me in an angry tone. Tahari looked at him in disbelief.

"I am not a witch, nor do I have any powers to control any person," Tahari stated plainly. The king looked back at his royal advisor, who was still cowering on the ground beside us. Concern for this man seemed to run deep.

"Back away from him! You will not harm any member of the royal house!" King Alabaster shouted. Tahari watched as the anger grew within the king's aged yet handsome face. Holding her hands up, Tahari calmly backed away from the royal advisor. Slowly Solarous climbed back to his feet. The king was instantly at his side, helping him up. After he made sure that Solarous was all right, King Alabaster turned to Tahari, brown eyes flashing with anger. "What is the real reason you are here tonight?" he demanded. The anger in his voice echoed throughout the grand hall. The crowd wisely stayed silent.

"Your majesty, please, let me try to explain…" Tahari began, but once again her voice was cut off by another obnoxious voice.

"Solarous speaks the truth!" As Tahari turned to see who it was coming to aid this evil man, cold chills ran down her back. Much to Tahari's dismay, the wiry form of Thera Dancar emerged from the crowd. She was beautifully clothed in an elegant red satin gown and a matching red shawl. She looked as noble and gracious as those around her. Her cold dark eyes stared at Tahari as she walked up beside Solarous and King Alabaster. Her glare hit Tahari like the taskmasters' whips. It felt like Tahari would never be free of her past. "This is no woman of nobility. She is one of our field rats who escaped from our plantation." If her appearance alone did not destroy Tahari's credibility, her vile words would. Tahari winced at her words. "She is wanted back on our plantation for the chaos that she caused a few nights ago. Many good men were killed, including my husband!" Thera's bitter words were adding to the accusation that was already in King Alabaster's brown eyes. They seemed to please Solarous, who had his arms folded and was nodding in agreement.

"If you do not believe my words, my lord, please heed the words of this noble woman: she is the wife of the late Master Dancar. They are respectable people who care for those most unfortunate," Solarous pleaded as he looked with great concern into King Alabaster's eyes. The king looked thoughtful for a moment.

"Lady Dancar, my judgment rests in your hands." King Alabaster spoke in a calm tone as he turned to Thera. "As a caretaker for this young woman, do you agree with my royal advisor? Would you go so far as to say that this woman is a witch, or is she just a very gifted individual?" At that moment, Tahari's heart sank. Her chances for escape from this place had just vanished. Tahari's only hope now rested in the very same woman who left her to be baked alive in the scorching afternoon sun.

Thera turned her cold gaze toward Tahari and stared at her until Tahari found the courage to look back at her. Then as if she had waited to look her directly in the eye, Thera smiled an evil smile.

"It is as Solarous has said. This woman is indeed a witch." Her harsh words cut Tahari to the quick. She managed to hide her hurt, however, for there was little surprise in Thera's answer. "If it were not for her magic, my husband would still be alive. Tonight I speak in his place. If it is your will, my lord, then I will gladly take this witch off your hands. We will deal with her properly." Thera managed to choke back her tears long enough to testify to Tahari's guilt and offer her execution. As Thera spoke, she quickly grabbed hold of Tahari's long braid and pulled her away from the king and Solarous.

"Hold!" King Alabaster spoke up with alarm as he watched Thera's sudden and unexpected attempt to take Tahari back to the plantation again. He was quick to summon a guard to restrain Thera. Tahari managed to tear herself free from her tight grasp. "If what you say is true, then she is a runaway and should be punished. If what Solarous says is also true, then the crime is heresy. Punishment for such a crime is death." The king's words stopped Tahari's ability to breathe for a moment. The king turned his attention back to Tahari. His expression softened just a little. "However, a fair trial would not be very fair if we did not at least hear what the accused has to say." Tahari began to breathe again. King Alabaster restored her hope for survival somewhat.

"Do not give her permission to speak, my lord!" Solarous gasped. "Given the chance, she will put a spell on us, and then she will be at liberty to kill us all!" he warned as he turned a cold look in Tahari's direction. She prayed that King Alabaster would keep his word and allow her to speak, but this was not to be.

"Very well, then," he said, renouncing his words and thinking for a long moment. The whole room awaited his decision in silence. Tahari felt the coldness of evil become almost overpowering. Her fate was sealed. "Guards! Seize this woman and put her in the deepest dungeon within Avdima." The darkly dressed guards within the room were quick to obey the king's orders. Palace guards took hold of Tahari as she heard her sentence proclaimed to the audience who looked on. "Tomorrow, this witch will be executed for the crime of heresy." The king's words were hard to take, seeing as she had just saved his wife and daughter from certain death. "Thousands of years ago, an evil spirit took possession of a man's body, becoming the greatest threat our world has ever known," King Alabaster said as he walked up to Tahari. "It has been rumored that this evil spirit longs to return to bring death and darkness back to the known world. Tonight would be a most fitting time to make that rumor a reality, and you might be the one who could be the start of this apocalypse. After what we have witnessed tonight, we fully believe that you are not to be trusted and that you would bring harm to all those around you." Hearing these words, Tahari felt her world come crashing down upon her. Tahari lowered her head in shame and defeat. "Guards, take her away.

The last thing Tahari saw as the guards dragged her out of the ballroom was a small servant boy watching on in horror. It seemed that no child's innocence was safe.

Chapter 55

The Great Dragon Comes Forth

Minutes before midnight.

After leaving the grand hall's boisterous festivities where hundreds of guests were still gathered for late-night dancing, King Alabaster walked down the quiet corridor leading to a private chamber where his family would meet him. Almost three hours had passed since his family had been attacked. It sickened him to have to reward the dark-haired beauty's honorable actions by throwing her into Avdima's dungeons. However, he knew that Solarous had been right in his counsel. With all the kingdom expecting the return of some ancient evil, people would try anything to scare the populace into believing such far-fetched ideas.

"Alabaster!" Elanza gasped, her green eyes quick to spot him quietly entering the private chamber, where candles and calming incense had been lit to comfort the queen and her daughters. The queen picked up her dark-green gown as she rushed across the room and wrapped her arms tightly around her husband.

"Where are Minta and Kosta?" Alabaster asked as his concerned eyes looked for them.

"They are fine. They fell asleep in the next room awaiting your arrival," Elanza reassured him as she loosened her grip on her husband. "What happened?" she asked as she looked at Alabaster with deep worry. Alabaster had noticed that Elanza had taken down her hair since the attack, for now her dark locks hung by her waist.

"The people who attacked us were subdued by a strange young woman in a dark cloak. It seemed as though she was trying to save us, but we were told that she was the one who orchestrated the whole event to promote the belief that the ancient evil was returning.

"Strange young woman in a dark cloak?" Elanza asked as her green eyes widened with realization. Her heart told her that this woman was not only innocent but also the same woman who had saved her from the beastly man in the street. "Then I do believe that..." Before the queen could offer her wisdom on this matter, the dark wooden door opened and Solarous slowly entered the room wearing his usual dark cloak and an expression of worry and concern.

"Your Majesties?" he began as his dark eyes looked upon them with a strange and deep concern.

"Oh, Solarous, this has been quite a night, has it not?" Alabaster welcomed his advisor in with a nod. Queen Elanza watched the advisor warily as he humbly entered the room.

"My lord, I believe it is not over." Solarous's voice was filled with worry, catching the king's attention. "In fact, it is only beginning."

"Surely you are jesting," King Alabaster replied with a smile, thinking this was merely another one of his advisor's pranks. "I have been through too much on this festive evening for our usual banter, Solarous." The King's voice was light and carefree, but Solarous's serious expression did not change. Elanza's face drained of all color as her heart told her that her husband was about to see his advisor's true side.

"This is no joke, my lord," Solarous said slowly as his dark button-like eyes bore into the king and queen. "This is a very serious matter. It will go easier for you and all you hold dear if you are compliant with my master's wishes." King Alabaster's smile faded, and he began to feel uneasy.

"Your master? Solarous, what are you talking about?" Alabaster's chest began to tighten as Solarous turned his head slightly back to the door.

"Please come in, master." A dark-red-cloaked figure quietly entered the room and stood just behind the deceptive royal advisor. "My lord, my lady, I would like to introduce to you my master, Lord Jarden." Silence filled the chamber for a long moment as King Alabaster struggled to decide if this was some out-of-control prank on Solarous's part.

"Solarous, seriously. Making a mockery of the incident tonight is no joking matter. Now, I order you to desist with your antics!" King Alabaster demanded as he tried to retain some control.

"You are right; it is no joking matter. Relinquish your kingdom peacefully and Lord Jarden will spare you and your family from the oppression of his coming revolution." Solarous's dark eyes and the seriousness in his thin face did not waver.

"You dare threaten your king and his family?" King Alabaster demanded, anger rising in his voice.

"My servant did not threaten you," Lord Jarden said in his deep, resonating voice. Without warning, Lord Jarden pulled out a black sword and thrust it into Solarous's back. Elanza screamed as she and Alabaster watched, frozen in terror. "I am threatening you!" The horror and shock upon the advisor's face was mixed with intense pain. His dark eyes were wide and screamed for someone to help him. The light faded from the balding advisor's eyes as he crumpled to the brown-and-gold-carpeted floor, sliding off the blade. Lord Jarden looked back to the king and queen, who remained frozen before him. "So, what will it be?.

"If Solarous was your servant, why did you kill him?" King Alabaster asked, finding his voice again. He watched the blood pool and slowly began to stain the brown carpet. The dead advisor's eyes remained open and filled with the horror that claimed his life.

"His usefulness to me was at an end," Lord Jarden reasoned simply as he knelt down and held a bony hand over Solarous's lifeless form. Moments later, Solarous's physical form disappeared from the blood-soaked floor and was replaced with the dark mist and bone that was the old body of Lord Jarden. His new body resembled Solarous, except that his fleshy features remained gray.

"If you have come back just to inflict more pain and misery upon this land..." King Alabaster began as he turned his back to Lord Jarden for a moment and tried to discreetly motion to Elanza for her to escape with their daughters. Even in her petrified state, Elanza summoned the courage to flee the room, grab her daughters and escape, as she took a deep breath. Suddenly, there were screams from the other room. Elanza started to whirl around and hurry to her daughters. Their screams were silenced just as suddenly, and Elanza felt her body go cold.

"Do not be concerned about your daughters now. Their souls will find their way to the realm of the dead," Lord Jarden spoke up calmly. "Still, I want you both to meet someone I am most proud of." The dark lord gestured to the shadowy image of a man dressed in a black chain-link suit and dark gray tunic who stepped through the inner doorway holding his own bloodied sword.

"Alon-Settie!" King Alabaster gasped. His dark eyes widened with horror as he stared in heartbroken disbelief at the face of his beloved son. His son only smiled back at him with an evil smile in response. "NO!" the King of the Shandel screamed, pulling out his own sword to protect what remained of his family. The intense battle did not last long, and when it was over, Alon-Settie simply disarmed his father. The dark lord would interrogate his prisoner at his leisure; death for Alabaster was only a matter of time.

While they battled, Elanza did the only thing she could. She quietly slipped into the other sitting chamber where her precious daughters lay in a heap on the brown-carpeted floor, slain by their own brother. Tears streamed down Elanza's white face as she gently touched their still-warm faces, searching in vain for some sign of life. She found none. Her beautiful daughters were gone. Ripping herself away, Elanza vanished into the secret passages that ran throughout the palace.

Chapter 56

Inner Strength

With the king's final words, Tahari was cast into a dark, cruel world of pain and torture. The guards dragged her deep beneath the castle to an interrogation room. Solarous had them shackle her to a stone wall and blindfold her eyes so that she could undergo his "just" treatment of a witch. It quickly reminded Tahari of her time within the Tomblock. The guards yelled at her and demanded that she answer their questions, but she remained silent. Their questions made no sense, but they kept asking them. Tahari's silence was rewarded by pain. After a long while, they finally decided they could not get any information out of her concerning her real plans. They decided to be finished with her. Tahari was unshackled from the iron cuffs that had restrained her and was dragged from the room down a long corridor. The sounds of metal cell doors echoed down the corridor. The air was musty and foul, and as they took her farther down the damp corridor, the smell became almost overpowering. Death had never been such a wicked and utterly terrifying thing as this.

When the guards finally ripped off the blindfold, Tahari could barely make out her surroundings. They had stopped in front of a cell that would be her sleeping quarters for the last night of her life.

"Walk, witch!" they shouted at her, but as hard as she tried, Tahari's feet would not respond, and she began to falter. Seeing that she was about to fall, they gave her an extra shove to push Tahari into the cell. She fell hard against the cold, damp floor. They slammed the door closed and left, but the echoes of their laughter lingered behind and filled the small cell. Tahari wearily lifted her aching head and looked around, her eyes adjusting to her new surroundings. Tahari quickly found that the interrogation room was much cozier than the grungy cell she was in now. Tahari painfully pushed herself to the cell door and put a hand on a mildew-riddled metal bar. Looking between the bars of her cell into the corridor, Tahari was left feeling cold and lonely. Across from her were at least ten iron-barred cell doors; she judged the same number on this side. There was but one torch placed upon the stone wall. Its orange flame did little to brighten the space. In the dim that surrounded her, Tahari could see that the stone floor was covered with damp dirt. The damp air that surrounded her was heavy with the stomach-churning smell of blood. Narrowing her gaze and peering into the dimness, Tahari saw the other prisoners who dwelt within the dark dungeons. Whether anyone knew of the treatment these poor souls had endured would not matter anymore. Death had long since taken them. There were three men and a woman chained to the walls of their cells. Two of the men still reached for a small tin plate with a single piece of moldy bread upon it. Another was reaching for a small leather canteen, but the woman remained propped against the wall to which she had long been chained. Of the three of them, only the woman still had most of her flesh. Their message to Tahari was painfully clear. Life's journey ended here.

As Tahari looked around her, she could not help but remember what had led to this darkened cell. Everything that she had done to save the royal family from the evil that threatened their lives had been slapped back into her face. Disgrace and shame weighed down her shoulders.

Tahari had just lowered her aching head to rest it against the metal bars when she heard the eerie echo of footsteps approaching her cell. A faint orange glow began to brighten the dim corridor as it came closer.

Judging from the slow approach and the malicious presence that she felt, Tahari knew it was not someone coming to aid her during her darkest hour. She ignored this newcomer until Tahari heard a whisp cut through the air and she felt something sting her hand that rested on the metal bar of her cell.

"Well, well, well. Is this not a perfect picture?" Thera's nasal voice was all too familiar, driving shivers down Tahari's back. Tahari slowly lifted her head and saw a pleased expression on her thin face. She held a torch in one hand and a thin golden fan that she had slapped across Tahari's knuckles in the other. She had covered her precious red satin gown with a gray cloak to keep the dirt off it. Although she had pulled her gray-streaked hair into a neat bun, several strands had escaped to dangle about her thin face. Taking in the gray surroundings of the dungeons, her expression was the same, smug and full of disgust. Of all the times that Tahari had seen Thera, this one pained her the most. It was her word that had persuaded King Alabaster to have her executed. Tahari saw laughter in her cold stare. This was where Thera had always wanted her, and her expression declared it.

"Master Dancar would be truly delighted to see this, but what delights me even more is knowing that it was I who put you here," Thera said with great pride, lifting her gaze from Tahari to the dark cell that she was in. "Now that is a pity," she said with a sigh of disgust. "Even this cell is too good for you." In spite of all Thera's hate for Tahari, she managed to find her strength again.

"Ahhh, I am deeply touched. Did you miss me?" Tahari asked with warm sarcasm. Thera quickly recoiled from this remark and shot an evil glare at her.

"You defiant child," Thera hissed coldly. "I am glad they are going to give you a slow and agonizing death," she added with a cruel smile. It was then that the guards called down to her. Her time for visiting the prisoner was up. As she turned to leave, another thought seemed to occur to her. "Just to let you know," she said as she turned around to face Tahari one last time. There was an evil look in her dark eyes as she looked upon her with immense pleasure. "I talked to the king and Solarous, and we moved your execution up. The guards will be coming to get you any time now." Her words were quite cold and harsh. With that, she put her nose in the air, whirled around, and stormed down the dark corridor. As she left, the light from her torch began to fade until only the dimness remained. Tahari listened as the sounds of her footsteps become faint and then a heavy metal door slammed shut. The loud noise echoed down the corridor and marked Thera's departure from Avdima's dungeons.

Tahari sighed sadly and rested her weary head against the door once more. Tahari's mind raced with everything that had transpired on this evening.

"My actions tonight may have only delayed the inevitable, and if so…I have failed," Tahari whispered to herself sadly as she painfully closed her eyes and tried to shut out the evening's events. Tahari's heart was further saddened by the fact that she had let Sala and Leondros down. They would have no one to translate the scrolls of the prophecy that would lead to Farro. Tahari's guilt was almost too much to bear.

Then Tahari was reminded of something very special. She lifted her head slowly as she remembered where she had lived for a majority of her life and what she had done thus far to save an elfin prince. As Tahari looked around the cell and peered through the metal bars to look down the corridor, she noticed that the security within Avdima's lower level was quite lax indeed.

"Am I free?" Tahari asked herself with disbelief. By seeing Thera one last time, Tahari had bid farewell to her old life and those who dwelt in it. There was truly nothing holding her to the world they had destined her to. "I *am* free," Tahari said into the darkness.

Everything was as before, with one exception. Tahari had remembered a key piece about herself which those who had imprisoned her had overlooked. "Slaves are most resourceful when freedom is within an arm's reach." Finding the strength to stand, Tahari looked through the damp bars of her cell. A sly smile came to her face as she remembered how easy it was to get out of the Tomblock plantation. As Tahari peered down the long dark corridor, she observed that the lax security in Avdima's dungeons greatly paled against the Tomblock's prison.

Chapter 57

Grave News Received

Midnight passed as Sala returned from Akendron. It had truly been a night of wondrous celebration. There had been much dancing, music, and refreshments to occupy the night. He had met with Queen Elanza just before the royal family was to make their grand appearance. Their conversation was relatively short, for she wanted him to enjoy the night's events. As the hour of eleven came, Sala had grown weary from the excitement and festivities and had decided to return home. In addition to his weary mind, the advisor felt that his presence was needed elsewhere.

Walking through the trees that led to Cypress Palace, Sala smelled the heavy scent of rain in the air. He caught flashes of lightning through the Misty Forest's trees and heard thunder in the distance.

"This looks to be a bad one," Sala said to himself thoughtfully as he pulled his orange cloak tighter and trudged for home. He wondered about the storm's significance on this night. He shook his weary head, dismissing these thoughts as paranoia, and continued on his way back to Cypress Palace. Yet a feeling of foreboding nagged at him, though no word had been sent from the palace about any major incidents. Try as he might to clear his weary mind, though, the feeling would not go away. Upon his return to Cypress Palace, Sala found it empty; he could not find Tahari anywhere. "Now where could she have gone?" he asked himself, the feeling of foreboding growing. Looking out a nearby window that faced Akendron, he saw fireworks light up the sky above Akendron. "You did not..." he said as he quickly turned and rushed down the long corridor and eventually to the front door. He had not known Tahari very long, but he already knew that she was a very determined individual. He did not doubt that she had indeed left for Akendron. This only added to his fear that something awful had taken place on this night.

Sala took up his walking stick and opened the heavy wooden door. He jumped back when he found a shadowy figure standing before him. He was quick to take up his staff and defend himself from the dark figure. Only through divine intervention did lightning flash overhead and light up the grounds around the Cypress Palace. Sala saw the familiar features of Leondros Goldendragon emerge from the shadowy figure. The elfin warrior, clothed in his brown tunic and silver armor, gave Sala a puzzled look as he watched the elderly prophet holding up the staff, ready to take a mighty swing.

"Expecting company?" Leondros asked calmly as his dark-brown eyes calmly studied the aging prophet before him. Sala lowered his walking staff and let out a huge sigh of relief. He took a moment to gather his thoughts and let his heartbeat return to a normal rhythm.

"I can feel that tonight has not gone by in peace," Sala said finally.

Leondros became concerned with these words and the look he saw in Sala's blue eyes. "Has anything happened within the palace?" he asked as he turned his concerned gaze back toward the capital city.

"Beyond the festivities and celebration that have enveloped the city, I do not know," Sala replied in a tone of uncertainty, but when he looked at his elfin friend's worried expression, he could not help feeling concerned. "What troubles you, my friend?" he asked, searching Leondros's weary face and sensing that he had already seen much trouble on this night.

"Our orders sent us to Endenbury, which a Draccen army had ransacked. Those who survived managed to escape to Akendron. When we rode out to stop the Draccen army responsible, we nearly found ourselves in an ambush. I have reason to believe that the siege upon Endenbury was premeditated by someone who wanted the Secret Alliance away from Akendron. Evil is closer than we realize. I believe it has already taken Avdima." Leondros began to explain the events of his journey and motioned back to Akendron as Sala listened on with great concern and interest.

"This is news to my ears. I was in Akendron for most of the night and there was not the slightest hint of trouble. Yet I..." Sala stopped suddenly as he watched someone materialize from the thick mist that surrounded the palace and rush across the wooden bridge toward them. He stepped closer to get a better look at who was approaching Cypress Palace at such a late hour. Deep within his heart, Sala hoped that it would be Tahari. When the figure emerged from the shadows of the Misty Forest into the heavenly light given off by the magical palace, Sala recognized who it was instantly.

"Elijah?" Sala and Leondros said in unison. They both recognized the servant boy, who was wearing an oversized gray cloak he had grabbed at the last minute before leaving Avdima. The elfin prince's heart sank as he saw the expression of horror and fear in the boy's face. The men were quick to meet the panicked servant boy before he reached the end of the large bridge. Leondros took hold of the thin child, who collapsed into his outstretched arms, fighting to breathe.

"Breathe, boy! Just breathe," Sala instructed him as he anxiously looked upon the weary child and waited for him to speak. Leondros watched nervously as Elijah tried to catch his breath enough to talk.

"I-I bring secret news from Akendron. No one knows that I have left with such news, or I would have been stopped," Elijah managed to say in a gasp. "Tonight, there was an assassination attempt on the royal family. Twelve people within the crowd gathered before the royal family went berserk. The palace guards, who tried to stop them, were killed. They nearly succeeded with their assassination attempt," Elijah explained as he continued to catch his breath, looking between Leondros and Sala. "Except there was a dark-cloaked stranger who stopped them—I have never seen anyone fight like she did," both Leondros and Sala picked up on the word *she*, and exchanged looks of certainty.

"She?" Sala asked with increased interest. Elijah nodded with assurance.

"I forget her name, but I think it was Tahari. She was like no person I have ever seen before," Elijah spoke with such reverence and admiration, but then a deeply grieved look washed over his face and he lowered his head sadly. "Why did Solarous have to show up, anyway?" Elijah asked bitterly.

"Solarous? What has he done?" Sala asked, a pit of dread growing within him.

"He convinced the king and the people that Tahari was a witch. They accused her of orchestrating the assassination attempt." fear and urgency radiated from the boy's eyes. "She was to be burned at the stake come first light." Elijah shook his head with immense grief for this brave woman. "However, the king and Solarous changed their minds. Her execution has been moved up to tonight." Sala and Leondros exchanged looks of horror for a second time.

"We cannot let her die because they lack vision!" Leondros exclaimed.

"Nor are we about to," Sala assured his friend with sheer determination as he had Leondros and the servant boy follow him back into the palace. The old prophet led them to a small meeting chamber to the right of the main entrance to the palace. Sala quickly strode past the table and chairs in the middle of the almost cozy room to an old wooden trunk in the far corner of the room. Pulling a thick leather strap, Sala unbound the trunk and threw the top open. Its creak momentarily filled the chamber. "Leondros, I need for you to go and bring Tahari back. It will be easier and safer if only one of us goes. As the General of the Secret Alliance, you should not have too much resistance," Sala said as he frantically rummaged through the deep trunk.

"At once," Leondros promised with urgency and turned to leave.

"Leondros! Wait!" Leondros halted and turned back as Sala pulled a dark cloak from the trunk. "Take this with you. Should things go badly, you can use this to ease your escape. It has been with me on many of my adventures," Sala said, presenting it to Leondros. The elfin prince quickly took off his own cloak and replaced it with the black cloak that Sala handed him. "I do not trust the guards that linger within the palace, and I believe that you are going to need all the help you can acquire," Sala continued as he thought about the evil that could be dwelling within the palace walls.

Leondros noticed the worry in Sala's blue eyes and knew that it was for his sake that this wise prophet was worried. "I will return, and with Tahari. I am not leaving Avdima until she is free," he promised his dear old friend as he put a reassuring hand on the old man's shoulder. Sala could only nod encouragingly. Leondros pulled up the dark velvet hood, which now covered his head and shadowed his face. He lingered a moment before Sala gave him a nod, allowing him to go. Leondros was quick to run out the main doors of Cypress Palace and disappear into the thick white fog of the Misty Forest.

Watching Leondros rush back out into the storm to save the brave warrior, Elijah felt that his mission was finished. Bidding farewell to Sala, the boy pulled his gray hood over his golden-blond hair. Taking a deep breath to calm his own anxieties, Elijah began to make his cautious return back to Akendron.

Long after Leondros had left for Akendron, Sala continued to watch for his friend. It was only right that Leondros should go after Tahari, for Leondros would outmatch any resistance that he would come into contact with. Yet as Sala's soulful eyes watched the skies grow more threatening and the wind began to pick up and the rain started to fall in torrents, he could not help but worry for his elfin friend.

"My dear one, we have been friends for such a long time, and though you have lived much longer than I, you seem like the son that I was never blessed with," Sala whispered with concern. It was in these later years that Sala found himself keeping a special eye out for his dear friend. "Be careful, my son; I feel you are right, and evil is closer than we realize. Be very careful," Sala said again as he heard thunder crack much closer now. The storm was almost upon them.

Chapter 58

Friends United

Emerging from the darkness of Avdima's dungeons, Tahari stepped out into a full-fledged thunderstorm. The wind howled mournfully, and the rain began to beat against her as if it wanted her to return to the dungeons. Refusing to be driven back, Tahari pulled her ripped cloak and dirty robe close and pressed on, climbing up a slippery bank of mud, for she did not want to return to Avdima. As Tahari made her way past the palace gates and into the darkened streets of Akendron, she half-stumbled over debris that was being blown into the streets. The storm grew with intensity and began to unleash its wrath of torrential rain, hail, and winds. Unable to see through the storm, Tahari managed to find shelter in a small doorway of a market that was closed for the evening. Lightning, flashed and she could clearly see the Misty Forest in the distance. Sala's concerned expression came to mind. She knew that he had to be greatly concerned about her whereabouts by now. With this burning in her mind, Tahari took a deep breath and stepped back out into the raging storm.

Making it to the middle of the city, Tahari ran across a street that was starting to flood. There was no way to see or hear anything going on around her, for everything was a mixture of wind and rain.

Suddenly, she felt a pair of strong hands grab her from behind and yank her back against the wall of a building. Tahari's skull made a sickening crack against the stone, and a hand quickly covered her mouth. Desperation and alarm filled her senses, and she began to struggle against this person.

"Shh! Do not move!" the strangely familiar voice spoke to Tahari in a hushed whisper. She looked at them but could not see clearly. "The enemy is close. Be still." Before either of them could move, an army of mounted soldiers rushed down the street. Tahari could only guess that it was the palace guard on patrol. They would have run straight into her if the stranger had not pulled her aside. When the soldiers had disappeared behind the palace gates, Tahari felt uneasy about their mission. She sensed evil within it. Then Tahari was released, and as she looked at the person who had kept her from being trampled to death, she froze.

"Almari!" Tahari gasped. Her familiar features were a welcome sight. Her light-brown and blonde hair was pulled back in a ponytail, soaked and hidden under the tattered dark-blue cloak that she wore. Her blue eyes sparkled as she looked upon Tahari again. "You are alive!" Tahari continued as she wrapped her up in a hug filled with enthusiasm. "Have you seen Senti and Rami?" Tahari pressed with wonder as she pulled her head back to look upon Almari's face again. The bright expression that Almari wore when she first saw Tahari drained into a solemn expression. She could only shrug and shake her head with uncertainty. Tahari nodded as she accepted her answer and patted her shoulder, still thankful that she was alive and with her now. Suddenly, a bolt of lightning flashed directly overhead, followed quickly by a heart-stopping clap of thunder. Almari lifted her tanned face and steady gaze to the stormy sky above and gestured to the storm raging on around them.

"I won't stay alive for long if we stay out in this. We have to find shelter quickly," she said, glancing down the street while debris from a nearby building rolled by. Judging by her weary condition, Tahari knew that she did not have the strength to go very far.

"Come. I know where we can go that will be safe from man and nature," Tahari said with assurance as she put a hand on her shoulder. Almari's expression of fear and anxiety slowly began to melt as she pulled her hood down over her wet brow and followed Tahari. Together, they fought the storm that seemed to grow worse with every passing moment. Tahari could only hope that no one else was caught in the middle of this storm.

Tahari led Almari through the streets and into the Misty Forest as quickly as the storm let them. Soon, they arrived at the palace and entered through the main door. Having seen them from a window, Sala had rushed to the door to greet them.

"Tahari! You're alive!" Sala exclaimed. His face brightened as he ran up and threw his arms around Tahari. He could not have been any happier to see her standing before him. When he stepped back and looked at the person who had accompanied her, deep concern emanated from his dark blue eyes.

"Sala? What is it?" Tahari asked, puzzled as she watched the concern in his face become fixed with worry.

"Is Leondros not with you?" he asked in growing distress as he quickly ran past them to peer out the front door of the palace. Tahari looked at Almari and then back at Sala as he stood upon the doorstep searching the stormy grounds for his elfin friend. She felt a chill shoot down her spine.

"He has returned from Endenbury already?" Tahari asked, feeling her heart sinking. Sala slowly walked back through the doorway and nodded. There was grave fear and worry in his blue eyes.

"Leondros returned not long before we heard about you being sentenced to death. He promised to get you out before any harm could come to you," Sala explained as he started to pace the floor. His arms were folded and his face twisted with worry. Tahari's mouth had gone dry. Horror filled her thoughts as she looked toward the open door and the raging storm that continued on outside. Something had gone wrong; she could feel it.

"Tell me that he did not," Tahari said in a horrified whisper. Almari stepped toward her and put a reassuring hand on her shoulder.

"Do not fear. When your friend finds that you are not there, he will return," she tried to assure her, but Tahari refused to clutch at such lofty hopes. Looking at Almari, Tahari shook her head with a guilty expression.

"Normally, I would agree with you, but we are heading into dark times. There is much evil at work tonight, and it is growing. It will not be so simple getting to and from Avdima now." Tahari spoke from experience, for she had felt a strange and chilling force within the walls of Avdima when she escaped earlier. "Leondros, I am afraid, is in grave danger," Tahari said as she agreed with Sala's suspicions.

"You are right. The evil grows stronger, even as we speak," Sala said as he turned toward the open door. His eyes gazed sadly into the storm that raged on around the palace. "I am an old man, and my strength is failing me, but I wonder..." he said softly as he looked down at his hands. Tahari saw the love that he had for Leondros. He would give everything at that moment to protect his dear old friend. She could see that he was summoning the courage and strength to go out into the raging storm after Leondros. Sensing that she was the cause for Leondros's disappearance and Sala's distress, Tahari was overwhelmed with guilt.

"*I* will go and bring him back," Tahari said with determination, pulling her drenched hood back over her head.

Sala turned toward Tahari with an alarmed expression. "Please, do not risk your life any more. If you go out that door, you will be killed. I cannot let you go!" he said with equal determination.

Tahari lowered her head for a moment and breathed a deep breath. "Sala, I made a promise to him, and I cannot fail him, nor will I abandon him to the evil that lurks within that horrible place. Besides, I am the reason he went back there," Tahari replied calmly as she looked at him with great fervor. "The evil that Leondros is about to walk into is growing stronger by the minute. The minds of all who reside there will be swayed to the darkness and will turn against him. Leondros is going to need help.

"Tahari, do not worry so for Leondros. He is a most cunning elfin warrior, and his keen senses will keep him from any such danger," Sala said optimistically, looking back out the open door. "You are needed here. Your mission is here before you now." Tahari looked at Sala in frustration and despair for her friend. She understood that she was on a secret mission that was of the utmost importance, and only she could find and read the ancient scrolls of the prophecy that Rafar had left them, but Tahari knew that a friend of hers was in grave danger and needed her help.

"Sala, I do not doubt Leondros's abilities as an elfin warrior, but I believe that everyone needs someone to watch their back from time to time. There is no shame in asking for help!" Tahari was almost shouting, her worry and concern for Leondros was so great. Suddenly, Tahari realized that Almari was no longer standing at her side. Looking around, Tahari saw only wet foot prints upon the marble floor. Almari had gone back out into the storm while Sala and she had argued.

"Where has your friend gone?" Sala asked with concern as he quickly scanned the grand entrance only to realize, too, that the girl named Almari was no longer standing quietly beside them.

"Almari goes to search for Leondros," Tahari said with worried realization.

"How will she know what he looks like? She has never met him before," Sala asked as they watched the raging winds tear at the surrounding forest. Out of the corner of her eye, Tahari could see deep concern in the aged prophet's face.

"She overheard us speak of him and that he is an elfin warrior. Currently there are not many elves within the Shandel, but her search will still be extensive. It will be a mission of faith, to be sure," Tahari said knowingly. She closed her eyes and prayed for both of her friends.

Chapter 59

Mission Amiss

The storm continued to rage over Akendron, the wind howling and the streets quickly flooding as Leondros fought his way toward Avdima Palace. Edging closer to the palace, he reached a corner of a building where he could take shelter for a moment. Peering into the rain and hail, Leondros sensed the evil was much stronger now than before. He remembered the chill of evil he had felt while walking with Alon-Settie through the long dark corridors of Avdima. It had taken great strength for him to break free from that icy grip. Now, he would confront it again. He did not dread this challenge, for someone awaited his help deep within the castle. Narrowing his eyes at the tumultuous road that awaited him, Leondros charged on ahead. He soon disappeared within the shadows that surrounded Avdima Palace.

Taking cover near a large oak tree that grew on the far east side of the palace, Leondros climbed through its branches until he came to an open window of the castle. Peering inside first, he made sure that no one was around to see him slip inside. It was almost one o'clock now. Leondros knew that most people would be heading off to sleep shortly, allowing him to move throughout the castle unseen. Leondros walked quietly down the long, dimly lit corridors of stone. He made his way through the palace toward the dungeons, listening for the sounds of anyone approaching. The palace was silent. He found that quiet unusual on a night of celebration. *This is most strange,* he thought, but he focused his attention on getting Tahari out of the palace as soon as possible.

When Leondros eventually reached the lower levels of the palace, he quickly found himself within Avdima's dungeons. Staring in horror at the network of cold dark cells, he saw that much had been changed since he had last seen this place. Gazing at the condition of the dungeons, Leondros felt chills run down his spine. Dampness hung in the air, and he guessed that it was not from the weather outside. The air itself smelled of disease and mildew. *Why would the king allow these conditions to exist within his own palace?* he thought as he stared a moment longer at the deteriorating conditions within the dungeons. Then, the thought of Tahari being held within this foul place drove him on. He made his way down the long, winding corridors deep underground. As Leondros searched, he became increasingly concerned, for he could not feel her presence anywhere close by.

After searching for some time, Leondros came to a particular cell that caught his attention. There was a small piece of black cloak caught within the metal framework of the cell door. He slowly reached up and touched the damp fabric. An image of Tahari flashed before his eyes, but he did not see where she had been taken.

She was here. Leondros was at a loss, for he had no clues as to Tahari's whereabouts. Before he could decide what to do next, he heard footsteps making their way toward the dungeon level. Leondros heard two guards talking as they came closer. What he heard left him frozen with shock, for they spoke of Alon-Settie's capture and death. Forcing himself to put aside his feelings, Leondros watched as the two guards approached.

The guards who approached were the same two who had brought Tahari to her cell. They had just been given the orders to execute the prisoner. Of the two, the younger guard was the more nervous about the task, for he feared what the witch could turn them into. Before opening the door to the dungeons, he took a deep breath and prayed that they would live through this. The older guard simply rolled his eyes and shoved his armor-plated partner through the doorway. Entering the dimly lit corridor, they walked down to the damp cell they had locked the dark-haired witch in. The younger guard trembled with fear, and sweat ran down his thin face. His armor shouted his fear throughout the darkened corridor as it rattled along with him, until his older partner grew frustrated and grabbed him by the neck.

"Would you stop that?" the older guard demanded in a gruff voice, his gray eyes glaring at his cowardly partner.

"I cannot help it," the younger guard replied in a quivering whisper.

"Well, you had better help it, or I will see to it that you get your armor oiled while you are inside it!" the older guard's threat carried the weight of being carried out on other young guards. His partner nodded fervently. As the rattling of the young guard's armor lessened, his partner lightly shoved him and shook his head as he turned back to their assigned task. Entering Tahari's cell, they found it empty. They stared into the cell for a long moment in disbelief.

"Do you think she...?" the young guard began to say, when his partner slowly turned to him with a cold glare.

"Be silent! She is gone. What more needs to be said? Solarous was as afraid of her as we are. He no doubt has forgotten that he had sent someone else to carry out the order," the older guard said angrily as he hit the back of the young guard's helmet with his worn gloves. He cautiously eyed the long corridor around them. "We'll just report that the witch has been dealt with. Now, let us leave this place. I..." the older guard stopped when he noticed a strange expression come over his young partner's face. "What is it?" he asked, his face slowly draining of all expression.

"I-uh..." the young guard slowly began to double over, holding his midsection. "Understood. I will pass this word along," the young guard said as he tried to straighten himself. A look of horror came over his face and he began running down the dim corridor. "Huh-oh! I must have eaten something..." the young guard's words faded with him as he ran for the privy located at the far end of corridor.

"Idiot." the older guard shook his head as he grumbled to himself.

Now alone, the remaining guard slowly walked back the way they had come. Before he could reach the dark wooden door, a shadowy figure jumped out at him, grabbed him, and slammed him against the metal cell door. The clatter of the guard's armor against the metal bars thundered throughout the entire level. The older guard froze for a moment in fear, looking into the cold and angry face of the elfin warrior who held him fast by the throat.

"What have you done with the prisoner Tahari?" Leondros demanded, glaring at the silver-armored guard. The older guard looked around this elfin warrior to see that he was indeed alone. Anger flashed through the elf's brown eyes as he slammed the guard back against the bars even harder.

"What is your business down here? Are you here on orders from Solarous?" the older guard demanded angrily, his gray eyes returning Leondros's glare.

"As the General of the Secret Alliance, it is my job to see that all prisoners are treated fairly. Now I ask again, where have you taken the prisoner known as Tahari?" Leondros carefully eyed the guard. The man's armor hid all distinguishing features of his body, but his cold gray eyes and aged face shouted that he would not be intimidated easily. His eyes studied the elfin warrior for a moment before a cruel smile crept into his angered expression.

"It would have been a waste of time, money, and wood to execute a slave in the morning, so some of the men took her to the cliffs outside of town and gave her a little push." the older guard's answer did not please Leondros as a look of hurt and fear passed over his face for a moment. He then tightened his grip on the guard's throat as his hurt expression turned into anger.

"You will die a very slow and agonizing death for that!" Leondros promised angrily.

Just then, Leondros heard the distant echo of clanking metal: soldiers running down the many levels of the dungeon toward his location. He watched as the pale man's lips curled into a sinister smile as if he knew what would happen next. Recoiling from the older guard, Leondros sensed that he had been betrayed, but by whom he did not know.

"Until such time, I would love for you to stay, General. We have been expecting you," the older guard said, an evil expression washing over his whole face as he drew his sword and pointed it at Leondros. The elfin prince had but one option now. Looking around for another exit, Leondros saw the soldiers enter the dungeons. His heart sank as he recognized the soldiers as his own.

"The Secret Alliance has been taken and is no more," Leondros said to himself in a tone of defeat. The pain of betrayal drove itself deep into his chest as he watched his men surround him with spears and swords. A voice spoke out.

"That is where you are wrong." the voice was muffled, but it sounded strangely familiar. Leondros turned to see a hooded man in a black cloak. Leondros slowly backed away from the older guard and the soldiers, positioning himself with his back to the only door out of the dungeons. "The Secret Alliance will continue to exist. It is you who will be no more. Tonight is a night of many endings and beginnings. The old kingdom has fallen, and a new one created by my lord has taken its place. The Tabor family line has passed into history, and you will join them." the man's words were hard to believe, but Leondros felt the great eruption of evil in the air. It was no longer silent and secret. Evil had come to take possession of this palace and all who lived there.

The man ordered two soldiers to restrain Leondros. As they reached him, he grabbed both men and rammed them into the stone wall.

"Be mindful of history. Without it, neither present nor future could exist," Leondros said as he drew his sword. The soldiers moved in to attack him. They did so without care that this had been their general, whom they had greatly respected and honored, only a couple of hours before. They attacked like ravenous wolves, but their prey was neither weak nor afraid. The corridor was wide enough to allow only a few soldiers forward at once. One by one, Leondros took down the soldiers, backing closer to the door. He did not, however, take a single life. Although he could have killed them, he did not. When the opportunity arose, Leondros bolted through the open door leading to a staircase that would eventually lead him out and away from the palace, soldiers on his heels.

Running down the long dim corridor toward the front hall that would lead him out of Avdima, Leondros felt the overwhelming presence of evil with every step. Its icy cold grip was everywhere. The great palace had been taken. Leondros's mind was a whirlwind of madness and thought, and he was now desperate to escape the darkening palace. He felt hurt and betrayed, but he forced these thoughts from his mind. He must think only of escape. He had to bring word of these tragic events to Sala and to his people. The ancient evil had indeed returned, and soon this darkness would spread beyond the borders of the Shandel. The very existence of Andora was in grave danger.

Reaching the front hall, Leondros came to an abrupt halt. Waiting for him was the rest of the Secret Alliance. These men had not accompanied him on the road to Endenbury, but they had been ordered to remain behind to guard the palace. Leondros was greatly outnumbered. Looking into the eyes of these men, Leondros again found no ally. He was very much alone.

The elfin prince refused to let his exhaustion dull his senses, for he needed them to survive the next few moments. The rearguard of the Secret Alliance charged forward to attack. Evil had taken their minds, and they no longer recognized their general. Leondros was the enemy. In the hour of Lord Jarden's rise to power, the minds of the Secret Alliance soldiers were taken. They were quick to receive instruction from their master from the mind control technique that Solarous incorporated with his soup. They had waited in the shadows until the time was right for them to strike. Leondros now fought the advancing swordsmen without killing a single man. He did not have to, for his movements were quick enough to evade his oncoming enemies. Those who died were inadvertently killed by their own. The battle had gone on for several long minutes when, all at once, the remaining men stopped fighting and backed away from him. They enclosed him in a circle and eyed him closely, making room for someone approaching the group. The cloaked man from the dungeons walked into the circle. This time, the man was carrying a sword. As the man entered the ring, Leondros felt the disturbing coldness of evil emanating from his opponent. This fight would be much more difficult, for he would be fighting forces of both man and evil. There would be no rest for Leondros; his opponent would show him no mercy.

The battle between Leondros and the dark-cloaked man started with great intensity. The mysterious man knew that Leondros was weary and wanted to use that as an advantage. Except, to this man's dismay, Leondros fought without showing signs of tiring. As they fought, Leondros noticed that this man's skills exceeded those of the men he had previously fought. He had been well trained for battle, for his skills nearly matched Leondros's own. Leondros then felt the powers of darkness grow. The darkness sank into his mind and body, robbing him of strength. If he was going to survive this match, Leondros would need to break this man quickly. Taking up whatever strength he had left, Leondros disarmed his dark opponent and drove him back against a stone wall, pinning him with his sword to the man's throat. He had only to drive his sword forward to finish the man and the evil that emanated from him, but Leondros needed to know where his friend had been taken.

"Answer me this and I may spare your life," Leondros said in an angry whisper as he fought to catch his breath. The man remained silent. "Where did you take the prisoner who was to be executed in the morning for heresy?" Still, the cloaked man remained silent. Angered by this, Leondros quickly reached up and ripped back the man's hood.

Leondros froze to see Alon-Settie staring back at him with a cold, uncaring expression. Studying his face, Leondros wanted to see his friend, but all he could find was pure hate in Alon-Settie's brown rage-filled eyes. An excruciating blow hit Leondros in the chest and he staggered backward. Tears stung Leondros's eyes as he looked back at Alon-Settie. His world came crashing down upon him, leaving him unable to combat the agonizing pain that tore through him.

Quickly, the remaining men of the Secret Alliance surrounded and overcame him. He did not feel the punch that threw him to the ground, nor the pain from the savage beatings that followed. Leondros closed his eyes as blackness washed over him. Never before had he known of such things. The world that Leondros loved tore him apart on the inside as the soldiers tore him apart on the outside. He refused to open his eyes again, for nothing but pain awaited him. Leondros welcomed the blackness coming over him.

Chapter 60

Hell's Dungeon

The storm raged on endlessly. Not everyone who sought shelter knew of the terrifying events taking place within Avdima; most were too afraid to venture out into the violent storm. Almari made her way through the driving wind and rain toward the palace. She had never seen the person that Tahari and Sala spoke of, but she had seen the concern in Tahari's face, and she could not help but also feel concern. Almari did not fully understand why it was so important that they get Leondros out of the palace, but the worry in Tahari's sea-green eyes had been enough to convince her to help.

Almari had not planned on going back out into the storm after she had barely escaped the Tomblock. She had found the one person most important to her, one she thought was lost forever. She saw no real benefit for doing such a crazy thing, but something told her to do this for the friend who had been brought back into her life. When Almari reached the edge of the storm-swept marketplace, she made her way into the shadows of a darkened alley. It was an alley filled with debris and, thus, a dead end to everyone who passed by it. Yet to a very secret few, this alley was much more. Beyond the rotting crates and garbage that lined the end of the alley was a narrow tunnel that led under the moat that surrounded the palace walls, past the walkways and temples of Avdima's grounds, out of sight of the Draccen soldiers that now guarded Avdima's high outer walls, and into the palace of Avdima itself. It was a path that she knew well, for while still a prisoner of the Tomblock, some of their nightly escapades involved secret missions to the subterranean tunnels of the Avdima. There were only a handful of palace workers who risked great punishment to sneak out food to the unfortunate people of Akendron, let alone to the workers of the Tomblock. As she traveled these tunnels now, she found herself thankful that she risked so much then to have this knowledge now. Almari finally emerged into a long, dim corridor. Glancing down both ends of the corridor, she quickly decided which way to go. Before she could go, Almari heard the sound of soldiers' footsteps approaching.

She looked around wildly for a place to hide. She noticed a heavy wooden beam just overhead and quickly scaled up the stone wall. Making use of the cracks within the walls, she pulled herself up onto the high beam. The beam was damp, and Almari felt her grip slip and then her body start to fall. She caught herself just in time and froze, hearing the guards doing their evening patrol. She clung tightly to the damp timber as the unsuspecting group of armored men walked beneath her. Then one soldier stopped at what seemed to be his post, for he took a moment to gaze down both directions of the corridor and then out the window behind him. After several long moments, Almari began cursing at this man silently, for her grip was slipping and she did not know how much longer she could hang on. Then a loud voice echoed down the hall.

"Soldier! Come! We need your help!" a man called from the doorway that led to one of Avdima's high towers. It was here that several men from the Secret Alliance were gathered in conspiracy. The work of the ancient evil was getting underway as they silenced members of the old kingdom. It was for this purpose that they summoned all the guards within the palace. The guard was quick to leave his post and head up to the high tower.

No time too soon, Almari thought as she dropped in relief from the slippery beam. Landing on the hard stone floor, she cautiously looked around for a sign of more soldiers. When she was satisfied that the corridor was clear, Almari focused her attention on the work at hand.

Finally able to take in the sights, sounds, and smells of the palace, Almari began to understand why Tahari was concerned with her friend's safety. Chills ran down her spine and cold dampness soaked into her body. Almari dared not speak aloud, for she could sense the great evil within this place. Its dark shadow was everywhere. All the goodness that had existed within this place was slowly being consumed. Turning toward the doorway where the soldier had disappeared, Almari surmised that if Leondros were free, he would have returned to Sala's palace by now. She silently crept toward the doorway. Almari had a sense about these things, and it told her that if she were going to find Tahari's friend, she would find him here. When she reached the dark doorway and gazed up into the dim and murky staircase of stone, she felt her heart sink. Besides the mournful wail of the wind, there were other sounds in the tower that caught Almari's attention, and they vividly reminded her of the Tomblock.

Never would I have imagined that any place could be worse than the Tomblock, but I think I have found it. Almari shook off the feeling of dread that threatened to overwhelm her and quickly climbed the damp staircase in her worn leather shoes. As she climbed higher, Almari noticed that the smell of decaying wood was growing stronger. It was hard to breathe the thick, foul air, but choking it down, she forced herself to continue on as silently as before. Climbing higher into the dark tower, Almari looked up at the winding staircase wrapped around the inside of the tower's exterior wall. Several torches lit up the stairwell, and she could see the door to a chamber halfway up the tower. Horrible sounds of someone being beaten emanated from this chamber. The sounds echoed throughout the tower. Swallowing hard, Almari forced herself to keep moving closer to the chamber. She winced at each crack of the whip and sound of a blow hitting its mark. She agonized with the men being whipped and beaten relentlessly. As their screams filled the night air, Almari's mind flash back to the people who worked within the Tomblock. She had watched how they had suffered and died at the hands of the cruel taskmasters. The weight of the moment overwhelmed her, for this grief was still with her, and she struggled to catch her breath and remain calm. Then the thunderous sound of a heavy wooden door being thrown open against a stone wall startled her and caused her to jump back into the dark shadows of the stairwell.

"What is your plan for him now, sire?" Almari heard a man's voice cut through the murky darkness. She found herself thankful that she had not yet reached the landing that lead into the chamber as two men came out of the torture chamber. The first man turned back to his companion to answer him.

"The master wants that we should finish him, and so we shall. However, I have much more planned for him before he reaches his end." when this man answered, Almari recognized the man as the Prince of Akendron. She had seen him when he came to ensure a fair order on the plantation, a duty given to him by his father. She narrowed her blue eyes at him, for he never fulfilled any such duty. The plantation masters had long since paid Prince Alon-Settie for his silence.

"When will we do this, my lord?" the second man asked with curiosity. Alon-Settie looked back into the chamber with an evil expression.

"Patience, Judeas; we wait until he wakes again," Alon-Settie replied.

Judeas turned back to the chamber. The expression that filled his face was one of great doubt. "Truly, he can't be alive. Are you sure he is not dead already?" he asked with a concerned tone.

As the two men talked, Almari peered closely at Judeas. His features differed from Alon-Settie's. When he turned back to Alon-Settie, she realized that Judeas was of the elfin race, just like the person she was searching for, but this elf was also very much a traitor.

"He lives still. It will take much more than that to break him," Alon-Settie said, speaking from experience. He stepped toward the door for a closer look. "But it will not take much longer," he said as if he were speaking to the prisoner instead. Then Alon-Settie grabbed hold of the door and slammed it shut. The thunderous sound caused Almari to jump again. The two men turned toward her, and Almari's mouth went dry. Her capture would not help Tahari's friend, so she began to back down the dark staircase. As she was on the verge of being seen, the two men stopped and then mysteriously turned and started climbing the stairs to go higher within the tower. Almari froze for a long moment, not daring to even breathe as she waited for the footsteps to fade away. She heard another heavy door being thrown open and slammed shut again. She took a deep breath. Now was her chance.

"Thank Adalai," Almari whispered as her heart pounded violently against her chest. Looking up passed the torture chamber, she pushed aside her fears of the two men returning and capturing her. She silently made her way up to the torture chamber's door. In the dim light of the stairwell, she noticed that the door was badly worn and had a barred opening at the bottom. It was nowhere big enough for a man to fit through, but just big enough to catch a glimpse of whoever was inside. Staring at it a moment, Almari did not know if the man behind this door was Leondros, but her search had to start somewhere. Dropping to her knees, Almari felt the night's chill hanging close around her. Ignoring this discomfort, she peered between the bars and into the darkness of the chamber. As her eyes adjusted to the darkness, she began to make out the room's features. It was a plain stone chamber with a small, barred window on the outside wall. The fury of the storm was driving wind and rain into the chamber, and the stone walls within the chamber were glistening wet. As lightning flashed outside, she saw a body lying motionless on the wet cold stone floor. Almari's heart sank.

How could anyone leave someone in these horrid conditions? she asked herself, but then shook her head sadly, remembering quite well that she herself had lived with such atrocities. *People such as these? Easily,* she thought as she crept closer to get a better look at the body. Almari had no idea what Leondros looked like, but she knew that he was an elf. With another flash of lightning, she saw the tell-tale features of an elf. His torn brown clothes were dirty and soaked, making him seem but a slave, yet Almari knew in her heart that this was Leondros. He was lying on his stomach, facing the door, and had been beaten badly.

Looking past the wet blond hair that almost covered his face, Almari could see a just and caring individual. "No one deserves this, you least of all," she whispered as she reached up to pull the door open. Just then, she heard the men coming back.

"Bring him at once. He will awaken soon, and I would not want to miss it." Alon-Settie's voice echoed down the staircase. The sound of soldiers' feet came marching down the tower stairs toward Leondros's cell. Almari felt her chance to get him out of here quickly pass her by. Torn by indecision, Almari froze for a moment as she gazed back into the dark chamber. Leaving now would give these men the chance they needed to kill him, but not leaving would mean her capture and thus he would perish regardless. Reaching out and taking hold of a bar on the small window, Almari wanted to leave him some word of encouragement.

"Please do not give up. Whatever awaits you may be horrible, but keep this hope in mind and try to endure. I will brin' word of this to Tahari. I know her well. She would never see any of her friends put through such peril. She will get you out one way or another," Almari whispered, hoping that he could somehow hear her. Looking upon him one last time, Almari then tore herself from the door and hurried down the staircase. As she did so, she heard the soldiers nearing the spot she had just left. Reaching the bottom of the tower, Almari heard a thunderous crash echo down to her. Stopping with a deep sense of regret, she heard them take Leondros out of the damp cell and carry him higher into the tower. Biting her lower lip, Almari finally tore herself from the doorway and ran back the way she had come. There was not much time before Alon-Settie made good on his promise.

Chapter 61

Betrayal's Agony

The murky cloud of silence began to shift and move as sounds became real again. The numbness of sleep lifted, and dull sensations became sharp pain, intense as the burning of an immense fire. Leondros opened his eyes groggily, blurred and distorted images coming into focus. He slowly lifted his head and realized that he was bound by his wrists and suspended off the floor from a timber in what he recognized to be a torture chamber. As his eyes focused on who was standing in front of him, all the pain that he was feeling paled in comparison to the pain of seeing his friend glaring back at him. Judging from Alon-Settie's cold look, their friendship was no more. Had it ever been true? The thought to ask for help quickly faded from Leondros's mind.

"It is about time that you awoke. I want you to meet someone," Alon-Settie said in an unconcerned tone, motioning for someone to enter the chamber where the elfin warrior was helplessly bound. Leondros studied Alon-Settie's face, and with every passing moment, the hard truth settled deeper within him.

"Why have you done such a thing?" Leondros managed to ask with an even whisper, masking the pain in his heart. Alon-Settie turned back to him and gave him a smug expression as three men came into the cold chamber. Smugness became an evil smile as the men entered. The elfin prince turned his attention to the men. He felt the cold sword of betrayal plunge deeper into his already wounded heart. The three men who stood before him had fought at his side near Endenbury. Looking into the faces of Gesson the dwarf, and Amon-yen and Judeas, the two elfin warriors from his father's army, Leondros thought for a moment that he might find some hope in their eyes, but that hope also died quickly. They watched him with cold expressions, expressions almost eager for his death. Alon-Settie whispered several instructions to them. Judging by their sinister grins, Leondros felt his end coming. "What great injustice have I ever done to you, friend?" Leondros asked in a raspy whisper, throat tightening and tears stinging his eyes.

Alon-Settie stepped close to him. "Friend? You have no *friend* here, nor do I see a friend before me. My father always found more favor with you than with me. It is time that you know what it feels like to be second to someone close to you!" Alon-Settie spoke angrily, but his voice was strained with immense grief. His cruel words drove the sword of betrayal soul-deep.

"If you believe that, then you know not who I am. I am second to my father's throne and one of four heirs within my family, but I am content. You will ascend to your father's throne. If that is not enough for you, I pity you." Leondros's testimony of reality enraged Alon-Settie. He pulled out his dagger and drove it deep into Leondros's left side. The intense pain kept Leondros from breathing as he felt warm, thick liquid run down his side. His brown eyes stared wide in horror at the man who had once been his friend.

"Save your pity for those who will join you soon!" Alon-Settie hissed. His malice-filled brown eyes did not waver as he watched the life within his elfin companion fade. The four men watched in delight as Leondros weakened before them. As the elfin prince's eyes closed and his head sank, they knew they had seen the last of this great elfin warrior.

"What is next, my lord?" Gesson asked gruffly as he looked over at Alon-Settie. The prince took a moment to admire their handiwork before he spoke again.

"There is still life within him; destroy it. Make sure that the son of Goldendragon breathes no more and then dispose of him. I would hate to run into him again later," Alon-Settie replied as he took his last look at Leondros. An evil idea entered his mind. "Amon-yen, I have a special mission for you, but know that it will not come easily to you.

"I am at your service; whatever you ask will be done," Amon-yen replied humbly with a bow as his long light-brown hair hung over his shoulders. He returned his gaze to Alon-Settie, who seemed pleased by the sight of such loyalty.

"The ship *Valora* is docked in the harbor of Seamara. Its captain and crew stand ready to do my bidding. I have need for you to return home." Alon-Settie's dark brown eyes were filled malicious intent; Amon-yen studied him carefully and then gave a slow nod before leaving the tower's highest dungeon with the prince. Gesson and Judeas stood for a long moment afterward, staring at the bruised and bloody body of their general.

"Well? Will you do it? Or shall I?" Gesson asked. Judeas remained silent; great disbelief filled his eyes as he reeled at the scene now before them. "All right, fine! I will do it!" the dwarf soldier hissed impatiently, quickly drawing his sword and raising it high over his head.

"NO! Wait!" he shouted suddenly, leaping forward to stay Gesson's hand from driving the sword through Leondros's neck. Gesson turned to his comrade and stared at him with wonder.

"'Wait'? What do you mean, 'wait'? What exactly should I wait for?" Gesson demanded angrily, narrowing his gaze at the black-haired elf. The elfin warrior looked at Gesson and then to the battered elfin prince. Judeas studied Leondros closely, looking for a sign of life within their former leader. A moment passed in silence, and then Judeas moved away from Leondros's body.

"There is nothing for us to do here," Judeas said in a hesitant whisper, gazing at Leondros with disbelief. "He has already passed into the realm of shadow and darkness. Let us leave, for if his spirit is strong enough, it will search for a kind soul to help him return," he said as he quietly made his way to the open door.

"Maybe Alon-Settie will prove to be a better general than you; it would not take much," Gesson said as he turned to go. His words added to the pain that still dwelt within the room. Thunder and lightning suddenly exploded overhead. The storm seemed to be growing to cataclysmic proportions. The wind's howl became even more mournful as the rain and hail pounded the earth mercilessly. Nature herself sensed that a great injustice had occurred. Man had taken something special and sacred from her. This deed would not go unpunished, and nature would bring down its fury as a result.

Chapter 62

Called to Fight

G azing out into the night from a large window in the grand entrance of Cypress Palace, Tahari watched and listened intently as if nature herself were speaking to her. As she watched the storm become stronger and more violent, Tahari knew something had gone terribly wrong. There was a great stirring within nature as if it had been greatly upset by a grave injustice. The mournful sound of the wind was as one who wept bitterly for a lost love. Tahari slowly began to understand, for she too felt a great sadness she could not readily explain. It took everything she had to keep the tears back.

"Why such a look?" Sala asked with concern as he walked over to Tahari. He had taken notice of how quiet and solemn she had become after Almari had left. "There is no need to worry. In a few minutes, your friend will return with Leondros. They will be all right; you will see," he continued encouragingly. Tahari turned from the window and looked at him a moment, trying to believe that he was right and she was merely worrying too much, but her instincts told her otherwise.

"I want to believe that they are safe and will walk through that door unharmed very soon," Tahari replied, feeling uneasy with worry and concern. Turning back to the glass window, she listened to the wind's mournful wail. "Yet I have listened to the wind, and it tells me that something terrible has happened tonight," she said, stepping closer to the window to listen for any more news the wind might have for her.

Sala looked at Tahari with disbelief for a moment and then nodded his head. "You speak like Leondros. Surely, you are a member of the elfin race," he said with reverent smile. "Many times I have watched him as he listened to the sounds of the wind, rain, and animals of the wild. He said that they can tell you much if you will quiet your mind long enough to listen to them." a faint smile came to Sala's face. "This sadness that you feel no doubt comes from the loss of your friends within the plantation," Sala said in a sad but thoughtful tone. Instantly, Tahari's mind returned to those whom she had become close friends with and had lost. This sadness ran deep as she felt hot tears sting her eyes.

"If I had not left that day, they might be alive this very moment." since that fateful day, Tahari blamed herself for their deaths, for the master's hatred for her ran deep. Master Dancar sought any means to hurt her, even if it meant hurting those that she cared about.

"Do not think such thoughts," Sala said in a compassionate voice as he stepped up to Tahari and put a reassuring hand on her shoulder. "If you had not done what you did, Leondros might never have arrived in Akendron alive. Fate may work in strange ways, to be sure, but it has spared you both for a good reason. A quest to save Andora from the ancient evil sounds like a perfect reason." Sala's reminder of the ancient prophecy put a small hope back in her mind.

Then the heavy wooden front door flew open and hit the wall, causing a thunderous crash that echoed throughout the great hall. Tahari bolted toward the entrance and awaited Leondros and Almari. She breathed a sigh of relief as she watched Almari stumble through the large doorway. She alone grabbed the door, however, and with all her strength fought the raging wind and pushed it shut again. Tahari watched her, feelings of confusion and fear gripping her heart. All hope of seeing Leondros vanished. Almari turned back to them, fighting to catch her breath. The worried expression on her face told her story.

"Almari?" Tahari asked as she approached her. Her blue eyes were filled with hurt and guilt but also hope. Tears welled within her eyes when she saw Tahari. Blinking them back, Almari forced herself to stand and control herself.

"Tahari, I know the news that I brin' is not what you hoped for." she spoke humbly, explaining what had happened. "A terrible fate has fallen upon your friend. When I left, he lived still." Tahari's face drained of expression as her heart sank as she heard these words.

"Almari, please, tell me what has happened to Leondros," Tahari insisted, taking hold of her shoulders. She looked at her with a defeated expression as if she wished that she could be spared from retelling what she had seen.

"Leondros was captured," Almari said and then gave a long, painful sigh. "When I managed to get close enough to hear what was goin' on, I realized they were trying to beat the life out of him.

Tahari froze to the spot on which she stood. Her mind could not even begin to image such a horrible fate falling upon Leondros. Tahari could only wonder who would even dare to inflict such harm upon a prince of the elfin people. "You said that he was captured," she began as an idea began to grow in her mind. Almari nodded in response. "Did you see the men who did this to him?" she asked.

"I did recognize one of the men clearly. Prince Alon-Settie. From what I heard from his own mouth, he was one of the men who captured Leondros.

At the mention of Alon-Settie's name, Sala gasped. "Are you sure that it was Alon-Settie?" Sala asked as he looked at Almari in horror.

"I am most sure. I would know the face of Alon-Settie anywhere. When his father entrusted the plantations to him, the prime masters paid him for his silence so they could do as they pleased. It was because of him that we suffered so.

As Almari told them of the real Alon-Settie, Sala was overwhelmed with grief. He slowly made his way over to a chair and sank into it. "Then Leondros has been betrayed by his best friend," he said slowly as the shock of what Almari had said slowly began to sink in.

Tahari remembered then something that gave deeper meaning to what was going on around them. She turned back toward the window and listened to the wind's mournful cry, aware now of what it had been trying to tell her and how it tied in with a line from the prophecy. "Betrayal and a tomb await a prince," she said, horrified, turning her gaze toward Sala. He understood the reference and lowered his head sadly. Tahari watched a father grieve for his son. Sala could not have loved Leondros any more than a real son, and for this reason, he wept. The thunder cracked loudly outside. Turning her head back toward the window, Tahari could feel from where she stood that the city had been overtaken by the ancient evil. Then she heard a faint whisper on the wind as it came through the window.

"I could choose no other to be the eyes that watch my back in battle."

The words that Leondros had spoken to Tahari upon their meeting seemed to drift through the window. She had clearly heard his voice on the wind. It was his plea for help. She could not let him down. Tahari would not. She quickly grabbed her cloak and threw it over herself as she marched toward the front door.

Sala looked up confusedly. "Tahari? Where are you going?" he asked in growing alarm as he rose from his chair and his grief. She turned back to him and saw the worry in his face. He did not need her answer, for he knew where she was going. "You must not go! You will be caught, and the same fate will fall upon you as it has Leondros!" he said as he took hold of her arm.

"Leondros has been brutally betrayed, and from what Almari has seen, he has been put through enough tonight," Tahari said with determination, but Sala did not let her go. "Did you not hear? He calls for help, and if someone does not answer, he will die." she gestured to the window, for she could still hear the mournful cry of the wind, and on it was Leondros's voice.

"What of the prophecy?" Sala asked in a raspy whisper.

Tahari looked into his soulful blue eyes and nodded with understanding. "I know that you would not dare risk my life for any reason, but the prophecy now calls us into action. How can we find Farro if we refuse to face the dangers that lie before us?" Sala's eyes went wide with momentary shock, but her words slowly sank in.

"Remember the line of instruction given after the prophecy?" she said, hoping he would understand what they needed to do.

"'Do not leave him in towers high but bring him home,'" Sala recited with a slow and understanding nod. Deep sorrow filled his face as the line of prophecy and the actuality of Leondros's betrayal hit him hard.

"If we are going to save our world from the ancient evil, then it is best that we follow the prophecy. Leondros is dear to us both, and it is for this reason as well that I go at the risk of persecution and even death." as Tahari spoke, she saw hope began to fill both Sala's and Almari's eyes.

Closing his eyes for a moment, Sala grieved for his friend, but he reopened them and found a hopeful smile. Letting go of Tahari's arm, he said "Bring him back, Tahari." the expression in his sad blue eyes was like seeing Leondros's own father asking this of her. Then, before Tahari turned to go, Almari walked up beside her.

"I am joinin' you, for there is much peril that awaits you in the palace, and I could not sleep now knowin' that someone was left to die in that awful place." she spoke with a determination equal to Tahari's own. It was clear that whatever she saw moved her enough to join her.

"I would not dare refuse such help. Thank you," Tahari replied with a warm smile as she put her hand on Almari's shoulder. Almari nodded in response.

Almari caught the lingering sadness in Sala's blue eyes. "Do not worry. I now fear for those who betrayed Leondros," she said.

"Why worry for them?" he asked, sounding quite puzzled.

"They did not know that Tahari was his friend. She is most protective of her friends. Let them be *very* afraid." Almari's words warmed Sala's face, and a bright, hopeful smile came to his face. With that, Almari and Tahari hurried out into the fury of the storm.

"Almari, you make me sound as if I am going to lay waste to every soldier we come in contact with," Tahari said, looking at her with a look of disbelief.

"Well, are you not?" she asked, smiling at her.

Tahari smiled then, recognizing the truth in her words.

Chapter 63

Phantom

The storm's raging winds began to die down, the torrents of rain slowed, and only occasionally did the lightning flash over Akendron. As a calm began to settle outside of Avdima, no such calm settled within the palace. Most of the royal family who still lived had been captured, including their loyal guards and servants. They had been taken to the dungeons within Avdima and tortured most horribly. Hope seemed but a memory to those poor souls.

The new regime had come to full power; the evil was free and did as it willed. Draccen soldiers that had been imprisoned within the mountains now walked upon Avdima's vast grounds and through its long corridors, guarding it from any attempt to overthrow the new order. The darkness that dwelt within the palace began to spread over the Shandel. The threat to Andora's fate was now very real.

Prisoners' cries echoed throughout the dreary, dimly lit palace. One by one, they fell silent as death came to them. Evil was stomping out all hope.

A Draccen soldier cautiously walked over the lush palace grounds and observed his surroundings closely. His scaly green skin blended perfectly with the soft wet grass that he walked upon. The grounds were covered in the hazy mist the storm had left. As the solider turned back toward the palace, he heard a scream emanating from the palace. It cut through the night air like a knife and hardly seemed human. A cruel smile came to the soldier's face, revealing razor-sharp teeth.

"Enjoy this time," he gloated with a harsh and raspy voice, "for we return to you everything that you have given to us." he turned away from the screams and looked past the outer wall. His smile grew wider as he heard more cries of pain, terror, and sadness coming from the city below. "Long have I waited to hear the sounds of revenge," he said.

Hearing a rustle in the trees to his right, he turned and quickly raised his spear. He heard a wisp behind him, and his horizon filled with bright stars. As the stars quickly faded, he felt warm liquid ooze down his face. The wet ground rushed up to meet him. He lay on the ground, feeling death's icy grip upon him, and a voice whispered in his ear, "Your time for revenge is *over.*

By the time the other guards discovered his body, the attacker had long since vanished into the mists surrounding the courtyard. Word spread quickly, and soon more Draccen soldiers were gathering in the courtyard to investigate this strange death. As they did, more Draccen soldiers were found slain throughout the palace, while others seemed to have vanished into the very stonewalls. No one, not even Lord Jarden himself, knew who was wreaking such havoc on his Draccen soldiers. Those Draccen soldiers left alive began to believe that it was a spirit who had been greatly angered and had come back to haunt the palace. A different kind of fear now gripped Avdima, for no one knew when this phantom would strike again.

Chapter 64

Life's Thread

Gazing cautiously down one of the many long corridors within Avdima, Tahari watched from a darkened doorway as several Draccen soldiers ran alongside the Secret Alliance's remaining soldiers toward the other end of the palace. The pleasant smell of freshly cut flowers and spicy incense that had drifted down these wondrous halls earlier had been replaced with the pungent smells of swamp and death.

Almari emerged beside her and took a peek for herself. "Do you think they suspect us?" she whispered.

Tahari smiled and shook her head. After listening closely to her surroundings, she looked back at her. "Fear has gripped them. They are suspicious and uncertain. They do not know what to expect anymore," Tahari replied with reason, gazing down the hall. "Now we must find Leondros. Where was he when you last saw him?" she whispered.

Almari pointed with her chin in the direction of one of Avdima's high towers. "There is the tower they have transformed into a torture chamber. That is where we will find him," she replied. As she spoke, Tahari saw pain in her eyes. It was not hard to imagine what she had seen, for she, too, had seen her share of torture, suffering, and death. Clenching her teeth, Tahari took another cautious glance down both directions of the long corridor before they silently made their way to the stone doorway that would lead them into the tower. Upon reaching the doorway, Tahari charged up the stairs and into the tower, prepared for the Draccen soldiers that they might encounter. They reached the first landing in the torch-lit tower unchallenged. Just as she prepared to climb higher, Almari grabbed her shoulder and stopped her. She silently motioned toward the wooden door they had come to. Reading the unsettling expression in her blue eyes, Tahari felt her heart sink, but she forced herself to reach for the black handle on the wooden door and made to open it. Tahari did not know what condition she would find Leondros in; she could only pray for the best but expect the worst. When she grasped the door handle, her hands went cold and her heart sank even further. Tahari ignored this and opened the door slowly.

The heavy wooden door creaked loudly and echoed throughout the tower. Tahari pulled the door wide open quickly to stop the noise. Dim light from stairwell's torches filled the dark cell, casting an orange glow upon the prisoner inside. Struck with horror, Tahari stepped back against the damp, cold wall of the stairwell. What Tahari's eyes had seen was beyond belief. Almari glanced at her face and quickly looked into the cell to see for herself. She looked back at Tahari, equally horrified at the mutilated body of King Alabaster.

"Poor King Alabaster. This does not look promising for Leondros," Tahari managed to whisper. "Where do we look now?"

Almari quickly pulled the noisy door shut and took her arm. "Go on. Look for Leondros up at the top of the tower. I will start checkin' the lower chambers. We must be quick now. If he is still alive, he will not have much time before they send him to join King Alabaster," she instructed in a hushed whisper, her blue eyes nervously eyeing the doorway below them. Tahari nodded in agreement, for they needed to find him quickly and splitting up their efforts was their best course of action now. Almari gave Tahari a reassuring nod and then quietly disappeared down the dim staircase.

Taking a deep breath of musty air, Tahari turned toward the dim staircase that loomed above her and continued on higher into the tower. She remained on edge, for she could hear the echo of the Draccen soldiers' armor jostling as they ran through the long corridors. Their footsteps echoed up the staircase, adding to her paranoia. *Whose path will I cross next?*

Tahari came across many heavy wooden doors, but none hid a single elfin warrior behind them, though many revealed others who were past suffering. Reaching the top of the staircase, she walked onto the last stone landing and saw the last wooden door before her. Swallowing hard, Tahari quietly walked up to the door and peered through the barred window at the bottom of the door. As she peered inside the darkened chamber, she could not distinguish any figure that resembled a person. Then as fate would have it, lightning flashed through the tower window. As the chamber's dank interior was revealed to her with brilliant light, Tahari saw what should have been only a nightmare: hanging by his wrists from a timber near the ceiling was Leondros!

Pulling the door open, Tahari quickly slipped inside. "My God..." she gasped as she felt her heart plummet into the deepest pit of her stomach. As Tahri hurried over to him, lightning flashed again, revealing Leondros's bruised face and his blood-stained clothes. It stopped her cold. He was soaking wet, bruised, and battered. Gone were his armor, weapons, and everything that had given him royal status—all that remained were the tattered brown clothes his captors graciously left him with. His head hung limply. Swallowing hard, Tahari pulled out her sword and sliced through the rough rope that held him suspended. With the rope severed, Leondros crumpled to the cold stone floor and remained limp and motionless. She sank down beside him and gently rolled him onto his back and cut his wrists free from the ropes that bound him still. His arms fell limply at his sides. Looking down on him, Tahari saw the full extent of what Alon-Settie had done to him, including a knife wound to Leondros's left side. Taking a piece of her dark cloak and tearing it, Tahari quickly fashioned a bandage and tied it around his waist. She began to realize that something was missing. She looked upon his lifeless face and gently took hold of his right hand, which was cold and clammy to the touch. A moment later Tahari knew what was missing. The soulful presence that she had felt when she first met Leondros was no longer there. Tahari put a gentle hand on his bruised forehead. "What have they done to you, my friend?" she whispered, but it came out weak and raspy. Taking in the coldness of the room and the condition in which he lay before her, she began to understand the great pain that he had endured.

From the palace below, the sounds of soldiers talking, amongst them Alon-Settie's distinctive voice, floated up to Tahari. Looking at Leondros, she glimpsed a vision of the great friendship that had existed between these two for long years. One could even have called them brothers. Then as lightning flashed directly overhead, it somehow changed her vision, for what Tahari now saw was not the warm remnant of friendship; it was the malice of hatred and jealousy that burned in Alon-Settie's brown eyes as he glared at Leondros. She saw only a fragment of the cruelty that Alon-Settie subjected Leondros to. All Tahari could do was watch painfully as Alon-Settie spoke to Leondros. She could not hear what was being said, but the hurting expression within Leondros's face said it all. Tahari then saw the black-bladed dagger that had been driven into the elfin warrior's left side. Tears stung her eyes as Leondros's soulful brown eyes filled with pain and utter devastation. She shared the moment of Leondros's heartbreak. The light faded from his brown eyes, and he weakly hung his head. When the vision faded, Tahari looked into his face and understood the loss that he had endured. Alon-Settie had meant more to him than most people knew, including Alon-Settie. The loss of such a friend is like losing a part of your own self. Not many people currently alive would understand such a deep concept, but Tahari had lived it. Try as she might, she could not stop the tears from coming. Lowering her head and resting it against his shoulder, Tahari grieved for her friend and his loss.

A long moment passed before a sound startled her. Sitting up and snapping her head toward the doorway, Tahari heard the sound of footsteps coming up to the door. She would fight to get Leondros out of this horrible place, but at this moment, her heart was not in it. Great relief washed over her as she saw Almari's familiar features slip through the open doorway. As Almari entered the damp, darkened chamber, she brought with her a torch, which brightened the chamber. Tahari smiled sadly as Almari looked at her. The hopefulness that had been in her face faded quickly. She stopped for a moment, horrified at the scene before her. Finally, she walked forward.

"What have they done to him?" she asked in a hushed voice as she slowly sank beside Tahari.

Tahari looked at her for a moment and then turned her gaze sadly back to Leondros. "The worst thing that anyone could ever do to another, something far worse than death; betrayal," she replied in a mournful whisper. Tears continued to fill Tahari's eyes as she looked at Leondros, for she could understand the pain that he had endured.

"Is he...?" Almari tried to ask, but her own voice got lost in the grief that she was feeling just by watching Tahari. She swallowed hard as she took her hand and held it in the air over his chest. Tahari closed her eyes and concentrated on finding any energy within him. After a long moment, she withdrew her hand and lowered her head. After taking a deep breath, Tahari raised her head again.

Tahari somehow managed to find her voice to answer Almari. "There is so little life here, but somehow he lives still. He is very far away, but maybe..." Tahari's voice trailed off. A thought of what they had to do came to her mind, and it would take both of them to do it.

Chapter 65

News Unexpected

The terrible thunderstorm may have passed on, but now a different darkness now lingered within Akendron, its source now firmly embedded deep within Avdima. All remnants of the old kingdom had been removed to make to way for the rise of the ancient evil. From a high tower window, Lord Jarden gazed out over the storm-swept city and marveled at the sight before him. All the things that he had spoken of and hoped for were now coming to pass. He now awaited the final word from his new general that the many loose ends had been tied up.

"Sire? Does something trouble thee?" The voice of Solarous's servant Zudoo came from the shadows of the dark wooden door behind Lord Jarden. As the door opened, it revealed a dimly lit stairwell that led down the tower. The young Draccen messenger had been informed of his master's death and of Lord Jarden's possession of the physical form. As the blood-red Draccen messenger entered the candlelit chamber, he looked upon his new master's red-cloaked figure and was gripped with an immense feeling of defiance. Zudoo quickly masked his true feelings. Turning, Lord Jarden noticed his small servant as he emerged from the dark shadows of the chamber. Zudoo bowed humbly before the dark lord.

"Not at all, Zudoo. Why do you ask such a question?" Lord Jarden asked as he turned back to the window.

Zudoo approached his new master cautiously, noting the concern in his gray face. "I can sense when someone is troubled, sire," Zudoo replied as he cocked his head slightly. There was a long moment of silence from Lord Jarden. For as much as he did not want to admit it, Zudoo was correct in his assumptions. Searching through the lingering memories of his former assistant, he noticed the magic and power within the strange woman who had protected the royal family from being assassinated. There was an equally threatening power within the elfin general from Adarah. Fearing the havoc these two could cause in his rise to power, Lord Jarden had issued the order that they must not survive the night. He now awaited final consolation about this pressing matter.

"There is talk from the soldiers that the mysterious woman has escaped from the dungeon. Is this the matter that troubles you, sire?" Zudoo asked curiously, searching his master's face with his bright green eyes. The dark lord looked down at him silently, his searing red eyes telling Zudoo of his great concern. Then, before Lord Jarden could answer Zudoo, there was a loud knock.

"Come!" Lord Jarden called out in his dark and gravelly voice, turning his attention to the person who entered the chamber. His expression turned into eager anticipation, for Alon-Settie had returned. "Alon-Settie! Your presence is most welcome. What news do you bring for me?" the dark lord asked as he clasped his new flesh-covered hands together over his waist. The darkly armored prince strode into his chamber and removed his helmet. The dark-haired prince looked almost edgy, adrenaline-fueled as he was after the events that led to Leondros's torture.

"All surviving members of the old kingdom have been sent to the dungeons and are now awaiting execution. Draccen soldiers are putting down any resistance within Akendron. The Secret Alliance is officially under my command and in your control, and we have men on their way to the distant kingdoms of Eden-Glee and Adarah to spread the wondrous news of your glorious rise to power," Alon-

Settie reported with an assured and proud expression. Lord Jarden listened carefully as he slowly lowered his red-cloaked head and paced the room in a deep and thoughtful manner. Alon-Settie began to feel uneasy, and he wondered about the soldier who had secretly set out for the other kingdoms within the tribunal. "What of the chance that these soldiers should be killed if the other empires refuse to join alliances?" Alon-Settie asked as he watched the dark lord stop at the window and look off into the distance.

"They cannot possibly be harmed by any force of light, for my power is with these men. They will sway the other kingdoms to join us or watch their kingdoms be destroyed," Lord Jarden answered confidently, but there was a hint of uncertainty in his dark voice. "However, we must keep a watchful eye upon them. I have not suffered millennia of imprisonment for nothing, and I will not overlook any minor detail now," Lord Jarden continued with an almost angry tone. "Tell me, what news do you have on our old general?" He turned his eerie form toward Alon-Settie and looked at the prince with his searing red gaze. There was a long moment of silence. "Well?" Lord Jarden asked with growing concern.

From the corner where he stood, Zudoo lifted his gaze and studied Alon-Settie's face. There was no hint of sadness or guilt within the prince's brown eyes. His hope in Alon-Settie waned; the prince clearly retained no memory of the friendship that had once existed between him and the elfin prince from Adarah. Zudoo recalled his memories of Alon-Settie as a child and young adult, though he seemed like a good child, he always saw the happiness other people had and became jealous easily. This dark trait only became more twisted as time passed. Zudoo now understood why the darkness of Lord Jarden could cause Alon-Settie to sever the friendship he had with Leondros. He had forgotten his former self completely, a sly expression of just revenge creeping into dark and handsome features.

"It is as you have ordered, my lord," Alon-Settie answered with a humble bow. A great wave of relief washed over Lord Jarden's face. "He died before my soldiers could inflict a last blow. Of course, the gift of the dagger kiss that I bestowed upon him did not help his chances," he explained callously.

"You killed him with the pain of betrayal," Lord Jarden said. "Such a thing is most difficult to do, especially to a being such as an elf." there was a moment of shock and disbelief on his face, and then a cold smile appeared. "A man after my own heart." The dark lord's pleased response brought a bright smile to Alon-Settie's face.

Zudoo also looked on with an expression of shock and disbelief, feeling the heart-wrenching malice of this deed. He had seen Leondros Goldendragon only from afar, but he had sensed the good within this elfin warrior. Zudoo never spoke a word of how he favored the prince from Adarah. Silently, he grieved to hear that Prince Leondros Goldendragon had been so cruelly betrayed. The Drac did not know why he was so strongly against such actions, but he knew that what had been done to the elfin prince was very wrong indeed. Lowering his head for a moment, Zudoo prayed that Leondros's spirit would be in good company now.

Unlike his race, Zudoo never took part in the burning and pillaging of villages or the murdering of innocent people. He knew that he was different from other Draccens somehow, but he did not know why.

My kind does not care about the safety of others, nor do they care about any other race that lives within Andora. Why am I so different? Zudoo had never found the answer while he lived in the dark mountains of the Serrigen, but as he watched the force of darkness spreading from Avdima into Akendron and on to the rest of Andora, the answer became clearer. I feel there are other forces at work here. *These forces want to help people like Leondros and all who would stand against this growing darkness,* he reasoned as he raised his eyes to Lord Jarden and Alon-Settie. A strange feeling of rebellion suddenly began to grow within him as his master and Alon-Settie continued to talk about Leondros's last moments. He narrowed his green eyes at them and listened to their conversation. *If there is one thing that I can do now, let me do it for Leondros's sake. His suffering will not go unnoticed. I promise.* He listened to the men conspire about the future of Andora. Zudoo knew then what he had to do to help the forces of good. It was something that he could do very well, for he had always done it. He deemed that from that time forth, Avdima's walls would have ears of goodness that would listen to every plot made by the ancient evil, and he would find some way to subdue this evil altogether.

"Now we can go ahead with the next stage of our plans..." Lord Jarden was saying when the heavy chamber door flew open and in stumbled a palace guard.

"Sire!" the out-of-breath guard rasped.

Lord Jarden glared at the newly recruited guard for a long moment. "Thank you so much for being considerate of my privacy. What news brings you so unexpectedly?" he asked sarcastically as he eyed the palace guard angrily. The guard saw the expression of anger grow in Lord Jarden's face and suddenly realized his error. He humbly dropped his blue eyes down to the cold stone floor, hoping to avoid any more consequences of angering the forces that now dwelt within the palace.

Lord Jarden waited for the guard to speak and became increasingly impatient. "Well? Have you lost the ability to speak?" he asked.

Shaking his head, the young guard finally found courage to raise his head again. "I hate to be the bearer of such unfortunate tidings, but I have made a discovery within the dungeon's lowest level. The girl that you wanted executed...She has vanished, sire." the young guard spoke nervously, eyeing Lord Jarden closely. Lord Jarden gazed at the new servant for a long moment.

"Thank you for bringing me this news straight away, but it is old news," Lord Jarden said as he walked over to the trembling guard. "I had the girl executed only moments ago. One of my most trusted servants took care of this matter personally. They have not reported any such failure...yet," the dark lord explained nonchalantly, escorting the nervous guard out of the chamber. "Return to your duties. There is nothing to be concerned about," he assured the guard. Lord Jarden closed the door and turned back to Alon-Settie with a sly grin upon his face.

"Is that not the guard whom you love to torture immensely?" Alon-Settie asked.

"The very same," Lord Jarden replied with a pleased expression.

"Given how much we have to celebrate today, I am feeling quite generous. I decided to spare him the usual torment. I was going to give him a pox before the day was out, but I like this much better." Lord Jarden had left the new guard with the uneasy feeling that *something* would be happening to him, only the young guard would never know when.

Alon-Settie looked back at the doorway and considered himself fortunate that he was not the new guard. Then he thought about what the guard had said. "Is that what become of the witch?" Alon-Settie asked as he looked back at his master.

"It is. Why do you ask?" the dark lord replied as he moved across the candlelit chamber and sat down in a wooden throne-like seat from which he could gaze out the window.

"It was said that Leondros spoke of her before we captured him. It surprises me that you were so eager to execute her," Alon-Settie said thoughtfully, wrinkling his brow in thought. There was an expression of curiosity on the prince's face.

"She had to be dealt with quickly. It was strange…I have sensed power like what Solarous felt from her before, but not since ages past and not as powerful as she was. When she looked at Solarous, he felt that her eyes didn't just bore right through his very soul," Lord Jarden explained, but Alon-Settie merely shrugged.

"There are many people who have that effect on others. Why was she so different?" he asked.

"Because she single-handedly took out all the people I had Solarous use to assassinate the royal family, and she nearly won the favor of the king," Lord Jarden retorted angrily, his gaze searing Alon-Settie.

The prince raised his eyebrows in awe. "That is most unusual. A single woman doing such a gallant deed," he said thoughtfully. "Her death, then, was necessary. If she had been in an alliance with Leondros, who knows what sort of damage they might have caused?"

"My point exactly," Lord Jarden said, lowering his gaze to his sandaled feet. He looked up at Alon-Settie, who was still deep in thought. "Do not strain yourself, my prince. These two threats have been eliminated. There is no more need to put such thought on the past.

"Maybe there is…" Alon-Settie said with concern as he raised his gaze to Lord Jarden. "How is it that this girl knew of your plans to assassinate the royal family?" he asked with suspicion.

"Who knows? Maybe she heard one of the guards talking," the dark lord said, gesturing vaguely in the direction of the grounds below the tower where soldiers patrolled. "It is no matter. Both she and Leondros have been eliminated. Now, let us talk about our future," Lord Jarden insisted eagerly. Alon-Settie was hesitant to let go of his worries, but he pushed them aside. "It is time that we begin our full assault on Andora and prepared her for the great dawn that awaits her." Lord Jarden's words caught Alon-Settie off-guard.

"Now, sire?" Alon-Settie asked, feeling unprepared for such an aggressive move so quickly after taking over Akendron.

"If we wait much longer, we will miss our chance to put down any small alliance that might be conspiring to attack us, especially after our siege upon Akendron," Lord Jarden said as he looked at Alon-Settie with an even and cold stare.

"Point taken, sire. I will ready the troops. I will have them standing ready for the order to strike as soon as word is sent that the other kingdoms have been taken," Alon-Settie said confidently.

"Very good. Begin with attacking the Shandel. Burn everything to the ground. Take prisoners to the camps we have prepared for them, but be sure that you are not swayed by compassion—execute all who threaten to oppose you," Lord Jarden instructed. He placed the tips of his pale fingers together, while his mind looked ahead at what needed to be done. His smile widened as he watched the concern grow on Alon-Settie's face. Lord Jarden wanted to see just how far this prince would go for him.

"If you are testing my loyalties, you can save your tests!" Alon-Settie replied in a raised voice. Anger flared within his brown eyes. "I turned the Secret Alliance against its own general. I betrayed my own best friend to his death. I betrayed my own family and killed my sisters with my own hands!" he shouted angrily.

The dark lord merely watched with a pleased expression. "Your deeds are well noted, and I thank you. If it had not been for your immense loyalty, we would not have made it this far. The hard work is over now. What lies ahead should come quite easily to you," Lord Jarden said reasonably. "I will have a dear friend of mine come to retrieve you. The great black dragon, Baldour, should make your travels around Andora much easier.

Still a little heated by the dark lord's words, Alon-Settie humbly bowed to the dark lord when there was a nervous knock at the door. Lord Jarden motioned for Alon-Settie to see who it was. After a moment of hesitation, Alon-Settie turned and opened the door; seeing who it was, he shut it again. "Unwanted company?" Lord Jarden asked in wonder.

"You might say that. It is your new guard," Alon-Settie said in a hushed tone as he shook his head with disgust.

"Let him in," Lord Jarden said half-heartedly as he waved his hand in the air. Alon-Settie opened the door again, this time enough for the nervous palace guard to enter. He hurried into the room in a panicked state.

"My lord! We have a problem," the young guard declared as he stopped in front of where Lord Jarden was sitting.

"Calm yourself. What is so urgent?" Lord Jarden asked as he studied the nervous young guard in front of him.

"Well, we actually have two problems..." the guard paused, lifting his blue eyes and remembered something else that posed a great concern.

"What are the *problems* that trouble you?" Lord Jarden rephrased his question as he fought to keep his patience with the fidgety new guard.

"Now that I think of it..." the guard began as an additional problem came to mind.

"Just spit it out!" Lord Jarden said angrily as he sat up in his chair.

"Many guards are missing from their posts. The few that we have found have been killed. The rest are still missing.

Lord Jarden's expression fell as the reality of the news began to set in. "Go on....

"The guards from the dungeons say that the woman whom you

had sent to be executed never reached the executioner's block. The soldier in charge of her execution has been reported missing. A search was made to find both the soldier and the woman, but so far neither has been found. There is also..." the young guard's voice began to fail him as he watched his master's face become fixed with a heated gaze.

"There is more good news?" Lord Jarden guessed.

"The rest is trivial in comparison," the guard offered meekly, lowering his eyes.

"Thank you for the news. Go and rest now, for these problems will be rectified," Lord Jarden replied in a surprisingly calm and relaxed tone, settling back in his chair.

"Yes, my lord. If there is any..." the young guard began to say when his voice trailed off and his face went white. Fear filled his blue eyes as he doubled over. "I...uh...will be around," he said as he darted from the room holding his stomach. Lord Jarden and Alon-Settie were left with expressions of wonder on their faces.

"I guess he had to go," Lord Jarden said with a sly grin as he looked over at Alon-Settie. The prince also had a sly smile on his face. "*Now*, it is time for you to begin your work within the tribunal.

"What about the girl? If she took out twelve of your assassins single-handedly, does she not pose a great threat to your plan?" Alon-Settie asked.

"Worry not; I will have some of the best Draccen trackers hunt her down. You just see to that task before you," Lord Jarden said in a serious tone.

"It will be in accordance to your will, sire," Alon-Settie said with a humble bow. Straightening up, he replaced his dark helmet upon his head, turned, and strode out of the chamber.

Zudoo cautiously slunk back into view. He eyed the doorway and shook his head. "The guards within this palace are quite strange," he commented.

The dark lord noticed him and nodded in agreement. "'Strange' is one way of putting it," Lord Jarden said in a slow and thoughtful tone. "Still, if these are the Shandel's finest, I can only wonder what defense could possibly stop the Secret Alliance from wiping out the Shandel and Andora," Lord Jarden said smugly. He rose from his chair and walked back to his desk to look over the plans that he had laid out. He sat at the desk and began writing on a blank piece of paper, speaking aloud his message.

"Dear King Jabberwrath,

"The revolution has begun, and it will not take long before all empires within this vast land fall..."

Zudoo watched and listened to his master while he composed the letter. The news Lord Jarden was going to be sending to the realm of Nod was not promising for Andora. After listening a moment longer, the young Draccen messenger slowly shook his head sadly and disappeared from the candlelit tower chamber.

I hope that the guard does not have too many problems with his bodily functions, Zudoo thought as he slowly made his way from Lord Jarden's tower to one of the long dim corridors of the palace. He had slipped a drug into the guard's food prior to the capture of Leondros. The guard had been put in charge of Tahari's execution, and whether he had assistance or not, his ailment would serve as a beneficial diversion. Zudoo had hoped to aid the girl in her escape, for he had sensed the same goodness within her that he had also felt within Leondros. Except, much to his surprise, the girl had escaped on her own. *Master underestimates this girl,* he thought as he walked to a nearby window and gazed out into the night sky. The presence of evil hung close enough to send chills down his spine, but within this same air Zudoo sensed something else. A sly smile came to Zudoo's scaly face. *She is an agent of light.* He knew then that Leondros would be well cared for. He did not know if Leondros had suffered enough to taste death, but either way, he would not be alone for long. *Light finds light.* He smiled and prayed for these two warriors of light.

66

The Rescue

In the gloom of the cold cell, Tahari knelt in silence next to Leondros. She was overwhelmed by the grief that had led him here. Tears continued to sting her eyes as she gazed upon his expressionless face. Gently touching his bruised forehead with her hand, Tahari longed to sponge away the painful scars and offer him some comfort. Almari looked on with a saddened expression; her blue eyes burned with tears and grief.

"Tahari, if there is life still within him, what must we do to help him?" she asked in a hushed whisper.

Tahari blinked back her tears and looked at Leondros with a hopeful and determined gaze. "We must get him out of Avdima. The evil within this place has grown powerful and will kill him if he is left here," she replied, feeling the chill within the room grow colder. "We must get him back to Sala's palace," she said, looking up at Almari. She nodded, and then a smile warmed her tanned face as she looked at Tahari. "What is it?" Tahari asked a little bewildered by her expression.

"He does not know it now, but there is an angel watchin' over him," she said in a gentle whisper. Tahari managed to find a moment to feel like a hero, but when the soldiers' voices drifted up through the tower, she shoved away such a selfish thought, for she only wanted to save her friend. Almari jumped to her feet and ran to the door to watch for the soldiers, and Tahari pulled the limp and nearly lifeless Leondros off the hard floor and over her shoulder. Almari had not questioned how they would get Leondros from the high tower cell to Sala's palace, for she knew only too well Tahari's immense strength. While at the Tomblock, Tahari was renowned for lifting as much and even more than most of the men who worked there. The challenge now was not carrying Leondros but how they would get him out of Avdima unnoticed by the palace guards. "All right, the coast is clear," Almari murmured as she cautiously scanned the stairwell below them and slowly crept through the open door. Tahari took a deep breath and uttered a small prayer before walking through the door with Leondros slumped over her shoulder.

They began to silently descend the stairs, listening to every sound that found its way up to them. They had descended halfway down when they froze at the soft patter of footsteps running up toward them. Almari turned to Tahari with eyes wide with horror. Then, determination filled her face; she took the sword from Tahari's free hand, which they had recovered from a Draccen soldier on their way into the palace. She did not have to utter a word, for her determined expression was easy to read.

They are not getting him or us without a fight. I just hope they're ready for it. Her thoughts gave Tahari reassurance and the courage to keep going. Almari turned and silently made her way down the staircase, and Tahari trailed just behind her. When Almari ventured just beyond Tahari's sight, she heard her run into the soldier who had been running up the stairs. The battle was over before it began, for when Tahari emerged around the corner of the stairwell, Almari was standing with the sword fixed against her opponent's throat, who stood with his arms spread out.

It was not a Draccen soldier but a young servant boy. His short blond hair was in a mess, along with the rest of him, and his tattered clothes were covered in soot. His skin was blackened from the soot, thus enabling him to blend in with the shadows of the palace. He was a frail boy, but there was something in his green eyes that was almost unsettling: hope.

"Wait!" Tahari gasped, seeing the fear in his eyes. He turned to Tahari and gaped at the load she was carrying. He studied Tahari nervously, his eyes drifting back to the body that she was carrying. The poor boy's eyes filled with great sadness as he recognized whom she was carrying.

"What business do you have here?" Almari demanded in a harsh whisper.

The frightened boy looked at her and then at Tahari. He slowly pointed at Leondros. "I-I heard what they did to him," he choked out, tears stinging his bright green eyes. The frail boy swallow hard and struggle to speak. "The whole palace has been taken. Everyone has been captured, and all are being executed. Th-they had not found me yet, and I could not leave without trying to help him." his small voice was riddled with panic and sadness.

"Why would you come back for him?" Almari asked harshly as if still sniffing for ambush in the air around her. "What is in it for you?.

The boy suddenly proved his worth. His eyes filled with determination and anger. "Just that I could rest knowing that I had returned the kindness that was once given to me. He is the only one who has ever shown me kindness. My freedom would be worth nothing if he was left here to die and I knew that I could have helped him." the boy stood up straight and faced Almari's sword with courage.

"How would you have gotten him out by yourself? Surely you would have needed help. Or is that your plan?" Almari continued, but as Tahari gazed into the boy's eyes, she began to see the loyalty and love the boy had for Leondros. The boy did not back down in defeat but rather engaged her in the argument.

"I would have found a way, even if it meant trading my own life for his." Tahari was moved by this young, frail boy's words. She reached out and laid a gentle hand on Almari's shoulder. She turned to Tahari and saw the warning in her eyes. She backed away from the boy.

"What is your name?" Tahari asked in a calm whisper. He turned to her, and she watched as his defenses softened.

"Elijah," he answered, still sounding uneasy.

Tahari smiled at him warmly and put a reassuring hand on his shoulder. "Elijah, right now, Leondros's life hangs by a thread. We are trying to get him out of here. Would you be willing to help us?" she asked in gentle and kind whisper.

A warm expression filled Elijah's soot-covered face. "Until my last breath," Elijah replied without fear as he put a hand over hers. "Come, I know of a secret tunnel the Draccen soldiers have not yet discovered," he said. Tahari smiled thankfully, and Elijah turned to lead them to another hidden passage.

While they followed him through the many darkened passages through Avdima, Tahari noticed the change within this servant boy. He might be a child leading them from peril, but she saw more than that. Tahari saw a friend helping another and giving no thought for his own safety.

When they came to the end of the long tunnel, Tahari could smell the sweetness of evening rain cutting through the musty smell that had been with them throughout the palace. The outside was close at hand. Although the night was dark, they could make out trees in the distance. On the far horizon, lightning continued to flash across the sky, giving some light to the darkness. Tahari peered through the darkness and saw the grass field before them. Looking closer, she saw a dirt path leading into the safety of the Misty Forest. The way for them was seemingly clear of danger, but something kept her from walking out into the darkness.

"Tahari? What is it?" Almari asked as she noticed Tahari's hesitation. She, too, had been cautiously scanning the horizon. As lightning flashed, her drying blonde-and-brown hair, still tied behind her head, was illuminated. Tahari wanted to answer, but something kept her from speaking. Looking on ahead, Tahari searched the grounds surrounding the tunnel repeatedly.

Noticing Tahari's hesitation, Elijah whispered, "Hold up." he slipped past Almari and Tahari and moved to the edge of the stone tunnel. Tahari watched as the boy's face took in his surroundings, and then his whole body stiffened. Slowly Elijah slipped back into the tunnel's darkness. He looked at to them without speaking as if he were contemplating what action to take next.

"Elijah? What is wrong?" Almari asked in a hushed whisper as her eyes filled with grave concern. Tahari studied his face for a long moment, and she felt the trouble he had seen.

"Trouble waits just beyond the tunnel, doesn't it?" Tahari guessed in a quiet voice. He looked at her with eyes filled with surprise, but he managed to nod his head in reply.

"The Draccen soldiers are all around us. If we try to make a run for the forest, they will see us and…" Elijah said dishearteningly before his voice gave out. Tahari watched as he swallowed the hurt that had to have been growing in his throat. Almari looked at Tahari with uncertainty and then looked over at Leondros with a hurt expression. In Tahari's heart, she knew what had to be done, for she was bound by her word to Leondros. Taking a deep breath, Tahari gently lowered Leondros from her shoulder and laid him against the tunnel's damp wall. She looked into his pale face and touched his bruised cheek; signs of life were weak, but they endured.

"Elijah," Tahari said as she sat back to think about her next course of action. The frail boy silently made his way over to her. He slowly knelt down beside Tahari, his sad gaze falling on Leondros. In his gaze, Tahari could see many things, and she knew then that Leondros would be proud. "If Leondros were awake now, I know what his words might be," she said. Elijah looked at her with wonder. "He would say that he has never met a truer friend than you," Tahari said with a small smile. "You have done everything that you have promised, and I believe that he would be very proud of you." as she spoke, tears welled up in the boy's sad eyes. "Now, I must do what I have promised," Tahari said with a deep sigh as she slowly rose to her feet and started toward the tunnel's opening.

"Tahari! Wait!" Elijah's voice called out from behind her and caused her to look. He whispered something to Leondros and put his hand on the elfin warrior's shoulder. Then he quickly rose to his feet and hurried after Tahari. When he reached her, she saw such a look of determination in his face that she was astounded. "Whatever has brought you here, it did not intend for you to walk out there without him. You are his guide now, and I know that you will lead him home.

When he wakes, tell him of his friends, so that he will know that they are with him still," he said, looking at Tahari with an understanding gaze. He held out his hand for hers. When Tahari took it, the smile grew on his face. "Our goodbye is not the end, for we will meet again."

With those words said, Elijah turned and faced the opening of the tunnel and darted out into the darkness. He ran into a rain-soaked ditch and headed into Akendron. His actions caught the attention of many Draccen soldiers, who had been waiting to capture any prisoners trying to escape. Almari and Tahari heard the sounds of many Draccen soldiers thundering after Elijah. Hearing the heart-wrenching sounds of the boy's capture would have broken anyone's heart, but this had been done for a reason.

"Come, he has given us our chance," Tahari said in a hushed whisper as she ran back to Leondros. Lifting him back over her shoulder, Tahari turned and joined Almari at the tunnel's opening. They listened to the thunder of footsteps fade into the distance. Almari looked at Tahari with a lost and concerned gaze.

"Will he be all right?" she asked with a look of disbelief and concern.

"Either way, Adalai will be watching over him, and that is the best protection anyone can ask for," she replied hopefully. Offering a smile of reassurance, Tahari silently slipped out into the night and started down the path that would take them into the Misty Forest and eventually to Cypress Palace.

Chapter 67

Sanctuary

Soaked and chilled to the bone, Almari and Tahari finally reached Cypress Palace with Leondros. Sala had left a candle in a library window to light their way. Almari opened the heavy front door to the palace, letting it slam into the wall inside.

As they entered the grand entryway, Sala quickly appeared at the top of a nearby staircase. Excitement and anticipation filled Sala's face for a moment, until the scene before him registered with him. He halted at the bottom of the stairs and stared in horror at them.

Everything seemed to move in slow motion as he approached them. When he looked upon the rain-soaked and badly bruised body Tahari carried, his face fell. There was no mistaking the face of his dear friend Leondros Goldendragon. He remained frozen for a moment as grief, sadness, and shock hit him all at once.

"Bring him," Sala said quietly as he motioned for them to follow him. Tahari could not help but see the hurt and disbelief within Sala's soulful blue eyes. He turned and hurried toward a darkened doorway under the long staircase. The dark-brown robe he had changed into since attending the festival hung to the floor, and as he walked, his feet kicked up the folds of the robe. He lit a candle at the doorway and held it up to an ornament on the wall. The candle's flame ignited the oil within the ornament, and a small trail of flame quickly snaked throughout a channel along the hallway, lighting their way.

Taking a deep breath, Tahari followed him. The hall was thick with incense, offering them some comfort. More than this, there was a strange mist floating to the ground. Tahari knew that it was the evil that followed them from Avdima sinking into the earth.

Sala led them to a small bedchamber on the first level of Cypress Palace. Upon entering the chamber, Sala lit several candles. Judging from the old wooden furniture, piles of scrolls upon a writing desk, and a wardrobe armoire within the small cozy room, Tahari guessed that it was Sala's bedchamber. The walls were deepest beige, with only a pair of burgundy tapestries upon them for decoration. The room had but one window, curtained with white gossamer, and the bed was covered with a black and burgundy quilt with an oak tree stitched in silver thread. The room gave off a warm, rich feeling. As Tahari neared the bed, Sala carefully laid Leondros's bruised form upon it. Sala's face was full of hurt as he looked upon his dear friend.

"There is still life within him," Tahari said softly as she sank into the wooden chair next to the bed. In spite of feeling exhausted, hungry, and cold, Tahari refused to leave Leondros's side.

"What grievance could have warranted this?" Sala asked in a voice full of sadness, tears stinging his eyes. He gently smoothed back Leondros's wet hair to reveal his bruised face. Sala shook his head slightly to break himself from the sad trance and went to the armoire to retrieve a white pitcher and bowl and a worn green washcloth. He left the room momentarily to fetch some water for the pitcher. He quickly returned and poured the water into the white bowl as Tahari took the washcloth and tended to Leondros's wounds. Sala pulled out another cloth and also began to tend to his friend's wounds. Looking at her sadly, he asked in disbelief, "Tahari, what happened?"

Trying to swallow the lump in her throat, Tahari watched as he Sala gently cleaned Leondros's wounds. She looked at his sad blue eyes for a moment and realized that it was as if she were looking at Leondros's father. It was not hard to see how much he loved Leondros. Somehow, Tahari had to find the courage to explain what she had seen. It was difficult to know where to start. Yet when she looked into Leondros's pale face, it was harder not to say anything.

"It was worse than we feared. The ancient evil has taken Akendron, and Avdima is his fortress," Tahari began. Sala's eyes widen in horror. "The people from the old regime are being tortured and killed. It is as if hell itself has unleashed itself upon the city." as Tahari spoke, she could see the horrors of the evening once again.

"What of the royal family?" Sala asked, full of dread. Tahari lifted her saddened gaze from her work to Sala, but the words would not come.

"Their fate was the same as Leondros's, or worse. Alon-Settie betrayed them to serve as Solarous's right hand," Almari interjected.

"Then they are both fools," Sala said fiercely. "They willingly serve Lord Jarden; however, his design for this realm does not include them." the aged prophet shook his head bitterly but found a weak smile as he looked back at Almari. "Continue, my dear," he encouraged.

"It seemed that none escaped except for a boy named Elijah. He refused to flee for his life until he knew that Leondros was safe." she shook her head slightly and managed a weak smile. "The boy seemed so frail and weak, but he said that he would have found some way to get him out, for Leondros had been the only person to ever show him any kindness. I believe that he would have, too," Almari said, sounding overwhelmed by the boy's actions. Sala's gaze drifted back to Leondros, a warmth and pride glowing in his bearded face. Tahari was deeply touched by what Leondros had done as well.

"When Tahari told him that we were trying to get Leondros out, he never gave it a second thought. He led us out of Avdima unseen. It was he who told us how everyone within the palace was being tortured and killed." Almari's voice trailed off for a moment as her eyes drifted sadly to the stone floor. "I cannot believe what that small child did for him and us. He let himself be captured to give us a chance to escape. Never have I seen such devotion and loyalty, except from Tahari." Almari smiled at her friend, tears glistening in her eyes. A look of sudden realization showed in Sala's blue eyes.

Pulling on a dark robe and hiding his gray-streaked hair with the hood, Sala said, "I will be back. If there is hope, then there is someone that I must try to rescue. Adalai willing, she is still alive and I am not too late. Please, stay and take rest yourselves; you have earned it." Then, before he turned to leave, he gazed down at Leondros once more. He stretched out his hand and laid it gently on Leondros's head. After a long moment, he looked up at Tahari. "It is good that you are here. He has been through enough for one day, and now he is very weak. However, his spirit lingers still, for now there is a kind and compassionate soul who truly cares for him. Please stay with him."

"I will," Tahari replied in a whisper, managing a small smile. With that, Sala silently left the bedchamber. Lowering her head, she closed her eyes for a moment and sighed deeply.

"Tahari, you are exhausted. Be mindful of Sala's words, and rest. After all, it was you who carried Leondros out of Avdima," Almari said as she looked at Tahari with concern. Tahari hesitated for a moment as she looked at Leondros. "I am sure he would want you to rest, too," she said helpfully. Looking up at her, Tahari smiled wearily.

"Almari, you are right. It is time that we both gather our strength while we can. Go and find a change of clothes and help yourself to food. Surely you are eager to eat something again," Tahari said. She nodded and silently disappeared from the room. Wearily looking at Leondros once more, Tahari could only hope that right now he was able to find some peace. Feeling too overwhelmed with exhaustion to care about being soaked, she rested her elbow against the wooden arm of the chair and laid her head upon her hand. As Tahari gazed around the cozy bedchamber, she saw a green candle on a writing desk. Its flame burned bright, giving light and warmth to the small room. As Tahari's thoughts drifted off toward sleep, she watched the wax glide down the candle. Tahari blinked once, but she never saw the wax reach the silver candle holder. Sleep washed over her tired eyes.

Chapter 68

Leondros's Light

The green candle continued to burn as did the other small candles within the room. Within the cozy bedchamber, Tahari saw herself still clothed in the soiled burgundy robe from her visit to Avdima palace and sleeping soundly in the wooden chair next to Leondros. Almari was there as well. She had returned wearing a warm green robe and carrying some apples, but sleep had also found her, for she sat in another chair near the doorway, fast asleep. Peace, it would seem, had settled over them at last. Tahari watched contentedly as everyone slept soundly. Then she noticed the gossamer curtains moving as if they had caught a slight breeze from the open window.

Walking toward the window, Tahari gently pushed aside the curtains to glimpse the thick forest that surrounded Cypress Palace. It was not as she had remembered it. A gloom completely covered the forest. No longer was there a heavenly glow about the palace or the surrounding mist-covered forest; now, only a dim gray remained. The gloom seemed to be draining the life from the forest. Its power was strong, for Tahari, too, felt weakened by it.

As she gasped for air, Tahari saw a ghostly image of Leondros watching her from the forest. There was deep concern within his brown eyes, and he seemed weak.

As she watched him with worry, she noticed something in the air over the Misty Forest. Raising her gaze, Tahari saw a pale orange light peeking through the gloom. The dark clouds that covered the sky were trying to smother that pale light.

Then a black dragon flew over the distant horizon near Akendron. Its shrill cry filled the air. It turned and began to fly toward Cypress Palace, its searing red gaze looking upon the window from which Tahari watched. She instinctively crouched down to prevent being seen. Tahari covered her ears, for its shrill scream was almost deafening. As it flew over the palace, a powerful wind came through the window and knocked Tahari backward, causing her to hit her head.

When Tahari had recovered her senses and slowly raised her head, a dead calm lay all around. She looked up to the green candle that had been burning so brightly against the dark. The flame had been extinguished, and now only smoke rose from its wick. Her gaze drifted over to Leondros. He had not moved, but the remaining color had drained from his face, a gray paleness remaining.

A mournful wail began to sound throughout the Misty Forest. Tahari returned to the window to search for the ghostly apparition, but it was gone. All that remained was the gloom that was deepening in the forest. Tahari struggled to breathe. The darkness had now come for her. Whirling around, she stumbled for the bedchamber door, but she was too weak, and Tahari collapsed to the floor. A voice called loudly, "TAHARI!"

Chapter 69

Return to Adarah

W aking with a start, Tahari jerked her head up from where she rested. Her heart pounded against her chest as she tried to catch her breath. Looking around, Tahari saw that nothing had changed since she had drifted off to sleep. Almari had returned and was sitting at the doorway, fast asleep. She was dressed in a warm green robe she had picked out for herself. Tahari's heart skipped a beat when she noticed Almari had found several apples to eat. Tahari looked over at the green candle on the writing desk. Its flame had grown dim and the green wax was spilling over the side of the silver candle holder. The candle was almost spent. Turning to Leondros, Tahari noticed that the color had drained more from his face. Holding her hand over his chest, Tahari sensed that his life was fading. Leondros needed to get away from the smothering evil that resided within the Shandel and return home while he still had time. Tahari now understood what Elijah had meant. She was his guide to lead him home.

"Almari! Get up!" Tahari called to her as she hurried over to her and shook her shoulder.

Almari opened her eyes groggily. She had taken the time to clean up, for her face was clean and her shiny blonde and brown hair was tied in a neat ponytail. "W-What is it? What is the matter?" she mumbled as she opened her tired eyes.

Tahari quickly jumped from Almari's side and ran over to the writing desk and opened the top drawer. "We must be on our way! Time is greatly against us," she said as she rummaged for a blank sheet of paper so she could write a note telling Sala where they were headed.

"What are you talkin' about? I thought we were to wait for Sala to return from Akendron," Almari said, sounding quite confused as she rubbed her tired face and watched Tahari with uncertainty.

"We do not have time," Tahari said, stopping to look at her with a grave expression. "Leondros does not have time. He is fading. The evil within the land will smother the little life that is left within him. He cannot stay here."

Concern filled Almari's features as she looked over at Leondros. She climbed to her feet and walked over to the bed. She gazed at him and then slowly turned to Tahari. As Tahari caught her doubtful expression from the corner of her eye, she knew that Almari could not see such a difference within Leondros.

"Even if he is, where can we take him?" Almari asked in a tone filled with uncertainty.

"We must take him home," Tahari said, thinking about where home for him actually was. "We have to get him to Adarah. His family lives in the capital city of Shoshon. They are the rulers there," she continued slowly as she recalled her conversation with Leondros and Sala. Leondros had not only reminded Tahari of her past, but he helped her to remember where home was.

"Shoshon, Adarah!" Almari exclaimed as she watched Tahari with a wide-eyed expression. "Just how are we supposed to get him to Shoshon, Adarah, when neither of us has been there before?" she asked with great concern, standing up straight. Tahari looked at her calmly for a long moment. "Right?" she asked, eyeing her with suspicion.

"Not exactly. I found out that I was born in Adarah and lived there a few years before I was brought to the Shandel as a child," Tahari admitted as she looked back down to finish writing the letter. "My father was an elfin judge and councilor for King Doran," she explained as she folded the letter and set it next to the half-spent candle. Tahari hurried to the window and looked at the dim horizon before her. Night was fading, but the dimness from the clouds passing overhead muted the morning's light.

"How is it that you learned of these things? Can you be sure that the source who told you these things was tellin' the truth?" Almari asked her as Tahari turned from the window and looked at her with a serious gaze.

"I learned of these truths from King Doran's son, and, yes, I believe what has been revealed to me, for he has already risked his life to see that I return home again," Tahari replied in an even tone, motioning with her eyes toward Leondros. Almari followed her gaze. Her eyes widened as the reality of what Tahari had just told her began to sink in. Her features quickly filled with guilt. "Come! We have a long road ahead of us, and I feel that the evil that has nearly killed Leondros and me will want to finish what it has started," Tahari said in a concerned voice. Deciding against taking the time needed to change into a clean robe, Tahari pulled her damp cloak off the floor and put it around herself.

"We will need provisions for the road," Almari reasoned. She turned to leave the bedchamber to gather food when something out of the window caught her eye. "Tahari? What is that?" she asked with a tone of dread. Tahari turned toward the window and joined her gaze. She saw the full measure of the ancient evil's work. Misty Forest was shrouded in darkness, and that darkness was spreading.

"That is the darkness of the ancient evil. Lord Jarden longs to cast Andora into the same darkness as he has Akendron, and little by little, his power will grow stronger. He gains his power by sucking the life out of the land and those closest to it," Tahari explained as she looked back at Leondros with worry. "This is why we must hurry. We are not safe here any longer," she said as she pulled herself away from the window.

"Then let us not wait here a moment longer," Almari agreed as she pulled the curtains closed with defiance. In the next few minutes, they hurried about Cypress Palace and prepared themselves for the journey to Adarah. When Almari finished packing food into a large leather knapsack, she headed outside to see if Sala had any horses in his stable to aid them on our journey. Meanwhile, Tahari found a dark hooded cloak that she could put around Leondros to offer him some cover from the elements and evil's eyes. He remained limp and lifeless. She felt a painful ache within her chest as she looked at him. He seemed so far from this world.

"Hang in there, my friend. You are going home, and I will not rest until I see that you are back amongst your people again. More importantly, you will be with your family again," Tahari whispered, gently pulling the dark hood over his head and carefully wrapping it around him. She lingered there for a moment, studying his expressionless face, hoping that he could somehow hear her and find the strength to cling to life. Remembering that time was not in their favor, Tahari pulled him to his feet and lifted him over her shoulder. Carrying him out of Sala's room, Tahari left no trace that they had even been there except for the neatly folded letter leaning against the silver candle holder. Tahari ignored the green candle as she raced out of the room, yet from the corner of her eye, she saw that the flame had gone out and only white smoke rose gently from the blackened wick.

Outside, Almari waited with two horses, one of them Leondros's. The white stallion walked up to Tahari and gently nuzzled his nose against Leondros. The horse could sense that his master was wounded, for he began to panic. Tahari reached out and gently touched the horse's nose and began to speak to him.

"Leondros is in trouble, but you can help him. Help us bring him home again. His life depends on it, for he cannot stay here a moment longer," Tahari said with concern as she gently stroked his head. The white stallion did not seem to need any more convincing than this, for he nodded his head in reply. He sank to his knees and allowed Almari and Tahari to get Leondros onto his strong back. Using a brown leather chord, Tahari fastened it around Leondros to prevent him from slipping from the horse's back. Tahari then quickly climbed on the white stallion's back and sat behind Leondros. He slumped back against her as she held onto him. Almari was quick to mount the black horse that she had found, and she stored their provisions in the saddlebags. She then nodded to Tahari, and with that, they set off for Adarah.

As they rode through the thick forest, they noticed that the rain had lightened up considerably. However, Tahari noticed that the rain fell like tears.

"Tahari? Why such a look?" Almari asked her as she studied Tahari's face.

Tahari looked at her with concern as she gestured toward the rain falling down around them. "The rain. It is weeping. It is right that it does so, for many have died and deserve to be mourned. But I can only pray that Leondros is not among them," she replied with a sorrowful tone, trying to swallow the lump in her throat but found it too painful. Almari and Tahari quickly disappeared into the dim of the Misty Forest and headed west for the elfin realm of Adarah.

Chapter 70

Not Alone

Their journey to Shoshon spanned two full days and into the morning of a third. In spite of the little sleep they had received before leaving, they pressed onward. Almari never questioned Tahari's decision to leave so early; the darkness growing over the skies and the shadow of death that now covered Leondros's pale face were warning enough.

On their first day, the road took them to the western edge of the enchanted Misty Forest, and it was here they came to the riskiest part of their journey. There was a large clearing that divided the forest and marked the boundaries of the Misty and Divervandon Forests. Crossing this clearing would be dangerous for they would not have the cover of the trees and vegetation to protect them. They would be targets to anyone hunting them.

"Wait here a moment," Tahari whispered to Almari as she carefully got off the white stallion and made sure that Leondros would not fall off.

"What are you goin' to do?" Almari asked with wonder. Tahari put a finger to her lips to caution her to be silent. She motioned to Almari that she was going to scout out their path before they passed through the open meadow. Almari nodded in understanding and rode up beside the white stallion to take his reins.

Tahari scanned the open field in front of her. Slowly stepping out into the green and grassy meadow, she took in her surroundings and studied them closely. There was no gleaming sunlight, for the gray clouds lingered within the area. The lush, grassy plain that stretched out around them seemed peaceful and undisturbed by the evil that was growing in the east. Sounds of birds and insects filtered through the fresh air. Late-afternoon breezes blew across the grassy clearing. The air smelled cool and clean. There was no sign of danger yet. They seemed to be ahead of it for now.

Tahari motioned to Almari that it was safe to come out of hiding. As she guided the horses out of the forest, Tahari noticed the exhaustion within her face.

"Tahari, we have to stop. We are both exhausted, and if we keep going like this, we will surely kill ourselves and Leondros," Almari said. Tahari walked over to the white stallion and looked up at Leondros. She felt a cold stab of pain in her chest. Tahari reached up and took hold of his hand, which dangled freely along the horse's shoulder.

"What hurt him has already been done. It is here where he will find refuge and healing," she reasoned softly as she held his hand. "Maybe for us, too." she looked up at Almari with a smile. Relief washed across her face as she stretched her aching body. Then something on the wind caught Tahari's attention. An eerie chill was scented with pungent swamp. She knew now who was following them. "Only not here. We make for the safety of the Divervandon Forest," Tahari instructed and quickly climbed back onto the white stallion.

"I was hopin' that we could make camp sooner," she said as she shifted uncomfortably in her leather saddle. "I do not know about you, but I am losin' the battle with these blisters." Tahari could understand how uncomfortable Almari was feeling, but she could not help smiling at her friend. Then Almari turned her attention to the east and sensed something that troubled her. Her blue eyes, filled with dreadful realization, met Tahari's. Tahari nodded in reply. "Whatever comes should have really taken a bath first," she said, making a face as she followed after Tahari.

They rode well after nightfall and did not make camp until

they were deep within the Divervandon Forest. When they finally stopped, Tahari sighed deeply with relief, for her body ached and her eyes burned with exhaustion. "About how much further is it to Shoshon?" Almari asked with a groan, painfully sliding off her horse. Tahari sat back on the white stallion and thought deeply about her question, for it had been many long years since Tahari and her mother had secretly made their way out of Shoshon on that one dark night.

"It took Mother and me about..." Tahari began when the gentle breeze that had been whistling through the tree branches above them became a dead calm. Silence fell around them, the creatures of the night refusing to utter a sound. Something dark and evil had entered the Divervandon Forest, and it was quickly approaching. Tahari froze and became very aware of her surroundings. Peering out at the surrounding darkness, she felt that evil was close. Tahari could not tell from which direction it was coming, but she knew it was near.

"Tahari? What is it?" Almari asked her in a hushed whisper. She had also frozen to where she was standing when she saw Tahari fixed in serious concentration. Tahari glanced at her and Leondros a moment before returning her gaze to the dark forest that surrounded them. In that moment, Tahari felt that her people had called upon her to keep these two safe from this danger. Quietly urging the white stallion to sink to his knees, Tahari eased off his back, gently picked Leondros up, and carried him over to the grass under a nearby oak tree.

"Danger is close. Almari, stay with him and let no harm come to him," Tahari whispered as she lay Leondros on the ground. Almari nodded, but Tahari could see the concern in her eyes.

"What are you goin' to do?" she asked worriedly as she settled on the grass next to Leondros.

Tahari looked down at them for a moment. "Improve our chances of getting to Shoshon alive," she assured her as Tahari pulled a dagger from her dirty leather boot and tucked it up the sleeve of her robe. Tahari also armed herself with a bow and quiver of arrows that had been carefully placed on the back of the white stallion's saddle. By then, the stagnant swamp smell had grown stronger. Almari's blue eyes filled with fear.

"Be careful," she warned her friend.

Tahari nodded as she put a hand on Almari's shoulder. "You also," she said encouragingly. She nodded in reply. With that, Tahari turned and quickly disappeared into the darkness of the surrounding forest.

Chapter 71

Bainen

A small band of elite Draccen soldiers, armed only with bows, arrows, and daggers, crept through the thick brush of the Divervandon Forest. Lord Jarden had dispatched them to track down and eliminate the slave girl. They did not have to know her name, for their master had created an image of her out of nothing but air. Finding her, however, was still a problem. Hence, the dark lord sent with them a highly skilled Draccen tracker. Bainen was known as a most cunning and savage tracker. His scales were such a dark green that they were almost black, thus enabling him to move like a dark shadow through the dark vegetation of the Divervandon Forest. It was said that he could even conceal his scent to keep his most cunning victims unaware of a pending attack.

Bainen eyed the surrounding forest with his charcoal-black eyes, and as easily as finding soot-filled tracks in freshly fallen snow, he picked up the trail of two horses heading westward toward Adarah. He and his men moved silently through the night. After journeying deep within Divervandon Forest, Bainen stopped them for a moment as he listened to the sounds of the forest around him. An evil smile came to his face, for he knew that they were gaining on the slave girl. Turning to his men, he silently ordered them to spread out so they could quietly and easily surround the slave girl and anyone that she had with her. One by one, the members of the elite band vanished like ghosts into the thick brush.

After passing through some thick brush, one of the soldiers saw two horses just ahead of him. Crouching low to the ground, he peered through the thick brush and saw a dark-cloaked girl kneeling on the ground, looking cautiously around her. Someone lay close to her. He pressed his way through the thick foliage to get a better look. Suddenly, something broadsided him. As he hit the ground, something covered his mouth. Then a cold blade sliced his neck, and he knew no more.

Nearby, two more Draccen soldiers were cautiously making their way through the brush when they heard this slight disturbance. They rose up for a moment to see what was going on. As they did so, they heard a wisp cut through the air. They looked down to see arrows protruding from their chests. They stumbled away to get clear of their attacker, but before they could gain any distance, a large shadowy figure rose up in front of them, blocked their escape, and finished them off with a long sword.

Disgusted, a fellow Draccen soldier lowered his sword and shook his head at the two soldiers who now lay dead at his feet.

"Idiots," the Draccen soldier hissed. He looked around, hoping that Bainen had not witnessed his deed. He swallowed hard, for he had just increased their chances of failure. They had been only thirteen when the dark lord sent them out, without counting Bainen. Suddenly he felt someone watching him from behind. Turning his head slightly, the soldier saw a figure behind him. He turned to face his watcher, who remained still. Studying the shadowy figure closely, the Draccen soldier only had time to discern how much shorter this person was compared to him before he noticed another Draccen soldier standing behind the figure. He, too, had seen this small figure and had an arrow aimed and ready to fire. He quickly took out his bow to fire an arrow also. Together, they could take this figure down from two sides. It would have worked, but when he fired his arrow, the figure was nowhere in sight. In the moments that followed, he heard the other soldier cry out in pain and realized that he had taken out yet another of his own soldiers.

He groaned, scolding himself for another misdeed. Then he felt something now looming behind him. Turning to look, he saw Bainen standing before him. The experienced tracker gave him a cold and malicious stare.

"Just whose side are you on?" Bainen demanded with a hiss. The Draccen soldier stood stupefied, staring back at Bainen. Bainen scowled at him and started to walk past him. "Any more soldiers die by your hand, and I will send you to join them." the words came out low and menacing. The Draccen soldier stood for a long moment, not really sure what to do next. On the verge of giving up this pursuit entirely and escaping with his own life intact, the soldier glimpsed something through the thick foliage. He moved closer and was surprised at what was in the clearing just ahead of him. An opportunity to kill the slave girl presented itself, but he had not intended to add an elf to his plan.

Chapter 72

Slave's Assault

Quickly and silently, Tahari made her way through the thick brush while she kept a tally of the Draccen soldiers that she had thus far eliminated. It was hard to say how many Draccen soldiers had been sent after her, but Tahari knew that she could not leave any alive. She would not be responsible for leading those foul creatures into Leondros's homeland. Then as Tahari passed through another thick hedge, she suddenly sensed a dark presence very close by. She froze as she glimpsed a Draccen soldier hiding in a tree. As Tahari turned her head for a better look, her world exploded into spinning stars. Staggering backward, Tahari felt cold, intense pain in her skull. Feeling herself begin to weaken, Tahari forced herself to remain standing. Lifting her gaze back to the tree branch overhead, Tahari realized that the Draccen soldier had been her assailant. Tahari sensed that he was no ordinary solider; he was more cunning and lethal than the others combined. There was great skill in how he held his bow, arrow training on her.

"Lord Jarden was right about you. You are not to be underestimated, but it seems I have figured you right," he said in a cruel hiss. "You are like me. You become part of nature and vanish from all sight. But I have found you now." Then nine other Draccen soldiers rose out of the surrounding brush to close in on Tahari. "I hope you enjoy this forest," he said as he pulled his bow taut, "because you are going to die here." then he fired the arrow aimed at Tahari's chest.

Quickly Tahari caught the arrow that was intended to kill her. Not knowing what to do next, the solider in the tree looked to his men for help.

"Finish her before she finishes you," he commanded as he fitted another arrow to his bow. The remaining nine soldiers charged Tahari, swords in hand. As she fought for her life, Tahari could see the boastful tracker trying shoot her while she was battling his soldiers, but he succeeded only in taking out his own men. When the last soldier fell dead to the ground, Tahari looked around for the leader. He had vanished. Her mind raced with uncertainty, for she feared that he would find Almari and Leondros. It pained her to think of this Draccen beast harming them. Then a cruel voice spoke up from behind her. "It would appear that I have a *slight* advantage over you." Tahari slowly turned around to see the leader perched in a tree above her, an arrow fitted and aimed at her.

"*Slight* is the correct word, for I could kill you right now with no problem," Tahari replied honestly.

The tracker seemed truly amused by her answer. "Ahhh, yes. You could, but then one of your friends would be very much dead. You would not risk their safety, would you?" he asked as he turned his gaze to the other side of the thicket. Tahari followed his gaze through the thick foliage, seeing Almari and Leondros. Almari was not aware of any danger they were in.

"I assure you, my best soldier stands nearby, ready to end their lives if you would like to risk them." before he could say more, however, a dagger lodged deep into his throat. He snapped his head back and glared at Tahari as he fought to remain within the land of the living.

"No, I would rather risk yours!" Tahari said as she slowly lowered her hand. "I would have to say that you and I are not alike at all. I care about those around me. I could not bear seeing them harmed, least of all by me." she watched the dark Draccen tracker begin to weaken. He stared at her a moment longer before he lost his balance and fell backward out of the tree, crashing into the thick foliage below. Tahari waited for a long moment. After she was sure he was not going to make a dramatic return, she prepared to rescue her friends.

Chapter 73

Fading Spirit

When Tahari returned to where she had left Almari and Leondros, she found Almari poised and ready to fight. She recognized Tahari through the brush and breathed a huge sigh of relief. Looking around, she saw something lying within the thick foliage. From where Tahari was standing, she could tell that it was a Draccen soldier.

"Did you have some company while I was gone?" Tahari asked as she slowly approached the motionless soldier.

Almari lowered her sword and shrugged. "He stopped in but ended up losin' his head," she replied as she wiped the blood from her sword.

As Tahari looked upon the Draccen soldier and at Almari, she could see that Leondros had been in good hands. Tahari smiled warmly as she looked back at Leondros and her. "Thank you," Tahari said softly as she walked over to her and put a hand on Almari's shoulder.

Almari nodded, a smile coming to her face. "It is no more than you would have done for me," she replied in a truthful tone. Tahari nodded as she looked down at Leondros. Her warm smile began to fade, however as those words took on new meaning for her. "Tahari?" Almari asked.

Tahari shook her head and found her smile again, looking up. "It is nothing. We can take rest and eat something now. The evil that was following us has been stopped for the time being," she said as she looked at the surrounding trees.

Almari had a look of concern in her eyes. "What about Leondros? Should we not keep on going for his sake?" she said.

Tahari looked down at him and weighed this decision. "We should take some rest, even if it is only for a few hours. If our strength gives out, then he will have no one to help him," she said thoughtfully. Almari nodded with understanding.

"All right, but only a *few* hours," she reassured Tahari as she turned and started collecting wood for a fire. Tahari watched her friend for a moment and found her ability to smile again. Almari never was one to speak openly of her concern, but it always managed to come through somehow.

The crackling fire's warmth was soothing and complemented their full stomachs, which for Almari and Tahari was a blessing never to be unappreciated. Finding this level of contentment allowed them to relax for a moment. While Almari slept under a nearby tree, Tahari sat close to Leondros. She remained awake and watchful. Her exhaustion was overwhelming, but she did not sleep. She had tried to doze off, but something kept her from drifting into a peaceful slumber. Tahari kept thinking about what Almari had said earlier.

"It is no more than you would have done for me."

As Tahari thought about this, she looked over at Leondros. He had not moved since she had laid him there. At that moment, she felt the guilt set in. Just seeing him in this condition reminded her that he had been horribly betrayed, and she felt responsible for what had happened to him. If she had lingered there a moment longer, he would not have been captured and forced to endure such a horrible fate. Tears stung Tahari's eyes, and her throat tightened with the hurt that she was feeling. Swallowing hard, Tahari leaned over and gently touched his forehead with her hand.

"I am sorry, my friend. It is said that I possess the ability of foresight, but for all my power, I did not see," she whispered in a mournful tone. Lowering her head shamefully, her long brown braid slipping over her shoulder, Tahari wept silently beside him.

Overwhelmed by her guilt, Tahari did not notice a presence approaching until she felt a warm, gentle breeze touch her face. Lifting her head, Tahari saw a column of heavenly light materializing in front of her. Before her was Leondros's spirit, dressed the same as his physical body. Seeing him, Tahari felt the air catch in her lungs. He did not speak, but looking into his brown eyes, she felt his grief. Tears welled in her eyes and she lowered her head.

"It was not my intent for you to suffer," Tahari managed in a raspy voice.

"Tahari..." she heard his voice, but when he spoke, his words were mingled with the warm breeze that surrounded her. Finding the courage to look into his concerned face again, Tahari lifted her head and found him kneeling before her. "Finish the journey that you have started. All that is left of me longs to be home. Please, do not leave me here," he pleaded with her as if he were lost. In spite of her guilt, Tahari saw that her friend still needed her help, and she would not deny him of that.

"Once you put your faith in me to be the eyes and ears that would watch your back in battle. Now let me restore your faith in me. I will not fail my part. I will lead you home," Tahari replied with assurance. She watched the sadness in his face be replaced with relief. He did not need to say anything more, for his expression said it all.

Tahari looked down at his body for a moment and noticed that something had changed. Reaching over and holding her hand over his chest, she felt her own heart leap. There was more life within him! When Tahari looked up again, his spirit had vanished from sight, but it was not gone. She looked back down at Leondros and smiled hopefully. "I promise, my friend," she said softly as she gently crossed his arms over his chest and pulled the dark cloak that he wore closer to his chin to keep him warm, for the night around them was still cool from the previous rains the land had received.

⁕

After Tahari woke Almari and got Leondros onto his horse only a few hours later, they set out again for Adarah. There was no threat of evil pursuing them, but the need to reach Shoshon was even greater now. Tahari clung to the chance that there was still hope for Leondros. She prayed that when they reached his home, he would be healed by the power of his people. Yet as they continued their journey, she could still feel the anguish within him.

They journeyed all of the next day and into the following night. Hunger was momentarily relieved by a short stop at a cool, emerald-colored pond. As they ate, Tahari found that this new life away from the Tomblock was most strange. They had food aplenty, yet troubles still found them. She stared off toward the eastern horizon.

Resting by the water, Almari looked at her with concern. "Do you sense trouble?" she asked.

Tahari continued to focus her gaze toward the land beyond the eastern horizon. "It is not trouble that I sense, but something... something that I had almost forgotten," she replied softly, feeling contentment wash over her. Looking over at Almari, Tahari could clearly see that she did not understand what she had meant. Tahari smiled. "Home." Tahari turned her gaze back toward the midnight-blue horizon and felt ever closer to home. Dawn was still several hours away when they packed up camp and began to near Adarah's eastern border, where their path would lead them into Shoshon.

The dirt road they traveled took them up to a tree-covered hilltop. As they drew near the top of the hill, Tahari's senses tingled with a strange energy. She stopped the white stallion, climbed down, and slowly walked ahead of Almari. Up ahead, two round pillars of gray smooth stone stood on either side of the dirt road like sentinels. On top of the pillars rested two iridescent glass orbs.

"Tahari? What is wrong?" Almari called to her friend with concern.

"This place is a gateway to Adarah. The magic that guards this gate will keep out intruders and evil, unless someone allows it," Tahari said, recalling her long-forgotten history.

"Why is it that I feel like we are intrudin'?" Almari asked with a tone of worry.

"Do not worry. You are helping two people return home; you are welcome," Tahari reassured her with a warm smile. Turning her gaze to the path before her, Tahari closed her eyes and recalled what her mother had done when she left Adarah, and repeated this ritual. Taking a deep breath, Tahari reached up, held her hand out, and touched the empty space between the two pillars. The air around her hand dazzled with blue energy, and a once-invisible barrier was now revealed to them. They could only stand and marvel at the blue shield of dazzling energy as it disappeared and allowed their passage into Adarah.

When dawn finally rose up over the mountains, Almari and Tahari gasped at the beautiful country that they had entered. They marveled at the endless miles of lush, green forest, misty waterfalls, and crystal-blue streams that were woven throughout the countryside. The gray clouds shielded the sunlight but could not take away the beauty that was forever locked within this majestic realm.

"I never realized what a beautiful place Adarah was," Almari commented as she looked about her with an awed expression.

"Nor I," Tahari replied with a half-smile. "My memories pale to what is before us now." she breathed in the cool, sweet air around her. She was beginning to recall her childhood in its every detail. "Come, we are close. Shoshon is just beyond those foothills and lies within those white mountains," Tahari said encouragingly as she nudged Leondros's horse onward. Several hours passed before they reached the ridge that overlooked the river valley below, where their breath was lost once again. There amongst the hills of lush grass and forest was a magnificent city of white. Its radiant white light gleamed as far as the eye could see. It was clearly heaven on earth.

"Tahari, you did it! I do not know how, but you did it!" Almari said excitedly, reaching from her horse and gripping her friend's arm.

Tahari smiled and took a moment to breathe a sigh of relief. "*We* did it," she corrected Almari as she gave her a warm smile. Almari rode ahead of her to get a better look at the majestic landscape that now surrounded them. As Tahari watched her, she felt a warm breeze blow gently against her face. Tahari smiled with relief as she looked at Leondros, who was still slumped against her. "We made it. You are home again, my friend," she said softly as she gave him a warm hug. Tahari did not know if he had heard her, but she felt that it was worth saying. Then, to her surprise, Tahari watched the color of life come back to his face. Leondros wearily lifted his head and opened his eyes. The realization that he was home again could be found in the warmth of the weary smile that came to his face. Only before Tahari could be relieved that he was going to be all right, something bizarre occurred.

Leondros gazed upon the white city of Shoshon, and then his eyes closed again. Tahari did not get worried until she felt a warm wind rush past her. When it had passed by her completely, Leondros had crumpled against her, limp and lifeless.

"Leondros!" Tahari gasped as she caught him and managed to look into his face. All color had faded; what remained was a grim paleness. She felt suddenly hollow and overwhelmed with disbelief. The life energy that had seemed restored within him was gone. It was hard to explain, but it was as if someone had pulled his spirit from his body. Tahari remembered then what he had told her back in the Divervandon Forest.

"All that is left of me longs to be home."

Chapter 74

A Son Brought Home

The realization of what Leondros had meant hit Tahari hard. He did not intend to come home to live but to die. The wounds that had been inflicted had cut Leondros deeper than she had realized, and now there was no pledge that could be made that he would heed or trust. His spirit was tired, wounded, and it longed for its heavenly home. As Tahari held onto him, she urged his horse onward toward the white city. Tahari did not know what words to speak that he would listen to. "Please, Leondros; hang on for your family. Surely, you have their trust and love," she whispered as she rode up to Almari. She looked back at Tahari with a warm smile, but it faded quickly when she saw her. They quickly rode down into the river valley. As they neared the white wooden gates of the city, Tahari noticed that guards had spotted them and were gathering to see who was coming.

"Are you ready for this?" Almari asked, glancing at Tahari nervously while clutching the reins of her black horse. Tahari understood her nervousness, but she merely looked at her with a saddened expression.

"I just hope his family and friends are ready for this," Tahari replied, feeling utterly disheartened as they approached the white gates of Shoshon.

When they reached the large gates of the grand city, armored elfin guards studied them closely. It was understandable that they did not know them, but they did not even recognize their own prince.

"What business do you have within the city of Shoshon?" one of the guards finally asked them in a suspicious tone.

"We have brought a member of the royal family with us," Tahari said loudly and clearly, so they would understand her at once. "He wishes to return home again," she added hopefully, for she did not know what else to say in order for them to understand the urgency of their need to enter the city. The elfin guards looked at each other and peered down at them with growing suspicion. Tahari sensed that their presence here was quite awkward, and with the threat to the east, they had every right to be suspicious. Only she did not have time to dispel their suspicions; Leondros did not have time. "How much proof do you need to allow your own prince back into his city and to be with his family?" Tahari yelled up at them as she pulled off the dark hood that covered Leondros's bruised head.

When the guards looked down upon their prince, their faces went white with horror. They were quick to open the thick white gates and usher Tahari, Leondros and Almari inside. As the huge wooden gates began to shut again, the guards ran up to meet them. Their armor looked familiar, for Leondros had worn similar armor when Tahari first met him. These soldiers were fitted with silver chain-link suits and dark-gray armor, which resembled the beauty of dragon scales.

"What has happened to him?" one of the guards asked. His blue eyes stared in horror at Leondros's lifeless form as Tahari carefully pulled the hood of the elfin prince's cloak back over his head. As Leondros's life hung between the realms of life and death, she felt that he still deserved the decency of being shielded from prying eyes who would exploit his downfall further.

Tahari tried to remain calm as people walked by to see the strangers who had entered their grand city. "It is a long story, and his need is most dire," she managed to say at last.

The guard finally realized how grave the situation was and offered them an escort into Shoshon. "Follow me; I will lead you to the palace," he instructed them as he leapt onto his beautiful white-and-gray horse and rode ahead of them. Tahari and Almari followed closely behind him, making their way deep within Shoshon.

Beautiful wood flutes, mandolins, and various other instruments played harmonious tunes throughout the city. In addition to the wondrous sounds that greeted them, they were momentarily mesmerized by the beauty of the buildings they passed by, but their main focus remained getting Leondros to the palace and to his family.

As they passed through the paved streets, people looked up at them from their work. It was as if the angel of death had arrived, for as they passed by them, their expressions fell into great despair and grief. Even the festive music that played throughout the city faded as they passed. It was not long before they began to hear the mournful wail of people crying behind them. Whether or not they knew it was Leondros did not matter. This limp and lifeless person, who leaned against Tahari as they rode through the streets, was one of their own; they could feel it. Tahari began to feel even worse than she had before arriving in Shoshon. It was one thing to arrive in a grand city such as this, riding beside a prince, but to arrive in the city carrying his body, unsure if he would last the night, drove a stake of fear, sadness, and uncertainty into her heart.

It was not long before the great white palace of Shoshon came into view, its main dome rising gracefully out of the glimmering city that surrounded it. It left the newcomers with a feeling of awe, for the dome's roof was covered with sparkling crystal.

As Tahari and Almari rode deeper within the city, Tahari began to feel an immense love and kinship for all around her. It was truly like coming home.

Looking at Leondros's expressionless face, she began to see into his past. There were so many years of happiness that he had enjoyed with family and friends; its remnants could be felt within the very walls of Shoshon. The bonds of love that existed within this place were beyond anything Tahari had ever felt. As she held Leondros in her arms and saw the palace gates come into view and looked upon its delicately designed brass bars, Tahari knew that his family was not far away now. Her heart hurt as she thought of what this would do to them and everyone else who cared for him.

The crowd behind them grew as people put aside what they were doing and began to follow them. However, Tahari was too tired and concerned for Leondros to care. They pressed toward Tahari and Almari to look upon the stranger they carried. As they neared the palace, the crowd became increasingly alarmed. Word had quickly spread throughout the city, for many more people than they had passed, thousands of people, had begun to slowly climb the hill toward the palace. The city guards greeted Tahari and Almari at the palace gate and stood between them and the people so that they could pass on through to the palace without interruption. Up until now, Tahari had managed to retain her composure, but what was to come would be utterly heart-wrenching.

When Tahari and Almari finally reached the front of the dazzling white palace, Tahari gazed up at the long, white staircase that led up to the grand entrance to the palace. His family would appear momentarily. Swallowing hard and taking a deep breath, Tahari tried to make her mind go blank. She watched the guard who led them through Shoshon quickly and gracefully dismount from his horse and run up the beautiful stone staircase.

Several moments passed before anyone emerged from the palace, but then the large wooden doors opened again and several people rushed outside. Their colorful gowns and robes fluttered around them as they raced toward Tahari and Almari. Their faces showed expressions of disbelief and great worry, but when they gazed down upon the newcomers, one by one, they each stopped in absolute horror. Tahari had no knowledge of what his family looked like, but that must be who was standing before them now. She watched an older couple hurry down the steps and guessed that these were Leondros's father and mother. Looking past them, Tahari saw three other elfin royals, whom she could only guess to be his brother and sisters. As she watched them approach and saw the immense sadness strain their kind faces, Tahari could feel her defenses start to give and her heart begin to break.

Leondros's father and mother reached Tahari. His father was dressed in a dark-blue robe with a black sash wrapped around his waist. A thick, elegant gold crown, adorned with radiant iridescent crystals, sat upon his dark-brown hair. He slowly walked to the white stallion and looked up at Tahari. She hoped he would not notice her ragged burgundy robe, dirty face, or tangled hair that lay in disarray over her shoulder; she prayed that he would only see the compassionate soul who had brought his son home. Looking into his sad brown eyes, Tahari could see that he still clung to a small hope that there would be some life left in his son. He slowly raised his strong arms and reached for Leondros. Gently lowering him into his father's arms, Tahari fought the stabbing pain within her chest. As Tahari looked on, she found herself watching everything in slow motion as she watched Leondros's father carry his body like a rag doll toward the queen. The king slowly sank to his knees before making it to the first step of the long stairwell as he became overwhelmed by immense grief.

Leondros's mother sank weakly beside her lifeless son. The white gossamer veil that was carefully draped over her head was held in place by her thin delicate gold crown, the edges of the veil falling past her shoulders. There was sadness in her face, but the reality of his condition had not taken effect yet. Her long, sky-blue gown spilled out around her as she knelt beside the king. Reaching out and gently placing the palm of her right hand upon his bruised forehead, she whispered something as she leaned close to Leondros. When there was no response from her child, the queen painfully closed her eyes as her face becoming wrinkled with immense grief. Tears streamed freely down her pink cheeks. She slowly buried her face against Leondros's shoulder, muffling her sobs. She clung to him as if never to let him go again. It took everything within Tahari's being to remain composed and not break down as she watched this bitterly painful scene.

However, when Tahari remembered that this was the same elfin warrior and prince who had humbly introduced himself to her, offered her his friendship when he learned that she had saved his life, and faced danger and death to fight for her freedom, Tahari felt hot tears stream down her cheeks.

After several moments, Leondros's father regained his composure enough to pick his son up off the ground and slowly carry him up the stairs toward the palace with the queen close at his side. Tahari watched as Leondros's family gathered around him and disappeared into the darkened doorway of the palace.

"Tahari?" Almari asked softly after a moment of trying to recompose herself. Wiping her own face, Tahari looked over at her. "What is to become of us now?" Tahari had not thought about such a detail, but Almari was right. Their journey here had been no easy task, to be sure, and the weight of the grief they carried had worn them down even more. They needed rest.

"I do not know…" Tahari answered with uncertainty. Her body felt weak and tired from their long journey. Taking a deep breath, Tahari gazed over at the guards, who still barricaded the crowd gathered in front of the palace gate. They did not know their story, but there was sympathy and acknowledgment in their elfin faces. As the crowd dispersed, the guards slowly turned to leave, and as they did, Tahari heard them start to sing a soft but bittersweet song. It sounded very old, and as she listened to the words, she began to understand their grief. They sang about all the warriors of the past that had died in battle. These warriors were remembered most by the deeds that made them great. When they spoke of Leondros, it was not his deeds that made him great but his heart.

"What was it that his mother asked him?" Almari asked quietly as she turned her gaze back up the staircase of stone.

"'Speak to me, my son, so I do not have to look for you in the realm of Mortu'us,'" Tahari translated slowly, her throat aching with sorrow. "Mortu'us is the realm of the dead. It's a vast realm of many islands. Half of it lies within Aura, or our world; the other half lies within Inferus." sadness and loss filled Almari's face as the reality of Leondros's fate hit her. However as she studied Tahari's pained expression, she seemed to discover something.

"You care a lot about him." Almari said in a hushed tone.

As she spoke these words, Tahari felt her heart ache a little more. She nodded. "Indeed. Leondros reminded me that I was a part of this race and that I did at one time have a true home among these people. The love that binds these people together is immense. They do not have to speak of it, for it is felt in the very air that you breathe. You can feel it, even if you are separated," she explained softly as Tahari gazed upon a beautiful garden not far from the palace. "Knowing full well how precious friends are and how fragile life is, I could not take such a wondrous thing as friendship for granted. Leondros offered me his friendship after he found out that I had saved his life while I was still enslaved within the Tomblock. I am honored to have brought him home again, but it still seems so little," Tahari managed to finish before she was overcome by her grief again.

"I sense that his trust in you runs deep," Almari commented as she studied Tahari's face and thought about their journey here.

"I hope so, but he was badly hurt by his best friend, Alon-Settie, and I fear that he will fade from life," Tahari said honestly as she lifted her gaze toward Almari. She looked at her friend with great concern, for she had never seen her in such a grievous state.

"Tahari, you have never let your friends down. Even when the worst happened, your heart never betrayed them. Such is the case now. If Leondros did not know what you have done, his spirit most surely did. And what remains true is that you did what you have promised. You watched over him, and you returned him to his loved ones. I pray Adalai reminds his spirit of this," Almari said gently as she gave Tahari an encouraging look. She was right, but Tahari felt that it was now up to Adalai to decide if Leondros would stay within the life realm or journey beyond to the distant isles of Mortu'us.

Then someone approached them. As Tahari turned to see who it was, she gasped for a moment. There seemed to be a vision of Leondros standing before her, but she realized that this had to be Leondros's sister. Judging by the close resemblance in features, Tahari discerned that this was his twin sister. Her long hair hung loose about her delicate form. The light-green gown that she wore was made from lightweight material that swayed gracefully about her as she moved. She did not bear a crown but rather a dark beaded rope from which strings of crystal jewels hung.

"Are you friends of Leondros?" the blonde-haired girl asked calmly, a trace of sadness buried deep within her beautiful voice.

"Yes, we are," Tahari answered in a raspy whisper. Just looking into her face, she could not help but see Leondros. Tahari could not help but show her grief. The girl smiled warmly.

"If your answer had been silence, I still would have known. I can see the answer within the grief that is in your face," she said knowingly as her brown eyes looked from Almari to Tahari. Then she noticed how weary they seemed. "Leondros's journey had taken him to the Shandel, so you must have travelled a long distance to bring him home to us. For this we thank you," she said as she bowed humbly before Tahari and Almari. "We would be honored if you stayed and took rest from your journey," she continued as she gestured gracefully toward the large wooden doors of the palace. Tahari turned to Almari, saw the reaction within her blue eyes, and knew full well what her answer was.

"We would be most appreciative," Tahari replied wearily. The princess continued to smile warmly as they sorely climbed off the horses and joined her. Servants appeared from the palace to take the horses to a nearby stable.

"I am Zation Goldendragon, Leondros's twin sister," she said. They walked up the white stone steps to the palace.

"I am Tahari of the Shandon, and this is my most trusted friend, Almari of Trensa," Tahari replied and gestured toward Almari. Zation led them through the warm wooden doors into the palace. They could not help but be overpowered by the magnificence of the corridor's jade walls and pillars and the black stone floor. The captivating scent of roses and other flowers seemed to refresh them, but still their minds were not far from the pressing matter at hand.

"How did you meet Leondros?" Zation asked as she led them down a warm candlelit corridor.

Tahari fought to sum up an answer for her. "Our first meeting was at the Cypress Palace, the home of Sala of Antioch, whom I guessed to be another of Leondros's close friends. It was most fortunate that we met, for I had no memory of my childhood. Leondros helped me to remember that this grand city was my home once and that Reymier of the Shandon had been my father," she explained softly as they passed through the heavenly lit corridors and chambers. Zation stopped and turned to her with an amazed expression.

"You are the daughter of Reymier of the Shandon?" she asked as if it sounded too good to be true. Tahari watched as a bright and hopeful smile washed over her face.

"I am," Tahari replied simply.

She gazed at Tahari for a long moment as if in disbelief. Her brown eyes widened and blinked several times as this news soaked in. "It is an honor indeed!" She took Tahari's arm in gratitude and exclaimed in a hushed whisper so not to let her voice carry. "It is no wonder that you were able to pass beyond Adarah's borders. It would be impossible for anyone to find their way into our lands unless they were elf in origin, had been here previously, or had been given permission to enter." as she spoke, Tahari felt reassurance in what Leondros had told her. Then a voice disrupted their conversation.

"Zation! Come quickly!" a man's voice echoed down the long hall. Tahari watched her face fill with alarm.

"Please excuse me. Our servants will see to your needs." she spoke hastily as she picked up her gown and hurried down the long corridor and soon disappeared from sight. Tahari and Almari remained standing in the long corridor for a moment in silence. Looking at each other, they did not know what was going on. Fortunately, they did not stand there for long. A dark-haired servant dressed in a white robe emerged from the room that Zation had disappeared into. He kindly led them farther down the hall, away from all of the commotion.

Upon being led to exquisite bedrooms, they found soft beds and carpets that lay in front of beautifully designed fireplaces with comfortable chairs to rest upon. Each room's colors ranged from warm browns to beiges, accented by fresh flowers.

After arranging a meal for them, the elfish servant then kindly dismissed himself. Almari retired to her room, but Tahari lingered in the large hallway a moment. Not a sound could she hear. All seemed peaceful and quiet. However, in her heart, she felt that things were not thus.

After cleaning up from the past few days and dressing in a black and gold robe, Tahari ate and then fell asleep. Just after the sun had set in the west, she woke again and in her bare feet slowly made her way toward the open patio beyond her room. The dark cherry doors opened onto a patio that faced west, for Tahari could see the remnants of the setting sun and the dim of evening beginning to settle over the lush landscape. In spite of the great sense of peace that she felt, Tahari also felt a great disturbance. A bell tolled in the distance. It was a deep, mournful chime that drove shivers down her spine. Something was not right.

Hurrying from her chamber, Tahari ran to Almari's door and knocked on it repeatedly. When she finally answered, Tahari could tell that she had still been sleeping.

"What is wrong?" she asked groggily as she stretched her aching muscles within the blue and green robe that she wore. Grabbing her hand, Tahari rushed down the hallway toward the long corridor where Leondros had been taken. "WHOA! Tahari!" she gasped as she kept herself from stumbling over her tired feet. "What—?" she started to ask.

"Something has happened, and it is not good. We must find out what," Tahari said as they turned a corner. They collided with someone. Stumbling backward, they were quick to catch themselves from falling. When Tahari looked up at whom they had crashed into, she froze to where she was standing. "I-I am really sorry," Tahari stammered. She recognized Leondros's brother, the crown prince, from earlier that day. He was dressed in a robe of red and gold and wore a thin gold crown upon his long dark hair. "I sensed that something awful has taken place and…" Tahari continued, trying to slow down her words so that he would understand her. The prince listened silently with a somber expression. There were few similarities between his appearance and Leondros's, for she saw more of his father's features in him. His dark-brown eyes looked down, and he gave a heart-heavy sigh.

"Your senses are keen, for something awful has happened," he said in a low and mournful tone. "Prince Leondros was on a quest to help the Shandel with something that would be a threat to all of our kingdoms. We fear that it was this quest that greatly wounded him." he spoke without emotion, but when he raised his gaze to meet theirs, Tahari saw such pain and sadness within his dark-brown eyes. "I wish I had better news to tell you, especially seeing how far you both have journeyed to bring him back to us..." His voice trailed off as grief took over. "Leondros died shortly after you brought him to us. Please, excuse me. I have to make arrangements for his funeral," he said as he bowed his head, turned, and disappeared down the hall.

Tahari stood frozen to the ground. The will to move had left her body. Almari finally helped her to move and pulled her back toward their chambers.

"Tahari, please, come back to the room. I do not wish to impose on such an occasion," Almari whispered as she led Tahari back to her own chamber door. Swallowing hard, Tahari silently retreated to her chamber.

The cool of night had fallen over the city. Everything was still around Tahari. There was no breeze, not even the soft sound of birds or the buzz of insects. Nature, it seemed, was also in mourning. It grieved for its child. She stood for a long time on the patio reliving the precious time that she spent as Leondros's friend. Tahari scolded herself relentlessly and went over all the things she could have done differently. Tahari questioned her role as his friend. Lifting her gaze, Tahari swallowed hard as she watched while Leondros's family carried his body through the crowded city streets and into the tomb of his forefathers. Tahari's heart caved in as she recalled a line from the scroll of the ancient prophecy.

III.) Betrayal and a tomb await a prince.

Tahari wept for her friend.

Chapter 75

A Father's Guilt

A single candle burned in the darkness of Paracity Palace's great library. Its flickering light offered only a small comfort to King Doran, who stood alone, shrouded in grief and despair. His heart was broken, and his mind was fighting a great battle as he pored over the scroll in front of him. Its message had been written long years ago but had only now come alive. He prayed to find some hope for his beloved son who now rested within the tomb of his ancestors. Over and over, King Doran searched to find some miracle within the cryptic text to save his dead son. But the grieving father found nothing and kept returning to the passage that haunted him as if to remind him of the tragedy that he could not keep from harming his child.

Betrayal and death will fall upon a prince of the Goldendragon House who is destined to be King. *Grant a brave soul permission to look in on the dead.

King Doran's grief ran deeper than most, for he had known of the prophecy for many years, but not once did he foresee any threat to his younger son. It was the older son, Prince Dreyhon, who was entitled to the throne. The threat of the prophecy seemed to point to Dreyhon, so he and the queen had done everything in their power to protect him while Leondros was left in the shadows to fend for himself. He should have protected *both* sons.

King Doran glanced up from the scroll and saw a face in the darkness looking back at him. Stopping dead, he gasped. Looking closer, he saw an oil painting of Leondros looking back at him. His heart ached as he gazed at the image.

"What have I done?" he asked aloud. The darkness that enclosed the library did not answer him, but the painted image of his son seemed to respond, Leondros's brown eyes staring back at him. Tears welled up in King Doran's eyes; his guilt festered within him. Turning away from the painting and slowly walking across the dark-red carpet to a large window that overlooked the cemetery and the tomb of his forbearers, King Doran walked out onto the small balcony. He remembered his last conversation with Leondros. His son had been troubled by the mission. As King Doran's brown eyes sadly gazed upon the tomb, he saw that night had cast a shadow upon his beloved son's resting place which the moonlight could not dispel. Leondros, it seemed, was destined to be in the shadows even in death. "I am so sorry, my son." the elfin king took hold of the wide stone railing before him, lowered his head, and wept bitterly.

"Father?" a kind voice called to him. Raising his head and wiping the tears from his eyes, King Doran looked around and froze for a moment when he saw an image of Leondros standing within the balcony doorway. Blinking the tears from his eyes, King Doran recognized Zation. She shared many characteristics with Leondros, and both bore a strong resemblance to Inya, their beautiful mother. They were his inspiration. He could not explain from where it came, but he felt an unusual power radiate from their faces. Even in the worst of times, they brought him hope. With Zation standing in front of him now, he felt that in some way his son was still alive.

"Is there something that I can do?" she asked with concern as she walked out of the shadows. She was dressed in a black gown and a black veil muted the brightness of her blonde hair, but it was clear that she still had a shred of hope. Around her neck was a crystal medallion that caught and amplified even the smallest amount of light. It seemed almost as if there was still some hope for Leondros.

He paused for a long moment, trying to think of something nobler to say, but, alas, he could not deny the guilt that ached within his heart. "I can think of only one thing," he said in a saddened whisper. Zation smiled encouragingly, trying to offer some way to ease her father's suffering. "Can you find it in your heart to forgive me?" His voice faded as he lowered his face.

Zation's face fell, and she embraced her father. "What is there to forgive?" she asked as her brown eyes began glistened with tears. She looked back in the library at the portrait of Leondros and somewhere found courage to be strong in such a moment of adversity. When she pulled back to look into her brave father's saddened face, Zation felt her own heart torn apart.

"We did not see that Leondros was in danger. All these long years, we believed that Dreyhon was the one the prophecy foretold of. We thought his life was in peril, so we tried to protect him—and by doing so, we lost Leondros." he spoke in a voice riddled with bitter grief.

Zation felt hot tears run down her cheeks as she listened to her father. "Father, do not blame yourself," she said as she took hold of his hands. "You did what you thought was right. The prophecy is only a vague glimpse into the future. We do not know if its events are near or far, so we do the best we can. You did not shut Leondros out of your heart or our family. He was content to be home when he lived here." her healing words sounded as old as time itself. "He did not die in vain. Upon his death, Leondros found someone whom we thought was lost to us." even though to speak of her own twin brother's death was heart-wrenching, Zation found her brother's strength to speak of the thing that Leondros had returned to them.

King Doran let go of her and looked at her a little perplexed. "Who was lost to us?" he asked, trying to think of someone they had been missing from their kingdom. A light of a faint hope glimmered in Zation's face.

"The daughter of Reymier of the Shandon still lives and is with us now," she said in a soft tone. She knew her brother well, and he had a mysterious way of doing things, but somehow it always worked itself out for the good.

Thinking back, King Doran remembered his dear friend Reymier. He had been his most trusted elfin counselor and closest friend. When Reymier had stood against evil itself to save Shoshon and his family, it was said that he, along with his entire family, had perished.

"How is that possible? Reymier was killed. And from what we were told, so was his family. How is it that their child survived?" he asked in disbelief. He searched Zation's face for answers to these questions.

"I do not know, but one of the girls who brought Leondros back from the Shandel said that she was Tahari of the Shandon. Later, she told me that her father's name was Reymier," Zation replied with a hint of enthusiasm. "Father, though this girl does not have elfin features, how else would someone not familiar with Adarah know how to get into Shoshon, let alone find their way through the magic barrier that protects our land?" Her questions made the king wonder about this mysterious girl. It somehow made Leondros's passing a little easier to know that his final hours had been protected by a kindred spirit.

Pulled out of his despair for the moment, King Doran looked up with interest and curiosity. "Is she still with us?" he asked, feeling a sudden sense of worry that he had overlooked the two young riders when he had seen his son's nearly lifeless body.

"She is. Out of gratitude for the compassion they showed Leondros and for bringing him to us, I invited her and her friend to stay with us. They looked quite weary and needed rest after their long journey from the Shandel," Zation said with a light tone of encouragement. Greatly pleased by this, King Doran was able to sigh in relief. He vowed that by his son's sacrifice, he would learn from his mistakes and try to be the man that his son had become.

"Please send for her. I know it is such a late hour, but I fear not many will sleep well on this night. Maybe we can find some peace yet," he said in warm tone as his smile returned. Zation smiled.

"Right away, Father," she said, but looked at him a moment more. "I believe that Leondros meant a great deal to them, otherwise they would not have gone so far or risked so much to bring him home." her words lingered long after she left the room.

Chapter 76

Remembrance

S itting on her room's balcony, night passed very slowly for Tahari. It was good to relax after their journey, but she could not bring herself to rest entirely. Tahari tried to lose herself in the peacefulness of the night, the calm sweet breeze that touched her face and toyed with her long, brown hair. The coolness of the night hung around her, and she could hear the sound of distant waterfalls, but the ache of Leondros's death was as acute as a wound to her body. In her attempts to put these painful thoughts from her mind, Tahari would glimpse someone walking in the streets below and instantly an image of Leondros's face came to the surface again. Coming to grips with his death was tough enough, but not having the chance to say goodbye bothered her even more. Tahari pondered why she was finding herself so lost over his death, for they had met only once before she found him in the tower. Then Tahari remembered the dream she had of the woman and who she said Tahari was. Tahari had been the great sphinx Shamira and as such she was more than Leondros's friend. Tahari was his guardian, and she had failed him.

Tahari lost track of the time and was unsure if sleep had taken her, but she was startled by a knock at her door. Half surprised and half dazed, Tahari jumped from her chair and ran to the heavy wooden door in her room. When Tahari opened it, she gasped. There in front of her, Tahari saw Leondros's face, but she quickly realized that it was Zation standing at her doorway. She had a warm smile on her face and looked at Tahari with concern.

"I am sorry to disturb you at this late hour; knowing the weight of your grief, I would have rather let you alone, but my father wishes to speak to you. It might offer you some comfort knowing what he has to say, and it may also offer comfort to him. It is not an easy night for any of us, but maybe we can ease its passing." she spoke soothing words, yet Tahari also found comfort from her mere presence. The resemblance she had to Leondros was unreal, and somehow it made Tahari feel better to know that he was in some way close by.

"Yes, by all means," Tahari replied as she wiped the tears from her face.

She shook her head lightly and smiled. "It is all right. Tears are a good sign. They mean you care deeply," she said. Tahari smiled but did not say anything in response. Tahari was not at all surprised by the King's request to see her. It was perfectly understandable that he would want to know more about his son's last few hours. Tahari only hoped that she could remain composed enough to tell him the entire story. It was not an easy story to tell.

As they walked down the long, wood-lined corridors, Tahari breathed deeply the burning incense. It had been placed throughout the castle, and its spicy aroma hung heavy in the air. The lights glow softly, casting shadows throughout the castle. Even more than the atmosphere of these great halls, Tahari could feel the sadness that loomed over the palace. It affected everyone.

Turning her head slightly, Tahari looked over at Zation. She watched her expressions and could feel her deep distress over her twin's death. "I just wanted you to know that even though I did not know Leondros a long time, I had the privilege of being his friend," Tahari whispered to her. She looked at her and smiled sadly. It was mixed with relief and gratitude.

"I loved my brother very much, and I was concerned whenever he left on one of his many journeys. Deep down, I feared that one of his quests would eventually get him into trouble, but this…" Her voice trailed off. Zation struggled to find her voice again. When she looked up at Tahari, her smile returned. "I am grateful that you were with him in his most desperate hour. If you had not been, he would have died alone, and we would never have learned of the Shandel kingdom's fall and of our own danger." her words encouraged her a little, but Tahari still felt undeserving of such gratitude.

Tahari followed Zation into a large, dark chamber musty from aged manuscripts and scrolls. In the thick of darkness, she saw a single candle lit near an altar that held a very old scroll. As Tahari followed Zation through the massive library, she saw the king dressed in an ebony robe, gazing out of a window. His hands were clasped in front of him. Tahari could see the sorrow weighing heavily on his shoulders. Hearing them approach, he turned toward them. Through the sadness in his face, Tahari could see features similar to Leondros's. He did not have his son's golden hair, true, but there was an age-old wisdom that radiated from his face. She sensed that he was a powerful ruler, but in this moment he thought nothing of worldly things. She felt that he was a good man and a caring father. He tried to mask his grief, but Tahari could still see it in his eyes. The love that he had for his son was beyond measure. Tahari grieved for him.

Seeing her, King Doran's face brightened. "Tahari of the Shandon, I presume?" he asked politely as he bowed to Tahari. She was surprised that a king would be bowing to her of all people, but she did not dispute this and returned the bow. His voice was strong and thick with an elfish accent, but it was still soothing and gentle.

"Yes, my Lord. I am she," Tahari replied.

He remained quiet for a moment and just smiled at her. "Forgive me, for you bear a strong resemblance to your father, and it was so long ago that he lived here among us," King Doran apologized for his long gaze.

Tahari shook her head slightly. "No apology needed, Sire. I fear that I do not remember my father, only what Leondros had spoken of. I am grateful to Leondros, for he helped me to remember much of my past that had been buried. I believe that if it had not been for the small amount of time we spent together, I would not have known how to return here," she said as her mind recalled the moment when she first met Leondros. The magic that Tahari felt between them on that first meeting took her breath away.

"Please, tell us how you came to dwell in the Shandel. After your father died, there was no word about you or your mother. It was believed that you both had perished," he asked with sincere concern.

"Mother sensed that what had attacked Shoshon was planning on attacking us next, so during the night, she took me into the kingdom of the Shandel. We made it just outside Akendron when she left me with a plantation family and went to fight the creature herself. Days later, it was said that both had perished that night. The family I had been placed with soon grew jealous of me and made me a slave," Tahari explained sadly. "The hardship I experienced caused me to forget my elfish roots, until the day that I saved Leondros from a Draccen ambush." these words caused both Zation and King Doran to look at her in surprise.

"There was an ambush waiting for Leondros?" King Doran asked with concern. Tahari nodded slowly.

"It would have meant his death, and for reasons that I do not know myself, I had foreseen this. Denying my own safety, I aided him during the ambush. Our meeting took place only after Sala of Antioch had kidnapped me from the Tomblock plantation, just before I was to be executed." the concern seemed to increase in King Doran's eyes.

"I am forever grateful for what you have done," he said with immense gratitude. "But what compelled you to save him if you did not know him?"

"Your son asked me the same question," Tahari said. "I told him that compassion does not need a reason to be given away. Our world has seen too much time without it." King Doran and Zation looked at each other with a warm smile. "It was later made clear to me that I am also a sphinx of the ancient world." these last words caused her audience to stop breathing as their gazes widened. "In a vision, I was told that I was the great and powerful sphinx Shamira. She was charged by Adalai with the task of protecting an elfin prince. I believe your son is that prince." as Tahari spoke these words, King Doran and Zation looked upon her with new-found hope. Tahari merely looked down sadly as tears stung her eyes. Struggling past the tears, she managed to lift her head again. "I was compelled to save your son in the forest, but for all my power, I did not see this in his future," she admitted as she hung her head shamefully.

King Doran was silent for a moment as he thought about what Tahari had said. After exchanging looks with his daughter, he looked at her with love and understanding. "In your short time with my son, you earned his trust and, in turn, his friendship. That is quite a feat to achieve in such a small time, but I take relief in knowing that his guardian was with him. I thank you." his words pulled hard on her heart as her thoughts drifted back to Leondros in his last hours of life. The ache in Tahari's chest grew even more painful.

"Beyond being my duty, Leondros was my friend. Friendship is not something to be taken lightly or to be abused. It is a treasure far beyond any value of jewels, gold, or anything that man can create. To have such a thing in your possession means you have a responsibility to care for that friend. More than my role as his sphinx guardian, this was my responsibility to your son as his friend, and I was honored to have that. Even now, I honor the memories that I still have," Tahari said as tears began to sting her eyes once again. Tears welled up in the king's eyes as well.

"You are unlike any other person I have ever known before. You are only a youth, yet you possess a wisdom that is older than time itself," he said with awe and wonder. He looked over at the portrait of his dead son. A reverent smile came to his face. "Adalai foresaw these moments long before we were even a thought. Everyone needs someone to watch over them at some point in their lives. Leondros was always watching over others with no regard for himself," King Doran said as if with regret. "It was right for you to come into his life when you did. Maybe Leondros did not know it, but Adalai chose you to watch over him, even if only for a moment." at his words, Tahari felt tears run down her face.

"I only wish I could have done more to keep him from such an end," Tahari managed to utter as her throat tightened up painfully. King

Doran's brow wrinkled as though a painful thought had come to his mind. "I know the question that is pressing on your heart," Tahari said as she looked at him with an understanding expression. Tahari took a deep breath and thought about how to say it without bringing them too much pain. She felt Zation take her hand and squeeze it. Looking over at her, Tahari saw her brown eyes fill with encouragement. Tahari's burden was hers too and not as hard to carry. "What happened to Leondros was far beyond my power to try to stop. He was betrayed by Prince Alon-Settie, whom I gather to have been his best friend," Tahari said with a mournful tone. She watched as King Doran sank slowly into the chair next to him and covered his eyes with his hand. She paused for a moment, for even the air refused to let her speak another word. Zation squeezed her hand again, urging her to continue, though she could not bring herself to speak.

"Such are the words also spoken in our prophecy," King Doran said as he slowly raised his head and looked at them with a grieved expression.

Tahari again managed to speak. "I got to your son moments after the betrayal occurred, and though the wounds on his body did not suggest his immediate death, I sensed that his spirit was far away and that death was close at hand. Knowing that the only place for him was amongst his people, I brought him here," Tahari said with a weak voice as she replayed the tragic scene over again in her mind.

"They killed him with the crushing grief of betrayal and everything else they could do to him. After that…" King Doran's voice trailed off. He looked at them with a defeated expression and shook his head. "There was no need to inflict physical injury." There was silence in the room as the sadness flowed through air.

Tahari fought to find some way to restore the goodness that was woven into the threads of this night. "I feel that Leondros hung on until he reached his home and was once again with his loved ones," she said with a weak but determined voice. "As we journeyed from the Shandel into Adarah, I could feel his spirit with us still. He even pleaded with me and asked for me not to leave him…" Tahari felt her voice fade. "And I did not." her voice was now barely audible.

King Doran smiled at Tahari kindly, rose from his red-velvet-covered chair, and took her hand. "You are most definitely Reymier's daughter. The light that he had about him shines from your face. Reymier was a wise and just counselor. Many looked to him for advice, and they depended on him. He was my best friend," he said with a tone of happiness. "He was not a selfish man and would gladly do anything for those he loved. He loved his friends so much, probably more than many realized. His life was love, which he gave without hesitation." as he spoke these words, Tahari could see images of her father in his eyes. "What you have told us tonight brings me great comfort. I look into your eyes, and I see my son," he said with a contented smile. Though King Doran was saddened beyond words that his beloved son was dead, he knew that Leondros had been looked after by an angel sent to him by Adalai himself.

"As it is when I see you. I see my father and what he was like," Tahari replied with a raspy whisper. He smiled warmly and took a deep breath. She looked down and found the courage to ask a favor that had been on her heart since she watched the funeral procession earlier. "If I may ask but one favor?" Tahari began.

"Anything, child." He smiled generously as he awaited her request.

"May I go and pay my last respects to your son?" Tahari asked humbly. Her request stunned him.

King Doran was silent for a moment as he seemed to be in deep thought. Judging from the delay in his answer, Tahari sensed that such visitations were extremely sacred and outsiders were not permitted. Then he looked up at her with a hopeful gaze. "Go; look in on your friend. If his spirit lingers, he will want to know that you are still with him." Tahari bowed to him.

"Many thanks, my lord. I bid you a restful night and pray that peace and joy will fall once again upon this house," Tahari said. Leondros's family missed him dearly, and she almost felt that she had the power within herself to bring him back. It felt like an old story of her past that was longing to be remembered, but she tucked this thought in the back of her mind as she quietly left the room, made her way through the palace, and walked outside into the cool night air.

Chapter 77

A Sphinx's Gift

T ahari was almost rushing to get to Leondros's tomb, so she forced herself to slow down. She came to an abrupt stop when she neared the burial grounds. The moonlight cast a heavenly glow over it and the hanging garden within it. It was a garden like none she had ever seen before. In the stillness of the night, Tahari could hear the thunder of a distant waterfall.

She forced herself to continue. Coming to a moonlit crystal gate, Tahari gasped in awe at the wonder and splendor of this place. Surrounding the garden, she could make out lush, green bushes with the most beautiful purple and white flowers on them. There were white stone statues of elves placed throughout the massive garden. This was a sacred place. A big part of her felt unworthy to pass through this heavenly garden, but her faithfulness to her friend was her key to entering this sacred realm.

Walking through this massive garden, the wonder of this place overwhelmed her. Tahari crossed an ancient wooden foot bridge, which led her over a small babbling brook. The stillness of the night brought a soothing peace to the land. Tahari, too, found a reprieve from the ache of Leondros's death. She made her way through the majestic garden by the way of a winding stone path that curved throughout the garden. The sweet fragrances of vanilla and lavender filled the garden and in a quiet and gentle way brought peace to her soul. This was Leondros's burial garden. Though Tahari could not explain it, she felt his presence close by. She stopped and listened. A smile came to her face as she looked around the enchanted garden. Indeed, he was here. Even though they were separated by the black veil of death, Tahari could feel that he was standing beside her.

Emerging from the shadowy garden, Tahari came to the entrance of Leondros's tomb. The monument was built of white marble, and its arched entrance was lit by torches. Suddenly, she felt the chill of death's presence. It felt as if her friend were trapped within these white stone walls and could not get out. She could feel him calling from beyond the grave.

"I am here, my friend," she whispered as she walked toward the tomb's entrance. Looking at the fine detail inscribed in the stonework, Tahari read the elfin script:

This is the house of the dead. Here within these sacred chambers lies the ancient line of the Goldendragon family. Faded from life, they now live on in our memories and hearts.

Tahari's eyes passed over all the names of the honored dead and came to rest upon a newly etched name; *Leondros Goldendragon*. She sadly touched the newly carved etching with her fingers as if to search through the realm of the dead, to offer him the comfort of knowing that he still had a friend who cared in this world. Closing her eyes, Tahari prayed that peace would find him, wherever he was, and that sadness would fade quickly.

A lavender-filled breeze blew against her hot face. Taking a deep breath, Tahari stepped inside the tomb. She let her eyes adjust to the darkness. Soon, the moonlit entrance faded into a ghostly gray corridor that led far within the tomb. Her path was not cast in total darkness, for small candles lit a trail. The small flames burned with a fiery glow but, strangely, did not flicker as soft breezes blew through the tunnel. The air was close and still. The spicy, heavy aroma of incense filled her nose. Following the candlelight, Tahari walked slowly to the end of a very long tunnel. Only the soft sounds of her footsteps echoed against the marble walls. Tahari moved slowly and cautiously. Approaching the larger chamber, anticipation grew within her heart.

Walking into the large chamber, Tahari froze for a moment. The magnificence of this place was astounding. Torchlight reflected off of the white marble walls, lighting the room with a heavenly glow. She noticed more elfin script on the walls. Accompanying these writings were beautiful carvings of heavenly beings watching over the honored dead. In the center of the octagon-shaped chamber was an altar stone with intricate designs carved into the gray marble. Upon the altar, dressed in a black burial robe, was Leondros Goldendragon. Tahari felt a sharp pain drive deep into her chest. There were no tricks here. This was not some illusion that her mind had generated. Her beloved friend was lying dead upon this altar. In that moment, a rush of memories hit her. Walking up to the altar where he lay silently, Tahari looked upon his face for the first time since she had heard of his death. The pain in her chest grew. Tahari took her hand and held it over his chest. She had to see for herself.

Unlike most people, Tahari could sense the spirit within a person's body. It gives off a special kind of energy. All living creatures have it. The life energy is what moves the living and gives the living breath. Tahari lowered her head sadly as she took her hand away. There was no life energy here. The bruises that had covered his face had all but faded, for his family's magic had done much to sponge away what had been done to him, but not all of it. Death remained. A sudden and terrible grief gripped her.

"This should not have been your fate," Tahari said softly, trying to remain composed. Looking at his gray face, she could feel the tears stinging her eyes. She smiled warmly. "Your father was right," she said in a whisper. "You always watched over your friends and cared for them. It was an honor to have such a friend." Tahari's smile faded as she saw a faint bruise remaining on his forehead. She covered the bruise for a moment with her hand as if to heal it.

Touching him, Tahari saw his whole life and the betrayal that led him here. She sensed that he had a great role in the mission to find Farro. More than that, she thought of his family and how devastated they all were. Deep down, Tahari wanted to do more than just wish him safe journey to the isle of the dead. As she hung her head to pray, Tahari received a flash of energy that awoke her senses and reminded her of the power she had as a sphinx. Although Tahari was very young for such power, she knew that she could do it. Tahari could defeat death's power.

A cool breeze washed over her face, seemingly from nowhere. Opening her eyes, Tahari saw a woman standing before her, dressed in a dark robe. Although a black gossamer veil nearly covered her face, it seemed familiar.

"I remember you," Tahari began, a little dumbfounded that she was suddenly before her, real as life.

"Tahari, I come to you to remind you of something that you may have forgotten." as she spoke, Tahari saw a warning in her sea-green eyes.

"What is it?" Tahari asked softly as she sensed that this woman would stop her from helping her dear friend.

"You are a very strong person, and stronger still is your power within the sphinx race. However, no one so young has ever turned back death before they had reached the fullness of their power. No one in the history of the sphinx race." her words were chilling. "If you bring him back, you will pay a heavy price.

"I am no stranger to persecution. Any price is worth a friend's life," Tahari reasoned. Then she remembered a line of the prophecy:

*IV. The key to finding Farro will lie within a tomb. *Be of courage to make a sacrifice.*

"Tahari, I cannot promise what favor you will find with the sphinx lords or Adalai himself, but once this is done, there will be no going back," she warned Tahari. "You must remember that you still have your role to play in the quest to find Farro." Tahari sensed the woman's worry, but as she looked down at her friend, Tahari was driven to go forward with her plan.

"I know, but so does *he*. It has been written in the lines of the prophecy," Tahari said, adamant about her decision.

"Would you sacrifice yourself for his sake?" The woman's tone was filled with fear. Tahari was then reminded who this woman was and why she was here.

"My life will not have been wasted," Tahari replied as she thought about all those that she had to watch die before her, powerless to do anything. Then as Tahari thought of her parents and the choices they made to save those around them, Tahari realized who she was. "I want to bestow the blessing that was taught to me once by my father and by you, Mother." Tahari's words caught her mother off-guard. She lowered her head and remained silent.

"Your road is before you now, and I have only one gift that I can leave with you," she said softly as if to keep anyone else from hearing. She walked over to Leondros's altar stone, knelt down, and touched a single intricately designed square stone upon it. Looking closer at the stone she had touched, Tahari saw that it was the crest of the Osarian Knights. Then Tahari remembered the last line of the first scroll:

*Look for a stone within a tomb that is marked with the crest. This is where you will find the second instructions.

Tahari heard the gravelly sound of stones scraping against each other. Her mother took two scrolls from the space that had opened up. One was radiant white and the other yellow with age. Replacing the stone, her mother rose to her feet, and handed Tahari the two scrolls. "Our ancestors are very proud of you. They look to you with anticipation," she said with tears in her sea-green eyes, a proud smile lingering upon her warmly tanned face. Then she vanished from all sight.

Tahari was again alone in the silence of the tomb. She set aside the yellowed scroll for a moment, sure that it was the second scroll of the prophecy. She looked upon the radiant white scroll with interest. It had a strange crest on its red seal. Tahari studied the crest for a moment and then realized that it was a sphinx symbol. It read:

Life Scroll.

Chapter 78

To Give a Life

Taking a deep breath, Tahari opened the white scroll. She was filled with anticipation and hope. Could she really bring Leondros back from the dead? Tahari thought about the decision that now rested upon her shoulders and the possible consequences, but then she remembered the line of instruction from the prophecy:

*Be of courage to make a sacrifice.

She unrolled the sacred scroll and read the incantations upon it. The words were written in the language of the sphinx. Tahari felt a twinge of memory from what she guessed was her past life, the life that had been Shamira's. This part of her was just starting to reveal itself, and it wanted to come back fully. Tahari was beginning to understand what Leondros and Sala had seen in her. Tahari, too, was awestruck by what she saw.

As she read the incantations, the scroll's energy was released. Tahari read the words a second time, and this time she felt her fingers tingle as her own power passed through them.

From dark to light, from death to life

Breathe once again, my friend.
Let a spirit return to your form,
So you may be alive once more.

Tahari could feel the power in the scroll. The tomb shook with it. It was as if heaven and earth had collided for a brief moment. She looked at Leondros to see the result of what had transpired. A cold pain hit her chest and drove her heart deep into her stomach. There lay Leondros, unmoving and just as lifeless as before. Tahari sank to her knees and hung her head, breathing in the air of disappointment.

Several moments passed before she could allow herself to move again. When Tahari did, she sat up and gazed over sadly at Leondros. Tears welled up in her eyes. Tahari felt defeated. Maybe she was too young to accomplish such a task. She slowly laid the white scroll on the altar next to him. The pain Tahari felt was ripping her apart inside.

"This should never have happened," Tahari said, full of sorrow. She realized that if she had stayed in the prison longer than she had, their places would have been switched. "This should be me lying here, not you. This world still needs people like you. Now more than ever." it was true. He still had a lot yet to offer this world, and no one had given him the chance to become the person that he could have been. Tahari took a look at her life and saw that she had lived it the best that she could, but it too was missing something. Maybe a moment to do something that was not for her but to do something much greater. The chance to do something good for someone else, someone who deserved to be given a great gift and not be asked for anything in return.

Looking at Leondros for a moment, a smile came to her face. Tahari leaned close to him and whispered softly, "If I have any power at all, I would gladly give it up to bring you back. If nothing else, let it be my life that is taken so that yours can return. You have a family that misses you terribly, and all I have in this world are three friends who mean everything to me. I am honored that you are among them." she was silent for a moment. Tahari noticed again the faint bruises on his face. They reminded her of Alon-Settie. "A man claiming to be your friend might have betrayed you to your death, but a stranger would have given up their life for you." tears rolled down her cheeks. Resting her forehead on the altar close to his head, Tahari began to pray for her lost friend.

When Tahari finished her prayer, she lifted her head and guessed that the hour was very late. She was weary and should be on her way. Tahari stood up to leave the tomb when she was suddenly overwhelmed with a strange fatigue. There was a higher power at work here; she could feel its presence, but no one else was in the tomb. Terribly weak and dizzy, Tahari crumpled against the altar and rested her head on it. She felt as if her life were fading from her. She did not know what was happening. Fearing that the coming blackness would be eternal, Tahari reached out and took hold of Leondros's hand. She wanted to cling to some form of reality. Then as day gave way to night, the darkness took her. Blackness and silence filled Tahari's world.

Chapter 79

Resurrection

Tahari opened her eyes and groggily looked around the tomb. A gentle radiance from dawn's light somehow made its way into the tomb's large chamber. She could hear the morning birds' songs and smell the fresh dew. Looking up at the walls, Tahari studied more closely the elfish script upon them. Though the words spoke of death, somehow that was not what she now felt. The room had a warm, heavenly glow about it as if death's cold presence had been eliminated. That was when Tahari felt her head still resting on Leondros's altar stone. All the events of the past few hours and days came rushing back to her. Tahari lifted her weary head and looked over at Leondros. He lay as unmoving and lifeless as he had been the night before. She let out a heavy sigh.

She attempted to climb to her feet, but Tahari felt something most strange, and she froze and to take in her surroundings. Tahari felt another presence in the room with her. Looking around cautiously, however, she failed to see anyone else in the chamber. Puzzled by this strange development, Tahari stood up slowly and looked at Leondros. She stopped breathing.

Tahari continued to watch him with anticipation but refusing to believe her own eyes. Life was returning to his face! An intense feeling of love filled the room, and the morning's light shone through the tomb's entrance and upon his altar stone. Sinking slowly back to the ground, Tahari watched him intently. Then, it was as if an angel placed her hand upon his chest; Tahari saw life begin to stir within him once again. He was breathing! Her hands slowly covered her mouth, and her heart skipped a beat.

"Oh my God," Tahari managed to say inaudibly. She was almost horrified to see such a wondrous thing. She did not even have to reach out to feel whether the life energy was really there because she could sense it from where she was kneeling. "You are alive," she murmured. Overwhelmed by the moment, Tahari lowered her head to the altar and thanked the sphinx lords and Adalai for such a miraculous thing to happen.

Tahari felt someone touch her hand. Looking up, Tahari saw Leondros looking back at her with a weary smile. He still seemed groggy and weak from his recent experience, but he was alive again! Her heart beat so hard she thought it would leap from her chest. Taking hold of his hand, Tahari held it tightly, resting her cheek against it. There were no words to express how thankful she was to see him alive again.

"Tahari..." His voice was very weak still, but she heard him just fine. Raising her head, Tahari smiled at him warmly, leaning closer to him.

"You came back," Tahari said, overwhelmed almost to tears.

He smiled as he squeezed her hand. "It was you who found me." his words caught her off-guard. Tears stung her eyes, and her heart hurt again, but this time it was a healing pain. Tahari found herself amazed that he knew that she was there with him in the tower and that she had carried him out, he had been so near death. Tahari looked down for a moment as she held his hand in both of hers. Fighting back the tears of happiness, she looked back up at him with a loving smile.

"I had a promise to keep to a dear friend," Tahari said as the tears still glistened in her eyes. "I could not let such a friend down." he smiled. She was overwhelmed that her dear friend was alive again.

Reaching over, Tahari gently wrapped her arms around him and held him close for a moment. "I missed you, my friend," she whispered to him. He seemed almost fragile in her arms, but she could feel his strength returning.

"Thank you, my friend. I am in your debt," he whispered to her. His words touched her heart.

"Seeing life in your face again is all the payment I need," Tahari replied as she let go of him and offered a warm smile. He then looked down and seemed uncomfortable. "Is something wrong?" she asked with concern.

"Your friend aches from lying on stone. Could I trouble you for a moment of aid?" he said in a soft whisper as he slowly moved his stiffened body. Tahari chuckled lightly as she took hold of his arm and put her other arm around his back to help him sit up again. He was still very weak and seemed quite stiff as he sat hunched over. She knew it would be some time before his full strength returned. She was content to be here with him, and she continued to thank Adalai and the sphinx lords for such a miracle. Tahari watched Leondros's face closely and could almost see the images of his last moments in the tower replaying in his mind. The grief in his face could not be missed.

"Such a look of memory; it haunts even my mind," Tahari said with a saddened tone. He looked over at her for a moment. She guessed that he was deciding whether to speak of such things with her. Tahari held his hand tightly and looked down at the floor. "I made it to your side only moments after your horrible ordeal; I saw the results with my own eyes…" Her voice trailed off as her mind flashed back to those horrible last moments. "Words cannot describe the treachery of that event." he dropped his sad gaze to the floor. Somewhere in all his confusion, he was trying to make sense of why it had happened.

"I do not know what I did to cause this change of heart in Alon-Settie." his voice was weak and filled with grief. Looking at him and recalling the vision of what he had gone through, Tahari could not know why anyone would want to hurt a friend so badly. Then she remembered the guards that she had to get past; they, too, seemed eager to destroy him—and her, for that matter. An image of the mysterious dark advisor who had her thrown into prison flashed before her eyes. Fear ran down her spine. Tahari now had a good idea of what they were up against. Her gaze went to the floor as she understood why Leondros had been killed. Just the thought of it pained her heart. He looked over at her. "What is it?" he asked in a soft tone.

"I do not think you are responsible for Alon-Settie's change of heart. There is something much more sinister at work here. I, too, have noticed a change, and it went far beyond Alon-Settie. The castle guards and now the Draccen soldiers who reside in Akendron have imprisoned the city and executed the royal family," Tahari said slowly as she worked out the purpose of the strange events that had happened within Akendron. Leondros listened intently. "The ancient evil known as Lord Jarden that Sala had spoken of..." She paused and felt the harshness of their reality. "He has come back to finish what he started. We are the only ones standing in his way, which is why we were made to suffer," she concluded as she looked back at him. Tahari knew he understood.

"How do we fight such odds?" he asked, sounding a little overwhelmed. It was a very real concern, but Tahari had hope from what she had witnessed already that morning.

"One step at a time. After all, you just came back from the dead," Tahari said with a sly smile. "I believe there is someone watching out for us. It is not every day that I wake up to a miracle," she said as she took his hand once again. Leondros's smile returned. Weakly leaning his head against hers, she heard him whisper, "Thank you for being the miracle in my life."

Tahari sensed a healing within him. The amount of love that she felt for him grew in that moment. Putting an arm around him, Tahari held him close. It touched her heart that he looked to her to be the one that lifted him out of his grief. He rested against her until they both heard someone entering the tomb.

Chapter 80

Reunion

In walked the tomb caretaker, clothed in a dark-gray robe. He looked quite a bit older than Leondros, and his features were a little worn. He had darker blond hair and steely gray eyes. Tahari guessed that he was a servant for the royal family. She could sense sadness in him. Just by looking at him, she knew that Leondros had meant a lot to him. Leondros and Tahari watched him prepare to begin his work when he suddenly noticed her.

"I am sorry; I will have to ask you to go," he said as if it were routine. Tahari looked at Leondros with an expression that said, *Ah, does he not see?* He seemed to understand her expression and smiled. He looked back at the tomb caretaker. The caretaker looked at her again after laying the heavy cloth bundle he had brought on the floor. This time he saw Leondros sitting next to Tahari, alive and awake. The man stopped in his tracks. No words left his mouth before he crumpled to the floor. Leondros and Tahari watched the man with great interest as he lay in a heap on the floor.

"I guess he does not get to witness too many resurrections around here," Tahari said teasingly. Leondros had been looking between Tahari and the caretaker. He smiled as he looked once again at the caretaker and shook his head. It was a blessing in itself to see Leondros smile.

Then she sensed someone else drawing near to the tomb. Looking up, Tahari could see Zation walking down the long tunnel. She was still dressed in her black robe and veil. In her hand, she held a small candle. When she noticed the body of the caretaker, she quickly rushed to his side. Dropping to one knee, she tried to wake the petrified worker. Then, a perplexed look came over her face as she realized someone else was in the tomb with her. Looking up at the two people sitting upon the ulter, she froze, a look of awe replacing the perplexity. Tears welled up in her eyes as a smile came to her face.

"Dear brother, tell me I am not dreaming still?" she finally asked.

He smiled at her. "Good morning, Zation. I am thanking the goodness of Adalai that this is not a dream," he replied weakly, but his words were heartfelt. Tears streamed down her face as she climbed to her feet, walked over to Leondros, and looked at him. Her smile was not to be missed as she reached over and held his face tenderly in her hands.

"My dear brother, what miracle has brought you back to me?" she asked, trembling. Leondros turned his head toward Tahari. Zation followed his glance until she saw her. There was a moment of bewilderment in her eyes. Then a smile came to her face, expressing awe and wonder. "How were you able to move heaven and earth?" she asked her astonished. Tahari smiled humbly, and Leondros looked at Tahari with wonder about the feat that had been performed, as well.

"It is a long story." Tahari paused for a moment as she pondered how to tell her account, but Leondros and Zation were patient and longed to hear her story. She reminded them of her sphinx past and how she realized her guardianship included Leondros. "After learning of your death," Tahari said, looking at Leondros, "I realized that I had failed. But I believe Rafar left me an enchanted scroll that helped make it possible for me to fulfill my oath," she explained slowly as she found her ability to smile again. Tahari finished her account with the reading of the scroll and the love it took to bring Leondros back. Zation's eyes glistened in the soft light of the tomb. She wrapped her arms around Leondros and held him close for a long moment. It was a comfort to see Leondros in the arms of his twin sister again. Tahari bowed her head humbly but could not help but admire the restored kinship between sister and brother.

In the short amount of time that had passed since his awakening, Leondros's strength was already beginning to return. He stood up and began to walk as before, although a little stiffly. Tahari watched his progress eagerly.

"Are you ready to see the family?" Zation asked with a reserved anticipation. Tahari knew that Zation could not wait to bring Leondros to the palace again. Tahari could already feel the celebration that would take place afterward.

"Yes. Let us not keep them waiting," he said with warm smile. Tahari could see that he wanted to see his family again. Then Zation turned to try to revive the poor caretaker. While she did, Leondros turned to Tahari. "I know that your being here last night helped me to find my way back, and I do not want to lose you now," he said. "Come and greet my family with me. They will be interested in knowing what you have seen." his invitation to accompany him as he went to see his family touched Tahari deeply. He offered his arm to her. She smiled shyly as she took it.

"I would be honored. Thank you." Tahari was looking forward to seeing him reunited with his family. Leondros leaned over and whispered in her ear.

"I may also need your help to keep from falling. My mother tends to be overzealous in her greetings." Tahari smiled and chuckled warmly as she pictured poor Leondros taken down by his own mother's hug. She hugged his arm and rested her cheek on his shoulder for a brief moment.

"It will be a moment to remember. I would not miss it for the world," Tahari said, looking at him with a reverent smile. They turned to see that Zation had been successful in reviving the poor elf who had passed out only moments before.

"I had the strangest dream," the caretaker said in a groggy voice. He looked up at Zation, who was helping him to sit up. "I saw your brother alive again. I swear, it almost felt real. Maybe it had something to do with the angel sitting next to him, but I could almost..." his voice trailed off as he saw Leondros now standing not far from him. Upon seeing Leondros alive and well, he passed out again in Zation's arms. A hopeless look came over her face as she shook her head.

"We will have to break this news to him slowly. Jeanpala has never witnessed a resurrection, even after 3,500 hundred years as the royal tomb caretaker." Zation's words struck them as funny. Tahari grinned at Leondros, who smiled back at her and patted her arm. Tahari looked at Jeanpala, wondering about what he had said about her. "I will send someone to come back here and get you. Rest well, old friend," Zation said. She patted his shoulder and then climbed to her feet. Zation stepped back into the tunnel, and Leondros and Tahari followed her out of the tomb.

It was if nature herself knew that Leondros was back from the dead. Morning's blindingly radiant light greeted them as they emerged from the tomb. They walked into the garden, and Tahari could feel the earth itself celebrating. Vividly colored flower petals fell from the trees above. The lush bushes and hedges seemed to stand just a little higher than before. Even the birds seemed to sing more brightly. Tahari leaned close to Leondros and whispered, "I think the word is out.

He smiled humbly. He did not expect to see such devotion from nature. Tahari looked at him for a moment and was almost startled by his features. The radiance of the sun shone down upon him and illuminated his appearance. His brown eyes dazzled in the sunlight. Even his blond hair glowed almost white. He seemed so much different from the first time she met him. It was as if a truer Leondros was returned to them. His regal features were amplified. She knew that it was Dreyhon who would by right be king, but in her heart, Tahari felt that somehow it was Leondros who was destined to be king.

They walked through the enchanted gardens and made their way through its crystal gates. Tahari could not explain the immense joy that she received from seeing the mountainous-looking hedges, the sea-green brook that flowed into pools of water, and the magnificent waterfall that loomed high overhead, shrouded in white mist. Tahari loved this garden, for there was a magic about it, but having Leondros alive and by her side made it so much more meaningful. She wanted to linger in the garden, but she needed to see Leondros with his family again.

They eventually made it to the palace. There had not been anyone walking around the courtyard, so the word of Leondros's return had not spread yet. Walking up the white stone steps into the grassy courtyard, Tahari looked up and saw his mother dressed in a black dress with a veil covering her face. Inya was standing quietly by herself and seemed to be in deep thought. She had not noticed them yet. Leondros looked at Tahari for encouragement. Tahari smiled and squeezed his hand warmly. Even though no words were spoken, he understood what she was telling him.

It will be all right. You were lost to them and they realized many things that they would give anything to change. Now they will have that chance. This is a blessing that people of the world pray for, but never see. Go. I will be right here. Tahari's warm thoughts stayed with Leondros.

Leondros took a deep breath and smiled. Turning to his mother, he called to her.

"Mother?" His voice was soft in tone. Inya stopped and turned toward them. At first, it did not sink in that it was Leondros in front of her. She lifted her veil and took a clearer look. Her eyes were reddened from crying. Her eyes brightened as she gasped at his presence.

"Leondros? Is it you, my child?" Inya asked in a yearning whisper. She slowly stepped closer to him.

"I am here, Mother," he replied as he stepped toward her. She walked up to him and looked into his eyes. She reached out and touched his face.

"My precious child..." She wrapped her arms around him and held him for a long moment. Tahari could hear her starting to weep again. Leondros tried to comfort his mother, but the fact in itself was overwhelming. Her child was alive and now safe in her arms again.

Zation walked up next to Tahari. The look that welled in her warm brown eyes said it all. Tahari had fulfilled her pledge as Leondros's sphinx guardian. The true effects of this miracle were beginning to extend past the confines of the tomb. Leondros took his mother's arm and they began to walk toward a small archway that was covered by vines and flowers and headed back to the palace. Zation took Tahari's arm, and they followed them through one of the palace's many doors.

"Adalai must have smiled upon you because such things have not been seen for thousands of years." her words stayed with Tahari, but she refused to take pride in what she did.

"Judging from what I have seen thus far, I can imagine no greater joy than to see Leondros alive and his family healed by this miraculous chain of events," Tahari replied as she gazed at Leondros with his mother, seeing how she held onto her son's arm as if never to let him go again.

Chapter 81

Price to Be Paid

It was not long until Tahari accompanied Leondros as he joined his family for a much-needed reunion in a small chamber lit entirely by candlelight. The room gave off a warm, cozy feel and was a haven for the family. Tapestries that hung from the ceiling were as green as the leaves of the forest. Woven into the velvet fabric was elfin script in silver thread. The words shimmered in the candlelight. They were poems and special messages left for the family from their ancestors. Tahari felt so much history in this room. It was as if their ancestors were here with them, watching. Tahari smiled with contentment.

The hours passed at a relaxed pace as this fortunate family welcomed back the son that had been stolen from them. Tahari sat silently among them, content to just listen and filled with relief. She had sensed the pain and anguish that Leondros had endured, and now she saw him safe with his family once again. She listened to the stories that told this family's history; they had shared many long years together. Through the stories, Tahari watched Leondros grow from a small child to the man he was now. She saw all the adventures that he had taken with his uncle, Tonious Goldendragon. It was amazing to hear about all the things that he had done in his 2,300 years. However, it seemed that he had been separated from his family during key moments in his family history. Still, fate had its own way of choosing people for a particular path. As Tahari watched the loving family before her, she was glad that fate had allowed them this chance to be reunited with a son that had been forgotten for so long. As she watched on, Tahari found herself gazing into the flame of a candle and soon became lost in a vision.

⸻ ❖ ⸻

She found herself walking through a misty forest, dressed in a silver and white gown. Her long hair flowed about her, and a small crown of silver and crystal sat upon her head. Tahari looked around, and as strange as this place was to her, somehow it felt like home. Soft voices sang sweetly, intertwining within the cool breeze that whistled through the trees and brushed her cheek.

Tahari walked through the lush forest until she came to an enchanted waterfall that towered high above her. Mist hung around the falls like a white veil as the water spilled into the sea-green pool below it. Tahari was immediately reminded of Leondros's burial garden. Now she knew why she loved being in that garden so much. It *was* like being home. Looking into the pool, Tahari saw her reflection. It took her breath away. It was the same face looking back at her that she had always known, but it was much different. It still had a few elfin characteristics, but there was something more that radiated from her face. Then Tahari realized that there was a second reflection in the pool. A woman was standing behind her. Tahari turned and looked up at her mother. She was wearing a flowing peach, gown and she almost glowed. She smiled and reached for Tahari's hand. As Tahari took hold of it and slowly rose to her feet, she remembered something.

"Anyi?" This was her name. It was like remembering a memory from long ago. Her smile widened. Tahari was captured by her appearance for a moment. She had sea-green eyes just like hers and long hair the color of mahogany. Her facial features were regal, and her skin was dark. Her beauty was not comparable to anyone Tahari had seen on Earth. There was a mysterious wisdom about her that seemed almost ancient. Startlingly, Tahari found all these traits in herself, too.

"How I have longed for this moment, my daughter," she said to Tahari at last. Her voice was calm and soothing. There was patience, wisdom, and much kindness in it, but more than anything, there was love. She took a hold of Tahari's arm and began to lead her around the pool toward the waterfall, where a rainbow shone in the spray.

"This is a place that I have witnessed only once before. Not here, but in the burial garden of my friend, Prince Leondros Goldendragon," Tahari said in awe at the splendor around her.

Anyi smiled a loving but sad smile. "That was a brave thing to do. Especially since you are so young," she said. Tahari tried to remember just what she had done. Anyi led her to a large rock by the waterfall and sat down. Tahari took her place on the rock in front of Anyi. She looked at Tahari a moment and then nodded her head. "You did more than just bring your friend back from the dead, but it is a memory that only your spirit remembers." turning her head toward the pool, she motioned for Tahari to follow her gaze. "Look into the pool and you will discover the gift that you have given your friend out of the love you have for him.

Gazing into the pool, Tahari saw an image of herself turn into the scene of her in the tomb with Leondros. Tahari remembered the words that she had spoken and shortly thereafter feeling very weak. She watched herself slump against his altar stone. Then a soft light lit up the dark of the tomb as though heaven itself glowed upon it. Tahari watched a source of light within her begin to glow brightly. The light left her body and went into Leondros. Then the heavenly glow faded and only the torches' light remained. It was then that Tahari realized what she had done.

"You have given your friend a very special gift, but in doing so, you broke a sacred rule of our people. You will walk your path until the sphinx lords decide what the consequences of your actions will be." she explained that the misuse of power was strictly forbidden by their sacred rules. Even to perform a wondrous feat of goodness meant unnecessary attention drawn toward the sphinx. Her mother's words caused a heavy feeling to wash over her. Tahari looked back into the pool and now saw the reunion between Leondros and his family. She shook her head and smiled anyway.

"It was a course I had to take. He risked everything to find me after my capture, and it led to his death. As his guardian and friend, I was compelled to do something. What is a friendship if you are not willing to make sacrifices for it?" Tahari said with a tone of defiance. "If the sphinx lords decide to pass judgment upon me and take me away, what will happen to Leondros and my friends?" Tahari asked.

Her mother looked at Tahari with a kind expression as she put her hand on her cheek. "Tahari, your friends care for you very much, and they would start a crusade if it meant that you could be returned to them.

Tahari looked back into the pool and saw Leondros with his family again. A smile came to her face as she watched them. She felt a wonderful sense of tranquility wash over her, for whether she was taken or left within the world of the living, Tahari was at peace with her decision. Tahari promised herself that she would make every moment count and commit them to memory. Tahari reached over the pool and held her hand over Leondros's image for a long moment.

"Your love will be with him always." her mother's words were warm and comforting. Tahari looked up and smiled as tears welled in her eyes. A single tear ran down her face and dropped into the sea-green pool, touching the image of Leondros. The ripples faded his image slightly, and the mist surrounded her. In that one moment, Anyi allowed Tahari to see how her sacrifice shifted fate's design for both her and Leondros.

Between the worlds of life and death, something magical stirred the fates. A special promise was made in the secrecy of a tomb that altered the courses of two destinies. Out of love and compassion for an unfortunate soul who had been lost to death's shadowy realm, a courageous spirit would pay the consequences of asking for this soul's return. Deeply touched by this courageous spirit, the sphinx lords would also grant a special opportunity. Both spirits would be allowed to walk the earth and continue their secret mission, but only for a short amount of time. The courageous spirit would eventually have to pay this debt.

Chapter 82

Reflection

As the orange sun slipped low into the vermilion western sky, Tahari slipped out of the palace unnoticed, making her way to a cobblestoned footpath that led south to a grassy hill high above Paracity Palace. She was still relieved that her dear friend Leondros was alive, but being surrounded by hundreds of people during the celebration, she began to feel claustrophobic. Tahari was beginning to understand the sphinx rule that she had broken to bring Leondros back. Such a demonstration of power would draw attention to a sphinx, which could lead to arrogance and egocentricity. Such things had been deemed forbidden amongst her people.

Tahari had to get away to breathe some fresh air again. Once free from the castle and the crowds of people who wanted to see Leondros, she made her way up the footpath, which turned into a narrow set of stairs that had been carved into the hill's rock. Beautiful green trees and bushes covered the hill carefully hiding the path that led to the hill's top. Tahari found her sanctuary in this place. Walking up the stairs, Tahari breathed in the fresh country air. It was filled with many wonderful scents. Lilac and jasmine caught her attention, and she could not help but take in their sweet aromas.

After a little trouble of climbing the narrow stairs in the midnight-blue gown and matching shoes that Zation had given to her, Tahari finally made it to the top. Still, it felt good to be in new clothes, for hers were in shambles from her journey here. Tahari had not realized just how long and beautiful her hair was until she was able to let it fall to its grown length. It now hung past her waist. When the rays of the setting sun hit it, she found highlights of reds, deep golds, and browns woven into it. Locks of hair were gathered from both sides of her face and pulled neatly behind her head and fastened. Tahari now found how well she fit in with the elfin culture. Although she did not carry the pointed-ear trait common among this race of elves, her other elfin characteristics, such as acute senses, shone through. Tahari loved this new life that she had found, but as she gazed into the horizon and saw that land and sky formed a wondrous whole, she began to realize that she symbolized this. Tahari had discovered her elfin half, but she had only just begun to scratch the surface of her sphinx heritage.

Tahari stood for a long moment taking in the warm sun sinking deep into the darkening sky, dropping slowly behind the tree-covered mountains far in the distance. The heat and light from the fading sun continued to warm her face. Her thoughts went back to what she had done to save Leondros. It was a moment that she wished could last forever. Closing her eyes, she breathed in the sweet, cool breeze that gently stroked her face.

Tahari lost track of time just listening to the hoot of the owls and gentle buzz of the insects bringing in the night. Then she felt a presence approach her. Tahari did not have to look to see who it was.

"Good evening, Zation," she said at last. Tahari believed that she startled her as she tiptoed up to her. At the sound of her gasp, Tahari opened her eyes and saw Zation staring at her in disbelief. She was still dressed in the sea-green gown with metallic blue and green beads that she had worn for the celebration. Her hair had been pulled up to form a blonde bun on the back of her head and long strands of hair hung by her cream-colored face.

After she collected her thoughts, Zation's smile returned. "I knew I would find you here. This is where I come to clear my mind and become one with nature again, especially after a really traumatic experience." her words caught Tahari's attention. Her soulful brown eyes filled with concern. "I am concerned for you." she spoke as if she knew more than she said.

Tahari smiled at her compassion for her. "There is no need to worry for me. I take strength in knowing that your brother has been returned safe and sound," she reassured Zation. "I saw what happened to him, and it hurt even more to know that it was his best friend who had betrayed him. My heart broke when I saw how much he had suffered. I could not remain idle; I had to help him," she said. Tahari still felt the twinge of pain pull at her heart as she visualized Leondros in the tower.

"At what cost?" she asked with a raise of her eyebrow and a tone that directed even more concern toward Tahari. Zation's question was innocent, but it would eventually lead her to Tahari's secret.

Tahari could not answer Zation as she looked over the darkening night sky before them. Stars of all sizes lit up the night. The evening's coolness had already begun to drift into the mountain valley. A ghost-like mist crept slowly over the land as if the night herself was putting the land to sleep and covering it with a blanket.

Zation stepped closer to Tahari and joined her gaze toward the cool night sky. Tahari had lost herself in the realm of nature again, but she knew that Zation would not let her go so easily.

"Long ago, a wise old man said that life is a circle. For something to live, something must die. This is the way of things." Zation's words were hauntingly true. "I am Leondros's twin sister. I felt him dying when you rode into the city with him in your arms. I could see it in your eyes; you had sensed the life leaving his body, too." she spoke in a whisper, but Tahari could tell that she was beginning to understand what she had done. "This morning when I awoke, something told me that he had returned. I was never so grateful to see Leondros again, but I know that you had to have done something…" her voice trailed off. She stared at Tahari with terrible realization. "What have you done?" she asked in what was now a raspy whisper. Tahari looked over at her and saw horror in her eyes. Zation knew Tahari's secret but did not believe it.

Holding on to the contentment that filled her, Tahari turned her head back to the wondrous starry horizon, taking in all the life around her. Peace filled her soul, and she took comfort in knowing that Leondros would always carry a part of her inside him.

"We do not write the script for our lives. If it were that easy, then we would never know of the miracles and blessings that can happen around us and how they can enrich our lives and the lives of others," Tahari finally said. "In the small amount of time that I have lived upon this earth, I know what the world's view is on slaves, for I was one. They see me as a flaw, or something that should be locked away, never to be seen again," she said with a sad sigh as Tahari remembered her time as a slave. "I am worn from these short, physically and spiritually draining years. My childhood after leaving Adarah was not a blissful one. It was spent working on the plantations surrounding Akendron. One could only pray they would see the next day, for our masters were cruel and petty. I never looked far into my future, for it was much too painful. Instead, I lived my life with an appreciation for all living things," Tahari said, feeling the draining effects of her old life. "Then the sphinx lords sent your brother into my life. For the first time in my life, I felt truly alive and of worth. Our meeting was short-lived, but there was magic in that moment. Holding dear to that one special moment, I vowed to befriend him on the journey that would take us back to Adarah. Then I was given a chance to do something very special for him. Not to do it because I found out that I was his guardian, but to repay the kindness that he had shown me. All too often, the good people of this world never get help they need when they really need it, like a true friend to be there when you really need them. I had a chance to help a friend and save his life, regardless of the consequences, and I took it." Tahari spoke with conviction, and it brought tears to her eyes.

Zation remained silent for a long moment. She joined Tahari's gaze and looked into the deep of the starry night.

"Dear God, what have you done?" she asked again but did not require Tahari to answer. She now knew the weight of what Tahari had done for her brother. She turned and slowly walked over to a gray stone bench and sat down. Tahari's news must have been staggering for her. Their history lacked such heroism and sacrifice. "Only once in my lifetime have I witnessed such devotion, but I can honestly say that I have never seen this in such a young friendship," she said thoughtfully. "You are your father's daughter. Reymier did this for us when we all were in danger. We honor his memory still. Your deed may not be known to the world, but Adalai has witnessed it. The amount of love that you have shown will not be forgotten. Love never dies. Your love will live on through those who remember it." her words made Tahari think about Leondros.

"I am glad that Leondros is with his family again, but the deed I had to perform to save him broke a law held sacred by my people. My actions will be judged. When the sphinx lords pass their judgment upon me, there is a chance I will have to leave this world," Tahari's voice faded with hurt. "What will become of him?" she asked with concern.

Zation looked up at her with sympathy and seemed to understand what she was saying. "I can see that Leondros already favors you, and this knowledge would crush him at this fragile moment. However, do not be troubled by this. The truth will make itself known when it is ready to come out," she reassured Tahari in a soothing tone. Climbing to her feet again, Zation gently took Tahari's arm. "Come, the night's events will be ending by now, and the guests will be returning home. You will have peace when you return to the castle," she said as she led Tahari back down the stone-carved staircase. "Besides, I think Leondros has been looking for you ever since you left." this made Tahari smile, but she also knew the reason for this. After being captured within Avdima's walls, Leondros had no memory of the events that followed afterward.

Chapter 83

Gathering of Friends

When Zation and Tahari returned to the palace, they found many people still lingering around the long corridors, enjoying good conversation. They made their way through the diminishing crowd toward the great hall that displayed a hanging garden within it. They stood on a balcony where they could overlook the hall and hanging garden from above. It was even more beautiful from above. The walls were covered with vines so green and thick that one could swear that the walls themselves were made of trees and bushes. The air was sweet with fresh flowers, and a magnificent water fountain in the center of the room bubbled with water that flowed into deep cracks that ran throughout the stone floor. Glass covered these cracks, so one might gaze upon the sparkling water as it flowed from the room.

Zation glanced at Tahari, motioning with her brown eyes toward someone in the room. Tahari followed her gaze and she saw amongst the small crowd of people Leondros standing with his father and brother. They were all handsomely fitted for this grand occasion. Leondros was dressed in a royal-blue robe with a white sash tied around his waist, King Doran in a silver robe with a black sash, and Dreyhon in a white robe with a red sash. Then Tahari saw his other sister, Gwenth, in a deep-rose gown, making her way through the crowd. She walked up to Leondros and gently took his arm. One could not miss the warm smile on her face as she said something to him. Leondros listened intently and nodded with understanding. Tahari smiled wistfully at the happiness in their faces.

"This still feels like a dream too good to be true. I have never seen my family so happy," Zation said as she watched her brother and Gwenth. "It has brought our family together. Granted, we were always close, but when we lost Leondros for that small span of time, we were suddenly reminded of how fragile life is, even for elves. Our race possesses the ability to live for eternity. It keeps us from tasting old age, even the darkness of death. Yet we have witnessed many of our kinsmen falling into the hands of death. It has been said that the life of an elf may be snuffed out only by the gravest perils of this world. We do not often see such horrible things with our race, but we have seen them." Zation's words gave Tahari insight into the elfin race. She looked over at her with uncertainty. "How can the mortals of this world endure so much pain and suffering when a loved one dies?" she asked as she looked at Tahari with confusion. She felt her heart ache for a moment as she recalled the all-too-familiar images of Leondros's death.

"The death of a loved one is not an easy burden to bear, but I believe that one should honor the memory of their loved one. Keeping the wishes of the dead that were made in life, you help their spirit find rest," Tahari replied thoughtfully. Zation looked at her with a hint of sadness.

"Did Leondros have a last wish?" she asked in a whisper. Tahari thought back over their journey. She remembered the details so clearly.

"He was not able to ask me directly, but his spirit was able to," she said.

"What was it?" Zation asked, gazing at Tahari with a sad expression. Tahari smiled and looked at her brother.

"He asked me to finish the journey that I had started. All that was left of him longed to be home. He did not wish to remain lost," Tahari said. Zation's brown eyes glistened with tears when she heard this, but as she followed Tahari's gaze and looked upon her beloved twin brother, she smiled. She put a gentle arm around Tahari and hugged her.

"You did so much more than honor his memory," Zation replied with a smile as a single tear ran down her white cheek. Tahari rested her head against Zation's for a moment, feeling slightly overwhelmed by the grandeur of what she had done. "You found him, carried him home, and then brought him back to us again. That is more than any friend has done for him in his long lifetime." as she spoke these words, Leondros looked up at them. When his soulful brown eyes met Tahari's, she smiled warmly. A soft smile came to his face in return. He then turned back to his father and bowed his head close to speak to him.

"I did only what a friend should do," Tahari replied humbly.

"Such are the words of a *true* friend," she said, reaffirming her point.

Tahari glanced behind them toward the staircase. *He comes*, she thought. As if Zation had read her mind, she turned to see Leondros emerge from the staircase. She looked at Tahari and smiled.

He comes to see his friend, she thought back in reply and left Tahari's side. She gave her brother a warm hug.

"What is it?" he asked, looking into her face with concern. Zation smiled at him warmly and then looked back at Tahari.

"Your friend..." she began to say but was overwhelmed for a moment. "She is like no one I have ever met before. When she speaks, it is like hearing the elders from the ancient times. However did you find her?" Zation asked.

"I believe it was she who found me," Leondros said.

Tahari blushed then and turned to look at the beauty of the hanging gardens. She lost herself for a moment as Leondros continued to talk with his twin. The celebration was beginning to draw to a close as people slowly filtered out of the large room. After a long moment, the lights were dimmed so that it looked as if the moon was shining within the garden.

"You linger here like a shadow in a corner of a room," Leondros said as he walked up to Tahari.

She turned to him and smiled contentedly. "After all that has happened, it is good to step out of life for a moment and count one's blessings," she said, gazing over the balcony railing at the heavenly lit garden for a moment.

"I can only imagine what you had to endure, but for me it remains a blank," he said, questions playing over his face. Tahari thought back to the details of her quest. Reading her face, he seemed to sense the extremes of her journey. Tahari wondered for a moment whether she should retell her story or not. She sensed that Leondros did not want her to carry this alone anymore, but more importantly, this was a piece of history that belonged to him.

"The memories of that journey are as haunting as what happened to you," Tahari began as she turned her gaze toward the waterfall below them. As Tahari retold the tragic events of the night Almari and she found him, Tahari could see his pained expression. "Our journey was not incident free, for we were followed by Draccen soldiers. They were tracking me, realizing that I had escaped from Avdima's prison." she saw alarm fill Leondros's brown eyes. "Do not worry. They did not make it to the borders of Adarah. Almari and I saw to that personally," Tahari said, and Leondros visibly relaxed again. "When we finally reached Shoshon and the palace, I was relieved that you were home and with your family again, but I could not help feeling guilty," she said slowly, lowering her gaze. Leondros looked at Tahari with a puzzled expression. Lifting her head again, Tahari continued, "I felt as responsible as those who betrayed you to your death. I blamed myself for leaving Avdima, for I learned that you had risked everything to get me out, and when you were captured, I feared that I had lost your trust." her voice grew raspy as she struggled to maintain her composure. Leondros watched her sympathetically.

"Tahari, let go of your guilt. Leave it where it belongs. Those who conspired against me also conspired against you. If anyone should feel the burden of guilt, let it be them," he said as he reached over and held her shoulders. "If I remember correctly, someone had promised me that they would lead me home, and when I awoke this morning in the tomb, that person was still at my side." Tahari took relief in his warm smile and grateful expression. "How could I lose trust in someone who risks everything to bring me home and then moves the heavens and the earth to bring me back to life? After all that you have done for me, a mere thank you seems so little."

Tahari lowered her head humbly as the tears welled up in her eyes. Tahari was so thankful to have her friend back and to know that his trust in her had not faltered. It seemed to have grown stronger instead.

Seeing how overwhelmed Tahari was, Leondros gently wrapped his arms around her and held her for a long moment. As Tahari laid her head against his shoulder, she could not help but thank Adalai and the sphinx lords for such a wondrous blessing.

The evening had grown old, but Leondros and Tahari had much to talk about. Their conversations led them into the hanging gardens that surrounded Paracity Palace. The night seemed perfect, with a mist hanging in the warm night air and the pleasant sounds of insects chirping and buzzing from within the gardens. They knew that with the fall of the Shandel, trouble would eventually find its way to Adarah, and it would have to be stopped. It reminded her of the second scroll that she had been given in the tomb, but before Tahari could mention it to Leondros, she heard riders on the mountain road high above the city. They were quickly approaching the large gates that protected the city. When Leondros saw the expression drain from Tahari's face, he did not have to ask her what she heard, for he heard it, too. He rushed from the hanging gardens and made for the wall that surrounded the palace grounds, and Tahari followed closely behind him. They ran up a set of stone stairs that led inside the large wall itself. Reaching the top of the stairs, they emerged from the torch-lit stairwell onto the catwalk that ran the course of the palace wall. By this time, the palace guards had noticed the riders approaching the city. Leondros and Tahari peered over the top of the wall. Looking past the moonlit streets of Shoshon, they turned their gaze toward the city gate. They watched in silence as the riders were allowed through and quickly raced toward the palace. Leondros recognized the incoming riders.

"My uncle comes; the news he brings is not good," he informed Tahari. His face was expressionless, but she sensed fear within him. Whirling around, they dashed back down the stairwell and made for the palace in time to greet the horse soldiers as they arrived.

Tonious Goldendragon's only words to them were "The evil that caused the Shandel to fall is closing in on Adarah's borders."

The next few moments were chaotic. Leondros dashed through the palace to find his father and brother while Tahari raced through the upper levels of the palace to wake Zation and Gwenth. They needed to get everyone together for an urgent meeting. The entire castle was weary with sleep, but with matters as pressing as these, there was no time for sleep. They pulled several people from the comfort of their beds to get them to the meeting chamber. Tahari ran alongside several members of the high council, who were still dressed in their nightgowns. As they filed into the large, terraced meeting chamber, Tahari saw a large crowd of people pour in from three other chamber entrances. The chamber's ceiling, flooring, pillars, and chairs were the color of ebony, with red intensifying the room's appearance in its chair cushions, runners, and carpets. The design caused one's eye to move to its center, where white marble stone made up the room's first terrace. Hurrying to join Leondros, Zation, Gwenth, and Tahari made their way down to the center of the chamber where Leondros, his father, and Tonious were already talking with the newcomers. Tonious faintly resembled Leondros in his face and stature, but he bore more of the dark features of his brother, King Doran.

Sala had told Tahari how Tonious took Leondros under his wing and taught him all he knew. They had spent many years together, traveling the wilds of Andora. As she watched Tonious's soulful face and how he carried himself, he reminded her of Leondros. It was as if Tonious had been Leondros's father, for she could see the bond between them was very strong. Tahari noticed that Tonious was wearing black armor, and as she listened to the unsettling news that he was delivering to them and the high council, Tahari was frozen to the marble floor that she stood upon and recalled one of the last lines within the first scroll:

V. A dark dragon will deliver unpleasant tidings.

Chapter 84

Coming Siege

"My news is grave, my brother, and it could have serious repercussions for Adarah and what is left of the Tribunal," Tahari heard Tonious say. Although his voice remained strong and firm, there was great concern in his eyes. His words sent chills down Tahari's spine, and as she looked around at the expressions on the other people gathered within the meeting room, she knew they were beginning to feel great concern. The chamber quieted down to hear what news he would reveal. Leondros looked over at Tahari, his expression matching her thoughts. This was a nightmare, and they could not awake from it. The prophecy was unfolding all around them, and nothing could stop it from playing out.

"What is this grave news that you bring?" King Doran asked calmly. Tahari studied Tonious's face, seeing the horror he had seen. It was but a reflection of what was to come if action was not taken immediately.

"Since the Shandel's fall, Draccen soldiers from the Serrigen have overrun its lands. They hunt all those not in allegiance with the dark lord. Prisoners are being rounded up throughout the Shandel, the Serrigen, and the Barrens and being imprisoned. Among the hundreds to have perished in the Shandel's fall are the Shandel's royal family, it is said. My spies have learned that this *is* the evil from thousands of years ago—this is Lord Jarden. Reports demonstrate that the Draccen people are loyal to the dark lord, and now new orders have been given, for their armies are amassing near Adarah's eastern border.

Apart from a few gasps of horror, the large chamber remained silent. Watching those around Tahari and Leondros, she noticed eyes widened and faces paled in fear. This news did not come as a shock to Tahari, but she was beginning to feel anxious about facing Lord Jarden's power again. It was as if her sphinx ancestors were trying to warn her of what was coming.

"He has returned for a reason..." Tahari began, her voice surprisingly steady. She walked to the center of the white marble floor and looked upon all the frightened elfish faces that looked at her strangely. She sensed that most were wondering if they should even take her seriously, for they knew not who she was. "Lord Jarden has returned to continue his mission," Tahari said loud enough for all to hear. "A mission that began in 2021. His king had sent him here for a dark and terrible reason. In coming back from imprisonment twice and turning Andora into a hostile landscape and torturing her people, he made us believe that he was little more than a tyrannical dictator. I believe that during this third appearance we will discover his *true* purpose for Andora and her people, and if we let him accomplish that," she paused momentarily to stare heavily at those around her, "then it is over for everyone. The Shandel is the beginning of the end, but we cannot let it happen. You *must* not let it happen! There is power in every soul here! Everyone here who draws breath, everyone who has a beating heart, has that power. As long as there is that, we can fight this!" she encouraged. Tahari turned to Leondros and silently pleaded for him to join her. The crowd seemed moved by her words, but most of them had never seen these horrifying spectacles with their own eyes. Of the elves that were gathered with them, the Goldendragon family and a few others were the only ones in this elfin council who had actually seen these things.

"Most of you know why we celebrate Rafar the Elder's honor every one hundred years," Leondros said, standing beside Tahari.

Those who were gathered around them began to nod their heads. "It is because Rafar faced Lord Jarden himself and kept him from completing his true mission here. Rafar was a kind and simple man who would have likely spent his remaining years upon the dragon isle of Nor, but instead he died protecting us. Would you continue to celebrate that one day in his honor while letting what he fought and died for triumph over us?" Leondros's words stirred the council uncomfortably. Glances fell to the floor in shame. He was right; most had never really taken Rafar's struggles to heart.

"If Rafar were here right now, how would you honor him?" Leondros asked as he pointed toward the crowd. The expressions upon the crowd before Tahari and Leondros were filled with great thoughtfulness; some were glowing with inspiration. "If the fall of the Shandel is only the beginning of what he has truly planned for us, then we must take action!" Leondros spoke from experience, his brown eyes charged with determination. He was desperate to keep his home from the Shandel's fate. King Doran listened intently to his son. However, Tahari sensed that the king was not about to put Leondros, or those who would not have the chance to fight back, in peril.

"Leondros and his friend speak truth," King Doran said. "They know what this evil is capable of—and Adarah as well as what remains of the Tribunal, stands within the shadow of this evil. We must prepare ourselves or fall like the Shandel. Tonious, take your army to the northeast passage to guard against anyone who might try to sneak into the kingdom. Leondros, take my army and patrol the perimeter surrounding Shoshon. In the meantime, I am putting Shoshon under a flag of emergency. All citizens living within the city limits are required to take what provisions they will need and leave for the safety of the city of Sion. Guides will accompany them. I will also dispatch riders to warn the rest of Adarah and spread the warning on to Eden-glee. I refuse to let this evil bring further harm to this land, its people, or my family," King Doran finished as he looked at his brother Tonious with an expression of certainty. He then looked over at Leondros and Tahari. She could not miss the look in Leondros's eyes as his father spoke. King Doran was a changed man, and he was not afraid to show it.

The meeting adjourned, and everyone scattered to prepare for the long night ahead. In the madness of the preparation as people were running about, a scout rushed into the castle to inform them that Draccen troops had penetrated Adarah's eastern border and were heading toward Shoshon. An attack on the city was imminent. Evil was finding its way even into this tranquil kingdom.

Passing by one of the meeting room's large windows, Tahari heard horns blaring out over the city. The evacuation was beginning already. This added to the commotion within the palace as people hurried back and forth. When the large meeting room was empty at last, Tahari stepped into the hall and prepared to find Almari. A strong hand took hold of her arm and gently pulled her back into the meeting chamber.

"Tahari of the Shandon," King Doran said. She looked up at him in surprise. "Forgive me for startling you, but I felt that I had to speak to you," he offered with sincerity. "I am honored that you are with us now and by what you have done for my family and me. I humbly ask, please watch over my son." his words were now a whisper, but the love and concern that were in his face stayed with her. Tahari put her hand over his and nodded.

"Your son has been in good hands since before I was born. It is a tradition I am honored to see through, to whatever end," Tahari promised. The King of Adarah nodded slowly in approval and relief.

"I thank you, Lady Tahari." the king bowed his head to her and quickly slipped into the crowd hurrying down the busy hall. As she watched him disappear, Tahari was touched to know that this time the king was indeed taking measures to protect his son. Her attention slowly turned to all the preparations being made to save Adarah. Everything seemed as if they would win this onslaught. Still, Tahari sensed something bitter in the air.

"Tahari!" a familiar voice cut through her thoughts. Looking ahead of her, Tahari saw Almari running toward her, her golden face wearing an alarmed expression. "What is goin' on around here?" she asked with a shaky voice as she fought to keep from being trampled by the crowd. Almari's blonde-and-brown hair was tied in a ponytail, and she still wore the blue-and-green robe she had been given upon their arrival.

"Draccen soldiers have been seen close to Shoshon and the elfin soldiers have dispatched several people to prepare for an attack," Tahari explained calmly. Almari's face went white.

"Would that explain why I saw Leondros jumpin' onto a horse, preparing to ride out?" she asked with great alarm and confusion. Tahari realized suddenly that she had not seen her friend all day. Judging by the sleepy look still in her eyes, Tahari sensed that she had slept through the entire day and had just awoken several moments ago.

"Do not be alarmed. There was a great miracle this morning. It is a tale for another time, but, yes, Leondros is alive and in good health," she replied with a reassuring smile. Relief filled Almari's face.

"That is wondrous, but I feel there is still a need to be concerned for Leondros. If he rides to protect Shoshon from the dark forces, will he remember the faces of the men who betrayed him in Akendron?" she asked. "Several of those men were elves. If they see Leondros alive, will they not try another attempt on his life?" Looking out the window, Tahari was filled with sudden dread as she watched Leondros ride out of the city with his father's army.

"Come. We have to warn them. I did not come this far for my friend just to watch him lose his life again," Tahari exclaimed frantically as she started running down the candlelit corridor toward her chamber. She needed a change of clothes and a few essential weapons before charging into battle. As Tahari heard Almari follow close behind her, she heard her comment.

"Count me in. I still have some frustrations to work out." there was sincerity in her voice; Almari was a woman of her word.

Almari dressed herself in a midnight-blue battle tunic with green trim, and Tahari put on a black battle tunic. They found suitable battle tunics made of leather, as well as boots and weapons for the journey ahead. Running outside into the still night air, they looked around and found that they were too late. All the armies had left for their assigned missions. Almari looked over at Tahari with worry. Determined to keep Leondros from falling into another murderous plot, Tahari glanced over at the stables and saw several horses inside. Almari and Tahari exchanged looks and ran for the stables. Almari found her black horse, and Tahari mounted a gray one. They did not have time for saddles, so they rode bareback. Before they could get out of the palace courtyard, someone yell Tahari's name.

"TAHARI!"

Tahari pulled hard on the reins and whirled her head around to see who called her. Zation was rushing down from the palace's main entrance to catch them. Something strange in her expression made Tahari turn her horse around. When Tahari got closer to her, she saw a long sword in her hands. Looking into her face, Tahari saw a hint of sadness and great fear in her brown eyes.

"Zation?" Tahari asked with great concern, jumping down from her horse.

"I need for you do to something very important for me," she said slowly as if she were choosing her words carefully. Tahari nodded her head in reassurance. "When you meet up with Leondros, give him this. Tell him that our spirits are with him always and that we will be watching over him," she explained calmly as she handed Tahari the sword. It was wrapped in black leather with gold trim. It seemed very old and must have great personal meaning for this family. Tahari thought that it might be a symbol of King Doran's love for Leondros, but something told her that there was deeper meaning in this sword. A chill of fear ran down Tahari's spine as she looked at Zation's defeated expression.

"Zation, if something should go wrong and you find your lives in danger, do *whatever* you can to survive. Flee if you must," Tahari said with an urgent tone as she took hold of her shoulders. Tahari hoped to inspire her into keeping herself and her family alive. There was no fear or worry in her face, just a strange sort of peace. "Please, do it for your brother's sake," she pleaded earnestly.

"I will," Zation replied softly as she bowed her head. Her answer might have convinced the royal bishop, but Tahari had a suspicious feeling that things were not as they seemed. She took that moment and gave Zation a warm hug.

"Do not worry about Leondros. I will watch over him," Tahari whispered in her ear.

"I know you will. As his friend, guardian, and angel, you could never let him down," she said as she pulled her head away and gave Tahari a warm and loving expression. Tahari was somewhat caught off-guard by this. She could only smile as she strapped the sword to her back and climbed back onto her horse. When Tahari and Almari started out again, Tahari glanced back over her shoulder at Zation. She lingered on the step where Tahari had left her. She watched them with a saddened but peaceful gaze. Then she put her hands together in prayer, her lips moving soundlessly. This was the last image Tahari had of Zation before ahe and Almari rode out of the palace gates.

Chapter 85

Friends Found

The moon shone brightly overhead as Leondros and his men meticulously searched the foothills and valleys that made up the perimeter of Shoshon. They watched for signs of approaching danger, but the night remained strangely quiet. In spite of this eerie calm, Leondros sent out scouts into the surrounding mountain ranges to search out any trouble that might be hiding nearby. When Leondros and his men reached the forested foothills just north of Shoshon, they remained silent, waiting to hear from their scouts. Each scout returned with the same report: no Draccen forces in sight. Yet deep down, Leondros felt that danger was lingering within the shadows.

A horse galloped in the distance, growing closer. Soon it was discerned that this was the last remaining scout, coming to report his findings from the range to the northeast.

The scout had a wary expression on his face, and he repeatedly glanced over his shoulder toward the dark mountains to the northeast from which he rode.

"What have you seen?" Leondros asked him.

"Smoke rises out of the northeast pass," the scout replied, motioning toward the northern range. "I heard the sound of distant thunder coming through the pass. Something is coming, my lord." Leondros's gaze fell upon the distant northern mountain range where the pass was located. "Your uncle's army was not supposed to reach the northeastern pass so quickly," the scout added with a thoughtful gaze back toward the dark eastern horizon.

"The northeast pass is secret to all outsiders. Even amongst our own people, there are only a few who know of it. Only those in my father's army..." Leondros mused to himself. As he thought of this, a few, dark memories from before his death began to surface. The images were blurry, but they gave him warning of some of the men within his father's own army. "We make for the northeastern pass!" he called out to his men.

Upon Leondros's command, the royal army followed after their prince, for they, too, sensed the trouble that was coming. The army could now see smoke rising from the pass that offered the only way between these two mountains. Making their way up the foothills and through the tree line, Leondros and the royal army neared the northeastern mountain pass. As they approached the pass, the soldiers managed to keep their horses quiet. In doing so, they could hear the strange thunder emanating from the pass. Emerging from the thick tree line, Leondros and the army stopped upon the wide rocky ridge that overlooked the entrance to the pass. They continued to listen, but the strange thunder ceased, leaving only an eerie silence. Leondros gazed suspiciously down into the dark pass, which looked like a huge trench between the two mountains that towered high above it. He felt uneasy about leading his men down into the dark pass. Before he could issue a command, one of his men called out and pointed toward the darkened pass below them.

"Look! Someone is coming!" Everyone looked where the elfin soldier pointed. Peering closely into the pass, they saw the shadow of someone running toward them. An elfish soldier was running from something or someone. Leondros kicked his horse and raced into the pass. Reaching the soldier, he recognized Theron, the elfin soldier who was thought to have been captured when they were nearly ambushed by Draccen soldiers near Endenbury.

"Theron! You are alive!" Leondros greeted him excitedly as he jumped down from his white horse and ran to meet the weary soldier. Theron looked ready to drop, but his dirty face broke into a welcomed expression when he saw Leondros standing before him. The worn soldier's armor was gone, only his torn brown tunic remained.

"What happened to you?" Leondros asked with great concern.

Theron took a moment to catch his breath and shift the cloth bundle that was strapped to his back. "Aceon and I were taken to a Draccen prison camp. Aceon did not make it," he said as he fought to get his air to speak clearly. "Sir, they are planning to invade Adarah as they did the Shandel." he looked his prince square in the eye. "They are coming…" He was interrupted by a voice coming from behind him.

"Theron! Wait!" The voice sounded to be in great distress. Leondros and Theron turned back to the shadow of the pass to see another soldier emerging from the rocky pass. As he got closer, Theron recognized him and breathed a sigh of relief.

"Judeas! We are in good company! Leondros has found us!" he called back to his friend. Leondros was relieved to see his men from the Secret Alliance still alive. When Judeas finally caught up to Theron and looked up at Leondros, he seemed momentarily surprised but also relieved to see that their general and prince had found them.

"Come quickly—if there is to be an attack upon Adarah, this is not the place to have a reunion," Leondros said in a hushed voice, gazing into the dark that loomed behind them. As he listened closely to his surroundings, he realized just how quiet everything had become. The uneasy feeling was now screaming at him. "Danger is close. We must hurry," Leondros warned in a hushed tone as he quickly climbed back on his horse.

They raced back for the rocky ridge as Leondros stayed behind them to ensure they made it out of the gorge. However as they ran, Leondros noticed something peculiar about their actions. They seemed too fearful as if desperate to get out of the rocky gorge.

When the threesome had climbed out of the shadowy mountain pass, Leondros watched in bewilderment as Theron and Judeas continued running toward the trees. They had almost reached them when an arrow whizzed overhead, driving itself into the ground just before Theron and Judeas, stopping them in their tracks. The soldiers of the royal army and Leondros immediately drew their own bows and arrows and aimed at the cliffs above them, from where arrow had been fired.

"My lord, what have we done that warrants being fired upon?" Judeas demanded as he and Theron angrily looked back at Leondros. There was fear in his voice.

"The order was not mine, but I will find out who authorized it and why!" Leondros proclaimed as he continued to look upon the darkened cliffs and studied their rocky features. It was then that he made out two riders standing in the shadows upon the rocky cliff face.

"Who are you? What business do you have here?" Leondros shouted up into the cliffs. There was no answer at first. As everyone waited for a response, an unsettled feeling spread over the whole army. Finally, a voice called out from the bottom of the cliffs. It was Tahari!

Chapter 86

Traitors Revealed

"Leondros, do not fire!" Tahari called out to Leondros as she and Almari carefully made their way out of the shadows of the looming mountain and down the rocky embankment. Riding out into the moonlight, they saw everyone looking at each other with disbelief. Leondros looked at them with uncertainty, for he saw Almari for the first time, and she had been the one who made the nearly fatal shot with her bow.

"Tahari, what is going on?" he asked as they approached the army. Tahari and Almari watched cautiously as one by one, the vigilant soldiers lowered their bows only after Leondros had lowered his.

"Leondros, beware of these men. I fear they were responsible for betraying you," Tahari said as she looked down at the two elfin warriors who remained still with Almari's arrow embedded only a few inches in front of them. They looked at Tahari with defiance and anger.

"I have done no such thing!" Theron snapped at Tahari angrily. "I have journeyed far to bring word of the dark things to come and risked my own life in doing so!" He glared at her, hoping to prove his innocence to his prince.

"But you surely have!" Almari yelled out with a steamy glare at Judeas. While perched on her horse, she quickly took out her bow and aimed for Judeas' throat. The elfin warrior continued to glare at them. One wrong move and he would be breathing out of his throat.

"Hold!" Leondros shouted as he jumped from his horse and ran in front of Judeas. "Please offer some sort of explanation for this!" he asked defensively as he looked at Almari strangely. Almari looked at Tahari and Tahari nodded. Lowering her bow and sliding off her horse, Almari stood before Leondros and his men and spoke without fear or hesitation.

"My lord, my name is Almari of Trensa. I am a good friend of Tahari," she began with a humble bow. "I would not otherwise ask you to remember the painful events that led to your death, but please hear me out. On the night of your betrayal, Judeas conspired with Alon-Settie," Almari said as she looked at Leondros with a soulful expression.

"Hang on!" Judeas shouted with a bewildered and astonished look as he pushed past Theron toward Almari. "I would never deny my lord, nor would I take part in any attempt to harm him!.

"But you did!" Almari shot back angrily at the elfin traitor. "It was you who wanted to know when you could finish off Leondros, but it was Alon-Settie who said, 'Patience, Judeas; we wait until he wakes again.'" As Almari recounted that dark night, Leondros studied her face. Her features were pained and fixed as if she were recalling a heart-wrenching memory. Leondros slowly stepped away from Judeas and looked at him with disbelief. "Your reply was, 'Truly, he can't be alive? Are you sure he is not dead already?'" As she spoke these words, Judeas's face drained of color and became riddled with guilt. He lowered his head in shame. While Almari painted the hauntingly vivid picture of what had truly happened, Leondros became lost in thought.

"She speaks truth..." Leondros managed to say in a tone of hurt and anger. He lowered his head for moment to think. Tahari could see that Leondros believed her and that she needed to say nothing more.

"My lord, please believe me when I say I would not wish any such harm on you or any of your family," Theron pleaded in a whisper as he searched for his prince's forgiveness. Tahari searched his face in the moonlight to see if he was really telling the truth. Then she caught a whiff of something most foul and pungent on the breeze as it blew through the group of elves Tahari was standing near. She slowly climbed off her horse and began to follow the odor. One by one, the elves watched Tahari with strange expressions. After scouting around for a moment, she discerned that the horrible odor was coming from Theron—or more accurately, his brown leather bag.

"What is in your bag?" Tahari asked inquisitively as she motioned her chin in the direction of his bag.

Theron turned to Tahari so that she could not see it. "Why do you ask? What great importance will a bag have in...?" Theron started to say when Leondros quickly drew his bow and fitted it with an arrow.

"Give her your bag, or I will give you something new to worry about!" Leondros ordered, aiming his arrow at Theron's face. The elfin prince had been betrayed enough for one lifetime; he was not going to have a repeat of it.

Theron tightened his jaw and looked at Tahari. He then slowly handed her his leather bag.

Tahari took it from him and stepped away from the group to open it. The moment she did, Tahari froze in horror. Her world seemed to stop. After a wave of nausea passed by her, Tahari somehow found the strength to close the bag again.

"Tahari? What did you see?" Leondros asked her with concern, noticing how pale her face had become. She looked up at him and then at Theron. Everyone awaited her response. Carefully setting the bag on the ground, Tahari took a moment to focus her thoughts. Then, without warning, she marched over to Theron and drove her fist into his lower jaw. The stunned elf was driven backward. He landed on the ground with a thud.

"Is this what happened to his army?" Tahari demanded as she grabbed Theron's ragged collar and nearly pulled him back to his feet. Theron did not answer.

Leondros sensed something disturbing in Tahari's words and actions. He quickly walked over to the leather bag. Sinking to the ground, Leondros gently pulled open the edges of the bag and gazed into it. Staring back at him was his Uncle Tonious's head.

After a long moment of silence, with all color drained from his face, Leondros lifted his gaze toward Theron and glared at him coldly. The expression that he saw in Theron's face was equal to that of Alon-Settie's and Judeas's when they betrayed him, only now it was his family that was suffering and dying. Leondros jumped to his feet and charged toward Theron. Seeing the rage that flared in the elfin prince's face, Theron tore himself from Tahari's grasp and ran toward the pass that he had just climbed out of only moments before. Theron tumbled into the rocky pass but was quick to get to his feet and run into the darkness. Out of the corner of Tahari's eye, she saw the rage that filled Leondros's face—he wanted to chase after the traitor and have his revenge. Reacting quickly, she reached out and grabbed onto Leondros to keep him from following suit.

"Leondros! NO!" Tahari gasped as she fought to keep a grip on him.

He struggled to break her grip. "He is a murderer! He must not be allowed to get away!" he shouted angrily.

"Leondros, his fate has already been decided. Do not make it yours," she cautioned as she kept him from moving any further.

As Theron faded into the darkness, Leondros continued to try and push past Tahari, until something caught all of them off-guard. They watched a hail of arrows come from deep within the pass. It came from both mountainsides and rained down into the darkness. Everyone watched in silence as Theron was slain by a multitude of arrows. Leondros froze in horror as Tahari held on to him. Together they watched the fourth line of instruction from the prophecy come to pass.

*DO NOT bring down his murderers.

"What cause would they have to kill Tonious or his army?" Leondros managed to ask in a raspy whisper. Grief filled his face as his uncle's death overwhelmed him.

"Perhaps in their continued quest for power, they will take out all threats to their plan," Tahari reasoned sadly as she loosened her grip upon him. She joined Leondros's pained gaze at the brown leather pack lying on the rocky ground at their feet. Anger filled Tahari's heart, for she hated seeing such suffering.

"You both were just the beginning…" Judeas spoke up as he crossed his arms and watched them with discontent. "However, we did not plan on Leondros coming back. It is no matter; Lord Jarden will deal with him in his own time." Leondros and Tahari exchanged glances of alarm and anger. Judeas seemed as though he was going to say something more when a strange whisp cut through the air. Judeas's expression filled with shock, his black eyes went wide with horror, and a small trail of blood oozed from his mouth. Acting quickly, Tahari grabbed hold of Leondros and dashed behind the rocky walls guarding the entrance to the pass.

"Everyone! Take cover!" Leondros gasped out the sudden order.

In the commotion of Leondros's men seeking cover near the south mountain, Tahari could only stare at the elf who had betrayed Leondros. Leondros joined her gaze. Looking upon Judeas, they could see that he had fallen to the same fate as Theron. An arrow from within the pass had been sent to keep him quiet.

"You were right. His fate was also already decided," Leondros reasoned softly as he looked back at Tahari. She could see hurt in his eyes, but he was thankful that she was there. Tahari spoke no words but simply took his hand in hers and held it. Tahari nodded with a warm and understanding smile. Their tender moment of understanding was short, for they were now staring into the face of a monstrous battle. Quickly taking cover beside them, Almari looked on with disbelief and confusion.

"What is going on?" she asked with great alarm. Cautiously, Tahari poked her head around the rock wall, and peered into the night, and discovered what lay hidden in the shadows. The sound of thunder rumbled out from the depths of the pass. Emerging from its depth was a dark ocean of Draccen soldiers, armored and ready for battle. Tahari swallowed hard.

"We have Draccen soldiers. A *lot* of Draccen soldiers," Tahari replied as she continued to eye the coming storm. Leondros tightened his jaw.

"A Draccen war party," Leondros said to himself thoughtfully, cautiously rising to his feet and discreetly making his way over to his men, who had also taken cover near the edge of the south mountain. "Draccen soldiers are coming! Hide yourselves within the surrounding tree line. Use your surroundings so they cannot see you. Fire only when you have a clear shot," he instructed as he kept a wary eye out to the approaching Draccen army. Leondros's men were quick to take this instruction and vanish within the surrounding trees and brush just below the northeast pass.

"Tahari," Almari whispered as she took hold of her friend's arm with worry. "Tell me we are not about to go into war?" she asked with a horrified expression, the color draining from her tanned face. Tahari looked to see the Draccen soldiers beginning to near the rocky ridge. Wasting no time, she grabbed Almari's arm and led her into the cover of some nearby trees along the thick tree line.

"War, no," Tahari said hesitantly as she thought of a way to give her some encouragement and prepare for the onslaught to come. "A mere battle," Tahari said with an optimistic tone.

Almari looked at her and rolled her dark blue eyes in disbelief and anxiety. Worry filled her features as the thunder from the oncoming Draccen army reached the trees.

Tahari turned to Almari and put her hands on her shoulders. "All you have to do is think of the taskmasters from the Tomblock," Tahari explained as she motioned toward the Draccen soldiers that were starting to emerge from the pass. They were now very close by and the battle was about to begin. "*They* are the taskmasters and *you* are to show them retribution," she whispered.

Cocking her head slightly, a complete change of expression washed over Almari. Gone was her fear, and in its place was the built-up rage from her time on the plantation.

"Well, since you put it that way," she replied with sly grin, straightening her dark-blue tunic. Then she carefully fitted an arrow into her bow. "Save a few for me.

Tahari smiled and turned her gaze back to the Draccen soldiers who were almost upon them. "Those poor souls have no idea ..." she mused to herself as she readied her bow and listened while the thunder of the Draccen army drew closer. Tahari pushed her own fears down by remembering the atrocity that had been done to Tonious and which this army now looked to do to Leondros and the rest of his family.

Chapter 87

Last of the Goldendragons

The Draccen soldiers closed in on the thick tree line that acted as a natural barrier between the mountain range and its foothills. Those Tahari could see through the trees were armored and well-armed for their attack upon the elfin empire. They crept into the surrounding territory, sniffing the air cautiously. The wind, however, was not on their side, for it blew out of the northeastern pass and rushed past them into the trees so that the Draccen soldiers were unable to detect the elfin army's whereabouts. Yet they prepared to fire into the tree line as if some supernatural source gave them the exact whereabouts of their enemy. Many of Leondros's men, and maybe they, too, would be seriously wounded or worse. Tahari aimed for the leader, who was eyeing the tree line closely. He turned to yell something to his men, but his words came out in an agonizing moan as her arrow drove into his neck. The Draccen army saw their leader fall and charged them.

Leondros, Tahari, Almari, and the elfin army rained arrows down upon the massive horde of Draccen soldiers who closed in on the tree line, while many more fought their way up the steep ridge that led out of the mountain pass. Many Draccen soldiers fell, but their places were quickly filled, and the army charged into the tree line.

Tahari's quiver was spent, and the Draccen soldiers were amongst them now. She drew her sword and began fighting in earnest. As she fought off Draccen soldier after Draccen soldier, Tahari noticed that the entire forest had erupted into a vicious battle. Battling fiercely with one Draccen soldier, Tahari was forced out of the tree line and near the ridge that overlooked the northeastern pass. Another large Draccen soldier crashed into her from behind, his immense weight knocking the breath from her lungs. The momentum knocked her off balance and sent her rolling over the edge of the ridge and into the northeast pass below.

When everything came to a stop, Tahari tried to catch her breath only to find that she could not. The Draccen soldier that had run into her had also taken the trip down the rugged rocky slope and landed on top of her, though he had not noticed that she had broken his fall. Shoving him off, Tahari gasped her first breaths of air.

When he realized that she was still alive, he struggled to get up and get a hold of his sword. As he swung his sword to kill her, Tahari drove her own through his middle. Bewilderment filled his dark-green eyes as the life drained from his face. Tahari angrily pushed him away and got to her feet, quickly adjusting her bearings. Then Tahari felt a cold chill run the course of her back; she quickly turned to see a Draccen soldier aiming his bow at her from up on the ridge. As he drew his bow taut, she heard a voice from nearby cry out in alarm, "NO!"

The Draccen soldier smiled and fired his arrow. A moment later the arrow found her. Tahari looked at it, and then lifted her gaze back to the Draccen soldier and smiled. The arrow was safe in her hand.

"Nice shot, but try mine," Tahari said in a low voice as she took up her bow, which had made the trip down the ridge with her, and shot the arrow back to its owner. Unfortunately, the soldier was less focused than she had been, and she watched him crumple to the ground. Tahari took a deep breath and wondered who had cried out before the shot had been fired. Scanning the area, she saw Leondros watching her from the ridge. There was warm relief in his face and a sly grin on his lips. Tahari returned a smile and a wink before she charged back up the mountain pass and into the fray above.

The Draccen soldiers who surrounded her fought as though some force gave them power against them and drove these soldiers to wipe out all who opposed them, but Tahari refused to give up. Beyond fearlessness and instincts, she had a greater purpose driving her. Her friends were here, and she could not let them down. Tahari fought not only for herself but for their sake as well.

After taking down the last Draccen soldier in her midst, Tahari finally looked around and found herself alone. The ridge was covered with the bodies of Draccen soldiers and some of their own. Tahari took a moment to breathe a tired sigh, for it had been a long night and a fierce battle. Light began to fill the eastern sky. Listening to the sounds from deep within the tree line, she realized that there was still some fighting going on. Despite her weariness, Tahari summoned enough energy to make her way into the surrounding forest. As she hurried over the fallen bodies that were between her and the dense tree line, Tahari noticed that thick, gray clouds were passing over the mountains and drifting toward Shoshon. Within the damp cool air, she sensed that things were worse than she realized. Walking through the forest, Tahari began to understand why. Like the Draccen army, the royal elfin army had also been reduced to nothing. Staring at the horror before her, Tahari wondered how this could have happened. She searched for any survivors, but try as she might, she could find none. A still calm settled over the forest as if to give peace to those who had died here. Her heart sank into her stomach. Where were her friends? The sound of soft footsteps caught her attention. Tahari lifted her gaze from the ground and looked around.

"Tahari!" By some miracle, she heard Leondros's voice calling to her. Turning her gaze toward his voice, Tahari saw him climbing out of a deep trench. He seemed quite beaten, covered in dirt and blood. She was concerned for him but found relief in the fact that he was alive. As she made her way over to him, Tahari could see the worn look in his face from the long night, but there was relief, too. "Are you all right?" he asked in a raspy whisper when he finally reached her. She managed to smile and nod, but her gaze wandered to the many that had fallen in battle.

"Tell me that we are not the only ones left?" Tahari asked fearfully. He looked at her quizzically, but as he followed her gaze, grief filled his face. The faces of the dead were fixed in horror. Leondros closed his eyes, seeming to sense the moment they were struck and the immense pain that claimed their lives. Out of the stillness came the sound of movement nearby. Hope inspired them to search for the source of the noise and brought them to another survivor. Tahari breathed another sigh of relief at the sight of Almari rising from a small creek bed. She had crawled out from under several dead Draccen soldiers that had fallen on top of her.

"Almari!" Tahari called out in a relieved tone as she raced up to her. She heard Almari grumbling to herself as she got to her feet. She looked up and saw Tahari running up to her with Leondros not far behind.

"I am all right," she said gruffly as she brushed off the dirt and mud that now covered her blue and green tunic. "Bumblin' idiots…" she was starting to say something more when she looked up at the terrific scene that now surrounded her. Tahari watched all expression fade from her dirty tanned face as she gazed over the blood-soaked landscape. "What happened?" she asked in a whisper. "I always heard that it would take a force greater than Draccen soldiers to overtake an elfin army," Almari said as she looked at Leondros, hoping to find the reason for such an atrocity.

"Evil resided within these Draccen soldiers. It made them stronger," Leondros replied softly. He sank to the ground and examined the body of a fallen Draccen soldier. He seemed dazed by what had happened here. Tahari lifted her gaze from the massacre eastward toward Shoshon. Peering closely at the distant city, it no longer radiated with glimmering white light. A looming shadow of gray had now descended upon the majestic city. She felt a great unsettling within her heart and a dire need to return back to the city.

"Leondros…" Tahari said slowly as she began to think back to Zation and her last words to her. "We must return to Shoshon. I feel that something awful has happened," Tahari said thoughtfully.

He looked at her and then followed her gaze toward Shoshon. His expression of concern matched her own. Rising to his feet, Leondros joined Tahari and Almari as they searched for their horses. Upon finding them, they rode hard out of the forest. Once reaching the outskirts of Shoshon, Leondros forced his horse to stop unexpectedly. Tahari and Almari quickly followed suit. Leondros seemed to be listening to something coming from the valley. Tahari listened too and picked up the faint sound of a bell tolling. It was coming from Shoshon. Looking at Leondros, Tahari saw great alarm in his face.

"A bell is soundin' from Shoshon," Almari said in an unsuspecting manner. Leondros seemed to have no reaction as he stared down into the gloomy valley.

"It is the bell in the Tower of Baron," he said as if he could not believe his own ears. It was not a pleasant sound for him. "That bell has not rung since my death, but before that not for a millennium. It is said that when the Bell of Baron tolls, an elf has perished and their soul has the people's blessing to be at peace. If it is not rung, the soul is doomed to walk the earth forever." Leondros listened again to the tolling. The longer he listened, the graver the expression upon his face. "Tahari, you are more right than you know. The Bell of Baron is supposed to ring only once per soul; it has yet to cease ringing." his words hung in the damp cool air. Tahari's stomach turned sour, for she sensed what awaited them. Spurring their horses down the road that led to Shoshon, they approached the city and could see signs that they were too late. When they reached the great white gates of Shoshon, they found them torn down and the guards who protected them slain. They found worse as they moved deeper into the city.

Many of the homes and buildings within the city had been set on fire or otherwise destroyed. Elfin people lay dead or dying in the streets by the score; those few who had survived were trying to comfort each other. As Tahari scanned the smoking ruins of the city, she began to wonder who or what agent of Lord Jarden had actually succeeded in taking the city. There were no remains of enemy soldiers to be seen anywhere. Was it really the Draccen who attacked this beautiful city?

"Did they not heed your father's warning?" Tahari asked Leondros as they made their way through the debris that lined the ash-covered streets.

"It seems that not everyone made for Rahara," Leondros replied sadly. He stopped his white stallion and dismounted, going over to three men and a woman who had survived the attack. He spoke to them in Elfish, encouraging them to leave for the safety of Rahara. They refused. Leondros nodded in understanding. He advised them to gather all survivors and move into the tunnels below the city. They would be safe there should any more Draccen patrols come back to the city. They nodded and turned to leave. The woman, dressed in a smoke-covered blue robe and veil, paused and walked up to Leondros and hugged him. She thanked him for returning to the city and prayed that Adalai would be with him on the journey that awaited him.

As Tahari watched on from her horse, she noticed that tears streaked the people's smoke-covered faces, and a forlorn expression shone from their eyes. Everything was in chaos now. Pain, agony, and suffering had seemed to wipe away all memories of faith, hope, and love, but the compassion in the kind woman's dirty face as she gently let go of Leondros told her that these things still remained.

Making their way to Paracity Palace, Tahari's heart sank once again. The once-beautiful castle was now black with smoke. Its welcoming white light had been snuffed out. It hurt to see such destruction, but it hurt even more to see the effect that it had on Leondros. Tahari could not even recognize his face for alarm and fear filled his features. Their approach had been a slow trot, but now they dismounted and raced toward the front door of the blackened ruins.

When they entered the palace, they came to a staggering halt. Debris and darkness filled the once-candlelit halls. Many of the treasures that had rested within these great hallways had been destroyed or stolen. Colorful hand-embroidered tapestries that had hung for centuries were torn and shredded across the floor. Age-old oil paintings had been stolen or burnt.

Leondros looked around wildly for any signs of life. When he moved again, Tahari and Almari closely followed him. It was hard to tell if there was anyone within the castle, for everything was as silent as a grave. As they turned a corner, Tahari and Almari nearly crashed into Leondros as he came to sa udden stop. There, lying in front of him, were several of the palace servants. They had been horribly slain and left in a bloody heap on the hallway floor. Leondros sadly sank to the ground before these servants, mourning their deaths. He looked down the long, dim corridor and noticed the door to the large family chamber slightly ajar. He stared at it for a moment before he rose to his feet and bolted down the corridor.

As they rushed after Leondros, Tahari began to get a chilling feeling. Seeing the damage on the large wooden door they were rushing for did not inspire hope.

When they reached the door at last, they saw an orange light emanating from within the chamber. Leondros walked up to the door and hesitated before he reached out to slowly push it fully open. The orange light from a single burning torch flooded over him as he walked through the doorway. Tahari and Almari followed him, but once inside the room, the threesome froze to the marble floor beneath their feet.

The chamber was in complete chaos. Broken furniture, torn tapestries, and shattered window glass lay everywhere. More than that, however, was Leondros's family, scattered about the room. They had all been slain. The air was thick with the scent of death and blood. They fell into a trance-like state as they stared at the gruesome scene. Tahari glanced over at Leondros to see him lost and alone. King Doran, Queen Inya, his brother Dreyhon, his sister Gwenth, and even his beloved twin sister Zation were all gone.

Leondros staggered farther into the room. Defeat filled his steps as he made his way toward Zation. Reaching her, he sank to the floor beside her. Tahari wished that somehow life would return to her face and she would awaken. After several long moments of silence, Zation remained still. The realization hit Leondros hard, the muscles in his jaw tightening. He closed his eyes and lowered his head. He began to whisper a prayer in Elfish. It was barely audible, but it was riddled with sadness.

Tears stung Tahari's eyes as she heard the grief within his voice. Swallowing hard, Tahari found the courage to walk over to him. She stopped beside him and slowly sank to the ground. She studied Zation's pale and lifeless form. Of all her family, Zation was the only one who had barely a mark to reveal her fatal wound. Looking up at Leondros's face,

Tahari sensed that he would not find any rest until he knew for certain what had taken place here. She tried to swallow the growing lump in her throat and concentrated on focusing her mind. Placing her hand over Zation's forehead, Tahari closed her eyes. Energy passed through her fingers and she saw into the last moments of Zation's world.

The palace had erupted into chaos and confusion. People were running and screaming, and no one seemed to know what was going on. Off in the distance, explosions could be heard bombarding Shoshon. Sensing great danger, Tahari watched Zation arm herself with a sword and hurry from her bedroom chamber toward the main family chamber, where most of the confusion was coming from. When she reached the large chamber and peered through a side door, a desperate scene awaited her.

Prince Dreyhon was wounded and dying in his mother's arms. King Doran was fighting the Draccen soldiers that were hell-bent on getting past him. Gwenth had been seriously wounded, but she was not going to die easily. "People will know what happened here!" the older princess yelled angrily at the Draccen soldiers who continued to storm the large chamber. Zation watched in amazement as her sister fought off several Draccen soldiers. For a moment, it seemed that she might actually drive back the oncoming Draccen soldiers. Then things went bad for all of them.

A Draccen soldier had climbed up the side of the building and found a window to the large chamber. He fired an arrow that caught Inya in the back. She cried out in agony. The soldier fired another arrow and the queen let out a gasp before collapsing over Prince Dreyhon. As Gwenth turned to aid her mother and brother, she was caught in the back by a dagger. She collapsed to the floor and remained silent. Enraged by this transgression, King Doran dove into the fray of incoming Draccen soldiers. He fought valiantly and strove to keep his family safe, even unto his last dying breath.

Seeing her family being brutally murdered before her, Zation as brave as Gwenth as strong as her father, and as loving as her mother, took up her sword and engaged the nearest soldier. She continued to fight and did not feel the spear that pierced her body. As death slowly swept over her, she did not fear it but was saddened that Leondros would be left without a family. Her hope for him did not die, however. She knew that Tahari was with him and that he would be all right. Her beautiful brown eyes silently closed.

Awaking from the heart-wrenching vision, Tahari lifted her head and gazed over the large chamber in front of her. Leondros glanced at Tahari and sensed that she saw something. He did not have to speak, for she knew the question burning within his mind.

"It was an army of Draccen soldiers that took Shoshon, but your family fought most bravely. Probably bravest of all was Zation. She was the last, but she fought with great passion, equal to that of any warrior in battle. Her only regret was that you would be without a family," Tahari spoke softly as she struggled to keep herself composed. The tears that had been welling in her eyes were now streaming down her face. Leondros had listened to her silently as Tahari told of his family's last moments.

"Leondros, your sister kept her word," Almari gently spoke up. She was now kneeling next to Gwenth's lifeless body, and she pulled a small roll of paper out of the tight cuff of the dead princess's sleeve. "Tahari envisioned Gwenth yellin' at the Draccen soldiers and saying that people would know what happened here." Leondros and Tahari turned to Almari with wonder as her dark-blue eyes quickly scanned over a small sheet of paper. "She wrote it down," Almari lifted her astonished gaze back to them. They all exchanged glances of surprise as Almari lowered her gaze and began reading the events that led to the fall of Shoshon:

To whomever reads this:

"We have been betrayed by one of our own—Amon-yen!

Moments ago he was seen leading an army of Draccen soldiers through Shoshon's southeastern gates. He invades from the harbor, for the one he calls master has now dispatched him by ship. We will die by his hand, of this we are certain, but he and the army he leads will not make it out of the city, of this I am also certain! Like the great elfin prophet, Sariff, who used his power to destroy an oncoming wave a thousand years ago to save us, so will the high scholars and councilors. I hear the thunder of the Draccen soldiers' footsteps coming for us, but they do not know what we have planned for them. When it is finished, not a single Draccen soldier's body will remain. Amon-yen's fate will be the same as those he leads against us.

Gwenth Goldendragon

After Almari finished Gwenth's testimony, she blinked back the tears that were stinging her eyes. Her head remained hung sadly for a moment as her long braided hair fell over her shoulder. Wiping a delicate hand over her tired eyes and the rest of her dirty face, Almari slowly rose to her feet and crossed the room where she kindly handed the note to Leondros, who was overwhelmed by both the betrayal of Amon-yen and the courage displayed by his people and his family. The expression upon his face alone as he graciously took the small roll from Almari and gazed upon his sister's own handwritten letter showed just how proud he was of his family, but the devastation of their loss cut him deeply. Lowering the small letter and gently holding onto it, Leondros looked back at his family and gazed at them with a look of confusion.

"This is a strange world indeed. I was returned to my family only to have them taken away from me," he said at last. "How does one deal with such adversity?" Leondros asked as his turned his saddened gaze toward Tahari. She looked at him and then back at the heart-wrenching scene.

"Do not do it alone," she replied weakly as she looked back at him and put a reassuring hand on his shoulder. They gazed at each other for a moment. There was such sadness in his brown eyes; it broke her heart.

He slowly shifted his gaze back to Zation and closed his eyes for a moment. He seemed to be searching for understanding, but there could be no relief for him here. How could one understand such senseless destruction?

When he opened his eyes again, Leondros reached over and took hold of Tahari's hand, gazing at her again. There was so much hurt in his eyes, but she knew that he was grateful she was there. He then slowly climbed to his feet and silently left the room. Tahari could not blame him for leaving.

"Tahari, what will happen to Leondros now?" she heard Almari whisper as she stood by her side. Tahari tightened her jaw as she realized something even more devastating about what had happened here.

"I do not know. And it is far worse for Leondros than it first appears," Tahari said softly as she gazed at his family. Almari turned to her with a confused look.

"How much worse can this be?" she asked in a tone of uncertainty. Tahari lowered her head sadly.

"Much, for now he is the last of the Goldendragons," she replied in a weak voice. Almari remained silent as she thought back over recent events.

"Surely there has to be some hope for him. Is there not?" she asked Tahari with a hopeful tone of voice. Tahari looked back through the doorway that he had walked out of.

"There has to be, for he is alive and in good company," Tahari replied quietly as she thought of the good things still within Leondros's life. There was not much, but he did have his friends.

Chapter 88

The Second Scroll

D ark rain clouds hung low in the sky as they passed slowly over the ruined city of Shoshon. The rain that fell was as gentle as tears. It continued throughout the day as Tahari and Almari helped Leondros bury his family. While walking the broken stone path that snaked through the ransacked courtyard, Tahari passed the place where the beautiful hanging gardens and fountains had been. All that remained was torn or burned. On her way back to the palace, Tahari looked out at the once-beautiful white city. It had been reduced to debris, smoke-charred buildings, and ash. No longer was the air filled with wondrous smells and sweet music. The few people who had survived the siege feared that the Draccen soldiers would return and had sought sanctuary underground as Leondros had suggested. Shoshon was little more than a ghost town.

As they returned to the palace, Tahari noticed two riders in the debris-covered street approaching the palace gate. She peered closer to see who had traveled to Shoshon. There was concern about pillagers and criminals who might take advantage of the elfin riches now that the protective shield of the country had come down. When Tahari stopped to gaze at these strangers, Leondros and Almari also stopped and turned to see who had come. When Tahari recognized them, she could barely believe her eyes.

"Sala!" Tahari called out, hurrying down to meet her dear friend. He stopped and slowly climbed off his gray and white horse, wincing in pain. She understood the soreness he was feeling, for he had indeed come a long way. Then she noticed the second gray and white horse and its rider. She wore a dark cloak and a dirty blue gown, so it was difficult to tell who it was. When Tahari got closer to them, she saw who it was. Somehow, Sala made good on his promise to Queen Elanza and saved her from the evil that took the Shandel. The horror of her experience was still vivid upon her face, but Tahari also saw relief when she looked upon them, for she knew she was with friends. "Sala, thank God you both are alive!" Tahari exclaimed in a relieved rush as she ran up to him and greeted him with a warm hug. He seemed glad to see them but even more so when his blue eyes looked upon Leondros up and moving around again. Great relief washed over his bearded, aged face.

"My queen is a most resourceful woman, to be sure," Sala said as he looked back at the saddle-weary woman. "I found her in what remained of Endenbury. She had taken down many Draccen soldiers who were trying to take her back to Avdima. Somehow, someone inspired her to fight her attackers without relenting." as Sala spoke, Tahari looked up at the queen, who humbly smiled at her with shining green eyes. Then Sala moved his gaze across the ruined palace before them all, his smile slowly fading. In spite of the smoky disarray and chaos that surrounded us, he still managed to find a shred of hope. "I see that your journey was successful," Sala said in a soft voice as he looked at Leondros with a relieved gaze. Happiness returned to Sala's blue eyes as he looked upon his friend, but he could not miss the lost look of sadness in the prince's eyes. Tahari smiled weakly and nodded.

"Our mission concerning Leondros turned into his resurrection, but not one for his family," Tahari replied softly as she slowly turned her gaze toward the tomb. Sala followed Tahari's gaze and then looked back at Leondros. The devastation of the news hit him square in the chest.

"There are no words in which to describe this tragedy…" Sala said in a soft voice as he looked up again. Compassion filled Sala's face, and he walked over to Leondros, who put aside the shovel he was using to bury his family and greeted his long-time friend. As Tahari watched Sala put a loving hand on Leondros's shoulder and offer words of comfort, it was as if Tahari was seeing King Doran back from the dead. Leondros kept his composure for only a moment before he was overwhelmed by his immense grief. Sinking to his knees, Leondros buried his head against Sala's robe and wept bitterly for his family. Sala held his dear friend close and comforted him.

Standing next to Tahari, Almari touched her shoulder. There was genuine empathy in her dark-blue eyes. Queen Elanza slowly walked over to the two women, watching the mournful scene before them. She seemed confused and lost.

"He lost his whole family in the siege," Almari whispered to Queen Elanza as she motioned to Leondros. The queen nodded slowly, understanding perfectly what that measure of pain felt like. Watching her expression fill with sad realization, Tahari knew that it broke her heart to see this fate fallen upon prince Leondros, but there was a glint of hope in her bright green eyes.

"Not all of it," Queen Elanza said softly. As she looked at them, an encouraging smile crept into her cream-colored face. They watched Sala take Leondros into the palace. The three ladies began to follow them. They were all weary with sleep and sadness. It was time to rest, if the world would allow them such a gift.

The day aged into early evening, the dark clouds lingering overhead. Paracity Palace had been left in ruins, but it offered enough comforts to allow them to clean up, eat, and find soft places to sleep.

When Tahari awoke late the next morning, she dressed in a black battle tunic with silver beads sewn around the shoulders and a black cloak with blue trim. Wandering from her old room, Tahari found the palace as eerily quiet as it had been when she fell asleep. Only the occasional mournful wind passing through the glassless windows broke the silence. Tahari slipped out of her room and entered the long, dim corridors. She wrinkled her nose at the foul smell clinging to the damp air. As she walked past several groups of windows, Tahari found that most of the windows within the palace had been broken and would no longer keep out the weather. Tahari stood for a long moment remembering what Paracity Palace looked like before the siege. She lost herself in thought as the events of the siege came back to her.

Then the sound of voices caught her attention. They were coming from the grand library that Tahari had been taken to earlier when she met King Doran. Making her way down the corridor, Tahari tried to identify the voices speaking. Almari was telling Sala about their trek through the Shandel and Adarah. Poking her head through the doorway, Tahari saw Sala at the far end of the large library, standing beside the fireplace. Almari sat to the right of the fireplace, dressed in her battle-worn blue and green tunic. Her blonde-brown hair was in a neat braid that lay over her left shoulder, and she now listened intently to Sala. Tahari felt another cold stab of reality as she walked into the library. A fire had destroyed much of the literary works that had been protected for thousands of years. Gazing at the wooden podium that now lay on its side, Tahari noticed that the large leather book that contained the elfin prophecy had the pages ripped from its thick binding. It seemed not even the prophecy had escaped harm.

"Judging from what we collectively know, all of Andora is under attack. Draccen soldiers are roaming the countryside, burning and pillaging as they please. They are taking prisoners—for some dark purpose, to be sure," Sala said with disgust as he paced the floor. As he lowered his head in deep thought, his straight brown hair hung over his shoulders and nearly concealed his face.

"Is there any place safe from these beasts?" Almari wondered as she looked at him hopefully. He thought for a long moment. Sala stopped mid-pace as he caught sight of Tahari out of the corner of his eye. He looked at her with a warm and welcoming smile.

"Any place near Tahari," Sala said as he chuckled softly. Almari turned toward her friend and smiled.

"This I would believe," she said. Tahari smiled humbly, acknowledging their praise, but as she glanced out of a window, Tahari saw someone who caused her to stop. There, standing all alone in the remnants of the hanging garden, was Leondros. He was clothed in dark-brown and green, a gray cloak, and leather boots. He looked ready for the mission that was ahead of them. His head hung sadly, his shoulder-length blond hair hanging limply. Seeing him put Tahari's pride back into check. She lowered her gaze sadly.

"Tahari? What is wrong?" Sala said with concern.

"What about those who have already been hurt by what has been done?" Tahari asked sadly as she looked back out the window at Leondros. "Where can they find peace?" she asked Sala as he walked over to Tahari and joined her gaze out of the window. Sala's expression saddened as he looked back at her.

"You are right. We need to retreat to a place that is shielded from Lord Jarden's spies, so we can decide our next course of action. Someplace peaceful and spiritually healing would be best," Sala said with sad understanding as he watched Leondros, wishing there was something more that he could do for the grieving prince. It was then that Tahari remembered something from the elfin prophecy.

"'The house of Goldendragon will be overrun with peril and grief as a grand city of white is turned to ash. Escape to havens north,'" she said aloud. Both Sala and Almari looked at Tahari with bewilderment. "I glimpsed a page of their elfin prophecy while in a meeting with King Doran and Zation," she explained as Tahari gestured to the very place where she had seen the aged text.

"There is no doubting your memory," Sala said in amazement.

Almari looked at Tahari with disbelief and then turned toward Sala. "There is no such place in the north—just desert and more desert," she said with certainty. Then she looked back at Tahari quizzically. "Is there?" she asked as she searched Tahari's face for the answer. Tahari nodded slowly and lifted her gaze toward Sala.

"Aye, there is. There is a place in the north that has been secret to the realm of man for thousands of years. Ever since it was created, no word of its existence has been spoken," Sala explained with renewed enthusiasm. Tahari listened intently, but she could not help looking out the window at Leondros. His pain was still with her, and she wanted to offer him some comfort. It was then she remembered the sword that Zation had given her before she and Almari had left to join Leondros in the mountains. Tahari's mind had long since wandered from the conversation with Sala and Almari.

"Tahari?" Almari's voice cut through her thoughts and pulled her back into the conversation. Tahari looked back at Almari and Sala. They were both watching her with concern. "Are you all right?" she asked with worry.

"I am all right," Tahari replied softly as she managed a weak smile. Sala looked out the window at Leondros and nodded in understanding. He put a reassuring hand on her shoulder and then turned and began to think. As he did, he started to pace the room. Then he stopped and looked back at Tahari with renewed curiosity.

"Tahari, did you happen to find the second scroll of the prophecy?" he asked.

"I did," Tahari replied, suddenly reminded of the scroll that she had carried on her since Anyi gave it to her in Leondros's tomb. Digging into her tunic pocket, Tahari pulled out the aged scroll and showed it to Sala. All at once, his eyes brightened as he motioned for her to come over to the small table in the middle of the room. Tahari laid the slightly damp scroll upon the wooden table and gently unrolled it. Sala and Almari gathered around her as she carefully worked at the aged scroll. They remained silent with awe as the ancient text was revealed to them.

"What is this prophecy that you speak of?" Almari asked softly, looking on with interest as Tahari studied the ancient text and slowly began to translate it.

Sala explained to Almari the history of the prophecy, Lord Jarden, Farro, and the Order of the Osarian Knights as well as the intricate details of Leondros and Tahari's mission to find Farro, who had been chosen to stop the ancient evil once and for all. Almari was in awe, but as she listened intently, her face was fixed with deep thought.

"I mean no offense, but why did Farro let Lord Jarden live so long when this could have been stopped so long ago?" Almari asked angrily.

"Those two forces never met. In 8021, Farro was captured and killed in prison, along with the rest of the sphinx race, and was not around for the second age of darkness. However, it is believed that these scrolls will lead us to Farro, who will be reborn to fight the evil. All we needed was the sacred messenger to translate the dead language," he explained as he motioned to Tahari. Almari looked at her with disbelief and then looked back at Sala. "Tahari was born to be the sacred messenger of this prophecy, for only a sphinx can read its cryptic language." Sala continued to explain the details that concerned this mission she was on.

"Then that would mean that Tahari is..." Almari's words faded as she thought about what was being said to her. "A sphinx? Legends say they have been extinct from the earth for..." Her voice trailed off again as she looked back at Tahari, feeling uneasy about what this meant for her friend.

"She is the last sphinx of the ancient world. Tahari is our only chance to find Farro," Sala said with a tone of conviction. "However, we cannot let her do it alone. This is why we must help her complete her quest to find the sacred scrolls of the prophecy." as he continued, Almari looked at Tahari in disbelief. She seemed overwhelmed by this news.

"How can this be? She was like the rest of us on the plantation. I believe that she is part elf, for I have seen how strong she is, but a sphinx?" She spoke in a hush, but her words still reached Tahari. She did not look up from her work, but she could feel the pang of jealousy that sparked within Almari. Tightening her jaw, Tahari continued to translate the scroll.

I. A black veil of death and destruction sweeps over Andora. Many will fall to this peril. *Do not let "one" bear the entire burden.

II. The armies of darkness will move in to surround the forces of good. *Learn the power of the sphinx ancestry in thyself.

III. A terrible position will force one to choose from among those near and dear. *Take a stand between them and a loved one.

IV. The darkness of a sacred messenger will threaten Andora. *A sacrifice will save the key to finding Farro.

* Look for the third scroll within the Barrens on the mount with the crest upon it.

When Tahari finished the translation, she sat back as a chill ran down her spine. She once again felt the prophecy speaking to her directly. There was still much ahead of them, and their future's finest details were uncertain, but she knew the time of her sentencing was close at hand. Still, Tahari had to wonder if there was another life still hanging in the balance. As she sat in deep thought, Almari and Sala peered over her shoulder and started to read what Tahari had written.

"What does it mean?" Almari asked as she looked at her with a confused expression. Tahari could not reply. Forcing dark and sad thoughts of her future from her mind, Tahari thought about those who needed her help now. Focusing her energies on what she could do, Tahari now saw her *true* mission before her.

"Excuse me," Tahari said quickly as she rose from the battered chair she had been sitting in. "There is something I must do." leaving the once-grand library, Tahari ran back to her room for the sword that Zation had given her and made her way to the hanging garden. The sky was heavy and gray. It made the mood even more somber. However, Tahari listened to the quiet that surrounded the city and knew there was more trouble approaching. Time was precious.

Chapter 89

Siege Upon Shoshon

Walking into the hanging gardens with the sword tight in her grasp, Tahari searched for Leondros. He was gazing over the sea-green pond, lost in thought, his expression set with grief.

Taking a deep breath, Tahari made her way down to him. She stepped to the water's edge and looked at the pond, yet she could find no comfort in its tranquil splendor. The weight of Leondros's grief was as heavy as if it were her own. There would be no comfort for her knowing that her friend was hurting so. Searching for her ability to speak, Tahari managed to get out a raspy whisper.

"I have not had the chance to give you something that was given to me before I went to find you in the mountain pass," Tahari began. Leondros slowly turned his gaze toward her. Out of the corner of her eye, Tahari saw the pain in his face and felt her heart break. "Zation said to give you this and to tell you that their spirits are always with you." as she spoke in a slow and soft tone, Tahari held up the sword so that Leondros could take hold of it. When his gaze fell upon it, she saw the memories come back rushing back to him. He reached out and took up the sword.

"This was my father's," he said quietly. "It was meant for Dreyhon when he became High King of Adarah." then he closed his eyes sadly as if remembering how he had found them.

Fighting to think of something to say, Tahari remembered the last moment she had shared with his twin sister.

"I believe that Zation knew how it would end for them. I could see it in her eyes," she said slowly as she blinked back the tears and swallowed the ache in her throat. "But she was calm in spite of what was coming." Tahari then remembered the strength in Zation's face and shook her head slightly with a sad smile. "No fear, only courage.

"Tahari?" Leondros began as he lowered his head and eyed the sword sadly. "Forgive me?" His request caught her off-guard.

"For what?" Tahari asked dumbfounded as she looked at him with concern, for the sadness in his face had deepened.

"I did not know the pain you felt when you lost those whom you cared about in the Tomblock." his confession reminded her of her own grief. He lifted his gaze and looked at her apologetically, while Tahari drew a labored breath of sadness as the memory of her own loss hit her again. Tahari looked at him with a sad smile.

"There is nothing to forgive," she stated clearly. "You might not have understood the loss, but you still had compassion," Tahari offered with a warm smile. There was relief in his expression, but she could still see the burden of his own grief in his face.

"How did you overcome the pain to carry on?" he asked as he shook his head. She turned her gaze toward the ruins of the hanging gardens and thought about all those she had lost along the way, including him.

"The grief that you feel from a loved one's death will always be with you. The loss runs soul deep. You cannot do anything more for the dead, but you can honor their memory by helping those in need." Leondros listened intently as if to soak up every word. "When I found that my new friend was in grave danger, it gave me a sense of mission. I would go to whatever ends to keep you from the same fate as my friends from the Tomblock." Tahari spoke with sincerity as she remembered how fearful she was for him.

"Adalai has sent my guardian angel to watch over me," he managed in a whisper as he seemed overwhelmed that someone would go so far for his sake. "You have taught me a lesson in friendship. They are not all the same; some are even better," he said in humble reply.

Tahari looked at him to see the spark of life in his face again. The grief that had existed there was fading. She smiled in return as he offered her a warm hug. "Thank you, my friend," he whispered as he held her tightly. When he pulled his head away, Tahari saw life return to his soulful brown eyes again. As Leondros gazed at her for a moment, he noticed something about her that brought concern to his face. "I sense that you are troubled. What is wrong?" he asked.

Tahari paused for a moment, but there was reassurance in his face. "The second scroll has been found and translated," she replied. This news acquired Leondros's full attention. As Tahari explained the unsettling details of the second scroll to Leondros, she felt evil suddenly very close. Thinking of what dangers awaited him and the others, she felt worry creep into her thoughts.

"Tahari, listen to me," he said as he held her shoulders. "I am here now because you believed in me enough to come back for me. I have never known a truer friend than you. Now let me repay the favor, for my debt is great," he said, with a gentle and soothing voice.

Tahari could not find the words to speak but nodded in response. Worry for her filled his face as he saw how much this concerned her. Leondros gently wrapped his arms around her and held her tightly again. Laying her head against his shoulder, Tahari held onto him as if never to let go. He began to whisper something in Elfish, and as she listened, she was greatly comforted. *In this day and age, there is much to be feared. Most hope for better times, but many really do not believe. It is a wonder that we have made it this far. Yet, for the first time, I have seen a faith like no other. Your concerns, fears, and worries are not for yourself but for your loved ones. I do not know where you find such strength, but I am inspired by it.*

In that moment, Tahari found courage to confront the perils that awaited her head on. There have been very few times when she had someone stand by her when she really needed them. However, Leondros had done more than stand close by her in her time of need. He also encouraged her, just as she had done when all life seemed to be caving in around him.

"Thank you, my friend," Tahari replied in a warm and grateful whisper in their native tongue. Tahari lifted her head and smiled at

him.

"No—thank you, my friend," Leondros said with a genuine smile of gratitude. The healing energy that filled that moment seemed as if it could last forever. Then the tranquility of the moment was shattered as a voice broke the surrounding peace.

"Tahari! Leondros! We have a problem. Come quickly!" Sala's voice was unmistakable. Tahari and Leondros looked at each other with a sense of alarm and then darted toward the front gate of the hanging gardens. Leaping over hedges and bounding up the long staircase that led to the front door of the palace, Leondros and Tahari made their way to the grand library. They found Sala nervously pacing the burnt floor of the library as Almari and Queen Elanza stood guard by the large window. When Sala looked up at them, they saw great alarm in his blue eyes. "Trouble has found us." he spoke with a quivering voice, and he wrung his hands nervously. "About an hour's ride east of here is a massive army of Draccen soldiers. It is hard to say just how many there are, but from what we can tell, there are at least a thousand, maybe more." as Sala explained the gravity of their situation, Leondros ran to the window to look for himself. He looked from an old-fashioned telescope that Sala had brought with him and studied the eastern horizon for a long moment before turning back to them. The expression that he wore was fixed with alarm.

"They are almost upon us!" Leondros gasped. In the moment when everyone exchanged looks of fear and uncertainty, thunder cracked overhead. They jumped from the sudden noise, but for Tahari something else began to happen as a result. It was not a vision, but she sensed another even greater danger closing in on them, and like the Draccen soldiers, it was almost upon them.

Tahari stood still for a moment as the sensation of knowing that something was quickly approaching grew stronger. Her eyes searched for the source of the new danger. Leondros saw the look of alarm growing on Tahari's face. She looked up at him at the moment she realized that she needed to leave the library. Whirling around, Tahari bolted out the door and down the hallway. Her name was called from behind her, but she could not stop until she knew what was coming at them. Hurrying down the stairs and out the front doors, Tahari ran into the middle of the ruined courtyard and started searching for the danger that she had felt. The only thing worse than a legion of Draccen soldiers was probably more Draccen soldiers. However, this was not what Tahari found, and it was not what she had expected. It was far worse.

"Tahari!" She heard Leondros call after her as he emerged from the palace. Tahari could also hear the others' footsteps behind him. "What is it?" he asked as he finally caught up to her.

"Oh, no..." Tahari whispered as she gazed out at the western horizon. It was dark and threatening. She looked over at Leondros. "Look to the west," she instructed with warning, pointing at the western horizon. He followed her gaze and cautiously studied the skyline. They were soon joined by the rest of their friends. They saw Leondros and Tahari watching the western horizon and followed suit. "It is coming, and we cannot stop it. We must escape before it reaches us," Tahari warned, looking back at the others.

"Oh, seriously—it is just a thunderstorm," Queen Elanza said, with a sigh of relief. "Our main concern now should be escape from the Draccen army," she continued, urging them to action. Tahari looked at Leondros and then turned her gaze toward the queen.

"I am afraid Tahari is right. This is more than just a thunderstorm," Leondros said, as he motioned with his chin back toward the western horizon.

"It is a fire!" Almari blurted out as her blue eyes widened with horror. Everyone turned back toward the western sky and started to see what Leondros and Tahari had discovered. The dark western sky was deceiving, for the thunderstorm that was passing over the area masked the black smoke rising out of the mountains to the west. Then they caught the thick smell of smoke within the air, just as red-orange flames started rising up from the western mountains. The alarm that had filled Tahari's eyes earlier now filled everyone's.

"That is more than a fire—it is a monster. Evil is rushing toward Shoshon, eager to destroy the one hope we have for a future," Sala said as he gazed at the western sky with contempt. Panic began to spread across everyone's face.

"Dracs to the east, fire to the west, and mountains all around. How do we get out of Shoshon?" Almari asked her voice rising to panic.

"There are several paths that lead out of the city. Two lead to the Life River, which flows north; another path is hidden underground and leads south," Leondros informed them calmly as he studied the grounds that surrounded the castle. He knew how to get out of Shoshon and refused to leave anyone behind.

"All right, everyone, to the stables. We will make better time on hoof," Sala instructed as he motioned with his hand toward the stables. This was their first sign of good luck in their attempt to leave the city. The stables had hardly been touched by the Draccen soldiers. As the others hurried down the grassy hill from the palace to a grand building of white marble that had large white pillars on its exterior, Sala looked at Tahari with deep concern in his blue eyes.

"Tahari." Sala gestured to her to come back to him as he glanced back down the hillside at the others with a watchful gaze. She hurried back toward him as the wind blowing into the mountain valley circled around them and caught his long, gray-streaked hair and wipped it around his shoulders. As she looked into his kind face, Tahari saw a serious concern in his normally relaxed face. "It is no doubt that what led you to Shoshon was of your elfin side, but from here on out, you will have to rely on your sphinx side. You will be heading into what used to be sphinx country; you will need to call upon the sphinx powers within you to protect the others. Besides Leondros, you are the best hope they have to survive this journey," he explained gently as he motioned with his head toward the others as they continued toward the stables.

Following his gaze and then seeing the danger that nearly surrounded Shoshon, Tahari felt fear grip her whole being. She did not know her sphinx heritage well enough to summon such powers to bend them to her will.

"I-I do not know how to call upon the sphinx powers," Tahari stammered nervously as she looked back at Sala with great uncertainty. "Even what I did to help Leondros was written in an incantation. I am completely unprepared." anxiety controlled her thoughts, and Tahari fought to hide her shame, covering her mouth with her hand. Sala merely looked at her with promise. "How will I know the difference between what is elfin and what is sphinx?" Tahari asked finally as she fought to summon the courage to battle back her fear and learn more about her other ancestry.

"Neither side will lead you astray," he affirmed with a nod. "You are but a child in the elfin realm, yet you already know that your senses are tuned into nature, the life force all around us, and the good and evil that exist within the world. These things are of your elfin side," he pointed out calmly. "Your sphinx side will most likely be memories of your ancestors, maybe even images of a past life. They will be potent and vivid, for the emotional bond between the sphinx people is much stronger than that between the elves. Let them be your guide into understanding the power of the sphinx." Sala's insight was a great help as far as what Tahari needed to know before setting out, but as she looked back down at the stables, she still was riddled with fear. Taking a firm hold of her shoulders, Sala looked at Tahari with understanding and knew that she was fearful of the responsibility ahead of her. "How did you get the three of you out of Akendron after Leondros was betrayed?" he asked.

"I really did not have time to think about it. I was more concerned for Leondros and getting him home," Tahari replied with a shrug, but as she looked at him, Sala beamed her a warm smile.

"Then let that same concern fill you and be your driving force," he encouraged with a look of inspiration. He motioned with his head back to their friends, who waited anxiously by the stable doors.

"All right," Tahari replied half-heartedly. She took a deep breath, closed her eyes, and focused her mind on what she needed to do. Opening her eyes, Tahari looked at Sala, nodded, and then headed back toward the stables. "Let's do this," she said to herself, but Sala overheard this and smiled slyly as he followed behind her.

When they reached the rest of the group, Leondros opened the large wooden doors to let them in. Almari and Queen Elanza were quick to run inside and find their horses as Tahari hesitated in the doorway.

"Tahari," Leondros called to her as he ran down the long wooden hall toward a particular stall. As Tahari followed after him, the thick scent of hay and horses wafted up to her. Upon reaching the stall that he had entered, she looked within and saw a beautiful black stallion. He seemed nervous and edgy but calmed down considerably when Leondros approach him. "This is Jade. He was Zation's horse. He is a spirited horse, but he always brought her back safely," he said in a soulful voice, so that Jade would not be alarmed by Tahari's presence. Leondros calmed the horse, which seemed to sense that trouble was coming.

Tahari slowly stepped up to the dark sleek stallion and looked into his deep brown eyes. Jade sniffed at her and eyed her. She offered him her hand, and he sniffed at it with curiosity. He allowed her to gently rub his head and she whispered to him.

A warm smile came to Leondros's face. "Amazing. Jade does not like strangers, but he seems to trust you. Zation and I were the only two who could walk up to him. He can usually tell what a person is like. It is as if he can see through to their soul," Leondros said, sounding a little surprised, but also reaffirming that Tahari was as true as her word.

"Trust is very important. It is a safety net. Without it, we fall one by one. I have seen too many people hurt and even perish from the lack of such a thing," Tahari replied softly as she gently stroked Jade's head. Leondros listened with great interest. Then before Tahari could say anything more, they heard cannon fire near the city. It shook the stables, and dust fell from the roof. Leondros and Tahari looked up at each other in alarm. The Draccen soldiers were getting close, and so was the fire. Jade jumped nervously and panicked. There was no time to saddle him, so Tahari quickly jumped on bareback. Leondros led Jade out of the stall and they soon joined their friends gathered at the entrance.

"Tahari, I need you to take Queen Elanza out of Shoshon using the north mountain trail," Sala instructed Tahari as he helped the queen onto her horse. "I believe that it would be best for us to ride out in pairs," he added with a tone of regret. Queen Elanza gave Sala a doubtful look. "Fear not, my queen; I would trust Tahari with my very life. Besides, with so much danger bearing down on top of Shoshon, it would be quite challenging getting out of Shoshon in a larger group. If we keep our numbers small and inconspicuous, the Draccen soldiers should not pay you any mind."

"Why do you send Tahari and Queen Elanza out with no other defense?" Leondros asked with concern.

Sala smiled with understanding. "We will cut down our chances of being spotted by the Draccen army if we travel in pairs. You and Tahari are the stronger riders; I need the stronger riders to accompany the other two, so you all make it out safely. I will meet up with you again deep within the Barrens, in the sacred realm of Rahara," Sala said. Leondros did not reply, but Tahari saw in his eyes that he still did not approve of this decision. Sala turned to them and nodded. It was time to leave Shoshon.

"Leondros, may Adalai see you out safely. We will meet outside the city," Tahari offered encouragingly in the Elfin tongue. Leondros nodded, but he still looked concerned. Then another explosion erupted, this time within the city limits. A plume of smoke rose into the air as the explosion violently expelled dirt and rock into the air. It was their signal to leave.

Rushing to his horse, Leondros jumped on his faithful white stallion, Aton. As Almari waited for Leondros to join her on their journey out of the city, he looked back at Sala with concern.

"What about you, old friend? How are you getting out of the city?" he asked with worry.

"Do not worry for me. I have my means. I will meet you all again, believe in that," Sala reassured his friend with a sly smile.

Leondros hesitated and then finally nodded. "Until we meet again. Safe journey, my old friend." Sala nodded in response and waved them on. Leondros and Almari turned and began galloping away.

"Safe journey, my friends. May the wind be at your backs and carry you all safely to Rahara," Sala prayed in a hopeful whisper. As he watched them disappear from sight, the thunder of Draccen soldiers' footsteps could be heard approaching from just outside the city, and the thick smell of smoke began to settle over the city. The ancient evil's siege had returned to Adarah and was about to finish what it had started. Sala glared at the atrocity that was about to consume this city. "Your time is coming." he looked out over the ruined city, then closed his eyes and spoke an inaudible prayer. Moments later, blue energy flashed, and he disappeared into thin air.

With that, Tahari urged Jade down the broken stone path that led away from the palace stables and began the dangerous mission to get out of Shoshon.

Chapter 90

Flight from Shoshon

In the distant foothills and mountains surrounding Shoshon, you did not have to hear the blood-chilling screams of the Draccen army closing in on the city from the east nor see the black smoke of the raging inferno approaching from the west to know that danger was near. You could feel it.

Emerging from one of the secret passages leading out of Shoshon, Tahari and Queen Elanza headed down a dirt road that led into the thick green forest that covered the mountainside. Judging from the path that they were on, Tahari knew they would weave through the mountain range surrounding Shoshon until they reached the northern part of Adarah. As they rode higher up the mountain, a bend in the path took them near an edge that allowed them to look south upon Shoshon. The view was breathtaking, but it was not wondrous beauty that took their breath away. The city was overrun with Draccen soldiers. Tahari's heart sank as she watched the soldiers destroy what was left of Shoshon. It was like watching a black flood washing over the ruins of the homes, buildings, and everything within Shoshon that made it home. Tahari watched helplessly as the soldiers leveled everything within their path. Their search for survivors would be in vain, for, thankfully, most of the survivors had been evacuated hours before, and those who went underground would never let themselves be found. The Draccen assault would eventually be followed up by a roaring inferno that would consume the whole mountain valley, including the grand city of Shoshon.

"Flame and spear will fall upon the kingdom of the elf. Escape will depend on all." Tahari spoke the last line of the first scroll sadly as she watched the predicted horror come to pass. Then as she searched the trail that ran along the river valley below, Tahari realized that she had not spotted Leondros or Almari yet. Stopping Jade for a moment, Tahari searched intensely for any sign of them. There was no one trying to escape from the doomed city.

After a long moment, Queen Elanza whispered, "I am sorry, Tahari, but if they did not make it out of Shoshon by now…"

Tahari tightened her jaw stubbornly. "You must have faith in us, for we are in this together. If they need help, then we will help them. If we need help, they will help us. That is how we are going to get out of here and reach Rahara alive," she said in a cautious tone, for Tahari did not want to hear that Leondros and Almari had died and they had done nothing to help them. Queen Elanza was about to say something but chose to remain quiet. Tahari looked back on the once-grand city of Shoshon a last time and prayed that someday she could help restore her wondrous beauty. Gently giving Jade a kick, Tahari pressed onward and continued on down the mountain trail.

Later, their trail overlooked a deep ravine just north of Shoshon. Tahari gazed into the ravine and saw another mountain trail that led up to a wooden bridge that crossed over it. Far below the bridge and overhanging trees was a long and winding river. It seemed deep and fast-moving. In the dimming light, it was spectacular to behold. Yet as she gazed at the scene before her, Tahari sensed danger. It was different from the danger that they were leaving behind. It was uncertain, but it lingered here waiting to strike.

"What is it? Why do you stop?" Queen Elanza asked, sounding confused. Tahari paused for a long moment, listening carefully to her surroundings.

"Something is wrong," Tahari whispered, continuing to eye her surroundings. She listened carefully, realizing that it was too quiet. Tahari longed to see Leondros and Almari riding out of Shoshon safe and sound.

"You worry for them," Queen Elanza said in a soft tone. Tahari turned back to her. She felt her heart plunge when she said this.

"I do indeed. They are my friends, the only friends that I have now. I have lost many loved ones already, and I do not want to see them hurt—or killed. I would gladly take their place if it meant that they would be alive and safe," Tahari replied as she thought of the promise that she had made to Leondros. A warm smile came to Tahari's face, for he was alive only because someone cared enough to make such a promise.

"It was you who helped my family during the attack on the Day of the Great Dragon," Queen Elanza said with sudden realization. Tahari did not answer, only smiled. "Why did you help me?" she asked curiously.

"We are all people. Flesh and blood. For someone to do something awful to someone else just because they want to is beyond my comprehension. Sometimes we have to remind others and keep them in balance. Everyone deserves a chance at life with no fear of living it," Tahari explained softly as she looked at Queen Elanza with determination and then returned her watchful gaze to their surroundings.

"People could learn much from your wisdom. Maybe when this is over, we can spread the word. I know that..." Queen Elanza was interrupted by a sudden explosion around them. Jade reared up, and Tahari felt her body go flying as light and thunder deafened her senses until only blackness and silence remained.

The soft sound of a heartbeat echoed through the thick darkness of Tahari's world. It was the only thing she heard at first, but slowly the sounds of reality drifted back to her. Tahari heard the openness of the wilderness around her. Then she sensed someone near her. Tahari heard their voice call to her as if from far away, but as it became louder, she realized they were panicked and yelling for her to wake up.

"TAHARI! Wake up! Please wake up!" Queen Elanza's voice was filled with fright.

Opening her eyes, Tahari saw a blurry image of the queen leaning over her.

"Tahari?" Queen Elanza asked with hopeful relief as she saw that Tahari was coming to. Tahari's vision cleared enough for her to see that she had been crying, tears having streaked her smoke-covered face. Her black hair hung loose and tangled from the explosion. "Are you all right?" Her voice was riddled with fear and concern. Her green eyes were full of a terror Tahari could feel as she held onto her. As Tahari's senses cleared and the buzzing in her head subsided, she realized how much she truly hurt. Looking down at her body, Tahari was covered in blackened smoke; she could feel the bruises forming already.

"I will live. What happened?" Tahari asked groggily as she looked around. Queen Elanza's horse lay nearby, dead. The forest around them had been cleared, and the road now had a gaping hole in it.

"The Draccen soldiers must have fired upon the mountainside. It looks like the whole valley went up! Thankfully, we were thrown clear of the main blast—well, except for..." her voice failed as she looked over sadly at her horse.

"What about Jade?" Tahari asked still fighting the dizziness in her head. Queen Elanza's face filled with grief.

"He shielded you from the main blast." she swallowed the lump in her throat. "There is not much left." her words made Tahari wince. Her heart began to ache as she remembered that he had been Zation's horse. Tahari suddenly thought of Leondros and Almari.

"Dear God, no!" Tahari gasped under her breath as she scrambled to her feet and rushed to the edge of the war-torn mountain trail.

"Tahari?" Queen Elanza called as she rushed after her. "What is it?.

"Leondros and Almari would have been on the trail that runs along the valley floor parallel to ours." peering through the smoke-filled air that now clouded the mountain range, Tahari glimpsed the areas that had borne the brunt of the attack. Then she saw the remains of the large wooden bridge that had crossed the Life River. It was in ruins, fire and smoke rising from the remnants of the beams and timbers. Most of the bridge seemed to have fallen into the river below. Looking across the ravine at the north bank, Tahari saw a dark horse standing alone, not far from the body of its rider. Through the haze, Tahari was able to make out the seemingly lifeless form of Almari.

"Good heavens!" Queen Elanza gasped, seeing what Tahari saw. "We have got to get down to her!" she gasped as she frantically rushed toward a narrow path that would take them into the valley below and onto the north bank. As she did, Tahari heard something terrible in the distance drawing closer to them.

"Elanza, wait!" Tahari yelled. She rushed over and tackled her just as another cannonball came whizzing through the air in their direction. Scrambling over to a large rock, Tahari dragged Queen Elanza behind it and shielded her. A second later, another explosion obliterated the mountain road leading out of Shoshon. When the thunder and flame had died, Tahari looked around cautiously. "Stay down. Let them think we are dead, or we will be," she whispered, motioning with her head toward Shoshon and the Draccen soldiers.

"What about..." Queen Elanza began to say, but Tahari quickly covered her mouth with her hand. Tahari waited a long moment before she dared even breathe. Listening to the sounds of the surrounding forest and nearby movement, Tahari made sure that it was safe just to whisper.

"Be silent and follow me. Watch for Draccen soldiers; they will be hunting us now. The dark lord will not take any chances. He will send them to ensure we are dead," Tahari whispered. She waited a long moment before she dared move. Taking a deep breath, Tahari led Queen Elanza down into the mountain valley and carefully over to the north bank.

They moved cautiously through the thick brush toward the bottom of the ravine, the ache in Tahari's heart growing as she now saw the full extent of the damage to the bridge that had spanned the immense ravine. Edging closer to the place where they had seen Almari, Tahari and Queen Elanza often jumped as parts of the bridge shifted and fell into the river below. Staying calm, Tahari hurried up the hillside where Almari had been.

As they crested the hill, Tahari discovered that Almari was not only alive but now awake. Before she could take relief in this, Tahari saw something in Almari's face that scared her. Almari was standing beside the ravine, staring into its depth. Her smoke-covered face showed panic and fear.

"Almari!" Tahari called out as she ran over to her friend. Almari turned around and broke down in tears at the sight of her.

"He was right behind me! I swear, he was right behind me!" she said hysterically as she pointed to the river below. Tahari peered over the ravine, but there was no sign of Leondros. Tahari's heart sank. Then she heard something just as terrifying as the Draccen soldiers coming to look for them. It was the roar of the inferno, now just outside of the ravine. It was heading in their direction! There was little time for them to escape, but Leondros was still lost. Turning to Almari, Tahari took a firm hold of her shoulders and looked directly into her scared blue eyes.

"Almari, listen to me," she said determinedly, making Almari meet her gaze. "I will go find Leondros, but I need you to get Elanza out of here.

Her friend could not stop shaking. "I am so sorry, Tahari." tears ran down her dirty cheeks. "I thought we could get out unnoticed, but then everythin' went wrong, and…" she continued to stammer as she trembled uncontrollably. "He was on the bridge when it blew up!" Almari's voice faded as she became overwhelmed with grief.

Tahari swallowed hard, starting to fear the worst, but she quickly shook such thoughts from her mind. "Almari," Tahari said calmly, and she held Almari's smoky face in her hands. Almari met her gaze and calmed down enough to listen to her. "I need for you to be strong now. Take the queen, and keep following the trail. Stay as close to the river as you can. The fire is close now; the river may be your only chance," Tahari instructed her calmly. As she spoke, Almari nodded with understanding. "I am going to look for Leondros," Tahari added with a note of confidence. Then before she could say anything more, more thunder caught her attention.

It was a different type of thunder—the thunder of heavy footsteps. They turned and saw a band of Draccen soldiers rushing over the hillside into the ravine. They hurried down the trail she and Elanza had been on.

"Are they trying to find us?" Queen Elanza wondered in a whisper.

"Or trying to outrun the inferno—either way, our time is quickly diminishing," Tahari said. "Almari, go now. I will meet up with you farther down river," she said.

Almari nodded slowly and managed to summon the strength to get back onto her horse. Tahari watched as Queen Elanza mounted behind her. They looked back at Tahari for a brief moment before they rode down the mountain trail.

After they had disappeared around the bend, Tahari took a deep breath and looked over the edge of the cliff into the river far below. She was not looking forward to what she had to do next. Tahari knew she had to do it for Leondros's sake, but getting herself to jump from the cliff into the ravine below was terrifying. Then Tahari heard the eerie whistle of something approaching. Lifting her gaze, Tahari could only watch in horror as a cannonball engulfed in fire headed straight for her.

Talk about motivation, she thought as she charged forward and leapt off the edge of the cliff. The explosion that erupted behind her was intense, filling her senses with heat and light. The last thing Tahari could remember was falling into a chasm of darkness.

Chapter 91

In Search

Seconds after plunging into the river below, there was only water and dark blurs around Tahari. When she finally broke the surface, she took a moment to refocus herself. Cannonball. The explosion's fire now combined with the firestorm that was descending into the river valley. Even the stormy afternoon sky was glowing red and orange from the raging inferno, which had grown to monstrous proportions. The fire, which had started in the west, was consuming everything in its path. As it drove them north, it also drove north the band of Draccen soldiers that had come in from the east. It would not be long before their paths crossed. Tahari could feel the intense heat radiating from the hillside, even from deep within the ravine. Thankfully, her search for Leondros was somewhere in the Life River, where they would be protected by its waters. Tahari only hoped that he was still alive.

Wasting little time, Tahari began swimming down the river, searching for Leondros. She looked up to find the charred remnants of the wooden bridge. Pieces of ash and wood continued to fall into the river. Her gaze drifted downstream, where she could see fragments of wood pieces floating upon the water. Images of the explosion and Almari, utterly horrified that Leondros had been caught in the explosion, flashed through her mind. Tahari swallowed hard and forced herself to focus on finding him. As thunder cracked overhead, rain began to fall. The rain would make finding Leondros more challenging, but it would also keep the Draccen soldiers from finding them.

As the river swept her further downstream, Tahari peered through the pouring rain and studied the shoreline, hoping to find some trace of Leondros. She would not let herself panic, but her search was not going well. It had been some time since Tahari had started her search for Leondros and, thus far, there was no sign of him. Her thoughts returned to what had happened to Queen Elanza's and her horses. Tahari refused to believe that Leondros had suffered the same fate. Then, out of the corner of her eye, Tahari saw something farther downriver. It was hung up on the rocks near the eastern bank shoreline. She strained to look through the rain and realized that it was not only a body hung up on the rocks but Leondros.

Swimming cautiously through the water, Tahari headed toward him. She could not afford to be noticed by Draccen soldiers. Reaching the rocks, she found that the current had forced him up against them. Thunder cracked overhead and lightning brightened the flame-lit sky. He lay face down upon the largest rock, soaked, bruised, and dirty from the explosion.

"Leondros!" Tahari whispered loudly as she gently touched the back of his head. He did not move, but he was alive. Sounds from overhead echoed down to her. Beyond the danger of the approaching fire, Tahari knew that the soldiers were getting closer. She scanned the eastern bank and found a good place to hide. Gently wrapping her arms around Leondros, Tahari pulled him off the rock. She locked an arm around his neck and under his arm and fought the current over to the other shore. Before they reached shore, however, Draccen soldiers emerged onto the shore from the forest beyond as they, too, were trying to get away from the inferno. It was clear that their search for them continued as well. They slowly patrolled the narrow beach. Tahari looked around quickly. There were no more large rocks in the river to hide behind. The beach itself was made up mostly of large, flat rocks. Then she saw something that just might save them both. There was a slight crevasse in some large rocks on the beach, not far from them, and it looked just big enough to hide both Leondros and herself. Quickly, Tahari dragged Leondros into the crevasse and draped her long dark cloak over the both of them. Their best chance for escape would be camouflaging themselves to look like the shadows of the beach itself.

As Tahari lay close to Leondros, she listened for the Draccen soldiers. Her nerves screamed as she felt their footsteps draw closer to them. She held her breath as the Draccen soldiers' search brought them closer to them. Then, much to her surprise, Tahari heard Leondros whispering.

"Tahari…" he whispered as he weakly opened his eyes. "You found me again." his voice was weak, but she understood and smiled warmly, reaching over to touch his cheek.

"Shh… There are Dracs close," Tahari whispered in reply. He closed his eyes and turned his head toward her. He was weary and exhausted, but he knew his friend was watching out for him. Tahari was glad that he was all right, but she had to remain focused on the danger around them. Several Draccen soldiers stepped unknowingly over the crevasse. Tahari did not breathe. As she heard them move on, she took a deep breath of relief. Tahari looked down at Leondros for a moment. The blast from the explosion had left him blackened with smoke, scratched, and bruised. He looked barely alive. Had this been yet another plot to put an end to the Goldendragon line? Whether it was or not, Leondros had survived. Tahari smiled thankfully as she lowered her head for a moment, glad that her friend was still with them.

The Draccen soldiers had passed by, but now Tahari heard a thunderous crash close by them. Snapping her head up, Tahari looked around and saw that part of a tree had fallen into the river nearby. It came from higher up the mountain. Lifting her gaze, Tahari watched in horror as the blaze started to rage out of control on the eastern bank. It had jumped the ravine via the trees that hung over it and was consuming everything in its path. Tree limbs were dropping into the river below. Staying put, they risked being surrounded by soldiers or having a tree engulfed in flames land on top of us.

"Leondros, come—we have to..." Tahari started to say as she looked back down at him. He had slipped back into unconsciousness. In spite of their impending doom, she was just glad that he was alive. She smiled down at him as she gently touched his cheek. "Rest, my friend; you have been through enough for one day," she whispered. Taking a deep breath, Tahari looked for the best possible path out of this death trap. Another tree came crashing down into the river, sparks flying at them. It was time to get moving. Tahari got to her feet, pulled Leondros to his, and then pulled him over her shoulder. Walking over the rocky embankment was no easy task, but Tahari pressed on toward a break in the rock wall. She could see a narrow path that led back into the forest above. There was not much time before the flames reached this part of the forest.

It was early evening when Tahari finally made it out of the ravine and began clawing her way up the grassy foothills leading toward the forest. Her back was warm from the inferno that now scorched through the ravine. When she reached the forest, Tahari stopped to recover her strength near a large oak tree, laying Leondros at its base. Her mind and body were both weary. Everything within her told her to continue on, but she needed rest for a moment. Sinking to her knees and closing her eyes, Tahari managed to drown out the distant roar of the inferno and the adrenaline that screamed for her to keep running. Several moments passed before she sensed something other than the inferno coming at them. Opening her eyes, Tahari remained on her knees close to the ground, listening to the sounds of her pursuers' approach. They were being cautious not to make too much noise, but even with the roar of the inferno, Tahari could still sense their approach. Slowly taking up her bow, Tahari fitted it with an arrow, thankful to still have both with her. Their pursuers were right behind her. Without warning, she whirled around and drew her bow, preparing to fire.

"WHOA!" Almari yelled as she held her hands out, her dark-blue eyes wide with alarm. Queen Elanza was nearby, standing beside Almari's black horse and Aton, whom they had found while fleeing. Tahari took a deep breath and lowered her bow. "We thought you could use some help," Almari said. She looked past her and saw Leondros on the ground. Her face filled with worry when she saw the state he was in.

"He is alive, but he needs to get out of here. We all do. The fire is spreading, and it will be here soon," Tahari explained as she knelt down next to Leondros.

"Pray that we do not get captured," Almari replied wearily as she cautiously looked at their surroundings.

"She is right, Tahari. The Draccen soldiers are everywhere. They are bound to capture us if they see us trying to escape the forest," Queen Elanza said as she approached them, gesturing to the surrounding forest. Her expression turned into concern as she saw Leondros lying unconscious. Their desperation was growing, and panic filled their eyes. Tahari could feel their chances of escape fading with each passing moment. Tahari lowered her gaze back to Leondros. He, like Almari and Elanza, was not going to get out of this forest unless someone gave them a chance. It reminded Tahari of what Elijah did for them, giving her an idea.

"Almari, I need for you to do something for me," Tahari said. "Get Leondros and yourselves out of here. I will lead the Draccen soldiers away," she said as she rose to her feet and walked over to Aton and led him over to Leondros.

"Come again?" Almari asked as she watched Tahari with a confused expression. "You are goin' to do what?" Tahari could not miss the concern in her voice.

"Almari, remember what Elijah did for Leondros?" Tahari asked turning to her, hoping to find understanding in her eyes. She nodded in response. "Now that is what I must do for him and for you," she calmly explained, but Almari would not let her friend go that easily.

"Tahari! That is suicide!" she cried as she grabbed Tahari's shoulders. "If you go out there alone, you will not have a chance!" she tried to find some way to reason with her.

"Almari," Tahari spoke up quietly as she lowered her gaze sadly. "There is more of a chance of your surviving if I go out there. It is the best chance he has—it's the best chance for you all," she continued as she took the scrolls of the prophecy from her pack and handed them to Almari. Much to Tahari's surprise, the scrolls somehow managed to escape being soaked. Almari froze for a moment before she let herself take the scrolls from her.

"Maybe you are right," Almari replied softly. Tahari stepped over to Leondros and knelt down beside him. "But one day these risky maneuvers will be the death of you," she said sadly. Almari's words caught Tahari off-guard, but as she looked upon Leondros's face, she was reminded of the life that was saved as a result of her daring. It also reminded Tahari of Shamira and how her mission to protect Leondros had become her own. In spite of Almari's words, Tahari smiled hopefully as she laid a hand on his chest.

"Eventually is not now," Tahari replied firmly as she looked back up at Almari. "I do not fear death in the battle ahead of me, for I have a greater purpose." Almari and Elanza exchanged a look of concern. Tahari knew they did not fully understand what she meant, but she knew they would do as she asked.

Tahari picked Leondros off the ground and carried him over to Aton, who looked concerned for his master as he knelt on the ground. When Tahari placed Leondros on his back, Aton rose to his feet.

"Keep the horses as quiet as possible; silence is going to be your greatest asset tonight. Ride for the Barrens; stop only when you must. Draccen soldiers may be dumb, but once they catch your trail, they will follow you with single-mindedness," Tahari instructed as she turned back to her friend and Elanza. "Almari, be careful," she warned as she looked at her friend with concern.

"And you also." she was about to hurry on her way when something came to her and she turned back to Tahari. "Do you know how hard it will be trying to tell Leondros what you have done, not to mention tryin' to keep him from coming after you?" she asked rhetorically. Tahari looked over at Leondros and smiled knowingly.

"Farewell, and Godspeed," Tahari said. She stepped back slowly as the two women climbed up on the black horse, Almari holding Aton's reins as well as her own horse's. They exchanged expressions of understanding for a moment. Then Tahari whirled around, jumped through the brush, and disappeared from their sight. She ran south through thick brush toward the inferno, making as much noise as possible. In a matter of seconds, Tahari heard the sound of the Draccen soldiers trying to cut through the thick brush to chase her. Tahari's plan was working, maybe, too, well.

Chapter 92

Enemy Revealed

The Draccen soldiers chased Tahari long after the sun had set, although the dark clouds and smoke concealed the actual sunset. She was not without a vermillion horizon, however, for the world around her had been set aflame by the inferno racing through the mountains surrounding Shoshon. Bright orange and red skies burned overhead as Tahari raced through the thick forest. Red embers were carried by hot winds as they blew into the untouched parts of the forest. Smoke filled the hot air and was thick and oppressive. This was looking more and more like some hellish nightmare.

Continuing up the eastern embankment, Tahari was running the whole group of Draccen soldiers toward the firestorm when it began to rain. A mere shower would have no great impact on the raging inferno that was hiding just behind the ridge to the south of the ravine, however. The wind within the mountain range had not shifted, preventing the fire from jumping onto this side of the mountain. This disappointed Tahari, for she needed the fire to overtake the Draccen soldiers and allow her a clean getaway. Instead she was going to have to lose them and make it to the river ravine and jump in—again.

When Tahari reached the war-torn trail where she had first found Almari after the cannonball attack, she readied herself to jump back into the ravine. The moment she did, a bolt of lightning shot right through her. Tahari was paralyzed with pain, and she hit the ground. After that, everything fell into darkness.

⌐⬦•⬥⌐

When Tahari regained consciousness, slowly, reality began to filter into her senses. As it did, she felt the painful extent of what had been done to her. Her body burned and ached from the blast. Tahari remained still. A conversation was going on around her.

"Why should we not kill her, master?" a raspy voice asked angrily.

"Are you aware of all the trouble that she has caused for us, not to mention what she has done to ruin your rise to power?" another raspy voice asked with intense hatred.

"I am fully aware of the blight that she brings to my new regime, but..." a deep and serious voice spoke calmly. Even still, that voice gave her the chills.

"Master, you of all beings surely do not want this creature to live!" still another gravelly voice interrupted, dripping with malice. "If you do not handle this matter, then I will!" the Draccen soldier continued, growing frustrated. "Why do you linger without action? Are you not the dark lord of legend? I will take care of this one, and as I take my time with her, you can pick up a few tips!" the Draccen soldier snorted, clearly enjoying the thought of what he was planning to do. He stepped over Tahari's body and was kneeling down when her arm suddenly moved. Before the soldier knew what was going on, she had driven a large sword through his groin.

"That's a tip for you!" Tahari hissed, glaring at the soldier. Looking around, she found herself surrounded by the large band of Draccen soldiers and the red-cloaked presence of Lord Jarden himself.

Amused by the display before him, Lord Jarden watched with fascination. The dark lord seemed to take great delight in watching the mouthy Draccen soldier fall to the ground, wailing in pain. He remained still, and his dark gaze told the remaining Draccen soldiers to do the same.

"Y-you stupid-!" the Draccen soldier spat, remaining doubled over on the ground. Tahari slowly rose to her feet and glared at him.

"Me stupid? You are the one who insulted your master, and you did it right in front of him. Then you try to assault me. Don't you know that you never anger those who have more power than you?" she explained with growing anger.

"What are you talking about?" he gasped with a pained expression. Tahari looked at him and shook her head. Tahari slowly walked over to him and leaned close enough for him to hear her clearly.

"In short, you stupid," she replied, mimicking his raspy voice. In the next second, she grabbed the sword still embedded within the Draccen soldier's body, yanked it out, and cut off his head.

Lord Jarden smiled at this proceeding, watching his men cringe in response to what Tahari had done to the insubordinate soldier. He leaned over to the soldier next to him and whispered. "Be sure this night's events are fully documented. This is good material for our training sessions." the soldier nodded but swallowed hard. He clearly was not looking forward to just how Lord Jarden planned to implement this into their training sessions.

"As for you—!" Tahari yelled as she lashed out at Lord Jarden with a speed that she had never known. The Draccen soldiers surrounding her were quick to restrain her, but not before she managed to lodge her sword into the dark lord's left shoulder. When Tahari was pulled back from Lord Jarden, she was surprised that she had lashed out so quickly and with such anger. In that brief moment, Tahari had felt as old as time itself, and the conflict with Lord Jarden was one that needed to be dealt with, immediately. It was as if she had known the ancient evil from a previous time when he had walked the earth.

"Release her," Lord Jarden ordered as he pulled her sword out of his shoulder without a wince. The tone of his voice suggested that this was business as usual. "So... you are the one my soldiers have been telling me about. A slave girl from Akendron," he mused an expression of delight filling his pale face. As he did, a Draccen soldier from within the crowd started to laugh out loud. Filled with rage, Tahari took up one of her hidden daggers and threw it into the crowd without even turning to see her target. Laughter turned into an agonizing wail as the soldier collapsed to the ground. Now the surrounding group of Draccen soldiers watched in humbled silence.

Lord Jarden smiled and tilted his head. "Solarous underestimated you. He never saw you as anything more than a slave—a slave with some guts, perhaps, but still a slave. But then, he never saw his own death coming, either." studying the pale face before her, Tahari suddenly made the connection. The traces of human that formed his body were the remains of Solarous. The other half of this horrid-looking creature had strange scales upon it, making Lord Jarden look almost more reptilian.

"You should be thankful that he did not see the real threat you bring to Andora," Tahari pointed out as she studied her opponent carefully. "If he had known even the smallest portion of what I know, he would have made sure that you could have never returned for a third time." the remark was not taken well as she had hoped. Lord Jarden's eyes turned from black to searing red as anger flared into them.

"Nor did your elfin friend. He let his best friend betray him to his own death. You would think that someone who has lived so long would have known better." Lord Jarden smiled evilly. Rage coursed through her veins, and Tahari charged forward; she intended to rush Lord Jarden, but this time the Draccen soldiers were able to stop her.

"Well now," the dark lord said, with a tone of surprise and realization. "It would seem that you have a bit of a soft spot for this elf." his words were as poison to a wound. Tahari felt as if her true feelings for Leondros had been exposed. It could mean both of their deaths, for Leondros had become her one weakness. Lord Jarden could turn this discovery into his tool and use it against her. As Tahari dropped her gaze to think, she remembered something that restored her confidence.

"It is only right that I have one," she replied calmly as she lifted her head and gave the dark lord a cunning smile. "I am sure you remember a time when there was a race that dwelt within Andora known as the sphinxes?" As Tahari spoke of this race, she watched the look of horrific memory wash over Lord Jarden's face.

"SPEAK NOT OF THEM!" he yelled. Rage and fear radiated from his entire being as he snapped his head back to her. "You know nothing of this, child! BE SILENT!" he commanded as he pointed a bony reptilian finger at her. Tahari's smile remained.

"Remember the name Shamira?" she asked with a cool anger. Lord Jarden had been fidgeting anxiously, but at the mention of this name, he stopped and looked upon her with a new-found fear.

"A vague memory, from long past," he began slowly, his voice riddled with fear. "A most powerful sphinx of legend..." The grandeur of the thought hit him for a moment before he totally dismissed it. "NO! Not possible! She died ages ago." he covered his ears with his hands to keep from hearing her story, but Tahari continued.

"Even still, she left you with a warning, did she not?" Tahari pressed as she eyed the dark lord. As Tahari spoke, her sea-green eyes fixed upon him, and he cowered away from her glare. "When you crossed her path in Lani some eight ages ago, you looked into her eyes, and you saw something. You saw the last battle you will ever fight. You saw the dark and mysterious warrior who would fight you. You saw your end. Am I right?" she said, forcing Lord Jarden to recall his past that predicted his future. Lord Jarden remained silent as he slowly looked up at Tahari with growing realization.

"Impossible! She died, and with her went all her power and promises!" Lord Jarden retaliated in defiant anger. Tahari, however, remained cool and composed.

"Shamira possessed much power, but she was also ordered to protect an elfin child born to a royal family," she continued her story without falter. "She was devout in her mission to protect the child, even after her death. The promises Shamira made still last, even today.

"That child is Leondros Goldendragon," Lord Jarden said in whisper. He seemed to suddenly realize who actually stood before him now. "Shamira?" his voice was small and frail, and his body seemed to tremble just a bit.

"You were behind the order to have Leondros killed, were you not?" Tahari gazed at him sternly. The dark lord seemed to cower in her presence. "I thought so," she said, nodding with certainty. Tahari then began to draw upon a power that she recalled from a past life. Raising her hands toward Lord Jarden, she prepared to put down this force for good.

"RESTRAIN HER!" Lord Jarden yelled as he pointed at her and backed away in fear. His loyal servants were quick to grab Tahari's arms and hold her in place. When he knew it was relatively safe to approach her, he stepped dangerously close. "A sphinx, huh? Well, I remember the last sphinx who tried to fight me in battle." he grabbed her head in his powerful hands with a sudden jerk. An evil look flashed through his searing red eyes, and they were now face to face. "After I break your neck, I will hunt down your boyfriend and anyone else with him."

As he whispered the remaining details of his rancid plan in Tahari's ear, she felt her heart race. Blood pounded in her ears, and she forced her eyes away from his, lowering them to his belt.

"Protector of a prince," he sneered. "You cannot even protect yourself." as Lord Jarden was about to break her neck, Tahari seized the dagger that hung from his belt and drove it into his side. "ARHHHH!" he wailed as the metal blade in his body began to sizzle and smolder.

"Know this: whether by my hand or by one who is even more powerful than I," Tahari said with certainty as she glared at him, "you will meet your end." Tahari grabbed the dagger and yanked it out, prepared for the next and final move, but his loyal minions were there to stop her. They dragged her away from their master and threw her on the ground near a cliff overlooking the river far below. One of the soldiers held her on the ground as he pulled out a very large sword as if just for the occasion.

"Our master has had enough problems with you. This will be the last time you interfer with his plans. Do not hope to leave these mountains alive. But don't worry; your friends will find you," one of them said, "just before they bury you." he raised his sword to behead her and said, "The pieces of you that they find!"

"You first!" Tahari replied, lifting her leg toward her head and kicking the Draccen soldier who held her down. The soldier stumbled forward, and she rolled over, grabbed his sword, and shoved him over the side of the cliff. Jumping to her feet, Tahari turned to the soldiers lined up to fight her. "What? You need his permission to fight me?" she taunted. Angered and infuriated, the whole group charged her. As Tahari fought these Draccen soldiers, she saw Lord Jarden watch for a moment before slipping away.

Thunder shook the mountains surrounding the ruined city of Shoshon, a great thunderstorm now breaking over the war-torn land. Rain was forced down to the earth by intense winds. Hail began to pound the earth. The storm's fury was just beginning and seemed to signal a major battle between good and evil. Many people within Andora had suffered from Lord Jarden's return to power, but like Solarous, Lord Jarden had also underestimated his enemy. The true face of their opponent had revealed herself, but they still did not know what she had in store for them.

Chapter 93

Deeper Understanding

The raging fire roared across the mountain range, and the thunderstorm unleashed its fury over Shoshon, allowing Almari and Elanza to get Leondros out of harm's way unnoticed. They had followed the Life River and traveled some ten miles before stopping to wait for Tahari to catch up to them. Almari knew Tahari's plan was successful, for it had been long since they had seen any Draccen soldiers. They had watched as the Draccen soldiers chased after Tahari, and, with reluctance, they had slipped away into the night.

After they had made camp in a quiet meadow along the river, Leondros regained consciousness. In spite of Almari's explanation and assurance that Tahari would be joining them momentarily, Leondros was concerned for his friend. He partly blamed himself for not being able to do something more, for he feared that something serious was taking place and Tahari was facing it alone. As the minutes turned into hours, Leondros stayed on guard while Almari and the queen slept. More importantly, he watched and waited for his friend's return.

During the long night, Almari awoke to the sound of something moving within the forest. She looked around the camp and found the fire still crackling and Elanza sleeping soundly. Leondros was still watching for Tahari's return at the shoreline. Although not as insightful as Tahari, Almari knew the face of concern well. She watched the prince for a moment, then decided to get up.

"Of all the people I have known in my life, Tahari is one of the few who has ever kept her promises," Almari said as she approached Leondros. He had not moved from the rocky shore since she had fallen asleep a few hours before. "She will be back," Almari offered reassuringly. Leondros watched the river for a moment longer before he looked at her.

"Tahari is out there now facing the evil that had been chasing us, and she is all alone." he spoke quietly as he slowly returned his heavy gaze back to the river.

Almari nodded her head in understanding. She joined his gaze for a moment, hoping that she would see her friend coming, yet there was still no sign of her. Almari thought about what Leondros had said and then thought about what Tahari had done. A faint smile came to her face.

"I pity any force that threatens Tahari's friends," Almari said, her gaze drifting off into the night sky. She looked at Leondros. "She was a true leader tonight. After the bridge exploded and all hell broke loose around us, she somehow found us and told us to ride on and she would go find you. I feared the worst, but she remained calm and hopeful. Not only did she find you, but she made it possible for all of us to get out."

As Almari recalled the evening's events, Leondros found himself overwhelmed by what Tahari had done for them. A weak smile came to his face, for Tahari had already proven that she would go to great lengths for her friends. Tonight was just the latest example.

"You know, there was a time when I feared that Tahari would simply fade away from life," Almari continued thoughtfully. Leondros looked at her with worry. "She has a very old spirit, and she has a passion to live life to its fullest, but there was a time when I feared that she would lose that. On the plantation, we endured so many long years of burden and torture and could imagine no chance for freedom. I saw the light in her eyes slowly diminish with each passing day. She tried her best, but I could see that she was fadin'," Almari said with a saddened tone. Leondros felt his heart ache at the thought of such a thing happening to his friend.

"On the night that most of the slaves of the Tomblock were scheduled for execution, I managed to escape, and I somehow found Tahari afterward. When I found her, I noticed that there was somethin' remarkably different about her. I could not explain it. The light that was missin' from her eyes had returned and was even brighter than before," she said, her tone changing into one of fascination. "I did not know what it was, but I do now. It was you," Almari said softly. "She has never spoken of it, but I have seen it with my own eyes. Tahari was inspired by you. She has always helped those around her, but now she fights even harder for her friends and struggles to keep them alive. She has embraced it—so much so, that she does not give regard for herself."

Leondros was warmed by these words and found himself remembering another person who had done the same thing for him once before.

"I have met only one other like Tahari," Leondros replied softly. "Her father, Reymier, taught us much. I am thankful for the lessons that he taught us, for now they mean even more, knowing that these lessons have not been forgotten." he lowered his gaze thoughtfully. "He would always say that people will walk with you on sunny days, but friends will walk with you on stormy days." he spoke in a reverent whisper, his gaze drifting into the stormy night sky. A warm smile came to his face as he studied the sky. "Tahari has illustrated this point perfectly." he spoke with such conviction that Almari lowered her gaze sadly, understanding why her dear friend risked so much for them.

"Truth be known, the taskmasters on the Tomblock were most cruel to Tahari when she grew up. Maybe more to her than to anybody else who was enslaved in that horrible place. They took away everyone she ever cared about, except for me. It is why she fights so hard to protect us," Almari explained in a soft tone.

"Did anyone ever show her a moment's kindness?" Leondros asked with concern. Almari hesitated a moment.

"All those who showed her any kindness, besides me and Sala, have long since passed into the realm of the dead," she replied sadly, but a hint of a smile lingered. "However, since the walls of the Tomblock have come down, I have seen many people show her kindness." she carried her wistful smile with her as she started back to camp. She stopped partway there and looked back at Leondros. "I am glad that she has a friend like you in her life."

Almari's words caught the elfin prince off-guard, and he watched her return to her place by the fire. Turning his gaze toward the surrounding forest to keep on guard, Leondros found that he could not help but think about his dear friend and wonder if she was all right.

Leondros had felt so undeserving of such a wonderful friend. He knew his debt to her was great, and many times, he had thought over how he was going to repay her kindness. However, with what Almari had told him about Tahari's past and from what Tahari had told him herself, Leondros knew that his debt to her had been paid in full already. All that Tahari required was his friendship. Yet Leondros felt compelled to repay the kindness back anyway. As these thoughts lingered with him, he suddenly remembered something that Almari had told him as they were leaving Shoshon. She had said that the second scroll of the prophecy had been found. He thought about two crucial lines of text from the prophecy. He sensed that these lines of text were meant for someone other than Tahari.

He hurried back to the camp, and reaching for her pack, he began to rummage through it.

"What is it?" she asked with growing concern as she sat up with a start and looked around wildly. Queen Elanza awoke at the sound of the commotion.

"We have overlooked our part on this mission!" Leondros said as he pulled out the two scrolls from her pack, finding the second scroll of the prophecy. After unrolling the age manuscript, he pointed out the crucial lines to Almari and Queen Elanza. The matter was serious and it called all of them into action:

I. *A black veil of death and destruction sweeps over Andora. Many will fall to this peril. *Do not let "one" bear the entire burden.*

Chapter 94

Friends Rescue

The battle with the Draccen soldiers who were desperate to carry out their master's decree to kill Tahari lasted until there was a change in the wind. At that moment, she turned and saw the inferno jump the ridge high above them. It took only seconds for it to charge down the mountainside. It would bear down on top of them within moments. Tahari could not understand how the fire could exist through a torrential downpour, but she pushed the thought aside and ran. Two soldiers rushed toward her with their swords held high over their heads. Tahari charged between them, jumped into the air, and grabbed their swords. When she landed, she drove the swords into their backs. Their screams brought their comrades to their aid. Watching the mob come at her, Tahari shoved the two dying Draccen soldiers at them, causing soldiers to fall over each other and the two dying soldiers. Tahari could feel the heat of the fire bearing down on them. Some of the more intelligent soldiers had seen the fire and fled, but those in the tangled mass were just now noticing the blaze before it consumed them.

Grabbing the dagger that Tahari had stabbed Lord Jarden with and making a mad dash for the cliff's edge, she dove into the ravine with the inferno's flames on her heels. Falling into the dark ravine, she heard the gut-wrenching sounds of Draccen soldiers burning to death. Tahari cared not for these Draccen soldiers, but it still burdened her heart to hear such mournful cries.

After hitting the dark waters of the Life River, Tahari found her world filled with chaos and intense pain. When she finally broke the surface of the water, she gasped for air. Tahari fought to stay on the surface, but her strength was draining away quickly. The Life River would be the death of her if she did not find some way to stay afloat. A log floated nearby. Using what strength she had left, Tahari swam for the log, pain searing in her right shoulder. Tahari lunged for the log and took hold of it. Wrapping her arms around it and resting her weary head against its rough surface, Tahari lifted her eyes toward the burning mountain. She mourned for the burning city of Shoshon. Violence had ruined this once great and beautiful kingdom, and now Leondros's home and family were gone. Tahari ached for his loss, for this place had also once been her home.

"One day, peace will come back to this land," she whispered in a raspy voice. "On my word, this will come to pass." Tahari's voice was weak and her strength was failing quickly, but her promise would not.

Tahari allowed herself to be swept away by the river, the raging thunderstorm tapering into a gentle shower at last. The cool rain soothed her burned skin. She did not know where the river would take her, but she held on to the hope that it would lead her back to her friends. Closing her eyes, Tahari did not feel sleep take hold of her, for her mind was weary and longed to rest.

Hours later, something jostled the log enough to wake her up. Tahari opened her eyes and found that her log had beached itself on a rocky shoreline. Tahari was several miles further downriver, the raging inferno now merely a reddish glow on the horizon. As she tried to get up, she discovered that her body was too weak to move. Adding to this, Tahari saw an arrow protruding from the back of her right shoulder.

"That might leave a mark…" she whispered, laying there a moment longer in hope that her strength would return. Tahari closed her eyes to rest only to sense that a hostile someone was approaching. Quickly, Tahari concealed the dagger, hiding it in the deep layers of her dark battle tunic. A menacing-looking Draccen soldier slowly approached the shoreline from the trees. His reptilian body moved sleekly through the darkness toward her, his dark eyes turned toward her.

"This is truly a sight that my lord should be here to see." as he spoke, he stepped up to Tahari and drew his sword from the leather strap that was tied around his muscular waist. "However, he is not here, so I will have to give him the next best thing. Your head…" he said as he raised his sword over Tahari's neck.

"Torga! Stop!" a woman's rough voice called out. Torga turned around as the woman emerged from the dense tree line. Tahari watched in growing alarm as this new Draccen soldier approached them. Judging from her armor, Tahari guessed that she was a superior in the Draccen army. She only looked at Tahari only for a moment.

"We can use her for leverage against the dark lord," the woman said. "How long will he have use of us once his war with the Andorans is over?" Her words caused Torga to lower his sword reluctantly, but he slowly nodded in agreement. "Bring her to our camp and make sure that none of the others harm her, or I will have *your* head." then with that, the woman Draccen soldier turned and silently disappeared back into the forest.

"I guess we will have to wait on our plans," Torga said half-heartedly. "Oh, let me help you with that," he continued as he ripped the arrow out of Tahari's shoulder. "As I promised my commander, you will be harmed no further," he laughed as he looked at the arrow as though it were a trophy. "I will hang on to this, if you do not mind.

"Just be careful with it; I hear they are quite sharp and hurt like hell," Tahari muttered evenly. He snorted angrily at her remark and grabbed her hair.

"Just know that I will have your head when all is said and done." he then grabbed Tahari's arms and yanked her to her feet. Finding the will to stand again took everything in her being. As Tahari was led to the Draccen soldiers' encampment, she felt her heart sink deep in her chest. Her friends were long gone, and she was to become a bargaining tool between two enemies.

When they finally reached the camp, Tahari was tied to a tall wooden pole with her feet barely touching the ground. As Tahari balanced painfully on her toes, she looked out at all the Draccen soldiers, who glared at her with intense hatred. Many of the soldiers who passed by Tahari cursed at her and would have taken the liberty of putting her out of her misery, but Torga was diligent in following his commander's orders, if only because he wanted to keep his head. As discussions between the Draccen commanders continued about what to do with their leverage in this battle, the attempts on Tahari's life also continued. Torga's orders were turning into a full-time job.

"You would do better to kill me yourself; save yourself the trouble of fighting off your comrades," Tahari reasoned with a tired expression. He stopped and looked at her with surprise.

"We know that you are not alone—you are far more valuable to us alive," he informed Tahari. "Finding you is our first big break. If we can get a hold of the rest of your band, freedom from the dark lord is within our reach. Once we give you and your friends to the dark lord..." Torga's words were cut short as an arrow shot into his chest.

"Like hell!" a familiar woman's voice growled from nearby. Suddenly, arrows rained down from the within forest. Draccen soldiers dropped one by one within the camp, while the Draccen commanders turned from their meeting to see several black-masked warriors charge into the camp from the surrounding forest. The masked warriors drew their swords and began cutting down all who got in their way.

"NO!" the woman Draccen commander yelled out angrily as she drew her own sword. "You will have to go through me to take our prisoner!" she shouted angrily as she charged at one of the masked warriors.

"Very well," one of the masked warriors said and took on the commander. The battle was intense, but the masked warrior was faster and stronger. Of the many advances that the Draccen commander tried against her opponent, the masked warrior merely stepped out of the way. The battle finally ended with the Draccen commander impaled on her own sword.

After that, those who were defending the camp found themselves at the mercy of these utterly mad warriors. They fought with such drive that it was breathtaking, yet there were only three of them.

Once the Draccen had been defeated, Tahari was not sure if she could relax. The masked warriors rushed over to Tahari and cut the rough ropes that burned the skin around her wrists, and she crumpled to the ground. One hurried to her side and pulled her off the ground, allowing Tahari to rest in their lap. Another one came up before her and sank to their knees.

"You do too much for your friends. Let them carry the burden from time to time, for you are just as important as they are." Tahari could not mistake Leondros's voice before her. She looked past the mask to see the welcoming sight of his soulful brown eyes. Taking a deep breath of relief, Tahari hung her head for a moment, thankful they had come.

"I thought you would be long gone by now," Tahari managed weakly, lifting her head as Leondros cut the ropes from her wrists.

"We discovered something after we left," Queen Elanza offered warmly as she took off her mask while she held Tahari in her lap.

"Leondros remembered somethin' in the prophecy that had great meanin' for us," Almari said as she walked up to them, mask in hand. "'Escape will depend on all,'" she quoted from the first scroll of the prophecy.

"Escape from Shoshon will depend on everyone within this party. You do not carry this burden alone, my dear." the queen looked upon Tahari warmly. Then Tahari watched Leondros take off his mask, and as he looked back at her, she could not miss how glad he was to see that she was safe again.

"It also said, 'Do not let "one" bear the entire burden,'" he said with a grateful smile. Tahari smiled, too as she closed her eyes wearily and lowered her head thankfully.

"Thank you," Tahari whispered weakly as she lifted her gaze to look at her wonderful friends. "You are right; this battle will take all of us.

"Tonight, you fought an amazing battle, and in doing so, you saved us all," he reminded Tahari. "Almari and Elanza told me what you did, and it amazes me still. Protecting our loved ones is one of the greatest things we can do." As Leondros gently spoke these words, he lowered his gaze to the ground. "I, too, have watched many friends fade from this life over the centuries, and long ago, I learned to value the time I have with them. I would rather lose ten kingdoms to such peril than lose one friend. Especially one as brave as you," he said as he finally raised his gaze back to Tahari.

She could not miss the warm smile on his face. His words were not only soothing to hear but also made her feel proud and humble at the same time.

"Of all the friends I have known in my lifetime, none of them have gone as far to save me and those dear to me as you have, and for this I am greatly honored," Leondros said reverently.

Tahari smiled at Leondros as she weakly reached over and wrapped her arms around his neck and clung to him. "Thank you for coming back for me," she whispered. He held on to her with no intention of letting her go.

"You are welcome, my friend," he whispered back.

"We had better cut this welcome short if we do not want to dance with any more Draccen war parties on this side trip," Almari said as she eyed their surroundings cautiously. Seeing that Tahari was weak from her ordeal, Leondros picked her up and carried her out of the camp, following Almari and Queen Elanza. Tahari was so relieved that her friends had not only read and followed the scroll's instruction, but also come back to save her. She allowed herself to relax enough to finally sleep.

Chapter 95

Evil's Pursuit

S moke and darkness surrounded Lord Jarden as he stumbled through the forest and out of the mountain range to the west. His dark-red robe was scorched from his brush with the inferno and covered in the soot and ash that the fire had reduced Adarah's beautiful forests to. Anger and pain overwhelmed his thoughts, which dwelt on the meeting between him and the slave-girl Tahari. He cursed as he looked down at the festering wound on his left side. That alone proved it. No one, human or elf or anyone else, could have enchanted a dagger with the power to scorch a being from the realm of Nod. Only a sphinx could do that.

It is just not possible that she is a reincarnated sphinx from the old world! he thought, denying the truth painfully obvious to him. He stopped and looked back toward the ash-covered mountains to the east. He remembered seeing the truth in her sea-green eyes. Worry and uncertainty filled the dark lord, and he felt his plan for Andora begin to crumble around him. *If she is anything like Shamira, then I am going to have a full-scale war on my hands.*

In the midst of his troubled thoughts, Lord Jarden felt the energy of another dark presence nearby. His worries seemed to diminish momentarily.

"Ah, my brother, Baldour. It is good to see a familiar face," Lord Jarden said with immense relief, watching a dark dragon materialize in front of him. Baldour was immense, his wingspan covering the distance of twenty-five horse lengths.

"It is an honor to have found you, my lord," the dark dragon said humbly, lowering his shimmering black head. Lord Jarden lifted his gaze saw that Baldour's rider was equally delighted to have found him. Although the night had no moon, Baldour's scales shimmered with a radiant light so that they almost glowed. The dragon noticed the wound in his master's side.

"I take it that your last appointment did not go according to plan," Baldour offered.

"My plan was torn to pieces and was tossed to the four winds," the dark lord said, shaking his head angrily. Then he looked up at the shimmering black dragon and noticed that he, too, seemed a little distressed. "What about you? You also give the appearance of someone who has something pressing to say," Lord Jarden said as he studied the dragon and wondered what news he had brought him.

"The Draccen band that you charged with capturing the rebels has been slain," Baldour reported half-heartedly.

"WHAT?" Lord Jarden exclaimed, his dark eyes popping wide open with sheer disbelief. "They were supposed to kidnap Tahari and get out of there." his mind raced as he stared at Baldour in disbelief.

"They followed your orders to the letter, my lord, but Tahari's friends came back for her. They tracked those who kidnapped her and followed them back to their camp. They slaughtered the entire Draccen band." Baldour's report greatly disappointed the dark lord. "It also appears that your second attempt to kill the heir to the Goldendragon line has failed. The Draccen troops pulverized Shoshon Valley when they spotted Leondros and several others trying to escape, but the prince eluded them.

"What is it going to take to kill that elf? I have killed him once already. He just keeps coming back." Lord Jarden paced the ground in front of Baldour, deep in thought.

"He must have someone watching over him," the black dragon offered humbly.

"A sphinx from the ancient world," Lord Jarden grumbled, kicking the dirt in front of him.

"That is most unfortunate. Any being that has a sphinx guarding them is truly blessed. They cannot be stopped with such divine protection." Baldour's wisdom about the old world needled Lord Jarden, who threw his hands into the air in complete frustration.

"Of course!" he exclaimed in frustration.

"It is, too, bad that there were not more creatures from the ancient world at your disposal," Baldour offered with sincere disappointment. Lord Jarden stopped suddenly and turned his hooded head toward the black dragon.

"What do you mean, 'at my disposal'?" Lord Jarden asked his curiosity piqued.

"There are many creatures from the ancient world that would prove quite helpful in defeating the elf and his protector," the dark dragon informed his master and then paused to dwell on his knowledge of the sphinxes and the task that needed to be done. "What kind of moral compass governs this sphinx's actions?" Baldour asked, cocking his head.

"She is guided by love and cares deeply for the well-being of others. She was a slave herself—she would see all peoples freed, and if left unchecked, she would raise a rebellion against me." Lord Jarden winced at the thought of his painful encounter with the sphinx.

"How powerful is this sphinx of which you speak?" Baldour asked with growing concern.

"Powerful," the dark lord answered with a disheartened tone, but then he smiled. "Powerful enough, to be sure, but I do not think she is so strong that she can be in two places at once," Lord Jarden said. A plan came to his mind, and the smile grew wider. He tore a piece off his garment, scribbled some instructions upon the fabric, and gave it to Baldour's rider. "Go to the Gortorro Prison with all haste. You will find it on the northern edge of the Serrigen Kingdom in the Barrens. Give them this and have them release one prisoner. Make sure that the prisoner finds the sphinx named Tahari and the rebel band she travels with. Let us see if she can fulfill her oath to that elf and still save her countrymen from annihilation. I will be in contact.

The rider nodded and then put his fingers to his mouth and whistled. Another dragon materialized before them. This one was not as big as Baldour, or as black, but he was *fast*. The rider leapt from Baldour's back just as the other dragon passed by. The rider's experience with dragon-riding was ideal. He could jump from dragon to dragon without them having to slow down or stop. The rider and the other black dragon had already blended in with their surroundings for the dark of night still held its grip upon the land. As they headed into the northern horizon, they vanished into thin air.

"What else do you have planned, sire?" Baldour asked as he looked down at his master.

An evil smile washed across Lord Jarden's face as he thought back to when he had been released from Zendro Isle. He remembered the creature that had stood watch over the isle for a thousand years. It had kept visitors at bay and killed anyone who had tried to get off the island to tell others of what they had found. "I need to return to Zendro Isle; I have a most important meeting awaiting me.

"As you wish, my lord," Baldour replied with a bow of his head.

"This might not stop you, Tahari, but it will certainly slow your quest to reach Rahara. I hope for your sake that you are prepared for what awaits you when you get there," Lord Jarden said as he climbed on the back of the mighty black dragon and took the dark night sky with all haste.

Chapter 96

"For the Love of One, For the Love of All"

When Tahari awoke again, she found herself in a camp set on a grassy cliff overlooking a beautiful forested valley. A river flowed gently nearby, and in the distance, a waterfall thundered. Lifting her gaze, she saw that evening was slowly approaching, which caused Tahari to wonder where this place was and where her friends were. Or had she dreamt her rescue? Then Tahari saw Queen Elanza make her way out of the forest, readjusting her slightly torn and dirty gown. She was muttering under her breath, which made Tahari smile.

"Try to find a moment by yourself where you can conduct your business, and something has to jump out at you and scare the life out of you…" Her mutterings carried on the gentle breeze that cut through the warm night. As Elanza looked up and realized that Tahari was awake, her face brightened.

"Well, it is about time that you returned to the land of the living." her voice was filled with genuine concern.

"How long was I out?" Tahari asked groggily.

"About three days." her words awakened her fully.

"Three days!" Tahari sat up to try to collect her thoughts and get to her feet, but before she could, Elanza gently laid a hand on her shoulder.

"Please, there is no need to do anything but recover your strength. When we found you, you were exhausted and wounded. Your body needed time to heal and replenish its strength," she reassured Tahari. Queen Elanza made sure she remained sitting as she examined Tahari's wounded shoulder. "Well, imagine that," she remarked with surprise. "You carry a great gift. The arrow wound has completely healed."

Tahari smiled in reply and looked at the lush landscape that surrounded them.

"Where are we?" Tahari asked.

"We are on the Adaran/Serrigen border. We arrived here earlier today. Leondros and Almari decided that we should take a day to eat and rest before leaving the safety of Adarah. He said that we are at least six days from Rahara, and the temple city of Sion is hidden within its jungles.

Understanding the long road ahead, Tahari nodded. She looked around the camp for Leondros and Almari.

"They are both on lookout. We had so many close encounters with Draccen war parties that it made us all uneasy. Leondros does not want any company following us into the Serrigen."

"Wise choice," Tahari said, turning her gaze toward the queen's. She was staring at Tahari with a wistful smile. "What is it?" she asked.

"I never got the chance to thank you for saving my life back in Shoshon Valley." sincerity filled her voice. Tahari bowed her head humbly, but there was something else. "But then you really saved all of us." she stopped for a moment to soak in the grandeur of Tahari's deed. "I have never seen someone so concerned, so passionate about their friends that they would go so far for them. You accept them, flaws and all. Why do you do it?" she asked.

"It is the way I would want to be treated," Tahari replied simply. Studying the older woman's creamy white face, Tahari sensed there was something more that Queen Elanza wanted to ask her. "Please, do not hesitate. Speak," she said.

"There is something very special about you." Elanza spoke with energy. "All your wondrous abilities aside, you have such strength of belief that it has empowered those around you with hope and courage." tears glistened in Elanza's eyes, and they sparkled in the campfire's light. "My world was shattered the night Lord Jarden came to power. He used my son to betray and kill Leondros and... my family." her voice was riddled with bitterness and grief. She was silent for a moment, her face filled with great sadness. "Sala reminded me that you were chosen to find the ancient warrior Farro. He said that Farro would be the only one who could stop Lord Jarden and destroy him for good." as she spoke, her eyes brightened with hope. "I do not know where I would start such a search, but as I look at you, I am reassured. Whatever it is that guides you gives me hope. One day when Lord Jarden is defeated and is no more, we will have our home back and our loved ones will be safe." as she spoke, Tahari could feel her revived spirit.

"Thank you, my Queen, but I am but a messenger on this journey. Your praise belongs with Adalai, for it is he that aids us in this battle. My strength in this quest comes from my friends," Tahari admitted honestly.

"You are a warrior like I have never seen. You have no weakness."

Tahari smiled sadly and shook her head. She decided to be totally truthful. "I wished for death after I was kidnapped by the Draccen soldiers," she said sadly as she revisited the feelings of dread that had overwhelmed her. "I believed that you all had followed my wishes and headed north to safety. I realized then that having you all in my life, since my time as a slave, was a dream come true. Knowing that my friends were gone, I felt that my mission was over. Death was close," Tahari said, watching the horror come into Elanza's face. "Seeing you all come back for me was a sight that will remain with me for the rest of my days," she recalled, tears coming to her eyes and a smile to her lips. Elanza's smile returned as well as she wrapped her arms around Tahari and held her tightly for a moment. Then she pulled back and looked at Tahari with wistful smile.

"I see something else, too, and I am glad," the old queen said sweetly. "Leondros never looked more relieved than when we found you. He has barely slept since we took you from that camp. He wants to protect us and you. He loves you." Tahari lowered her gaze, feeling greatly overwhelmed, but the old queen merely took Tahari's hand and found her gaze again. "Do not wait and keep your feelings for him a secret. You already know how short life can be, even for an elf." Tahari was reminded of his death. She nodded and pondered these things as the queen rose and bade her a good night.

Tahari rose, too, and wandered into the forest. She followed a path that led her to a grass-covered cliff overlooking the dark horizon to the east. Although the night was warm, Tahari felt a cool breeze stirring. She lost herself in nature's calm surroundings, for they brought her peace from all that weighed on her mind: the mission to protect the others, the quest to find the scrolls that would lead to Farro, and now her feelings for Leondros. Closing her eyes, Tahari cleared her mind of all her worries and focused on what Sala had insisted that she learn: the lines of instruction from the prophecy. Tahari meditated heavily on the next part, for she felt that a time was fast approaching when she would need to call on her powers:

II. The armies of darkness will move in to surround the forces of good. *Learn the power of the sphinx ancestry in thyself.

Time passed without her realization as Tahari meditated on Shamira, her powers, and how she used them. At some point, Tahari realized that by meditating upon her and the other sphinxes, she could tap into their vast mystical world, the power they possessed, and most importantly, how they governed themselves in the use of such great power. Tahari now understood why her ancestors fought to keep this power secret from those who would use it for harm against others. It connected all living things. This power was available to all sphinxes who could train themselves to calm their minds and tap into it. The greater powers were achieved only by the grand sphinxes. Those powers, of course, required even more focus and training. As she focused on unlocking the mystery that surrounded her powers and finding out what they were, Tahari sensed someone approaching her. Realizing who it was broke her concentration.

"Tahari?" The familiar voice reached down into her deep thoughts. With closed eyes, Tahari smiled as Leondros approached her where she sat on a rock overlooking the forested valley below. She sensed concern.

Tahari took a deep breath and opened her eyes. "Do not worry, I am all right," she replied. He stopped for a moment and looked surprised.

"You knew my thoughts," he said with a smile. Tahari nodded slowly with a smile. Leondros stood near her rock and lowered his heavy gaze to the ground as if in deep thought.

"There is something else on your mind. What is it?" Tahari asked encouragingly.

"I have not had the chance to ask what happened after you pulled me out of Shoshon Valley and sent us on our way to Rahara," Leondros said with a tone of curiosity and a hint of worry. Tahari looked at him for a moment and managed a deep breath before she began her tale.

"I met up with Lord Jarden and some of his Draccen minions," she began slowly, watching alarm fill his soulful brown eyes. "He has taken full possession of Solarous's body and is now flesh and blood once more. He was testing me to see just who he was up against. He had correctly reasoned that there was more to me than even Solarous knew. Solarous never believed that I would be much of a force to contend with," Tahari said.

"You proved Solarous wrong and put fear into Lord Jarden, did you not?" Leondros asked with a hopeful smile. A faint smile came to her face.

"I reasoned that if Solarous had known Lord Jarden's true purpose here, then we would never have lived to see a third age of darkness." Tahari's words caused a smile to grow on Leondros's face. "Angered by this, Lord Jarden insulted you for not knowing that Alon-Settie was planning on betraying you." A hurt expression washed over her elfin friend's face. "After that, I tried to attack him and it was revealed that I harbor deeper feelings for you than I was letting on. I could not let him use you against me, so I told him it was only right that I do, for I was the sphinx chosen to protect you." As Tahari spoke these words, a soft smile came to Leondros's face as he continued to listen with interest. "It was about then that he tried to kill me but succeeded only in getting a dagger in his side. I found that he is most fearful of the sphinx Shamira." With this, Tahari reached into a deep pocket of her robe and pulled out the dagger she had stabbed Lord Jarden with.

"You actually were able to wound him with this?" Leondros asked with surprise.

"Apparently, I am able to enchant weapons that can be used against him, even his own," Tahari said as she handed him the dagger. "Keep this; I sense you may need it on the road ahead." Leondros looked at it with an excited smile and then lifted his gaze to her.

"It was a risky move. Thank you." He studied her face and saw her concern for what Lord Jarden had gleaned from their confrontation. A look of understanding washed over his face and he wrapped his arms around her. "Tahari, you need not worry. Your feelings for me only add to the fear that Lord Jarden now has for us.

"I guess love is the best armor anyone can bring with them into battle," Tahari reasoned as she lifted her head from his shoulder and looked at him warmly. Leondros smiled and nodded. They remained like that for a moment, staring at each other, holding each other. Tahari was comforted by the warmth of his presence. She smiled as she reached up, touched his cheek, and moved her head closer to his. A commotion erupted from the camp. "Save this moment for later," she whispered as she looked at him.

"Definitely," Leondros said, returning the smile. He looked at her for a moment with a relieved expression. "The life of royalty in Adarah is not easy when it comes to love interests." He shook his head wearily. "I watched Dreyhon as he went through it. Too, much public gossip and meddling. Since my lifestyle never kept me close to home, I never really experienced it. Zation did tell me once that the life ahead of me holds great adventure, but there would be love, and I would find it. I would get to experience it far from what our family knew." Tahari was saddened that Leondros had seen so little love but pleased that it was happening now as his sister predicted.

Leondros took her head in his hands and rested his forehead against hers. "When I first met you, I was overwhelmed to learn that you were a sphinx of the ancient world and that you had already saved my life. I felt blessed that you were my friend. Now I am overwhelmed again that you are my friend and more." Tahari closed her eyes and took in his words, trying to hold on to this moment forever. He held her close for a moment longer before another noise carried up from the camp. It was time to go.

Opening their eyes, they looked at each other with an expression of promise before they allowed themselves to hurry away. Taking her hand, Leondros helped her off the large rock, and together they hurried back through the forest to camp.

Back at camp, they saw an angered Almari holding on to a dark-haired, wiry-looking man dressed in ragged sackcloth. His appearance would have stopped anybody cold. Blood soaked through the rough cloth against his back from repeated whippings. He was sunburnt and worn out. His dark eyes were wide with terror. Tahari and Almari looked at each other with horrible realization.

"What is going on?" Leondros asked Almari as he looked between her and the frightened man.

"I found him lurkin' around the trail to our camp. I grabbed him before he could get away," Almari said, eyeing him with suspicion.

"Please, do not kill me! I meant no harm," he squeaked. He folded his hands and prayed for them to spare him, wildly searching for someone who would hear his story. He saw their weapons and grew even more nervous. As Tahari studied him, she knew full well what he had been through and felt empathy for him.

"Let him speak. You have seen the inside of a prison work camp, have you not?" Tahari asked calmly. The slave looked at Tahari with surprise, but he nodded. "Please, calm yourself. We will not kill you. You are safe with us. Now, tell us your name and where you are from," she said gently as she nodding slowly and continued to analyze him.

"My name is Bakari of Mansee; I am from the kingdom of the Shandel. I was taken from my home a little more than two weeks ago in the dead of night by these despicable beasts called Draccens and given to the dragon Baldour, who brought me to this horrible camp on the border between the Serrigen Kingdom and the Barrens. There are thousands of us there. Many come from the other kingdoms, and all of us are prisoners of the one they call Lord Master Jarden. He forces us to manufacture weapons for the war he is planning against the rebel bands that are forming against him. Food is scarce, water is limited. Many have died already from the guards' brutality, but as we grow weaker, more of us are in danger of following the first ones who were brought there." As Bakari spoke, those who listened exchanged looks of disbelief and horror.

"You were released to bring us a message," Tahari gleaned as she analyzed this slave's features. He looked at her with surprise.

"H-how did you know?" his voice trembled as he spoke.

"You do not bear the wounds of someone tryin' to escape with their life," Almari retorted angrily, glaring at him.

"What does this look like to you?" he demanded as he turned his back to them to reveal three bloody scabs across his back.

"Punishment, but not for trying to escape," Tahari said, pointing to Almari. Reluctantly, she pulled up her black leggings to reveal jagged scars that had torn her skin from above her knee to her ankles.

"This is what happens when you stumble and fall into barbed wire in an attempt to flee. This was before they dragged me back to the plantation by the barbed wire and then used it to whip me as punishment for my escape." Almari's voice was low and filled with the graphic memory of that horrible night. Shivers passed down Tahari's spine. Silence filled the air when she finished as everyone slowly looked back at Bakari. He looked between Tahari and Almari and decided not to trick them any further. He dropped his head and nodded slowly.

"I was released to deliver a message to the one called Tahari. Lord Jarden waits for you at Gortorro Prison. You are to come and prove that you are powerful enough to take him on and protect the elfin soul that was entrusted to you. If you succeed, he will give you your life, the elfin life that you protect, and the lives of all those in the prison." A rush of anxiety washed over Tahari and was quickly replaced by anger.

"If I do not agree to these terms, what then?" Tahari asked, glaring at Bakari. A real and terrible fear came over his face.

"Then Lord Jarden will kill one person every hour until you show up for your duel with him. He says that you are supposed to be accompanied by the elf, Leondros Goldendragon. If you should choose to come alone, he will still kill those within the prison." Bakari's message brought the one thing Tahari feared most from accidentally letting on that she loved Leondros.

"When is this meeting supposed to take place?" Tahari asked reluctantly as she crossed her arms and looked down upon the burnt orange dirt in front of their campfire.

"Midnight, tomorrow," Bakari answered firmly.

"How in name of all things holy are we supposed to reach this camp by midnight tomorrow night? Even if we start now, it will still take us three days! The Serrigen Kingdom lies between us and the Barrens. You cannot just stroll through those dark mountains!" Queen Elanza exclaimed angrily as she glared at the prison-weary man. Tahari put a calming hand on the queen's shoulder to keep her from attacking him.

"Lord Jarden wishes it. He said that if you do not want these people to die, you will do as he tells you." The man's words enraged Almari, who was already fuming.

"You lying sack of..." Almari growled as she saw the terrible position this put Tahari in and was about to drive Bakari to the ground with her fist.

"I speak truth!" Bakari cried out as he backed away from an enraged Almari. "I had to come, or they were going to impale my wife in front of me and my children!" His words caused everyone to go still in the camp. Although Tahari sensed worry in his voice as he delivered his message, the situation was much more serious than they had realized.

"They have children there?" Queen Elanza's green eyes went wide with horror, her face paled. Bakari nodded sadly. Tahari lowered her head to think of her next course of action.

"Tahari, you cannot take me with you. It will be playing into his plans. There is a trap awaiting us," Leondros reasoned. Tahari saw concern in his brown eyes, but it was more for her sake than his. As Tahari stood pondering, she glimpsed Bakari fidgeting nervously as he lowered his gaze to the ground.

"Lord Jarden should be given a taste of his own medicine. Give him a test and see how he fares!" Almari spoke up with her usual spunky attitude. Her words gave Tahari an idea as she studied the differences between Almari's appearance and Leondros's. She then thought of what powers she had at her disposal and saw a grand opportunity.

"Then that is what we will do," Tahari said. Everyone looked at her in disbelief. "There are other ways to reach the Gortorro Prison without having to walk." She looked at the group that surrounded her. The people who looked back at Tahari looked a little puzzled.

"Care to enlighten us on what this other way is?" Queen Elanza asked with a tone of doubt.

"My way." Tahari looked at her friends with a sly smile. "There is a special trick that my people could do when they needed to cover great distances in a short amount of time. You will see this when I send two of you to Mt. Somerset. I have seen, too, many slaves suffer in my lifetime to let any more perish. I will accompany Bakari back to Gortorro Prison. I accept Lord Jarden's challenge, but we will go on *my* terms. Is that *clear*?" Tahari announced to the group as she turned back to Bakari. He nodded slowly as he watched her with uncertainty, but there was hope in his dark-brown eyes.

Looking back at everyone else, Tahari received the same acknowledgment. As Tahari looked over at Leondros, Almari, and Queen Elanza, she found herself feeling guilty that she had not practiced more with her sphinx powers. Tahari looked at them with apology. "You will have to trust me about what I have planned for you,.

"We already do," Almari and Leondros said in unison.

Queen Elanza looked at him and Tahari with raised eyebrows and shook her head reluctantly as if to *Young love.*

In the moments that followed, Bakari gave them the vivid and grim details of what awaited them in Gortorro Prison. As he explained the extent of the suffering and cruelty that went on there, Tahari distantly recalled something similar. She thought it was a memory of the Tomblock, but this memory was much older and very different. Tahari sensed that it was from her past life—something that Shamira had experienced just before her death. Tahari felt it as if it were her own memory as if she had been there herself. Tahari shuddered from Bakari's account of hatred, horror, and cruelty that dwelt within that horrible place.

"Tahari?" Leondros asked, breaking through her thoughts. His voice was filled with concern. Everyone looked at Tahari with wonder. It took her a moment to find her voice to speak.

"I know of what Bakari speaks. The sphinxes endured the same savage cruelty; Shamira was among those who died in a camp like Gortorro," Tahari said, explaining that she was Shamira, reincarnated. "One lifetime is a lifetime too many to have to endure such atrocity," she said, fighting the chilling memories that now haunted her mind. "This has to end!" Tahari looked at everyone with anger and determination.

"If there is a place worse than the Tomblock, then Lord Jarden has decided to taunt the wrong people with such a cold-hearted trick. This will end!" Almari promised, stepping up to Tahari and putting a reassuring hand on her shoulder. "What is your plan?" she asked her with determination.

Tahari and Almari exchanged expressions of fueled enthusiasm. Now was the chance for two slaves to turn the tables on the likes of the Tomblock. They pulled out an old map of Andora that Queen Elanza thankfully had upon her person and planned a course of action that would not only save Tahari from a horrible choice but would also save the many who had become prisoners of war.

Chapter 97

Just Betrayal

The next day was spent preparing for the aftermath of the prison break. The timing would be essential to the plan succeeding. When evening finally settled upon the land, it brought relief from the hot day, but it also brought hints of severe thunderstorms later in the night. This would help in concealing their escape.

As Tahari and Bakari walked from Mt. Somerset in the Barrens through the scorched red sands of its deserts and moved west toward Gortorro Prison, he looked at her in amazement.

"Remind me again how you got us here?" he asked with disbelief. "One minute we were on the forested cliffs that overlooked some of Adarah's lush rainforest, and the next we were walking through the orange sands that surrounded the base of Mt. Somerset."

Tahari smiled as she reached her hand in front of her and moved her arm in a single wide arcing motion.

"It is one of many hundreds of tricks that were used by my people. It was especially useful during times of war." Then within the motion of her circle, a ring of mist formed from the dry air. As the ring materialized, one could see through it to the Serrigen mountains and the dark horizon.

Suddenly, something appeared that Tahari was not prepared for.

Gortorro Prison was before them, its flaming torches mounted at each guard tower outlining its features against the rugged earth that it sat upon. "Let's do this," she mumbled as she found the courage to face this new fear. A moment later, Tahari and Bakari passed through the ring of mist and appeared hundreds of miles from where they had been only moments before.

"Extraordinary!" Bakari exclaimed in delight as he looked around him.

"Once everyone locked within Gortorro is safe from Lord Jarden, I will share that sentiment," Tahari replied.

The wiry-looking man's excitement drained with sudden realization, and they quietly ascended a large cliff that overlooked the desert valley. Shrubs and cacti were scattered scarcely throughout the area. Gortorro Prison's walls were constructed of weathered wood and reinforced with barbed wire and thorn bushes. What they hid were thousands of people.

"Why do we stop?" Bakari asked.

"I need to get a feel for what I am dealing with. Besides, we are hours early," she reminded him with a sly smile, turning her attention back to the prison below. As he nodded, Bakari's face still wore a look of confusion.

"I do not hold any judgments about whom you brought to assist you in this mission, but wouldn't your friend have been more beneficial in what we are about to tackle?" he asked with uncertainty. "They do have extensive experience in dealing with prisons, it would seem," he said as if to hint that she should rethink her plan.

Momentarily ignoring his questions, Tahari's focus moved to a shadowy pit just below their position. Tahari was hit with the reality of something much more sinister.

The brutality inflicted on men, women, and children caused Tahari's heart to sink into the depths of her stomach. Then as a bitter, foul stench drifted up to her nose and hung there, she felt her stomach churn.

The night sky had clouded over by the time they reached the cliff, but lightning cut a sharp streak in the sky overhead as if to expose the true atrocity of Lord Jarden's regime. Tahari and Bakari were witnesses to hundreds of sunbaked corpses that had been maimed, dismembered, and cleaved by the Draccen guards. Tahari closed her eyes and turned her head away, in hopes of blocking these graphic images from her mind. Instead, these disturbing images brought back a flood of horrible memories, memories from Shamira's life. Tahari crumpled to her knees and held her head in her hands as images roared into her mind in a heated frenzy.

Many days of atrocities flashed before her mind's eye in seconds. Tahari saw a compound of brick and barbed wire. Generals and soldiers from the realm of men cursed, screamed, and beat the sphinx people. Enraged demands were shouted. The sphinx people trembled and wept bitterly, but they resolutely refused to answer the generals' and soldiers' demands. Their rage exploded, and Tahari's people's blood spilled, mingling with the orangish-red desert sand. Some sphinxes ran for their lives only to be savagely cut down and slain. A few remained standing in spite of the horror that came at them. Fewer still stood in the place of others and were brutally beaten to death or set on fire.

Then Tahari saw a vague image of Shamira: a dark beauty with a torn and dirty burgundy robe and desert-brown eyes that burned with anger. She yelled something from amongst the crowd she was with. Tahari watched as she took down several soldiers as well as a general before succumbing to her own wounds. She watched Shamira's death as people from outside of the gates stormed into the compound to stop the madness. Screams filled the air as Tahari forced these terrible images from her mind. Atrocities that plagued their world some two thousand years ago were now beckoning to be remembered. Tahari felt that Shamira's life held great meaning and needed to be remembered.

"Tahari?" Bakari's voice reached her ears as though from far away. His hands were on her shoulders, and he was shaking her. "Wake up!" he demanded with fear in his voice, now sounding close by. Opening her eyes and looking around, Tahari saw the relatively calm night that still clung close to them.

"Dear God," she gasped as Tahari found herself almost too weak to even kneel. A whole realm of emotions hit her: fear, pain, anger from what had transpired.

"What is wrong?" Bakari searched her face in the dim light, hoping to understand. His strong hands held Tahari's arms tight, thus keeping her from falling to the ground again. She paused to regain control of her emotions and senses before she answered.

"I am beginning to remember my sphinx heritage. I am a reincarnated sphinx from the ancient world. She was called Shamira. I inherited her powers, but something else came with it," Tahari explained weakly.

"Her memories?"

"Yes. I saw the death of my people…" Tahari managed, her head still aching from the memory of what had happened so long ago. "But there was also the reason we need to keep fighting for ours. We need to keep Lord Jarden from doing the same thing to our people."

As she caught her bearings and her breath, Tahari recalled Bakari's questions from before, which suggested he doubted her and those dear to her. Anger filled her, and she rose up to face him and look him dead in the eye.

"Everyone I have traveled with on this mission is equally qualified for what awaits us in there, but my decision remains. The only thing we need to concern ourselves with is what *we* need to do to pull this thing off. Are we agreed?" Tahari asked him with a tone of authority. He nodded quickly. Tahari heard the thunder rumble and lightning lit up the western horizon once more.

"Your people should not have been forgotten. I wish they were with us now," he offered kindly.

"They are not forgotten, and they are with us still," Tahari corrected him, eyeing him with continuous suspicion. Then she turned her gaze back to the prison below.

With midnight nearly upon them, Tahari and Bakari made their way down to the prison. Tahari took the time to cover her head with a black-and-blue scarf that she had fashioned out of her cloak to hide her hair and face. Just before they reached Gortorro's outskirts, Bakari took a hold of her arm.

"Tahari, wait," he said with urgency.

Turning back to him, Tahari saw something in his suntanned face that worried her. Lightning flashed overhead, and she caught the nervousness in his dark-brown eyes. Tahari narrowed her gaze as the wind blew through his thick, dark hair. His real reason for acquiring their help was about to reveal itself.

"You are fearful. Why?" she asked.

"I need to speak truth to you," he said nervously. "I do not have family in Gortorro Prison, but there are children in there that are suffering. My family is already dead. Lord Jarden killed our parents and children just before he sent me to find you." He told his story in a gush. "They were killed to remind me of what would happen to me if I did not deliver you.

"You hold your life in more regard than that of your family?" Tahari spoke with a tone of anger.

"No...I-I have a young wife. They did not know she was my wife at the time they planned to entrap you, but they knew that she was of importance to me when they took us from our village in the Shandel. They used that against me because I refused to betray you. They want me to betray you now to save her life, but I have seen the hope that you bring to those around you, and I am encouraged to help you win back our freedom. I will do whatever I can to see that Lord Jarden's rule is undone." As Bakari spoke, though his words suggested defiance, his voice quivered with fear and revealed his terror of turning on Lord Jarden. Tahari's stare at him did not waver. Leaning closer, she bore her gaze into his soul.

"I know that you will betray me, regardless," Tahari whispered angrily. Alarm filled his eyes. "Lord Jarden has entrapped you into his service. If Adalai grants me the ability, I will see if I can sever that hold."

Whatever the truth of the situation, it was too late now. An eerie feeling of danger crept all around them. Evil was closing in when all peace and serenity around Tahari vanished.

A stench-filled wind washed over Tahari as a heavy force drove her to the ground and pinned her there. A second later, a huge black dragon materialized over Tahari, its sharp black claws digging into the sand around her, imprisoning her. The dragon looked down on Tahari with its huge, red eyes.

Looking over at Bakari, it said in a deep, resonating voice, "Master Jarden will be pleased that you brought him the sphinx Tahari." As he spoke, his razor-sharp teeth glistened with saliva. "However, you did not bring Leondros Goldendragon. This does not bode well for your wife. The judgment will be left to Master Jarden to decide, but do not be hopeful." Bakari's expression filled with fear as he looked down at Tahari.

The dragon looked back down at Tahari with a sneering smile and said, "Come." She could see the lightning rip through the stormy sky through the thin flesh of his black wings as he spread them wide. "You have a meeting with Master Jarden." The dragon wrapped a giant claw around her, snatching her from the sandy earth and flying her inside Gortorro Prison. Bakari hung his head and made the long walk on foot alone.

Chapter 98

Duel Within Gortorro

Tahari was dropped unceremoniously unto the sunbaked earth of the prison yard, and her breath rushed from her body as pain coursed through it. Before she could move again, a Draccen soldier pulled her up by her hair, ripping off the scarf that was still tied around her head, revealing her face to all who looked on at Baldour's newest find. He held onto her tightly.

The scene around Tahari was hauntingly familiar. Barbed-wire fences decorated the wooden border of this dreadful camp. Barracks and warehouses were made of weathered gray wood. She had just escaped her own prison camp not long ago, and Shamira's memories were bubbling up, adding another layer of horrible familiarity. The smell of death was mixed with those of dirt, sweat, and human waste and carnage that ran rampant amongst its inhabitants. Even the swift winds from the incoming thunderstorm did little to clear it out.

Prisoners stared at Tahari with empty lifeless expressions, and her lungs refused to work, seeing them. The weary eyes that watched her looked out from bodies that seemed to have lost their will to live. The soiled, ripped clothing these poor souls wore mirrored the trauma they had been through. They saw her as another poor soul brought here to die. Then Tahari heard something even more dreadful.

"Look who has decided to join us!" His painfully irritating voice was not hard to miss. As Lord Jarden walked out to the center of the prison yard, his dark-red cloak danced in the breeze. The metallic black designs and symbols stitched on the sash that ran down the red robe beneath the cloak added to Tahari's sinking feeling. His rise to power was close to complete. Stopping, the dark lord turned to her and looked out from under the large red hood that was draped over his head; his face was in shadow, but his red eyes pierced through the darkness. He hardly looked at Tahari; his focus was on the soldier behind her. He motioned with a slight nod of his head for the soldier to do something. Then the Draccen soldier who gripped the back of her neck shoved her forward and drove Tahari to her knees.

"Kneel before your lord!" his deep voice ordered harshly. On her hands and knees, Tahari looked up at Lord Jarden. He looked back at her with a smug expression. Everything within her was repulsed.

Bringing one of her black leather boots forward unseen, Tahari sprang up into the air, flipped her body backward, and landed behind the Draccen soldier. Acting quickly, she disarmed him and ran him through with his own sword. The soldier didn't even have time to call out in pain. Tahari leaned in close to the dying soldier.

"He is NOT my lord!" she corrected him. A moment later, the life within the Draccen soldier faded, and he crumpled to the ground.

Stepping coolly past the body of the soldier, Tahari looked at Lord Jarden. "Now that we have that clarified—you wanted to see me?" she said calmly. Lord Jarden looked at her with slight anger, but there was something in his eyes that seemed to bore right through her.

"What is missing from this picture?" he asked, glaring at Tahari. "Or should I say who?"

"I did not come alone. My friends are with me," Tahari replied simply.

"Ahh, but the condition was for you to bring only one other person. Leondros Goldendragon. Do you know what happens around here when you do not listen?" Worry filled Tahari's heart as he spoke these words. He snapped his fingers.

Instantly, a Draccen guard emerged from a guard tower with a woman who began screaming and struggled to escape from her captor. Her brown hair, wild and loose, caught the wind the moment she was brought outside the wooden barracks. The simple sackcloth she wore was cut off at the shoulders and below the knees, revealing sunburnt skin.

A second later, Bakari tried desperately to tear through the crowd to reach the woman. His rescue attempt was cut short by another prison guard who restrained him easily.

"No, master! She brought the elf! I have seen him, and he lingers near!" Bakari shouted at Lord Jarden.

"Bakari, you do not belong to that monster. You owe him nothing! You are a free man!!" Tahari yelled at him, trying to keep him from saying too much. The enslaved man could not hear her as he watched his young wife about to have her throat sliced open. The soldier behind her was dressed almost like a hangman, with a dark leather hood covering his beastly head. Tahari could still see that he had but one eye, and that eye watched for his master's signal.

"Master, please! Leondros waits on the cliff overlooking the camp. He is there now!" Bakari beseeched Lord Jarden in a last attempt to save his wife. Lord Jarden watched Tahari in silence. The only sounds at that moment were the coming thunderstorm, the dirt and sand being shifted by the wind, and the bitter weeping of Bakari's wife.

"I warned you," Lord Jarden said with a serious glare, pointing to Tahari. She responded with her own glare. He nodded. Bakari looked from Lord Jarden to Tahari, then to the Draccen soldier behind his wife. The large soldier quickly pulled out a large silver blade that gleamed in the torchlight. He pressed its sharp blade against the tanned skin of the woman's neck, and she closed her eyes, tears running down her dirty face.

"NO!" Bakari wailed as he managed to knock his captor backwards, grabbed his sword, and attempted to slay Tahari. "You want to me to betray the sphinx, so be it!" he yelled frantically at Lord Jarden as he moved with reckless desperation. His Draccen captor was quick to regain his bearings and his hold on Bakari. The wiry slave continued to fight the soldier.

As the excitement from this outburst subsided and attention went back to the slave woman's execution, the gathered crowd could only watch as the large Draccen soldier who held onto her dropped the shiny blade and released the fear-stricken woman. Only those who were standing near could have heard the whisp that cut through the air. The woman took her chance at freedom and ran over to Bakari, who was quick to wrap his arms around her when his own captor released him in shock. The masked soldier was left lying in the reddish sand, dead from the arrow that had been driven through his forehead.

"You did this!" Lord Jarden accused Tahari, angrily turning to her. She looked at the dark lord for a moment, aware of the throngs of people who looked on. Surprise and amazement replaced the dead expressions that had emanated from their faces.

"See, he is here," Tahari replied calmly. "Leondros is the only elf I know who could have made that shot." her defiance tore at Lord Jarden.

"You push me too far!" he spat angrily, clenching his fists. Then he seemed to pull himself together, and another sinister look came to his face. "You will never leave this place. What I have in store for you… you will wish you had obeyed me. Look out there and tell me what you see." he motioned toward the stormy southwest horizon.

Cautiously, Tahari turned her gaze to the southwest. She could see only the darkened desert beyond the barbed-wire fence. Tahari looked back at him confused.

A smile came to his face. "Look again." this time he signaled a guard in one of the south towers. The guard lit an arrow on fire and shot it into the night. The reaction that followed took her breath away. Moments later, one by one, torches lit up across the southern horizon. It seemed like a wildfire stretching across the desert floor. A massive Draccen army waited there for their lord's next signal. "Because of your defiance, I will have them run over this place and rip it apart. Every man, woman, and child will be laid waste for the vultures." he sneered as he pointed to all those who watched on helplessly. "They will have *you* to thank for their fate because you would not give up one lone elf.

"Remember those words, for they will forever haunt you," Tahari said knowingly. Lord Jarden was silenced by the remark for a moment and then began to laugh hysterically.

"You think you can just walk out of here?" he said when his laughter had subsided. Tahari smiled. "No, I think not," he said with an even tone of certainty. "You will pay. Of this, I am certain." his voice was low and menacing. For a moment it seemed like he was going to attack her in hand-to-hand combat, but he merely stood still, closed his eyes, and stretched out his arms, palms up. Lightning flashed overhead, lighting up the whole prison camp. The people's expressions were filled with horror, almost as if they knew what was going to happen next.

Thunder shook the earth as it blended with the bellowing of a dragon. Then, a large double-headed dragon materialized in front of Lord Jarden, its angry gazes finding Tahari as its target. It spread its large wings, which took up almost the entire path between the barracks as if to leap into the sky. The beast was double the size of the black dragon that had brought her to this place. If its claws were not dangerous enough, this massive beast had sharp black barbs protruding from its heads, necks, tail, and leg joints. This must be the Gradon, the last of a race from the ancient world. Shamira had to be familiar with it. It was a deep emerald blended with the black that ran along its back and wings, with a band of light green along its underbelly. The dragon-like creature eyed Tahari, growls rumbling deep within its throats before emerging as thunderous roars. Tahari looked back at Lord Jarden, who seemed very pleased.

"Coward," she remarked. "Not strong enough to take on a mere woman by yourself?" Anger flashed through his red eyes. "Who is your friend?" Tahari continued to bait him, carefully backing away from the approaching Gradon.

"Why, do you not know? It kept me company for nearly a thousand years. We know each other well." Lord Jarden was clearly pleased with himself. The challenge was set. Tahari had only a second to think before this beast from the ancient world attacked.

The Gradon swiped at her with its mighty tail. Tahari jumped clear of it just as one of its mouths opened and shot blue ice at her.

Tahari rolled out of the way and stood in time to see the other head unleash its flame.

Tahari dropped to one knee quickly and held up a hand to split the flame in two, forcing the flames to pass harmlessly around her. She had done it without thinking, and she trembled with surprise as she discovered yet another power gifted to those of her race.

Lifting her head and staring into the Gradon's enraged golden eyes, Tahari began to speak. "What magic has possessed you to do this evil creature's bidding?"

Surprised that she was acknowledging it, the Gradon head that could spout flame ended his assault on her. "You acknowledge me enough to speak to me?" he asked with a beautiful voice. Tahari smiled to assure him that she did. "I was under the belief that sphinxes were too haughty even to look at our kind.

"I tell you, my friend, your race was beautiful and brought wondrous variety to the ancient world. My people cherished your wisdom as well as your humor." Tahari recalled the memories of her past life with clarity. She smiled at the memories of these beasts and the magic they brought to the world. "It saddens me that time, the greed of man, and those like Lord Jarden have brought both our races to an end. Your kind deserved better." as Tahari spoke, both heads listened to her with great interest. The rage and anger that had consumed it for many long years diminished, and its golden eyes now glistened with tears.

"Humanity—I missed that." much to Tahari's surprise, the head of the Gradon who could spout ice spoke with almost a female voice. She looked at Tahari with reverence and understanding. "Too many long years have we heard that one speak such falsehoods." she lowered her head sadly. "You are right; there was peace and laughter between our races. Thank you, Lady Tahari." Tahari's eyes widened with surprise.

"You know my name?" Tahari asked with astonishment. Both Gradon heads looked at her proudly.

"Yes, my lady," the male replied humbly. "You are known to us. The evil one has talked much about you since he raised us from the dead after his servant slew us upon Zendro Isle. I am Amon-Ra and this is Adrasteia. Forgive us for our actions; we have been deceived," he apologized and lowered his head.

"You hold great power and by your mere words freed us from his," Adrasteia informed Tahari and glared over at Lord Jarden, who now stared at them, open-mouthed.

"Go then and be at peace. You have endured much," Tahari encouraged them as she felt the hardship they had had to bear for so long. They smiled at her thankfully, but Tahari sensed there was something more they had planned.

"We will, and we thank you, but first we must take care of something that is long overdue." Adrasteia nodded to Amon-Ra and gave Tahari a wink. Then, before Lord Jarden could react, the Gradon took him up by its tail and leapt into the air, vanishing into the dark clouds, leaving Gortorro Prison in the care of the Draccen soldiers. Judging from the prisoners' expressions, Draccen control would not last long. Hope and life now shone in the eyes of all who looked back at Tahari.

Chapter 99

Gortorro Overturned

In the stunned silence that followed Lord Jarden's sudden departure, a Draccen soldier seized the opportunity to take control before the prisoners could. He charged up to Tahari with a wicked-looking club.

"You defiant witch, your power will not save you from the Draccen," he informed her. He looked around to his subordinates in the guard towers and ordered them to shoot Tahari with their arrows. But before the archers could follow his command, they were struck down by arrows themselves. A look of disgust came over his face, and he turned back to her.

"Freedom is theirs now," Tahari said. "We are leaving this place. Do not stop them, or it will be your lives at stake." Anger flared in the soldier's brownish-green eyes. Then he smiled as he watched something happening behind her.

"So certain of that, are you?" he asked in his gravelly voice. Tahari turned to see what was going on behind her when something dark and heavy collided with her head. Multicolored stars blinded her, and she felt her body fly backward to the ground.

Tahari did not know for how long she was passed out, but when she managed to open her eyes again, the pain of her world crashed in on her. Looking up from the hard ground, Tahari felt a cold, throbbing pain course through her head, and Tahari had to force herself to stay conscious. The Draccen soldier with his nail-studded club now stood over her with a proud gleam in his dark eyes. He was joined by his friend, who was nearly double the size of him. "He thinks you should stay, and so do I." His very large friend had his own club, which only made her head hurt worse. Looking around, Tahari noticed that all the Draccen guards from the prison were now in the courtyard. Some of them surrounded her, and all of them had brought their swords and clubs for the fight they knew was ahead. However Tahari saw something they didn't that brought a weary smile to her face.

"I think we are all leaving, and there will be little that you can do about it," Tahari said in defiance, propping herself up with her elbows.

"I think you will be dead," the Draccen soldier stated firmly. He leaned over and whispered something to his friend. A cruel expression came over his large friend's face as the Draccen soldier took up his massive club and prepared to finish Tahari with it.

"So certain of that, are you?" a voice behind his large friend asked. The moment the soldier looked around, his large friend opened his mouth wide and wailed out in agony, the tip of a sword appearing from his chest. Blood spurted out as the sword was withdrawn and ran down the dark leather tunic. A second later, the very large Draccen soldier hit the ground next to his friend with a terrible thud, dead. Standing in the large Draccen soldier's place was Bakari's wife.

"You? Where is your sniveling husband?" the Draccen commander asked, caught off-guard by her sudden appearance. She remained silent, but her rage flared through her hazel eyes as she gripped her blood-stained sword.

"Who are you calling sniveling?" Bakari shouted from across the courtyard. A smile spread across his wife's face as they turned to see him standing in front of the army of slaves that had now banded together. "FREEDOM IS YOURS! GO GET IT!" he shouted at the sackcloth-covered army. As thunder exploded overhead and lightning flashed through the sky, the slaves charged the Draccen soldiers in the compound, armed with the anger and desperation that had burned within them for too long.

"You might want to run," Tahari kindly suggested to the Draccen commander, who stood totally baffled at seeing Gortorro being overrun by its prisoners. He dropped his club and scurried away, joining the other Draccen soldiers running for their lives who could not escape the enraged prisoners. The prisoners spread through the entire compound like an angry flood.

"Are you all right, Lady Tahari?" Bakari's wife asked, concern filling her eyes. She offered Tahari a tanned hand to help her up.

"I am, and I am very thankful," she replied. Tahari took her hand and inquired after her name.

"I am Freya," she offered kindly, helping Tahari to her feet. "It is I and all of us who are thankful. You and your friend have not only spared my life, but that of everyone here." she spoke with immense gratitude, and her tear-filled eyes looked out at the thin people who fought vigilantly to take back their lives. Following her gaze, Tahari nodded in understanding. In these people, Tahari saw something else: Tahari saw her friends from the Tomblock as well as Leondros's family. Their deaths were not in vain.

"My friend and I have already witnessed the terror Lord Jarden brought to our loved ones. Today, we vindicate them," Tahari reasoned softly as she watched the people of this prison fight back and win their freedom.

"We were dying and desperate and needed to find a way to even the odds. Most were too scared to fight back after those who did were impaled as punishment. The darkness of Lord Jarden's grasp made us believe that no one could stand up to him," she confessed as she lowered her gaze. When she returned her gaze to Tahari, there was the light of hope shining out from it. "We only needed a reminder that we were strong still." she smiled at Tahari and then took her arm. Bowing her head humbly, Tahari took her arm in return. "We thank you.

"You are most welcome, but this is not done." Tahari looked at her with a firm gaze. "Please, I ask you, what has become of the people from the Shandel?" She searched the tanned woman's face for the answer to the question that had pressed on the back of her mind since they left the Shandel with Leondros. The forlorn expression upon Freya's desert-swept features caused Tahari's heart to sink.

"Many are dead," she said in a disheartened whisper. "Thousands more dwell in camps like this one. We even heard a rumor that cities within Adarah have also succumbed to our fate."

Her words caused Tahari to lower her gaze. Tahari brought a hand to her lips as she fought to come to grips with what was happening to their world. It was happening quickly, too quickly. Then as Tahari lifted her gaze back to the battle that went on around them, Tahari saw a worn old woman fall. A Draccen guard caught up to her, gripped his spear tightly, and was just about to finish her off, when she rolled onto her back and drove a sword that she had been hiding into his midsection. She let out a furious yell as she shoved him away from her, got to her feet, and continued on with the uprising. A smile came to Tahari's face. These people still possessed spirit.

"The war with Lord Jarden is only beginning," Tahari said. She pulled her hand away from her lips, clenched it into a fist, and shook it as inspiration filled her heart once again. Looking up at Freya, Tahari could see that she shared the same indomitable feeling. "Take these people and continue what we started today. Free those imprisoned throughout Andora. We have to rally all those we can to fight against him, or his regime will continue and pave the way for his people to take possession of Andora." As Tahari spoke, a renewed spirit filled Freya's eyes as she nodded in understanding.

"We will, and we will follow you and your friends into that war," Freya promised with an excited smile. A tremendous yell of victory sounded throughout the grounds of Gortorro just then. Its prisoners had overrun it, had driven out or killed the Draccen soldiers who had guarded it, and had claimed their freedom.

Celebration quickly sobered as the thousands of weak and malnourished realized that a strong, well-fed Draccen army was advancing toward them. Bakari joined them, concern filling his eyes.

"The Draccen army marches on Gortorro. They will be here within the hour," he began, sounding slightly out of breath. Tahari turned her gaze to the south to see the ocean of torches flickering against the stormy darkness. "They are too many for us, even if we were armed and ready.

"They come to overtake an empty prison?" Tahari asked herself aloud. Bakari and Freya looked at each other and then at her with confusion. Tahari smiled, shook her head slightly, and then turned to them. "Gather everyone together. Prepare them to journey to Eden-Glee," Tahari advised calmly. The couple stood dumbfounded, but she nodded confidently, and they hurried off to gather the multitude. Moments later, the whole courtyard was overfilled with all the souls who waited anxiously for Tahari to speak. She looked among the many faces of the men, women, and children who had been imprisoned here. Tahari made her instructions clear and brief.

"Pass through the ring of mist; you will find yourselves in Eden-Glee. Be ready. Lord Jarden's minions may have reached the realm of the dwarves already. You have won your freedom—be ready to defend it.

As Tahari spoke, she felt as if this were an entirely different group of people. They were no longer dying prisoners but warriors who had tasted their freedom.

As lightning flashed over the compound and rain began to fall upon the dry earth at last, Bakari and Freya and Tahari exchanged looks of courage and understanding. Tahari created a ring of mist, and her new friends led the multitude through, vanishing without a trace. Gortorro was now empty, except for Tahari. She studied the many barracks and warehouses that had imprisoned so many souls while she waited patiently for the Draccen army.

An hour later, Tahari watched from beyond the abandoned compound, using her acute hearing and eyesight to her advantage. She then dropped on the Draccen soldiers and enjoyed their dismay at finding the compound empty. No prisoners could be found anywhere: not within the barracks, not within the warehouse. The army's intense search turned up nothing but the slain bodies of their comrades who had guarded the compound. General Sabin was beside himself, taking in the emptiness of the facility that had once held well over five thousand prisoners from all over Andora.

General Sabin was a seasoned officer of the Draccen armies. Although Tahari did not know about his wondrous military background, she could see from the numerous scars that covered his body that he had survived many battles. This included a gaping slice that had nearly taken his right eye. Adding to this from her memories of Shamira, Tahari knew that as Dracs age, their scales turn from a vibrant green and black or brown to a paling gray; the general's scales were almost white.

He stood for a long moment trying to determine what had transpired within the confines of this prison camp. Then one of his men called for him to join him at the back barbed-wire gate.

"My lord, LOOK!" the soldier cried out as he pointed to the north. The general was quick to join his soldier at the back gate. Beyond the surrounding storm, darkness, and desert, they detected Tahari's presence. Between the lightning flashes, they realized that it was a woman with dark-brown hair pulled back into a braided ponytail. The braid lay over her left shoulder. She was dressed in a black tunic and covered by a black and blue cloak. She was no slave but the sphinx they had been looking for. Tahari looked at them with a smile and wave. Then she turned and, with another wave of her hand, she disappeared from sight, another trick she had learned from her people. Standing invisibly, Tahari continued to watch the army's dismay as she waited for her friend to accompany her back to Mt. Somerset.

"Was that not the sphinx that Lord Jarden wanted us to make sure was dead?" another soldier asked. The consequences set by Lord Jarden were uttered by the soldiers surrounding the general. Failing to kill this lone sphinx meant death to any soldier given the chance to do so.

"The very same," General Sabin replied with frustration.

"She heads to Mt. Somerset—do we pursue?" the soldier at the gate asked, sounding a little bewildered by the strange event that they had stumbled across. The general turned to the soldier with an expression of repulsion and slapped him on the back of the head.

"If I can walk away from this one with my head, I will be lucky," the aging general began angrily as he turned back to his men who waited in the prison courtyard. "But if I do not, I can at least say that I took that sphinx down before Lord Jarden brings the ax down on me." His words were felt and understood by his men as their lives also hung in the balance. Their orders were clear and strict: kill the sphinx and everyone within Gortorro, or be killed yourselves.

"My lord, Lord Jarden is nowhere to be found," another soldier informed his general as he came running up to the general from across the compound. General Sabin seemed perplexed as he searched the prison with a studious gaze and then realized that Lord Jarden's pet Gradon was also gone.

"His plan with the Gradon must have backfired," he said aloud as he turned back to the out-of-breath soldier. "Summon Baldour's rider to call his winged friend and have them search for the master. We need to regroup and send a messenger for our other men. We will have need of them on Mt. Somerset. The sphinx seemed to be heading deeper into the Barrens toward that cursed mountain— we need to cut off her retreat before she leads her little band to the barrier that is located on the north side of Mt. Somerset," he instructed firmly.

"What is past the barrier?" the soldier asked with curiosity. The general stopped and looked back at his soldier as if the soldier's words caused him pain.

"Death. No agent of the dark lord can pass through that barrier. It is sacred ground," the general answered knowingly as his light-brown eye drifted north. In his words, there was a sense of something he had experienced himself. "My first mission for Lord Jarden was to take a regiment of men through that barrier—other than a couple of men and myself, no one survived. I can still see their bodies burning until not even the bones were left." this story added to their urgency to find the sphinx for Lord Jarden.

"What do we report to Lord Jarden about the prisoners?" one

soldier asked nervously as he looked around the empty compound with worry. General Sabin turned back to him, looked over the entire compound, and then replied simply.

"They are gone." the general's gaze was fixed with a weary fatigue and frustration. In this response, there would be no lie, and it would require no punishment.

Chapter 100
Mission's Success Tahari

After being sure that the Draccen army would pursue her, Tahari took leave of the Gortorro Prison and began to run back to Mt. Somerset. She realized that her plan had worked even better than she had hoped. When Tahari stopped to take a breath, she felt that she was not alone. Turning back to the south, Tahari watched the lightning flash periodically through the dark storm clouds and breathed in the refreshing scent of rain as it brought relief to the parched earth. The lightning flashed again, this time closer to where she was standing, and Tahari saw a silhouette of someone running toward her. Their features seemed almost elfish, but their true appearance was concealed by a dark cape.

As the figure joined Tahari and pulled off their hood, she offered, "I am thankful that you brushed up on your archery skills before you left Adarah.

"No, *I* am thankful that I brushed up on my archery skills before we left Adarah," Almari replied as she fought to catch her breath. "If I had let one of those Draccen beasts pull off a shot and get you, I would have had to answer to Leondros." she was exasperated and frustrated. Tahari could only smile.

"Knew you could do it," Tahari grinned. Giving her a look and shaking her head, Almari's smile returned.

"Adalai help you," she laughed and then hugged her friend. Their mission had been a great victory. "How did you know Bakari would betray you?" she asked as they began walking northwest.

"He seemed to be hiding more than what he had told us at camp. Besides, Lord Jarden would not freely let someone stroll out of a prison camp to give us warning," Tahari said as she thought back on Bakari's actions when he first came to them.

"Then how did you know he would be so willin' to lead a rebellion against Lord Jarden?" she wondered. "I mean, things looked a little hairy back there for a moment. They nearly killed you," she said with a look of concern.

"Remember how it was for us?" Tahari asked her, recalling their time as slaves. A look of deep memory came to Almari as she slowly nodded her head with sudden understanding. "We were desperate, starving, and angry at those who mocked us when we were barely able to stand, let alone work in the fields under the hot sun. They laughed as they watched us die before them. These people were where we were not too long ago." the people who dwelt within the Gortorro Prison gave Tahari and Almari the chance not only to free others from the bondage they had been in once but also to put hope back into their world.

"There is something I still do not understand," Almari said. "You let yourself be taken captive by a dragon, beaten down by Draccen soldiers, and nearly killed. You could have ended this whole thing and freed the prisoners by just usin' your power." Tahari listened and nodded in understanding.

"I could have," Tahari said softly as she reached up and tenderly rubbed the large bump that had now formed beneath her thick hair on her skull. Then she looked at Almari with a warm smile. "But these people needed hope for what is to come. They needed a *human* example of hope. If they are to find the will to fight what is to come, they have to believe in themselves. They also needed to be reminded of their humanity—and in that, compassion. Magic and the power of the sphinx cannot give them that." in Tahari's explanation, Almari gained understanding as well as her own inspiration. Tahari could see it radiate from her face.

"What is it about you, my friend?" She looked at Tahari through a teary-eyed smile as Almari put a comforting hand on her shoulder. "You move more people than anyone I have ever known.

"I do not know, myself; I just remember the vague lessons from my past life. I would want to live my life so that it may please Adalai," Tahari said simply, shrugging.

Almari smiled in reply. She looked at the long road ahead of them and then looked at her with a sad expression. "Your lesson in humanity and belief allowed those people to believe in themselves and taught them to find the will to rise up and challenge the forces of darkness. Does this also mean we have to walk all the way to Mt. Somerset by foot?" she asked with a weary expression. Tahari chuckled and shook her head.

"Your sense of belief is amazing." Tahari grinned as she created a ring of white mist in the humid air in front of them. Its white coloring seemed to almost glow in contrast to the black night that closed in around them. The rain began to come down harder now as if encouraging them to keep moving. They walked through the driving rain and felt the wind blow hard from the west until they reached the portal to Mt. Somerset. The wind began to roar distantly, low and menacing. Chills drove down Tahari's spine, for she was sure something had seen them. But in the next moment, they had passed through the ring and had left the desert sands just north of Gortorro Prison. Tahari and Almari's next steps were on the dirt and sand that covered Mt. Somerset.

Chapter 101

Lord Jarden's Opportunity

After being whisked out of Gortorro Prison by his pet, Lord Jarden had no other choice but to kill the Gradon he had planned would bring down the sphinx Tahari. Shaking the creature's dark-red blood from his torn robe, Lord Jarden looked at the mountainous wasteland surrounding him and shook his head. He figured that the Gradon had taken him somewhere deep within the Serrigen. His anger was momentary, for as he lifted his gaze to the stormy night sky, he saw aid coming in the form of Baldour.

"It is good to see you again, my friend," Lord Jarden said, relieved. He approached the large black dragon after he landed gracefully. There was no thunder in Baldour's landings, only a sudden rush of great wind. "Please tell me what has transpired within Gortorro. I am hoping it favors us," he requested as he studied the dark dragon's face.

"A majority of the news is not good," Baldour began slowly. Lord Jarden's bony body went limp with the burden of knowing there was indeed bad news. "The sphinx managed to incite the prisoners into rising up against the Draccen soldiers. After, she helped them to flee the area, before the Draccen army could carry out your orders." the news was worse than Lord Jarden could have imagined.

"Was no attempt made to kill the sphinx?" Lord Jarden demanded angrily.

"Many. But her archer took out many of the Draccen archers before a shot could be fired in her direction." Lord Jarden grew more frustrated.

"Of course, she had the elf positioned on a cliff outside the compound where he could snipe the enemy at his leisure while remaining safe," he reasoned aloud, gaining an understanding of Tahari's plan. He had to admit, this girl knew what she was doing, and she did it well.

"Only part of that is true, my lord," Baldour offered as his voice gave the hint of some good news. Lord Jarden turned back to his faithful dragon with curiosity.

"The elf of which you speak was most likely safe from any assault from within Gortorro, but he was not the archer whom Tahari brought to assist her at the compound." Baldour began to fill in the dark lord on what he had seen while he conducted his search for his master. He began to tell him of the two figures he spotted in the desert as they fled Gortorro. This news brought a slight smile to his master's scaly reptilian lips.

"You don't say," Lord Jarden said as he urged the black dragon to continue.

"In my search for you, I spotted two figures leaving Gortorro. One was Tahari and the other was a cloaked figure whom she would have had you believe was Leondros." as Baldour revealed his findings to the dark lord, his rider, who had been listening in, finally pulled back his dark chain-link hood. Lightning flashed through the stormy night air and revealed the tousled black hair and short beard of Prince Alon-Settie.

"It was Tahari's friend, the one she calls Almari," Alon-Settie said confidently as he looked down upon the dark lord. Upon seeing the athletic prince dismount from Baldour's back, Lord Jarden was suddenly very relieved.

"You have done well, my prince—and you as well, my friend Baldour," Lord Jarden commended them with praise, taking this news in with great thought.

"Tahari purposely ignored your order and brought her friend

Almari instead of Leondros. She deliberately went against the bargain you made with her," Alon-Settie stated, anxiously waiting for the dark lord's next course of action.

"It is what I was hoping for," his master began with a tone of delight. "I knew that she would not truly give up the elf or even put him in harm's way purposely. It is against everything she has been ordained to do. She is his guardian," he explained as his thoughts were overrun with cruel intentions.

"Then why did you ask for such an arrangement?" Alon-Settie wondered as his dark-brown eyes studied the reptilian master closely.

"It was a test to know just how far she would go to protect him. We now have found a weakness we can use against her." Lord Jarden smiled back at Baldour and Alon-Settie.

"Her love for Leondros," Alon-Settie sneered, shaking his head. Lord Jarden shot the youthful prince a serious look.

"It is precisely that *love* that has given us a closer look into the motivations that govern the sphinx and all who accompany her on this quest. These rebels have shown to us that they hold all those dear to them in such high regard that they would sacrifice anything for the sake of one so cherished. This is a weakness I am more than willing to exploit. A chance opportunity for us exists because of the love between them; do not sneer at such a fortunate gift," the dark lord glared. In his anger, Lord Jarden's black eyes turned searing red. His gaze held Alon-Settie's for a moment, until the young prince nodded in understanding.

"You are right; using their feelings for each other against them is a very clever plan," Alon-Settie said as he began to understand Lord Jarden's mindset. "I am willing to do whatever you ask no matter what your next plan of attack will hold." the prince bowed humbly. Lord Jarden thought for a moment as an evil look flashed through his deep-red eyes.

"Seeing how General Sabin keeps failing me, I have a special assignment for him and his men," he said, his tone telling how less-than-pleased he was. "I have something special in store for the rebels." Lord Jarden lifted his gaze toward Mt. Somerset and clasped his hands behind his back. "This will entail your engaging your old acquaintance in a duel once again," the dark lord offered as he turned toward the young prince. An evil smile came to Alon-Settie's face, but a look of wonder quickly replaced it.

"If the rebels should make it beyond the boundaries of Rahara and into safety, how do we get them to return?" Alon-Settie asked. Lord Jarden seemed pleased at his young apprentice's foresight.

"Thinking ahead—I like that," the dark lord noted with a nod of approval. "As I said before, we will use any bond of love or friendship to accomplish my plan." he spoke with intense determination.

"I hold no allegiance to anyone within the rebel band that we are hunting; I will uphold any task you give me." Alon-Settie bowed humbly before the dark master of Nod. Pleased by this youth's loyalty, Lord Jarden decided to award him a special honor.

"If you follow my orders to the letter, I will make you High King of Andora to rule over this realm in accordance with the laws of the Nodarian Kingdom. King Jabberwrath would be most pleased by your efforts." at the utterance of this possible promotion, Alon-Settie was overcome with realization and excitement. Tears stung his eyes, but he looked back at Lord Jarden with wonder.

"My lord, I would be honored, but it is you who have fought for so long to make Andora yours. This honor is yours, to be sure." Alon-Settie shook his head.

"I will take my place as ambassador to this realm; the rewards that are to come will be sufficient payment for the many long years spent trying to attain this realm," Lord Jarden explained kindly as he put a reassuring hand on the young prince's strong shoulder. "My lord, however, has told me personally that he detests the name Andora. After our victory, we will rename this land Goratha." Lord Jarden accompanied Alon-Settie and Baldour back to Gortorro, where the preparation for the final battle with the sphinx, Tahari, and her rebel band would be orchestrated.

Chapter 102

On the Mount

Towards morning, the thunderstorm had become a gentle shower. Soaked and weary from a lack of sleep, Tahari and Almari made their way up the rocky path toward the cave that they had discovered upon reaching Mt. Somerset the previous day. Torches had been set out for them. As they neared the mouth of the cave, they beheld a wondrous sight. Although exhausted herself, Queen Elanza remained awake and waiting for them. Hearing their footsteps coming up the rocky trail, she shielded her eyes with a delicate hand and watched for them like a mother waiting for her children to return home again.

"Oh, thank goodness!" Elanza gasped in relief as she ran down to greet them. Her dark hair now hung loosely about her. The wind pick up long strands of it to play with as Elanza clutched at the sides of her blue gown to keep from tripping over it. Half slipping down the mountain path, the kind woman did not care. She quickly wrapped them both in warm, welcoming hugs. "You are both safe!" Her green eyes were quick to examine Tahari and Almari for any injury.

"We are fine—there is no need for fuss, but thank you," Almari insisted, acting almost more like a teenager than a road-weary warrior.

Still, the queen clung to them as she escorted them back to the mouth of the cave.

"How did your plan go?" Elanza asked Tahari with warmth and concern, desperation clearly emanating from her eyes.

"Gortorro Prison has been emptied, and the prisoners are free and safe from the Draccen army," Tahari reported wearily but happily. A large smile came to Elanza's face. Putting her hands together in prayer as she lifted her gaze to the heavens, Elanza could not stop the tears of joy that stung her eyes. In spite of the atrocities and hardships she had seen and experienced herself in the last ten days, Queen Elanza's heart was not callous. She was thankful that the people of Andora were surviving this dreadful coup d'état.

"The Draccen army is half a day behind us, a day at the most," Almari informed the concerned woman. "I believe now would be a good time to—

"Get you into some dry clothes and give you some food and rest," Elanza finished for her, giving Almari a motherly look.

"But there is an angry mob of Draccen soldiers, and…" Almari began through her exhaustion. Elanza stood unfazed by the weary young woman's plea. Instead, she slowly crossed her arms and gave Almari a serious motherly look. "Oh, all right," Almari gave in as she half-heartedly hung her blonde head and trudged past the two torches that framed the cave entrance. Tahari fought hard to hide her smile. When Almari had disappeared inside the cave, the queen and Tahari turned to each other and laughed.

After they had calmed themselves, Elanza took Tahari's arm and walked with her into the cave. "How are you, my dear?" Elanza asked Tahari.

"Tired but glad to be back," Tahari said. Looking around, she wondered where Leondros was, but Elanza was way ahead of her.

"Leondros is on watch. He should be up the trail on the southeastern face of the mountain; he will need to be relieved in a few hours," she said with a warm smile and a wink. Tahari smiled and nodded knowingly. "I believe we have made all the necessary preparations for our guests.

"You made good time," Tahari remarked with disbelief and approval, for three of the mountain's trails needed traps to keep their guests busy and put the odds in their favor. Elanza's bright-green eyes opened wide and looked back at Tahari.

"*We* made good time? You two are the ones who covered about fifty miles of desert in mere seconds. Where I come from, that is most definitely a record." Elanza's quick wit caught Tahari off-guard, and she flashed her a smile and began laughing. Tahari joined in her laughter. Tahari changed into a dry black-and-brown tunic, grabbed some stew that was keeping warm in a small black kettle over the crackling fire, and eventually got some sleep. Although they had only blankets upon the hard floor, it still felt good to rest. Tahari watched as Elanza finally gave in to her own exhaustion and took her place in the circle they created around the small fire.

"Good night, Elanza," Tahari managed with a weary smile. She looked over at Tahari with a tired smile.

"Good night, sweetheart. Sleep well," she said. She turned to offer Almari a "good night" as well, only to find the weary warrior was already asleep. They exchanged tired smiles and lay down to join Almari. Just before Tahari drifted to sleep, a cool breeze drifted into the cave. As it washed over their sunburnt faces, Tahari remembered the smell of fresh air mixed with musty desert. It reminded her of what they had accomplished thus far—it was good.

After a few short hours of sleep, Tahari awoke to morning on Mt. Somerset. Even from within the cave, Tahari was able to see that the morning was cool and overcast. She loved mornings such as these, especially when she worked in the Tomblock. They were heavenly, for they brought such relief from the previous days of scorching heat. Tahari pulled on her boots to go find Leondros. Braiding her hair as she made her way out of the cave, Tahari turned back to see that both Almari and Queen Elanza were still curled up in their blankets, fast asleep. Tahari took in this moment, this shred of peace and tranquility.

Climbing up the rugged mountain path, Tahari eventually made it to the last part of the trail, which gave way to a cliff that looked over the grandeur of the Barrens' wilderness. The horizon before her was the deepest reds, most vibrant oranges, and rich browns of sand dunes and mountains. The cloud cover and lack of sunshine hardly took anything from this masterpiece. It was breathtaking. It was then she saw Leondros, watchful at the edge of the cliff. He leaned on his bow and seemed to be in deep thought. The morning's soft breeze caught in his shoulder-length blond hair, making it dance gently behind him.

"This is a good morning for sleep; you should take some more rest," he offered softly as he gazed out at the horizon before him. He turned to her with a warm smile. The morning's pale light caught the silver thread and beads that were sewn into his brown and green tunic.

"This is true, but I could not, for I know that you have been awake all night," Tahari smiled in return. A faint smile came to his face as he seemed to be reminded of something.

"How did the meeting at Gortorro go last night?" he asked with a hint of concern.

"Very well—Lord Jarden had intended to use the Gradon to kill me, but it turned on him and whisked him out to the wilderness somewhere. After that, the prisoners took back their freedom." Tahari recounted the evening's events, still vivid in her mind. Relief filled Leondros's features as she explained the other details of Almari's and her escapade.

"Any chance they saw you leave to come back here?" he asked with a tone of concern.

"I certainly hope so—Almari and I waited as long as we dared. Though I doubt Lord Jarden will be too happy that he lost all the prisoners within Gortorro," Tahari said. She looked down at the three mountain trails. Leondros and Queen Elanza had done very well constructing the traps needed for their assault on the approaching Draccen army. Tahari then realized that he was strangely silent; when she turned to him, she saw worry in his soulful brown eyes. "What is it?"

"Maybe nothing. I keep thinking about the last lines of the second scroll. Their meaning does not bode well for the one to whom they are addressed." he spoke quietly as worry settled into his warm voice. Tahari felt the words he spoke and understood them well.

"This is true—but Leondros, what I saw last night was a sight like no other," Tahari began as inspiration filled her once again. She smiled hopefully and gently took hold of his hand. "I saw people desperate and dying still fighting to take back their freedom. Old and young alike fought without fear. The expression of life that was in their eyes could not be missed. This land will not fade under Lord Jarden's regime so easily. He definitely has a fight on his hands," Tahari said encouragingly. Leondros's look of worry faded into a warm smile.

"I thank Adalai for you," he began softly. She could hear weariness in his voice. "I know what is ahead, and I sense the long road that awaits us, but you inspire me, my friend," he said as he took a labored breath, but Tahari saw life sparkle in his brown eyes.

"I am glad," she said as she reached up, held his face in her hands, and rested her forehead against his. "And I am thankful for you, too." after a long moment, Tahari sensed the weariness within him. "You are weary with sleep—go take rest. I will be here," Tahari ordered gently.

There was something he seemed to wish to say, but he only smiled and replied, "Save this moment." he looked at her with a promise and a smile.

"I will." Tahari watched him slowly head down the mountain trail.

In the moments after Leondros left to return to the cave, Tahari wished that they were already in Rahara and safe from the Draccen army. As her thoughts wandered and she thought of Sala and meeting up with them again, Tahari remembered that the third scroll of the prophecy was still waiting for them. The instructions had read "Look for the third scroll within the Barrens on the mount with the crest upon it." Mt. Somerset was within the Barrens, Tahari reasoned. Was there a crest somewhere?

She looked around the rocky cliffside but found nothing. Tahari grew desperate, and her search intensified. Surely it was here. Finally, she moved a smaller rock near the base of a rock wall that reached high into the sky, causing the morning's light to bounce off the wall brilliantly. Tahari had found it. Before her the crest of the Osarian Knights had been etched into a bright stone and fitted snugly into the wall of the mountain. Gently setting the small rock aside, Tahari pushed on the crest with her thin fingertips, and it moved with a gravelly sound, giving way to a hole. Reaching deep inside the hole, she touched the aged material of the third scroll of the prophecy and pulled it gently out.

It was tightly sealed, its crest in deep-red wax. Looking at it for a long moment, Tahari realized that she had not yet had any word from her mother or the sphinx lords as to the decision they had reached. It had been a week, and a lot had happened. Dare she hope that the judgment was in her favor and no action would be taken?

A gentle wind blew about Tahari's face, causing her to look up. Standing before Tahari was her mother. She was dressed in a beautiful deep-blue robe accented by a white sash with ancient metallic-blue symbols that she wore across her right shoulder to her left hip. Her long mahogany hair was pulled up and away from her face, only a few locks dangling around her dark face. The moment Tahari looked at the solemn expression she carried in her sea-green eyes, Tahari knew the verdict: *guilty*.

"One does not need to be a mind reader to know what they have decided," Tahari spoke half-heartedly. There was sadness in her soulful eyes but also pride.

"Yes, their judgment has been passed; the laws of the sphinx are absolute. It was an amazing feat that allowed you to call on the power of resurrection at such a young age, but it was a true miracle when it actually worked. No young sphinx was ever able to accomplish this before; only the grand sphinxes were able to perform such an accomplishment.

Still, the high judges are bound to the laws of our people. They cannot stray from them, for the powers that have been entrusted to our people are too great to take lightly or to use for our own gain. If they were lenient about the laws that govern our powers, the sphinx people would become a plague upon the world. They would truly do far worse to the world than what Lord Jarden could do, but they wanted you to remember that you carried yourself as a true sphinx of the ancient world. You have made the high council as well as the sphinx people and your family, very proud." Anyi spoke with reverence and a hint of pride.

"I appreciate that," Tahari said slowly as she waited to hear her reveal the sentence. Her mother smiled warmly as she looked at her with great pride and said nothing more. "Not that I am a glutton for punishment, but what is their sentence for me?" Tahari asked with dread. Anyi walked up to Tahari with a warm smile and put her arms around her daughter and held her tight.

"It will be as you decide," she whispered. Tahari became confused, and she pulled her head back to look at her mother. But the moment she did, Anyi vanished from sight. "I love you, my daughter." her warm voice came through on the cool breeze that filtered through the mountain crevasses.

"Love you, too, Mother," Tahari replied, standing alone with the aged scroll in her hand. "Most unnerving," she commented. Tahari hung her head and took a deep breath as she thought about the verdict and the mysterious sentence that was to follow.

Overwhelmed by the thought that she had wronged the honorable people who had given her direction in her life, Tahari felt the agony of her action, but when her thoughts drifted to Leondros and being taking from him, Tahari's heart ached. She sank weakly to the ground and wept bitterly for the friend she had grown to love.

In Tahari's delusion of grief and sadness, she was granted another vision of Shamira.

In a large, dark room, Tahari saw her weakened form displayed for the soldiers and generals on a wooden cross, her burgundy robe ragged and stained with dirt and mud. Her long dark hair hung matted and dirty around her face and shoulders, and her head hung wearily. She had been beaten and tortured. A general in a green and black tunic, whose repulsive appearance was amplified by the bulge of his large gut hanging over his belt, walked up to her. His loud footsteps echoed throughout the room as he approached her. His small eyes, like tiny black buttons, glared out from his pasty-white complexion.

"How much longer are you going to resist me? All I ask is just something useful from your people. Do you not want us to be able to protect ourselves?" His voice had a fake sense of warmth about it.

"It seems you can already protect yourself," Shamira said a moment later as she slowly lifted her head and glared at him defiantly. Anger flared through his cold eyes. He backhanded her, and Shamira's head whipped back to her left shoulder.

"If you want to play around, so be it!" he said in a voice that was riddled with anger. "GUARDS! Take her outside!" his orders were carried out promptly, and soon Shamira was back outside in the prison camp's courtyard. The blinding hot sun caused her to stumble, but she fought to stay on her feet. When her eyes had adjusted to the light of the hot afternoon, Shamira saw that ten soldiers surrounded her to keep her from leaving the courtyard. She watched as the general walked toward the middle of the courtyard. There was a cruel smile upon his face, and judging by the forlorn expressions on the crowd of prisoners who had gathered in the distance, this might very well be her last interrogation.

"You will get nothing from me!" Shamira yelled in frustration and anger. She glared at the general and the surrounding soldiers, who watched her almost playfully.

"I know you protect someone—but I know it is not yourself or anyone here," the ruthless general teased as he slowly paced back and forth over the almost-orange earth. He looked out at the emaciated people who watched with a deep concern for Shamira. Their strength was almost spent, but they gathered to watch still. "My sources tell me that there is someone you are protecting in the elfin kingdom." his words caused Shamira's eyes to open with horrible realization. She slowly stood to her full height and looked at the general. "Do you mind telling us who this particular elf is?" Shamira clenched her teeth, her fists balled up under her torn robe, but she uttered not a word. After a moment, a menacing expression twisted his seemingly calm face. The general turned to one of his officers and whispered something. The younger man nodded and marched away. The general's cruel order spread like wildfire as the guards within the camp began executing prisoners. The general watched in sincere pleasure as horror filled Shamira's face as the sphinx prisoners were quickly being slaughtered. "It is no matter. We will find out who this elf is, and we will do to them what we are doing to you. Maybe then you will talk." he turned and started to leave the camp.

"I was wrong," Shamira called out in a hoarse voice, pleading for the general's attention. He stopped and stood with his back turned to her for a long moment. The few sphinxes within the camp, who were close enough to hear her astonishing words even with the terror that was beginning to sweep through the courtyard, stared at Shamira in horror, but they remained silent, watching in agony. Shamira's face was pained with fear as her body seemed to shake with terror. "There is something I am willing to give up." the general turned back and watched with pleasure while the ragged young woman weakly walked up to him. He scanned the faces of his men and took pride in his work; they were already revering him as the one who had gotten this sphinx woman to talk. Shamira wearily lifted her face to the bald general and looked at him with an expression of sincere hope.

"What are you willing to give up?" the general asked, almost scoffing. Shamira smiled weakly as she leaned closer to him. In less than a blink of an eye, Shamira had snaked her arm around his large waist, grabbed his dagger, and drove it through his heart. A second later, she kicked his feet out from beneath him and shoved him to the ground.

Watching the large man as he gasped his last breaths of air, Shamira saw fear wash over the man's already pale face. The terrified expression that Shamira had worn moments before melted into searing anger. Kneeling down on one knee, she leaned close to utter her answer as she saw the guards running toward her.

"I give up my life, so that the elf I protect and many more will survive," Shamira hissed into his ear. A second later, she belted out a resonating yell that echoed through the courtyard and with all the ferocity of an enraged lion, leapt into the air and took on the ten guards, who by now were advancing toward her. She cut them down fluidly, gracefully. Her strength was all but spent, yet something else coursed through her veins keeping her from going down.

She was able to take down seven more guards before a large spear pierced her body. Overcome with pain and weakness, Shamira weakly sank to her knees.

The final act of rebellion from Shamira had caused an uprising within the prison camp. The sphinx people enslaved here were given a choice: die quietly or go out fighting. The chaos that followed was historic. She looked out at the devastation around her. The remaining people who struggled for freedom received only death. The bodies of the slain sphinxes now lay scattered around the camp. The survivors of the riot were being executed by the prison guards left standing. Shamira grieved for the loss around her, but she knew that no matter what the guards said or did, these people had received *true freedom*.

A tremendous crash shook the earth as the prison's gates were breached and a band of elves and men finally got through. Seeing these brave souls rush into the compound of wood and barbed wire, Shamira felt wondrous relief. It was justice enough for Shamira.

Those who found her encouraged her to hang on to life. Lifting her gaze to the hot sun overhead, Shamira smiled weakly, and a cloud passed over her as if shielding her from the intense heat.

"I give my life in service—do with it as you see fit," she whispered to the sphinx lords and Adalai, closed her eyes, and took a last breath. A strange cool wind came in from the desert and blew against her.

Warriors who had come to see this brave woman saw her strong body impaled upon a spear, still kneeling, the life within it gone. Yet her secret was safe as was the elf she protected.

Waking from her vision, Tahari wiped the tears from her eyes and looked out over the vast desert that surrounded Mt. Somerset. She found the strength and courage in Shamira's last moments to face her unknown fate, for they had the same mission. She decided to make peace with her sentence, whatever it would be. Tahari would not let it trouble her, for she did not regret the action that had led her to this sentence. It had saved her dear friend's life, and she was glad that she had been able to keep the promise she had made to him in a dream long ago.

Looking down at the aged scroll that had yet to be translated, Tahari realized that she still had a purpose here, and she was greatly needed. *I will protect you, my friend, to whatever end.* It was then that Tahari felt a cool morning breeze against her face. Tahari's task as the sacred messenger and Leondros's protector was almost complete.

Upon finishing the third scroll of the prophecy, Tahari rolled the aged manuscript up and with it, a smaller paper that held her translation. Placing both in a leather pocket in her tunic, she felt this scroll was meant for Leondros. Its meaning brought the great weight of another immense journey over her head, but Tahari cleared her mind and looked out at the midmorning sun and watched it as it broke through the thick blanket of overcast clouds and shone upon the vast desert before her. Tahari took comfort in nature's splendor, but she sensed that the Draccen army was on its way, and her focus needed to be on what was coming.

Chapter 103

Draccen Assault

The cool morning gave way to a hot and humid afternoon as Tahari continued her watch from the rocky cliff. She saw clouds building in the west, and she knew that another night of storms was ahead. She refused to leave her post, for their plan required them to know the precise moment when the Draccen army arrived. Still, Queen Elanza made sure Tahari did not miss lunch, sending up more stew made of meat, potatoes, and other vegetables via Almari.

After her meal, Tahari continued to meditate on what lay before her as she stood watch on the high cliff of Mt. Somerset. She sensed that the night ahead would call for everything she had to give.

In the late hours of the afternoon, Tahari noticed dust clouding the blue horizon to the southeast. She heard someone climbing up the rocky path behind her. Out of the corner of her eye, she saw Leondros coming to join her. He looked alert and ready for action.

"We are not alone anymore," he reasoned, joining Tahari's gaze to the southeast. Together they spotted the first signs of this Draccen company. Thanks to their sharp eyesight, they were able to see across the great distance to about sixty to ninety Draccen soldiers that made up the horde headed toward them.

"It is time," Tahari said as she took a deep breath and tried to calm her anxieties. Sensing this, Leondros took her hand reassuringly and offered a comforting smile.

"Come, Almari wanted to make some last-minute preparations within the passes. Honestly, her methods scare me a little," he confessed gently. The warmth of his smile helped Tahari find her own again.

"Almari is one of a kind, there is no denying it," she said in agreement as they made their way down the steep mountain trail and went to find Almari.

In spite of being so outnumbered, they had prepared a few surprises to put the odds back in their favor. As they searched for Almari, they double-checked the traps within the passes—traps that Leondros and Queen Elanza had worked diligently to install. When they finally caught up to Almari, she was nailing spikes into the logs that were braced at the high end of a pass. When triggered by the Draccen soldiers, the logs would roll free and fall upon them. Leondros approved, but he still eyed her with wonder. He leaned closer to Tahari, eyeing Almari cautiously.

"Where did you get these plans?" he whispered. Tahari looked at him and then back at Almari, and could not help but smile.

"The spikes are Almari's idea, but as for the rest of it, my people used these techniques thousands of years ago when they had to defend themselves and Andora against intruders," Tahari explained. "These were just a few of the plans that worked a little *too* well, but I believe they fit our situation perfectly," she said quietly, watching Almari check the trap they had set. "If luck is on their side, they will not feel their death.

"What will happen if luck is not on their side?" Leondros wondered.

"They will feel it," she said with certainty. Stealing a look, Tahari caught a glimpse of Leondros's unnerved expression. He seemed a little overwhelmed by the savagery of their ideas, but still, a cunning smile came to his face. Leondros and Tahari exchanged looks of certainty. They alone might not stop the rest of the Draccen army— Lord Jarden had been raiding and pillaging other cities and villages within Andora—but this group might have difficulty repeating past transgressions. This was especially true if they journeyed to the realm of the dead. Turning her gaze toward the southeast, Tahari felt the Draccen soldiers approaching. "Let's move into position," she called out to Almari.

"What of Queen Elanza?" Leondros wondered as he turned his gaze back toward their camp.

"She has been given a special task for tonight. Almari passed along my request at lunch," Tahari explained with a wink. "She waits for this company of Draccen soldiers to enter the passes.

"Are you sure the Queen is up for such combat?" Worry and concern filled Leondros's face. This concern was expressed just as Almari joined them and brushed her hands free of dirt. "The Draccen soldier is a formidable opponent." Tahari and Almari exchanged a look.

"I do believe Elanza has been itchin' for some retribution since the fall of Akendron," Almari said with certainty. "Let the Draccen soldiers be afraid, *very* afraid." they then each headed to a pass, positioned to watch for Draccen soldiers entering their pass.

Chapter 104

Enemy on the Move

To the west of Mt. Somerset, dark storm clouds grew and moved toward the mountain, the smell of rain thick on the air. But to the southeast, dust formed an eerie haze that hovered over the dreaded Draccen soldiers who came west.

Once night fell, they used the darkness to disappear into the mountain, focusing their sights on the bright flame the rebels they were chasing burned at the top. Many of the soldiers laughed and snickered at the rebels' foolishness, for they knew they could easily reach the summit unnoticed. However, the second-in-command eyed the mountain cautiously as he looked for the best way up the mountain. He saw four paths: three slightly obscure to the naked eye and another that led straight up the mountain. The latter looked very accessible and well-traveled. Torches had been placed as if to light a safe path up the mountain. Figuring this fourth way for a trap, the second-in-command quickly divided his group into three teams of twenty and sent them on the three obscure passages with their orders to use extreme caution and to kill first. These rebels were notorious for outwitting their enemies and leaving none alive.

The first team quickly made its way up the western slope of Mt. Somerset. The soldiers were silent, moving like shadows over the rugged terrain. Victory was theirs, they thought as they closed in on the summit. They cautiously approached the orange flame that supposedly lit up the rebel camp. Then they turned a rocky corner of a narrow passage. A wall of dry desert brush and tumbleweeds spanned the width of the passage to the summit. It was minor problem which could be breached without much effort.

They began climbing over the wall of brush. They did not see the dark figure rise from the large rocks ahead of them. One soldier looked up for a moment, glimpsing the figure, who now held a bow in their hands and an arrow, whose head was aflame. But by then, it was too late. The figure shot the arrow into the dry brush and followed it quickly with four more. The entire wall was soon ablaze. Draccen soldiers fought each other to get free of the prickly brush, but the fire was now out of control, and the soldiers were the flames and smoke.

The second team of Draccen soldiers took the eastern slope. They had heard about the treachery that took place in the mountains of Shoshon. Many of their comrades had been incinerated by the intense inferno Baldour had set to kill the rebels. Prior to reaching Mt. Somerset, these soldiers had made a pact to watch for any signs of the rebels. They would shoot them on sight and take their bodies back to Lord Jarden. As they continued their ascent to the summit, some of them noticed flames emerging from the western pass. They all stopped and stared in horror at the raging inferno on the western side of the mountain. Faint screams could be heard from near the blaze. The soldiers turned to each other and exchanged looks of terror.

"What do we do now? It is happening again!" one of the soldiers cried out, his dark eyes filled with horror. He started to back away from the others.

"He is right! This is a trap," another said, he too, backing away.

They were about to retreat down the mountainside when their leader stopped them.

"Do not run! Do not be cowards! We are so close to reaching the top!" he shouted at his men angrily. "We can still get..." The rest of his words were drowned out by a loud rumble. He whirled around to see that one of his soldiers had accidentally tripped over a large log. His gaze went from the stunned soldier on the ground to the rock wall behind them. Fear raced down the leader's spine as he watched the rocks that towered over them shift and move.

"RUN!" the leader screamed as he whirled around, dug his claws into the rocky earth, and bolted back down the mountainside. The remaining soldiers quickly followed their leader's example.

Fleet of foot though they were, the Draccen soldiers could not outrun the monstrous rockslide behind them. Their screams were quickly silenced by the thunder of the slide and the crushing weight of the rocks bounding down the mountainside.

None of the soldiers had seen the shadowy figure watching over them all the while. Leondros looked on in disbelief. The Draccen soldiers had inadvertently taken themselves out. He slowly scanned the remains of the soldiers. He replaced the arrow he had drawn, for no one had survived the rockslide.

As he looked over the entire mountainside, Leondros could see that both he and Almari had been successful in holding back the Draccen soldiers trying to sneak up to Mt. Somerset's summit. It was time to check in with Tahari and Elanza. There was no real worry, for he sensed they were both fine. Leondros only wondered how the Draccen soldiers would fare against them.

The third team of Draccen soldiers dispatched into the mountain passes made its way up the center of the mountain, soon realizing that the terrain was more treacherous than first anticipated. The dusty trail started out as flat rock that wound up the mountain in a gradual incline, but now it had narrowed, had grown steeper, and was covered in small pebbles. Each step was more taxing than the last. Even with their razor-sharp claws digging deep into the rocky surface, a soldier could misstep and find himself tumbling backward down the pass. Worse, up ahead the trail seemed to disappear, leaving them with a towering rock wall to climb. Having no other choice, the Draccen soldiers clawed their way up the pass.

As one soldier looked back at their leader and cursed at him for choosing this particular pass, an arrow caught him square in the back. His body convulsed in pain, and he cried out in agony. His grip failed, and he fell back into the murky pass below.

Before the remaining soldiers could react, another arrow was released and another soldier tumbled back down the pass. It was clear now that it would be suicide to continue any farther, so they began to scramble back down the rock wall. More arrows rained down upon them, and some of the soldiers felt there was no other way to avoid being hit, so they decided to take their chances and let go of the rock wall.

Before long, only the second-in-command remained. He turned his head and glimpsed their attacker. Sheer surprise made him lose his grip and fall back into the rugged pass below. Surviving his fall, the second-in-command slowly climbed to his feet. He saw that ten soldiers from his team had survived the fall, so he decided to attack the mountain from another way. He had secretly motioned to his men to follow him back down the pass when one of them tripped over a long, thin log that had been wedged into a large crack in the rock wall. The soldiers waited and listened for a suspenseful moment. They did not know if this was another trap set by the rebels. Only silence filled the humid air around them.

When nothing happened, they took a deep breath and began to hurry back down the mountain pass. They were not going to waste their good fortune on waiting around; as they ran down the pass, however, they heard and felt thunder all around them. Soon the ground beneath their feet began to shake. They didn't know where the danger was coming from, but a couple of soldiers stole a glimpse of what was going on behind them. Horror filled them, and they screamed in panic. "RUN! ALL OF YOU!" one of the soldiers cried out as the horror that followed them filled the dark features of his face.

Large, weather-beaten timbers with barbarous points protruding from them chased the soldiers down the pass, quickly caught up to them, and rolled over those not lucky enough to dodge them. Other soldiers were actually impaled upon the giant barbs and taken with the logs as they continued to bounce down the pass.

The second-in-command was knocked back against the rock wall and watched in dismay as a log landed on his lower half, crushing it. Pain tore through his mind. Looking up, he saw another cruel log bouncing toward him. In the seconds he had left, the second-in-command turned his gaze to the far end of the pass, where a silhouette stood watching. He knew who this must be and realized that Lord Jarden had been seriously wrong about the girl from the Shoshon Mountains.

Chapter 105

Trap's Bait

During all of this, Elanza remained at the base of the mountain. Her task was to stop any Draccen soldiers coming back down or any stragglers going up to join their companions. Long though it had been since her combat time at Endenbury, the old queen assured her comrades that she was not without her wiles. In addition to having been in battle in her youth, Elanza had lived on the streets of Akendron. Such a living was anything but easy, and she learned to be as swift and cunning as an alley cat.

Elanza watched silently from the shadows of a cave while the three groups of Draccen soldiers made their way up the passes. When they had gone, she came out, watching the last of the soldiers enter the center pass.

"Tahari will be seeing you shortly," Elanza said. She turned her attention to her surroundings, watching for signs of her first target. She picked up choice stones for her slingshot. *The sharper the stone, the better*, she thought. Some might have sneered at this choice of weapon, but two things could not be debated. There was always an endless supply of ammunition to be found, especially in a desert, and given Elanza's sharp eyes, there was no target that she could not hit.

While she eyed the base of the mountain, Elanza saw signs of movement coming back down the eastern pass. She hoped that it was Leondros returning, but instead, it was survivors from the Draccen party. They looked barely alive, but they would still cause a huge big problem if they got back to their army. Creeping closer to the battered soldiers, she readied her slingshot.

If Elanza's word was gold, her aim was a diamond, for none of the soldiers reached the bottom of the eastern pass alive. The few who did not go down from the sudden strike to the forehead, Elanza finished with a quick slice of her dagger.

Taking care of the soldiers, Elanza did not notice the eyes that had been watching *her* the entire time. They had been watching from scattered brush within the desert, and they, too, had waited for the right moment. When the signal was given, two soldiers crept out of the desert brush and moved toward the unsuspecting queen. One soldier rushed up to her from the front, surprising her so that she resorted to the tactics learned from watching her son as he trained for combat as a child and tried to take this soldier on, while his partner came up behind her and covered her mouth to keep her from screaming.

Using the great strength in his arm that he had snaked around the queen's delicate neck, he caught off her air until she passed out. Once she did, the soldiers were joined by the rest of their band of twenty. Suspicious of their surroundings, they kept a cautious eye out for the rebels they pursued. They were tying the queen up when a shadowy figure came out of the desert and studied the scene with his lone eye.

"What are your orders now, my lord?" one soldier asked General Sabin.

"We have only part of our bait," he said. He lifted his steely gaze to the mountain passes. Darkness had overshadowed the mountain, and rain had begun to fall. The general smiled, knowing the storm would work to his advantage. "Take her to the rebel encampment and wait.

When Almari had returned from the western pass to rendezvous with her friends just outside of their camp, she knew immediately that something was not right. Looking around, she did not see any signs of them. As her search deepened, Almari spotted Leondros making his way up from the eastern pass. He, too, was searching for the others. Almari whistled like a dove. Leondros was quick to reach her; his expression of concern matched hers.

"Have you seen the others?" Almari quietly asked, shielding her eyes from the rain that was pounding the mountainside.

"I was hoping that you had," Leondros replied, sounding worried. He continued to scan the rugged terrain through the heavy downpour for any signs of Tahari and Elanza.

"I do not like this," Almari said as she cautiously eyed her surroundings.

Leondros noticed something out of the corner of his eye and pointed. "Look over there!" he said. Someone was lying among the rocks close to their camp.

Almari looked in the direction he had pointed as Leondros hurried over to the body just outside of their camp. Dread crept into their hearts, quickly replaced by sorrow as they made out Elanza's motionless form.

When they reached the queen, Almari examined her for serious injury while Leondros traded his bow for his sword and searched the surrounding mountainside, sensing that danger was still close. The wind had picked up; it blew fiercely against them and drove the rain even harder. Leondros shielded his face and fought to keep his bearings on the enemies that he knew were lurking nearby.

"Elanza has been knocked out but otherwise seems unharmed. What could have happened?" Almari wondered as she strained to look up at Leondros through the driving rain. The torrential downpour had already soaked the entire mountainside as well as Leondros and Almari.

He continued to eye the mountain around them. "A trap has been set," he said, his keen elf hearing picked up footsteps moving over rocks nearby. The rocks scraped and shifted against each other as someone moved over them.

"A trap for us?" Almari asked in alarm, her blue eyes wildly searching the stormy surroundings. The ferocious wind tore at her soaked blonde hair and kept her from getting a clear view of what danger was coming.

"A trap for Tahari," Leondros realized sadly as his dark eyes bore into the sweeping rain to see something moving, coming at them. "We are only the bait." then as lightning flashed overhead, he spotted something toward them. "But not if I can help it," he said decisively as he dove into the heart of the storm.

"Leondros! Wait!" Almari called after him, but the howling wind only whisked away her words. She watched as Leondros disappeared into the storm. "You are only playin' into their hands," she finished helplessly. Victory now rested with her; she took up her bow and arrow and readied herself for anything.

Silence slowly replaced the deafening roar of the wind that had howled across the mountainside as Almari waited uneasily for Leondros to return. Now only the gentle sound of rain dripping off of nearby trees could be heard. Almari stepped out from under the rocky ledge that she had pulled the still-unconscious Elanza under to escape the storm's wrath.

The rain had cooled the mountain from the day's heat, and a musty smell lingered. A seemingly peaceful night was ahead, but Almari refused to accept this. Her body was still rigid and on guard.

Evil is still close. Scanning her surroundings, Almari spotted a Draccen soldier standing on the mountain trail leading into their camp. Startled, she did everything in her power to keep from screaming. A dark cloak concealed nearly his whole appearance. Rather than running from fright, Almari had another thought. "Peep at me, will you!" she muttered under her breath, and she took aim at him with her bow.

"I would not do that if I were you," said a deep, gravelly voice from the trees to her left. Almari saw a pale, one-eyed Draccen soldier standing beside a large oak tree. His arms were crossed over his battle armor, and it seemed as if he had been there longer than a moment. The soldier's battled-scarred expression gave her warning, and he motioned for her to look to his right.

Behind him in a small clearing, Almari saw something that caused her heart to sink deep into her gut. Leondros was on his knees with his arms bound behind his back, a dark-brown hood over his head. His brown and green tunic was soaked and mud-covered. Behind him a Draccen soldier stood at the ready with a shiny silver saber. The moment he was given the order, the soldier would slice his sword's sharp blade across Leondros's neck.

Almari was caught between anger and anguish. She turned her bow on the executioner behind Leondros, desperately wanting to take a shot with her bow and help her friend.

"Being noble now will just get your friend killed. And while I am sure you are prepared to die, what about him? How will you ever explain that to the sphinx?" the war-torn soldier asked with an eyebrow raised over his single eye. He smiled with pleasure at the position he had put her in.

Anger filled Almari's blue eyes as she bit down on her lower lip. Finally, she withdrew her arrow and, with angry frustration, threw aside her bow.

General Sabin nodded, signaling his men who had been lurking in the shadows to take Almari and the unconscious queen. Now he had all of his bait.

Chapter 106

Decision

Seeming pleased with his work so far, General Sabin slowly walked up to Leondros while his soldiers bound Almari's arms behind her back and threw her next to her elfin companion. Elanza had just begun to awaken and found herself helplessly tied up and on her knees next to Almari. Ripping the brown leather hood off Leondros's head, General Sabin glared down at his elfin prisoner, who blinked to refocus his eyes.

"Where is the sphinx?" he asked in a tone that sent chills down the captives' spines. Leondros and Almari looked at each other with concern. They did not know where Tahari was or if she even knew that they were in trouble. "Come now. I do not want to be kept waiting. Trust me, you will not have long before I lose my patience," he said with assurance. General Sabin's light-brown eye studied his prisoners. They merely stared back at him He realized then that their answer was defiance, among other things. "Very well. You force my hand," he said as he motioned to his soldiers for something.

Leondros heard the heavy footsteps of two Draccen soldiers walk up behind them. He did not dare turn around, but when he heard the sound of three large war bows being drawn taut directly behind them, Leondros felt his blood go cold. He could almost feel the sharp edge of the jagged arrowheads being aimed directly at their backs. Shifting his gaze to Almari and Elanza, Leondros saw their fearful looks. They were looking to him, hoping that he had a plan to escape this.

"A little overkill, don't you think?" Leondros piped up, stalling for time. Their only hope was for Tahari to find them and get them out of this mess.

"I do whatever the job requires," General Sabin offered evenly, watching Leondros closely.

"What happens to you after the job is finished?" Leondros pressed him. General Sabin was a little taken aback by the question, for he sensed genuine concern from the elf.

"If it is done right, then I will retire with all the spoils of this war. If not, I will be dead." the general's answer did not surprise Leondros.

"What if you were given another choice?" Leondros asked with a hopeful tone. "Leave Lord Jarden's command. You will have a better chance of surviving, and even when death finds you, you will have restored your honor, and your people will have a better chance for a future where all can be prosperous." the general stopped to think about Leondros's proposition. It seemed enticing, except for one thing.

"A future for my people does sound promising—very promising. In fact, there is only one problem with your proposal," General Sabin said slowly as he paced back and forth in front of his prisoners. He stopped in front of Leondros and set his searing gaze upon the elf.

"And that would be?" Leondros answered warily as he watched the Draccen general's body become rigid with anger. The muscles of the general's jaw twitched as he clenched his pointed teeth.

"Your kingdom has fallen; your people are dead, dying, or prisoners in prison camps governed by Lord Jarden—and you, *Prince* Leondros Goldendragon, are the last of your family's bloodline. You are in no position to promise anyone anything." these painful reminders were accompanied by the general's heated tone as he glared down at Leondros. Looking thoroughly pained, the elfin prince remained silent. Elanza looked anger as she knew how Leondros felt. However, it was Almari who refused to take the general's pessimistic view of her elfin friend's fate.

"May the Lord have mercy on you," she hissed under her breath as she kicked out one of her legs and tripped the general as he walked in front of her. He landed on the rocky ground with a thud. Before he could regain his feet, Almari pounced on him, bound though she was. She had quickly slipped her arms under her legs from behind her back and put General Sabin into a head lock. "For I have none!" she continued in a low hiss as she tried to snap his thick neck.

"ALMARI!" Leondros and Elanza cried out, hoping to keep her from getting killed. A Draccen soldier quickly ran up and grabbed Almari by her wet hair, pulling her off the general. She screamed and hollered at the soldier, and the soldier put a sharp dagger to her throat.

"ENOUGH!" General Sabin boomed, finally getting on his feet. Shrugging off the feeling of nearly having his neck snapped in two, he glared at Almari and then shot Leondros a look of death. Two more soldiers took their places behind Leondros, preparing to carry out their next order as another soldier prepared his own arrow for Elanza. Everyone was quiet, waiting for the general's next words. "I do not have time for this! You two have nothing I want or can use. You are of no further use to me. I will just have to hope that your dead bodies will lure out the sphinx," General Sabin said strongly. Waving his strong hand, he spoke his decree. "Kill them!" the cold words echoed in the prisoners' minds, the last words they were to hear before feeling the agonizing death that was awaiting them. Their expressions paled with horror, and the Draccen soldiers started to follow through with the execution.

Then as if Adalai himself had shown up, a thunderous voice filled the small clearing where the execution party was gathered. "STOP!" All turned to see who had put a stop to the execution. Most of the Draccen soldiers were gripped with a sudden intense fear. A figure in a dark hooded cloak seemed to emerge from the very air before one of soldiers. The soldier was wary and wounded, and the dark-cloaked figure held a sword just inches from his throat. The other soldiers sensed that this person was a force to be reckoned with, but their general remained defiant. The captives, however, were overwhelmed with relief, for they knew this dark-cloaked warrior was none other than Tahari. Tearing back her dark hood, Tahari made her anger most clear as one could see it in the seriousness of her sea-green eyes, the set of her jaw. But her rage had yet to be felt.

"You are good, I have to admit. However..." General Sabin said slyly. He pulled a crossbow from beneath his cloak and shot an arrow straight at the soldier and Tahari.

Chapter 107

Rescue

T ahari watched helplessly as General Sabin shot an arrow straight into the heart of the Draccen soldier she held prison in front of her. The soldier jerked in great pain and sank helplessly to the ground. Everyone stared in horror. "I am better," the Draccen general boasted in an unsettling tone.

The shock of his deed left Tahari vulnerable to his soldiers, who grabbed her and brought her face to face with the general. Tahari gazed coldly at him for a moment before she found her voice again.

"You are better? You would intentionally let the people of Andora die to serve scum like Lord Jarden and you? You murder them," Tahari pointed out with a disbelieving voice. "I never thought it was possible to meet someone more black-hearted than Lord Jarden himself, but you proved me wrong," she stated with a clear voice. His men looked at each with horror and uncertainty.

"Thank you; I am deeply honored to hear this. I was compelled to try something new after that stunt you pulled in Gortorro and the fine situation I am now in with Lord Jarden," General Sabin explained, flashing Tahari a look of animosity. "Since I am being held in such high regard by a sphinx of the ancient world, I am willing to offer a token of my generosity," he said slyly. Tahari narrowed her eyes, for she did not trust what he was going to offer her. "I am going to release all of you," he said almost sincerely. Looks of amazement passed between Tahari and her friends.

Tahari glared angrily at him. "At what cost?" she demanded, for she sensed an evil twist within their chance at freedom. The Draccen general remained silent for a long moment and studied each of them. His light-brown eye flashed with a sinister idea, a cruel smile forming across his lips.

"One will stay behind to pay the price for the others' freedom. One of you will have to die." as the Draccen general spoke these words, Tahari looked over at her friends. They exchanged looks of horror. Then he strode up to Tahari, took hold of her arm, and marched her directly in front of her friends. "You will decide who it will be, and then we will take care of the rest," he said in a cold tone, pointing a large muscular finger at the three who knelt before them. "Now take your time and choose carefully. I would hate it if you chose someone you did not want dead," he said maliciously as he stepped away.

Standing there, Tahari found herself frozen with uncertainty, faced with a strange and horrible decision. Equal expressions of horror and dread swept over her friends' faces. The guilt in Elanza's face was impossible to miss. Tahari knew that she felt awful for letting herself be taken by surprise, which put the rest of the group in danger, and she wished for death. While Tahari was still standing at the top of the center pass, she had a good view of the bottom of the mountain where Elanza had been overtaken—an action not of her making, but her guilt would not let her believe that.

Tahari's gaze fell next on Leondros. His head was hung low, his blond hair falling past his shoulders. She felt his shame, too, and her heart broke again. She had had a good view of what transpired within their encampment as well, and he had been helpless to do anything more for his friends or for himself with his hands bound tightly behind his back and the soldiers keeping a close guard on him. His actions, along with Elanza's incapacity, had been the tool the Draccen general needed to capture Almari, thus entrapping her in this terrible position.

Tahari looked over at Almari. She looked at her with her deep-blue eyes and then lowered her head sadly, an equal expression of guilt and sadness filling her face. She had let her temper get the best of her and had nearly had all three of them slain moments before.

Confusion hit Tahari hard. As she looked upon the faces she had grown to love, Tahari had to decide which of them must die. She tried to swallow the lump in her throat, but it was much too painful. Tahari felt the full weight of the prophecy crashing down on her. She now understood what the second-to-last line of the scroll meant:

3.) A terrible position will force one to choose from among those near and dear.

Chapter 108

Honoring a Promise

Tahari's chest felt as though it were about to cave in from the intense grief. Her dear friends were on their knees before her as if she were their executioner. For one of them, Tahari would be. They did not speak a word, but she read their eyes. Their pleas for help were deafening. Tahari felt their pain as if it were her own. It was her own.

"Take your time. We have all night. If it has to take that long," General Sabin scoffed, his last words coming out in a mumble. He crossed his thick, muscular arms over his chest and waited for Tahari to make her decision. She shot him a dangerous glare, and then she slowly turned her gaze back to her friends. These three were more than just strangers she had met during the course of this journey; they were her family. Tahari loved them all. How could she kill or even harm one of them? Tears stung Tahari's eyes.

Looking at each one, Tahari could see into their pasts. She knew their stories. One person was not more important than another. This was a choice that she could not make.

Her gaze met Leondros's for a moment. He looked into her eyes and saw into her thoughts. He knew that she could not bring herself to harm any of them, for it was against everything that she believed.

He had a look of understanding in his soulful face, but also knew that a decision had to be made or they would all die. He turned to the Draccen general and spoke.

"I will be the one. Kill me so that the others can be free," Leondros offered humbly. "I brought this peril to my friends; the least I can do is rescue them from it." shock spread through the group like wildfire. All except for General Sabin—he seemed glad that they had finally reached a decision.

"About time," the aged general said. He gave Tahari a sinister smile while he motioned for the archer standing behind Leondros to prepare for the execution. When they saw him, they all gasped.

The archer looked his part of executioner. Dressed in thick, dark material, he was ten feet tall and massive. He carried a large, black war bow tightly and fitted it with an arrow about an inch thick! Two other soldiers standing next to Leondros were shorter but no less threatening. They picked Leondros up by his arms and dragged him backward away from the rest of them, throwing him to the red dusty ground only a few feet from the archer.

The elfin prince slowly managed to sit up and position himself upon his knees once more. Leondros looked at the archer with an angered expression that clearly said, *Let us have this over with*. His gaze stayed upon his executioner. The life within his handsome face drained as he knew death was near.

Tahari watched in agony, her mind a whirlwind of confusion. She was his protector, so why was she letting him do this? Then Tahari remembered the line of instruction from the prophecy:

Take a stand between them and a loved one.

"Let it be as he has said," Tahari began with determination, finding the will to walk in front of Leondros and stand firmly between him and the giant executioner. Everyone watched her with uncertainty. Most, she was sure, did not understand what was taking place here. However, this gave her courage. Walking into the path of an arrow is difficult, but walking into the line of fire for a friend is easy. "But only if you can get the arrow past me," Tahari finished in an even tone, glaring at the oversized archer. He looked perplexed. Even General

Sabin seemed caught off-guard.

Finally Sabin said, "If that's how you want it, so be it." he studied Tahari's face closely as if to discover her true intentions. "Lord Jarden would have wanted you as a prisoner, but your being dead will have to suffice." he seemed almost disappointed as he stepped back to let his monstrous archer carry out the execution.

Standing before the archer, Tahari mentally blocked out everything else and focused all her energies on the archer. Watching him as he drew his bow taut, Tahari narrowed her gaze first onto the bow and then onto the arrow. Finally, Tahari concentrated on the arrowhead itself. All that existed in her world now was her and that arrowhead.

When the arrow was released, Tahari felt as if it were moving in slow motion. She watched it glide through the air, and as it came close to her, she grabbed it. The air rippled around her hand, and she held on to the arrow. Tahari fought to breathe normally again. Raising her gaze, Tahari saw the astonishment in everyone's eyes.

"Now, we are *all* free," Tahari said in an even tone, glaring at General Sabin and holding up the very large arrow in her hand. He seemed frozen to the ground and unsure what to do next. At long last, he threw down his sword in anger.

"FINE! So be it!" he shouted angrily. "Go free, for all I care!" The general's order traveled throughout the entire band of soldiers like ripples on a pond. The soldiers began to lower their weapons, for they had indeed won their freedom.

Almari quickly managed to stand up and turned towards the Draccen soldier behind her. She used the blade of his sword to cut her bonds and then turned to help Elanza free herself.

Finally allowing herself to move again, Tahari turned around and looked down at Leondros. The expression on his face was one she would never forget. He seemed so overwhelmed with emotion that there were tears in his warm brown eyes. He looked both confused and deeply touched by her actions. Tahari could read every thought within his mind as she looked at his face. Tahari managed a smile as she sank to my knees and took out a dagger to cut the ropes that bound his wrists.

"Are you all right, my friend?" she asked in warm whisper. He pulled his wrists free and rubbed the soreness out of them, looking at her with confusion and wonder.

"Why did you do it?" he searched her face for the answer to what she had just done. "The fault was mine; I put you all in danger. I deserved death." he spoke weakly as if undeserving of such a blessing. He had fully accepted responsibility for his deed and was ready to take his punishment. However, the punishment intended for him was taken away by someone who loved him. As he spoke, Tahari just listened with a warm and understanding smile.

"Three reasons. First, I took an oath to be your guardian, an oath that spans thousands of years already—I am to protect you, to whatever end. Second, I would not be a true friend if I did not find it in my heart to forgive," Tahari said as tears stung her eyes. As she spoke these words, the great weight that had borne down on Leondros melted, and his smile returned.

"What was the third reason?" he asked softly.

"Real love," Tahari said warmly. "Such a thing covers many transgressions; it makes it so the deed itself never happened, and the only thing that matters is the one I hold dear." too overwhelmed for words, Leondros weakly lowered his head, tears running down his dirty face. Tahari smiled and wrapped her arms around him, holding him tight.

"Thank you, my friend," he managed softly. He held onto her and rested his head against hers. The tenderness of the moment turned into a victorious celebration, for Almari and Elanza had jumped to their feet and were hugging each other and yelling in delight.

When Tahari finally let go of Leondros and looked at him, she noticed the second the warmth in his face drained. Tahari snapped her head around to see what was coming at them. In her horror, Tahari watched General Sabin charging at them like a madman. His shrill scream filled the night as he sliced through the air with his very large sword.

In his rage and attempt to come at Leondros and Tahari, he didn't see Elanza in his path. The queen was trying to get out of his way when she tripped over a root. She fell, screaming, but her screams were cut short when General Sabin came upon her with his sword. She raised her delicate arm to shield herself. The world seemed to stop as they waited in agony for the blade to shred her body.

"OH NO! NOOOO!" General Sabin cried out suddenly as he literally stopped his attack on Elanza mid-swing. Everyone, rebels and Draccen alike, stood absolutely still. The large sword fell from the general's muscular hands and clattered harmlessly to the ground. He was in the grip of absolute fright, holding his head in his hands and trying to refocus himself. He looked up at everyone and screamed. They looked at him dumbfounded, and Tahari wondered if he had lost his mind completely. The aged general looked around at everyone with eyes that were large and full of fear. He saw the massive sword lying at his feet and went into a state of panic.

"Now, feel what it is like for those who had to bear your wrath!" Tahari said with a cold anger as she slowly rose to her feet with her hand stretched out toward the General. "Feel their fear!" Tahari commanded him.

A second later, General Sabin cried out with a nightmarish yell as he whirled around and fought to get away from them. Half falling, half scrambling, the Draccen general tore out of their encampment and fled into the night. Although hesitant, some of his men followed him out of camp. They heard him long after he had vanished from sight. His screams faded down the mountainside.

"What the *hell* was that?" Almari asked, helping Elanza back to her feet. Leondros looked over at Tahari and cocked an eyebrow, a sly smile coming to his face.

"You turned our fear on him and made him believe it was his own," he said knowingly.

"You can do that?" Almari asked as she turned to Tahari in surprise. Tahari offered a soft smile as she bowed her head humbly.

"He will never hurt those who fight against Lord Jarden ever again," Tahari promised with certainty. "That fear will always be with him now as a reminder of what we have endured.

"I heard how the grand sphinxes of the ancient world could use their empathy and other emotions to confront enemies in battle. I just never thought I would see it with my own eyes," Leondros said. Tahari smiled humbly, but then as she looked out at the darkness that surrounded the small encampment, she saw something unsettling. The remainder of General Sabin's company had regrouped and were coming back.

"I think we are going to need a little more in our arsenal," Tahari said. "Look at what is coming for us." She pointed to the torches that spread out from the desert floor and up the mountainside.

The remaining Draccen soldiers were accompanied by about forty additional soldiers, all following one of the last sane orders General Sabin gave them, "*Search out and find the rebel band and deliver them to Lord Jarden, or it will be all our heads!*"

Their hearts raced with anxiety, but they were angered, too. Leondros did not hesitate to take up his bow and prepare himself for the battle ahead. The rest of these valiant-hearted friends followed his example. As Tahari readied her bow, she overheard Almari mumble under her breath as she, too, prepared.

"Oh, you have got to be kidding me! Have they all gone mad? Or are they afraid we just might reach Rahara, where they cannot attack us? Well, if they want a fight, I would sure hate to disappoint them." Tahari stopped, looked at her dear friend with a dumbfounded expression, looked at the mountain behind them, and then back at her friend.

"Almari, you are truly brilliant!" Tahari said with renewed energy.

"Huh? How so?" she asked, confused.

"You have just given us our way out of this!" Tahari offered excitedly. She picked up her gear and indicated to Leondros and Elanza that they needed to follow her. A look of sudden understanding filled Leondros's road-weary face. After a nod, he quietly put away his bow and helped Elanza gather the few supplies they had carried with them. They silently left the encampment, making their way up the winding mountain trail. Almari watched with disappointment in her deep-blue eyes.

"But..." She seemed a little lost that she could not have one more go at the Draccen soldiers. "But I was so hopin'..."

"Right now we need to find shelter and protection," Tahari said, keeping an eye on the mountain trail below them.

"I need neither shelter nor protection," Almari said firmly. Her body went rigid with anger as she gripped her sword tightly. Tahari smiled and shook her head slightly.

"Our need for shelter and protection is not for defense against the Draccen army. There is a force on the north face of Mt. Somerset that protects all agents good and just. It is not a force to be reckoned with. No evil should dare pass through it," Tahari clarified and winked. A sly grin came to her lips, and she picked up her bundle of supplies.

"Very well," Almari finally agreed in a tone of disgust. "But you owe me the chance to throttle them good!" Her words were accompanied by a determined look.

Tahari smiled as she looked at her friend who had once been a slave and was now a powerful warrior. She was tough, but there was something good and just that shone out of her whole being. Tahari thought of her role in this mission and felt saddened that she might have left her out. Tahari's smile faded slightly; she shook her head as they hurried up the rough terrain that led them over the mountain.

"What is it?" she asked when she saw the sadness in Tahari's face.

"I know during this journey you must have felt a little left out, but I have seen the warrior you have become, and I sense something grand in your future," Tahari said warmly as she put a comforting hand on her right shoulder. Almari stopped and turned to her friend. An expression of warmth came to her face.

"This mission was not about me—it was about somethin' much bigger. It called you to be its sacred messenger, and I accept that. Besides, I am no longer a slave; I am free. I hold no resentment." she shook her head as she explained. Tahari found her ability to smile again as a weight was lifted from her shoulders. "You said you sensed something about my future?" Almari asked with intrigue.

"As bold and strong as you are, I sense you will be a guardian—a guardian who will surely become as great and powerful as a knight of the Osarian Order. You may even earn Sala's favor to become one." Almari dropped her gaze as it filled with guilt.

"Tahari, forgive me. I do not deserve such an honor. I nearly got Leondros and Elanza and me killed just moments ago." her voice was filled with regret as Tahari watched her deep-blue eyes glaze over with tears and her face fall. "All because of my stupid anger," she confessed with great remorse. Tahari looked at her for a moment and then put a reassuring arm around her shoulder.

"Anger is good," she said thoughtfully. "It can keep you alive. You just have to know when it is best to display it." Almari lifted her gaze and looked at Tahari with hope. "I hold no grudge, and my trust in you is not broken." Tahari's smile allowed Almari's whole posture to lighten. "What is ahead will require us to think as a whole and not as parts. Think of everyone, and not just for yourself." Almari listened carefully and nodded as they kept walking up the mountain path.

They felt the stormy night air hang close to them as they fought to keep from slipping down the wet terrain. Suddenly, lightning flashed in the distance, and thunder rumbled across the mountainside. The storm, it seemed, was returning. They heard someone holler behind them.

"I SEE THEM! HURRY!" a Draccen soldier shouted, his voice echoing across the whole mountainside.

"Thinkin' of the group, we should step on it," Almari reasoned quickly as alarm filled her face and she broke into a dead run.

"No debate from the group," Tahari replied as she ran alongside her. They were quick to scamper over the summit of the mountain and down the other side, where they met up with Leondros and Elanza.

Chapter 109

Heaven Gates

Tahari and Almari soon made it down the soggy mountain trail and rejoined Leondros and Elanza. They all looked out at the darkened landscape. The winding path before them led to what looked like a dark, barren wasteland beyond Mt. Somerset. Almari and Elanza looked at Leondros and Tahari in doubt.

"Wait for it," Tahari said simply as she continued to lead the group toward sand dunes, scrubby brush, and cacti. Out of place were two obelisks of gray granite that seemed to resemble a gateway of sorts. Tahari walked up to the gateway and slowly raised her hand to touch the dark space between the two obelisks. As soon as her fingers passed beyond the space between the obelisks, they disappeared! Tahari's smile widened as she felt the humid atmosphere on the other side of the gateway.

Looking back to her friends, Tahari held out her other hand and smiled with excitement. Leondros took her proffered hand, then Almari reached out and took his, and Queen Elanza took hers. Pushing forward with no fear, Tahari passed through the gateway and led the others from the sands of the Barrens to the mystical land that lay beyond.

They were greeted by a lush rainforest with wondrous smells of grasses, flowers, and heavy dew. Tahari could hear a waterfall's roar in the distance. She could feel the magic in this realm, for she felt safe as soon as they left the shadow of Mt. Somerset. On the trail that led north from Mt. Somerset and descended past the two obelisks into the thick lush forest below them were three walls that stood side by side made of white and gray granite. The walls were twice as tall as Leondros and were spaced evenly apart so that only two people could pass side by side.

"The two obelisks that we passed through and these walls are the sentinels for Rahara's southern gate. The magic that protects this gateway lies within them. No evil can pass through them and survive. It will protect the good and just from evil's harm," Leondros explained to them as he motioned to the walls with his hand.

"You said that your people created this realm?" Almari asked still in shock at the serene beauty of the land around her.

"Yes, my father wanted to create a haven for those who needed sanctuary from the evils of the world. It was felt by all my people that the Barrens would be the perfect place to conceal just such a paradise. It was a chance for us to restore the splendor that was Lani and honor our friends the sphinxes," Leondros replied, a look of memory washing over his face as if he were reliving the good times he had had with his family and friends long ago.

"Why can you not see this realm from the desert surrounding Mt. Somerset?" Elanza asked. Lightning flashed overhead.

"The magic keeps the sacred land of Rahara under a shield of invisibility. Agents of evil might have the good fortune to look upon the gates and even the landscape of Rahara itself, but they will not be alive long enough to enjoy it," Leondros said.

Though his voice was filled with warmth and wisdom, they felt uneasy about the doom that was in store for any transgressor. The sounds of the rainforest seemed to ride on the warm breeze that swept past them, and birdsong welcomed them into this land. Their weary minds were already beginning to take comfort in being here, but the tranquility that surrounded them was rudely interrupted by a brash voice.

"DOWN THERE!" the cruel voice boomed down the mountain

trail, and the four friends whirled around to see the Draccen soldiers filing down the mountainside.

"Everyone," Leondros announced as worry washed over his face. His brown eyes nervously studied the charging mass of Draccen soldiers. He slowly moved toward Elanza, but his gaze remained on the soldiers charging down the mountain trail toward the southern gates of Rahara. "GET DOWN! BEHIND THE WALLS!" he cried out in great alarm, and he pulled Elanza behind the middle wall and shielded her. Tahari and Almari grabbed hold of each other and huddled behind the wall to the right of Leondros and Elanza. They did not know what was about to happen, but they braced themselves for the worst.

Chapter 110

Dissention

The remainder of General Sabin's company of ruthless soldiers had combed the mountain's southeastern side for the rebel band. However, the trackers had begun to suspect that the band had moved on and was now on the other side of the mountain.

"You do not intend to follow them over the summit, do you?" a Draccen soldier asked the new commander. The new commander was silent for a moment as the company looked to him and waited. He remembered very well the command that Lord Jarden had given to General Sabin.

"I will not let superstition govern my actions!" he barked back in anger. "There is nothing magical about this worthless piece of rock. I plan to chase after these rebels, even if I have to drive them to the very edges of the Barrens!" he proclaimed as he angrily took up his sword and began to march forward toward the mountain summit.

"What if the legends are true?" the soldier called after the commander, nervously eyeing the rugged mountain with anxious brown eyes. "What if the elves have actually enchanted this mountain? It would mean death to pass beyond its northern face." as he spoke these words, other Draccen soldiers looked at each other and then back at the commander with uncertainty.

The commander stopped and slowly turned around. He glared at the soldier from out of a leather mask that ran down his forehead and between his pointed ears. Long strands of leather decorated with silver beads hanging from his dark leather mask seemed to add to his ferocity.

"I should kill you where you stand!" he glared at the soldier and then at those who surrounded him. The commander could see they were debating whether to stay or to follow him to hunt down the rebels for Lord Jarden. "If you decide to stay, then that will be your course, but I march to bring the rebels back for Lord Jarden. He, no doubt, will be gracious enough to reward those who capture the rebel band." he stared at them a moment longer and then turned and charged up the mountain trail that would take him over the summit.

"Go, any of you that want to share in his glory—I am choosing my own path!" the soldier announced to the rest. A moment later, all but ten soldiers charged after their leader. They yelled out as they charged up the trail.

The forty-seven Draccen soldiers were quick to catch up with their commander. As they thundered down the trail together, the commander caught a glimpse of a black dragon in the distance flying down to join them. Pride and excitement coursed through his veins. He let out a howl of animal joy as he pressed forward, and his men followed.

"We are not alone. Lord Jarden comes. We rush to victory!" he called out to all his men, and he took up his spear. The Draccen soldiers who followed him returned the howl. The excitement fueled the company as lightning flashed across the sky. They wanted to charge into whatever lay ahead of them, but when they reached the bottom of the mountain trail and passed between two odd-looking obelisks, the Draccen soldiers stopped dead in their tracks.

After passing beyond the two obelisks, the charging Draccen soldiers noticed that the wastelands' sandy trail had changed into soft, white sand. When they looked out ahead, they looked upon the legendary land of Rahara. The commander and his company were quick to take in the land's splendor, for no one of their race had ever looked upon it. Then the Draccen commander saw the rebel band and remembered their mission.

"DOWN THERE!" a soldier cried out, pointing to something below them. The harshness of the soldier's voice woke them from their trance. The commander looked upon the sphinx and remembered his chance for reward and riches.

"There is no land where you will be safe from us!" he swore as he raced down the white sandy trail toward her. The Draccen company quickly refocused itself and followed its leader.

Before they could reach Tahari and her friends, however, the three massive walls that protected them began to glow blue. Then, from the walls that shot an intense beam of blue light shot straight into the stormy night sky. The light formed a barrier that stretched east and west of the walls as far as the eye could see. Its energy glowed brightly in the night's darkness.

Fear struck the Draccen commander, but he could not slow his descent to avoid hitting the barrier of light. His scream filled the night as he and his men ran full speed into the barrier. An explosion of blue light and thunder ripped across the base of Mt. Somerset's northern face. The earth shook, and its roar drowned out all other sound as the Draccen commander and his men were obliterated before Rahara's southern gates.

Chapter 111

A Son's Mother

When all was quiet again, Tahari waited a moment before she opened her eyes. Shaken from the explosion, Tahari and Almari clung to each other and fought to breathe normally again.

"It is safe now," Leondros's gentle voice broke through their panicked thoughts. Leondros cautiously stood in front of the large wall he and Elanza had hid behind. He was looking toward the northern face of Mt. Somerset. "The Draccen soldiers are no more," he said with a sigh of relief. "Our journey into Rahara will be protected by the land's magic and will be free from Lord Jarden's evil," he said reassuringly. He took a minute to lean back against the granite wall and close his eyes to calm his mind.

Elanza finally rose to her feet and stepped past Leondros to look upon the enchanted mountain. Seeing for herself that the soldiers in fact had vanished, Elanza brightened considerably.

"Thank you, my child!" Elanza said in a rush of relief as she threw her arms around Leondros, nearly smothering their elfin friend. Tahari and Almari chuckled as Leondros struggled to regain his bearings and return the hug.

"I cannot believe it," Almari said, sounding astounded. "We made it! We *all* made it!" She took Tahari's hand and squeezed it.

There were no words that could describe the new sense of life Tahari was filled with. Almari was right. As the whole of their journey flashed back through her mind, Tahari remained in awe at what they had triumphed over. A new-found enthusiasm gave strength to her road-weary body and made her look forward to seeing Sala again and finding a way to stop Lord Jarden once and for all. Looking down and finding the scrolls of the prophecy that were safely tucked away in her saddlebag, though, something occurred to her.

"Strange," Tahari said, half to herself. "It has not played itself out yet. Something else remains..." Tahari stared at the three aged scrolls, each now bound with dark leather string. Tahari slowly lifted her head and saw Almari walking down toward the dense tree line of the rainforest, admiring the breathtaking view before them. Her thoughts drifted for a moment before they were shattered by Elanza's blood-curdling scream.

"ALON-SETTIE!" Elanza's scream snapped all of them back to reality, and Tahari turned just in time to see the queen race back toward Mt. Somerset. Tahari looked at Leondros in alarm and hurried toward the opening between the two large walls. Leondros and Almari were quick to join Tahari.

"Alon-Settie must have been following the Draccen army on the back of the black dragon we've seen. Lord Jarden must have made him a dragon rider," Leondros reasoned quickly. They watched on in horror as Elanza raced toward the dark-armored body of her son, who lay sprawled on the red sandy mountain trail, just a few feet from the obelisks.

"Looks like his dragon had more sense than he did," Tahari said as she pointed to the black dragon flying a distance away.

"The dragon avoided flying into the barrier by quickly changing his course, but Alon-Settie must have fallen off," Almari said.

"Oh, no," Leondros said as his brown eyes went wide with horror. "The barrier is trying to bar Alon-Settie from passing through," he continued to comment as his pace quicken as he headed for Queen Elanza. "She must not pass back through the energy barrier while Alon-Settie is on the other side. It could mean death for her!" He broke into a run, desperate to stop the distraught queen. "ELANZA! STOP!" Leondros hollered after her, struggling to catch her before she reached the energy barrier, but it was too late. The moment that Elanza passed through the blue barrier, thunder filled the air and a flash of blinding light enveloped everything around it, including Elanza. The force of the blast knocked everyone from their feet.

Chapter 112

Enemy Engaged

Regaining consciousness, Elanza opened her eyes and looked up into the dark sky. As the pain from the blast subsided, she slowly sat up and took stock. The blast had blown her shoes off, and her already ragged gown and cloak were even more ragged, if that were possible. As the ringing in her ears faded, Elanza remembered Leondros trying to stop her. Looking around, she felt her heart sink as he was nowhere to be found. Tahari and Almari weren't nearby, either. Perhaps the blast had blown them into the tree line further downhill—or at least, she prayed it had. Strangely, the blasts had no effect on the land itself. The white sand on which she had been deposited was completely untouched by the violent explosions. Turning her gaze back to the mountain trail, Elanza saw the body of her son still lying in a heap on the red sandy ground.

"Alon, what have you done?" Elanza asked in a hurt whisper, slowly picking her bruised body off the ground and painfully walking back toward her child. This time as she walked over the sandy ground where the barrier had stopped her before, nothing happened. She did not care why—all she cared about was reaching her son.

She passed through the gate and over to him. When she reached his battered body, she knelt beside him. "Why have you let yourself be misled by such a creature?" she asked him pointedly.

Before she could react, Alon-Settie's eyes popped open and he took hold of her arms with an iron-like grip. He forced them both to their feet.

"I was not being misled. I have a new sense of awareness—and with it, I can see fools and their feeble attempt to use power!" he said strongly. "Lord Jarden may be only a messenger for his people, but his mission is most sacred. The time of his people is coming. How long do you think this feeble nation will be able to hold off his kind?" Alon-Settie's harsh words caught Elanza off-guard and broke her heart.

"War comes to all nations, and the life of a nation rests with its people, but you have betrayed your own family. Riches or glory will not erase the travesty that you have committed!" But Elanza's words held no meaning for the man standing before her. His brown eyes did not waver. "No," she said sadly as she shook her head. "You are not my son. He would have defended my family with his very life.

"Alon-Settie! Let her go!" Leondros's angry voice echoed up the mountain trail and caught their attention. They turned to see a slightly battered-looking Leondros Goldendragon coming toward them. The anger in his face was as hard as stone. As he slowly walked toward his one-time friend, Leondros drew his sword for the fight ahead. The sharp sound made Alon-Settie eager.

"Come! I am waiting!" An evil expression filled Alon-Settie's face. As he waited for Leondros to join him, he looked back down at his mother as if for the last time. "Goodbye, Mother—now you are free to be with your family!" he said in a tone of voice that was a mix of hurt and anger. Then he shoved her backward and watched her small form tumble to the ground. The aged woman lay there, limp and unmoving.

"So where is your precious barrier now?" Alon-Settie asked with a scoff as he spitefully passed between the obelisks and kicked the sacred white sands of Rahara. Leondros's answer came in the form of a heated glare as he slowly made his way closer to the prince of Akendron. "Is it not true that the barrier is supposed to stop any transgressor? Anyone who would bring harm to this sacred paradise?" Alon-Settie pressed, the mockery in his brown eyes teasing Leondros.

"The magic of this place cannot contend with something even more sacred: the love of a mother for her child," Leondros calmly explained as he lifted his soulful brown eyes to the surrounding night air around him. Leondros was reminded of his own mother. A sad smile came to his face and tears stung his eyes.

When he lowered his gaze back to Alon-Settie, Leondros's anger returned, washing away the brief warmth. "Elanza felt her child in danger and was driven to try to protect him." Leondros studied Alon-Settie for a moment and then nodded his head slightly in understanding. "Only the son she knew died on the night that Lord Jarden took over Akendron. He died in a torture chamber along with his friend." Leondros's words brought back vivid images of that terrible night. A sad anger now filled the elfin prince's face.

"Touching story. I will make sure it is written in the walls of your tomb." Alon-Settie said coldly as he pulled out his own sword.

"How generous of you!" Leondros narrowed his eyes, watching his enemy's movements and preparing for the first attack. "Your name will never be found on any wall or tomb. It will be found only in the pages of this country's history, along with all the others who brought it to ruin." the sad reality of Leondros's words hit Alon-Settie, forcing a lucid moment of clarity onto Akendron's prince. The realization of all his actions tortured his mind, and there was only one course before him now. "You have no kingdom, no country—and most of all, you have no family," Leondros said angrily, cocking his head slightly as if to drive home his point.

"Then I will deprive you of what is left of yours!" Alon-Settie said, enraged as he rushed at Leondros. Their swords clashed and rang in the night air as lightning illuminated the fight.

Chapter 113

Defending Mt. Somerset

"Tahari!" The distant sound of Almari's voice broke through Tahari's unconsciousness. The sensation of the damp forest around her and someone shaking her shoulders became real. "TAHARI, WAKE UP!.

"I am up—really. There is no need to yell," Tahari mumbled as she fought to open her eyes. When the blurry images around her slowly came into focus, Tahari saw an intensely worried Almari kneeling on the moist earth beside her. Her blue-and-green tunic, along with her dark cloak, had become wet once more in the gentle rain that passed through the rainforest. Her long blonde-brown hair hung in a soaked braid and was draped around her shoulder as beads of rain glistened in her hair and on her face. In her dirty face Tahari saw great worry. "What happened?" Tahari asked in a groggy whisper.

"Elanza walked back through the barrier. Her first attempt knocked us all back, but on her second attempt she made it to Alon-Settie's side." Almari relayed the previous events to Tahari in a panicked rush.

While doing so, she noticed something on Tahari's head that caused alarm to fill her face, and she quickly rummaged in her pack for a handkerchief. She gently placed it against her aching head. "You were thrown against one of the walls. You seemed to have hit your head on it." the worry in her eyes was replicated in her whole posture.

"Oh, is that all?" Tahari mused as she fought to shake the pain and dizziness out of her head. Almari shot her friend a serious glance, and she took the handkerchief off to re-examine the gash in Tahari's head. It had already become soaked with blood, but Tahari refused to let it worry her.

"Tahari, this is serious!" she scolded, and then gestured toward the Barrens. "Leondros went to confront Alon-Settie. He is going to need our help." Almari replaced the handkerchief on Tahari's forehead and then looked for her sword and daggers.

Tahari held the handkerchief to her head for a moment. After a brief meditation, Tahari removed the handkerchief and cautiously looked around the granite wall to see the fight that she overheard going on. It gripped Tahari's heart to see Leondros in another match with Alon-Settie, and not far from the fight was poor Elanza, who lay unmoving, no doubt as the result of Alon-Settie's handiwork. Tahari could only lower her head wearily.

"Yes and no," Tahari said quietly as she continued to watch the ferocious duel transpiring just up the hill from them. Almari stopped and looked at her friend strangely.

"Do you not want to help him?" Her words were riddled with disbelief. Tahari ignored her question for the moment, looking from the fight to the tree line behind Leondros and Alon-Settie and listening carefully. Upon the warm and humid air, Tahari noticed an elusive presence as dangerous as the former prince of Akendron. Chills ran down her spine for the elusive threat closing in on them.

"He needs help, of that there is no question. But not with Alon-Settie. There is more danger coming toward us," Tahari explained calmly as she gestured with her head toward the trees. Tahari then turned her gaze back to the fight. "Leondros will have to fight Alon-Settie on his own, or he will never be free of the betrayal that claimed his life," she said with sad certainty. "That leaves us to deal with the coming danger."

Taking a breath to refocus herself, Tahari picked up a sword, a brown leather whip, and her remaining few daggers. She jumped to her feet and scurried to the far end of the west granite wall. She stayed low to the ground to avoid being seen.

Almari lingered for a moment as she watched the intense fight between her friend and the former prince before joining Tahari at the wall.

"What is this danger that you speak of?" Almari asked when she had caught up with Tahari. She followed her intense gaze to the mountain before them.

"Draccen soldiers—not many, but nonetheless dangerous. They must have broken off from the main group just before they were obliterated by the energy barrier," Tahari said slowly as she shook off the unsettling vibe of their essence.

"Lucky buggers," Almari grumbled under her breath, sounding annoyed.

"Come," Tahari said as she watched Almari pull up her dark velvet hood to better blend in with their surroundings. "We need to fix that. Now is your chance to hunt those 'lucky buggers,'" she said with a sly smile. In giving Almari permission to go to war, Tahari saw the side of her that she loved.

"You may call it huntin'," she said as she took out a dagger and studied it for a moment, "but I call it sport." nodding in approval, Tahari gave Almari the signal to move up the mountain to the east as she checked out the western side. Together, they disappeared into the surrounding mist that had moved over the lower half of Mt. Somerset.

From Tahari's hiding place, she could see and hear the Draccen soldiers easily. They were a small band of 11. The leader scanned the area cautiously, listening to even the faintest sound that came from the mountain. They looked determined to succeed where their previous commander had failed.

"How do you plan to lead an assault against a sphinx from the ancient world?" a soldier asked the all-black leader humbly. "They are beings of immense power and…"

"Do not dwell on what you think, for you will end up losing the battle before it even begins. She is still a creature of flesh and blood, and we are born of a clever and cunning race, too. Dwell on what is only," the new leader instructed in a hushed voice as his warm brown eyes continued to study the rough terrain of the mountain.

"My lord, do you hear that?" another soldier asked. At that moment, all ears within the war party twitched and turned in unison and strained to listen against the howling wind. As Tahari strained to listen through the wind, she could hear metal swords clashing against each other. As the leader listened, a smile grew upon his dark face.

"It sounds like Prince Alon-Settie has found the elfin prince from Adarah. Lord Jarden has something special planned for the elf, but we need to ensure that Alon-Settie comes out victorious, or Lord Jarden will have all of our heads," he said as he faced the ten others who watched and listened. "We will split into two teams, each team taking one side of the mountain, and move toward Alon-Settie's position. Remember to stay under the hood of your cloaks; they will conceal you when lightning flashes overhead. If this sphinx and whoever else she has with her are as good as we believe, they will be watching for us. The rain causes our skin to glisten; we need to stay concealed," the leader carefully instructed as he pulled his dark cloak over himself and covered his head with the large hood. The remaining soldiers did the same. As they did, they became one with the shadows. Then the all-black leader pointed to five of the soldiers who stood before him. "You five patrol the eastern side; the rest of us will take the west. Be cautious and on your guard."

The five Draccen soldiers nodded and then quickly and quietly turned to start their mission. Moments later, they had disappeared into the night, headed toward Almari. Tahari almost felt sorry for the soldiers.

Meanwhile, the remaining six Draccen soldiers headed west and south through thick trees and rough rocky terrain that covered the mountain. Tahari followed them until she was certain of her advantage.

Coming to a ridge on the southeastern edge of the mountain, the soldiers had a clear view of the intense fight between the two princes. No senseless words were spoken amongst them; for everything that was at stake, they felt they needed to be on their guard and ensure that Alon-Settie walked out of this battle by any means necessary.

"When you have a clear shot, fire upon the elfin prince!" a greenish-brown Draccen soldier instructed as he quickly pulled out his bow and readied an arrow. Four other Draccen soldiers followed his example. All they waited for now was a clear shot.

The leader, however, reached slowly for his bow, watching the elfin prince fighting for his life. He lowered his arm and shook his head. "If he dies by our hand, then we are no different from those who locked us away for thousands of years or the master we serve now." with that, the leader backed away from the ledge.

"Have you gone completely soft and useless?" the greenish-brown soldier asked with a heated glare. "Do you know what will happen if we do not kill him? We die!"

No sooner had he finished uttering this when the chance the soldiers had been waiting for presented itself. Alon-Settie grabbed Leondros, who was reeling from a blow to the chest, and threw him over his shoulder. The elfin prince landed on the hard ground with a thud, and lay still. The five Draccen soldiers drew their bows to fire in unison. The greenish-brown soldier looked at their leader from the corner of his dark eye and hissed, "Coward!.

It was time.

From seemingly out of nowhere, three daggers came flying from the surrounding dark foliage and met their marks in back of the three middle Draccen soldiers' necks. Intense pain washed over their faces as their bodies went stiff. In the second moment as these soldiers crumpled to the ground and aroused the suspicion of the two remaining soldiers, a whip came out of nowhere and latched onto the far right Draccen soldier's arm, which held his war bow firm, and with a sudden jerk, swung him left.

"HOLD YOUR ARROW!" the Draccen soldier on the far left cried out instinctively, but to no avail. The stunned Draccen soldier on the far right tried to free himself from the whip that had wrapped itself to his wrist and, in doing so, shot his companion.

"What just happened?" the far right Draccen soldier managed to get out before a dagger met its mark as well. This soldier fell to the hard ground as the dagger that lodged in his forehead remained.

The last remaining Draccen soldier knew that his time was at an end, so he sank to his knees and lowered his head submissively. From the corner of his eye, he watched the black silhouette of a woman approach him.

"Do to me as you will. I want to be done with this life, for my life ended when I woke to find myself in the service of Lord Jarden," the lone soldier spoke up calmly as he raised his head and looked at Tahari. She had been poised to behead him with the black-bladed sword.

"You chose not to fire upon the elfin prince and suffered the discontent of your men. Why?" she asked.

"He is where we were and, in truth, still are. He fights for his life. I do not have the heart to take my own life, nor his," the lone soldier answered simply. "When we awoke, we thought Lord Jarden had freed us. But he did not. He only put us in a different type of bondage, much like a slave's life. We want freedom, too. As for my comrades, their discontent is over now."

Tahari watched the all-black Draccen soldier with great caution for a moment, but then she lowered her sword and pushed back her hood. The soldier had given her hope.

"If you were given the choice to fight with the elfin prince who now fights for his life and possibly lose your life anyway, would you do it?" Tahari asked him. The question caused him to look back at Leondros before replying.

"I would, though I do not know why I would. I would be moved to aid him." the soldier's answer pleased her, and she felt the tension melt away.

"What is your name, soldier?" Tahari asked.

"J-Jax," he replied.

"Well, Jax, I am Tahari, and I sense there will be a day when you will have to decide between your allegiance to Lord Jarden or the strange path that is presented to you. I cannot help you choose your path, but know that the path that takes you closer to Lord Jarden will never bring freedom to you or your people. Adalai be with you." Tahari bowed her head then, pulled her hood back over her head, and silently slipped back into the darkness of the thick trees. She watched for a moment as Jax simply walked away from the intense battle that was still going on at the base of Mt. Somerset.

Chapter 114

Elements of Surprise

Battered and bruised from his fight with Leondros, Alon-Settie summoned enough strength for one last effort to finish his one-time friend who had become nothing more than a meddling elf. He had managed to knock Leondros off his feet by running straight at him and jumping feet first at the elf's midsection. The force of the blow caused Leondros to tumble backward onto the rocky ground and lay still for a moment. Rolling to his right, Alon-Settie quickly snatched up his sword and hurled it at Leondros. Leondros looked up just in time to see the blade coming at him and, acting reflexively, he grabbed a small dagger from his leather belt and threw the dagger while ducking out of the way of Alon-Settie's sword. The dagger's silver blade caught Alon-Settie in his right shoulder, driving him to the ground.

"If you are merciful, you will kill me," Alon-Settie grimaced. He winced in pain as he angrily pulled the dagger out of his shoulder and threw it aside. The only trace of blood that could be seen on the black tunic that Alon-Settie wore was the glistening wet patch on his right shoulder. He lifted his gaze to Leondros, who still had his eyes trained on him. The elfin prince slowly began to climb back to his feet. He looked at Alon-Settie and shook his head in weary frustration as he picked up his sword and slid it back into its sheath.

"I am not a murderer. You have come to believe that I am many things that I am not," Leondros offered simply. Alon-Settie painfully sat up enough to prop himself up on his bruised elbows. He slowly wiped the blood that oozed from his nose and mouth with his hand and spat the bitter taste from his mouth. Alon-Settie was a sight with his torn tunic and haggard looks, for he had not fared as well as his former friend. He looked upon Leondros with his dark-brown eyes as if he might have taken in what Leondros was trying to tell him, but instead, a sinister smile formed upon his lips. The evil expression that grew upon the young prince's dark-bearded face caused a cold chill to wash over Leondros.

"Too bad. I did not wish to look upon your death myself." Alon-Settie delivered his words coldly, but before Leondros could understand their full meaning, a dark shadow stood directly behind him. Leondros reached for his sword and spun around to take on the new opponent, but before he could actually grip his sword, a blast of radiant blue energy caught him square in the chest. The blast knocked him off his feet and threw him backward, causing Leondros's world to go black.

Walking up to Leondros's unconscious form, the dark-cloaked figure looked over at Alon-Settie. The figure appeared to be a massive Draccen soldier. He only shook its head in disappointment.

"This is still your responsibility—let nothing stop you now!" the Draccen soldier grumbled as he took out his own sword from its black leather sheath and tossed it at Alon-Settie. The prince painfully pulled himself to his feet as the metal sword clattered at his feet. Alon-Settie looked up and scowled at the dark figure. The prince from Akendron slowly bent over and picked up the sword.

"I have not lost my fervor for this mission. Make no mistake, Andora will come into the glory that awaits her when the Nodarian people finally take possession of it," Alon-Settie said simply as he gripped the sword, walked up to Leondros, and prepared to drive the sword into the unconscious elf's heart.

"Not in my lifetime!" a young woman's voice yelled from nearby. In the split second that it took for both the Draccen soldier and Alon-Settie to look up, Almari raced out from the surrounding trees and tackled Alon-Settie. She ripped the sword from his hands. Before she could do anything with it, the Draccen soldier released another blast of blue energy from his palm. Almari fell listlessly into the prince's arms. The blast had not driven her to unconsciousness, but she no longer had the strength to stand.

"Now as you were before we were so rudely interrupted," the cloaked soldier said with growing impatience as he snatched up the sword again and shoved it into Alon-Settie's free hand. The soldier turned to Almari, leaned over, and ripped off the hood covering her blonde-brown head. "Woman, you are out of your league here. You should not have come to this place." the Draccen soldier's words caused a wave of infuriated anger to flash through her dark-blue eyes.

"The same is said of you!" she hissed in a heated rage as she glared up at him.

"Of this I am sure," the soldier chuckled as he playfully waved his hand and stood up again. He then turned his dark gaze back at Alon-Settie and was silent a moment. "Well? Are you going to wait until there is another disruption? Get rid of him!."

"No!" Almari managed to get out, fighting the paralysis that plagued her limbs. Her feeble attempt was still no match for Alon-Settie's strength.

"It is over. This has to happen. A new empire is almost upon us now; these few remnants of the old kingdom are all that stand in its way," Alon-Settie reasoned. He continued to restrain her as he pulled her to her feet.

"Forget the new empire and save what is left of that old kingdom— it is the only good that can come from your actions!" Almari pleaded, still fighting Alon-Settie's iron-like grip. He paused, thinking about what she said, every dark deed that he had done rushing back into his mind. But the Draccen soldier let out a growl of frustration.

"Fine! I will do it myself!" he grumbled angrily, taking back his sword from Alon-Settie and lifting the sword above his head. The Draccen soldier gazed upon his target with immense pleasure.

Chapter 115

The Nodarian Conquest

"Where is your sphinx protector now?" the Draccen soldier asked smugly as he brought the black sword down that would end Leondros's life. As he did so, another black blade erupted from the midsection of his own body, forcing him to cry out in pain.

"Always watching!" Tahari hissed in reply. The soldier did not bleed. Instead, the wound began to sizzle, and smoke curled up into the humid night air. The soldier groaned in pain and was silent for a long moment, breathing heavily, before he spoke again, but when he did, the words he uttered were not what anyone was prepared to hear.

"Foolish sphinx, I would have to be amongst the living for you to truly kill me," he said, turning his head and looking at her for the first time. A twisted smile of pleasure formed upon his dark-green leathery lips as he studied Tahari. He grabbed hold of her and threw me against a rocky wall.

Tahari's body hit the wall with a sickening crack, which echoed in her head and overwhelmed her body with pain. Tahari slid down the wall and landed on the hard sandy ground. When she had managed to open her eyes and breathe again, she looked warily up at the strange soldier, who now gazed at her with delight. He carefully pulled her sword out of his own back before returning his gaze to Tahari.

"How did you get so lucky to have the dark lord himself grant you the power of invincibility?" Tahari asked in a labored breath, fighting to gather her strength again.

"The dark lord would never be so gracious to grant one of those hideous beasts such power. So it is a good thing that I am not a member of the Draccen race," the dark-cloaked soldier said with a tone of disdain, shuddering. Then this strange creature began to give off a reddish glow, transforming before Tahari's eyes. She could see Leondros awakening nearby. When Tahari looked back at the creature, dread washed over her. It was none other than Lord Jarden himself!

Tahari looked into the searing red gaze of Lord Jarden as he stood with his hands on his hips and looked upon her with amusement. Leondros and Almari were now aware of Lord Jarden's dark presence, too. Victory was all but his, and he knew it. Looking past Lord Jarden and upon the southern gates that led into the sacred land of Rahara, Tahari was reminded of the men who had brought the sphinx realm of Lani to ruin, and now she was on the verge of witnessing it again. Thus, a simple but pressing question came to mind.

"Why would you drive life and goodness from a land just to suit your own purposes?" Tahari asked in a weak and raspy voice, managing to prop herself on her elbows. "Was your own kingdom so awful that you could not find contentment there?" Tahari's words caused Lord Jarden to be silent a moment as though deep in thought. Then with a nod of certainty, he plunged his sword into the ground at his feet.

"Very well, I will tell you, seeing how there is nothing you can do about it anyway," Lord Jarden began. "Long before your forefathers came to dwell upon Andora, my people lived upon the island nation of Nod. They were very much like your people. They lived together in relative harmony; they worked their lands for food and rejoiced at the simple things in life. All was in a delicate balance, until that one fateful day.

A traveler came to our shores from another island realm near the bottom of the world. He was very dark and handsome. He was roguish, to be sure. During his stay, it is said he saved the king and queen's daughter from a horrible sea creature. Overwhelmed with gratitude, the king and queen invited the traveler to a dinner banquet.

"At that festive occasion, however, his true purpose was revealed. His alluring presence found favor with many of the women of court, but he was taken by the beauty of the queen. During the festivities, he stole her away from the main party to be with her. Rumor quickly spread throughout the realm of their love affair, which continued and went unnoticed by the king for some time. When the king discovered that his most honored guest had greatly dishonored him and his queen, the man was put to death. Before being run through by a sword, the man spoke one word: 'Tartarus.' No one understood what it meant, so they quickly forgot about it.

"The hope that life would return to normal faded in a single moment when, one night, the queen awoke feeling most strange. She looked upon her reflection in a mirror and screamed. Her fair skin had turned deathly gray, and her eyes had become dark and lifeless. Upon hearing her scream, the king had quickly risen from his bed and hurried to her side, but as he tried to comfort her, she was compelled to bite him, thus spreading her condition. Soon, the whole island realm became what we called gray walkers. The madness of the Tartarus that followed after people were bitten greatly varied. In worst case scenarios, a person's physical appearance changed and was most unnerving. The sickness caused a person to bite someone healthy, thus diminishing their intense craving to bite anymore. Some, like the queen, were immune to the full effects of the disease; instead they retain their sanity and only display the insatiable need to bite someone, until bitten. But their condition is permanent. They are forever changed into a gray walker and no longer desire food or water.

Lord Jarden's horrifying tale of his people gripped them, and they listened in silence.

"If your people are truly the dead walking, why do you try to take a land that has creatures alive and healthy?" Tahari asked as she shook her head in confusion.

"The Tartarus," Lord Jarden offered simply. "It means hell, and in this there is no lie. All who have yet to bite someone are consumed by madness until they are able to infect another person. When I left

Nod, many people were fully consumed by the madness, for it had been some time since the last healthy person had been bitten, and with no one else left alive, there was no way to quench the need of this madness. That was more than eight ages ago—I will not even begin to imagine what sort of chaos dwells within the realm of Nod now." As Tahari listened to the chilling details of Lord Jarden's story, she began to study his very being and demeanor.

"For all the damage that you have done to our realm, you do not strike me as someone who is itching to bite anyone," Tahari said as she continued to study his graying form.

"I, like the queen from long ago, retained my original senses after my time under the madness and I bit my one person," the dark lord answered simply. "For this reason, coupled with the fact that I was a general in my king's army during my natural life, King Jabberwrath has ordained me as one of the ten soul finders. It is our secret mission to find new realms for our people to live in and to fulfill their need. Granted, my mission has dragged out a little longer than I had anticipated, but Andora is a precious jewel that I am not going to relinquish anytime soon." as he spoke these words, Tahari looked over at Leondros. Their expressions of horror mirrored each other's.

"If you need people alive and healthy to quench this madness of which you speak, then why have some of our people been butchered and left in mass graves?" Tahari asked pointedly. As she spoke of this atrocity, fear washed over Leondros's and Almari's faces. Lord Jarden was silent a moment as his searing red gaze watched her with a contented expression. A cruel smile came to his lips.

"Those 'poor souls,' as you call them, are to us as fine wine to you. The longer they decompose, the more flavorful they are." Lord Jarden's repulsive answer made Tahari's stomach turn and her anger swell. They now saw the horrible plan that Lord Jarden and his people had laid out for Andora, and it was in this moment that all Tahari's sphinx senses screamed for her to fight.

"So, you are a sacred messenger to your people?" Tahari asked in a tone riddled with anger. Tears burned in her eyes as she put her dear friends into Lord Jarden's terrible plot. She then remembered the last line from the second scroll of the prophecy:

*IV. The darkness of a sacred messenger will threaten Andora. *A sacrifice will save the key to finding Farro.*

Everything within Tahari's being drove her to stop this plague coming to her home. Searching deep within herself, Tahari found the will to stand again. She slowly rose to her feet, ignoring the pain that coursed through her battered body.

"Well, yes, you could say that I am," Lord Jarden replied.

"Well, then, you have met the sacred messenger for my people." standing now, Tahari glared angrily at the dark lord. He looked upon her in disbelief.

"You? You are jesting me," Lord Jarden replied.

"As such, I make you this offer. Spare these people, spare these lands, and in exchange, I offer myself as your prisoner," Tahari said calmly. The reaction of her words crashed over her friends like a giant wave.

"NO! You cannot!" Leondros and Almari cried out in unison. Leondros fought the paralysis to stand as Almari fought against Alon-Settie's grip upon her. Lord Jarden now wore an expression of surprise, and he put a single foot on Leondros's chest to keep him on the ground.

"Now, that *is* an offer. You, my dear, will be the first sphinx ever to visit our shores during this age," Lord Jarden began, sounding impressed by her offer—so much, in fact, that his dark, lifeless eyes actually brightened. "King Jabberwrath will be most pleased by this. He will have many uses for you, and it will definitely grant me some forgiveness for my tardiness in this mission."

As the dark lord thought to himself aloud, Tahari could see the hurt and loss growing in Leondros's and Almari's faces. In her silence, Tahari remained fervent in her decision.

Then, after a long moment of thought, Lord Jarden lifted his head and looked at her with assurance and a pleased expression. "I accept your offer." Lord Jarden took his heavy foot off Leondros's chest. The silence that followed his words was deafening. Leondros slowly sat up and looked upon her with tears in his soulful brown eyes. Almari lost all will to fight Alon-Settie and sank sadly to her knees. Although they, like Andora, were now free from the coming plague, they were about to lose something just as important, or maybe more so.

"Take this time to say goodbye to your friends, for we make for the realm of Nod with great haste," Lord Jarden patiently instructed as he took a couple of steps back, crossed his arms over his chest, and waited while he looked upon Almari and then Leondros, who was now slowly climbing to his knees. As Leondros looked upon Tahari, there was understanding in his face but also great loss and sadness.

"Although, there is something I do not understand," Lord Jarden began subtly as he put a thoughtful finger to his lips. Deep thought washed over his graying face as he looked first upon Tahari and then upon Leondros with wonder. Then, without any warning, he strode forward and, grabbing Leondros, put a black-bladed sword to his back. "In the prophecy that guides every action you make, how could it be that this mere elf could be the key to finding the one your people call Farro?" Lord Jarden's words were as startling as his sudden grip upon Leondros. Leondros looked at Tahari with horror. "Yes, I know of the prophecy; it is no secret. Now, answer my question," he demanded with a tone of rising anger.

"If you know of the prophecy, then let fear be your guide now. Take this knowledge and leave our shores, for no matter what course you take to overcome Andora, you will be defeated. Make no mistake," Tahari managed to reply calmly as she ignored the thunder of her racing heart.

"You offer very sound advice, and I thank you, but I must ask you this," Lord Jarden said. "How can this elf be the key to finding Farro if he is *dead?*" Upon uttering these words, Lord Jarden drove the sharp edge of Tahari's black sword into Leondros's back.

Her heart stopped as did her world as Tahari heard Leondros cry out in agonizing pain. As she watched the expression of traumatizing pain twist Leondros's facial features, Tahari also watched all the people whom she had ever loved and who had died by the cruel hands of some taskmaster or intolerant force. Everything in her being wanted to save them somehow, and it broke her heart to see such heart-wrenching suffering.

The dark lord then looked upon Tahari with his lifeless eyes and smiled cruelly. "If you are his protector and guardian, how will you save him now?" His cruel smile widened as he ripped the sword out of Leondros's back and stepped back to admire the chaos of the moment.

Tahari's eyes quickly shifted back to Leondros, who fell to his knees in agony as Lord Jarden loosened his grip upon him. Looking into the agony in his face, she felt the intensity of the pain that coursed through him; Tahari felt the cold chill of death seeping into his hands and feet. Something deep in her soul stirred her to take a step forward and reach her hand out to Leondros.

"I take your pain as if it were my own," Tahari said calmly and warmly. The magic in that moment was in the very words that she spoke, for as soon as she closed her eyes, Tahari was hit with an overwhelming sensation. The sword wound that had impaled Leondros had now torn through her body. When Tahari opened her eyes and looked upon Leondros, he was still on his knees but no longer in pain. He had dropped his head down to look at his midsection and put a hand to his chest to inspect the miracle that had just transpired. Tahari heard him breathing easier now. He had been saved.

Lifting her gaze back to Lord Jarden, Tahari glared at him, for she was now fueled with a rage that drove her to charge at him. Running at him, she grabbed him by his neck. "You have your answer. Now, leave before the rest of my kind come to hunt you down," she said bitterly. The horror in Lord Jarden's lifeless dark eyes was incredible. He saw great truth in hers and was truly gripped by fear. Then, before he could utter another word, Tahari remembered something Shamira needed her to know. It was her knowledge that told Tahari to summon the radiant white energy from the palm of her hand, an energy used by all sphinxes in combat. The intensity of the blast caught Lord Jarden in the chest and blew his dark-cloaked form from the northern steps of Mt. Somerset back into the dark wilderness of the Serrigen. When the blinding white light from Tahari's blast faded, so did her strength. As the wound she had taken from Leondros took her power and strength, her legs buckled beneath her. Tahari weakly fell to her hands and knees upon the hard, rocky ground.

Chapter 116

Oath Fulfilled

Watching Lord Jarden be blown off into the Serrigen drove Alon-Settie berserk. He felt suddenly overwhelmed by the opposition that surrounded him. His and Lord Jarden's plan for Leondros had failed, and the true power that dwelt within the sphinx, Tahari, had won. Determined to see the darkness of his master's grand design carried out, the prince of Akendron took up a dagger and was about to slice it across Almari's neck when he was overcome with agonizing pain as a sharp blade was driven into the back of his shoulder. Whirling around, Alon-Settie was taken aback by the sight of his own mother standing before him. The anger and rage that coursed through her fair, delicate features were a new and strange sight.

"This is my last gift to you, my son," Elanza said in a low, angry voice. "Leave here. Leave this land and never return, and you shall keep your life. For if you decide to stay, the only course I foresee in your future is death." gone was the bright light in her brilliant green eyes. All that shone out now was a heated rage.

Alon-Settie could clearly see that it took everything in her being to keep herself from lashing out at him. He looked upon her for a moment. Then, holding his shoulder, Alon-Settie turned and rushed up the gravelly footpath that led to the summit of Mt. Somerset, where his form disappeared into the night.

Kneeling on the hard rocky ground, Tahari sat hunched over as the intensity of the wound stole her ability to breathe normally. Tears of pain rolled down her cheeks as she slowly sat up enough to look at the realm of Rahara that lay just to the south. Leondros dropped to his knees before her. There was a look of horror in his soulful brown eyes as he gently held her head in his hands.

"Tahari, what have you done?" he gasped.

"Long ago, Shamira promised to watch over you and keep you from the darkness that would try to bring harm to you and kill you," Tahari whispered. "Today, that oath has been fulfilled." even though tears ran down her cheeks, Tahari was content, for he was alive and kneeling before her.

"Tahari, tell me what I should do?" he stammered in panic as he held onto her arms to keep her from falling over. *"Please!"* Refusing to let Tahari succumb to her injury, Leondros used a portion of her dark cloak to bandage her wounds. Tahari gently took his hand to get his attention as he frantically fought to stop the bleeding. When he stopped trying to bandage her and looked at her, Tahari looked at him and shook her head.

"I am finished," Tahari said simply, and Leondros slowly put down the bandages, his face devoid of all expression.

"The third scroll has been found and translated," Tahari said softly. "You will find the scroll along with its translation in my saddlebag. The quest that lies ahead belongs to you, Almari, and all who would take up the call to find Farro." Almari had sat stunned for the longest time, but now Elanza helped her to her feet. Together they stood nearby to look on in horror and silence. Sad realization struck Leondros as tears burned his brown eyes.

"But you are my guardian. What will I do without you?" he asked as he tried to smile in spite of the sadness that crowded his voice. Tahari managed a weak smile as she looked upon his bruised face.

"It is up to Adalai and the sphinx lords now," she said sadly. "But fear not, for you were watched over long before I was free from the Tomblock and even before I was born as it will be again." in spite of the numbing cold that was settling into her hands, Tahari slowly reached up and gently touched a bruise on his left cheek. A disheartened sadness washed over his handsome face. "You are still in good hands. You have carried a part of my spirit within you since that day you woke in the tomb of your forefathers. The fullness of my spirit will be with you." there was a slight hint of confusion in his face, but she had faith that he would come to understand what she meant. The energy that gave strength to her body drained completely, and Tahari could not stop her eyes from closing. She felt herself collapse against Leondros, who caught her in his arms and held her tight. As her head came to rest on his shoulder, Tahari heard him speak.

"I love you, my friend." his words were as close as the air within Tahari's failing lungs.

"And I love you...my friend," Tahari mumbled under the blanket of heavy sleep that overwhelmed her wounded body and made the warmth of this moment last forever.

Chapter 117

Into Rahara

Holding Tahari's lifeless body in his arms, Leondros felt a great rush of wind blow against him. Life had fled from her beautiful face. Tears ran down his bruised face as he closed his eyes and gently buried his face against her shoulder. Leondros wept bitterly for his dear friend.

Nature itself seemed to recognize the tragedy that had happened, for a gentle shower began to fall upon the southern face of Mt. Somerset. It settled any lingering dust that had been kicked up during the earlier disturbances that took place upon the mountain. Although nature itself was willing to pay homage to the brave warrior who had paid a heavy price for her friends and the freedom of the Andoran people, this did not mean that outside forces would be so understanding. As Almari and Elanza tried to wipe away their tears, they heard something or someone moving toward the gate from Rahara.

"Elanza, quick!" Almari cried, jumping to her feet and taking up the dagger that Alon-Settie had dropped. Almari forced herself to concentrate on the danger that now approached. "Danger approaches from the south," she whispered as she quickly positioned herself behind the west-facing obelisk. Elanza took up her own dagger and positioned herself behind the east-facing obelisk. They looked at each other in growing alarm as they listened to the soft sounds of someone carefully walking toward them through the thick brush. Almari could not imagine what force they would be contending with now, but as she looked up at Leondros who remained unwilling to move from Tahari's side, she took it upon herself to watch over him in Tahari's stead.

Vigilantly listening to the sound of danger coming closer to the gateway, Almari nodded to Elanza and clutched the dagger against her chest. As the footsteps walked through the gateway, Almari let out an angry yell, and both she and Elanza jumped out at their opponents, daggers firmly in hand.

"WHOA!" Sala yelled in fright as he jumped backward, narrowly escaping being slashed by both daggers. At his cry, an accompanying band of elves quickly took a defensive position around him with their deadly bows and arrows.

"Stand down, everyone!" he called out in alarm as he suddenly realized who they had found. He spun around and held out his arms to keep his bodyguards from firing upon Almari and Elanza. "They are friends," he informed the company of elfin soldiers. They reluctantly lowered their bows but remained suspicious of their surroundings. When Sala turned back, he looked upon the road-weary women; he judged from their dirty and torn clothes many exciting events that had transpired since Shoshon. The heated rage that had filled their dirty faces was now replaced with immense sorrow and relief, and they lowered their daggers.

"I am glad that it was you I found," he began in a welcoming haste. "The elves that have reached Rahara and dwell upon the mountain of Sion alerted me to an evil force trying to penetrate the barrier by the southern gate. We feared that it was Lord Jarden trying to breach the borders of Rahara," he explained, still trying to relax from his startling experience. As he studied them with his blue eyes, a welcoming smile came to his tanned, bearded face. "Thank Adalai that you have made it! You are safe now," he assured them.

Almari and Elanza could see that the prophet had indeed reached the safety of Rahara already and whatever civilization that was found there, for his long dark hair had been neatly combed and now hung just above his shoulders They could tell that while in the mountain city of Sion, Sala had a chance to clean up and tend to his appearance. He wore a new white robe and a dark-brown leather coat that hung down to his dark boots. It was refreshing to know that there was a wondrous place of sanctuary ahead, but it did not overshadow their current grief. Almari walked up to him and gently put her arms around his neck and held onto him, just thankful that he was there.

"Yes, we are here, and we are safe, but not all of us made it," Almari explained softly, and then let go of Sala and looked at him sadly. Stepping aside so he could see past her, Almari gestured across the barrier.

Raising his gaze, Sala looked upon a scene that stopped his heart cold. He saw his dear friend Leondros sitting on the rocky ground, cradling Tahari's limp body in his arms. Sala tried to convince himself that he was not actually seeing this, but Almari softly began to tell her account of what happened.

"We would have made it if Alon-Settie had not shown up. He and Lord Jarden must have planned for this." as she recounted the events just past, anger washed over her sad face, and tears filled her eyes.

When Almari spoke of the disease Lord Jarden's people suffered from, Sala seemed to know of it. "The Tartarus," he said in a whisper filled with great dread, and his blue eyes widened with horror. He was reminded of a bad memory. Almari looked stunned, so he nodded his head slightly, saying, "My master never really spoke of it, but he mentioned the word *Tartarus* and a plague that had consumed the realm of Nod.

Almari finished her story with tears freely running down her face and Sala's arm around her for comfort.

"A sacrifice will save the key to finding Farro," Sala said slowly as he recited the second scroll's last line of instruction. Lifting his solemn face to the dark cloud-covered skies, Sala found the strength to smile. "Tahari, you were good as your word. You went to whatever ends necessary to save those around you. Thank you." swallowing the soreness that threatened to choke him, Sala put a consoling hand on

Elanza's shoulder and then walked over to Leondros. Elanza gently wrapped a comforting arm around Almari.

Leondros had his head hung in deep prayer and meditation, his blond hair hanging limply over his shoulders. Sala slowly sank to his knees beside his friend and looked upon the pale face of Tahari. Her lifeless expression, combined with the immense grief of Leondros's, caused the old prophet's heart to break.

"I now know what she meant," Leondros said in weak whisper as he slowly lifted his sad gaze to Sala. "She said that I had carried a part of her spirit since the day I woke in my forefathers' tomb." despite his sadness, there was a touch of wonder in his voice. "When I died, she had found some way to bring me back. In that way, I realize now, she had to give up a part of herself." as he took a labored breath, the elfin prince looked upon his friend. "Now she has given up the rest of it."

The gravity of Leondros's realization also overwhelmed Sala; tears stung his eyes and he lowered his head in deep sadness. However, it was these very words that formed the basis for their next major course of action.

"Tahari's spirit is within you now fully," Sala said with sudden realization. He looked down at Tahari with some strange sense of understanding. The expression that grew upon his aged facial features was energized with an immense sense of hope. He looked at Leondros and put a comforting hand on his friend's shoulder. "Come, my friend. In this mission, I believe there was a higher purpose for Tahari than just her sacrificing herself for our sakes, but we will not find it here." Sala rose to his feet with a new-found energy and turned to Almari and Elanza, who were standing beside them still shrouded in their grief. "Come, we make for the mountain of Sion.

The elfin prince's devastation was somewhat lessened as he looked back upon Tahari. Finding the will within himself to get to his feet and gently pick Tahari off the wet, rocky ground, he put hope in what Sala had said. When Almari and Elanza looked at Sala, they were weary with fatigue and the heaviness of grief. He was compelled to encourage them with the insight of the hope that he suddenly realized.

"Almari said that Lord Jarden called Leondros the key to finding

Farro. I remember now—it was vaguely noted, but in the journals that my order passed on to me, they did speak of an elfin child who would become the key to finding Farro," the prophet said as he put a hand to his chin. He paced back and forth as his aged, bearded face became fixed in deep thought. "I never truly understood this, but I still accepted it. Now I understand fully." tears came to the aging prophet's eyes as he looked back upon Tahari. "The sacred messenger's mission was not yet complete, for not all the scrolls of the prophecy have been found and translated," Sala explained.

At these words, Almari remembered Tahari's last words to Leondros about the third scroll's translation. As Sala spoke, she quietly went over to the dark-brown saddlebag and rummaged through it until she found what she was looking for.

"In Tahari's sacrifice, Leondros was gifted with her spirit. He has now become the key to finding Farro, because of the hope that he carries within him. That hope is Tahari's spirit," the old prophet explained with passion. But sadness and uncertainty still lingered within those who lingered around him. Even Leondros looked overwhelmed at what was now expected of him.

"Sala, you are right," Almari said softly as her voice began to fill with hope and anticipation. "Tahari was not finished with her quest, and she didn't just leave us the third scroll. There is somethin' else with it: it gives us a separate note of instruction." as she spoke, her blue eyes quickly studied the small piece of cream-colored paper that had been tucked inside the scroll. She slowly rose to her feet, reading. Tears ran down her dirty, tear-stained cheeks, but Almari lifted a hopeful gaze to the others, who waited impatiently to hear what she read within the small note. She read:

> *Let the spirit within the key be your guide now. Do not be disheartened because of what has been taken; this spirit is still with you as it always has been.*

Almari lifted her hopeful gaze to Leondros, who took reassurance from what she read.

Sala, too, found reason to hope, and as his gaze looked upon all of three of them, a smile of encouragement came to his face. "This quest is not over, and Tahari is not lost.

After gathering their things, Leondros, Almari, and Elanza followed Sala and the elfin soldiers through Rahara's southern gate and deep into the land's dense tropical jungles. A stretcher was fashioned out of tree branches to carry Tahari's body; her dark cloak now covered her lifeless form. Leondros and another elfin soldier took up the honor of carrying it on their journey to the mountain upon which the city of Sion had been built.

The dirt trail that entered the southern edges of the lush jungle led the travelers to a wide, gently flowing river that ran diagonally through the kingdom. The group split up into four dark mahogany-carved longboats and started paddling down the river, which flowed through the seemingly endless jungle. The tranquil river bent and curved around thick tree-covered hills. A heavy mist hung thick in the air and morning's soft first light beamed through the jungle's thick canopy overhead. The warmth of the sun's rays shone upon the longboats and warmed the passengers, who were chilled and soaked from the night's heavy rains. Finally the three weary and grief-stricken travelers were able to sleep. Although the boats helped to expedite their journey to Sion, the journey still took them until early evening.

As the four longboats quietly sailed around the foothills that surrounded the mountain in which an entire city dwelt, Leondros, Almari, and Elanza looked on with great interest, for the sight of the mountain alone brought peace to their souls. Despite of the closeness of the surrounding darkness of the jungle, they were still able to steal glimpses of the oncoming mountain. Once the boats drifted around the last bend in the river, the three weary travelers were breathless when they were able to look upon the beautiful city of Sion—even Leondros, who had seen the city before on a few occasions. Before them, shining out of the coming night, were tens of thousands of flaming torches which lit up the entire mountain. At the base of the mountain, a fine layer of fog silently drifted just above the water near the river port, and elfin soldiers stood watching for their arrival.

"Welcome to the city of Sion," Sala said as he motioned to the majestic city built into the mountain itself. The mountain had been specifically chosen as a site for Sion, for it was an extinct volcano and served as a natural fortress. Although the night concealed many lovely parts of the city, the mountain still emanated an overwhelming sense of serenity.

As the four longboats pulled along the wooden docks, the elfin soldiers were quick to greet them and kindly assisted them from the boats and up into the city. There was no need to carry lanterns as they walked the streets paved with stone, for lanterns had been strategically placed all along the city. Each lantern was intricately crafted and gave off a soft enchanting color of either blue, purple, or cream. As Leondros, Almari, Elanza, and Sala climbed up the mountain streets, they were greeted by the soothing aromas of chamomile and lavender. They were reunited along the way with the elfin people from Shoshon who had decided to leave when King Doran issued the evacuation order, bringing a small measure of relief to their troubled minds.

On the last stretch of the journey, the group's road turned into a footpath of wooden planks that led deep into a forest. The forest had grown along the base of a wide crevasse that had split the volcano's western rim and formed a doorway into the volcano's deep crater. The dark trail was lit by more tranquil lights of blue, purple, and cream. As they drew deeper into the crevasse, they could feel the cool night air become damp, and they could smell a lake nearby. When the group finally came to the opening on the other side of the crevasse, they saw a truly fascinating world that had been hidden deep within the rim of the extinct volcano.

A large, crystal-blue lake had formed within the crater just a few hundred feet from the rocky rim. The dark rock walls of the entire crater were speckled with blue and iridescent glowworms, which shone like stars against the darkness, casting the whole crater in a heavenly blue-and-white glow. Amplifying the view was a rocky island that rose from the center of the lake with a castle glowing blue and white upon it. Two stone bridges led to the castle from opposite sides of the crater, also dotted with the lanterns that were all over the city. The only sounds that came from within this mystical cavern were the gentle waves lapping against the rocky base on which the magnificent castle rested. Finally, Sala dared to break the silence with his warm and gentle voice.

"Welcome to the palace of Seymoura."

Chapter 118

Requiem

Midnight came, and though Sion slumbered peacefully, the newcomers did not. They had been welcomed into the palace of Seymoura with open arms and were well cared for. They had been given bedchambers to take rest and replenish their strength in, but when they heard that the palace priests were holding a candlelight ceremony in Tahari's honor within the castle's main tower temple, they forgot their weariness.

As Leondros, Almari, and Elanza stood in their new black robes, they found themselves overwhelmed by the immense power of the scene. The round ceremonial chamber, which sat at the very top of the tower, was a wondrous sight in and of itself. It had no walls: only nine beautiful pillars of white marble encircled the temple chamber's black marble floor. Beyond the chamber, the dark walls of the volcano crater glowed and glittered like blue and white stars.

Standing in darkness and silence, Leondros, Almari, and Elanza watched with solemn expressions as flame-lit torches were carried into the chamber by the elfin priests dressed in silver-accented black robes. The priests slowly went around the chamber and placed their torches upon the nine pillars, thus giving a dim light to the room. Tahari's friends instantly noticed a black marble stone, round and flat, in the middle of the chamber. Three large terraced stairs encircled the stone. Despite the lack of walls, no breeze filtered through the tower; all was quiet.

Then a wood flute's deep music began to float throughout the temple as four more elfin priests processed into the chamber carrying an elegant black and gold stretcher on which Tahari lay. She wore a black and sea-green velvet robe, and white beads had been woven into her long brown hair, which now spilled out neatly around her shoulders. Her hands were delicately folded across her stomach. Across her entire form lay a translucent black veil, which seemed to represent her fate. The four elfin priests gently set the stretcher upon the center stone; three of them turned to stand at the back of the large chamber while one remained at the stone. He pulled out a small black velvet bag from his dark robe. From the bag, the priest took several small white candles, which he placed around the stone just beyond where Tahari lay. He placed one large white candle at Tahari's feet. He lit all the candles before humbly bowing to Tahari and slowly retreating to the back of the room with the others. The high priest gracefully stepped out of the crowd now gathered throughout the open chamber and took his place before the large stone on which Tahari lay. He began speaking a prayer in elfish. As he spoke in a gentle and low voice, all who gathered lowered their heads. When he had finished, he placed his hands together and humbly bowed his head. Then he slowly knelt down and placed a golden cap upon the large candle, extinguishing its flame completely.

Leondros looked on sadly as the smoke from the large candle gently curled into the warm night air. His thoughts were crowded with the mission that was still before them, what had happened, and what they had all been through. He knew that Tahari's spirit was with him, he knew that he would find a way to walk in her place, but something within him refused to let him move on. He had witnessed hundreds of people over the course of his lifetime pass on to the realm of Mortu'us, but he refused to let go of Tahari.

When the ceremony had ended and most of the people had filed out of the chamber, Sala and three priests came forward to carry

Tahari's body from the chamber. They were removing the candles that encircled Tahari when the large candle suddenly flickered to life again. The four men stopped and stared at the candle and then turned to each other in disbelief. They looked around the chamber, but the only other souls within the room were Leondros, Almari, and Elanza. Shaking his head, one of the priests carefully knelt down and blew out the candle. He stood up, and Sala and the priests began to move aside the candles in order to carry Tahari out. Again the large candle flickered to life. This time the priest did not get the chance to extinguish the candle before a woman's voice filled the chamber.

"Would you extinguish the miracle that could save a multitude?" the woman's warm voice asked pointedly. Everyone within the chamber froze. A small but radiant light appeared on the steps near Tahari's body and became a tall, thin woman. Her stunning features were hauntingly familiar; though she seemed older, she resembled Tahari: dark-brown flowing hair which hung in beautiful locks, sea-green eyes, warm, tanned skin. She wore an elegant blue and white velvet gown with a hood that she gently pulled off her head. The dark-haired woman looked at the audience before her for a moment, and then she looked upon the priest who had put out the candle the second time. The heat of her gaze warned him not to repeat this act, and he shrank back from the altar.

"Anyi?" Leondros gasped, stepping forward in disbelief at her sudden appearance. The woman turned to the elfin prince and a warm smile of memory came to her face.

"Leondros, you know her?" Almari asked softly. She cautiously leaned closer to Leondros and stared at the haunting image of the woman.

"Yes, I do," Leondros replied gently, overwhelmed by memory. "She is the sphinx who watched over me and my sisters and brother when we were children." Almari and Elanza looked back at the woman with understanding. Leondros bowed his head humbly before Anyi. "It has been ten and five years since news of your death reached Shoshon; forgive us for not knowing that you were also in danger," he apologized with deep regret. Anyi's face filled with empathy and understanding as she stepped down from the altar and walked up to Leondros, who looked upon her with a guilty, sad expression. She wrapped her arms around Leondros and held him tight for a long moment.

"There was nothing you or anyone could have done. What happened had to transpire," Anyi said gently as she let go of Leondros and faced him and those around her. "I was an immortal sphinx, but I chose to give it up for something more important. But it is not the past that brings me to you now. I have been sent by the sphinx lords and Adalai himself to bring you all two very important messages. You must begin your journey throughout western Andora to unite all peoples for the coming war." in uttering these words, Anyi noticed looks of sudden confusion and uncertainty from her audience. A disheartened expression crept into her tanned face, and she lowered her head for a moment before speaking again. "In a very short time, Tahari had mastered many of the magical tactics used by our race, but unfortunately, her power was not enough to stop Lord Jarden. Some of my kinsmen have reported that he has sought refuge within the Serrigen city of Romulus. He will be most adamant in his conquest of Andora now. He will also rally many agents of darkness to hunt you down." the warning in Anyi's voice was clear to the group. Almari and Elanza were alarmed by Anyi's news, while Leondros managed to put aside his grief and focus on what they needed to do next.

"You are right—unifying Andora is our only hope, and it must begin quickly," Leondros said and looked at Sala, who nodded in agreement. "We should begin with Graven. If we are going to unify this realm, we should start with the outlying lands first. Since the Serrigen splits Andora in half, Graven is all but cut off from the three southern kingdoms. The people of Graven are said to be savage and ruthless, wanting nothing to do with outsiders. These lands may be the most difficult to unify, but if they are unified, others will follow more quickly," Leondros offered as he reflected on his vast knowledge of the different kingdoms within Andora. Although he was now eager to begin this quest, he looked to Anyi and waited for the second message she had for them.

"The second message may have come from the Adalai and the sphinx lords, but it also comes from me," Anyi began humbly, clasping her hands together and seeming almost distressed. "*I* need to ask this favor of you, all of you." worry seeped into Anyi's sea-green eyes as she looked upon Leondros and then upon Almari, Elanza, and Sala. "In your plans to save Andora—please—will you also save my daughter?" Everyone except Leondros looked between Anyi and the lifeless body of Tahari in disbelief.

"You are Tahari's mother?" Almari asked kindly as she studied the features made familiar to her through her friend.

"Yes, she is," Leondros said with a sudden realization from deep within him. His heart stopped for a moment, for the hope of Tahari's resurrection seemed impossible. "Is it truly possible that Tahari can return?" he asked hopefully, his throat dry in anticipation of Anyi's answer. Anyi smiled slightly.

"While you continue Tahari's search for Farro and unite the peoples of Andora, you must also take Tahari's body to the small Isles of Rane, which lie just off Adarah's eastern coast. There you will find an abandoned sphinx temple, which held great importance for my people." as Anyi spoke, Leondros's brown eyes widened with understanding.

"You speak of the temple of Vestigia," Leondros said softly. He did not have to see the looks of confusion within the company to know that they had no idea what he was referring to. "Long ago, the sphinx people had built temples and other places of sanctuary around Andora to perform the sacred rituals of their culture. The temple of Vestigia was where certain sphinxes were taken to be resurrected after they had been killed or had died." at the word *resurrected,* everyone was filled with hope. Almari's and Elanza's eyes widened in growing excitement.

"Such a place sounds too wondrous to comprehend. But if this is true, you said 'certain sphinxes' were resurrected. Why not all?" Elanza asked, her bright green eyes looking at Leondros.

"Not all the sphinxes of the ancient world were guided by morals that were good and just," Leondros said briefly, and Anyi nodded in agreement.

"When a sphinx of the ancient world was born into the living realm, they were born mortal. They were guided by the laws that brought stability to our race. They were encouraged to learn of their ancestors and of the love and compassion that these honorable people used during their lifetime, but in the end, it was up to each sphinx to decide how they would govern their own life. If a sphinx chose to reject the ways of their race and adopt the dark parts of life—greed, jealousy, murder—then at death, when the sphinx's soul was taken to the shores of Mortu'us, Adalai would pass judgment upon them and cast them into Aetus. Once they entered into Inferus's realm of the dead, these souls were lost to the memory of all who ever knew them. But if a sphinx had chosen to live by the laws of our people and had embraced the love and compassion that existed within our race, Adalai would bless them with immortality so that they could be resurrected back into the living realm to begin the next stage of their sphinx life and continue to guard the world as you know it." Anyi's explanation was both fascinating and haunting. As Elanza listened, she seemed greatly intrigued by the wondrous tale of spirituality that governed the sphinx people.

"If you are born mortal with the ability to become immortal," Elanza said as she thought deeply about Anyi's explanation, "why deny your children the truth that existed within your race? This truth could have saved those who were lost to the realm of Aetus. Why were they not told that if they led righteous lives they could gain immortality?"

"For this reason alone," Anyi began with growing passion as a serious expression filled her sea-green eyes. "The righteousness that existed within our race would have been lost. All would have sought out this blessing for their own selfish reasons, and the sphinx would have become a plague upon the world." In some way, it seemed that she was speaking from experience. "Adalai himself gave us this warning: 'No child born within the sphinx race was to ever hear the word *immortality*.'" Elanza lowered her gaze humbly and nodded in understanding. As Almari listened to what was spoken, she looked back upon Tahari's lifeless form; she felt her own heart twinge with fear for her friend.

"What if a sphinx child is born and no one is there to teach them of your people's laws or the love and compassion that you speak of?" Almari's question caused a moment of silence. Anyi looked at the young woman before her and then at the body of her daughter. A warm smile came to her face.

"The sphinx laws are not the only righteous laws that one can follow. Sometimes one needs only listen to the whisperings of one's own heart to follow the right course. Tahari did just that. When Leondros was fatally betrayed, as his guardian, Tahari was bound to find a way to save him. Though it meant giving up a part of herself to do it, she chose to resurrect Leondros. In doing so, she broke a sacred law of our people, and her actions carried a heavy penalty." as Anyi spoke of the burden that Tahari faced, Leondros looked upon his friend under the black gossamer veil. Tears came to his eyes as he was taken aback by the burden she had faced since the day that he awoke in the tomb. There was a long pause from Anyi as she, too, had tears in her eyes, and for a moment her head dropped.

"Anyi?" Almari asked gently.

"I spoke with her about the consequences of disobeying the laws of our people. Although I was disheartened by her actions against her own people, she was certain of what she had to do," Anyi recalled thoughtfully. A tear ran down her tanned cheek. Lifting her head, a warm smile came to her face. Anyi looked at Leondros. "She had no regrets. In fact, I watched her as she went forth from that moment with courage. In the face of possible incarceration or even death, Tahari walked forward, boldly, because it was not for herself that she was fighting; it was for those whom she loved—her friends." Anyi's smile widened proudly as she looked upon the four souls Tahari had deeply cared about in her life. "As I said, Adalai himself sends this message to you. Although Tahari was guilty of breaking a law of her people, the reasons for which she broke it and the sacrifice that claimed her life have greatly touched Adalai. She has been granted immortality." everyone gasped in delight. Anyi smiled and breathed in relief, but there was still a look of concern on her face.

"Do not worry; we will see to it that Tahari's body is taken safely to the Isles of Rane," Sala interjected with sincere promise as he stepped from the shadows.

"About this, I have no worry," Anyi began slowly as she struggled to find the right words. "What worries me is what you will encounter on the road when you leave this place." her words were spoken in a tone of seriousness that filled the room. "Tahari was the last sphinx of the ancient world. This was possible because I am from the old sphinx kingdom of the Far World before it vanished. Each sphinx was a guardian over one element in life. Rarely, a sphinx guarded more than this. Tahari was such a sphinx. She had inherited two elements from Shamira and the elements that she received from me. From Shamira, she could call upon all sphinxes from all the ages, living or dead, calling them to battle with just a whisper; she was also Leondros's guardian. From me she had yet to learn that she could create fire and become invisible. But Tahari had yet to learn what element *she* held guardianship over.

"Surely Tahari was entrusted with a wondrous element. Nothin' to be feared, right?" Almari said in an attempt to sound hopeful. Anyi smiled slightly, but then she lowered her head slightly and shook it.

"*Wondrous* is used only to describe what the world looked like when Tahari was alive and the element she unknowingly guarded remained in check," Anyi gently corrected her. "Long ago, before Andora was settled, plagues ran rampant throughout Aura and Inferus. Of all the plagues, seven were the most feared, for they would bring utter chaos and catastrophe anywhere they went. It was decided by Adalai and several sphinx lords that these seven plagues would be locked away from the known world and put under the protection of a sphinx. When the sphinxes were all but annihilated in 8021, the sphinx who carried this guardianship was also killed. This sphinx's power passed on to the only sphinx who survived the holocaust that wiped the sphinx race from the face of the earth: me." Anyi's words were ground breaking. "I oversaw a dear friend as they died trying to protect me. In dying, they passed on this power to me, and I passed it on to the next sphinx child born. Tahari was that sphinx." the silence within the chamber was deafening.

"What should we expect to encounter?" Leondros asked when he finally managed to find his voice again. He was determined to take on the challenge that now loomed before them, for it was what Tahari would have, no, *had*, done for him.

"In the plagues that are to come, look for a plague of rain, drought, mammals, storms, darkness, spirits, and death. When the last plague descends upon Andora, I pray that you are close to resurrecting Tahari, for the death plague will mean death to all within Andora and within Aura, giving Lord Jarden and his people new lands to settle in." the plagues were chilling, to be sure, but Leondros listened carefully and looked upon the lifeless body of his dear friend to help him believe that the impossible could happen.

"This will be done," Leondros said with confidence. "I will go forth, unite the peoples of Andora, and raise the army needed for the war with Lord Jarden. And above all else, Tahari will live again. I cannot fail her. I *will* not," Leondros said fervently. His fervor was infectious, for Almari found her reason to believe again as well and put a reassuring hand on Leondros's shoulder.

"Then you will not be alone. I will join you," she said as great determination filled her face and her blue eyes sparkled with renewed strength. "If Lord Jarden doubted the power of friendship, then he will not see this comin'!" she promised emphatically.

Elanza stepped forward. "We are with you, Leondros. Tahari suffered too much and paid too high a price for us and Andora for us to stand by idly and watch everyone and everything she loved come to ruin," she said as her gaze went from Leondros to Almari and Sala. An angry determination filled her whole being, and the strength of her confidence could not be missed, for her bright-green eyes dazzled in the flickering orange light of a torch that burned nearby.

"We are all with you, Leondros. This will be done. If this be Adalai's will, then as the lone member of the Osarian Order, I will fight what lies ahead until my last breath. I swear." Sala promised as he also stepped up and was counted among those willing to start this crusade. Anyi looked on proudly, a warm smile upon her lips.

"Your path is before you all. Now go, and Adalai be with you!"

Her words adjourned the ceremony that had started out as a farewell to their dearly beloved friend, Tahari of the Shandon, and had become a christening for the mission that would restore her life and begin the war that was to come.

Chapter 119

A Crusade Begins

In the preparation for the coming war with Lord Jarden, Leondros and the remaining rebel band took a few short hours to eat and sleep before setting out on their new quest. This time, the rebel band would be parted in two. Leondros and Almari would travel to the west toward Graven to unite the peoples of Andora, while Sala and Elanza took Tahari's body by ship to the Isles of Rane. Leondros and Almari were to meet them at the temple of Vestigia, for Leondros needed to resurrect Tahari as he carried her spirit within him.

Morning came gradually to Sion's tree-covered mountain, the warm sun gradually breaking through the night's fog. The damp chill and heartache that had accompanied the night gradually melted away, and Leondros and Almari took several moments to meet with Sala and Elanza upon their ship, the *Milagros*. They spent a tender moment to celebrate the life that had been sacrificed. Anyi graced them once more with her presence so that she could bestow one last blessing upon her daughter, whose body now lay upon a wooden altar that had been prepared for the occasion. The elfin captain had heard little about who Tahari was or the deed that took her life but still felt compelled to speak a few words to the five souls who stood before him. Ironically as he spoke, his words carried and caught the attention of the ship's crew, who stopped and slowly gathered near the altar, out of respect. Leondros, Almari, Elanza, Sala, and even Anyi watched in awe as the elfin crew came forward one by one and placed a single red-tipped white rose around the wooden altar upon which Tahari lay. One of the crew members gently and quietly explained to the mourning group of friends that news of Tahari, the last sphinx of the ancient world, had reached Sion early that morning; their captain had received word that they would be escorting her body back to Adarah. They had sent a crew member into the market place and had him bring back the roses for all the crew to bestow their respects. It was all they could do on such short notice.

During this small ceremony, the stillness of the balmy morning was broken by a gentle breeze. It drifted across the peaceful river's waters and through the grand ship. The *Milagros's* large sails caught it, and the ship swayed back and forth. The breeze blew onshore, causing the palm trees and ferns that grew thick there to sway gently, bringing peace to the weary souls about to embark on the next leg of their journey.

All looked on silently as Anyi slowly walked up to Tahari's body. When the sacred messenger had been placed upon the wooden altar, a white gossamer veil had been placed over her body. Her mother now offered a prayer to Adalai and then gently waved a delicate hand slowly over her daughter. As she moved her tanned hand over her daughter's still form, the air filled with millions of white sparkles. The onlookers watched in awe as the white sparkles gracefully descended upon the veil and robe that clothed Tahari. Then Anyi lifted her hopeful gaze to the four friends.

"Now Tahari's form will be preserved from time and nature until you are able to restore her life when you reach the Isles of Rane," Anyi said gently, smiling weakly through her sadness. Leondros nodded gratefully. There was still sadness in his features as he stepped forward, dressed in a new green and brown tunic for the long road ahead. He knelt down and gently put a hand upon Tahari's forehead. He lowered his head to hers for a moment and closed his eyes in prayer.

"Tahari, you fought for me; now I will fight for you. Hang in there, my friend—I am coming." taking a deep breath, Leondros lifted his head, stood to his full height, and looked upon Anyi one last time. He gave her a nod of promise and certainty, and then silently turned away. He and Almari bade farewell to Sala and Elanza, and they took their leave of the *Milagros* to start their journey to Graven.

Leondros and Almari rode on horseback from Sion for most of the day. The elves who had escorted them from Mt. Somerset had managed to retrieve Aton and had gifted Almari with a beautiful black and white stallion for her journey with Leondros. It was evening once again as they were about to pass the sacred border of Rahara and return to the desert plains of the Barrens. Before reaching the twin gray obelisks that oddly rose out of the rainforest in the west, taller than their southern counterparts, Leondros stopped Aton and turned the white stallion to face toward the east. The elfin prince looked back upon the dark eastern horizon with a sad and seemingly lost gaze. Almari stopped her horse and watched Leondros, unable to miss the sadness in his face. She knew the reason for his grief, but she sensed that something more was troubling him.

"Leondros? There is somethin' more wrong, is there not?" she asked with concern as she rode up beside him. He remained silent and almost distant for a long moment.

"I do not know..." Leondros managed to say as he continued to gaze on the eastern sky. "I feel like I am leaving a part of my own soul behind," he said half-heartedly. Almari watched him for a moment before joining his gaze to the eastern sky.

"Maybe so, but I am certain that you will find it again when you reach the Isles of Rane," Almari replied. She said it with such strength that Leondros was inspired to refocus himself on the task that lay before him. He found courage in Almari's tanned face as she gave him an encouraging nod. Then a warm and gentle breeze came from the west and blew softly against them. Leondros and Almari turned to each other knowingly. The warm wind was filled with a calming presence; they knew that Tahari was with them still, and she urged them on with hope.

"Come, we must not linger here. Tahari waits for us," Leondros said, inspired to press on. Gently nudging Aton, he and Almari began down the damp grassy hillside and passed through the western barrier that shielded Rahara. The cool damp grass beneath their horses' feet changed into cool, reddish sand. Ahead of them was the Barrens' high desert. They continued on without hesitation and made their way to the treacherous lands of Graven. Almari remained at Leondros's side, for she refused to be parted from the friend who would need help in the journey ahead, or from the friend who now waited between worlds, longing to be with them once again. The ancient prophecy had yet to be completed, and their search for Farro went on.

To Be Continued…

ACKNOWLEDGMENTS

To those in my life who continue to be the voice of encouragement in this wondrous undertaking. I would like to thank Justin P. R. & Bridget B., Cecilia S., Rikki S., C. J., Sara K., Ta Louis M., Tine S., my family, friends, and fans.

SPECIAL TRIBUTE

To the people, places, and events that come into our lives that help inspire us to dream and long to keep the vast realm of imagination alive within all of us!

If you enjoyed this story and want to read more about how these gripping events play out, look for Spirit in the Darkness, the next book in The Chronicles of Farro Series.

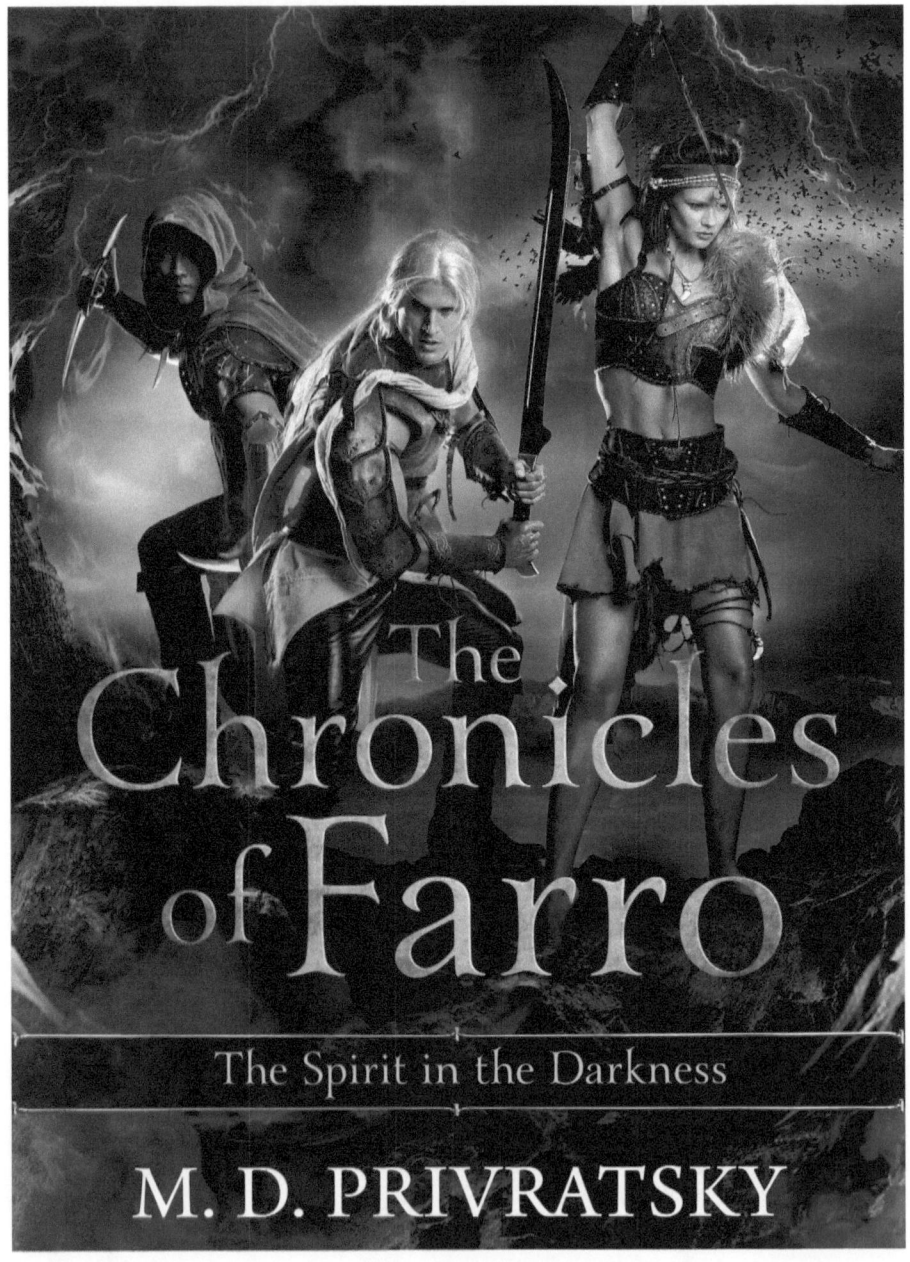

APPENDIX A
The Timeline

The timeline assumes that year 1 was the year sphinxes arrived in Andora and on dates mentioned throughout manuscript. For the sake of keeping the timing straight, in the style sheet the date changes at dawn rather than midnight. The timeline assumes that Aura's months have same number of days as their Earth counterparts (e.g., Juna (June) has 30 days, Jeli (July) has 31).

Ages

First Age (1–999): Sphinxes arrive from the old kingdom (Far World from across Great Ocean) to settle the area (ch. 44)

Second Age (1000–1999)

Third Age: (2000-2999):2015–2021 Age of Decimation, First Age of Darkness: Sphinxes abandon old ways in 2015 & Lord Jarden attacks for the first time. He rules for a thousand years.

Fourth Age (3000-3999):3012–3021: Age of Affirmation 3022 Revolt against Lord Jarden, led by Berecyntia the sphinx; Jarden banished to Ice Island. (ch. 44)

Fifth Age (4000-4999) Age of Enchantment: Farro establishes his Order.

Sixth Age (5000-5999)

Seventh Age (6000-6999)

Eighth Age (7000-7999)

Ninth Age (8000-8999) Age of Set: 8021-The sphinx race annihilated.

Tenth Age (9000-9999): Second Age of Darkness (9000–9022): Lord Jarden rules. Rafar the elfin prophet and member of the Order banished Lord Jarden to

Zendro Island prediction of the coming evil and the Phoenix Age

Eleventh Age (10,000-10,999) Age of the Phoenix (encompasses 10021, book's opening): Current time of the book.

Events

2015: Sphinx revolt against Far World teachings. (ch. 44)

2021: Andora is attacked by Lord Jarden for the first time. (ch. 44)

3012: Berecynthia and 9 other general-prophets sent to Andora to restore order. (ch. 44)

3018: Sphinx generals land in Andora and take back Lani. (ch. 44).

3018–3021: Sphinxes join with elves & dwarves in revolution to defeat Lord Jarden. (ch. 44)

Seprice 10, 3021: Final battle at Grimlock. Andoran Army wins, but Berecynthia dies. Farro takes on Berecynthia's power, takes on mission from Berecynthia to protect sphinxes.

5800: Draccen first come down from the mountains to look for food. (ch. 10)

6897: Draccen raiding party was captured in White Tower and forced to lead their captors back to the Serrigen, where the Draccen people were sentenced for their crimes against the lower kingdoms. (ch. 10)

6904: The Draccen are put to sleep by their guards through amulets. (ch. 10)

7721: Leondros is born.

8021: Shamira dies.

Abril 27, 8021: Date on Farro's first scroll. Farro dies.

Abril 28, 8021: Date on Sariff's scroll, enclosed with Farro's.

Sometime after the death of Rafar the Elder: Hosea takes over the Order, destroys or hides descriptions of Farro.

10021: Year of the Great Dragon

Juna 10, 10021: the old man's warning, the king & queen consult their advisors. The queen is attacked and saved by a young woman. Solarous is taken over by the green mist. (ch 1–6)

Juna 11: The queen confides in her son. (ch 6)

Juna 13: Solarous & Zudoo prepare to leave Akendron and bump into Sala on their way out. Sala attends meeting at the palace. (ch. 7)

Juna 15: Solarous & Zudoo land at Zendro and release Lord Jarden. Zudoo has until Juna 17 to put together an army. (ch 8 & 9)

Juna 16: Zudoo frees the Draccen people held prisoner in Romulus in the Serrigen. Lord Jarden assigns a group (lead by a military leader) to kidnap low-class people from the Shandel and imprison them in the buildings the rest of the Draccen will build. (ch. 10)

Unknown day between Juna 16 and 19: Tahari climbs a tree to watch the night sky. (ch 11)

Next day: Tahari works in the fields, has a vision, attacks 3 taskmasters, and is punished for it. (ch 12-13)

Unknown day between Juna 16 and 19: King Doran finds a new page of one of the sacred scrolls. (ch. 14) This is probably Juna 16.

Next day: Leondros returns home and learns that he has been conscripted. Zation has a nightmare/premonition. (ch 15-17) This is probably Juna 17.

Next day: Leondros leaves at dawn. (ch.17) . This is probably Juna 18.

Return to day Tahari is tied to pole between Juna 16 and 19: Evening falls, and after a taunting, Tahari almost escapes to the southern end of the Divervandon Forest. Instead she warns everyone of the tornado & is visited by a mysterious woman who tells her she is a sphinx. (ch 18-19)

Juna 16-18: Solarous returns to Akendron on horseback (ch. 20), is killed, and resurrects (ch 21-22).

Juna 19: Five days before the Great Dragon celebration; Alon-Settie kills his mother's attacker in the evening (Ch 23); Sala has visions about Tahari and goes to rescue her. (ch. 24+25). Tahari escapes to the forest & takes out some Drac soldiers. (ch 26); Leondros is attacked, but he successfully defeats them with Tahari's help (ch 27). Tahari is then brought to the prison and later the cave, where she is to be killed (ch. 28). Sala rescues her (ch. 29); Tahari wakes briefly in a bedchamber, presumably in Sala's house (ch. 29). Solarous meets with General Sabin (ch. 30). Leondros arrives in Akendron & meets Elijah (ch. 36); Leondros attends the high council meeting (ch 37).

Juna 20: Tahari sleeps soundly at Sala's palace. (Ch. 29) The high council meeting finally breaks up; Leondros sleeps fitfully. (ch. 38)

Juna 21: Tahari sleeps soundly at Sala's palace. (Ch. 29) Leondros spends the day trying to make plans for the Secret Alliance. (ch. 38).

Juna 22: Tahari dreams of the royal family's murder at the celebration to come and awakens (ch. 31); Tahari & Sala speak & he gives her the scroll to read (ch 32); she translates the scroll (ch. 33); the queen tells Sala of the slave uprising (ch. 34); Sala shares the news with Tahari (ch. 35); Leondros wanders the palace until he meets with Alon-Settie; the princes visit map room (ch. 38). Leondros visits Sala at his palace (ch. 39); Alon-Settie meets with Solarous (ch. 40 & 41); Tahari meets Leondros & Sala tells them the story of the First Age of Darkness (42-46); Tahari and Sala have a training session (ch. 47); Leondros returns to Akendron and leads his army toward Endenbury (ch. 48)

Juna 23: The Secret Alliance rides through most of the day. Toward the end of the day, the battle with Dracs (ch. 49) and then begin their ride back.

Juna 24: The Day of Great Dragon Celebration. The Secret Alliance continues to ride toward Andora. They break briefly in the afternoon and then continue their ride, anxious to reach Andora at nightfall. (ch. 50) Tahari sneaks off to help Sala stop Lord Jarden (ch 51). Solarous prepares for his master (ch. 52). Crazed people try to kill the king and his family, but Tahari stops them (ch. 53). Tahari is arrested for witchcraft (ch. 54). The princesses are killed by Alon-Settie; Solarous is killed by Lord Jarden, who takes over his body; the king is taken prisoner, and the queen escapes (ch. 55). Tahari is tortured and thrown in a cell; Thera confronts her; Tahari realizes how lax the security is in the dungeons (ch. 56).

Juna 25: Elijah tells Leondros & Sala that Tahari has been arrested (just after midnight), and Leondros goes to rescue her (ch 57). Tahari escapes, meets up with Almari, and goes to Sala's palace. They realize Leondros is gone, and Almari goes off to rescue him (ch. 58). Leondros fails to find Tahari and is captured by Alon-Settie (ch 59). Almari finds Leondros, who has been captured and is being tortured but she cannot rescue him (ch. 60). Alon-Settie confronts Leondros, who is in chains; Alon-Settie stabs Leondros in the side and leaves. Leondros appears to have died (ch. 61). Almari reports to Tahari & Sala; Almari & Tahari leave to rescue Leondros (ch 62). They kill several soldier to get into the palace (ch 63) and search for Leondros in the tower. Tahari finds him in the torture chamber, all but dead (ch 64). Lord Jarden makes plans with Alon-Settie, learns that Leondros is dead and Tahari has escaped; it's revealed that Zudoo poisoned the guard in hopes that Zudoo could help Tahari escape (ch. 65). Tahari & Almari rescue Leondros (ch. 66). They bring him to Cypress Palace, where Sala and Tahari care for him; Sala leaves to rescue one more person (ch. 67). Tahari dreams Leondros is dead (ch. 68).

Juna 26: In the early morning hours, Tahari & Almari leave the palace to return Leondros to Shoshon (ch. 69).

Juna 26–28 (morning): Tahari & Almari travel with Shoshon with Leondros (ch. 70). On Juna 26, they fight 14 Draccen soldiers; all (?) of them die, including Bainen (ch 71-72).

Juna 28: Tahari & Almari make it to within sight of Shoshon (ch 73). They deliver Leondros to his family, where he finally dies. By evening, his family escorts Leondros's body to the family tomb as Tahari looks on from her room (ch. 74). King Doran feels guilty as he looks over the scroll predicting his son's death; Zation tells him of Tahari's lineage (ch. 75). Tahari requests to visit Leondros's tomb (ch 76). Tahari visits the tomb, and sees her mother. Her mother gives her the second prophecy scroll and the life scroll (ch. 77). Tahari attempts to bring Leondros back with the white scroll (ch. 78).

Juna 29: Tahari awakens in Leondros's tomb to find him alive (ch. 79). Jeanpala and Zation find Leondros & Tahari in the tomb; they go back to the palace and greet Leondros's mother (ch. 80). Leondros is reunited with his family & Tahari has a vision of her mother, finding out the cost of her gift (ch. 81). At sunset, Tahari sneaks off; Zation follows her and figures out what Tahari sacrificed (ch. 82). Leondros tells Tahari to let go of her guilt, and they watch Tonious ride into the city (ch. 83). The council convenes with Tonious announcing that the Dracs are coming (ch. 84). Leondros and his men are in the northeastern mountains; Theron and Judeas emerge from a pass. (ch. 85); Tahari reveals that Theron and Judeas are traitors and the Dracs emerge from the pass (ch. 86). Tahari, Almari, and the elves defeat the Dracs in battle overnight (ch. 87).

Juna 30: Tahari, Almari, and Leondros, the only survivors of the battle, head back to Shoshon, which appears to be in trouble. They find the city destroyed and few survivors. Leondros's family are all dead and Leondros is the last of his line (ch 87). Tahari, Almari, and Leondros bury Leondros's family; Sala arrives with Queen Elanza and all sleep in the ruins of the palace (ch. 88).

Jeli 1: Tahari translates the second scroll (ch. 88). Tahari gives Leondros his father's sword. The group discovers an army coming from the east and a massive fire coming from the west; they leave on horseback for the north toward the sphinxes' land (ch. 89). Tahari and Elanza make their way up the mountain and narrowly miss being killed by an explosion. They find Almari. Almari & Elanza ride the remaining horse away, while Tahari jumps off the cliff to the river below to escape another cannonball and to search for Leondros; it's now afternoon (ch.

90). Tahari finds Leondros hung up on rocks in the river, unconscious. They sneak past soldiers and hide in a crevasse until they leave. Tahari carries Leondros into the forest and rests a moment. She nearly shots Almari with an arrow. They have found Leondros's horse. It's now early evening. Almari & Elanza lead Leondros away from the fire, while Tahari heads toward it to lure the Dracs away from her friends (ch. 91). Tahari scuffles with Lord Jarden, revealing that she is a sphinx, and then defeats all his soldiers while he escapes (ch 92). Almari, the queen, and Leondros get safely away and make camp to wait for Tahari; they realize they have a role in the latest prophecy too (ch. 93). Tahari finishes off the soldiers and jumps into the river to escape the fire. She grabs hold of a log and floats along the river as weariness overcomes her and she falls asleep. It is now night. She awakes hours later and is captured by the Dracs. Her friends rescue her (ch. 94). Lord Jarden is walking west, away from Shoshon and the fire; it is near dawn now. He sends a dragon and rider to release a prisoner to slow down Tahari, and he rides Baldour to Zendro Isle for revenge. (ch. 95).

Jeli 4: Evening. Tahari awakes after being asleep for three days; the queen points out that Tahari & Leondros love each other; Bakari of Mansee appears in their camp and presents Lord Jarden's challenge, which Tahari accepts (ch. 96).

Jeli 5: Tahari and her friends prepare to meet Lord Jarden by midnight; Bakari & Tahari arrive first & find the mass grave; Tahari remembers Shamira's death (ch. 97); Tahari is betrayed by Bakari & captured by Baldour; Tahari wins over the Gradon, which carries away Lord Jarden (ch. 98). Prisoners take over the prison, defeating the Draccens; Tahari sends everyone to Eden-Glee & lets the army, led by Gen. Sabin, see her run northwest toward Mt. Somerset (ch. 99). Almari meets her out there, revealing she was the one who shot the arrow; they use a ring of mist to reach Mt. Somerset (ch. 100); After being carried away to the Serrigen mountains by it, Lord Jarden kills the Gradon. Baldour & Alon-Settie meet him there and report (ch. 101).

Jeli 6: Dawn. Thunderstorm ending in mountains as Tahari & Almari reunite with Queen Elanza; they clean up, get something to eat, and sleep a few hours; Tahari relieves Leondros on guard duty and finds the third scroll; she has a vision of Shamira's death; she translates the scroll but doesn't reveal its contents (ch. 102).

Tahari, Almari, Elanza, & Leondros spend rest of day preparing for attack. Dracs approach by evening (ch. 103). The Dracs enter the mountain area that night, with three teams of 20 taking the three paths; all the men are killed (ch. 104). A huge rainstorm kicks up; the remaining team of 20, including Gen. Sabin, capture Elanza & leave her at her camp; they then capture Leondros (off stage) and Almari (on stage). The storm is over now, too (ch. 105). Gen Sabin has all three captive somewhere (his camp) and after a brief scene is going to have them killed; Tahari shows up & Sabin shoots an arrow at her & a soldier she holds hostage (ch. 106). The arrow kills the soldier; Tahari must choose one of her friends to die (ch. 107). Leondros volunteers; Tahari puts herself in front of him & catches the arrow & they all go free; Sabin comes back, almost killing Elanza; Tahari transfers their fear to Sabin & his men disperse; his men regroup, bringing reinforcements (19 remaining men from original band of 80 + 40 new men = 59 men total); Rebels head up the mountain (ch. 108). The rebels cross over to Rahara via the southern gate (ch. 109). Back to the 59 Dracs chasing the rebels: 11 decide not to go over the summit; the remaining 47 spot Baldour in the distance and charge down the mountain and through the gate; the walls emit a blue light, which creates a barrier that the Dracs run straight into and die (ch. 110). Elanza spots Alon-Settie and runs into the blue barrier to reach him; the barrier erupts, knocking everyone off their feet. (ch. 111) When Elanza comes to, she runs to Alon-Settie, who grabs her. Leondros comes after her, sword drawn. Alon-Settie pushes Elanza down the path, where she lies limp. Alon & Leondros begin a sword fight (ch. 112). Tahari comes regains consciousness after the explosion; she & Almari head back to the mountain, where Tahari has sensed more Dracs (the remaining 11); Almari takes out 5 on the eastern side; Tahari takes out 5 more, sparing Jax, the original soldier who decided not to go over the summit (ch. 113). Leondros defeats Alon-Settie but doesn't kill him; a cloaked figure knocks out Leondros & orders Alon to finish him; Almari bursts in to stop him but Alon restrains her; the cloak figure decides to do it himself and is poised with the sword over Leondros (ch. 114). Before he can kill Leondros, Tahari skewers him with a sword from behind, but it doesn't kill him because he is Lord Jarden; he explains that his people are zombies and need healthy people to feed upon (better if they've suffered first); Tahari offers herself in place of her friends and all of Andora; Lord Jarden runs Leondros threw with a sword; Tahari takes on Leondros's wound and then blasts Lord Jarden into the Serrigen and collapses to the ground (ch. 115). Elanza stabs Alon in the shoulder and forces him to leave; he escapes up to the summit of the mountain; Tahari reveals that the 3rd scroll has been found and translated and then dies in Leondros's arms (ch. 116). Sala and a band of elves come out of Rahara; Almari tells them of Tahari's death; they discover that Tahari's spirit is within Leondros & Almari reads the additional instructions in the thirds scroll; they cross over into Rahara and enter the jungle; the board 4 riverboats to go to Sion (ch. 117).

Jeli 7: Morning comes as they paddle down the river toward Sion; they travel on the river until early evening; they arrive in Sion, walk up the mountain to the palace of Seymoura (ch. 117). After they rest a while, Tahari's friends meet at midnight for a candle light ceremony for Tahari; after the ceremony, Anyi appears before Sala, Leondros, Almari, & Elanza and tells them they must unify Andora, find Farro, and bring Tahari's body to Vestigia (ch. 118). The rebels eat and sleep; Leondros & Almari will go west to unite the Andorans while Sala & Elanza go to the Rane Isles with Tahari's body; L&A will meet them there to perform the resurrection (ch. 119).

Jeli 8: Leondros & Almari meet with Sala & Elanza on S&A's ship, the *Milagros*; they have a small ceremony & separate; Leondros & Almari go by horseback to the western border of Rahara toward Graven; they cross over at night (ch. 119).

APPENDIX B
The Prophecies

First Scroll of the Prophecy (Content revealed in chapter 33)

I. The Secret Alliance will go forth in battle. *Do not look for lost men; search out your friends.

II. A long-awaited night of celebration turns foul. *Rise up to stop this assassination.

III. A betrayal and a tomb await a prince. *Do not leave him in towers high, but bring him home.

IV. The key to finding Farro will lie within a tomb. *Be of courage to make a sacrifice.

V. A dark dragon will deliver unpleasant tidings. *DO NOT bring down his murderers.

VI. Flame and spear will fall upon the kingdom of the elf. *Escape will depend on all.

*Look for a stone within a tomb that is marked with the crest. This is where you will find the second instructions.

Second Scroll of the Prophecy (Content revealed in chapter 88)

I. A black veil of death and destruction sweeps over Andora. Many will fall to this peril. *Do not let "one" bear the entire burden.

II. The armies of darkness will move in to surround the forces of good. *Learn the power of the sphinx ancestry in thyself.

III. A terrible position will force one to choose from among those near and dear. *Take a stand between them and a loved one.

IV. The darkness of a sacred messenger will threaten Andora. *A sacrifice will save the key to finding Farro.

*Look for the third scroll within the Barrens on the mount with the crest upon it.

Third Scroll of the Prophecy

Extra note of instruction, rolled within the scroll (Content revealed in chapter 117)

Let the spirit within the key be your guide now. Do not be disheartened because of what has been taken; this spirit is still with you as it has always been.

APPENDIX C
The Seven Plagues

(Outlined in chapter 118)

1.) The Rain Plague- (Chapter 6) (Each plague begins and ends on the following dates: Jeli 8th-28th) This plague is not be to confused with random flooding. Never before in Andora's history has every kingdom within the realm ever experienced the same catastrophic weather related occurrence at the same time.

2.) The Plague of Drought- (Chapter 10) (Augo 1st-20th) This plague has several names, but nevertheless it is quick burn away the green lush earth and turns Andora into a burning desert wasteland. Travel is not advised, but some have no choice.

3.) The Plague of Mammalian- (Chapter 17) (Augo 23rd-30th) As the duration of the plagues shorten, they also worsen. As the animals of the entire realm of Andora become wild and ultimately crazed, if the plague isn't stopped, it's only a matter of time before it crosses over to mankind.

4.) The Plague of Storms-(Chapter 46) (Seprice 3rd-10th) This plague does not only dominate Andora with a ceaseless thunderstorms, but it is also brings with it blinding snowstorms and a finale of a twister no one could have possibly anticipated.

5.) The Plague of Darkness-(Chapter 76) (Seprice 13th-20th) It occurs near the hour of noon as a strange murkiness overtakes the mid-day sunlight. Blinding darkness so black that even blazing torches offer little solace.

6.) The Plague of Spirits-(Chapter 85) (Seprice 23rd-27th) There is far more to this plague than mere haunting eeriness and mournful winds, for the first time in Andora's history, the veil between life and death has been pulled back and the dead are allowed in the living realm.

7.) The Plague of Death- (Chapter 93) (Octor 1st) It begins at the lonely hour of midnight as a green fog makes its way upon Andora's southeastern shore and spreads far and wide, this deadly fog strips away life within a single breath.

APPENDIX D
Physical Realm

World: [unnamed]

Aura: Upper World; top half of the hemisphere. Made up of many island nations.

Inferus: Lower World; part of the bottom half of the hemisphere.

Mortu'us and Aetus: together the island of the dead. Mortu'us is in Aura, while Aetus is in Inferus. Aetus is a kind of hell.

Nod: Far off, across the sea; Lord Jarden's home. Island kingdom. Nodarians

Ice Isle: Where Lord Jarden was first imprisoned; far off, off Adarah's southern coast. Half the island remained lush and green; the half Jarden was imprisoned in was frozen.

Adarah: Elfin kingdom, west of Misty Forest & Sala's palace (ch. 69). It is three days' ride from Misty Forest. Unknown how far it is from Akendron.

Andora: chief kingdom in the book, located on Aura

Zendro Isle: Far off; where Lord Jarden was later imprisoned. Rocky shoreline, turbulent waters surrounding it

Akendron: There is a harbor to the east of the capital city of the Shandel; to the north is a thick forest *and* mountains (ch. 30); to the west is Misty Forest (ch 44). The city can't be seen from Sala's palace but is in relatively easy walking distance (perhaps an hour?).

Avdima: in the east is a large oak tree (ch. 59)

the Tribunal: the three lower kingdoms of Andora.

the Tomblock: The Dancar Plantation, which Tahari grows up on; borders the southern end of Divervandon Forest. Slaves live in the barracks; a jail is in the central yard; past the main house to the east are bunkers for protection against tornadoes. Wooden post Tahari is tied to is close to forest's southern border as is rock pile where she spends a day breaking rocks and the cave where the taskmasters try to kill her. In the south of the plantation is a prison where slaves do not return from; Misty Forest is south of the Tomblock.

Divervandon Forest: near Endenbury; borders the Tomblock to the south; road goes through it, east to west. Forest covers half of the Shandel (ch. 27). *On which side is Adarah?* Borders Misty Forest to the east; divided by a large clearing.

Misty Forest: Where Sala lives; from the palace, must go through city to get to the edge of the forest. Border is south of the palace & the city. Borders Divervandon Forest to the west; divided by a large clearing.

Seamara: Harbor near Akendron
Shoshon: Capital city of Adarah; a moat surrounded the city when Tahari is 3 (10006). Surrounding is a range of mountains; to the northeast there is a secret pass that is the only passage between two mountains (ch. 85).

Kingdom of Lani: Farro's homeland

Far World: Island origin of sphinxes before first age.

Great Ocean: Separates Far World from Andora

TERMS AND CHARACTERS

A

Abalan Dancar, Master Dancar's son

Aceon, Adarah soldier

Adalai: The god or deity of Andora; also the god of the sphinx race.

Adarah, elfin kingdom

Adaran: of or related to Adarah

Adrasteia: female head of the Gradon advisor

Akendron, Andora (capital)

King Alabaster

Almari: light-brown and blonde hair; blue eyes

Prince Alon-Settie, Alabaster's son & heir; has a dark beard (ch. 114)

amidst

Amon-Ra: male head of the Gradon

Amon-yen: elfin soldier; 2,000 years older than Leondros; dark-blue eyes, light brown hair

Andora

Andoran: one from Andora

Anyi: Tahari's mother; sea-green eye, long mahogany hair, dark skin;

Aton, Leondros's horse; white

Avdima: Alabaster's palace in Akendron, Andora

B

Bainen: Draccen tracker; dark-green scales; able to conceal his scent; black eyes

Bakari of Mansee: slave Lord Jarden sends to Tahari (ch. 95); sun-tanned, dark-brown eyes, thick, dark hair;

Baldour: large, black dragon. Wingspan: 3 massive oak trees wide (ch 95). Sides with Jarden

the Barrens

Berecynthia (sphinx): 1 of 10 general-prophets sent to free Andora from Jarden; dark-red hair, green eyes, black & silver armor

burnt

C

Celebration of the Great Dragon

Cypress Palace, Sala's home

D

dark lord: Lord Jarden

Dialogue: thoughts and mind-to-mind speech is italicized, no quote marks.

King Doran, ruler of Andora

Dornos, Eden-Glee soldier

Draccens: glisten in the rain (ch. 113)

dwarven

dwelt

E

Eden-Glee: a far-off dwarf kingdom

Endenbury: Elanza's hometown

Queen Elanza, Alabaster's wife

Elfish: language of the elves

Elijah: young messenger from Avdima Palace; small, weak; green eyes

F

failsafe

Farro of Aiden, founder of the Osarian Order (3rd age)

Freya: Bakari's wife; hazel eyes; tanned

skin (ch. 99)

G

Gesson: A dwarf soldier from the kingdom of Eden-Glee; black eyes; black hair, brown skin, stocky

Goratha: What Andora is to be called under Lord Jarden's rule

Gortorro Prison: one of Lord Jarden's prison camps, on the northern edge of the Serrigen, in the Barrens

Gwenth: Leondros's sister

the Gradon: two-headed dragon-like winged beast; last of its kind; emerald green & black, with light green underbelly, black claws & barbs; golden eyes; one head shoots blue ice (female, Adrasteia), the other fire (male, Amon-Ra);

Graven: north of the Tribunal kingdoms, cut off by the Serrigen

Great Dragon Celebration (Juna 24): celebrates Rafar the Elder

Grimlock: during 3rd age, Lord Jarden's last stronghold

Tonious Goldendragon: Leondros's uncle

gray walker: a zombie.

H

High council: 200 councilmen, plus the king & Alon-Settie

Hosea, Osarian Order

I

Ice Isle (where Jarden was imprisoned the first time)

J

King Jabberwrath, high king of Nod

Lord Jarden: takes over Solarous's body, looking exactly like him at first (ch 55), but becoming more reptilian (ch. 92, ?)

Jade: Zation's horse; black with brown eyes

Jaran, soldier from the Shandel

Jax: all-black, brown-eyed Drac soldier that Tahari spares (ch. 113)

Judeas, elfin warrior/scout; long black hair; light-brown (tanned) skin

Jeanpala: royal tomb caretaker for 3,500 years; dark blond hair; somewhat wrinkled; steel-gray eyes

K

Princess Kosta, Alabaster's daughter

Kutalas, Eden-Glee solider

L

Lani

Life River: flows north out of Shoshon

M

the *Milagros*: Sala's & Elanza's river longboat

Princess Minta, Alabaster's daughter

Misty Forest: faces the southeast portion of the castle

Months: see Appendix

N

Nor, dragon island & Rafar the Elder's home

Numbers: spell out numbers zero through one hundred

O

off-guard

the Osarian Knights

P

Paracity Palace, Shoshon, Adarah: library & Tahari's room have views of family cemetery; to the south is a hill that overlooks the palace. Stairs are embedded in the hill.

prime master: the one who has charge of the slaves on the Tomblock (an overseer)

Q

R

Rafar (elf), from Nor

Rahara, sacred sphinx realm; rainforest; southern gate is on Mt. Somerset

Randye of Corpse (Jarden takes over his body in 9th Age)

Rane: collection of small islands off east coast of Adarah

Reymier of the Shandon: Tahari's father

S

General Sabin: general of Draccen army that comes to overrun Gortorro prison camp; one eye (brown); battle-scarred face

Sala of Antioch: blue eyes

Sariff the Wise, Osarian Order (lived during the 9th age)

Seamara: harbor near Akendron

Seymoura: palace in the city of Sion

Shamira: ancient sphinx that Tahari once was; dark; beautiful, desert-brown eyes the Shandel (part of Andora)

Sion, temple city deep within Rahara (ch. 96)

Mt. Sion, mountain within Rahara (ch. 117)

snuck, not sneaked

Mt. Somerset, the Barrens, bordered by red desert to the west; Gortorro lies beyond it to the west

sphinx, sphinxes

spirits for *alcohol*

sunburnt, not sunburned

T

Tabor, Alabaster's family line

Tahari: slave; almost 18 when introduced (ch. 11)

Tartarus: spoken by the Traveler in Lord Jarden's story (ch. 115)

Taskmaster: a slave driver and guard. Those employed by the plantation masters to take charge of the slaves

The Tamrika: ship on which Solarous sails from Akendron to Zendro

Theron, Adarah soldier

Thoughts are italicized

torch-lit

Torga: Draccen who almost behinds Tahari (ch 94)

U

V

Valora: ship Alon-Settie hires

Vestigia: sphinx temple on Rane Ilses

W

wormish

"wisp": sound a whip or arrow makes when travelling through the air

X

Y

Year: 10,012 Age of the Phoenix

Z

Zendro Isle (Rafar imprisons Jarden there)

Zudoo: small Drac; blood-red scales; green eyes

ABOUT THE AUTHOR

My journey to be a self-published author didn't begin with the first paragraphs of "The Chronicles of Farro" series. In truth, it began when I was old enough to pick up a pencil and write my name. At that young age, I realized the true power hidden within the small tip of my pencil; it had the power to tap into the unknown of the human imagination. It began with simple child stories, but it already had the potential of being so much more. All the while enduring a rough childhood of being bullied in my school, writing became my outlet to escape into a larger world where my pain became inspiration for my stories. With the movies I watched and the music I listened to, I began to feel this epic story in the far reaches of my mind just waiting to be recognized and brought to life.

In college, I allowed a fellow classmate read over my work. She strongly encouraged me to compile my stories into one genre and form a novel. The search for my genre began, but it wasn't too long before "The Lord of the Rings" movies came out did I ultimately realize that I had found the genre to tailor my novel around. So it began: In 2000 the epic quest for writing "The Chronicles of Farro" series initially began. It took one year to write out the basic concept of my trilogy and many more years to hone the series. All the while life as you know has a tendency of grabbing a hold of you and taking you for a wild ride. One that I am still on...

In 2008, my father passed away due to a massive heart attack and it was then I decided to go full throttle and blaze the trail to publish my work. At the time, North Dakota was hardly known for its authors or writers. I remember talking to a representative of a large book company and them specifically telling me, "All we want from North Dakota writers are stories about prairie dogs and wheat grass." Now the positively determined part of me thought, "Oh no, you didn't just say that!" North Dakotans as any other state not known for its writers are an untapped resource of incredible inspiration, just give us a chance. So I charged ahead until I discovered a self-published author who lived in Jamestown, ND, who gave me the tools I needed to cross the bridge into the publishing world.

This journey was far from perfect and yes there were more trials, hurdles and setbacks than I care to recall and no; it doesn't happen overnight (THANK GOD!). The financial price tag...well let's just say numbers are still scary, but now as my book has been refined by the talents of so many great people, that I have met along the way, I have reaped my losses and in fact, I have been handsomely rewarded already. My reward has come in so many forms. First, I immensely enjoy this undertaking and would not have done it any differently. Secondly, every time someone comes up to me, who has read my book 1, "The Chronicles of Farro- The Sacred Messenger" and looks at me with eyes that are alive with intense inspiration or seeing the grateful reaction from a father who purchased my book 1 in hopes to help his son who is paying for a lifetime of bad choices which ended him in prison, I am bountifully rewarded. Of all these things, I am and will always be immensely honored. I give all that I am and all that I achieve and I give it back to my Lord and Savior, Jesus Christ. Thank you for the good and bad days, for they in themselves are inspirational and when channeled through the fine tip of a pencil, they can and often times do have the power to change the world. Agape my dear friends, my story is far from finished...